cath·ar·sis

[kəˈθɑːsɪs]
NOUN
1. the process of releasing, and thereby providing relief from, strong or repressed emotions

I

It was no secret that King Dyran was getting old. He'd been more reserved these last few years - more careful and reluctant to make public appearances. Next month would mark his 215th year on the throne as the monarch of Klaevr - and although none of his staff would dare say it, they were all aware that it was about time he retired.

That was the issue, he supposed. His retirement would leave a vacant throne, and a vacant throne needed to be filled.

Filled by an heir.

Klaevr was a relatively nice place to live. Or rather, to die. It was on the west side of the underworld - protected by a large forest which opened up onto neighbouring Kingdoms of Hell. Those who lived as normal in the underworld were shadows of mortal lives - of those who hadn't quite made the cut for an eternity of happiness.

That's *why* it was a nice place to live. Some other kingdoms looked down on it; they called the residents weak and uncommitted. They weren't bad people, not really. Just those who made a few mistakes in the short time they had consciousness on Earth.

The royal bloodline was different.

They weren't, aren't and can't ever be mortals. Royal children were born of pureblooded demons in the kingdom, and that's where they stayed. *Of course* King Dyran was reluctant to retire, to pass his legacy down to his children. He'd kept the kingdom in order these past few centuries - and no amount of training can prepare a child to inherit such a land.

The monarch's royal advisors had been strongly against the idea of crowning Dyran's firstborn.

"He's still a boy!"
"He doesn't understand the responsibility!"
"He needs to undergo more training first!"
It was ironic that the Crown Prince was perceived in this light. He had recently completed his final year of formal schooling and, *boy*, had it been a long eighteen years of life so far.
The advisors had carefully suggested that someone a little older and closely trusted by the King take over until Prince Theo had grown more. The King thought it was ridiculous to make assumptions about a person's character or ability to perform because of external factors like age.
So it was decided.
Theo was sitting cross-legged on his bed when his door was knocked on. Sitting may have been the wrong word, but he was perched about six feet above the bed itself, surrounded by dark-coloured particles of light as he read to himself. It had been a long day; he'd had to wake up at the crack of dawn for 'swordsmanship training' (which he *personally* didn't think was necessary).
It was only midday now, and Theo was more than ready to collapse into sleep. He wanted desperately to finish the chapter of the book he was preoccupied with. The novel floated in front of him, and he'd reach forward every few minutes to turn the page. Behind his bed was a wide open window that looked over the forest, which was just behind the kingdom, and arched round slightly towards the border with other kingdoms either side of it. The castle was at the head of the kingdom on a very slight hill that made it raised above the villages, only enough that your legs began to ache when walking up it, but not enough that it was a strain to traverse. The forest was dark, but there was a gentle red glow of light illuminating the boy's bedroom - cast by the ruby sun.
When the knock sounded out, Theo dropped himself down onto his bedsheets, letting his book fall shut as he stood from the bed and made his way over to the door.
Upon noticing himself in the mirror, the boy hoped more than ever that this wasn't someone important wanting to speak to him. He looked tired, and his appearance was sleazily uncared for. Light grey porcelain skin lay underneath wistfully dotted darker freckles that traversed the bridge of his nose and cheeks. His eyes were completely black - like unending pools of naivety.
The eyes. That was one of the easiest ways to distinguish a pureblooded demon from an ex-mortal. Those who were visiting from Earth changed significantly after settling into life in Hell. In fact, they were given their

demon forms by the guardian of the kingdom. Their skin became monochromatic - ranging from snow white to ink black depending on how their mortal body looked. People kept their original hair too, although it wasn't at all unnatural for people to change the colour of their hair either. Theo actually quite liked how his hair was naturally - a deep auburn that bordered on black in certain light.

No matter how much someone's body adapts to life in the underworld, their eyes always stay the same. The eyes are the key to the soul, and you cannot lose your soul.

Theo's eyes were completely frosted over with darkness - no pupil, no iris, nothing. Although he could still see out the them perfectly well (if not better than an ex-mortal), they were very different and obvious to spot.

He was wearing a dark blue, long-sleeved shirt made out of a light material. The sleeves were only reaching his elbows, and there were black bands of leather criss-crossing down his arms to hook in between his fingers. They left enough clearance so that the faint grey markings on his arms were visible, taking the form of various jagged shapes. Below his shirt sat a pair of black ripped jeans.

Theo inherited his deep green shaded horns from his mother, who hadn't been around for a while.

One of the greatest misconceptions that mortals created about demons was that they abided by a strict 'red and black' colour scheme. No, in fact, quite the opposite. In actuality, horns and tails of all the colour spectrum existed in Klaver - some even being as noticeable as highlighter yellow.

Of the same viridian green, also honed a pointed tail which waved itself anxiously behind him as he glanced to the mirror. The Prince ran his tongue along his teeth, tracing over the sharpness of his two fang-like canines to ease his worries.

He pulled the door open to be met with Sir Nikoliah - his father's self proclaimed 'favourite ex-mortal' and right hand man. He was a knight, a soldier, and an advisor. He had short, ear-length light brown hair that seemed to always magically be styled perfectly. His horns and tail were a cotton blue tone that brought out his eyes of a similar shade. His jawline was sharp and his features were slender. The man had a good three inches of height on Theo; he looked pretty much like your typical soldier. There was a slight waft of tension in the air that silenced them both for a moment.

Theo raised his eyebrows at the man, who was significantly taller than himself.

"I'm waiting for you to address me before I speak to you, My Prince." He smirked, half-heartedly being irritating just for the sake of it.

"I think you were supposed to start this interaction on a knee, bowing to me, Sir. Don't talk to me about status." Theo replied, calm and calloused. He didn't even care about it - that was what made it even funnier to him. He really didn't care whether or not the castle's workers bowed to him. If he was actually being honest, he saw it as outdated and weird. It was just this particular man that always managed to get on his nerves. He always had. And if Sir Nikoliah was so concerned about formal addressals, then the Prince mused that he could be too.

"I bow for your father - not for you."

Persistent and arrogant as ever, he supposed. Theo used his left foot to kick the door aside further, creating a few metres of open space either side of him. With an eased movement of some muscles in his back, a pair of large, forest green feathered wings emerged from behind him.

That was the second way to distinguish a pureblooded demon from an ex-mortal. Only the royal bloodline had the luxury of flight.

It was also very intimidating to have a two-metre wingspan presented to you. Nikoliah took a step backwards as the Crown Prince gestured for him to go on.

The older man had to muster a lot of self control not to roll his eyes at the heir. Instead, he opted towards just spitting out what he came here to report.

"Tomorrow. Sunset."

"What's happening then?" Theo asked, a little more curious. They didn't have scheduled events often.

The advisor looked to his right, sighing. "King Dyran's retirement ceremony and your subsequent coronation."

Theo's eyes widened, his wings folding back in on themselves and fading back into invisibility. He pulled his hands backwards towards his chest, face and eyebrows contorting into one of fear and confusion.

"Tomorrow ?! He... he hasn't said anything about this to me- I, I can't-"

Nikoliah straightened. "Well, he decided last month that he would take his retirement tomorrow. It is tradition for the heir to only be informed twenty-four hours before the coronation, unfortunately for you."

That felt unfair. Theo shook his head, bringing one of his black-painted nails up to his mouth to bite on it anxiously.

"Can I... talk to him about this at all?"

"In the same alley, it is tradition for you to not speak to him from now until the coronation."

The boy stepped backwards, becoming slightly more erratic. "I can't- I can't be the King. Not yet, I'm- I'm barely an adult! Why doesn't he wait a few years more?"

"Don't shoot the messenger, Your Majesty." Nikoliah shrugged.

Theo recoiled. "Don't call me that. Oh my god."

"Look, you've got the whole of today and until sunset tomorrow to prepare yourself. A lot of people are going to want to speak to you to sort out the coronation. That will begin tomorrow, today is yours to process this."

Theo nodded, keeping his gaze to the ground. "Um, yeah. Thank you." He nodded, eyes flickering back up to the man still standing in his doorway. The advisor took this as his queue to exit, so he did - making his way back down the corridor and out of sight.

He took another step backward, shaking his hands out in front of him to relieve some of the tension coursing through his veins. The door of his bedroom had eased its way closed now, and the Prince was left standing alone in the expanse of his bedroom.

He stood still for a few minutes, trying to contain the racing thoughts in his mind. I mean, he knew that his father was nearing retirement but he'd had no warning at all. Maybe if he'd shown up to more 'family dinners', then he would've heard about it. In Theo's defence, he didn't even see King Dyran much. Monarchy duties and all.

Oh, God, his life was over, wasn't it?

Or maybe it was just the beginning. He was about to become the most important person in the largest Kingdom of Hell. That had to entail a world of possibilities. Or maybe not, but he entertained that only time would tell.

He had to tell Laine. Of all people, she'd definitely be the most excited for him. Theo's sister was only two years younger than him, and they'd always had a running joke going that she'd probably never get her hands on the throne because of their close age gap.

Swinging his door open, the teenager bounded out of the room on excitedly apprehensive feet. He was surrounded by stone walls, lined with torches and paintings of previous monarchs. Theo really hoped he wouldn't be expected to sit for one of those.

Despite his discontempt about wanting one of himself, he had to admit that they were really nice. It was almost reassuring to him.

Inside of an ornate gold frame, on the wall in front of where Theo stood was a painting of his father and mother. This was from before they had children, and they were both sitting in the foreground of the ballroom. Dyran's wife, Aster, was a princess from the neighbouring Kingdom of Stonbrin. Their marriage had originally been arranged, but they did end up genuinely falling in love after a while. Aster was depicted with gentle brushstrokes, a mid-toned grey as her skin and dark hair. She had sharply pointed horns the same colour as Theo's.

He stared at the image for a good minute. Turning his head down the corridor, he looked across the centuries of previous kings and queens. His grandmother sat alone in her painting - without a spouse like most others had. She'd only had one son: the current king - who wasn't the result of a marriage, so had been considered dirty and unfit to be a prince when he was born. Theo was glad that times had changed.

His grandmother was the queen for quite a while, being reluctant to retire, much like her son. She now lived in the Kingdom of the Ancient, where most older demons stayed to have peace after serving themselves to Klaevr for centuries beforehand.

The Prince carried on his stride down the hall, feeling a little like the paintings were watching him. Judging him. Expecting him to be perfect, just like they were. He was snapped out of his thoughts when he noticed that a patrol of royal guards was heading down towards the throne room, led by the chief of defences for Klaevr: Sir Oliver Garrah. The man halted his squad, stopping on the accord of seeing the Crown Prince.

Theo paused his walk , recognising that he would need to speak to this man. The chief bowed his head slightly to show respect, placing a hand on his belt which rested atop a grey-coloured tunic. Theo responded by standing up straight and saluting the dark-horned general with his right hand and a syllable of 'Sir'. The Prince had no issue giving respect to this man because he gave it back. That was how respect was supposed to work.

The whole squad of soldiers had dropped to kneel on their left knees at the same time that the chief had bowed.

"Thank you." Theo said, showing that he had accepted the gesture and allowed them to stand once more. They did so in quick succession.

"I've heard the news about the King's retirement. Congratulations, My Prince. You'll make a great king." He said, seeming somewhat nostalgic. Sir Garrah himself had been working for the King for years. Long enough that he'd been in the castle the day that Theo's father was born, and then Theo afterwards, and now, here he was. Being crowned king tomorrow.

Time really does fly. The general had a thought that Theo's mother would be proud of him, but he decided not to voice it simply because he worried it would upset the young man to remember she wouldn't be at his coronation like he'd always imagined.
The Prince nodded.
"Thank you, Sir. I... hope so."
Reaching out and placing a hand on the Prince's shoulder, the man smiled. "I know you'll be excellent. You just let me know if anything or anyone is bothering you, alright?"
Theo nodded. He felt way out of his depth in this situation, but surmised that it was okay because what the chief had said *was* true. He had a lot of support. Everyone wanted him to succeed. It added a lot of pressure.
The heir must have gotten a little lost in his head, because when he looked back up to meet eyes with the general again, the man and his parade were gone - far down the hallway. Theo shook his head to regain his thoughts before turning and carrying on his stride towards his sister's room. Soon enough, he reached the main staircase with the intention to walk right past it. It was a large ensemble, with a glass chandelier hanging and two wide mahogany bannisters either side of a carpeted staircase large enough to fit 10 people in a line.
It overlooked the entrance hall to the castle, which consisted of some large double doors, stone-constructed walls and other various wall pieces like paintings and murals. From the top of the staircase, Theo noticed some people walking along the bottom of the stairs. More notably, his father and four guards that he was lightly having a conversation with. Bingo. Theo knew that he wasn't *meant* to speak to his father, but how could he not?! Especially when he'd been given no warning about any of this.
The Prince moved over to the top of one of the smoothly sloped bannisters, perching on the edge of it with both of his legs on the outside. He used his hands to push off and began sliding down the bannister pretty quickly. His hair blew backwards with the momentum. He wasn't worried about falling because he'd been doing this since he was old enough to walk - it had worried his parents consistently.
When he reached towards the bottom, Theo pushed his arms downwards to propel himself upwards slightly, jumping off the bannister and practically landing on two feet in front of his father, who sighed.
"Well, that was a regal way to get down the stairs." He slighted, scrunching his face up a little. "Very becoming of a future king."
Theo dismissed the sarcastically charged and slightly rude comment,

being quick to make eye contact with his dad. The man had very traditional dark hair and red coloured horns that were very swirly compared to how Theo's were. He had the same skin tone as his son, but rather broad shoulders - whereas the Prince's were a lot narrower.
"Dad, can we talk about that-"
"No, we cannot. I've made a decision and I want you to respect it."
Theo's eyebrows furrowed together in annoyance and slight anger.
"Yeah, I'd be more than happy to respect your decision if it didn't impact my *whole life*! Maybe if you'd asked me first-"
"Enough." Dyran boomed loudly enough that the guards beside him all straightened, and even Theo recoiled in fear a little. "If I did not think you were ready, I would have chosen for someone else to rule until I thought you were. Despite what you think of yourself, Strythio, I am more than confident in your ability to be king. I love you a lot and it is never my intention to upset you. I believe in you - I only hope you can believe in yourself."
Theo sighed, shoulders deflating. King Dyran only ever spoke to him like that when he was really serious about something. He supposed he could concede.
"Now," The King began again. "Get back up those stairs and show a little excitement, hey? You're going to be crowned king tomorrow, Theo. Most people would be ecstatic." He chided, smiling sympathetically. "Have you told Laine yet?"
The Crown Prince shook his head. "I was just on my way now, actually."
"Well, you'd best do it soon or she'll be upset with you for not giving her adequate time to choose an outfit for the ceremony tomorrow." The King laughed, making the mood flush back to its lightheartedness. "Oh, and I think she has that angel friend of hers over."
"Raphie's my friend too, dad."
King Dyran waved his hand dismissively. "Now, I'll see you tomorrow evening. And pretend this conversation never happened. I'm not meant to speak to you until then."
"Okay. Thanks..." Theo nodded, a little disappointed with the conversation but satisfied for now. He stood watching the King walk away and into a side corridor with his royal guards. Theo knew that he definitely did *not want* his own guards. He turned on the heel of his brown leather buckle boots, beginning to trek back up the stairs with the intention of heading to Laine's room.
Maybe she would be excited for him, even if Theo wasn't.

8

II

Theo placed his hand on the handle of Laine's bedroom door, which was a dark brown but had her name scrawled onto it in a silver paint that she'd done at quite a young age.
He could preemptively hear the chatter of the two girls before he saw them. They were both sitting on the bed; Laine being cross-legged and Raphie having her legs tucked to the side as she leant on an arm. Both of them turned to look at him when he walked in.
"You realise you're meant to knock, right?"
Laine looked up at him through her black pools in place of eyes. She had shoulder-length hair which had been kept a natural brunette colour - slightly lighter than Theo's but still similar enough that you would recognise them as related because of it. Her hair was slightly wavy, and she had two strands at the front which are shorter than the rest of it, and dyed the same deep red as her horns. Her skin was, again, the same pale shade as her brother's, but dotted with significantly less freckles. She had very wide eyes naturally, and an angular jawline complimented by thin lips. She was wearing a pair of dark grey shorts and a lacey, long-sleeved red shirt - the two being connected by a black leather belt. Her outfit was accessorised with red gemstone earrings and subtle wings of eyeliner - the same colour as her septum piercing.
A lot of young girls in the kingdom looked up to her.
"Guess what?" Theo asked, dismissing her comment on his intrusion.
"You're gonna leave us alone?" Raphie gasped sarcastically, bringing one of her hands to sit in front of her mouth in mock surprise.

She was naturally very different-looking to Theo and Laine, simply because she was an angel and they were not. In retrospect, not much actually varies between the way that angels and demons look respectively. It's mainly colour palettes.
Raphie's hair was pretty long - straight and split dyed in a mix of bright mid-blue and pastel pink. Almost like candy floss. When she was a mortal living on Earth, her parents had never let her dye her hair - so she did so with a lot of pride in the afterlife. She had hazel coloured eyes - the kind that she would say were green on about five days of the year, but everyone around her could tell they only had little flecks of green in them if you squint at them for long enough.
Her facial features were illuminated by the glowing halo hoving an inch or two above her head. Most demons would call an angel insane for actually *opting* to spend time in a Kingdom of Hell, especially one as demon-infested as Klaevr. But, Raphie had never considered herself one to conform and she'd found better friends in Laine and other Klaevrian girls (and sometimes Theo if she was in a good mood) than she ever did in The Heavens. Of course, she still lived there, King Dyran not being too fond of hosting an angel in their castle most of the time, but she liked to hang out with the Princess a lot.
Her skin was a very light blue - so much so that it looked grey or white from a distance, and she had very long naturally grown nails. She was wearing a pair of sage green jeans and a light pink t-shirt. Raphie liked to consider the clashing colours more of a 'fashion statement' than most would.
The two girls were each holding a small hand of playing cards. Laine had set hers on the bed in favour of whatever Theo had to say.
"Ha, ha. You wish." The Prince countered, scrunching his nose up a little and pushing the door closed behind him so that he could lean on it. "Now, actually guess."
"I have a feeling that you're going to tell us anyway." Raphie hummed as a response, slightly over the intrusion and just wanting to return to her hand. She was only two turns away from winning.
Laine's bedroom was a very similar size to Theo's area wise. Rather than being a rectangle like her brother's, her's was more of an L-shape, with the part of the room extending around a corner hosting a vanity and clothing rails, whereas her bed sat against the back wall where a window was placed in a similar position to that of Theo's - with the exact same view.

Theo groaned, flapping his arms around a little in exasperation. "This is actually really important news, guys!" He frowned, moving to sit down on the edge of the bed in a semi-sulk.

Laine turned to face him, shifting her cross-legged position slightly. She gasped. "You aren't scared of dogs anymore?! I never thought the day would come-"

She was interrupted when one of her pillows hit her in the head. Laine and Raphie both laughed at Theo's fed-upness. The dog thing was a one-time situation. And, to be fair, it was a big dog! And it had multiple heads!

After a few moments longer of laughter ruminating in the air, both girls stopped.

"Alright, we're done now. What's so important?"

"Father is... retiring," Theo began, the words slowing trailing out of his mouth as if he was learning to pronounce them as he spoke. "Tomorrow."

Laine stared at her brother for a moment. She wore an expression of confusion.

"Retiring as in...?"

Theo placed his hands onto his lap, breathing out anxiously. "As in, my coronation is tomorrow at sunset." He clarified.

Both girls' mouths hung open in shock. Laine practically pounced onto Theo, pushing him off the bed and forcing him to stand. She squealed, her wings extending outwards and wrapping themselves around the Prince along with her arms. "That's amazing, Stryth! Why aren't you bouncing off the walls?!"

She pulled away, her wings moving to sit behind her so that Raphie could now see the two of them again. "Sorry, Theo, but there is no way I'm ever going to be able to look at you and think of you as a powerful authority figure." She teased, standing up to engulf the young man in a hug, similarly to how her friend had.

Theo smiled at the contact, and when they had both stepped away (and Laine was still bouncing on the balls of her feet from the excitement) he spoke.

"Firstly," Theo raised an eyebrow, meeting eyes with his sister. "Don't call me that ever again."

Laine snickered as he continued. "And secondly," He inhaled. "I'll probably be excited this time tomorrow. I only got told like ten minutes ago."

"Awh, and you came to tell us first!" Raphie smiled slightly annoyingly, lightly hitting Theo on the arm.

"Don't be flattered, I'm not sure who else you expected me to tell." Theo countered, placing his hands on his hips and looking to the ground. Laine reached out, grabbing the King-to-be's hand. She giggled, pulling the door to her bedroom open. "If you won't be happy about this, I will for you, you moron."

The corridor was pretty empty - a few staff members were milling around idly. Raphie followed the two of them out. "Laine, whatever you're doing - don't." He warned, still being dragged to the top of the staircase despite his protests.

About twenty to thirty people were in the foyer that the staircase led onto. They all looked busy. Laine smiled, dropping her brother's hand. She cupped her hands over her mouth, her wings still visible to show her status. She was sixteen but still able to project her voice well.

"Hey! Guys!" She called. Everyone milling around turned to look up at her. Theo just about wanted to die from embarrassment on the spot. Raphie smirked, moving to lean against a wall so she wouldn't be in the view of all those looking up.

"My brother is gonna be the King! The King! And he's not even excited about it! Isn't that ridiculous?!"

Half of the spectators looked amused, and the other half looked annoyed to have been distracted from their tasks. Theo placed his hand over his face in embarrassment, and then Laine grabbed the Prince's hand and raised it in the air.

"My brother! Everyone! Crown Prince Theo Virzor, is going to be the King! Can we show some sort of enthusiasm please!" She chorused. When nobody on the bottom floor moved, Laine waved her hands around in the air a little. "Raphie...!" She whispered, looking off to the side.

Raphie's eyes flickered to the two of them. Then, she brought her hands in front of her and started clapping wildly. "Woo! Yeah! I'm over the moon for you! Woo!"

One of the younger castle workers grinned. He joined in with the clapping, which led a few more to do the same.

Laine smiled. "Thank you! Are you happy for yourself yet, Theo?" She still spoke loudly. Theo kept his mouth shut, looking a little angry as he shook his head at her.

She sighed. By this time, almost all of the workers in the foyer were clapping - some adding in their own hollers. They didn't get fun moments like this at work much.

"Cheer the hell up!" She said to Theo. "Make some noise if you think Theo should screw his head on and be delighted about this!"
The crowd made some more noise, and now people from other rooms of the castle had walked out upon hearing the commotion. Laine wrapped her arm around Theo's body, shaking him slightly. He cracked a smile, deciding to concede.
"Fine, I'm so goddamn excited to be the King! So happy!" He mused, replicating the energy of the rest of the room.
"That's the spirit!" She reached in again and hugged her brother. "Thanks everyone! Please keep this same energy for the coronation!" She exclaimed with a curtsy, turning and grabbing Raphie's hand in the one she wasn't pulling Theo with. When they got back into Laine's room, she burst out laughing.
"Oh my God! You should've seen the look on your face, Tee!" Both girls were laughing now. Theo considered brooding and keeping up his sarcastic act. Any self-control he had over that melted away when he saw how happy the two of them were. He let himself smile, laughing with them as he flopped down onto Laine's bed and looked up at the ceiling.
 "Why were you only told today?" Raphie sat up, planting her hands either side of her and looking at Theo through her blue eyes.
"Tradition." Theo scoffed, his position unmoving as he continued to stare at the ceiling.
Laine's eyes lit up. "What are you gonna wear?"
Theo sat up at that, bringing his legs in front of himself to cross them. "To the coronation?"
"No, for your afternoon walk." She slighted, rolling her eyes.
"I don't know- just, whatever they want me to wear, I guess." He shrugged, running one of his hands over the other in nervousness. He hated 'dressing up' for formal events.
"This is the most important day of your life, you realise that, right? Maybe other than your wedding or the birth of your children if you do either." Laine stood, walking over to her dresser and opening the top drawer as he spoke. She pulled out a small necklace and threw it at Theo. "Wear that." She closed the drawer. "Wear it with whatever they make you wear."
Theo looked down at it, running his fingers along the golden chain until his skin brushed over the charm on the end of it. It was a flower with a yellow centre and long, spindly light purple petals branching off it in all directions. The charm itself was only about the size of his thumb - the

kind you wouldn't be able to recognise from any more than two metres away.

"Oh," he breathed, eyes not yet disconnecting from the item itself. "You- who gave you this?"

Laine turned herself around, leaning backwards onto the dresser. "Um, father did. He told me I should wear it at my wedding."

"Why... why didn't he give me anything?" Theo asked, more to himself than the others in the room. His voice was quiet and hurt.

"I'm sure it wasn't personal, Theo. You know how he is about masculinity."

"It's not girly, though. It's a flower."

Laine reached forward and grabbed Theo's hand, letting the necklace stay in the other. "Hey, don't wear it if it's going to make you upset. I just know you want her to be there, and she would've wanted to be there too."

Theo nodded. Laine was, of course, talking about their mother again. Her name was Aster, which had been chosen after the same flower as on the necklace he was holding. It was almost like she could be there. Almost.

"Thank you." He whispered, averting his gaze from the item to look at his sister. She smiled softly, reaching up with her spare arm to pull him in for another hug.

A loud, fake-retching sound came from behind them, and both demons turned to face Raphie, who was looking at them boredly. "I get it, you love each other."

"We tolerate each other." Laine shrugged, smiling as she moved to sit back down. "What are you gonna do now, Theo?"

The Prince didn't reply, placing the necklace in his pocket.

"If you're anxious about tomorrow, you can speak to dad about it surely."

Theo shook his head. "No, he doesn't want me to. Tradition, apparently."

"So, speak to Grandmother." Laine countered smoothly. "She has the exact experience that he does, if not more."

Theo raised his eyebrows. It wasn't a bad idea. "I'd have to travel all the way to T'kota for that, though." He replied. 'T'kota' was what most residents of Klaver used to informally talk about the Kingdom of The Ancient. It was a lot easier to say.

"She'd appreciate the visit. And it's not exactly a strenuous journey to make."

"I suppose not." Theo said.

Raphie uncrossed her legs. "Just don't disappear for the rest of the day. Laine will need you to approve her speech." She laughed, looking at her friend, who paled.

"Oh God, I have to write a speech, don't I?"

Theo smirked. "Yeah, and if it's bad my first act as king will be to banish you." He said, shrugging apologetically before giving a chuckle and opening the door to leave.

"Have fun with your game of cards then." He said, walking out and closing the door. He only walked about ten steps down the corridor before he stopped, leaning against the wall and exhaling.

His right hand found its way into his pocket.

Theo pulled the necklace out, using his thumb to push the clip back, and wrapping it around his left wrist. It draped over the grey marking of a zig-zag on his arm - it was one of his biggest. They were almost like birthmarks, but they glowed when whoever had them was performing magic.

He clipped it into position and shook his arm a little to ensure it wouldn't fall off. Having that security, the heir began heading back to his bedroom, where he entered quickly, just grabbing a small leather day bag and putting in some basic items that he would need to take to visit T'kota. Some money, water, etc.

"Going somewhere?" Nikoliah asked from the doorway, blue-coloured tail swishing behind him cockily. Theo sighed. He must have left the door open. "I hope you aren't running away." He said, amusement in his voice. Theo groaned, turning his head to face the man as he slung his bag over his shoulder.

"I'm going to T'kota for like, an hour. I'll be back in two hours at most; it's not a long journey."

"You'll need a passport if you want to cross kingdoms."

Theo stood. "I don't need a passport, everyone knows who I am."

Sir Nikoliah raised his eyebrows sarcastically. "Alright, alright. I can tell you're not letting this whole 'king' thing make you big headed at all."

Theo sighed, his shoulders deflating. "Fine. I'll take it, don't get too jealous."

Nikoliah snorted. He had only been twelve when he had died, and was now about eighteen (nearly nineteen, he would add) if you were to equate him to human lifespans. Because he was young, he felt a little more comfortable back talking to the Prince a little. Maybe there was another universe where they were friends.

"Are you going to get the train?" The older man asked, running his hand down the side of the sword on his belt.

"Yeah."

"I'll walk you to the station. Your father wouldn't be happy with me if I let you go alone."

They called it a 'train station', mainly because the overwhelming majority of residents of Klaevr used to be mortals, and were accustomed to calling it a train station. It hadn't always been that way, but, after transport like trains had been invented on Earth, the overwhelming majority of ex-mortals in Hell had brought the system there. It was just another thing they had adopted from Earth's culture. Something that had happened a lot to Hell. Theo's grandmother called it gentrification, but Theo just thought that, hey, if having things in the afterlife mirror what they have on earth helps people adjust, then so be it. It was also just a natural process that over time, Hell developed to keep up with the standards of living on Earth.

Theo walked into his ensuite bathroom with a water bottle, turning the tap on to fill it up as he replied. "I don't need babysitting or guarding as part of a five-minute walk."

"You're going to be crowned king tomorrow, My Prince. What if somebody tries to assassinate you?"

Theo left the bathroom with a full water bottle. "If someone tries to assassinate me, Sir Nikoliah, then you can have the throne after I'm gone." He teased, stopping to tilt his head at the soldier, scrunching his nose up as if mocking him.

"I'll come with you so that you can get used to being guarded. As of tomorrow I'm no longer in the service of your father, but yours, so you should probably get used to having me around, kid."

Theo rolled his eyes. "Whatever, you can follow from a distance." He walked out of the room, allowing Nikoliah to turn and shut the door behind him, following the boy out of the corridor, down the stairs and towards the exit of the castle.

III

The sky was a mid-afternoon red, bordering on the darker side. The station that would take Theo to T'kota was quite grand - it being the central transportation method of the kingdom. There was a series of steps leading up to it that were all made up of a white stone. They met an open doorway in front of a large light blue rug that stretched across the large area of the hub. It was quite busy, but not busy enough that it went unnoticed when Theo and Nikoliah walked in.

The whole atmosphere completely faltered - everyone in the building was completely stiff. People would usually get antsy when someone like Sir Nikoliah was around, simply because of his status. So, you can only imagine the shock of some ex-mortals when the Prince, or better yet, *king-to-be* arrived.

Their fear was more than justified. Theo knew he was intimidating to random people, it had always been that way.

The tension broke when a small child, maybe aged 5, with long flowy blonde hair and pale purple-coloured skin approached. An angel, Theo recognised. Probably down here visiting someone. You didn't get many children down in Klaevr - young people who died usually hadn't lived long enough to do anything bad enough to warrant Hell.

She ran up to Theo and wrapped her arms around his legs, squealing. "My momma said it's an honour to touch the King!" She smiled, looking up.

"Not yet, squirt." He laughed, bending down to be eye level with the child.

A few metres away, an older woman was stepping over slowly. She was a demon, unlike the child, and had dark, curly, black coloured hair and deep-grey toned skin.
"Sorry about her," She began sheepishly. Theo looked up and his smile didn't falter.
"No, that's alright."
Theo hoisted the girl up into his arms and stood to make better conversation with the woman.
"And, sorry if she's a little clingy. It's only her second day here."
The girl nodded. "I like it here better than up there, cus momma's down here!" She said, referring to her placement in The Heavens.
Theo frowned, ignoring the girl for a moment and looking to her mother. "I'm sorry you were separated." He said softly.
"That's alright - not your fault. I just hope they take care of her up there."
"They do." Theo nodded.
The truth was that he didn't know first hand. He'd never been to any of The Heavens, but he'd heard from Raphie and various other angels that it's nice. Nicer than Klaevr, at least.
The rules were that angels could come down to any of the Kingdoms of Hell whenever they wanted, regarded they had the right passports and everything. They often formed little charity groups when coming down, and, although every demon knows they mean well, it's really patronising. Demons aren't allowed to pay visits to any of The Heavens. It had always been that way. Something to do with safety or biology or whatever. The Prince had always wanted to change that rule when he became king, but it'd take a lot of debate with many people of much higher power than him.
Nikoliah cleared his throat.
"I'm going to head back to the castle, My Prince. Have a safe journey, alright?"
"Um, yeah, yeah I will, thank you." Theo stuttered, yanked from his thoughts somewhat abruptly.
He turned back to the woman, who he handed the child back to as they continued to talk.
"Where are you headed then, Prince Theo?
"Um, I was hoping to get to T'kota."
"Ah, see, we're going to Stonbrin. Leila's grandfather is there and she hasn't seen him yet."
Theo nodded. "Yeah, I hear it's nice over there. ...Alright, well, I best be going. It was nice to meet you."

He began to walk away, but found that his arm was grabbed. He turned his head and made eye contact with the woman again.
"Theo?"
"Yeah?"
"You need to do something about these angel-favouring legislations once you're coronated." The woman spoke solemnly before turning and striding off, child in arms.
Theo stood for a moment longer. He nodded, more to himself than anything, and began to walk over to where he would board his train. Previous monarchs had never done anything about the inequality, simply because it always seemed too big of an issue to deal with. Maybe it was. Speaking of previous monarchs, it was only a short train journey before Theo found himself standing on the doorsteps of his grandmother's house.
Wrapping two hands around the strap of his satchel, he stood for a minute anxiously. This kingdom was peaceful - almost eerily so.
On his walk from the train station to the tall, pillared building towering over him, multiple people had stopped him for a conversation. A few had heard the news of his coronation tomorrow, and wanted to congratulate him.
Theo really liked how casual T'kota was. Hardly anyone bats an eye when the Crown Prince walks through the centre of the town, nobody bows or salutes or is overly-formal with him. Theo assumed it's because they're all older and have had plenty of time to respect people when they were in their primes. Despite that, most people are very kind.
Most people.
Theo hadn't seen his grandmother in a few years. When he knocked, it took a few minutes for the door to open. Cordelia was a tall, broad-shouldered woman with incredibly pale white skin - accompanied by dirty-blonde curly hair that fell to her ears. And, much like her grandchildren and their father, her eyes were complete pools of black, with turquoise-teal horns.
She frowned.
"I see you've finally decided to visit. What's the occasion?"
"Hey Grandma, it's really good to see you." He smiled. "I was wondering if I could come in-"
"You may not." She interrupted quickly. "But, if there's something you'd like to talk about I can go and grab my coat and we can walk to a nice cafe or similar. How does that sound?" Her voice was quick and dripping with sugar. Lively and clear, despite her age.

Theo nodded. "Yeah, that's great."
Cordelia smiled and abruptly slammed the door, making Theo flinch backwards a little. His eyes downcast to the floor and he took a few steps away, backing off the porch and turning to lean against the outside wall. The sky was still the same red shade as it was earlier, but it was now populated by considerably more clouds, so much so that it almost felt dark.
The door opened again, and the woman was now wearing a long, light blue coat and had a small handbag draped over her shoulder. She began to walk and whistled for Theo to follow, which he did, scampering behind like a puppy being dragged on a leash.
When he did catch up to her and her long legs, he had to walk at an exaggerated pace just to keep in par.
"So, what's going on that makes you so inclined to pay me a visit after two years?"
Theo sighed. "I'm sorry I didn't visit. I've been really busy with training and all."
"I'm somehow not convinced." She replied quickly. Then, she laughed a little. "I get it, Strythio, I do. You're young and free. You don't have time for decaying old things like your grandmother. But, I encourage you to remember that I was young once too. I got up to just as much mischief as you have been, if not more."
She kept walking at her brisk pace, but turned to face Theo while doing so.
"And one day you'll be old and your grandchildren will ignore you as karma."
Theo grumbled a little. "I'm sorry, I'll visit more, but I really need your help with something right now."
"Let's wait until we actually get sat down at a cafe first, hm? Just make small talk with me for a moment. How is Elaine? Please tell me she didn't dye her hair that horrendous shade of green she wanted to last time we spoke."
"Laine is fine and you know she dislikes the 'E'. And, no, she didn't... but she did get a few piercings. Just ears and septum."
"I suppose I can live with that."
The woman placed a hand on her hip. "I just don't get what it is with your generation and shortening your names. It makes you sound like mortals."
"You say that like it's a bad thing."

"Maybe I just favour tradition. Or, traditional names. Your name is so beautiful, for instance, but you keep cutting the first four letters off. For what? Convenience?"

Theo shrugged. "Maybe, I don't know. I think the advice I would give you here is that if someone is happy with their name it's none of your business."

"Yikes, you're in a touchy mood, huh?" She observed.

"Just a little stressed today." Theo replied quietly.

The streets were relatively empty as they walked through them, considering that it was that awkward time between lunch and dinner where cafes weren't all that populated. The one they ended up finding didn't have any customers other than them.

The man working at the cafe floundered over to their table. "Ooh, a young'en! And how old are you, young man?"

Theo smiled. "I'm eighteen."

"And I take it that this is your grandma here?"

Cordelia smirked. "Unfortunately."

They made easy work of ordering drinks and pastries. The interior of the cafe was homely - shelves lined with all kinds of menus and spices and plants. After a few minutes, the owner of the cafe disappeared into the back and their conversation resumed pleasantly.

"So, why've you visited then?"

"I assumed you would've already been told."

Cordelia shook her head. "Your father doesn't tell me much these days. Is anyone dead?"

"He's retiring." Theo replied quickly, wanting to get it over with.

The ex-monarch's eyes widened significantly. "Really?"

"Yeah."

"That's a shame, he has at least another decade in him."

Theo stayed silent, staring at the table.

"I see, so, you must have found out this morning and Dyran won't talk to you, so you've come to me for advice about this? You're being crowned tomorrow?"

Theo nodded. "Yeah, pretty much. I would've liked more time to prepare if I'm honest."

Cordelia sighed. "Argh, come here. Let me give you a hug."

She stood, and so did Theo. They met in the middle of the table, and Cordelia wrapped her arms around her grandson, who lent his whole body into hers and melted to the touch. The older woman extended her wings and wrapped them around his body along with her arms.

Laine had done the exact same thing earlier, but it somehow felt nicer coming from his grandmother. He felt safe, which wasn't a feeling he had the luxury of experiencing much.
"I know it's scary, Theo. But I know you're going to do amazingly."
They broke apart and Theo smiled. "Thank you." He choked.
Once sat back down, Cordelia smiled as if nostalgic. "You know, I was only told the morning of my coronation that it was happening."
"What? Why?"
"My parents had wanted to tell me the day before, but I had gone to a friend's house for the night. It was the most stressful twelve hours of my life, but it was certainly worth it for how much joy being the Queen gave me."
"What was your coronation like?" Theo asked quickly.
"Beautiful." She replied. "I was only young then, so I didn't appreciate it as much as I should have. The actual ceremony was very quick, but I then had to mill around and socialise for hours on end."
"Yeah, I'm not looking forward to that."
"Trust me," She reassured. "There will be queues of people wanting to speak to you, and you won't have to do much of the talking yourself, just nod and agree."
The cafe owner walked past and placed their food in front of them, to which Theo thanked the man and he then left once more.
"Do you have your eye on anyone?" Cordelia asked while sipping her coffee.
"Huh?"
"You're going to be expected to marry someone pretty soon."
Oh. Right.
"You never did." He argued.
"Yeah, and I went through Hell because of it. Your father will arrange someone for you if you don't get into a serious relationship soon."
Theo's eyes glanced to the door.
"I doubt that. Wasn't he super penalised in childhood for not being born of a marriage? Surely he would understand."
"That's exactly why he's going to want you married, Theo." She hummed. "Dyran doesn't want any kids of yours to be treated the way he was."
Theo cleared his throat uncomfortably.
"Are you going to come to the coronation?"
"Of course I will. I'll attend just to spite those who dislike me."
Theo laughed. "Tomorrow at sunset, alright?"
Cordelia nodded. "Noted. Tomorrow at sunset."

"Tomorrow at sunset!" Laine groaned, flopping down backwards onto her bed. "And I'm yet to figure out anything about how it's going to go!"
Theo raised his eyebrows, standing a few metres away from her - arms crossed. "Can I at least read your speech?"
"No," She pouted. "It's going to be a surprise."
"Oh God, what have you written?"
"Nothing bad, don't worry. How was grandma?"
Theo snorted. "Same old."
"Unsurprising... What are you wearing tomorrow then?"
Laine sat up and crossed her legs underneath her. It was just her and Theo now, together in Laine's bedroom as they were most evenings, usually playing board games or something, but tonight discussing the arrangements of tomorrow.
"I don't know, probably the same thing I usually wear for those formal events that dad drags us to."
Laine stood up abruptly. "There is no way I am letting you get away with that. We'll have to figure something out."
Theo ran a hand down his face. "I'm more than certain that there'll be tailors with an array of stupid-looking outfits for me. We'll let Jaymie and Kougan figure it out."
"Hey," Laine warned playfully. "I'll have you know that their outfits are nicer than whatever you throw on yourself in the morning."
Theo looked up and down himself, wearing the same dark-coloured ensemble that he was this morning. He gave a playful "Rude!" in response to his sister before sitting down on the bed next to her.
"You think I'm gonna be a good king, don't you?"
"Yeah, of course I do. Why do you ask? Did someone say something?"
Theo let his head fall into his right arm, which he propped up on his knees. "No, no, they didn't. I just... It feels like a lot of pressure."
Laine wrapped an arm around his shoulders. "Of course it feels like a lot, because it *is* a lot. That doesn't mean you won't be good at it." She reassured.
The Princess was never the biggest fan of emotions. Of showing them, of consoling others when they showed them - the lot. She'd found that it was easier to keep your head down and get through life, which was probably true, but not necessarily healthy.
Theo snapped his head to make eye contact with his sister.

"When are you gonna be getting married, Laine?"
She laughed. "I'm sixteen, Theo. Seventeen next month. I won't be thinking about that for a while." She replied, stretching out the world 'while' for some kind of attempted dramatic affect as she subverted the question. "Why do you ask? Have you got your eye on a pretty-looking girl?"
Theo laughed nervously. "No, that's the problem. I'm worried Dad's going to arrange something if it doesn't happen naturally."
Laine sighed. "I mean, our parents were arranged and they turned out fine. All the girls from this kingdom are generally lovely, Thee."
Theo swallowed. "Would dad be upset if I didn't marry a girl?"
"I can't tell you what he'd be thinking," She paused. "But, his own mother never married and he turned out fine so-"
"No, I mean-" Theo interrupted his sister, stopping for a few seconds. "I mean if I married someone that wasn't a girl."
"*Oh.*" Laine pursed her lips. "A boy?"
Theo swallowed. "Yeah." He breathed, feeling so incredibly stupid for even bringing it up. Laine looked deep in thought for a moment.
"I'm not sure... *what* our father would have to say about that, but you know that you don't need his support, right?"
"Yeah, I guess."
Laine rolled her eyes. "You're so stupid." She said affectionately, bringing one of her arms to ruffle his hair. "Stupid for caring what our dad thinks." She said, and then after a brief pause, she looked at the bedsheets.
"Thank you for telling me."
Theo rolled his eyes. "Don't feel too honoured." He countered, leaning in a bit as she gingerly wrapped her right arm around his shoulders to hug him.
She smiled, and Theo felt content. He was lucky to have a sister like her. He stood and exhaled loudly, glancing out over the darkened sky. "Is it too late to go to the kitchen?" He asked, glancing back at his sister.
"Not too late to *sneak* into the kitchen. And steal some food." She smirked, standing. "Come on, Theo." She said to her apprehensive looking brother, standing and opening the door to her room. "One last night of being mischief-making kids?"
And Theo could only follow her.

IV

The Prince was all-but swarmed with attention from the moment he woke up the next morning.

He was unpleasantly awoken by knocks to his bedroom door, and ended up having about five minutes to get ready for the day before he was supposed to be doing things. It would've at least been nice if someone had told him what time he had to be up so he could've prepared himself a little.

Theo supposed it didn't matter now, as he hurried himself down the stairs dressed only in a pair of dark-coloured cargo shorts, an emerald green tank top and his signature fingerless brown leather gloves - the same material as his boots.

His outfit meant that the markings along his arms and shoulders were very visible, which did get him a lot of stares. They were only a few shades darker than his skin tone, and all pureblooded demons had magical markings. Theo's were pretty excessive and he was often insecure about them, which was weird because most people were incredibly intimidated by them.

"Ah! There you are, perfect timing. Try on this jacket for me."

One of the stylists all-but threw a dark blue coat-looking thing into Theo's arms the minute he walked into the room. He was very familiar with all the castle staff, so knew this woman as Jaymie. She was in charge of pretty much everything that Theo and Laine wore to any formal events (much to Laine's dismay, as they didn't quite agree on most fashion points).

Theo laughed a little at the suddenness, but slipped his arms into the sleeves of the jacket nonetheless. It was a little baggy, but could definitely work.

Jaymie groaned. "I told you it'd be too big, he's only a skinny little thing!" She communicated to one of the other stylists. There were about five in the room, all but the two of them in question pre-occupied in something else.

The woman turned to Theo and placed two hands on each of his shoulders. He wobbled a little - it was far too early for this.

"We're trying to find measurements for if we want to put you in a coat of some kind."

"Which we're not going to do!" The other stylist called from across the room, hanging some clothes on a rail. "Because it would look stupid." He clarified, turning to face the two of them and smiling.

"He's in a bad mood." Jaymie nodded, taking her hands off Theo and walking over to her desk.

The other stylist, Kougan, could only roll his eyes.

Theo smiled at their playful dynamic, and his smile only widened when his sister walked in from a side door. "Okay, be honest." Laine began, bringing her hands in front of her as if touching a wall at a slant. "Do I look like one of those mannequins in the window of a party-costume shop?"

She was wearing a toned-down fuchsia- coloured dress with an accentuated waist and skirt going down to her ankles. The top of the dress had very thin spaghetti straps, and a criss-cross of the straps at the back.

Black platformed boots matched an array of bracelets up and down her arms, as well as thin wings of eyeliner. Theo thought she looked really good, but he must have stared in silence too long for Laine's liking.

"I knew I did! Argh!" She exclaimed, turning and marching herself out of the room.

At this point, all the stylists apart from Jaymie and Kougan had cleared out. It was only a few seconds after Laine left that they continued their rambling.

"Do you know why this outfit is so exciting for us, Theo?"

"Um," He stuttered. "Because most of the kingdom is going to see it?"

"No!" Jaymie replied. "Well, yes, but that's not the reason I was after." She approached him, leading him onto one of the room's sofas and sitting beside him. "It's because we get to do stuff with your arms!"

Ah, right.

This was another thing related to the markings. They were a very recognisable symbol of power or status, and so, when attending an event in which you are not the centre of attention, it was considered very disrespectful to have visible markings.

Every single formal event (be it a meeting or party or whatnot) Theo and Laine had *always* had to keep their arms covered out of respect for the host or person the event was for. Of course, for the coronation tonight, Laine would still be expected to have her markings covered. It was typical for males to do this with long sleeves, and for females to wear elbow-length gloves, or higher ones if their marking presented themselves as such.

However, this time, Laine really wanted to wear something sleeveless, so had asked Theo in the kitchen last night if he'd be okay with it. Of course, she'd have to have her markings covered with makeup or something so that they weren't visible, but it was something she thought she should ask Theo about anyway.

Naturally, he'd said he was more than okay with that. He wasn't at all worried about his sister 'disrespecting' him by showing that she has magical abilities. If Theo was honest, he thought it was a stupid expectation.

"You have so much stylistic potential, but it's always been smouldered by sleeves. Today is the day of liberation for you, young man." Kougan kneeled in front of Theo and placed a hand on one of his knees.

"I've worn sleeveless shirts before, you realise that, right? I'm wearing one right now."

"Not in front of the entire kingdom, you haven't. Most people have never seen how beautiful your arms are. It is now our duty to make sure people do."

Theo smiled while sighing playfully. "Alright then. What did you have in mind?"

A whole three hours (and a lot of arguments between Jaymie and Kougan that Theo did *not* want to interrupt) later, his outfit was finished.

As he eyed himself up and down in the mirror, he had to admit that he did look good.

The outfit consisted of a black-coloured dress shirt with the top two buttons undone, and a deep green satin scarf-tie-whatever-it-was wrapped around the collar and draping about half way down his torso. It was the same colour as his horns, tail and wings (if he decided to show them at any point this evening). The sleeves of the shirt were made of a very thin, white - practically clear - mesh which allowed every inch of his arms from the mid-upper arm down to show, only stopping to turn back into the black fabric of the shirt at the cuffs of the sleeves, where he was wearing a mixture of tight, silver bracelets and rings layered on each of his fingers.

Well, only his right wrist had multiple bracelets. He'd asked Jaymie and Kougan if we could leave his left wrist plain and only have the bracelet with his mother's symbolism on it showing. He wanted it to be effective. There was also a pair of two silver necklaces hanging around his neck, and the whole look was accompanied by some black semi-formal jeans. A little bit of himself.

Theo was also wearing an elaborate belt with silver chains on it, and although the belt itself wasn't visible under the untucked shirt, the chains spilled down the side of his legs. He'd also been given some white leather platform boots (that he was totally keeping after this, by the way) with similar silver chains to match the white of the sleeves of his shirt. Jaymie wanted him to wear white and green coloured eyeliner or some sort of eyeshadow at the least, but apparently it wasn't something that would be 'appropriate' as Nikoliah had told them after being sent to ask the King about it.

Either way, he was pretty happy with how it turned out. Apparently, so was Raphie, who had arrived at some point and was frequenting between Theo and Laine's dressing-rooms.

"You look so good!" She smiled, squealing as she ran up to Theo and hugged him tightly.

"Ack! Get away, you're going to crease his shirt." Jaymie scolded, using her hands to push Raphie away from Theo. She pouted.

Theo laughed softly. "How does Laine look?"

Raphie smiled. "She looks amazing, you'll have to wait until tonight to see though." She teased, ending her sentence on a purposeful high note as she walked out of the room.

"Oh God, look at the time. Right, well, you'd best let me hang this stuff up for you so you can head off to wherever you're meant to be next. Busy day for you and all." Kougan said, not actually looking to check the time anywhere as he said it.

Theo nodded. He felt a little overwhelmed at the sudden influx in attention. After changing back into regular clothes, he managed to sneak himself back into his bedroom - even if he knew the solitude wouldn't last long.

He shut the door behind him and breathed out heavily. He was already exhausted. It wasn't at all that he didn't appreciate all this, or appreciate

Jaymie and Kougan's presence. It was just... A *lot*. A lot in a very little amount of time.

Well, now he did have a little more of that, Theo supposed he could change into something more ideal. He decided that he'd keep the shorts, but had now shown his markings off too much and changed into a long-sleeve shirt. He felt a lot more comfortable this way, too.

The next task of his day was 'approving' the decorations and set up of the dining hall. There would be a lot of guests for the main ceremony, but, much like a wedding, there was going to be a meal afterwards. The meal would only have about two hundred people in attendance - family and people of importance from other kingdoms.

It was going to be a big deal.

The actual event was taking place in a wing of the castle that was literally only used for this type of thing. The last time it had been used was for the 'funeral' of Theo and Laine's mother. Although there was never any conclusive evidence as to where she was, most people accepted that she wasn't coming back after a few years of her being missing, and so, a funeral was held. She was the Queen, after all - it was only customary. Theo hadn't been very old, maybe five. He didn't remember it well. He remembered it being a bad day, because his father was very upset, and that had meant that there was no chance of play-time before bed.

To be blissfully ignorant, oh, what Theo would give.

He felt disturbed when he entered the event hall. It was a little strange, he hadn't been here in a very long time, since there was another, smaller hall for less important things.

Only three things ever happened in this one. Weddings, coronations and funerals. It was an incredibly large room. The kind of thing you'd envision a typical church to look like, but on a much bigger scale. There were stone pillars along all the edges, and rows of benches resting atop a mahogany-coloured floor. At the front of the room were four thrones. Two next to each other in the centre, both quite large and full of ornate patterns and gemstones.

The one on the right was traditionally the King's, and the one on the left the Queen's. Of course, only one of the two had been in use for the past few years. And when Cordelia was Queen, only hers was ever used. On either side of the two larger thrones were slightly smaller versions, meant to the Princes and princesses. At this point in time, there were only two, because there were only two heirs. If Dyran were to have another child, another would be added, and when he was growing up as an only child, there was only one, on his mother's side.

There was a large glass chandelier hanging above the thrones, illuminating the whole room. Just the thought of all the chairs that would be filled made him feel anxious. It was now about midday, and guests were due to arrive from 5pm, for a sunset and ceremony beginning at around 7:30pm.

The atmosphere of the room was making him tense, so Theo decided to leave and head into the dining area. It was a short walk along the corridor for convenience, and inside the space, a lot of workers were milling around. One of them saw him enter and immediately dropped onto a knee and bowed their head.

"Thank you for coming, Prince Theo."

The room was full of round tables with white tablecloths, half of the vases with roses dyed dark-green in them. It was a pretty consistent theme that the same shade as Theo's wings was used for accentuation. This was always done when a specific demon was the centre of attention. The other half of the vases had red roses in them - the same colour as the current king's wings, since it was also his retirement ceremony.

"That's alright, thank you for, um, you know, organising all this."

The employee smiled. "Of course! This is the most exciting thing that's happened around here in a long time." They replied, standing to now be eye level with Theo. The room was decorated with banners and candles. If it were up to the Prince, he would not have decorated it so traditionally. He supposed it's what his dad wanted.

The person must have noticed Theo's gaze, and turned to look too. "It's nice right? Your father likes it, so at least we have his approval."

Theo nodded. "Yeah, yeah. It's really nice."

Two minutes of idle conversation later, Theo managed to worm his way out of the social interaction and was now traversing the corridors in the general direction of the castle gardens. Along the way, he managed to run into Sir Nikoliah, who looked very stressed - holding a lot of mixed fabric, papers and a few metal items.

He stopped. "Please don't salute me or anything because I will have to do it back and everything I'm holding will go all over the floor."

Theo smirked. "Dad isn't treating you well today?"

Nikoliah kept walking and Theo followed as the older man replied. "He's stressed. Giving me a lot of grief for random things that he wouldn't usually care about." He complained. "I just, argh, I feel like I'm going to get all the blame if anything goes wrong today."

"Of course, King Dyran is a great man. He changed my life and all, but he does expect *a lot*."

Theo raised his eyebrows. "I'd lower your voice if you're going to disrespect the King on his retirement day." He smirked.

Sir Nikoliah groaned, stopping for a moment. "I'm being unprofessional, forget it."

"Where are you sitting tonight?" Theo asked quickly, prompting the man to continue walking as they chatted.

"I'm not." Nikoliah responded bluntly. "I work for you, I'm not your friend. I wasn't invited."

"Oh." Theo hadn't assumed that he wouldn't get an invite. "You'll be around though, right?"

"I'm in charge of security. Meaning that it's incredibly likely I'll be standing outside the venue for the whole evening."

Theo placed his hands into his pockets and hunched over a little. "Well, you're in charge, right?"

"Much to most of my staff's dismay." The soldier replied quietly. He was pretty young, and so, most of the people he was in charge of were older than him - some by decades; some by centuries. Nikoliah wasn't exactly sure why he'd been appointed his position as King Dyran's right-hand, but to be fair, he had earned it. He'd spend pretty much all of his life (or lack of, rather) in Klaevr. It was a very big kingdom, so naturally there was work outside of the castle, but he'd ended up here. The first job he'd had in the castle was as a dish-washing boy, but Nikoliah was quickly able to work his way up the ranks and into the throne room of the King.

"Then, get them to do it." Theo suggested easily.

"I wish it were that simple." The soldier replied. "It's fine, really. Word travels quickly amongst us castle workers, so I'm sure I'll hear all about it from the catering staff. They do like to gossip."

Theo followed Nikoliah into a side room, where he placed his things down on a desk and began sorting through them. He turned around. "I need to get some stuff organised." He placed a hand on the handle of his sword. "My Prince, if I don't see you before tonight, then good luck."

Theo smiled somewhat fakely. "Thanks." He replied, turning and continuing his journey down the corridor towards the gardens. Rows of flowers spouted from dead grass, lining the edges of the rectangular area. Once outside, Theo stretched his wings out and pushed his shoulders backwards. It was nice to be able to do that, since the corridors were often narrow and his wings were prone to scaring people sometimes.

Finally having a moment of peace, Theo sat down on the grass and crossed his legs. He crossed his legs and placed both of his hands onto the grass. He closed his eyes and tilted his head upwards, spinning his wrists around and dragging them upwards. As he did so, his body rose around a metre above the ground. The glowing outline of his jagged markings were illuminated from under his shirt, which also created a slight emission of light coming from the young man.

Theo sighed contently, opening his eyes and bringing his hands in front of him. He twisted his hands and formed a ball of golden light, the same shade as the markings that were very visible through his shirt. The light created a lot of warmth. Theo felt content for a moment. He loved getting time to himself, where he could ascend into the air and forget everything on the ground.

Considering the absolute chaos that would become of the evening, Theo actually felt pretty peaceful here.

V

All the seats of the hall were filled, and people were crowded at the back of the space too. Theo watched everyone from the backstage area, behind the thrones. They couldn't see him but he could see them.
The front row was full of the most important people. Monarchs and their children from other kingdoms, people ranked highly in King Dyran's government, and, most intimidatingly, angels. Only three or four were in attendance - and they were powerful. The current king and queen of Menphe (the Kingdom of Heaven that Raphie was from), Raphie herself and a very strong political figure from Menphe, who Theo *did not like*. He was a very firm believer that angels and demons were *supposed* to be separated and different from each other. He was pretty well known for his incredibly strong views. If there was anyone that the future king needed on his side to make changes, it was this man. His name was Lord Beckett.
Theo shook him from his thoughts, turning away from where he could see the crowd and walking back to find someone he was familiar with. The ceremony was due to start in only a few minutes time, and the Prince didn't think he'd ever been more stressed.
He looked around for a few minutes and was able to find his sister. She had her hair straightened so that it now fell to touch her shoulders rather than being slightly above them. She was wearing a beautiful, deep red silk ball gown with a v-shaped neckline and thin straps. The skirt was flowy but reached to her mid-calves in the kind of shape you'd expect a Disney Princess cake-topper to have.

Her arms were very much visible, but her markings were not - covered by some kind of makeup that Theo didn't care about enough to think about. She wore a lot of silver jewellery, the same kind as Theo's, and had changed her piercing out to an equally as nice silver version of the one she usually had in.
She blinked at him through her accentuated wings of eyeliner, smiling also. This was the first time that either of them had seen what each other were wearing. It was pretty clear that Jaymie and Kougan had coordinated their outfits to have small parts of eachother's in them without them looking too 'matching'.
Neither of them said anything as they looked eachother up and down. Then, Theo suddenly found himself wrapped in Laine's arms. "You look amazing, Theo." She said, pulling away from the hug and snorting. "Well, a bit extra but you make it work."
"You look really good too. I can tell you aren't trying to upstage me or anything." He commented sarcastically. Laine rolled her eyes.
"Whatever."
"There you two are!"
They both turned to face their father, who was dressed in his usual dark-coloured suit that he wore for formal events, as well as his crown. He glanced them both up and down for a moment before smiling.
"We need to get to the back doors so we can head in. Are you ready?"
Theo didn't feel like the situation would change if he said no, but luckily he didn't have to because Laine answered for him.
"Yeah, we're ready."
Theo walked somewhat uncomfortably behind his dad, shoulders tensed. This would work very similarly to weddings in that the three of them would walk down the centre of the pews and then take their positions on their thrones.
"This is the first day of the rest of your life." Dyran said, walking pretty briskly as he spoke.
"I know." He replied softly.
When they reached the entrance to the hall, the doors were closed and it was just the three of them, as well as Sir Nikoliah, who was standing outside on guard.
The King straightened. "Nikoliah, come here."
He turned his attention to them, quickly making his way over to the King - having to ignore the other two for the time being, even though he really did want to let Princess Laine know that she looked really nice.

Nikoliah moved down to a one-kneed bowing position. "Sir?" He asked, looking up.

Dyran smiled. "Well, this is the last time you will ever be in my service, and you have been for a good few years now, so I just wanted the opportunity to thank you for your loyalty before I hand my kingdom and your service over to my son."

He nodded, standing up and reaching his hand out for the King to shake. "It's been a pleasure, Your Majesty."

The soldier then returned to his post, squaring his shoulders back and having his right hand resting on his weapon like before.

Laine was the first to enter the room, as it was supposed to be in order of status, from the least powerful to the most powerful. The doors to the event hall opened, Laine supposed that it was now or never.

She walked into the room, and all of the eyes were immediately on her. Some people started to cheer and clap for her, mostly younger girls that saw her as their idol. She grinned widely, and it took her about twenty seconds for her to reach her throne on the left side of the main two.

Once she was sat down, King Dyran gave his son a reassuring pat on the back and sort of pushed him inside.

Theo felt like his heart stopped for a moment. Everyone had their eyes on him and it felt a little claustrophobic. He made anxious eye contact with Laine, who smiled widely and beckoned him forward with her right hand. Theo brought his hands behind his back and held them there as he was meant to when walking. Much like they did for Laine, there was clapping from the people in the audience. Theo even thought he heard a few wolf-whistles.

It was hardly any time at all before he was sitting on his throne, on the opposite side as Laine.

Once the noise had died down, the whole hall stayed completely silent for a further thirty seconds. This was something that always happened when the royal family made appearances. After Theo, it was supposed to be his mother's turn to enter, and although she wasn't with them, they all still had a thirty second silence after the Crown Prince's entrance as if she was here.

Theo stared at the ground for the whole time, trying not to let it get to him that his mother wasn't attending his coronation. It just felt like it was being unnecessarily highlighted.

He didn't have to feel that way for long, because his father entered the room. This time, when the man entered, practically everyone in the room stood to clap for him. To be fair, he had served the kingdom for centuries. Once the man had sat down, it took a good ten seconds for everyone to have sat back down too.

Theo fidgeted with his shirt sleeves anxiously as his father stood again. "I'll make this short and sweet as I'm sure everyone wants to get on with eating and I'll deliver a much longer speech later with the rest." He said, addressing the kingdom for his last time as monarch.

"I did not serve this kingdom very long compared to my ancestors before me, but, considering that my eldest has recently come of age and my rule has been quite eventful, it feels appropriate for me to pass my legacy on." He turned to look at Theo, who was watching him intently.

"I think that the last thing I have to say is thank you to all of my staff and thank you to the people of this kingdom for putting up with me." He joked, and a few people laughed. Theo smirked slightly, a little too stressed to give any other sort of response. Theo saw his grandmother in the front row, on the left, and she appeared to give a quiet chuckle.

"Okay, well, without further ado, I suppose it's about time that I hand you over to the officiant, and my kingdom over to my son, Theo."

The audience clapped, and it sounded out incredibly loudly in Theo's ears. The officiant was a very old man, who had been the person to coronate Dyran *and* his mother. He walked to the front of the elevated platform, standing in the front of the thrones with the current king on his right. Beckoning for Theo to stand on his left, he cleared his throat.

"Today we see the leadership of Klaevr passed on from King Dyran Virzor to Crown Prince Strythio Virzor." He began, smiling and then turning to Dyran.

"The kingdom thanks you for your service." He said, placing his hands on either side of the crown atop the King's head. "I hereby relinquish you from your monarchy duties."

Theo turned his head to look over to Laine. She smiled in over-exaggerated encouragement and stuck both her thumbs up at her brother.

"I can't help but remember your baby shower, Prince Strythio. It was held in this very room, and now, here you are eighteen years later." The officiant said, holding the crown in front of him now.

Dyran smiled to himself a little. It was kind of reassuring for Theo.

"But, I digress." The man sighed happily. "Do you promise to uphold the duties, standards and responsibilities of Klaevr and the position of king ruling over it for as long as you decide to keep the throne?"

Theo swallowed, eyes dancing around the crowd as ran his thumb and index finger over the aster-flower charm on his bracelet.

"Yeah, yes, I do."

"And do you promise to act in the best interest of the kingdom, to protect and serve your people for as long as you keep the throne?"

"I do, yeah." Theo nodded once more.

The officiant grinned widely, placing the crown on Theo's head. It rested nicely in-between his horns, and the first thought the newly crowned king had was that it was really heavy. He hoped he wouldn't be expected to wear it much.

"Then I am honoured to coronate you, Strythio Virzor, king of Klaevr."

Theo had been the monarch for about thirty minutes and he was pretty sure he was already exhausted by it.

He looked around the dining room and exhaled in relief. At this current point in time, nobody was approaching him with the intent to talk or congratulate him. It wasn't at all that he wasn't grateful for people's interest, but he was just *so* tired.

He watched his father laughing while speaking to Lord Beckett on the other side of the hall. Theo reached into the centre of the table he was sitting at and refilled his wine glass, hooking his hand under it and bringing the alcohol to his lips.

"Easy there, tiger. You might wanna slow down with that stuff." Laine planted her hands on Theo's shoulders from behind him, bending her torso around the right side of his chair and looking at him judgmentally.

"I'm the King, I can do what I want." He replied lazily, setting the glass back down in front of him. "You're just jealous that you can't."

Laine pulled her chair from the table (it was a round table with five seats, and she was sitting next to Theo) and sat on it, tilting it to be facing her brother's chair.

"We're going to start the speeches in like five minutes, and when that happens you'll be stuck sitting here for a while. So, may I suggest that you get up and start voluntarily talking to people? You look like you don't want to be here."

"Just tired." Theo declared, turning his head effortlessly to face Laine. "But, fine. Only if you promise to come with and assist me when my social battery inevitably runs out."

She nodded, grabbing his wrist. "Alright then, up we go."

They walked a few metres across the carpeted floor before their father caught their attention. All of the other guests were still mingling, and Dyran approached with Lord Beckett behind him.

"Children, come here for a moment." He said, gesturing widely with his whole arm for them to proceed. Theo and Laine shared a knowing glance. This guy was trouble. Nonetheless, they walked themselves over, and Lord Beckett smiled. He was an average height man with light bluey-purple toned skin and a glowing halo hovering atop his head. He had a stubble beard and shaven, light-coloured hair.

"Amadeus, these are my prodigies: Theo and Laine." Dyran said, as if the man beside him would have absolutely no clue who they were and hadn't just sat through an entire ceremony centering them.

Lord Amadeus Beckett was not a nice man. Theo had heard some of his speeches, and had seen the effects of his ideology first hand. He was not a nice man, and did not deserve the newly crowned king's respect in his eyes. Theo wondered what his father saw in this guy.

He'd been knighted as a Lord after twenty years of working his way up the ranks of Menphe's political system, as a thank you for 'dedicating his life' to the kingdom.

Lord Beckett smiled, reaching his hand out towards Theo. "It's nice to meet you, King Theo."

Theo looked at the man's hand, outstretched for him to shake. He looked to his father, who shot him a dangerous look - fire resting behind his glare.

Finally Theo looked Lord Beckett directly in the eyes, and after a few seconds of disrespectful indecision, he shook the man's hand. "Yes, it's alright to meet you as well."

The angel narrowed his eyes, pulling his hand back after a moment and re-applying his smile. "Of course, the same applies to you, Princess Laine. It's a pleasure to meet you."

Laine shook his hand easily. "You too."

Amadeus tilted his head towards Dyran. "Do you at all mind if I speak to Theo alone for a moment?"

Theo looked over to his dad quickly and began to rapidly shake his head. "Yes, of course." The ex-king replied. "Come on Laine, we shall go and get ourselves sat down for the speeches to begin."

"Follow me then." Beckett said smoothly, spinning on a heel and marching himself to a corner of the room that was very difficult to see from any other place. Theo did *not* like the implications of being dragged somewhere unseen. Despite himself, he followed.

He felt incredibly cornered, leant against one of the marble walls - the angel towering over him intimidatingly. "Look, Strythio."
"Don't call me that."
He gave a little eye roll before continuing. "I need you to understand that I have a good thing going on here." He spoke in almost a whisper, dangerous. "And I'm not going to let a naive, barely-adult little thing like you ruin it."
Theo raised his eyebrows. "And, let me clarify," the King began. "By 'good thing going on', you mean discrimination, right?"
Beckett's eyebrows furrowed in frustration. "You would be banished in my kingdom for that kind of disrespect towards a Lord."
Theo smiled cockily. "Well, I suppose it's a good thing that this is *my* kingdom. And, I'm not all that sure that I want a disgusting person like *you* in *my* kingdom."
Theo's whole body fell to the ground from just the force of being slapped across the face. He was lucky that he was no longer wearing his crown, because it would definitely have been launched off his body and probably damaged. Theo planted his hands in front of him to catch himself, having fallen sideways so that he was now lying on his back, pushing himself up on his elbows and watching Lord Beckett with a shocked expression.
The man leaned down to his level, saved by the seclusion of where they were meaning that nobody saw him, and snarled. "You need to learn your fucking place. Don't you dare try and mess with me or what I do."
Theo looked up, eyes watering as he blinked away his weakness. "That was unnecessary." He groaned, using the side of his right hand curled into a half-fist to rub his cheek where he'd been hit.
Lord Beckett reached his hand out to help Theo up, which the King reluctantly took. "Oh, so now you're inclined to take my hand? I think you should apologise."
Theo suddenly felt very small standing in front of this man. He was a good six feet tall, and his halo added more to his figure - also existing as a constant reminder that this man *was* better than him.
"I'm not going to apologise to someone like you." Theo protested, squinting at the man through still-forming tears. "I need you to know, Mr Beckett, that you aren't welcome here, and I'm not going to be passive about it."
Amadeus practically laughed out loud. "That's a lot of nerve for a child who looks like he's about to run off crying to his mother." The man sighed dramatically. "Sorry, poor choice of words." He nodded while smiling in sarcastic, mock sympathy.

The King narrowed his eyes. He had never felt more inclined to punch someone in the face than he did at that exact moment. He didn't quite get the opportunity though, (which was probably for the best) because the angel seemed to have more to say.

"I haven't made the journey down to this wasteland to bullshit with you." He said, eyes fiercely locked onto Theo's intimidated stature. "I've been at the highest rank I can get to in Menphe for almost a century now. About five times the length you've been alive. You're frail, and weak, and you have something that I want."

Theo raised an eyebrow. "And what's that?"

"A kingdom."

Theo didn't say anything back.

"Yours, I should clarify. All of the others have monarchs that are far too strong and respectable." He drawled. "If I were you, I would watch your back." He said, and then he shoved Theo backwards into a wall with a quick mutter of "Stupid kid", smirking and turning on a heel to return to his seat.

Theo swallowed, straightening his posture and diving his hands into his pockets. He didn't have the energy to deal with this right now. He followed the man out from the secluded area, and now pretty much everyone was sat down - all still talking and mingling. On his table was his father, his sister, his grandmother and his friend Raphie. Well, to be fair, she was more Laine's friend, but since Theo would consider Laine to be his best friend (as well as sibling), it was kind of a package deal.

Raphie looked really nice too. Her split dyed hair was tied up into a nice bun behind her, a single strand forming a plait and leading into her hair-tie. She had two strands of hair out of the style, and was accompanying the look with a pastel yellow-coloured, long-sleeved lacey dress that looked really good against her pale-blue skin.

She would admit that she did feel a little out of place, being one of four angels in attendance *and* sitting on the same table as the literal royal family.

Theo trudged over to the table and slumped down in his seat. Laine leaned into him and whispered, "Yikes, you look like a puppy that's been kicked."

Theo rolled his eyes. "Right about one of those things." He mumbled, again, quiet enough that only Laine could hear.

Her eyes lingered on his face for a moment, trying to decipher what he meant. Then, her eyebrows raised in shock before furrowing in slight anger. "He hit you?!"

Her brother didn't move his head, but his eyes flickered to Laine. "It's fine, I was kind of being really rude to him."

Laine was not at all satisfied with that being the end of the discussion, but she had to lean away from Theo and back to sitting up properly in her seat when her father stood and clinked on his glass with a spoon. The Princess quickly turned to Raphie, who was sitting on her other side, getting close and relaying the information to her friend. The angel frowned, leaning forward and making eye contact with Theo. Well, it was kind of difficult to make proper eye contact with him or Laine, because their eyes were all completely one colour, but she knew what she was doing.

"*Girls...!*" Cordelia whisper-shouted across the table from where she was sitting opposite Theo and next to Raphie. They both leaned back into their seats. Laine shook her head subtly at Theo, as if to say 'this conversation isn't over'.

VI

"To directly quote one of my supervisors," Dyran began, having the whole room's attention as he began his speech. "'Giving your entire kingdom to an eighteen-year-old would be like shooting yourself in the foot with a rifle you worked for your whole life to afford.'"
There was an eruption of laughter from around the room, and a few cheers sounded out. Theo himself smiled slightly, having an idea himself of which person had said that.
"Despite that gentle advice, my son is..." Dyran turned his head to look at Theo, who was sitting in his seat, watching with slight worry. "...a really good kid." The man smiled. "I think that everyone here is aware that he didn't have the most straightforward upbringing. But, I have absolutely no doubts in Theo's ability to take good care of this place. Just like he takes care of his sister, and just like he's going to have to take care of me when I'm too old for all of this."
Another round of chuckles, and the ex-monarch was raising his glass and encouraging others to do the same. Once he had sat down, Laine stood from her seat. She was holding a series of five or so small cards, which she was not even trying to hide the fact that she was reading off.
"When I was seven, and Theo was eight, there was about a six-month period where he had developed his wings and I hadn't yet. In light of this, he convinced me that if I jumped off the top of our staircase, my wings would appear and save me from hurting myself when I hit the ground."
Theo could still remember it well. She'd gotten really excited about the prospect of having wings like her brother, and had all-but launched herself down the staircase the moment she heard this rumour.

"So, a broken ankle and sprained wrist later, I was made to stay in bed for a week or so to recover. During this time, our dad made Theo do *everything* that I asked him as a punishment. And he spent the whole week getting me snacks whenever I wanted and doing my school work et cetera."

Laine had a very good speaking voice, and Theo had to admit that it made him a little jealous. She was standing with her shoulders squared back, jewellery rattling a little as she moved the next flashcard behind the other. She glanced at Theo fondly.

"During that week, I spent more time with my brother than I had for the rest of our lives that far combined. And, it was in that seven-day period in which he had to bring me breakfast in bed every morning that I had a bit of a revelation about Theo; maybe he wasn't so bad after all."

"Awh." One of the guests cooed, semi-loudly so that the whole hall heard and began laughing as a result. Laine inhaled while giggling slightly, looking to the ground and then back to her flashcards. When everyone was silent once more, she carried on.

"And then the next week he spent three hours trying to make me believe I was adopted." She nodded, grinning to herself. "My point is that I was raised with this young man, and although he can be a little bit of a moron, he's a very mature, responsible moron who I know will take great care of this kingdom." The guests applauded and Laine sat down. Raphie leaned into her and whispered something incoherent - Theo assumed it was a congratulatory remark or similar. He then realised that it was now his time to say something to everyone for the first time this evening.

He stood (maybe a bit too quickly) and looked around. "Um, I don't really have much to say. I'm not sure what kind of magic goes on behind the scenes to make events like this happen but thank you to everyone who was involved in organising this and thanks to everyone for... You know, showing up."

It was pretty quiet, almost awkwardly so. "When I was younger I imagined this day a lot. I imagined that maybe there'd be fireworks, or a unicorn for decoration. Although I had high expectations of this in my childhood, it's been all I could ask for and more. I didn't even know this was happening until yesterday afternoon, so it has felt a little rushed, but I think it's going to be a great start to my time serving Klaevr."

He paused, looking around.

"I'm not really a public speaker, but, um, if you do actually want to talk to me, I promise I'm a lot better with words one-on-one. Okay, I hope you

all have a good rest of the evening." He finished, sitting back down. It was silent for a few moments before Laine began clapping wildly.
"Woo!" She called, clapping at a quicker pace. Theo was pretty sure he wanted to melt into the floor.
Slowly, other people in the room became amused by the Princess, and joined in until pretty much everyone was clapping.
Dyran looked over to his son and smiled slightly reassuringly. Theo smiled, back staring at the table as his sister patted him on the back. It wasn't long before food was brought out, and the King ended up just tiredly shovelling the food around his plate with a fork, feeling a distinct lack of appetite that probably boiled down to anxiety.
God, it was going to be a long night.

"Nikoliah!"
The soldier turned around, noting the five foot seven angel standing at the end of the hallway. He raised his eyebrows at Raphie.
"That's sir to you."
She walked a little faster, dress flowing behind her. It was about one in the morning now - a lot of guests had gone home and most people still hanging around were partying and everything.
"Can you do Laine and I a favour? It's for Theo."
"King Theo."
Raphie stopped, placing a hand on her hip. "Come off that, just help us out." She bargained, now only a few metres away from the demon.
"I can't help you out unless you get on with it." Sir Nikoliah replied, straightening his posture upon realising he was still technically on duty despite wanting to have gone to bed hours ago. He was wearing the usual soldier uniform that was pretty uncomfortable, especially this late at night.
"Theo's drunk. *Wine drunk.* He's being all giggly one moment and then crying the next. Can I trouble you with dragging him to bed? Laine and I wanna stay down here dancing and such for a few more hours."
Nikoliah sighed exaggeratedly. "I suppose so. Lead the way then."
Inside the main hall, where the speeches and dinner had occurred about four hours ago, the lights were now dimmed and coloured spotlights were illuminating a dance floor. About thirty people were on it, and some mindless music was on in the background. It was mainly young people still around, Dyran and all the people his age were long gone.

Laine was sitting on a bench on the side of the dance floor, holding one of his brother's hands in hers and talking to him steadily. She must have made a joke, because both giggled for a moment. The Princess' eyes lit up when she saw the two of them returning.

"Alright, Sir Nikoliah is gonna make sure you get to bed now, okay?" She asked, and the King nodded.

"Mhm, gonna go to sleep." He slurred, wobbling a little as he stood.

"Yep, careful now." She said, holding onto one of Theo's arms until the young adult leant onto Nikoliah. Laine mouthed a 'thank you' to the soldier and the two girls walked off onto the dance floor, completely forgetting the previous interaction in favour of the music.

"I'm sorry, I'm ruining your night, aren't I?" The King said, stumbling in the hold of the soldier as they began to traverse the corridors.

"It was never a night to begin with."

Theo frowned. "Oh my God, that's so sad, Niko." He said, his words merging together slightly as he spoke.

"Don't call me that."

"Sorry." The King giggled. "It's just like, you didn't even get to have any fun...! That's so unfair."

"Life is often unfair."

Of course, Sir Nikoliah wasn't actually upset about this being his job - he took a lot of pride in it. He was just very tired and really wanted to go to bed, and his mild exhaustion was fueling the way he was talking to the King. He would never be so blunt if he knew Theo was sober, but he also knew that the man wouldn't remember it tomorrow morning, so it didn't *actually* matter.

"You know what else is unfair?" Theo asked, sounding a little more sad this time as they continued to walk. "I'm gonna have to get married to someone probably."

"Yeah, people do that sometimes." The soldier replied, picking the pace up a little as he dragged the other man along with him.

"You know, you're pretty attractive, Niko."

"I am?"

"Mhm... but don't tell me that I said that because nobody is meant to know." He whispered, even though it was a completely empty corridor. Nikoliah cringed, feeling a little guilty at the admission that he probably wasn't meant to hear.

"You're drunk." The knight countered, finally reaching the staircase that led to Theo's room.

The newly crowned king laughed kind of loudly, before shushing himself. "Shushush... We gotta be quiet, people are sleeping."
Nikoliah took one step up the stairs with Theo in hand before the King tripped over his own feet. The soldier sighed dramatically, before looking to his left and right and hooking his own arms under the King's and literally dragging him up the stairs backwards.
Theo stared up at the ceiling before pushing himself up to stand as the soldier also pulled him at the same time. "Good, there we go. Not far now." He reassured, once again tugging the younger man along.
Much to Sir Nikoliah's relief, he managed to get to Theo's room without any other inconveniences (other than the King himself). He directed the man towards his bed, taking the empty glass from his bedside table and quickly filling it up in the en-suite bathroom before placing it back full.
"Okay, sleep well now." He said, turning and walking towards the door.
"Mhm." Theo mumbled into his pillow, already pretty much asleep as Nikoliah flicked the light off and shut the door.
He made his way back to the hall that the coronation took place in, but rather than standing outside this time - he considered that it was probably okay for him to go in and enjoy himself. I mean, all of his superiors were fast asleep by now - other than Princess Laine, who he knew for a fact would not care if he was off duty.
By the time he had returned, there were only about five people still milling around. Six, if you included his presence.
"Theo's sleeping?" Raphie asked, walking up to meet the soldier at the door.
"Like a baby." He confirmed. The angel nodded while smiling and led the other towards the dance floor where her friend was waiting for her. The Princess smiled and headed over to where the older demon was standing.
Nikoliah was a little apprehensive towards the idea of taking Laine's hand when it was offered to him. Firstly, Laine was a princess. He was not royal of any kind. He was not royal when he was alive on Earth. It would surely be wrong for him to take her hand. He would easily lose his title and job for it if Dyran was here.
But, *she looked gorgeous.*
And, he supposed, that she was the one initiating the contact, so he couldn't *technically* get in trouble for it. Not like Laine or Raphie would tell anyone, but still, the concept was there.
"Are you going to come and dance with me or stand there looking like a deer in headlights?"

So, Sir Nikoliah glanced to the door of the now decrepit hall and then back to the Princess, still in her deep red dress, the same colour as her horns and tail and strands of dyed hair. He smiled amusedly and took her hand, being dragged onto the dance floor while Raphie mingled with the remaining people.

Laine must have noticed Nikoliah's apprehensiveness, as she grabbed both of his hands, smiling at him widely. "Stop worrying, nothing is going to happen. Enjoy yourself for once."

"Fine, okay." He replied, laughing a little. He was slightly caught off guard when Laine wrapped her arms around his waist and tucked her head into his chest, swaying herself side to side and bringing him with her.

He placed his hands on her shoulders, not wanting to overstep the Princess' boundaries as they continued to hold each other close. It was really nice, and for once, Nikoliah would admit that he felt comforted. He allowed himself to smile and hold Laine closer.

The coloured light reflected on their bodies as the musicians started to play a slower song. Raphie turned away from her conversation and noticed the two of them. Usually, she would report any gossip like this to Laine, but since it was Laine involved, she would definitely have to tell Theo.

Laine might not want the first person to know about her attempts at romance to be her brother, but Raphie understood that he would find out from Nikoliah anyway - considering he was going to be the King's right hand and would spend significant time with him.

Raphie, in all honesty, didn't know all that much about Sir Nikoliah - considering they were from different realms and Nikoliah worked for the castle and Raphie was only ever a visitor. What she did know was that Laine thought he was nice, and she supposed that was enough - for now at least.

It was incredibly likely that tomorrow morning the two of them would regret all of this - and then awkwardly stand around each other pretending that this evening had never happened. They both mutually decided that that was half of the fun. And for that night, nothing else mattered apart from the slow, rhythmic beating of Nikoliah's heart that Laine could hear with her ear pressed to his chest.

To be young.

VII

It had now been two months since King Theo's coronation, and much to the eighteen-year-old's surprise, the kingdom was prospering. And, by prospering, it was doing just as well as it was under King Dyran's rule. Theo classed that as a win.
He was sitting alone in the throne room, one leg lazily resting on top of the other. It was quiet, almost annoyingly so.
 Since being crowned, Theo was expected to spend a lot less time in his bedroom - so his only other option was the throne room.
It was a large room with a long red carpet lining the centre, leading from the two thrones down to the double doors. They were a different, less expensive set of thrones than the ones in the event hall, but it was a grand room nonetheless.
It was just about the afternoon at this point - Theo had spent two hours of his morning in a meeting about relaxing the border control, which he wasn't really interested in.
Theo had tried his best to get through to Lord Beckett these past few months. It had served to be a lot more difficult than he wanted, considering that he couldn't go up to any of the Kingdoms of Heaven, so if he wanted to talk face-to-face to the man, he would have to convince him to come down to Klaevr, which he was not showing any interest in doing as expressed through the letters that Theo had been receiving. He hadn't told anyone about the slightly distressing threats that Lord Beckett had made to him on the day of the coronation. The implication that it would be easy for his kingdom to get snatched from right under

his nose had been shameful. And, it had been far too long now, regardless. He was doing fine as king, and he would keep doing fine.
As per one of Theo's duties, he was sometimes asked to certify whether or not someone deserves to have been placed in Klaevr - whether they should be somewhere more extreme or maybe he'd have to write an appeal to get them transferred to a Kingdom of Heaven.
The doors to the throne room eased open, and Theo straightened himself, moving his leg off the other and placing his elbows on his knees in order to seem more composed.
"Good afternoon, Theo." A staff member of the castle whose name Theo didn't know bowed his head slightly towards the King as he spoke.
"Afternoon." Theo replied. "What's up?" He said, leaning further forward in his sitting position.
"Same old." The worker continued. "Got someone who thinks they were placed wrong."
Theo groaned, placing his head into one of his hands before sitting back up and smiling. "Alright, thanks. Send them in."
The demon being spoken to nodded before scurrying out of the room, and about half a minute later, a woman walked in. She had mid-length blonde hair and was wearing a very simple jeans and tank-top combination - looking about nineteen to twenty years old. Her horns were a lovely salmon colour, Theo briefly thought that it'd be a shame if she transferred to Heaven and she had to lose that lovely shade.
"Come here then." Theo said, beckoning the girl forward. She walked quickly. "What makes you think you shouldn't be here?"
"Well, I was murdered. Brutally. I've been told by a few people that getting murdered is meant to give you a free pass to Heaven."
Theo grimaced. "Not necessarily. That's more of a rumour."
"So what then?" She asked, raising an eyebrow. Theo decided that he did not like her attitude.
"Well, tell me a bit about yourself." He said standing from his throne and walking towards her.
She looked around for a moment. "Okay, well, I grew up in a pretty small town, and went to college at-"
"I'm kidding, don't tell me about yourself, I don't care." Theo interrupted pretty bluntly, and the woman frowned, being caught off guard when Theo pressed the palm of his hand to her forehead.
The markings on his arms glowed for a moment as his skin connected with hers.

A young girl, excited, running through a playground with her brother. They were racing to get the last swing on the swingset. The young boy got there first, and the blonde-haired girl shoved him off, onto the ground, where he burst into tears.

The girl blew out the candles on her birthday cake. She was twelve now - big year. She spun to her side and hugged her mother. She'd gotten a new phone, the newest phone. She couldn't wait to show her friends.

"What are you, like, poor or something?" The blonde girl teased, looking down on a shorter brunette girl, who sniffled. The blonde girl laughed and shoved the other girl, watching her fall onto the ground as she scoffed and walked off.

She smiled from the stage. Her whole school was watching her, blonde girl, win prom queen. She was off to college next year, and decided that this was the perfect way to end her time at school.

"I want to dedicate this award," She began. "To all the girls who just weren't pretty enough to win. Like Gracie Prendal. Gracie, I'm sure there's another universe where you don't look so much like a disgusting animal."

The blonde girl was having her first day of college. She was meeting the people in her form class - the people she would spend the morning of the next few years with. A boy with dark brown hair sat next to her. She smiled at him.

"What were you like in highschool?" The boy asked. It had been a few years. They were now sitting on blonde girl's bed, having just finished working on their project for this month of college.

"Oh, I was great in highschool! Prom queen and all." She giggled sheepishly. "Why do you ask?"

The boy smiled too. "Do you remember Gracie Prendal?"

Blonde girl's face fell. "That weirdo? Yeah, why?"

The boy's smile faltered. "She was my sister."

Blonde girl laughed, loud and obnoxious. "No way that's true! You're gorgeous, and she was... Well, she was Gracie."

"Do you know what happened to her, Kiara?"

Kiara shifted uncomfortably. She didn't know where this sudden change in attitude had come from - they'd been friends for years, and now this boy was acting like she was some kind of criminal. "No." She whispered.

"She killed herself, Kiara." The brunette boy said, eyebrows furrowing in anger. "Shortly after graduation. Because of the things you put her through. You made her feel worthless. I read her note; she named you in it." He scoffed.

50

The blonde girl, Kiara, didn't respond. She didn't speak, not when Alex started yelling at her. Not when he got up from the bed and clicked the lock on her bedroom door. Not when he pulled a knife out of his backpack.
"If she doesn't graduate college, neither do you."
Theo stepped backwards.
"What was that?!" Kiara asked, holding her head with one hand. Theo shook his hands out in front of him to relieve the tension he was feeling.
"You're right. I don't think you deserve to be here." Theo judged, stepping further away from the girl.
"Finally someone with some sense!" Kiara exclaimed. "You really think so?"
Theo nodded. "Oh, yeah. Someone up there must have really messed up." He confirmed, walking past the girl and towards the door of the throne room. He found the same worker that had escorted Kiara in waiting outside.
"Hey, she needs to go somewhere else. I don't want her in my kingdom."
"Where do you mean by 'somewhere else'?" The staff member asked.
"Somewhere for people worse than the people that end up here. She drove a kid she went to school with to suicide and has the audacity to stand in front of me and ask if she can get up there." He said, gesturing to the sky as he finished the sentence.
"Oh." The worker replied. "Right, I'll take her away and we can figure out which kingdom is best suited."
Theo nodded solemnly. "Thank you very much." He said, turning and heading back into the throne room, telling Kiara that the man who brought her here would escort her to where she should be.
The blonde girl thanked him profusely and walked out with confidence. Theo almost laughed.
He sat down back on his throne. He hated doing things like that - it was really stressful to have a person's whole life played for you like a fast-forwarded highlights reel of a football match. He'd seen a lot of them - some really heartwarming and some incredibly heartbreaking.
This whole thing was just part of his duty as king apparently - not that he'd known that when he was coronated. Theo sighed, deciding that he wanted to get out of the throne room for a moment - maybe for a walk. Except, when he opened the door, he wasn't met with an empty hallway as he had expected. Nikoliah was walking down the hall semi-quickly. He stopped and sighed when he saw Theo.
"I was just looking for you. We have a tiny issue."

Theo looked back into the throne room before shutting the door and leaning against it. "How so?"

"Well, you know how when people die, they typically show up in their demon forms?"

"Um, yeah?"

"There's a human. A boy, a young man. A random person found him wandering around and sent him to one of the guards of the castle, who sent him to me, and now I'm sending him to you because I don't want to deal with it."

"Sorry?" Theo questioned, leaning himself forwards and raising his eyebrows.

"Yeah." The soldier replied bluntly. "Anyway, I'll send him over in this direction and-"

"No you won't, what the hell? I've never spoken to a human before, I don't know what they're like!"

"You realise that literally every person here that isn't related to you is technically a human? You're speaking to one right now. This is your job, man."

Theo grimaced and Nikoliah smiled cockily. "Think of it as a favour to me, just figure out what to do with him." He said as he walked off back in the direction he came. As evident from their conversation, Theo and Nikoliah had become significantly more relaxed around each other - in fact Theo had managed to abolish almost all formality between him and his staff. His father had been pretty uptight with all of the 'respect' things, like bowing, or addressing him as the King. Theo did not care for it at all, and he found that talking to his staff like he would talk to his friends made for a generally much more relaxed environment around the castle where people were happier. Of course, if his dad did decide to visit from T'kota any time soon, they'd have to revert back to how it was for the day or however long he stayed just to keep him happy.

Theo probably got lost in his head, because he was incredibly harshly pulled back to reality by the mortal standing in front of him, waving his hands in front of the King's face.

"Hello? Anybody home?" He teased.

Theo flinched away before regaining his composure and looking down at the slightly shorter man.

Much as Nikoliah had described, it was a person. Not a demon, not an angel.

A boy.

A normal-looking, human who seemed to be about Theo's age. He had medium-brown skin and hair of a similar, slightly darker colour. His eyes were a piercing green, body muscular behind a grey t-shirt and teal-coloured hoodie. He was extraordinarily handsome - at least Theo thought so. A flutter rose in his chest, and it made a thrum of anxiety pound in his chest.

He was very caught off guard, not saying anything to the human, but stepping backwards through the door of the throne room and ushering him to follow. He closed the door behind them.

"Your eyes are sick! Why is nobody else's like that? Are you, like, soulless or something? Oh my god! This room is cool. Maybe a little too fancy for my personal taste, but if you like it then that's alright I suppose. What are we gonna-"

"Oh my God, shut up for one minute!" Theo yelled, chest rising and falling pretty quickly. He looked to the floor and then back up to the other person. "Sorry, it's just… Just chill out for a minute, please." He said, quieter this time, using his hands to gesture downwards.

"Sorry." The brunette cringed. "This is very new to me, I've never died before."

"I would hope so." Theo replied, running the palm of his left hand over his face. The room lulled in silence for a moment as Theo started pacing.

"So… you're in charge here?" The boy asked. He had a light Northern English accent underneath a pretty deep, scratchy voice. Not that Theo would recognise the region he was from based on how he spoke.

Theo stuttered in trying to find a response. How was this guy being so casual? He was- well, he was royalty. No strangers ever really spoke to him like this.

"Um, yeah, you could say that."

"Right, well, I'm hoping you're going to tell me what I'm supposed to do now." He said, shrugging as his eyes continued to follow Theo's stressed paces around the room. The King didn't give an answer, so the boy changed the subject.

"I like your horns, can I touch them?"

Theo didn't even get to reply before the boy had both of his hands hooked around the King's deep green horns, causing him to stop his movement. He reached his arms up and grabbed the brunette by his wrists, pulling his arms away.

"You don't remember dying?" He asked, holding the boy's hands at the level of his head. The contact was original, beautiful. He quickly let go.

"No, I guess not. I remember coming home last night, tomorrow's my birthday. Oh! Is today my birthday? Do I stay the same age I died? But I don't remember dying. Am I meant to look like you?"

Theo blinked. "Usually that tends to happen." He said, reaching his hand out to touch the boy's forehead in order to figure out what about him made him so special as to not have turned into a demon upon arrival.

"Why are you doing that?" He asked, laughing a little in confusion at being randomly touched on the forehead. Theo removed his hand and frowned. Nothing happened. That was also another first for Theo.

"Um, nevermind." Theo said, not wanting to scare this person into thinking something was wrong with him.

The guest raised his eyebrows. "What's your name then, Your Majesty?" The boy mocked, walking over to Theo's throne and flopping down on it. Theo thought it was a little disrespectful, but he supposed this whole situation was a much bigger issue.

"It's Theo."

"Boring." The boy snorted, now lying horizontally on the throne, his head resting on the left armrest and his legs dangling over the right. "That's not a very demon-like name, is it?"

Theo walked to sit down on the second throne, since his was kind of pre-occupied by this bumbling idiot.

"My full name is Strythio if that satisfies your need for a 'fancy' name more."

The boy laughed. "Yeah! That's more like what I was *expecting* you to say."

"Is that a... compliment?"

"Kinda. Not really." The boy replied. "It's a bit pretentious."

Theo frowned. He might not actually use his full name, but it was still his name.

"Do you have a middle name?" He pried some more.

"No." Theo lied quickly. The boy grinned widely.

"Is it bad?" He giggled.

Theo just rolled his eyes and scrunched his nose up. "Okay, well, if you're the chief of name-judging', what's yours then?" He diverted the subject, raising his eyebrows expectantly at the visitor.

The boy jumped up out of Theo's throne and pranced across the gap between the thrones, standing in front of the King and reaching his hand out for the King to shake.

"Julian." He stated, smiling. "Wait, is my name meant to change when I become one of you?"

Theo allowed a smirk to slip onto his face. He was kind of charmed - or more entertained - by this lad. "Not unless you want it to." He replied, taking Julian's hand and allowing the stranger to shake it.
Touching Julian's skin made Theo's ignite with electricity, not literally, but he felt like magic was coursing through his veins for a moment. Okay, so that's three new experiences today.
"Maybe I could have a 'Jude' moment? You know, like the Beatles song."
"Who?" Theo asked, raising his eyebrows in confusion.
"The Beatles? I'll have to play some of their music to you later." Julian stated, sitting down next to Theo on the same throne as him. He must've seen the look on the King's face, as he rationalised. "There's plenty of room, don't worry."
Although it wasn't a lie, and there was plenty of room on the throne, Theo still thought it was a little strange. "You've got a bit of a personality, haven't you?" Theo mused.
"Yeah, I guess. People sometimes think I'm annoying, but my mum tells me I'm just excitable."
"Your mum?" Theo questioned, turning himself in his sitting position to be more facing Julian, who hoisted himself up to be perched on the right armrest of the throne.
"Yeah! She's never gonna believe me when I tell her about this." He lamented, eyes downcast and a small smile on his face. Theo cringed.
"Is she... um, is she still alive, Julian?"
Theo watched as his face fell. "Oh. Oh, I'm not going to see her again, am I?" He asked, looking like a puppy who had been denied food. "Oh my God, I have to go home. I have to go home Theo, you have to let me go home!" He almost yelled, gripping onto Theo's shirt and breathing heavily. "This is a lovely town, really, but- but only to visit. I want to go home now."
"I'm sorry, Julian, you can't. You die once and that's that." He replied. He'd given this speech to many people who have begged him to get back to Earth, so it didn't deliver it with much sympathy. That *was* until he got a second look at Julian.
"What if she died at the same time I did? We spent a lot of time together - didn't have any place else to go. Could she be here?"
Theo sighed. "I'll... I'll write letters to the monarchs of the other Kingdoms of Hell and ask them if she's there. It might be a little harder for me to get through to The Heavens, but I'll see. What's her name?"
"She won't be in Heaven, definitely not. Her name's Vanna Thompson."
Theo felt the need to ask a little more about the first statement, but then

he realised that they literally have all of eternity for those kinds of discussions.

"Okay, I'll do that later for your peace of mind. Let's just, let's find you somewhere to stay while I figure this out."

The King stood from the throne and began to walk back down the middle of the throne room, Julian standing and following in a scurry.

"This place is massive, you own it?"

"I guess I do. I don't really think of it like that, though. It's more of a shared space for the people that work here and my family."

Julian nodded, following Theo down the corridor and through a few doors. They quickly managed to reach the corridor which Theo and Laine's bedrooms were on. Theo had been given the opportunity to switch to a larger bedroom after his father moved out, but he found that he quite liked his.

Laine exited her bedroom, wearing light grey joggers and a black tank top and holding an empty bowl with milk pooling at the bottom and a spoon sticking out of it.

She gasped.

"Is that a human? What the hell, Theo?" She exclaimed. "How is that even possible?"

The King stopped. "I don't know either Laine. Neither does he."

She raised her eyebrows in amusement. "And you are?"

"Julian." He said, again reaching his hand out for her to shake, which she did. "You're Laine?" He asked, having inferred it from what Theo called her.

"The one and only. What are you gonna do with him, Theo?"

Theo stepped backwards and leant against a wall. "I don't know! It was *your* boyfriend that dropped him in my hands."

"Shush…!" She replied, beginning to walk with her bowl towards the stairs. Theo followed.

See, over the last two months, Laine and Nikoliah's relationship had progressed into the stage where they were calling eachother partners but it was still on the down-low. They had told Theo about a week into their relationship, since Laine didn't like keeping secrets.

The more people that know, the more chance Dyran would find out - and that was *not* what they wanted. Theo was also a lot more independent in his rule, so he didn't actually need Nikoliah around for much - allowing him more time to spend with his girlfriend. Now that Laine was seventeen, she felt a lot more free to do what she wanted - even if it meant pursuing a romantic relationship with a man who was meant to be working for her.

"Just, what do you think I should do?"

"Do you know how he died? Could be related."

"I don't know, neither does he."

"Well, maybe you should start by figuring that one out." She said, beginning to head down the stairs and leaving Theo at the top of them, looking down in disappointment. He turned back around to face Julian, who was standing awkwardly behind the King.

"Your sister's hot. Have you ever realised that?"

"No." He replied bluntly, grabbing Julian by the wrist and continuing to trek him down the corridor. "Let's just find you a bedroom and we can go over what our plan of action is tomorrow. Sound okay?"

Julian smiled a little. "Yeah, sounds good, sparkles."

Theo turned. "Sparkles?" He asked, and the other man laughed.

"Yeah, you're all glitzed-up in like jewellery and an expensive palace. So, sparkles."

"It's a castle." Theo laughed, not too upset about the playful nature of the nickname.

VIII

Theo sat down at the table for breakfast. It wasn't very often that he found himself up and eating at the same time as his sister - but, today that seemed to be the case.
"Oh, good morning." She smiled, looking up from her toast. "How's that human you're smuggling around?"
He'd found a guest bedroom up a single flight of curved stairs on the end of him and his sister's hallway. Julian had been left from then to figure himself out and sleep, and Theo supposed it was pretty early to expect to have already seen him.
He stayed silent as he started to cut up one of his eggs. "Haven't spoken to him this morning. But we're going to do some digging as to how he might have died later today."
Laine raised her eyebrows in apprehension. "You gonna have time for that?"
"Why wouldn't I?"
The Princess put her food down, leaning backwards in her chair. "Dad's coming over today, he didn't tell you?"
Theo's mouth fell open. "No! No, he didn't tell me." He groaned, letting his head drop into his hands. "Well, I'll need to keep Julian out of the way then - I wouldn't want Dad to do anything with him."
Laine nodded. "Don't get too attached to that kid, okay? He's gonna have to go the second you figure out what's up."
"I'm not gonna get attached, Laine. I just care about his safety like I do all the people that live here."

The Princess laughed. "Whatever you say. Now, if I were you I'd take a shower and change into something nice, or else Dad will get upset at you for your personal presentation."

"Mhm, will do. How long until he gets here?" This was going to be a pretty big deal, Theo realised. It was the first visit that the ex-king (who now had the title of 'Sir Dyran', given to most retired monarchs) had made since he moved out after his retirement began, and the new king really wanted it to go well - at least for the validation.

"An hour, give or take." Laine replied, standing with her own plate. "Oh, and Raphie is coming over in thirty minutes also. She wants to quote on quote, 'experience Theo getting ripped apart by your Dad'."

"Good to know someone believes in me." Theo exhaled sarcastically, standing up. "Right, an hour then." He said, already halfway out of the door.

He put his plate away and immediately headed up to his bedroom, showering and getting changed into a nice outfit with a black, semi-formal blazer over the top in just under twenty minutes - which was pretty quick for him.

With his hair still wet, Theo left his room and practically jumped up the spiral staircase towards the room he gave Julian. He dragged his hand along the bannister, more out of habit than desire for safety. The area at the top of the staircase was small, maybe five by five metres with two doors either side. One led to an empty bedroom, and the other a bathroom. This space of the castle had a mirrored version the same on the other side of Laine and Theo's corridor, and they were both traditionally used for bunk-beds for servants or maids to stay in if they wanted to be close to the centre of the castle.

However, they hadn't actually been used in a long time, not since a previous monarch gave all castle staff members their own spacious bedrooms. Now, they were *always* empty and nobody ever traversed the spiral staircases.

Theo knocked on the door twice in quick succession, waiting for a moment. When he got no response, he slowly opened the door.

Julian was asleep, lying on his right side, face pressed against the pillow and legs splayed around the bed. He was wearing a pair of Theo's joggers and an old t-shirt of the Kings that had been given to him to sleep in comfortably. His clothes he was wearing during the day were folded neatly on a chair to the left of the bed.

Something about this boy wearing Theo's clothes made his heart jump a little, and he smiled, walking over to the bedside and kneeling down to be at eye level with the sleeping guest.

"Julian?" He whispered, tapping him on the shoulder. "Julian?"

"Mhmph?" The man in question groaned, eyes fluttering open to look at Theo. "Go away, 'm tired."

"Yeah, good morning to you too, sunshine." Theo replied, wanting to laugh at the other's grogginess. "I'm not asking you to get up or anything, but, my dad's coming over in like half an hour and he can't know you're here because he'll blame it on me. Just, stay here and be quiet, okay?"

"You have a dad?" Julian replied, ignoring the rest of the statement and wiping his mouth where he'd been drooling with the back of his hand. "I assumed you didn't have parents because you're the King."

"No, I do. Just retired, and he's coming here today so do me a favour and don't get in the way." He said, and Julian snickered.

"Yeah alright, don't get all worked up over it. Now leave so I can get back to my beauty sleep." He grumbled, adjusting the pillow and rolling over.

Theo rolled his eyes playfully, walking to the door of the room and slipping out of it quietly, hearing the soft click of it shutting behind him. He trampled down the stairs and back into his hallway, past all of the portraits of previous monarchs and towards his bedroom. He got to the door, but didn't enter just yet, because he saw Raphie making her way up the staircase.

"Hey Theo. You would not believe how busy the train stations are at this time of day." She said, stopping at the top of the stairs to talk to the King, who turned to face her. "I'm kidding, they aren't usually busy, it's just that your dad is travelling and decided he needs the whole population of North America to guard him."

Theo gave a light chuckle. "Yeah, he does that. Sorry. I heard you're praying upon watching my downfall."

"Only slightly." Raphie joked. "I've just been missing your Dad and his..." She looked over to the window at the end of the corridor. "...Really bad taste in curtains. Are you gonna change those?"

"Bigger things going on than mismatched textures."

"Oh yeah? Like what?"

"Dead person who's appeared here still in his human form is upstairs. No idea what's going on with him, hoping Dad doesn't find out and blame it on me."

"Oh, really? Is he cute?" She teased.

"Shut up and go paint your nails with Laine, or whatever you two do." He replied humorously.

"Actually, we'll be gossiping about you, Dyran, Niko and various other men in our lives. You should try it, it's very therapeutic."

Theo nodded in sarcastic interest. "I'd love to, but I actually have big things to take care of like, oh, I don't know, running a kingdom."

"Yeah, and that's going great for you, as evident." She laughed, opening the door to Laine's room and entering, closing the door behind her and leaving Theo alone in the hallway very briefly.

"Did I hear my name?" Nikoliah asked, appearing out of one of the more disused servant passageways.

"Yeah, the girls are gossiping about us apparently."

"Damn." He replied, perching on the edge of the landing bannister. "You treat a girl like a princess and this is how you're repaid."

"She is a princess, so that statement is redundant." Theo mused, running a hand through his hair to feel how wet it still was. "You on duty today?" He asked, considering that Nikoliah was not dressed in his usual soldier attire; he was wearing a pair of black basketball shorts and a grey tank top. Theo had been giving Nikoliah two days off a week where he wasn't at all expected to be working, considering he was dating his sister and if they ended up getting married Niko would be honorary royalty anyway.

"I should be. Will be, I mean. Don't want your dad to think I've gone soft."

"You have gone soft." Theo ridiculed lightly. "Now, go get changed. Dad'll be here in like twenty."

Nikoliah braced up. "Sir, yes sir!" He mocked, doing an about turn and marching back through the servant's passage towards his bedroom. Theo snickered to himself, finally turning into his bedroom.

He flicked the lights that he had left on off as he blew out his candles and drew the curtains, collapsing backwards onto his bed and sighing, eyes hooked onto the ceiling. He managed to stay there relaxed for a grand total of thirty seconds before his anxieties got the best of him and he convinced himself he didn't have time to relax right now.

Theo sat up, and his eyes fell onto his desk. There was an untidy pile of envelopes inside of them, each saying pretty much the exact same thing - asking the monarch whom it was addressed to if they had Julian's mother living in their kingdom.

If the King was honest, he wasn't optimistic that Vanna (Julian's mother) was also dead. Surely, most people would be happy that their relatives are alive, but something inside of Theo really wished she had died with Julian just so he could deliver good news.

He should probably get those sent off. So, he picked up the stack of letters he'd written last night and left his room, the lights still off and envelopes in hand. The issue *was* that by the time he'd made it to the bottom of the staircase, it appeared that his father had just arrived. Early, or earlier than Laine had told him.

He huffed, turning to his nearest staff member, who just so happened to be Kougan, the stylist. He leaned over to the other man, whispering because Dyran was being greeted by other people.

"Hey, can you do me a massive solid and get these posted?" He asked. Kougan looked at the King with interest. "Yeah, if you give me a parade and then afterparty for being such a kind soul." He joked, taking the letters from Theo's hand and walking away.

"Are you doing business or something?" Sir Dyran chucked at his son, who quickly turned to face him upon hearing his voice - only a few metres away. Theo smiled, deciding to play it cool.

"Yeah, king stuff. You wouldn't get it." He spoke softly. Dyran laughed and pulled Theo in for a hug, which he will admit was a little embarrassing in front of most of his staff.

"I've heard it's going well." The ex-king whispered, not because he was talking in secrecy, but because he was very physically close to his son and didn't need to speak any louder. Theo replicated the same tone of voice in his response.

"It is, yeah."

They pulled away from the hug, and now staff members were starting to dissipate. "Theo, I'll be honest, I came here today because I need to discuss something with you. Can we find somewhere private to talk, like the dining room?"

Theo's heart rate immediately sped up. The one thing you never want a parent to say to you is 'can we talk in private', that's like the number one worst thing ever. He nodded, trying to keep composure. "Yeah, we can... we can go there."

They weaved through some corridors, Theo tapping his leg anxiously as he walked. This was the same room that he and Laine had breakfast in this morning - a long mahogany table in a room that allowed only a metre or two on each side of the chairs. Theo entered first and Dyran shut the door behind them. They sat opposite each other on the end of the table.

"So, Theo." He began, hands linked in front of him and elbows on the table. When Theo and Laine were younger, they would get told off for having their elbows on the table, but the King assumed it was a 'do as I say and not as I do' moment. "I'll make this really short."

"Did I do something wrong?" Theo whispered.

"No, no! Not at all. See, in T'kota, I met a lovely couple of ex-monarchs from a neighbouring kingdom with a beautiful daughter. And, upon speaking to her myself, she expressed a lot of interest in the possibility of marrying you, son."

Theo hesitated. "Um, I don't really think-"

"Her name is Serenity, she's twenty - so, not much older than you. A princess too, so no controversy with bloodlines. She's really kind as well, I really think you're going to love having her as yours, Theo." Dyran continued, nodding and smiling subtly as he spoke.

"What do you mean, I'm 'going to love her'...?"

"Well, I've agreed for you to marry her. Arranged for you to marry her, per se. A week today is the wedding. It'll be amazing for our politics - me and your mother were arranged and it was perfect for both of us. I know you aren't much of a traditionalist, but as your father, I know what's best for you, and it's this."

Theo felt like all the air surrounding him was pushing inwards, constricting his ability to breathe or even form a coherent sentence. All he could muster was to shake his head in disbelief.

"I'm aware there's been a lot of giving you short notice for your major life events recently, but we need to get you two married off soon before Queen Luciana, her sister, decides that she doesn't want Serenity moving away. That would mean that you might have to move to her kingdom to live with her - and the last thing that Klaevr needs is to lose a monarch so soon after I left."

Theo's chest tightened and he gained that horrible feeling that you get in your throat before you cry. His hands were subtly shaking and he couldn't stop a choked sob from escaping his throat. This wasn't what he wanted. It wasn't anything close to what he wanted. He didn't know much about what the hell he even wanted, but he knew it wasn't this. Theo felt his dad's hand touch his wrist. "It's fine, she's a lovely-"

"It's not fine!" Theo yelled. "It's not fine, don't say it's fine! You don't care about me, just what's best for you or for the kingdom or whatever!" He ran a hand over his face, pushing away the tears that were now falling. Dyran watched his son's outburst in disbelief.

"Theo, calm down." He instructed sternly. "Where on earth has this come from?"

"Don't tell me to calm down, fuck you." He spat, standing from the table and walking towards the door.

"Strythio Lucretius Virzor, you will sit back down here right now or else!" Dyran argued, eyes narrowing in anger at the way his son had just cursed him out so rudely.

Theo ignored him, leaving the room and making a point to slam the door like an eight year old having just been told he can't stay up past his bedtime. He slipped through one of the servant's passages so as to not have to walk past any of his staff in his state. Now crying hysterically, Theo hurried his way up the stairs and out of the same passage that Nikoliah had used earlier. From there it was only about twenty seconds before he was in his bedroom, lying face down onto his bed. He screamed into his pillow, not even caring about how much noise he was making.

This was literally the worst thing that could have come of Dyran's visit in Theo's mind, and it felt like his whole reality was collapsing. He was only just an adult, it was horrific that his father expected him to marry so soon. And to a girl. A random girl he'd never even heard of, let alone met, let alone loved!

Again, much like a child would, Theo pulled his duvet over his head and cried softly into his arms. His dad, of all people? The person who was meant to love him the most and always have him in his best interest. Somehow the notion that his dad didn't actually care about his feelings hurt more than the idea that he'd have to marry a random princess from another kingdom.

He heard the sound of his bedroom door creaking open, but did nothing to make any notice of the person walking in.

"Um, you okay?" Julian asked, peeling back the duvet and frowning. "Is your dad... that bad?"

Julian sat down on the edge of the bed, still wearing Theo's clothes from last night. He looked a mix of tired and concerned. The King sat up, sniffling. "Yeah, apparently."

"Do you wanna talk about it?" The human asked, shuffling along the bed to sit next to Theo. He shook his head, barely able to see Julian through bleary eyes. "You're okay, it's gonna be okay."

Sure, Theo had *hated* when his father had told him it was fine, but hearing it from Julian was different. The King leaned into Julian's body, accepting the comfort of the touches. Julian wrapped his arms around Theo's shaking form.

Something about the affection must have set off a trigger in Theo's senses, as he quickly found himself erupting in a new fit of tears and sobs as his shoulders jerked up and down and he buried his head into the other man's chest. He gave a few incoherent pleas of misery about the idea of being wed... This was wrong, this was all wrong. He was the King; he was meant to suck the bad parts of life up, and yet, he was crying like an inconsolable child into someone's arms. A boy's arms.

Of course, Julian was a little foggy on the context of this upset, but he figured that there was time to ask the King about it when he was in a little bit less of a distressed state. For now, he just rested his hand on Theo's back, offering a gentle but not overwhelming touch. Julian hadn't shut the door upon entering, so he wasn't all that surprised when Nikoliah ended up awkwardly hovering in the doorway.

"Is he... okay?" The soldier asked in almost a whisper once the other man acknowledged his presence.

Julian shrugged. "Something about not wanting to marry someone, I'm not sure." He countered, just as quiet as to not distress Theo any further.

Nikoliah paused for a moment. Then his face went from an expression of confusion, to realisation, to shock and to anger all in about two seconds.

"Has Sir Dyran arranged for him to marry someone?" He asked in a fierce tongue.

Theo looked up from where his head was buried in the other man, tears visibly staining his cheeks but no longer flowing so violently. He nodded.

"Oh my God, really? You're so young though."

"Politics." Theo sniffled, sitting up and crossing his legs. "Sorry, I don't mean to be all unprofessional and upset... It's just... so much."

"Yeah, of course it is." Nikoliah offered sympathetically.

The conversation didn't have the opportunity to progress any further, because Theo's eyes widened at the sound of heavy, unmistakable footsteps on the stairs.

"My Dad." Theo interjected quickly.

"What?" Julian and Nikoliah asked at the exact same time.

"I've grown up with him, I can recognise his footsteps." Theo said, standing up from the bed and practically grabbing Julian's arm. "Get under the bed right now." He hurried, practically pushing the poor human to the ground.

"Yeesh, okay, okay!" He argued, crawling under the bed. Just as Theo looked up from the ground, he could see the figure of his dad in the doorway. Nikoliah braced himself up.

"Sir." He said, avoiding eye contact with the man.

"Oh." Dyran responded. "Sir Nikoliah. Is loitering in my son's bedroom part of your employment? Or are you just feeling lazy today?" He chided condescendingly, but he spoke with a soft and threatening tone.
Nikoliah's face fell, expression shifting to one representative of a child that's been yelled at. "Um, no Sir, it's not. I'll leave, I apologise." He said, staring at the floor and then looking at Theo worriedly before leaving the room. Dyran sighed loudly, walking over to the door and shutting it.
"I do not want to be the bad guy in your life, Strythio. But there are some things that you need to understand. Maybe you're too naive, or too prideful to make sacrifices for your people, but every monarch has to do it."
Theo almost rolled his eyes.
"I apologise that this decision has upset you, but I *do not* appreciate you raising your voice at me, and I *especially* don't appreciate you swearing at me. Do you understand how rude that is?"
"Yeah, I'm-"
"I'm not finished, Strythio, let me finish."
"You asked me a question, I was answering it."
"Are you back talking me?"
Theo took a deep breath and sat back down on the edge of his bed. He decided that he couldn't win in this scenario, and just accepted the grilling he was receiving.
"Right." Sir Dyran began again. "A week today, you are going to have a lovely wedding ceremony to an incredibly perfect Princess from the Kingdom of Vaemunt. You're not going to make a fuss, you're going to be professional about it. She's going to move in with you here, and she can be crowned Queen of this kingdom after two years of loyal marriage to you. After that, you can think about children. I don't want to hear a word about it to anyone or from anyone. This is the kind of thing that you have to get over."
"I have to 'get over' marrying a girl I don't like?" Theo whispered.
"Yes. I did the same."
"Doesn't make it okay, and you ended up liking her anyway."
Dyran grumbled. "I've told all the staff about it. You're lucky I didn't tell them about your outburst towards me. Just, put on a face for the wedding. Trust me, it'll be easier once you've met her and realised she's a real person." He talked a little softer this time. "Now, come and give me a hug and apologise for swearing at me, and I can go back home happy."
Theo's shoulders deflated and she stood, shuffling over to his dad and allowing himself to receive a hug. "I'm sorry." He admitted, even though

66

he wasn't. He wasn't going to be sorry for getting angry at his dad over this.

After a few moments, Dyran pulled away and nodded silently, smiling and exiting the room. Theo breathed out and flopped back down backwards onto his bed. In a matter of moments, Julian was sitting on the edge of the bed, offering him the comfort that Theo so desperately needed.

IX

Theo had to sit through a whole dinner with Dyran later that day. A dinner in which his sister was also there, not yet aware of the wedding that had been arranged. Nikoliah had wanted to tell her, but he'd scampered off to his bedroom after being told off by his old boss. During this time, Julian had gone back into the room that Theo had allocated him as well, to avoid anyone seeing him.
"So, Laine." Dyran said, putting his knife and fork down to indicate that he was going to start a conversation. The Princess looked up while half-way through chewing a mouthful of pasta. "Some exciting news, do you want to tell her, Theo?"
Theo huffed. "Yeah, okay."
He put his own cutlery down and ran a hand through his hair, waiting for Laine to finish eating so as to not catch her off guard. "Our loving father has so very kindly arranged for-"
"Theo." Dyran interrupted strongly.
"Fine, fine." He whispered. "Um, Laine, I apologise because this means you might have to spend another afternoon with Jaymie and Kougan, but, um, I am getting married next weekend."
Laine dropped her fork that she was holding, and it clattered onto her plate loudly. "What?" She asked, looking more at her Dad than Theo, who she was sat next to as opposed to being opposite Dyran.
"Yeah. Her name's Serenity."
Laine furrowed her eyebrows, turning to face Theo this time. "But you don't even like-" The words fell out of her mouth before she could finish the sentence. "You don't even like formal events. Um, dad, why doesn't

he just let her move in and they can date for a while. Nothing too... Hasty." She corrected, cringing at her own words.

"No, that's not how it works. I was expecting you to be a little happier for him." The King frowned, wondering if his children knew something he didn't. Laine swallowed.

"Yeah, no, of course. I'm super happy for you, Theo!" She said, awkwardly hugging him from their seated position. Theo hummed in agreement, accepting the hug with a slight smile.

Theo picked up his cutlery and continued to push his food around his plate before taking a mouthful in order to avoid having to speak anymore.

"I don't get why you don't just tell him. Then he'll call it off and it'll be fine." Laine said, perching on the edge of the vacant Throne next to the one that Theo was sitting cross-legged on. Raphie, Nikoliah and Julian were all in various degrees of attendance too. Dyran had gone home, so the five of them were having a bit of a mother's meeting about the circumstances.

"Because if I tell him then he's going to turn you into his reproductive prodigy. He'll have someone to marry you the day you come of age and will be expecting heirs within a few years. I'm not going to put that on you, that's why." Theo spat.

Laine sighed. "Well, you- ugh, okay. Okay, well we have a week. We can figure it out."

"Okay, how about this." Raphie proposed, sitting down on the small set of stairs that lead up to the thrones. "You tell her. Tell Serena or yknow, whatever she's called."

"Serenity." Theo whispered.

"Tell Serenity, and you two can get married but just... without being in a relationship. I'm sure she'll understand."

Theo rolled his eyes pessimistically. "Yeah, I'm sure she'll be super happy to marry someone who tells her he's never going to love her the first time they speak." He slighted sardonically.

Julian shoved his hands in his pockets. "Sorry, um, what are we telling her?"

Theo leant back in his throne. "That I'm gay. I don't like girls and I'm getting married to one next week."

Julian raised his eyebrows. "Your dad isn't supportive?"

"He doesn't know." Nikoliah said, walking over to the throne that Laine was sitting on the armrest of and flopping into it. "And as far as Theo's concerned, he isn't going to know."

This time a year ago, or even six months ago, Sir Nikoliah would not have dared to get within ten metres of the monarch's thrones, and now here he was sitting in one as if he had any sense of entitlement to it. For a moment he imagined a future where he might share a set of thrones with Laine.

"Okay, um, then sorry if this is insensitive at all, but you can't really get upset at him for arranging for you to marry a girl if he doesn't know." Julian voiced.

"It's less that I'm upset that it's a girl and more that I'm upset he didn't even *ask me* first." Theo indicated, leaning forward now, elbows resting on his knees.

"Either way, nothing is going to change by us sitting around and talking about it. We need to figure out what's up with you, Julian. I got those letters sent so I'm expecting responses by tomorrow morning."

Julian smiled. "Thanks."

"So, we're trying to figure out how he... died?" Raphie asked.

"Yes," Niko said, pulling a notebook out of one of the seemingly-endless pockets in his trousers. "Where are you from, Julian? Like, where did you live?"

"Stockport." He said.

Theo and Laine shared a confused glance. "Where?" The King asked.

"Um, like, Manchester?"

"I'm not a geography expert, I'm gonna need you to be a bit less specific."

Nikoliah almost laughed. "England, Theo. He's from England."

"In Europe, right?" Laine asked, and all three ex-mortals in the room nodded. It was almost comical how the two of them, being young adults and old teenagers respectively, couldn't recite much about basic geography, but to be fair to them, they'd never been on Earth before.

"Only geographically now though." Julian said, raising his pointer finger as if delivering a crucial fact.

"What?" Raphie questioned.

"Yeah, they like, left a few years ago."

"How do you leave a continent?" Theo said.

"No, just the European Union. It's political, I don't know, I was too young to care when it happened."

Laine looked around. "Sorry, how does this relate to Julian dying?"

"It doesn't. Let's get back on track." Nikoliah said, sitting down on the carpet with the notebook. "I'm hoping we'll say something that will spark a memory."

"It's not to do with Julian's memory." Theo said, sitting up straighter. "I tried to do that palm-to-forehead-life-course thingy that monarchs can do and it uh, it didn't work. Which is weird."

"That palm-to-forehead what?" Raphie glanced between the Virzor siblings.

"It's a thing that we can do once or if crowned monarchs. We can see the whole duration of someone's life on Earth in like, five seconds tops." Laine replied.

Julian sat down on the floor. "Why can't we just go to my hometown and nosey around? It's not an everyday thing that an eighteen-year-old drops dead."

"Yeah, that's great in theory, but we can't go there. Like I told you yesterday, death is death. No getting back to Earth." Theo replied.

"Well, we don't actually know that. We've never tried." Laine replied.

"And how would you go about trying?"

The room lulled in silence. Theo inhaled sharply, standing up from his throne. "It's late. I'm tired. We can reconvene tomorrow, alright? Julian, your room is the same but if you can't be asked to get up that staircase just crash on my floor."

The King didn't wait for a response, just walking down the corridor and out of the Throne room.

What Theo had failed to see in his hindsight about the next day, was that a girl would show up at his doorstep. Not just any girl, but Serenity. The girl he was going to marry.

He didn't even register who she was, because before Theo could actually look at her she had thrown herself onto him in a hug. She only stayed there for about three seconds before pulling away, keeping her hands on the King's shoulders.

Now, as he got his first look at her, he had to admit that she *was* beautiful. Fiery, curled ginger hair falling to her elbows. She had the same blacked-out eyes as Theo, Laine and Dyran, as well as freckles running across the bridge of her nose - similarly to her fiance . She also had navy blue coloured horns and tail that looked really good against her red hair.

"Hi, Strythio. It's really good to meet you." She smiled, almost so quiet that Theo couldn't make it out. He offered a hand for her to shake, which she took as he replied.

"Yeah, you too. Serenity, right?"

She nodded, shoving a backpack into his hand and marching off towards the main staircase. Theo faltered for a moment before spinning on his heel and following her hastily.

"Where's our bedroom, then?"

Theo caught up to her easily, having pretty long legs. "Um, well, my bedroom is just on the right here. I was assuming I could get you your own for now?"

Serenity stopped, turning only her head to face the monarch. "We're engaged, Strythio. We're sharing a bedroom."

"Theo."

"What?" She asked, continuing to walk briskly.

"My name's Theo."

"Right, okay." She accepted, swinging the door of Theo's bedroom open and flicking the light on. She stood for a moment, staring at the space. "This is... nice."

Truth be told, the room did not look nice. Theo would have definitely tidied it if he'd known he'd be meeting his fiance today. Julian had slept on his floor like he'd offered, and so there were also messy bed sheets on the ground. The curtains were drawn still, light seeping out from the bottom of them. His floor had clothes on it, and the bathroom still had water on the ground from when Theo had showered this morning.

She inhaled sharply. "Let's go out for lunch. Just me and you, while your servants move my stuff in here and tidy our bedroom."

"I don't really call them servants, they just work here." Theo replied. "But, um, I'm kind of busy today."

Serenity looked at Theo as if he was joking. "Do you even want to get married? You're acting like this is a chore for you!" She laughed. "You are taking your future Queen out to lunch, okay?"

Theo bit back admitting that it was a chore, and just nodded, trying his best to look guilty. "Okay. Let's go then."

"Good morning, King Theo!" Someone shouted cheerily from the streets as him and Serenity were walking. They were walking at the same pace, but about half a metre apart.

"Morning." He smiled back.

One particular person walked directly up to the two of them, the crowd that had formed watching. "We heard about the royal wedding, is this the lucky girl?" They asked, gesturing to Serenity, who smiled.

"Yeah, I'm his fiance. Serenity." She smiled, loving the attention.

That was until she heard the murmurs.

"He's not even holding her hand."

"I'd bet my life he doesn't even like her."

"We can all tell this is arranged."

"He's way out of her league."

Theo heard this, not caring too much until he saw the devastatingly upsetting look on Serenity's face. He groaned inwardly, reaching down and grabbing Serenity's hand, raising it about their heads with his own with newfound confidence. He couldn't allow his people to talk so rudely about her.

"This is my beautiful fiance, Serenity." He began, speaking loudly in a tone that shushed the whole crowd. "The circumstances of our engagement are none of anyone's business, and if you have an issue with it you can come and speak to me in private because I am *not* going to have this."

There was a silence for a moment before Theo brought his and Serenity's hands down. "Does anyone have any issues they want to address while I'm here?" And when there was only silence and murmurs of 'no', he continued. "Good. Have a nice rest of your days then." He finished, still gripping the other royal's hand as he pulled her along the street. Once they were out of the way, he stopped.

"I'm sorry if that embarrassed you, I just can't deal with them talking about you like that and-"

Serenity interrupted him by putting her hands on the collar of his shirt and pulling him forwards and stealing his lips in a kiss. Serenity's tail floated behind her happily as they did so, and Theo found himself kissing back out of obligation. It made him feel a little bad for leading her on like this, but he supposed there wasn't really a solution other than to play along.

After five or so seconds, Serenity pulled away and smiled really widely.

"Thank you for doing that." She whispered, endorphins still heightened from the excitement of the kiss. "I've never had a guy protect my honour like that, I just, I appreciate it."

"Yeah of course." Theo whispered back, chest elevating and descending up and down as he spoke.

Serenity looked to the ground, linking her hand back with Theo's.
"I'm sorry for acting all entitled. I was just worried that you didn't like me because our parents sorted this out. I really appreciate the reassurance." She smiled, hugging Theo once more, with more gentle care than she had when they first met.
This time, Theo felt genuinely guilty. "Serenity, I really need to be honest with you about something-"
"Come on, let's get sat down at a cafe or somewhere and we can have a proper conversation about anything you like, alright darling?"
Theo swallowed. "Alright." He said softly, smiling. "Alright, let's go find somewhere."
And so they walked down the street further. Serenity felt a lot more peace of mind towards the people looking at her now that she felt protected by Theo. They eventually made it to a restaurant, in which they sat in a closed-off booth in the corner.
"I like your kingdom. It's nice." She commented, picking the menu up. "Mine's not as nice."
Theo looked up from where his eyes were scanning the options. "Really? What do you mean?"
"I don't know, you have loads of prospering businesses here, and nice scenery. I suppose this is the kingdom for the best of the worst, so it makes sense that it's nicer than Vaemunt."
Theo frowned. "I'm sure it's really nice. You'll have to take me there someday." He added, not because he was actually interested in his fiance's kingdom, but because it seemed like the kind of thing that would cheer her up.
Her shoulders deflated and she smiled to herself. "Yeah, I suppose you could visit. What are you getting?"
"Um, steak, probably. We have the teeth for it." Theo laughed, reading over the options of how he could have his steak cooked and seasoned and all. Serenity laughed too. "Yeah. Show me yours; every pureblooded demon I speak to seems to have slightly different canines."
Theo smiled, leaning in closer to Serenity and using his thumb to hook back his mouth in order to show his teeth. They were normal, except for two fang-like pointed teeth in the position of his canines. It was another of the traits that pureblooded demons had that ex-mortals didn't. Serenity all-but gasped.
"Woah, Theo! Those are like, sharp. Bet you're fun in bed." She joked lightly. "Mine aren't as cool." She said, smiling widely to show her own teeth to the King. True to her word, they weren't of the same slim

sharpness as Theo's - more rounded but still sharp enough that they'd impress an ex-mortal.

"Nah, they're great. You could do real damage to a well-done steak if you're up for it."

"I'm more of a medium rare kind of girl." She added, tilting her head in pleasant surprise when the server walked over just as she said it.

So, a steak and glass of rosé each later, Theo and Serenity found themselves walking back towards the castle through town. It was now maybe 1pm, and the streets were a lot more lively now than earlier. Which is why Theo wasn't all that surprised when they bumped into Laine and Nikoliah going out for a walk, or food, or whatever they were doing.

Laine saw Theo and waved, dragging her boyfriend over to the King. Her eyes glanced over to the foreign princess and she smiled.

"You must be Serenity! It's lovely to meet you." She said, sticking her hand out for the other to shake. Rather than doing so, Serenity giggled slightly and just engulfed Laine in a hug.

"Yeah, nice to meet you too." She said, pulling away. "God, you're so pretty. Must run in the family, huh?" Serenity looked over to Theo as she said this, smiling widely. "Laine, right?"

"Mhm! And, this is Niko." Laine added, turning to the soldier and noting the impatient look on his face. "...liah. This is Nikoliah. My boyfriend." She corrected, finding it semi-adorable that he only really allowed his girlfriend to call him by that nickname.

Serenity raised her eyebrows. "Oh! I assumed you were a guard or something." She said before leaning into Laine. "You don't find it weird to date an ex-mortal? What about bloodlines?" She whispered, looking at Nikoliah as she did so.

Laine's smile faltered before reappearing. "No, I don't really think that matters so long as we love each other. Why? Would you not date an ex-mortal?"

"Well," The Princess began. "I suppose I don't really have to worry about that, huh sweetheart?" She grinned, wrapping her arm around the back of Theo's shoulders.

Laine smiled and nodded. "Yeah, um, Niko, did you wanna speak to Serenity for a moment alone? Maybe you can tell her about that time you tripped while carrying a bowl of soup and it went all over you?" She suggested. Nikoliah raised his eyebrows and tilted his head as if to say 'what?', but it only took about two seconds after that for him to catch on.

"Um, yeah, okay. Yeah, let's chat over here." He motioned, beckoning Theo's fiance over. She glanced back to the King as if to ask permission, to which he encouraged the action as well. Once they were a good five metres away, Laine's disposition turned slightly annoyed.

"Theo, do not tell me you are leading her on."

Theo sighed in exasperation. "I'm not leading her on, I just-" He groaned. "She keeps talking like she was so miserable in her own kingdom, and this is the best thing that's ever happened to her. I only kissed her once, and *she* initiated it, so-"

"Theo." Laine warned. "I love you, but she's going to get hurt, you need to tell her the truth."

"Agh," Theo whined. "I tried. I tried, but she seems so happy to be marrying me."

Laine reached forward and took Theo's hand. "Look, I'm not going to tell her for you - but you're both going to live deeply unhappy lives if you don't, and I mean that."

Theo exhaled. "No, you don't mean that, Laine. I'm not going to have you stand here and lecture me on romance. You haven't the faintest clue what I'm going through!" He spoke kind of loudly, and Laine worried a little that he was being too loud.

"Yeah!" She whisper-yelled. "I don't know, but what I do know is that you're going to break her heart if you keep this up."

"What would you do then, Mother Teresa?" He stressed.

"Not whatever you've got going on, that's for sure." She spoke angrily. "I get that this is difficult for you and all, but you have to think about her."

"Stop saying that! Stop saying that you get it, you don't. You don't get shit about what it's like, because you have your perfect little boyfriend that you're *allowed* to date!"

Laine raised her eyebrows as if to give the notion of a sarcastic 'really?'. "Your fake girlfriend just made a dodgy comment about his species about two minutes ago. Get your head out of the gutter, it's difficult for all of us and it doesn't justify what you're doing to that girl!"

Theo rolled his eyes. "I think you'll find it's actually none of your business."

Laine was about to reply, but Nikoliah stepped in between them.

"She went to look at one of the market stalls and I've been listening to you two for the last minute or so. Maybe you should have this conversation in private." He suggested.

"No, that's okay." Theo grinned sarcastically, his nose scrunching up as he did. "I think we pretty much finished this conversation, didn't we? Have a nice little date." He said, looking at both of them. He walked off towards where serenity was gazing at some jewellery on a stand.

"Hey, sorry about that." He said, standing next to her.

"Oh, that's alright! That soldier kid is very... interesting." She said, smiling a little judgmentally.

"Yeah, he's alright when you get to know him, don't worry."

Serenity nodded. Her eyes kept dancing over the rings.

"I was thinking that maybe we could buy engagement rings. What do you think?"

Theo paused. "Um, yeah, I'd love to - I just, I left my money at home."

"You just paid for food." The Princess snorted. "You're so forgetful, don't worry, my dad's like that too."

Theo laughed awkwardly. "Alright... What were you thinking?" And Serenity smiled.

"Well, see these little gold ones with the gems on? I was thinking that you could get the little blue gem, and I could get the same one in green, because you know, your colour is green and mine is blue." She nodded, gesturing to their horns as she spoke.

Theo reached down into the ring holder and picked them up, agreeing awkwardly. "If that's what you want."

X

When Theo and Serenity arrived back at the castle, rings on fingers, the first thing they did was head up to Theo's (or, their, he supposed) bedroom. They were exhausted from walking around, and Theo definitely felt like slipping into a food coma.
To his surprise, his bedroom *was* actually tidy now. Which was weird, because he hadn't asked anyone to. Serenity must have. It made him feel a little violated that someone had nosed around his room. What if he couldn't find his stuff later? Well, too late now, he supposed. He sat down on the edge of his bed and brought his right ankle on top of his left knee to unbuckle his leather boot, planning to repeat the action with the other foot afterwards.
Serenity just slipped her heels off by the door, flopping down onto the bed backwards and exhaling in relief. "This is so comfortable, how do you manage to stay awake when you're just sitting on it?" She asked, body melting into the thick duvet, hair splaying out behind her.
Theo pulled his second shoe off, throwing them aimlessly in the direction of the door, where the other demon's were. He laughed, looking back at the comfortably peaceful girl. She, however, sat up.
"No wonder your room was a mess." She scolded, sliding off the bed and marching over to the pile of his shoes, picking them both up and straightening them next to hers. "Don't worry, I can fix you." She chucked.
Theo felt a little ill.
"Take your jacket off, I wanna cuddle." Serenity pouted, standing in front of Theo and smiling lovingly. Theo slipped his arms out of the jacket.

"I really need to talk to you about something, Serenity." He said, gesturing for her to sit down beside him. She frowned and looked like a sad puppy.

"Did I... did I do something wrong?" She asked, a slight whine on her voice. "I can- I can do better, please don't leave me Theo, you're the love of my life. I know I haven't known you long but *I love you*." She pleaded.

Theo swallowed. Ouch. She *loved* him? That felt like... a lot.

"No, I just, um. I was wondering if..." He thought, deciding that there was no way he could do what he was planning on now she'd confessed her love to him. "Maybe if you wanted to go out this evening. Um, by yourself. Just to explore the kingdom. I just have some business stuff to take care of here, wouldn't wanna bore you." He fumbled, fidgeting with his hands.

Serenity grinned. "Yeah, okay. That sounds alright. Sorry I got emotional, I just, I can't believe you're real." She sighed. "Now, come and cuddle."

The moment the door closed and Serenity left that evening, Theo felt a wave of relief wash over him. He sighed in exasperation, heading back up the stairs to his room. When he got there, though, and sat down on his bed, he felt overwhelmed.

His bedroom smelt like her. It smelt like her hair, and her clothes and her skin and- agh. He groaned, leaping up off his bed and leaving his bedroom, slamming the door behind him and leaning against it, panting heavily as the smell of his fiance wafted away. God, it was too much.

It was too much, all of this. He'd only known this girl for the better half of a day and it was too much.

Laine hated him over it, and he hated Serenity over it, but he mostly hated himself over it. This was horrible, so horrible, and Theo felt tears pool in his eyes as he gasped for breath. He couldn't live the rest of eternity like this, he just couldn't. His body slipped down the door and his knees folded into his chest.

He couldn't breathe, he felt like he was dying. Was he dying? Was that even possible? No, no it wasn't, that's stupid. Stupid. Just like he was for doing all this. His fingernails dug into his right wrist in an attempt to ground himself. It was too much, he needed it to be over. He needed it to be over.

"Hey, hey. You're alright." Julian coaxed. Theo hadn't noticed him appear, but he had somehow, now wearing some of his own clothes that Nikoliah had bought him earlier in the day. He looked a lot more like himself now than he did in Theo's clothes - wearing an oversized coral-orange coloured t-shirt with pink and white flower graphics on it, and light blue jeans. The clothes fit his body a lot better, and displayed his natural essence. He looked beautiful.

Theo shook his head through tears and jagged gasps for breath.

Julian reached out and took his hands, pulling him away from the harmful behaviour of digging his nails into his skin. The extra contact was calming, and it immediately slowed his breathing to a slightly more regulatable pace. Theo felt his heart beat faster from just holding his boy's hand.

He was royally screwed. This guy would be the death of him.

The King tightened his grip on the human's hands. Gasping for air, he placed his head in between his knees.

"Do you want me to talk you through this or are you good?"

Theo coughed, trying to speak. "Talk." He choked.

Julian nodded. "Alright. Just breathe all the way in for me, I'm going to count in my head and I'll let you know. Okay, one." He lectured softly. "You know, when I was twelve I was in one of those Christmas-time shops. That's four, now just hold it. And, I was fooling around like kids do, and knocked a whole display of glass snow globes over - and they smashed all over the floor." He told the story casually as Theo focused on his breaths.

"That's seven, now just breathe out slowly. And so, they asked my mum to pay, but she had like six quid on her card, so after it declined she just picked me up and ran, and it was like, the most adrenaline-rushing moment of my life. The security guard chased us for six blocks, but we got away. Oh, shit, sorry, you can breathe again now."

Theo laughed, wiping his eyes of the remaining tears. His chest was still rising and falling steadily, but at a more manageable pace that made him feel alright.

"Thank you." Theo smiled, still holding onto Julian's hands as he crossed his legs.

"Yeah, don't sweat it. I can imagine this is... a lot for you, huh?"

Theo sniffled, pulling Julian closer to him as the human rested his head on the King's shoulder. "Yeah." He breathed. "I don't wanna talk about it more than that."

"Then we don't have to." Julian offered. "Just forget about all of it. I'll sit here with you for as long as you need."

Theo hummed in response, a hand moving to absentmindedly comb through Julian's hair. The mortal sighed, relaxing his body into Theo's further, so that he was practically lying against the other man. Their bodies stilled in bliss for a minute. Theo wasn't sure what love was supposed to feel like, but he was pretty certain this was close.
"Did you get those letters back?" Julian murmured into Theo's chest.
"I'm not sure. I haven't checked yet today." He replied. "We can go now. You're gonna have to get up." Theo chided, planting both hands on Julian's shoulders, who groaned.
"We can check later it's fine, I'm comfy here."
"We should maybe get out of the hallway anyway, Julian."
"Why? Would it be bad if someone saw us?" He replied in a tease.
"Yeah, it would. I'm engaged."
Julian snickered. "Are you implying that you're attracted to me? Is this scandalous?"
Theo faltered, only just registering what he had said a moment ago. He stuttered, lightly shoving Julian away from him and standing. The other man pouted, reaching his hands up to signify that he wanted pulling to his feet. Theo obliged, sighing, and Julian smirked. "Is that a no?"
"Shut up and let's go check the mailbox."
They slinked through one of the servants' passages, giggling slightly like children playing spies. The corridors were narrow enough that they had to walk single-file, and when they got down the stairs near the castle entrance, Theo turned around to face Julian.
"You wait here, okay? I'll be two minutes." He instructed, not waiting for a response before he opened the door and left the passageway, striding confidently towards the mailbox. There was a stack of letters in it, and he smiled, glad he'd been written back to.
He retrieved it hastily, not wanting anyone to see him and speak to him. So, two minutes later he and Julian were sitting on the bed in the latter's temporary room since Theo had decided he wasn't ready to go back to *his* room just yet.
"Do you want to open it, or shall I?" The King asked. Julian shrugged.
"It's your mail, you can open it, just tell me quickly."
And so, Theo carefully opened the envelope of the first letter, and then the second, and then the third and so on. Each time he read one, it was a pretty brief 'no Vanna Thompson here', which he expressed to the other.
"Sorry." Theo said, not really knowing what else to offer.

"Nah, it's fine. I'm happy she's still alive. I think... I think it'd be worse if she was dead and in another kingdom that I couldn't get to." He confessed, fidgeting with his hands.

"Do you, um," Theo began. "Do you miss her?" He asked, trying to sympathise.

"I've only been dead, like, what? A day?" Julian laughed a little sadly. "I mean... Of course I miss her. She's my mum, and, and we were close." He lamented.

"Yeah, of course." Theo said, suddenly regretting that he'd brought it up a little.

"Is yours around?" Julian said, looking up. "I know your dad is, I've heard, but, is your mum?"

Theo swallowed. "Uh, no, she's not."

"Is she still alive like mine?"

"She never was - she was pureblooded like Laine and I am. Was never on Earth."

Julian paused. "You never lived?" And Theo shook his head.

"Oh." He breathed. "I just assumed you were like a really special deceased person or like a dead monarch or something."

After a moment of silence, he continued.

"Is that why you're so hopeless at geography?"

Theo laughed. "What, did you think I was just a bit thick?"

"You are a little bit." He replied. "I guess I thought you'd just died young."

"Wait, I am not hopeless at geography." Theo argued, only just then registering the other's previous statement.

Julian smiled endearingly. "We'll see about it, considering you didn't know where Manchester was."

"Is it a capital city?"

"Well, no, but-"

"Then there is literally no reason I should know it." He debated. "I'm not from England. Could you name a random city from a random country you aren't from, let alone never been to?"

Julian only smiled wider, happy to be having an energetic debate.

"You're literally speaking English right now!" He exclaimed, raising his right hand towards the King who smiled back playfully.

"No, I'm not." He said.

"What do you mean?! We are currently having a conversation in British English, am I wrong?!" He half yelled, smiling while he did, thoroughly amused by this.

"We are in the afterlife, Julian, it's kind of magical." Theo lectured. "I don't speak English, but when I talk to you, or anyone talks to you in a different language, you'll hear it that way because that's what you can understand." He said.

Julian's eyes widened in disbelief.

"What language are you speaking then?"

"Latin." Theo replied bluntly.

"Latin?!" Julian laughed. "That's dumb as hell. Why do you speak Latin?"

"Traditional." Theo smirked slightly.

"Seriously?" Julian asked. "I literally can't even describe how pretentious that makes you seem. How does that even work? Latin? That's so stupid, nobody speaks that. You realise that nobody speaks that, right?"

"Julian-" Theo laughed, trying to interrupt.

"AND! And, I swear they don't even have words for most modern stuff! How do you ask someone for a sheet of paper when they don't have a word for paper!"

"Julian." The King smiled widely.

"What?" The other grumbled.

"I'm fucking with you. Of course I'm speaking English." He grinned.

"That's just for calling me thick."

Julian's face contorted from one of disbelief to one of amusement.

"Asshole." He joked. "So, you *should* know where Manchester is."

"Maybe I should." Theo conceded. "I wasn't kidding about the language thing here though, I just speak English. And I can speak Latin by the way, so watch your mouth about it."

Julian rolled his eyes with playful content. He shifted his position in sitting so that he was completely facing Theo, but pretty closely now compared to when he was a little further away.

"Hold on, I'll get you to do one of those 'name the country' tests." He said, reaching into his jean pocket. He paused, and then placed a hand in the other one. His eyebrows furrowed in confusion as Julian continued to pat himself down as if looking for something. "That's weird, I can't find my phone." He stated.

Theo raised his eyebrows. "Have you had it since you got here?"

Julian thought for a moment, then he realised. "Oh. No, I suppose not. Do I not get my phone in Hell? Is this my eternal punishment for a slightly skewed moral compass?"

The demon simpered. "This kingdom has been around a lot longer than your mobile devices. Here we kind of believe in conversation, I know your generation has some issues with it." He said cockily.

Julian gasped in mock offence. "You're part of my generation, you realise that, right?"
Theo shrugged. "Not really. It's more of a socialisation thing, and I've never even used a phone."
"Yeah, and you're missing out. I bet you don't even know what a phone is."
"I know what a phone is."
"It's like," Julian began, ignoring the previous statement. "A metal box of wires and chips and glass and stuff that you can use to communicate all around the world, and post things and-
"I don't need you to mansplain what a mobile phone is to me, thanks though."
Julian snickered. "Alright, I'm sorry, love."
Theo's head tilted to look at the other. He blushed slightly, body heating up at the use of the nickname. "Love?" He asked.
Julian smiled, leaning his head into Theo's body, similarly to how they were in the corridor earlier. "Yeah." He confirmed, and that was all.
Theo sighed, lifting Julian's head off his chest and looking him in the eyes. "You're giving me pet names now. What's... up?" The King asked, not exactly sure how to phrase it. Julian raised an eyebrow.
"What's what? English would be nice."
Theo exhaled. "I mean, I guess. What's going on between us, Julian? What are we?"
Julian smirked, shifting himself to be all-but sitting on Theo's lap. "What do you want us to be?" He whispered, and Theo felt more alive in that moment than he had all the rest of his life.
It was strange, he thought, as this human breathed down his neck. It had been a few days at most and yet he found himself so helplessly infatuated with this boy. Not even just aesthetically. Sure, he was incredibly attractive, the dazzling green of his eyes against his dark skin were surely enough to hypnotise the monarch, and he didn't think he would mind if that were to happen.
Is this what Serenity felt about him?
He hoped not, because in this moment, if Julian had told him that the feelings weren't there, he might have to barricade himself in his room for months, only coming out for water and food. But, considering how forward this dead boy was, sitting on the King's lap, heavy breaths lingering in the air, eyes enrapturing the other's soul as he waited for a response, Theo was pretty sure the feeling was mutual.
He wasn't sure what to reply.

He was engaged. He had a girlfriend, this was wrong. He knew it was wrong but it somehow made the adrenaline coursing through his veins move at a rate of a hundred times faster than it was. His thoughts raced with love, love and passion and care and hope. Hope that maybe this was something more than a flirtatious comment. Hope that maybe this was his chance at the happiness he'd spent his whole life seeking.
Holding onto that hope for dear life, Theo smirked lovingly. Julian placed a soft hand on the underside of Theo's jaw, tilting his head upwards and plunging their lips together in a kiss.
And this time, Theo kissed back out of genuine admiration and sentiment. It wasn't about pleasing his dad, or not breaking a girl's heart. It was about himself. Himself and this man he'd become so accustomed to. It felt the same kissing Julian as it did Serenity, physically at least. But, emotionally, the leap between the false romance and genuine connection was strong enough that Theo felt more at home than he'd ever felt before. In the safety of this boy, *his boy*.
His body felt electric, and it was unlike anything he'd ever felt before. It was like a new sense of self, a sense of his own personality and a sense of independence. Theo placed his right hand on the back of Julian's neck, left hand steadying himself on the bed as they deepened the kiss, it turning into more of a make-out that was blinded by sudden impulse and delicate love.
Theo didn't think he'd ever felt better.
He wanted it to last forever, didn't want it to ever stop. He wanted to feel like this all the time. To feel this cared for, this loved, this head-over-heels for one person. It was more magical than any spells he'd ever performed.
Julian had now practically straddled Theo's lap - it being a more comfortable position to offer himself in. It felt so incredibly right, even though there was that looming voice in the King's head telling him how wrong he was. He didn't care for it at this exact moment. He didn't care for anything other than Julian. Nothing else mattered apart from his whatever-they-were. He assumed that this was what it was meant to feel like.
"I thought I told you not to get attached."
Theo pushed Julian off him, more than upset that they'd had to break the kiss. Both men's heads snapped to the door of the room, where Laine was leant against the doorframe with a partially judgemental, partially amused smirk adorning her lips.

"Oh my God! Oh my God, get the fuck out!" Theo yelled, standing from the bed and wiping the saliva off his mouth. "That's why you knock!" He continued.

Julian's eyes remained downcast at the bedsheets guiltily. Laine took a step back, not liking the way that her brother was raising his voice.

"To be fair, Theo, I wasn't expecting you to be at first base with a random mortal." She quipped.

His breathing exaggerated, and he used his sleeve to wipe his mouth again for good measure. "For God's sake, Laine." He breathed.

"I'm not going to get upset at you, Theo. I'm happy for you." She assured, although it didn't quite make its way into the King's head, who remained looking distressed.

The Princess looked away, feeling a little guilty about ruining whatever moment they were having. "Well," She said, swallowing. "On an unrelated note, your girlfriend is downstairs waiting for you. You're lucky I volunteered to come get you rather than her."

Theo shook his head. "God." He panted, turning to Julian. "I can't do this, we can't do this. I'm sorry, I'm really sorry, we can't- we can't do this. It's too much." He panted, tears forming in his eyes. He didn't even take the time to register the betrayed look that pushed its way onto Julian's face. Instead, he hurried to the door of the room, shoving past his sister and leaving his upset mortal behind, to go and find Serenity like it was his duty to do.

Laine didn't try to stop him, but her head followed him, watching as he descended the stairs. She sighed. "Did you kiss him first or did he kiss you first?" She asked.

Julian sniffled, flopping his body backwards onto the bed. "I kissed him." He confessed. "But he's been flirting with me all day." The man pouted. Then, Julian sucked in a harsh breath. "Why did you do that? You could've just left after you saw us." He accused.

"And how far exactly would you have gone if I hadn't interrupted? Serenity is downstairs, it would be suspicious for him not to show up." Laine criticised as she closed the door behind her, sitting on the edge of the bed. "I need you to understand that his life is more complicated than just fooling around with whoever he wants. If I had been *anyone* else, you would probably both end up banished to a harsher kingdom - maybe even Nesbryn. Do you know how serious affairs are taken here?" She asked condescendingly.

"It doesn't even matter anymore." Julian frowned, pulling his knees up to his chest to comfort himself. "He's made it clear he doesn't want me, thanks to you. You're stressing him out."

Laine stayed silent for a brief moment before speaking. "I'm sorry if I squandered your chances with him." She said, "but, *he is* engaged."

"He doesn't want to be." Julian replied. "If you actually cared about him you'd be helping him get out of it." The man scoffed, sliding off the bed and walking towards the door. He opened it, holding it in that position and gesturing for the demon to leave.

She nodded. "I *want* to support him, Julian. I'm just worried about the consequences of all this."

"It's not your issue to worry about, it's ours. Thanks for the concern though." He replied sarcastically, once more gesturing for the Princess to leave.

She sighed, standing off the bed. Her head turned towards the human and she gave him a few last words before leaving.

"Whatever you do, just- please be careful with it."

XI

Sure enough, when Theo got to the bottom of the stairs, he saw Serenity sitting on the top step of the grand staircase, not paying much attention to his footsteps. In fact, she didn't seem to notice his approach until he sat down next to her.
"Hey." He said.
"Hi." She replied quickly, taking one of the King's hands in hers.
"How was the town?" He asked.
She pursed her lips. "It was nice. I felt a little lost without you knowing where we are, though." She laughed to herself. "Didn't get to see all that much, it started to look like it was going to rain."
Theo looked out the window at that. He hadn't realised it, but the weather had turned a little since earlier. The sky was a lot darker and there were small drops of humidity grazing the surface of the glass in the window frame, also creating a versatile layer of condensation.
"Oh yeah. Well, we can go to the kitchen and get some hot chocolates if you wanna warm up at all?" He suggested, running his thumb over her knuckles endearingly.
She smiled. "Yeah, that'd be great. Where are the kitchens?" She asked, standing and pulling her fiance with her. Theo stood, following as he explained.
"Just down here to the right, through that hallway and past the dining rooms." He instructed, picking up his pace to be slightly ahead of her in order to show her the directions.
The kitchen was completely quiet when they arrived. There was hardly any kitchen staff anymore, as Laine and Theo found themselves more

than capable of cooking their own meals. It was a completely empty room with a marble island in the centre and industrial sinks, countertops and fridges all around the edges.

Serenity smiled, drumming her fingers on the countertop as Theo sifted through the cupboards. After trying a few, he found the ingredient he needed and got started on making the drinks, some idle chatter occurring as he did. Just as he was stirring them, another voice made itself clear.

"Oh, Hello you two!" Jaymie said, walking over to the sink with her empty water glass. She gasped, turning to Serenity. "You must be the fiance! It's so great to meet you!"

Serenity smiled back, giving one of those over-exaggerated smiles that you give when you have to greet a lot of people. "Yeah, you too. Serenity." She told the other. "What do you do around here?"

Jaymie shook Serenity's hand excitedly. "Well, my name's Jaymie. I'm a stylist, which basically means I do all of his," She began, pointing to Theo who paid no mind, "outfits for special occasions, and I'll also probably do your wedding dress or whatever you wanna go in." She fussed.

Serenity looked confused. "You work here?"

"Mhm!"

"Why didn't you... like bow when you came in, then?" She asked, not really judgemental, but just a little lost. Theo tapped the spoons on the edge of their mugs and placed them in the sink.

"We don't really do that here," He said. "I'm not any better than them, I just have a different job."

Serenity considered this for a moment. "Oh. I see, that's kinda cool. Progressive, even." She stuttered, a little dumbfounded. "Well, it's nice to meet the girl who's going to design my wedding dress. We should talk styles." She encouraged, leaning over the counter to face Jaymie.

"Alright! We have a lot of stuff to consider, do you wanna go traditional white or a different colour? Other monarchs *have* deviated before. How long do you want it to be? Short sleeve or long? What kind of neckline?" Theo allowed the endless stream of questions to fade into the cool air. The steam from the hot drinks was rising up from them, and he watched intently. After a moment, he realised that the two girls were now deep in conversation, so he picked up the mugs and turned to them, placing them on the counter.

"Um," He interrupted. "Sorry. I have some more business stuff to do outside of the castle today, can I leave you two to it?"

Serenity frowned. "Do you have to? I just got back."

"Yeah, don't run off, Theo. If we're figuring out her dress today we'd be best to do yours too to make sure they match." Jaymie persuaded. "The way I phrased that made it sound like you're going to be wearing a dress." She giggled.
The red-headed princess smiled, exhaling in amusement. "Business can wait until after your wedding, come on." She instructed, reaching to grab his hand.
Jaymie stood up a little straighter. "Do you wanna go to a lounge or something to chat about this? Then I can get my notebook and sketch out some ideas. I might have to fetch Kougan if we're doing this now, but I think he said he was having the day off." She rambled, her first question being kind of lost as Serenity smiled to herself at the enthusiasm, excited to design her dress.
"Yeah, let's go." She beamed, following Jaymie out of the room. Theo stood in the kitchen for a moment. He closed his eyes and took a deep breath in before exhaling, then he began to follow the two girls down the corridor towards one of the lounges.

The sun had just set when Theo got another moment alone. Serenity wanted to get an 'early night' and was showering now so that her hair had enough time to dry before they went to bed or something, Theo wasn't really listening.
The designing of Serenity's dress had gone really well, and she'd ended up with a traditional white style that she really liked. Much to his own distaste, she'd had her heart set on Theo wearing a suit, and so he agreed and Jaymie had said she'd get to work to have them both done in a few days' time.
He was now sitting on the edge of his bed, wearing just joggers and a t-shirt now as he planned to shower after the Princess. The idle sound of the water spraying from the bathroom lulled in the background of his thoughts, and was only interrupted when there was a knock to his bedroom door.
The King stood, assuming it was probably his sister or someone that worked at the castle. However, when he opened the door he was met with Julian, standing before him with puffy eyes.
"Can we talk?" Julian stuttered, nervous and caught off guard.

Theo blinked. "Not now, you need to go back to your room." He warned, peeking his head out of the doorframe and scanning the corridors for witnesses.

"For how long?" Julian countered. "Are you even trying to get me home? I refuse to stay there when it's convenient for you."

Theo furrowed his eyebrows in anger. "You realise I don't *have* to let you stay here, right?"

"But you will."

"Will I?"

Julian smirked. "Yeah, I think you will, Theo."

"Mhm, and why's that? What's stopping me from kicking your needy ass onto the street right now?" He asked somewhat harshly, eyebrows raised and shoulders squared back. Julian deflated a little at the insult, hoping it wasn't sincere but just for the sake of making a point.

He frowned, rolling his eyes before looking back up to the King, a determined look crossing over his face.

"Because you love me, Strythio Virzor. I know what it looks like, and it looks like the way you were looking at me earlier when you kissed me."

"Shush, shush, please." Theo pleaded, looking back at the bathroom door.

"Have you ever even had a boyfriend before, Theo?" The other man asked.

"No, obviously not."

"So, you're scared because this is new to you. But it doesn't have to be scary, I promise. I can show you what love is meant to feel like, if only you'll let me." He said, exasperated. Theo shook his head.

"You've had boyfriends, or girlfriends, or whatever, before, right?"

"Right." Julian confirmed easily.

"So you aren't going to have any trouble finding someone that can treat you right and doesn't have to hide you." He said, voice breaking a little.

Julian's shoulders deflated and he looked around the hallway before back to the other man. "I've had girlfriends and boyfriends, Theo, but none like this. This is different. This is real. You- you make me feel more alive than I ever felt when I was *actually* alive."

Theo blinked in realisation. Julian made him feel alive too. And he didn't even know what being alive felt like, but it was something like he feels when he's around Julian. Any words that the taller man had died on his tongue, and he was only able to gaze longingly at Julian. Someone he wanted so badly, but he couldn't have. He was leading Julian on by doing this. It couldn't work, and the longer he let them entertain the idea that it could, the more it would hurt in the end.

Julian swallowed. "It's just- you love me, and I love you. I don't care what your dad thinks. We can make it work, I promise! But, you have to want to make it work."

"That feels kind of naive, Jude." He sighed.

"This is your sister talking, right? You didn't care about it until she did. Theo, I don't see what-"

"Shut up!" Theo yelled, slapping a hand over his mouth once he recognised his lack of volume control.

He waited for a moment, cringing, listening in the direction of the bathroom. After about ten seconds of silence he relaxed, slowly peeling his hand away from his mouth. He downcast his gaze to the ground, voice dropping to a whisper.

"Just... just go back upstairs, Julian." He said, once again getting that uncomfortable feeling that holds in your throat right before crying.

Julian shook his head, looking upset. "Theo, please don't do this. We just need to talk. I'm sorry if I came on too strongly, but, how I feel about you is genuine, and I'm not going to let you throw it away because you're scared."

"Go back upstairs." Theo said, voice louder now, eyes darting in the direction of the staircase.

Julian scoffed, shaking his head. "Fine, fine whatever. But don't say I didn't try, because I did. It's your grave." He grumbled, shoving his hands in his pockets and walking away.

Theo wanted to tell him to wait. There was a feeling tugging at his chest telling him to chase after the boy. But he didn't. He didn't because the water in the shower turned off and he was suddenly dragged back to the prospect that he had responsibilities.

The door to the bathroom opened, and Serenity stood in the doorway with a towel wrapped around her torso. Her grey skin contrasted nicely against the white of the towel, and her hair was still dripping wet, altering the brighter orange colour to be more of a brown-looking shade.

"Who were you talking to just now?" She smiled, sounding more amused than accusatory.

Theo pulled the door shut. "Oh, um, just someone that works here."

"Right," She laughed. "Did you wanna shower?"

Theo shook his head. "I will tomorrow morning, I think." He replied pensively. He wasn't in the mood to do anything anymore.

Serenity sat down on the side of their bed after pulling on a pair of her pyjama bottoms and a light blue tank top.

"Is something bothering you? I know I don't know you that well yet but you seem really tense."

He nodded. "It's fine, just the wedding and all. It's important."

"Well then I suppose it's a good thing you're stressed about it. Shows you care." She reassured, beckoning her fiance to the bed. He smiled, walking over and sitting beside her. "Come on, let's cuddle a little before bed."

It took approximately four days for Theo to break.

He hadn't meant to, but it had been four days of uncomfortable torture for him. He'd been totally avoiding all four of the people who had been in the throne room last Saturday supporting him, because he knew they were all mad at him.

Well, Laine and Julian were mad at him. Laine being mad at him meant that Nikoliah and Raphie were too, though. He'd been getting dirty looks from random staff members all week; he had no idea what his sister had been saying about him, but he knew it couldn't be good. He'd tried to speak to Julian, but had consistently found himself turned away by the other boy, who claimed to be busy or 'not in the mood'. He regretted pushing Julian away pretty much instantly after he did it, but, like the boy had told him, he had dug his grave.

He was receiving all of this isolation from the people he *really* cared about, and yet was gaining all the attention in the world from Serenity. It had been late on Wednesday evening, so three days before the wedding. They'd adopted their usual routine of getting into bed together, but somehow, all of Theo's thoughts caught up to him. He'd spent the whole day worrying about everything he could possibly think about.

The foreign princess wrapped her arms around his torso, pulling herself into his chest in the pitch darkness of the room. One of her legs moved to wrap around the King's own, and he felt horribly overwhelmed. The duvet was too heavy, feeling like it was a sheet of metal pressing down on him.

"We can't get married."

Serenity looked up. Theo could see her in the darkness that his eyes had now adjusted to.

"What?" She asked, pushing herself away from his body and flicking on their bedside light.

She sat up, looking more confused than anything, and Theo only then registered what he'd said.

"Fuck, I didn't mean-"

"Is this why you've been acting weird?" She asked, now pulled out of her groggy state. "What's going on, Theo?"

He swallowed, taking in her form. "I'm gay." He stated, looking up for her reaction. She didn't have one immediately, so he continued. "My... father arranged this without even asking me before he'd already signed me off to you, and I'm sorry if I lead you on or if you like me, but I can't pretend like this any longer."

It was silent for a few seconds after the King's rambling.

"No... no, Theo, you're not. You- you love me. You've *told* me that. You're confused." She argued, voice breaking as she fought back her emotions.

"I didn't want to upset you." He whispered, suddenly feeling a lot smaller than he had before. "I'm sorry."

And then Serenity started sobbing *loudly*, and Theo had to fight back the urge to shush her at this hour of the night. She plunged her face into the pillow, dampening it quickly.

"I was so stupid for thinking anyone could love me." She wailed.

Theo cursed to himself, reaching an arm out to comfort her. She pushed it away as quickly as she could. "Don't fucking touch me!" She cried, standing up from the bed.

"I'm sorry." Theo repeated in a whisper.

"No you're not! If you were, you would've told me the first day we met! I would've been fine with it! We could've figured it out together, but you had to wait long enough to make me fall in love with you, didn't you?"

Theo swallowed, not knowing what to say as guilt flooded his senses.

"Does your sister know?" She asked, wiping her soaked face.

Theo frowned. "Yeah, um, yeah."

Serenity nodded. "We're still getting married." She said, sniffling. "Our kingdoms need it."

Theo raised his eyebrows. "What?"

"Our wedding, Theo, is gonna benefit me, and it'll benefit our kingdoms. The only thing it won't benefit is you. That's what kings are supposed to do: good, selfless things for the sake of their kingdoms."

"Serenity, I'm sorry that you're upset but-"

"No, save it." She said, starting to cry again. She walked towards their bedroom door and opened it.

"Just come back to bed," The King pleaded. "We can talk about it more in the morning."

Serenity was lit up only by the dim glow of the nightlight as she shook her head, and Theo could visibly see the tear tracks on her face, still flowing.

"Don't follow me." She whispered, stepping outside and clicking the door shut.

Theo couldn't tell how long he stared at the closed door for.

He really considered hurrying to follow his fiance, but eventually decided that it was probably the last thing she wanted. By the time he'd come to that conclusion, she could have been anywhere in the castle, though.

He flopped backwards onto his back, staring up at the ceiling as he sighed. This was great. Now *everybody* hated him. How in hell had he managed that? Theo audibly groaned, flopping his arms down onto his face to shield himself from his shame. He rolled over onto his side, bringing his knees up to his chest.

He didn't even realise he was crying until he felt the dampness of his pillow pressing against his skin. He hadn't thought he would feel this horrible about it. It was like a gaping emptiness that ruminated through his chest, grabbing at his body and forcing a headache and stream of tears.

He sat up, deciding it was too much for him to go about alone. As much as it was something he was reluctant to do, he needed the comfort of someone he cared about.

The lights in the corridor were off and Theo was a little worried he'd trip or something, but, to be fair he'd been traversing this corridor his whole life. He made it to the spiral staircase and now that his eyes had readjusted to the dark, he could easily make his way up until he was standing anxiously outside Julian's room.

He pressed two knocks in quick succession to the door and waited, bouncing on his toes. A moment later it opened.

Julian's hair was a mess, and he was blinking tiredly. He was only wearing a pair of dark blue plaid pyjama pants, yawning. Theo's eyes widened as he scanned over Julian's shirtless figure.

"Oh, Theo." He said, smacking his lips together and wiping the drool off his mouth.

"Sorry, did I wake you up?"

"Yeah," He nodded. "It's fine, though. What's so important?" Julian asked, now rubbing his eyes. Except, when he looked back up at Theo, he raised his eyebrows. "Oh, shit, have you been crying?"

"I told Serenity."

"She didn't take it well?"

"Not really." Theo shrugged.

Julian grumbled, reaching for Theo's wrist and grabbing him, pulling him into his bedroom and allowing the door to shut.

"I'm still upset at you." Julian said. "But I understand that you're upset, and I *care* about you. How can I make you feel better?" He offered.

Theo felt even more upset by the formal tone, just wanting casual comfort. He choked on his words slightly, voice breaking as he spoke. "A hug would be nice."

And Julian nodded, an invisible force tugging on his heart as he opened his arms, allowing the monarch to dive into them. He wrapped his arms around Theo and let all of his anger melt away as he embraced the other. The genuine comfort was overwhelming, and Theo began crying again, into Julian's chest this time.

"There, shh, you're okay. It's alright, you're alright, darling."

They moved onto the bed, Julian sitting on the edge of it and Theo basically in his lap as he continued to release his emotions. It might not have been much, but it was exactly what he needed. Julian ran a hand through his hair, hushing his sobs.

"You're okay, you're gonna be okay."

XII

Theo blinked, tiredness encapsulating him as he awoke. His right hand came to rub his eyes, but he kept them shut a little longer to adjust to the morning light.
Oh. This wasn't his room. He looked up at the ceiling as the events of the previous night came flooding back to him. He'd somehow allowed himself to fall asleep in Julian's room, which became pretty apparent when he realised that the other male had his slumbering arms wrapped around the King's torso. He stayed for a moment, exhaling to allow himself more time to process what was going on.
Theo had no idea what time it was, so he wiggled himself out of Julian's grasp and stood. He felt a little dizzy and like his head was stuffed with cotton. He looked a mess if he was honest; his hair was scruffy and sticking up a little. He looked relentlessly tired and was still wearing his sleep clothes, which on this occasion consisted of a pair of grey joggers (only slightly lighter than the colour of his skin) and a black t-shirt.
He looked back at Julian, who hadn't even stirred. The boy was still wearing the same as last night, and Theo was suddenly jealous of how blissfully unaware and peaceful he looked - like he didn't have a care in the world. And then quietly opened the door to his bedroom and began to descend the stairs.
It was very quickly apparent to Theo that it was significantly later than he thought it was. There was an array of staff members milling around. He walked over to his bedroom door and placed his hand on the doorknob, rotating it clockwise to enter his room. He expected Serenity to be there, but she wasn't.

The next place he wanted to survey was his sister's room, so he started to walk along the hallway in that direction.

"Your Majesty." A voice said, and Theo turned to look in its direction.

It was a chief. The same man who had spoken to him the day he'd been told he'd be the King. This time, he was alone. Theo was a little caught off guard, but demonstrated his usual routine of saluting for the man. Sure, he'd kind of abolished that whole kind of practice towards *himself*, but that was because he'd not done anything to earn his title, and this man had, so he deserved the respect.

"Sir." Theo greeted, feeling a little embarrassed about not really being dressed for the day yet.

"Do you think we could have a word or two?" The chief asked. "In private."

Theo's breath hitched. From his experience, that never meant anything good.

"Yes, yeah, of course." The King replied, eyes scanning the hallway for where they could go. Luckily for his racing mind, he didn't have to make a decision because the chief, Sir Garrah, began to march off down the grand staircase.

Okay, Theo supposed. He'd have to look for Serenity later.

They ended up in one of the drawing rooms, which was empty. Garrah sat down on a sofa and Theo took the one adjacent.

"As much as I hate to have to, King Theo," The chief began, sighing. "Every day that passes I feel an increasing need to tell you off about what you're doing around here."

Theo swallowed. "How so?"

"I really respect that you're young, but you're careless. The state of our affairs has rapidly declined these past months. I don't think your focus is in the right place."

When Theo didn't reply, he exhaled loudly. "I mean, it's past noon and I've found you - the King of the biggest kingdom in Hell - wandering around in your bedclothes."

Theo's shoulders slumped. "Um, yeah, I'm sorry, I just-"

"You don't need to apologise to me, My King." Garrah interrupted. "It's your people that are being hard done by as a result of your laziness."

The chief's eyes glanced around the room. "I received a letter a few days ago." He said, capturing Theo's attention. "You're familiar with Amadeus Beckett, yes?"

The King swallowed. He wondered if now was a good time to tell someone about what had happened at the coronation. He decided against it. "Yeah."
"He sent me a letter asking for details about how you're running the kingdom. He wants to know your social and political motives, but doesn't want to engage with you directly."
"Right, okay."
"Now," The man continued. "I can tell him what he wants to hear. Which would be the truth that you've been slacking immensely and I'm concerned about the future of our kingdom."
Theo frowned.
"Or, I can tell him something more ideal. I thought I ought to ask you."
"Do you know if he'll be attending the wedding?"
Sir Garrah raised his eyebrows. "He will be. As far as I'm aware."
"Then don't respond. It got lost in the post and he can come see the kingdom on Saturday." He bargained. "I need to get about my day, thank you for this." The monarch said, standing.
"Strythio." Sir Garrah called, loudly. The King turned. "You have to promise that if this gets too much, you'll swallow your pride and come to someone for help. Klaevr isn't worth your insecurity, and all of us more experienced adults *want* to support you."
Theo pursed his lips and then nodded softly before returning back to the door and abandoning the conversation. He immediately headed back in the direction of Laine's room, and knocked twice on the door.
"Come in!" He heard, and pushed the door open.
Laine was sitting up in her bed, duvet over her lap and Nikoliah laying on her stomach, appearing asleep. She raised her eyebrows at Theo.
"He had a long day yesterday." She rationalised, looking down to her boyfriend. "I assume you're after your fiance?"
"Yeah. Did she come here?"
"She did, but that was like twelve hours ago. She was really upset and I comforted her for a little and then showed her a guest room in another wing. She wanted to be 'as far away from Theo as possible.'"
Theo's jaw dropped and he stood in shock.
"Her words, not mine."
"Laine, you told me to tell her, and now you're upset at me for telling her?"
"I didn't say I was upset at you." Laine sighed, standing up off the bed and adjusting the sleeping soldier so that his head was on a pillow. She held her arms out. "Come and give me a hug before I change my mind."

Theo softened, wrapping his arms around his sister as she did the same.
"Thank you." He whispered.
"I'm proud of you for telling her. It must have been difficult."
"Yeah, it was."
After a moment, when the two royal siblings ceased their hug, Laine asked if the wedding was still on.
"Seems so," Theo said. "She said it was last night, at least."
"Well then, I suppose you'd better find her and begin your preparations. Let me know if anything changes." Laine instructed, moving to sit back in her bed. Theo nodded in affirmation and left the room, now in search of the girl he was marrying in a day's time.

"She doesn't want to see you right now." Jaymie said, standing with her arms crossed outside one of the bedrooms. Theo had finally managed to locate Serenity, but found that there were some issues with actually getting to speak to her face-to-face.
"Please?" Theo begged. "How are we going to get wedding preparations done if she won't speak to me?" He pleaded.
"Sorry, Theo, but she said not to let you in."
Theo grumbled. Fine, he could play that game.
"Jaymie Newman, as friendly as I might be, I'm the King and I'm asking you to move. So move."
Jaymie stuttered. "She's a princess, and she asked me-"
"That was an order. I'm of higher status than she is, and quite frankly, until we're wed you don't even serve her. Move before you lose your job." He threatened. The stylist almost gulped. She hated when Theo acted like this.
"Sorry, Serenity. I tried my best." She admitted to the door before moving away. Theo pushed open the door and shut it behind him, closing the stylist out.
Theo neglected to say a word as he stared at the red-headed girl. She just looked at him, eyes showing a thousand thoughts. She smiled sadly.
"I love you."
Theo nodded. "I know."
"I've decided that for our sake, we're going to pretend you never told me what you did last night." She stated plainly, hands coming to rest on her lap.
"Serenity, that's not fair."
"Don't talk to me about fairness. Not after you pretended to love me."

"I didn't have a choice."

"You always had a choice, you're just claiming that you didn't to make yourself appear anything but the selfish dick you are."

Theo frowned, body still unmoving from his position against the door. "That's harsh." He swallowed. "Who did you tell?"

Serenity rolled her eyes. "Nobody, Theo. I didn't tell anyone, I'm not a horrible person." She bargained. "However..." She trailed off, crossing her right leg over the other as she batted her eyes at Theo. "If you don't get married to me... people might find out." She shrugged.

"You're blackmailing me?"

Serenity's expression suddenly dropped. She looked like she was about to burst into tears. "I'm sorry." She sniffled. Theo didn't reply to her. "I was gonna... But now you're standing here in front of me looking at me with those innocent eyes that I love. Just, please can we still get married?"

Theo sighed, walking over to sit down on the bench next to Serenity. He took her by the hand, placing both of his own hands around her left hand and bringing it into his lap.

"Um," He started, rubbing circles in the back of Serenity's hand. She sniffled, clearly anxious. "I don't know if I can live a lie."

"It doesn't have to be a lie, we could be like... like best friend roommates that just so happen to be married." She suggested.

"Serenity, I can't get married to you."

"Please!" She cried. "You're all I have. If we don't get married, I'll have to go back home. I can't- I can't go back home, it's miserable. I don't have anyone."

Theo's features dropped into guilt.

"And, Theo, if you call off the wedding there's going to be a public scandal. Do you want to address the kingdom and tell them you're incapable of loving a woman?"

Oh, God. Theo hadn't thought about that. The whole kingdom (and others) knew about this wedding, considering it was a royal one. If he announced that it wouldn't be happening he'd be expected to provide a reason. He could just say that the marriage was arranged and he didn't love her, but that wouldn't really be considered seriously since it was a very long standing tradition for royal marriages to be arranged.

"Oh, um." Theo stuttered, unsure of how to answer. Then he came to his realisation, and it hurt much more than anything else that had been said to him over these last few days. "I suppose I am marrying you then." He nodded to himself.

Serenity smiled, but she still looked upset as she interlocked her hand with the King's and pulled it onto her own lap. "I'm sorry it has to be like this, but I promise we're going to make it work."
Theo swallowed. He doubted that.

Clasping a maroon-coloured cloak around his neck and hanging his satchel over his right shoulder, Theo left the castle. It was slightly cold, hence the extra layers of protection that also meant gloves. He'd gotten dressed now, and had a mission to attend to.
He was not getting married.
Now he just had to figure out exactly how he was going to go about that. He needed to disappear, he'd decided. He was pretty content with his life here, but he had to get away for long enough that the whole 'engagement' thing would blow over.
Also, there was the Julian problem. Theo did not want to get married, but there was also no way in hell he could be with Julian, despite the way that the mortal constantly plagued his mind. Theo recognised that it was too much, and he and Julian could never be, despite the clear feelings of infatuation that he was suppressing.
So, he wanted to go in search of someone who could help him get Julian back to Earth where he clearly belonged - or maybe even help them decipher what was going on with him so they could get it over with. Having him around was too dangerous, especially at a time like this. The most logical way to begin the endeavour of sorting the mystery of the mortal out was figuring out *how* he had died and then maybe *why* he'd appeared in Klaevr the way he had.
So, there were two objectives that he was trying to achieve. A: flee the kingdom, and B: find out how Julian died.
To make a long mission short, the King wanted to get to Earth. Specifically, the town that Julian was from. He'd escape his incoming marriage and could snoop around for clues about the boy he was unfortunately head-over-heels for.
His black leather boots clicked against the stone of the ground, overcast by the red sky as he made his way out of a side gate. The wind ruffled his hair untidily as he headed through a more desolate path that avoided most people into the town. Except, he wasn't looking for the town.
There was a small one story house up on the outskirts of the town. It was semi-run down, but obviously still in good living condition. The bricks

were painted in a cream colour and the building itself was supported by wooden beams. It stood alone, but with a wooden gate and fences surrounding a lovely garden.

Theo glanced back down at the torn-off piece of parchment paper, with the address of this house scrawled on it.

He pushed the gate open, taking around ten steps down the path before knocking. He bounced on his toes as he waited for the homeowner to answer.

When the rustic-looking door did open, he was greeted by a short, though aged, woman with ear-length blonde hair. Her eyes widened. "Oh my god." She exclaimed.

"Who is it?!" A voice called from the hallway.

"The King..." She murmured, turning around to the narrow corridor.

When the other person in the house came to the door, Theo immediately recognised her as the same dark-haired woman whose daughter he'd met in the train station those months ago. He smiled. "Um, Hello again." He waved awkwardly, one hand resting still against the leather strap of his bag.

"Come in, come in! Do you want a cuppa or anything?" The blonde woman began, stepping backwards. Before the King could respond, she turned to her wife. "Darling, I think we should make him a cuppa."

Their hallway was rather small, painted pastel yellow with an array of pictures framed along the wall. They walked along the oakwood floors and into the kitchen. It was small, and was an open-plan kitchen and dining room. The table was round and only had two seats. Theo sat down in one of them, and so did the woman from the train station. The blonde woman flicked the kettle on.

"I'm Elsie, by the way, and the blondie over there putting too much sugar in your tea is Hettie." She stated. "What can we do you for, King Theo?"

"Well, um," He began, as Hettie placed a cup of tea in front of him, and one also in front of her wife as she pulled up a stool from their kitchen bar and sat at the table. "Thanks," The King muttered in between his confession. "I was given your address by someone that works for me, um,"

The women eyed him expectantly, although they both had an inkling what he needed.

"I need to get out of here."

"This about your wedding day after tomorrow?" Elsie asked.

"Something like that."

The wives shared a knowing glance. "You'll be after my father." Hettie said.
"Your father?"
"Well, he isn't really. But he's an older guy that lives with us and treats us like his kids." She clarified, and then looked up from the cup of tea. "Why are you so desperate to get away?" She asked, before backpedalling. "Oh, I'm sorry! That was intrusive, you don't have to answer that."
Theo chuckled. "No, no, it's alright. You're helping me, so you ought to know. My father arranged the marriage. He doesn't know I'm gay. Serenity does, but she just wants me to marry her anyway for politics or something."
Both homeowners looked at him sympathetically. "You'll come back to Klaevr, right?"
"Of course I will. Just after it's been long enough that my fiance wants nothing to do with me."
Elsie pointed in the direction of a little staircase in the corner of their dining room. "He's downstairs. I'll let him help you on one condition."
Theo nodded, already wanting to agree. "Yeah, what is it?"
"I need you to promise that you can get my daughter to live with us. She's staying in a communal home in Heaven because both her parents are down here. We miss her so much, Theo."
Theo grimaced. That was tricky. "I, um, I can't promise anything concrete. I'll really try my best, though, I swear."
The hosts looked to each other. Theo felt very bad about their situation, of course he wanted to help. "Alright, thank you, Your Majesty."
Theo took a sip of his tea. He stood. "I'll speak to your 'dad' then. Thank you so much for your help."
"Anytime." Elsie smiled, and Theo took the tea and began to slowly descend the stairs. They creaked, and the light in the room started to fade away. It was darker in the basement.
"Um, Hello?" He called into the abyss.
It really caught him off guard when the light suddenly flickered on. The room had a bed and a desk, and that was about it. The floor was the same oak as upstairs, but the walls were also made of wood. It made the room feel kind of intoxicating and scary. Sitting in the desk chair which was now facing the staircase was a man with blonde hair and purple horns. He had a blonde layer of stubble grazing his chin and part of his neck. He was tall, almost unnaturally so, and his features were very accentuated. He had an average frame, but the clothing he wore made it appear

differently. The man almost looked like a pirate, wearing a white shirt and a black pair of cotton trousers as well as an array of silver jewellery.

"Good afternoon." The man said, and his voice was raspy and thoughtful. He sounded old, but the man didn't particularly look it. "Come, take a seat."

Theo's feet connected with the actual ground, no longer on the staircase. He walked over to the bed and perched on the edge of it.

"So... how can I be of assistance to you, young man?" The man said, twirling around to face Theo on the chair.

"I want to get to Earth."

"You want to get to Earth? Well, you came to the right person."

The man crossed his legs on the seat. "I worry about the implications of allowing a royal to travel there." He stated, gesturing towards the monarch. "I'd probably be banished for such a crime. Although, I've done this many times and nobody has been caught yet."

This man had an indescribable presence. He seemed old and young at the same time, and his whole body displayed an inquisitive feeling.

"Please?" Theo asked.

"I suppose so. How much are you offering me?"

"However much you want. But um, I'll be able to get back here, right?"

The man nodded, bringing a hand up to his chin. "You should be. You're sure about this?"

Theo nodded. He was slightly relieved by the way that this man didn't ask any questions.

Wait. *Was* he sure? He would admit that he'd been pretty hasty about this whole thing. Maybe he was just overwhelmed and these feelings would brush over. But, before he could manage to rationalise these thoughts, the man spoke again.

"Good. Come back here tomorrow night then." He said, before detailing an amount of money that made Theo's jaw drop.

Theo stood and was ushered back to the staircase, still holding his undrunk tea. He finished drinking it upstairs and thanked the two women before making his way back home.

It was only after he was long gone that he realised that he'd neglected to catch this mysterious man's name.

XIII

Upon his return to the castle, the King was immediately whisked away to choose the flowers that he wanted on the tables at the wedding. He thought that all of this detailing was a little silly, but both Serenity and the staff seemed very passionate about it, so he supposed he could entertain the fantasy.

It was late when the day's work had finished. Tomorrow, the day before the wedding, was traditionally a day of rest where the engaged couple have a break from the preparations and spend the day together. Kind of like the exact opposite of a bachelor/bachelorette party, but significantly more formal, and it had been around a lot longer than earth's custom.

It ended up being Theo, Serenity, Laine, Nikoliah and Raphie at the start of the day. Theo had suggested that they'd be very busy after their marriage and wanted to spend time with their friends beforehand. Julian had wanted to be there, and had put on a very strong pout when Theo told him that they couldn't kick his fiance out of her own pre-wedding celebration.

"Ooh! I'm a dog, then."

"No!" Laine laughed, looking back up to the post-it-note stuck to Raphie's forehead. *Hedgehog*: it read. "Someone help me out!" She pleaded, almost lost in a fit of laughter.

"Well, ask another question!" Serenity smiled, a post-it-note of her own on her forehead, the same as everybody else in the room.

Raphie paused. "Um, am I a mammal?"

Theo exchanged a confused glance with Nikoliah. "I don't know, is she?"

Laine raised her eyebrows. "Yes, she's a mammal, you idiots."
It took a few minutes of further grilling before Laine came to her conclusion. "The little thing with the spikes. Agh, um." She said, clicking her fingers. "Porcupine."
Everyone in the lounge groaned, utterly fed-up with this. "The other little thing with spikes, Raphie." Theo warned.
"Hedgehog!"
"Oh, thank the lord." Nikoliah breathed. "Alright, I think this game is frying my brain." He confessed, pulling the post-it-note off his own forehead and looking down at it. "How the hell was I supposed to guess 'baby turtle'? Why was it a baby?"
Again, everyone started laughing. Serenity exhaled through her own chuckle. "Argh, I need a glass of wine. You want one while I'm in the kitchen, love?" She asked, standing.
Theo shook his head. "I'm alright. Don't wanna be hungover at our wedding."
"You wouldn't be hungover from one glass, but alright." She turned and pecked a quick kiss to Theo's mouth. "Do either of you two want one?" She asked, looking at Nikoliah and Raphie, who were both also over the legal age.
"I'm alright, thanks." Raphie said, and Nikoliah agreed. Serenity nodded. "Be back soon." She spoke softly before exiting the lounge.
Raphie faltered. "She knows you don't love her, right?" She laughed.
"Hey." Theo warned, voice dropping an octave. "She's still coming to terms with it, cut her some slack." He scolded.
"Ooh, you're in a bad mood." His sister slighted. Theo just gave her a predatory glance. He was dismissed, and Laine started a conversation with her boyfriend while they waited for Serenity to return. Raphie stood from the sofa she was on and moved to where Serenity was previously sitting. She leaned into Theo with a hushed voice.
"You're okay, right? Not gonna do anything impulsive, are you?" She asked with a kind voice.
"What?"
"Don't tell her I told you, but Laine's worried you're gonna run off, or kill yourself or something."
"Oh. Um, um, no, I'm not."
Raphie frowned. "You hesitated a bit there. You sure?" She asked. "You know there's always another way-"
"I'm not going to kill myself, Raphie. I don't even think that's possible."
The angel didn't deflect her serious expression. "I mean it, Theo."

Laughing, the King replied. "I'm fine, I'm not going anywhere. Now, let's pick the next game we're gonna play." He instructed, standing from the sofa.

Laine slapped her hands on her knees, the same way that dads tend to do when they announce they're leaving the family gathering. "Right, we've been at this all afternoon. Niko and I are gonna go upstairs, you coming Raphie?"

The angel hesitated for a moment, eyes glancing back to the King and then her friend. "Yeah, alright. May as well give those two some time together." Theo wanted to protest, but he didn't have time to because Serenity returned from the kitchen, holding a glass of white wine and passing the other three in the doorway, saying a quiet goodbye to them. Serenity sat down on the sofa, reaching her glass out to Theo, who rolled his eyes, taking it from her and having a sip before passing it back to the woman.

"Enjoying our last day of unmarried life?" She asked, smiling as she leant back on the couch.

Theo hummed in agreement. "Nothing's really gonna change after tomorrow though. Just legal stuff. I feel like people make weddings out to be this massive thing, when really they aren't." He complained, huffing slightly.

"You're just telling yourself that, you need to get out of that head at some point."

"What do you mean?"

Serenity grimaced. "I shouldn't have said anything, sorry."

Theo leant forward. "No, go on."

She placed her glass down on the table and continued with apprehensiveness. "It's just... you're constantly preoccupied with something that isn't really in front of you. You're always; '*oh, I'm thinking about this*' or '*this is going to happen next week*'. I really wish you would pull yourself out of your head for once and actually focus on what's going on around you. You know, like our wedding. We're getting married tomorrow and you keep staring off into space like you can't even think about it."

Theo was surprised by this little outburst, and he could see it on Serenity's face that she was also surprised. She stuttered. "I just- I wish you would pay attention to me."

The King's face dropped into a frown. "I'm sorry, just busy."

"Yeah, that's what you always say."

The air was thick with tension, and Theo couldn't find it in himself to reply to that. He cleared his throat, leaning back on the couch and avoiding eye contact with his fiance. "Um, I can pay attention to you now?" The King suggested, eyes now connecting with Serenity's.
"Fine. Fine, sure." She said, allowing her head to rest on her 'boyfriend''s shoulder. She held his hand strongly, head tilting so that her face was leaning against his neck. "And after the wedding tomorrow I'll be all yours forever, hm?" She suggested, and the implications made Theo feel sick to his stomach.
"Yeah." Theo breathed, eyes fluttering shut as the two rested in their comfortable position.

It was late at night now, so the sky was dark and the air was cool and eerie. Theo had just managed to slip his way out of Serenity's arms, so that he was now standing on the floor of their bedroom, staring down at her. He'd just quietly shuffled out of his pyjamas and into a suitable outfit.
Was this really the right decision?
He decided that he'd already made this decision, and quickly pulled a sheet of parchment paper from his desk drawer. This was the difficult part, and it was enhanced by the darkness. He couldn't turn the light on because it would wake his fiance up. Eventually, with a messy scrawl, Theo managed to write just five words on the sheet.
'Sorry. This isn't your fault."
He sighed, tearing off the corner that he'd written it on and taking the rest of the paper with him. Serenity was subtly snoring, and the sound only weighed on his guilty conscience more. Luckily for him, though, he'd packed a bag the previous night. It was just his satchel with some essentials in the form of water, snacks, and a large heavy handful of gold. Gold wasn't the currency in Klaevr, but Theo opted to bring it over their money because he could sell it on Earth for their cash. And of course, he had the money to pay the man who was helping him get away in the first place.
He also had no idea how the world worked.
Theo turned back to his bedroom. He wished he could take a few more sentimental items, but there just wasn't room for it. The only personal item he had on him was the bracelet that Laine had given him on his

coronation day. She'd forgotten to ask for it back, and he didn't want to remind her because it was a great comfort to the King.

He shut the door to his bedroom, and walked once again down the corridor to Laine's room. He wrote the note against the wall. This one came a lot easier than the one he left for Serenity.

'I'm sorry. I can't stay here. Laine, you're in charge until I get back. You and Nikoliah better look after each other. I'm okay, don't worry about me. Love, Theo.'

He couldn't stomach the idea of going into his sister's room to leave it on her own dresser; it would surely make him too upset. So instead, he bent down on his ankles and slid the paper under the door in one quick motion. He now had one small torn-off piece of parchment left, and it was for Julian.

Each time the staircase creaked, Theo cringed horribly. He was only able to feel any relief when he got to the top. This time, he pushed the door knob and walked into the room. Much as he expected, the mortal was fast asleep in his bed, covered in a tangled array of his duvet. Theo thought he looked whimsical.

While leaning against the chest of drawers, Theo pulled out his pen. Taking a few moments to formulate his words, he wrote his message.

'I'm going to find out what's going on with you. I love you so much. I'll be back, but I need to get you home. Love, Theo.'

He paused for a moment. What if they got seriously worried and needed to know what had happened to him? He took a moment to think, and then messily scrawled down Elsie and Hettie's address at the bottom of the page. He left the note and the pen there, and turned one-hundred-and-eighty degrees to face Julian. He leant down and pressed a soft kiss to the man's forehead.

Then he left.

He left Julian's room, and then the hallway. Then he left the castle building and eventually the whole grounds. He had his gloves and cloak on again for pure warmth, as the air was harsh this time of year, and he had no idea what it would be like on Earth.

Praying that nobody would see him, he kept his head down as he quickly scurried to the outskirts of the town, fleeing from his existence and the burdens that come with it.

He made it to the approach of the house just before midnight.

For a fleeting moment, Theo was unsure whether or not he was supposed to knock. It was incredibly late, and he didn't want to wake the homeowners. Luckily for his conscience, he didn't have to debate long, because the door opened.

"We can hear you pacing from our living room." Hettie said, smiling as she leant out of the door. Theo's head snapped up to her, and he stopped his onslaught on the pavement.

"Sorry."

"You're leaving tonight then, I assume?" She asked, sadly.

Theo swallowed, nodding. "It's either now or I get married tomorrow." He shrugged.

She nodded, stepping out of the door frame. "Dad's downstairs still, come on straight through." She said as the King trekked through her house. The sound of Elsie humming a song could be heard through their closed living room door, and it stopped when the woman shouted a muffled 'Good luck Theo...!' from her seat on their sofa.

The lights in the house were off, and after giving a goodbye to one of the women who owned the house, he began to make his way back down the stairs into the basement. This time, the lights were on already, and the man who he'd spoken to before was sitting cross-legged on the fleeting area of floor space between the bed and his desk.

"I was beginning to assume you weren't going to follow through." He commented, looking down at his nails, not even paying any visual attention to the monarch.

"Had to leave some notes to some people, sorry if I'm later than you expected."

The blonde man began to stand. "No worries. You're sure you want to go through with this?" He asked, eyes now meeting his visitor's. Behind them, it appeared that there was an inkling of anxiety. Theo supposed he was worried about getting caught.

The man was wearing a light grey, long sleeve dress shirt and a purple waistcoat, and Theo wasn't sure if the look was comforting or intimidating.

"Um, yeah."

"Alright, well, there's a few things we shall need to go over first. I'm going to just tell you all of it, and you can save questions for the end." He instructed.

Theo nodded, and the unnamed man walked up to one of the wood panels on the back wall of his room and pressed both of his palms against it. Immediately, a bronze-tinted glow of light began to ruminate from his hands, revealing a complex of light-up symbols that even Theo couldn't recognise.

It astonished him to begin with. Nobody outside of the royal bloodline could perform magic in the underworld, or at least, that was how it was supposed to be. But, with this blonde, bearded man standing with his hands against the wall as it lit up, Theo began to question what he'd been taught. He watched through apprehensive eyes as the wall completely dissipated, revealing a larger room behind it. The man turned around and used his eyes to gesture that they were going to go in that room.

Theo glanced back to the exit of the basement, and then he followed the mysterious man through the newly formed doorway and into his now revealed space. The second he stepped through, the wall reformed, and the King turned back to it.

This new room had a very different atmosphere.

It was dark, very dark; that was the first thing that Theo noticed. The only light sources were in the form of a candle in each corner, and a single torch sat on a wooden desk in the centre of the room. The carpet was actually a dark red, but in the light it appeared more brown. The walls were all coated in a dark blue, flower-patterned wallpaper. Theo looked around it, a little confused at where the door he'd just walked through had gone.

"This is nice... You put this wallpaper up yourself?" He smirked, and the man's expression morphed into a thin line.

"Rule one, no witty quips. I'm doing a service for you, the only words I want to hear are 'please' and 'thank you'. Got that?"

Theo swallowed. "Yep."

"You've somehow already failed." The man frowned. "Just, sit down."

"On the chair?" He asked. It was a small wooden piece, set in front of a long rectangular table of the same oak. Both looked a little unstable.

"No, on the floor, while you look at the chair." He scoffed, walking behind it and pulling it out as he looked at the King expectantly.

Theo held his hands up in mock surrender, walking over and sitting down, bag still over his shoulder. The strange man paraded around the table and then leant forward onto it so that he was looking down at Theo.

"I'll start with the basics." He instructed. "Do you have the money?" He asked, and Theo nodded. "Good, I'll ask it of you after I finish explaining all this."

"Right," He began, not even blinking at the monarch. "You won't be able to die on Earth, because that's reserved for people with souls. Only mortals have the privilege of death, I'm sure you know. Having said that, you can get hurt. You won't have a pulse, as you normally don't, so don't go passing out on any street corners because you might wake up to an EMT performing CPR on you."

"Secondly, you can't be getting yourself involved with any legal matters because you don't exist. Oh! And you'll age normally there. I know that here you royal family members like to stay on the throne for literal decades because nobody can die. Therefore, you age a lot slower. That doesn't apply on Earth, so if you stay there for eighty years it won't age you the same as it would here."

"When you want to return, you'll know what to do." He said, raising his eyebrows. "Got all that? Good. Next, you obviously can't go there looking like that." The man continued, gesturing at Theo in a circular motion. "Do you know what a human looks like?"

"...Vaguely."

"Right, well, I'm going to perform a spell on you that will allow you to flick between how you normally look and a human-lite version of it."

"Um, sorry, I didn't catch your name?" Theo prompted expectantly.

"It's not relevant to this."

"How do you know... magic?"

"Theo." He boomed. "I've been doing this for longer than your grandmother has been alive. I promise I know what I'm doing. Don't ask so many questions." He smirked, standing up straight and walking to a corner of the room, where a large set of drawers was held. He pulled the top one open and brought out a small goblet and a glass beaker with a cork in the top.

"Okay, I want you to drink this, and just really focus on the intention of human-like attributes."

Human-like attributes, huh? He could think of a lot. Julian's eyes, in their emerald green shade. His hair, in a curled co-ordination. His skin, smooth and dark as it presses against his own and-

"Theo."

"Sorry?"

"I asked if you were gonna take this cup from my hand in the next ten minutes?"

The man held his hand outstretched towards the King, holding the goblet full of the clear, water-like liquid. Theo took it while muttering a vague apology.

"So... you're having an affair?" The man asked, laughing a little as he walked back over to the drawer.

Theo was half way through drinking the liquid, and all-but spat it out back into the goblet.

113

"What? No." He bluffed. Who was this guy? Some kind of mind reader?
"Really? That hickey on your neck kinda suggests otherwise." He smiled, and Theo immediately clapped a hand over the side of his neck, eyes wide as he blushed. The man snorted. "I'm messing with you, but you did just confirm my suspicions with that reaction."
"Well- no, my fiance could have-"
"If your fiance gave that to you, you probably would have said 'My fiance gave that to me, you nosey asshole...!' instead of trying to hide it."
He brought a small book out of the drawer and walked back over to the table, opening it up as Theo stuttered. "Also, literally why else would you be running off the night before your wedding? Drink up."
Theo frowned, bringing the cup back up to his lips.
"Did you want him to come with you? Seems weird you'd run away because of him and leave him here."
Once he'd finished drinking the beverage, he wiped his mouth and looked back up.
"Um, no, he doesn't know I'm leaving."
"Oh, sorry. So he's being left here? You need to come back for him eventually."
"I will. ...Probably."
The man gave Theo a cursory glance, looking extremely judgemental as he licked his finger, using it to separate two pages of the book and smiling at it. "Stick your hand on here." He instructed, and Theo apprehensively did as he said.
The page of the book began to glow for about five seconds before it stopped completely. "Now, I want you to focus again on the intention of forming human-like attributes."
When he opened his eyes again a moment later, he felt the same. But when Theo looked down at himself, the skin of his arms had shifted from his usual light grey to a more pale, white, human skin colour. The man handed him a mirror, and the King looked at himself.
He had eyes. Like, regular eyes. They were a light blue colour and Theo smiled, exhaling. "Woah."
He looked the exact same as usual, except with a human skin tone and lack of horns or tail. It was incredibly strange, he'd literally only seen one human before in his life and now he looked exactly like one. He had freckles dotted across his face, and his hair was still the same dark shade.

"Cool, right?" The man asked, placing the mirror back down. "Now, close your eyes again and focus on your regular attributes." He instructed, and not a moment later Theo was back to looking exactly how he had before. "You should be able to perform that at will, but I *very strongly* suggest that you don't drop your human facade when on Earth." He lectured, flicking to a page further on in the book. "Alright, now you can give me the money. So- um, are you okay, kid?"

Theo sniffled, fiddling with his hands as he looked at the ground. "Yeah, I just... This is my home, you know? And it's meant to be my job to protect it but now I'm just abandoning everyone."

The man rolled his eyes. "I'm not gonna stand here and convince you to stay, if that's what you want me to do. I'm not going to convince you to leave either. It's getting late and I want to go to bed quite frankly. So, figure it out please?"

Theo took a deep breath inwards, and then out again. Just like Julian had told him the other day, then he nodded.

"Okay, I'm ready."

The blonde man's eyes flickered with indecision for a moment, and then he nodded.

XIV

Julian stirred, waking with a groan. He sat up, sighing. Today was gonna be the day that the man he was in love with would get married, and he had not been looking forward to it. Theo hadn't even been paying attention to him recently.
He slid to sit on the edge of his bed, reaching for his glass of water that he took a large sip of. When putting the drink back down, he noticed a sheet of paper that wasn't on his desk before last night.
'I'm going to find out what's going on with you. I love you so much. I'll be back, but I need to get you home. Love, Theo.'
His eyes widened at the implications of the note, quickly snatching it off the table and reading over it again. He quickly turned and pushed the door to his bedroom open, trampling down the spiral staircase and towards Theo's bedroom. He stopped when he noticed a bunch of demons milling around, remembering that they weren't meant to see him. He leant back around the corner so that he was out of sight. About twenty seconds later, Laine walked around the corner.
She looked very stressed and stook about two steps up the staircase before noticing Julian leaning against the wall. She turned to him abruptly.
"Julian. Is Theo with you? Like... possibly in your room?"
"Um, no. I came down here hoping he was with you."
The Princess groaned loudly, before grabbing Julian's hand and dragging him along the corridor. "I told Raphie this would happen! I told her! But, no, she had to convince me it'd be fine! And now, I have to take care of this mess!"

"Um, Laine-" He protested as he was dragged along, noticing all of the castle staff staring at him in surprise. When they got to Laine's bedroom, she pushed the door open and all-but shoved Julian in.

Nikoliah was sitting on the bed, fidgeting with his hands. Serenity sat on one of Laine's oval chairs, knees up to her chest and tears running down her face. Both looked up to Julian when he entered with the Princess, and she shut the door behind them.

Serenity raised her eyebrows at the human.

He smiled awkwardly, not having been expected to have to perform social interaction in his pyjamas at like 7am.

"You must be... the girl! Um, Stephanie?"

Serenity sniffled. "Who is that?" She asked.

"Julian, Serenity. Serenity, Julian. Um, Julian is our friend." She said.

"Why is he...?"

"We were trying to figure it out."

Laine walked over and sat on the bed with her boyfriend, who wrapped an arm around her shoulder, leaving Julian standing awkwardly in the middle of the room. He looked around and shrugged, before sitting down on the ground.

"Where's Theo then?" He asked, feeling pretty small from sitting on the ground. His question made Serenity erupt in another fit of cries.

"He's gone somewhere. Run off, I don't know. We don't even know where he's gone." Nikoliah told him.

Julian paused for a moment. "Oh, I might have an idea. He, um, he left me a note about it."

"Yeah, he left all of us notes. Vague, though."

Julian nodded, pulling the piece of paper out of his pocket and un-scrunching it. He read over the words again, before handing it over to Theo's sister.

"He's totally gone to Earth." She realised, voice on a whine. "This is bad."

"Let me see." Serenity instructed, standing up off the chair and plucking the paper from Laine's hand. She sat back down and read over it.

"Why did he write '*I love you so much*'?" She questioned. "And, how come you got a '*Love, Theo*'?! I didn't get a '*Love, Theo*'." She frowned, looking down. Then, her eyes widened significantly and her tears almost evaporated, replaced with a conditional anger.

"Oh my God, you and Theo! You were... What the fuck?!" She exclaimed loudly. "Seriously? This whole time?"

Julian looked over to Laine and Nikoliah, unsure of what to answer. When they only gave him blank faces, he blinked. "Well... technically he broke it off a bit ago because he was stressed about... you." He said, cringing immediately afterwards. "Well, I mean, not *you*, you, but like, the wedding and... He was worried about getting caught, like Laine caught us one time and it was stressful for him so-"

"You knew?!" She yelled, looking over to Laine. "I literally cannot believe this. Fucking find him on your own." She scoffed, standing up and storming out of the room. The moment the door closed, the three remaining could hear an array of cries as the woman went further down the corridor.

Julian looked at the door, grimacing.

"Well, you may as well sit where she was sitting." Nikoliah grumbled, gesturing to the vacant seat. "What's our plan of action?"

"If he ran off he probably had a reason." Julian stated plainly as he sat on the chair. "He's an adult, he can make decisions."

"Maybe, yes, but he can't just leave the kingdom, it's meant to be his job. Running away was kinda selfish, and we need him back." He suggested.

"Ooh!" Laine exclaimed, smiling sarcastically as she looked between the two of them. "Maybe two lads who haven't been close with him for longer than three months should stop trying to speak for him...!"

"Um, sorry."

"Yeah, sorry."

The Princess raised her eyebrows, glancing between the two men. She nodded slowly at Nikoliah, who stuttered.

"Um, Laine, what do *you* think?" He bluffed, and she responded with a thumbs up.

"Well, he said that he's going to find out what's up with Julian, right? And I wanna get involved helping with that, and I certainly don't wanna look after this kingdom while he's gone."

"Oh, right, so you're suggesting the same thing I was?" Nikoliah asked playfully.

She ignored him, turning back to Julian. "Did he write anything else?"

"Just an address."

"An address?"

"Mhm."

The door to their bedroom suddenly had knocks rapped against it, and whoever it was didn't even wait for them to respond before barging in. It was Kougan, the stylist - he looked stressed.

"Hey, I'm sorry, but, Laine, your dad's here and Serenity is talking to him and he seems really *unhappy* about something." He said, words in quick succession. "Something being that Theo has run off because he's... gay? She's yelling a lot of words but that's what I could make out."

Laine flopped backwards onto her bed, groaning. "I suppose you want me to come and speak to him."

Kougan nodded. "Yeah, either that or Princess Serenity is gonna keep calling your brother some really insulting words that I don't want to repeat."

She sat back up, nodding. "Let's go." She instructed, standing up off the bed. Nikoliah followed her, and Julian stood up, but she turned back around. "Sorry, I don't know if you're the best person to help defuse this situation." Laine said.

"Right, yes. Well, I will be... Here." He nodded, sitting back down.

Laine and Nikoliah followed Kougan down the hallway and towards the main staircase. At the bottom of it, Dyran stood with Serenity. The former was in the middle of what appeared to be a very strong-worded sentence.

Laine descended the stairs in somewhat of a hurry, and when the redhead saw her, she gasped.

"There she is! She knew the *whole time* that your son, my fiance, *the King*, was fucking some random boy on the side!"

Sir Dyran looked absolutely appalled, and he immediately turned his whole body to face his daughter's - shoulders raised.

"Woah, can we just calm down a minute?!"

He raised his eyebrows. "Is this true, Laine?"

The Princess frowned, glancing back to her boyfriend for any sign of hope of what to say in this situation. She found that the whole of the room was looking at her expectantly. There were about twenty staff members in total, as well as her father and boyfriend and Serenity, of course.

She sighed, conceding. "Yeah, but-" She began, before being completely interrupted by a large uproar from the crowd. Laine didn't think she had ever seen her dad look this angry before. She raised her voice, shushing everyone effectively.

"But he wouldn't have had to, if you'd made him feel like he could tell you!"

"He could have! I would have been fine with it, but I'm not a mind reader! And now I have to tell a whole kingdom (plus more people...!) that no wedding is happening because he's run off somewhere."

The ex-king sighed. "I suppose you're in charge then, Serenity. As the future Queen."

Laine bit her lip. "Um, sorry, he left me a note saying that I was in charge, so…" She told them, and the King frowned.

"You know what, why don't we take this conversation somewhere more private." He suggested, looking around. "Ah! Sir Garrah!" He called, and the soldier turned to face the other man. "Could you announce to the kingdom that the wedding is postponed. Tell them that Theo has fallen ill."

The soldier paused. "Respectfully, I don't feel comfortable deceiving the kingdom, Sir."

"Fine. I'll do it. You two," He turned to face Laine and Serenity. "Go and sit down in the west wing lounge. I'll be out shortly."

Before either could protest, he walked off in the direction of the central balcony. Laine reached her hand out towards Nikoliah, and he took it, following the two of them. He felt a little like he was intruding on something personal when they sat down and immediately began arguing again.

"You're a lying bitch, huh?" Serenity accused, eyes narrowed to slits as he leant forward.

Laine rolled her eyes, leaning into Nikoliah's body for comfort as she grumbled. "I'm not going to engage with you." She said, pressing her face into her boyfriend's chest.

"Yeah, hide, just like your brother. Cowardice must run in the family."

Laine looked up. "I get that you're upset, but you don't have to take it out on me."

The door opened, and Sir Dyran walked in, shutting the door behind him. The ex-king raised his eyebrows. "Sir Nikoliah, what are you doing here?"

The soldier looked over to his girlfriend. "I'm kind of involved so…"

"No you aren't, this is a family matter, get out." He instructed angrily. Nikoliah swallowed, nodding as he stood. Laine reached her arm out and pushed him back down onto the sofa next to her.

"He's staying."

"He's not family."

"Neither is Serenity."

"She's with Theo, so she is." The King said, hands on his hips.

Laine's eyeline roamed over to Nikoliah's and she asked him a silent question which he nodded as a response to.

"Okay then. Dad, Sir Nikoliah is my boyfriend. I'm his girlfriend, he's my boyfriend and has been for months. So if Serenity can be here because she's 'with Theo', even though he never loved her, then Nikoliah is going to stay because we *do* love each other." She smiled pettily.

120

Dyran exhaled angrily, and Serenity's eyes had begun to water from the insult. "Nikoliah, you're fired. Get out."

"I don't think you can fire me - we're actually equal in rank now, so..."

"What the fuck has happened to you?!" He yelled, using his full-on king voice. "This time last year I would have called you the best soldier I have and now you're lounging on this sofa with your arm around my daughter while talking back to me? I'm not sure what's gotten into you these past few months but clearly I was wrong to give you a knighthood. Get out of this room before I strip you of your title *and* your job."

Nikoliah bit his lip and nodded, standing and walking out of the room with his head down. Laine tried to grab his hand and tell him to stay but he just ended up murmuring that he'd see her upstairs later.

The door closed and Dyran sat down next to Serenity. "Laine, I'm going to want to talk to you about that later. But for now, we need to figure out who is ruling this kingdom in Theo's absence, and how we are going to retrieve him."

Laine inhaled, looking towards the ground and then back up as she spoke, jaw firm and eyes determined.

"I'm going to get him." She instructed in a voice that didn't leave any room for argument. "I'm going to get him, and he left *me* in charge, and I'm leaving Nikoliah in charge until I get back, okay?"

"Sir Nikoliah is not royal, he cannot possibly take charge over this kingdom." Sir Dyran rambled, one eyebrow raised in scepticism. Laine looked over to Serenity, who stared back at her with completely black eyes. That was the thing that Nikoliah lacked.

"He can if I say he can, and I do. As next in line it's quite literally up to me."

He found it in himself to want to argue. Dyran sat with pursed lips, particularly proud of the assertive tone that his daughter had used. Theo had never been very good at sticking up for himself, hence the whole 'fleeing the kingdom' debacle.

Laine glanced all around the room when nobody responded, and her father seemed pretty content in not getting involved any further.

Serenity had her the gaze downcast to the floor, and Laine couldn't help but feel a little bad for her. She sighed. "I'm sorry it had to turn out like this, Serenity. I am, but you're beautiful and I'm confident you'll find someone without it having to be arranged."

Serenity frowned for a moment. "Yeah, okay, whatever." She muttered before standing from the sofa and walking out of the room. The door shut behind her with an irate slam, and it made Laine flinch a little. She sighed, but didn't start talking quick enough before her dad could intrude.

"Do I get to meet this boy that Strythio has been sleeping with?"

"The boy that Theo has been dating, dad. You make their relationship sound dirty, and it wasn't." She criticised. "And, no, you don't. He's coming with me to find Theo, you stay out of this."

"Elaine."

"Father."

They locked eyes in a tense staring contest, and Laine knew for sure she wasn't going to let up to this man, not after what he said to her boyfriend. After about thirty seconds of this silence, the Princess stood.

"Right, well, there's no wedding clearly, so you can go home, dad. I have a kingdom to address."

Dyran held the smirk off his face until after his daughter had left the room. When in solitude, he smiled to himself, because he was genuinely a little proud of the way she was acting like a leader. He didn't want to tolerate that kind of behaviour, of course not, but he could admit it was impressive coming from her. That was the kind of leader he had hoped to raise, and maybe deep down he was a little glad that she was getting her five minutes.

Laine made her way up the staircase and barged back into her bedroom, where both Nikoliah and Julian were sitting. Nikoliah looked upset, which was expected.

"Julian, we're going after Theo. Niko, you're in charge of the kingdom in my absence."

"What?!" Nikoliah exclaimed.

"You're the only person I trust other than Raphie, and she can't rule the kingdom because she's... you know, an angel. And I need Julian with me because he knows his way around England."

"Well- not, not the whole of England." The man protested weakly. Laine waved her arm around in dismissal.

"My point is that I love you, and you're going to be fine. Julian, we're gonna go visit that address this afternoon."

The door to the room was already slightly ajar because of the abrupt nature of Laine's entrance, but Raphie knocked on it anyway out of courtesy. After doing so, she walked in, wearing a beautiful summer dress that matched her eyes.

"Sorry, I've been standing outside this door for the last thirty seconds. I want to come with you guys if you're going to Earth to find Theo. I have some unfinished business there and…"

"Yes, you can come, yes!" Laine smiled. She thought she'd never ask. "If we figure out how to get there. I think we need to start with the address." She nodded.

"Laine, can we talk about the whole 'ruling the kingdom in your absence' thing for a moment?" Nikoliah asked from the bed, and the Princess turned around.

"Of course we can, yeah. Um, Raphie and Julian, I want you back here for 2pm so we can go investigate that address." She told them as the two of them left.

Laine turned back to Nikoliah and moved to sit back on their bed. "What's up?"

He sighed. "You *really* think I can do it?" He whispered, and Laine pulled him into her body.

"You were the King's personal soldier and right hand man for years, Niko, you know exactly what the duty entails. And nobody would be expecting you to be perfect, darling, I just need to know that should something happen Klaevr will be in safe hands." She said genuinely.

"Do *you* want to do this?" Laine asked upon a breath.

"Yeah, I do. I just worry I won't be good at it. You have to promise me you'll be safe on Earth."

She nodded, rubbing circles on Nikoliah's back in a comforting manner. "I'll be safe. I'll be really safe, I promise. I believe in you so much, you're going to do great, okay?"

"Okay." He whispered, smiling in a direction that Laine couldn't even see. They wrapped their arms around each other tightly, each other's warmth bleeding into their bodies. Nikoliah buried his face in Laine's shoulder. "Okay."

XV

Theo's arm was uncomfortable. That was the first thing he noticed. He must have slept on it funny. When he awoke himself properly he realised that he *definitely* must have slept funny, because he was lying on the ground in a wooded area that overlooked a path lined with more trees and short cut grass... How had he let himself fall asleep in a park? How much did he have to drink last night?

The next thing he noticed was that the sky was blue. There was grass below him. Real, living grass - not the dead stuff that he's used to. Oh, shit. Shit, fuck.

He was on Earth.

The realisation hit him like a truck and Theo scrambled onto his knees, coming properly out of his post-sleep haze. Upon inspection of his own body, he could pretty quickly tell that he was in his human form, so that was a relief. He still had his satchel slung around him, and was also wearing the same clothes that he had been in the underworld.

He spun around a few times like a dog chasing its tail, trying to absorb his surroundings. He was by a black metal fence with loops in it that extended up to his knees. He stepped over it and ended up on a concrete-looking path. He turned his head left and right, trying to decipher which way he was meant to go.

He wanted to find somewhere he could sell the gold he'd brought. It was weighing down on his shoulder and he knew he would need some form of money if he was going to be on Earth. Theo couldn't see any particular buildings, so he just set off in the same direction as a person who had just walked past him, hoping they were local and maybe knew where they were going.

Within a few minutes, he'd managed to make his way to a break in the black fence surrounding the area and onto a street, which directly had a small unused road in front of it. Once he crossed it, he was fully out of the park and was standing on the pavement of a busy-looking street.

It was instantly incredibly overwhelming.

Theo took a step back from the road at the flurry of cars driving along it. They were ridiculously loud and when the traffic lights turned red and they stopped moving, Theo had to cough because of the horrible petrol-like smell that flooded his senses. He took another step backwards. Those things could definitely kill someone. Is this why so many people die so young nowadays? Big metal death traps disguised as transportation? Theo missed home.

There were also so *many* people. He'd never seen so many humans before. Granted, before he met Julian he'd never even seen one and now there were at least fifty in his eyeline. He clutched the strap of his satchel tightly and began to continue walking down the road. He kept his head down.

He got to a section of the pavement where it broke off and there was a road in front of him. It felt like a river that was far too wide for him to even consider crossing. Standing on the edge of the pavement and looking out into the road worriedly, Theo tapped his feet on the red bumped surface of the ground. Someone walked up beside him and pressed a small light grey button on the bottom of a yellow rectangle. It caused a light to go on, but other than that nothing happened and that confused Theo more.

He apprehensively turned to the woman standing on his right.

"Um, hi, sorry. I'm not from here, do you know where the town centre is?" He asked. The woman turned to him.

"Yeah, doll, just cross over this road and continue right so that you go under the viaduct with the railway over the top. You can follow the road where it curves along past the bus depot and then carry on the road to the junction. On the right from there you've got all the dodgy shops like laundromats and pawn brokers. If you just turn left there you'll find the entrance to the shopping centre, and the town centre is just around that area."

Theo nodded absentmindedly. "Okay, thanks- um, when you say 'junction', which direction did you-" He tried to ask, but the traffic lights started beeping and the woman walked across the road.

He stopped talking and started following her, assuming this might have been what the button did. But why did humans have to wait until beeping to cross the road? It seemed dumb, but it also made the cars stop, so Theo assumed he wasn't really in the position to criticise human traditions.

Okay, follow the road to the right. He could do that. There weren't many people on this side of the pavement, which allowed him to follow the route in a mostly stress-free manner. It wasn't a particularly sunny day, but even he would admit he was getting to overheat in his gloves and cloak.

Theo made a silent decision that he needed to get himself some different clothes that were more typical of this area. He looked incredibly out of place and it did make him feel a little self-conscious. Most people were wearing jeans and hoodies, or tracksuits. Theo was wearing leather gloves and boots, as well as dark-coloured cargo trousers and a tight-fitting shirt with long sleeves and of course his cape.

A loud metallic noise pulled him from his thoughts. Theo's head snapped up and he looked up.

There was a purple and blue coloured train making its way swiftly across the train tracks that sat on top of the viaduct. Oh! Right, that's what a train was. It was cool, seeing the idea that their underworld transportation system was based upon. Now that he saw one in person it made a lot more sense why the ex-mortals in Klaevr called their carriage transport system a train. He thought theirs was a little more classy though, smoother in its movement. That thing just kinda looked like a metal tube that slid along more metal. The thought of the scraping made Theo's skin crawl.

"Move, you tosser." Someone grumbled as they walked past Theo, strongly shoving him with their left shoulder as he'd stood still to watch the train. He stumbled forward a few feet and then steadied himself, watching the puffer-jacket wearing person stride along the street further. He huffed, not even knowing what the insult meant. He looked back up and the train was gone, but he stood there on the pavement for a few moments following in order to distance himself from that person. This time he walked quickly and kept his head down as he made his way under the viaduct. There were more vehicles past it. They were tall and rectangular, and Theo didn't even make an attempt to task himself with recognising what they were. There were about twenty of them all in the same area.

He walked past the edge of the bus depot and under a much smaller bridge, which made him come out onto a crossroad area. There were five roads in total, and they all met in the centre. To Theo's right was a lane of shops, like a Superdrug and a Card Factory. There was also a triangular canopy in front of a set of multiple doors. Theo recognised this as the shopping centre entrance. And then, directly in front of him was a road that looked a little more run down, with a boarded up theatre-looking building on the right and a row of shops on the left. This must have been what that woman meant when she was talking about the more run-down shops.

He made his way across the road again and switched to that side of the pavement. They had shops in Klaevr, of course. They were all those cute mom-and-pop type joints - there weren't any big businesses, so in that respect this little narrow street reminded him of home.

True to what that person had told him, there was a small laundromat and then about two consecutive boarded-up shops, as well as a closed jewellery store and a pawn shop.

Bingo.

He had to check to see if it was open, and when he realised that it was in fact open for business, he hesitantly pushed the door ajar.

All of the walls were lined with random items, so that he only actually had a few metres of walking space. It was mostly books and boxes. The shop was long and narrow and looked incredibly unkept. There were cobwebs and the floor was scuffed. Nobody appeared to be in the shop, and Theo took a few steps towards the mahogany counter at the front. A white doorway lead into a backroom that the demon couldn't see properly, so he leant against the wood and glanced around a few times before slipping out a hesitant "Hello...?".

"Coming!" A voice called, and then made themselves apparent about twenty seconds later. They were a short person who looked to be about twenty-five to thirty, with jaw-length mid-brown hair. "Hey there! Sorry, I've been meaning to put a bell on that door." They confessed somewhat awkwardly. "You looking to buy or sell?"

Theo stuttered. Their northern accent was pretty strong and for a moment the King was worried they'd say something and he wouldn't be able to make it out.

"Um, selling. I've got some gold." He explained, opening his satchel and pulling it out. It consisted of about three gold goblets, two plates and a bag with about a handful of coins in it.

The shop owner's eyes widened a little. "Damn, dude, okay. Let me get my scale from the back and I'll check out how much you'll get for it." They said, not waiting for a response before they turned back into the back of the store. Theo drummed his fingers on the counter and used the time to investigate the space he was in a little further.

The whole shop had a colour palette that consisted of owly browns and greys, mostly wood and cardboard too. It was homely, if anything. Theo had no idea how much money the shop made, as it didn't appear that customers were too frequent if the owner made time lounging around in the back.

"Where are you from? I can't put my finger on your accent, kid." They asked, walking out with a scale and a metal bowl.

"I just, um, I moved a lot growing up." Theo bluffed, shrugging as he avoided eye contact.

The shop owner hummed as they placed the scale on the counter, then the bowl atop it. They set it to zero and quickly placed all of the items in the bowl before reaching down under the counter and bringing out a hot-pink binder, flicking to one of the pages.

"I'm just checking out my chart for how much this is worth." They said lazily. "It only looks to be about nine, maybe ten karat."

They ran their finger along the paper of the binder, clearly accounting the amount of weight to a price.

"I'll give you fifty-three hundred pounds for it all." They offered, looking back up to Theo. It was only at this moment that he realised he had no idea how the currency here worked. How much was five-thousand pounds worth in the English economy? Was food for a day gonna cost him like three thousand pounds or like ten?

He swallowed. "Um, how much does a loaf of bread cost here?"

The person looked at him with an incredibly confused glance. "Uh. Maybe a quid? Quid fifty?" They said hesitantly, and Theo blinked.

"And, um, what's the difference between a 'quid' and a 'pound'?" He asked, hoping that a quid wasn't like two hundred pounds or something.

The shopkeeper snorted. "You aren't British, are you?" They asked, a smile cracking on their lips.

"Uh, no." Theo confessed.

"It's all the same thing, lad. They're called pounds. A hundred pennies in a pound, and that's literally all you need to know. Quid is just slang for pound. You got a card or do you want cash for this gold?"

Theo nodded at the information, hardly retaining it. Good thing though, it seemed that five thousand pounds was definitely enough to last him for at least a week, he hoped. "Cash, please." He said, and they nodded, opening their till.

A hundred fifty-pound notes were placed onto the counter. "Right, so, these are fifties." They said before pulling out a singular pound coin. "Worth fifty times this. This is a quid, alright?" They asked, and Theo nodded. "You've also got fives, tens, and twenties, which are self-explanatory. I'm going to give you your cash in fifty pound notes, but it's likely you'll get the other notes and coins in change. Oh! And this is a penny. A hundred of these for one of these." They said, pointing to the penny and then the pound coin.

"Um, yeah, thank you." Theo said, as they took out six more fifties and added them to the others, rolling them and putting a rubber band around them. "I appreciate that."

They laughed. "You look like an emo Pokemon trainer, you know that, right?"

Theo squinted. "Who's Pokemon?" He whispered, and the shop owner smiled widely.

"Don't worry, just, lose the cape unless you wanna get your ass kicked." They nodded, and Theo did the same, unclasping the cape and folding it up. "I mean that in the most loving way possible, you look like a prat."

Theo took the money and shoved it in his pocket. "Oh, while I'm here." He moved on. "Has anybody, like, died here recently? In this area? Potentially under suspicious circumstances."

"Oh God, you haven't killed anyone, have you?" They asked, grimacing, and Theo jumped to defend himself, not really recognising their jokey nature.

"No, no! I just... I have an interest in... crime." He nodded.

"You're a true crime podcast lad?" They questioned, smirking, and Theo didn't even know what they meant, but he nodded. "Well, not that I'm aware of, but I don't keep up with things like that."

"Alright, thanks anyway." He replied, walking away from the counter.

"Good luck out there." They offered their wisdom as they watched Theo leave.

Okay, good. So, he was now about five grand richer and his bag was much lighter. He turned and walked back in the direction he came from. He got back to the junction, where a large chunk of the road was painted red. Now that he had money, actual English money, he felt a little more able to tackle this large building.

There were a lot more people here, and it genuinely shocked Theo how quickly the area can go from completely barren to full of life. He entered and was immediately met with an arcade that meant shops were lined either side of the covered walkway. It wasn't until Theo laid his eyes on a food store that he realised how hungry he was. It had been very physically demanding travelling here from the underworld, and he hadn't eaten since dinner the night before.

He got a waft of a lovely pastry smell from one of the shops, a 'Greggs', though he thought that was a weird name for a store. Either way, he wandered into it absentmindedly, eyes scanning over the cold goods on the left as he joined the queue. Nothing interested him from there, not until he noticed the glass case of warm pastries.

Sausage roll. That was something he'd had many times in Klaevr, and he sighed internally at the relief of something, anything, familiar to him. When he got to the front of the queue, that was what he ordered, as well as a small black coffee.

The worker was a teenager, maybe about four or three years younger than Theo. She looked tired and like she didn't want to be working.

"That's gonna be two eighty-nine," She said. "Cash or card?"

"Cash." Theo said, pulling out his roll of cash and removing one of the notes from it. He handed it apprehensively to the cashier, who gave him a look that said 'I'm literally going to kill myself'.

"Seriously?" She asked, looking down at the fifty pound note.

Theo shrugged. "Sorry." And she groaned, pressing it into the machine and then raising the note to the light to check its legality. After confirming it was real, she put it in the machine and started to pull out notes and change. It felt like she was purposely taking ages.

"Right, that's forty-seven pounds and eleven pence change." She said after a long time, handing the change back to him in a really awkward way that meant he had to kind of catch it. "Just wait over there." She instructed before turning behind her. "Kev, black americano, small."

Theo stepped over to the other side of the shop and leant against the wall.

Ten minutes later, he had finished eating the sausage roll (which was really good, by the way) and was now only holding his coffee. Now that he was surrounded with loads of other people, it reinforced how weirdly he felt he was dressed.

He looked for the nearest clothes shop and made his way into it, following all the signs that led him to the mens section. It was at the point where he stood in the centre of the section that he realised he'd probably have to compromise on his usual style. He walked over to the more casual section and picked out a deep cotton blue t-shirt with some kind of animal logo on it. He also needed shoes, but all of his had always been tailor made for him so he hadn't the faintest clue what size he was. He picked up a pair of black trainers and chucked them on the ground then placed his foot next to them and then nodded when it was good enough.

And his trousers were probably good enough that he could keep them, they weren't too eccentric. He walked towards the counter, wanting this to be a pretty simple transaction, but was pretty effectively distracted by an accessories section.

There were loads of necklaces and cool bracelets, and it was nothing like he'd ever seen back home. Usually he had to go to jewellers and get things that he wanted custom made. The only product that was really sold in bulk were rings, which he had enough of already.

He scanned over the necklaces and pulled two or three off the stand, knowing he could afford it. He then did the same with some particularly nice silver chain bracelets. Since they were on the way to the counter, he kind of had already put himself in the queue as he selected them out. Before he knew it, he was being beckoned forward by a cashier and placed his items on the counter.

Theo was actually a little surprised at how similar Earth was to Klaevr, but he also knew that their whole system in Klaevr was based upon and was mostly formulated by ex-mortals, so it made sense.

Much like the last cashier, this one seemed pretty exhausted and on minimum wage. Luckily for Theo, the total was just over thirty pounds, so when he handed the person a fifty they weren't particularly upset like the previous encounter.

He was going to ask if he could use their fitting rooms, but eventually decided that would be way too awkward and started looking for the bathroom so he could get changed.

Then, after he'd properly settled into Manchester, would he start looking for Julian's mother.

XVI

Laine looked around slowly at the royal council. Here she was, having to explain to everyone the idea of leaving her boyfriend in charge of the whole kingdom while she went on a wild goose chase. Nikoliah sat *very* apprehensive on the throne beside her. Laine was sitting in Theo's throne, and had insisted that the other sat with her. He felt incredibly wrong about it, and so did most of the council, but what she said had to go because she was the acting Queen.
The room had been configured to fit a bunch of seats, and all of the knights and even low level soldiers of the castle were in the room. Hundreds of pairs of eyes.
"Does anybody have any questions?" She asked, using an intimidating tone.
Immediately, about ten hands shot up. Laine decided to work left to right, signalling the first noble to ask her question.
"Crown Princess, exactly how much experience in leadership does Sir Nikoliah have?"
Laine leant forward. "More than me, Ma'am. I don't want anybody in this court to forget that he was also my father's right hand man for a number of years. He knows much more about running this kingdom than I or King Theo do."
"Does he have a plan for if we are attacked?"
"Our kingdom hasn't been attacked in centuries, I'm not all that worried, Sir."
"Sir Nikoliah, do you mind if I ask *you* a question?" One of them shouted out.

"Um, yeah, yes, of course, Sir." He said, sitting up at attention.
"What makes you feel that you have the ability to lead this kingdom in the absence of both the King and Princess?"
He blinked a few times. "Well, Sir, I'm older than King Theo and I have a lot of knowledge because of my position that I've held in Klaevr. And mostly, Princess Laine thinks that I can. The royal family have looked after this kingdom forever without any doubt, and I think that she's grown to consider me one of them. Hopefully I will be one day." He said, smiling to himself at the thought of marrying Laine.
"So is it love that makes you competent enough to run a kingdom?" Someone hollered, and it caused the whole hall of people to erupt in their own shouts of agreement or otherwise. Nikoliah turned to Laine and leaned towards her, making a plea with his face.
She turned to him and mouthed something along the lines of 'I don't know!', but the soldier had never prided himself on his ability to lip read. It got really loud in the duration of about thirty seconds, and before she knew what she'd done Laine stood from her seat and yelled.
"Can everyone please be quiet!"
And they were. Within a second of the call, everybody was silent and looked towards her with a sense of direction.
"I'm taking it upon myself to find the King, and there is not a single person in the underworld or anywhere else that I trust more than Sir Nikoliah to take care of the kingdom. Does everyone understand that?!" She asked, now angry with the way they were being treated.
A few mumbles sounded out.
"I said, does everyone understand that?!" She asked again, an eyebrow raised.
A mixed variation of yeses came from the court, and Laine smiled. "Good. You all know Nikoliah, and you all know that he's a great guy with a great ability to lead. If you're jealous that he's made something of himself you can ask him for tips instead of being upset with him." She instructed, looking around the room.
Laine sat back down, exhaling at the now broken tension. "I'll be leaving later today."

"Are you sure this is the way?" Julian asked, squinting as he panted from traversing the uneven path up the hill.

"I've lived here for seventeen years, I know where the houses are." Laine slighted back, following Raphie, who was further up the hill than she was. They'd all decided to dress pretty practically, which was something that Theo had neglected to do.

Laine was wearing a pair of light grey joggers and a red hoodie. Raphie had a jumper in her backpack and was only wearing a pastel green t-shirt with some leaves on it with a pair of wide-legged light blue jeans. Lastly, Julian had some black jeans and a magenta-tinted shirt under a patterned jumper, so that the collar and ends of the sleeves stuck out. Once the house got in their view, Julian stopped. "Oooh." He chorused, eyeing the yellow-painted building up and down.

"What?" Laine asked, turning back around to him.

"This is where I got here from." He processed, and Raphie looked at the human and then back to the house.

"What do you mean?"

"Like, when I first got here I had to come through this house. At first I thought I'd been kidnapped but then this kooky guy told me I was dead." He explained, looking at it somewhat nostalgic as if it wasn't only a few months ago.

"Oh! Like the entry hall? We have that in Menphe, that's where we got our angel forms and all."

"Right, well," Laine began as a response to this new information. "We know this place has ties to Earth, so that's a good start for chasing after Theo if that's where he went." She said, walking down the path to the house and knocking on the door. Upon doing so, she took a few steps backwards so as to not seem invasive once the homeowner responds to the knock.

Elsie answered the door - her hair was down and she was wearing a nice summer dress. She huffed playfully, and then smiled endearingly. "Is this about Theo?" She asked, knowing wholeheartedly that it was. It seemed appropriate to give some kind of interest in their misadventures. The three of them nodded. "You'd best come in then. Don't bother taking your shoes off. You lovelies want tea or coffee?" She spoke as she walked down the corridor, her voice projecting away from them.

"Just after Theo for now, thank you though." Julian said, following the other two through their narrow hallway. They made it into the kitchen and Hettie nodded, turning to face the staircase leaning down to the basement.

"Zero! Get up here, you have visitors!" She yelled.

After a few seconds. Some cautious footsteps sounded out as well as an annoyed grumble. "Elle, you're running my anonymity, I told you to send anyone *down* to me, not-" He stopped, coming face to face with the three of them. "Oh, this is about your brother isn't it?"

Hettie walked out of their living room holding a cup of tea, having been drawn out by the commotion. She clicked her tongue. "Oh! Yes, why not have the whole royal family in my house within twenty-four hours?" She said sarcastically. "...And a person, good." She nodded at Julian.

The old blonde man smiled. "Good to see you again." He said, then after a beat he widened his eyes. "Oh! You're the King's boyfriend? That's you? He told me about-"

Laine scoffed. "The only thing that we need to clarify about Theo is where the hell he went." She said in an accusatory way.

"Well," The blonde man, whose name had now been revealed to be Zero, spoke with a huff. "He went to Earth to escape his fiance, obviously." He said, then he paused, looking at Raphie. "You're not the fiance, are you?"

She rolled her eyes. "No, I'm not the fiance!" She said exasperatedly. "I'm like the emotional support." The angel nodded.

Zero turned back around. "Right, well, questions answered, I'll be downstairs."

"Don't you dare!" Laine exclaimed, grabbing him by the shirt. He yelped. "Take us to him." She instructed, and he stuttered.

"Now?"

"Unless you're busy." She shrugged.

Raphie blinked for a second. "Wait, why do you two let this guy live in your basement?" She asked.

"Oh, it's his house; he rents it to us." Hettie answered quickly. "He's like my dad."

"He is *way* too old to be your dad." Julian said, eyes flicking between the two of them.

"He's *like* my dad. Took me under his wing when Elsie and I died." She explained to the cramped kitchen space. Zero was already half way down his staircase at this point, and he popped his head back up towards the kitchen.

"Are you three coming or not?" He asked impatiently and they nodded.

"Thanks for letting us walk through your house." Julian nodded to them, the last to make his way down the stairs. The couple laughed a little and headed back to their living room, having seen this so many times that it didn't really phase them anymore. The rent was cheap.

Laine, Julian and Raphie got to the bottom of the stairs and into Zero's abode. It was never a very big room to begin with, but with four people in there it felt even smaller. "Stand back a moment, kids." He instructed in a semi-patronising manner, but the three young people all did what he said anyway.

He did the exact same thing that he had for Theo just the night before, opening the door in the wood panels into the next room and allowing them all to walk through.

Twenty minutes and a few sarcastic comments from Julian later, they'd all (bar Julian) been given their human forms. Laine had kept her exact hair, and she had adopted a pair of brown eyes as well. Raphie was a brunette naturally, but kept her dyed hair when given her human form. It was weird to her, she'd never seen herself with the coloured hair as a person, her parents hadn't approved of it during her life.

"You alright, Raph?" Laine asked, noticing that her friend was staring off kind of absentmindedly.

"What? Yeah, I just, this is weird. Seeing myself as a human again, I never thought I would." She shrugged. "I didn't really have the best life so... um, it's weird." She repeated.

Zero turned around from his set of drawers. "Don't worry, angel, a lot of people feel that way during this process. I once let someone go back to Earth who'd been here for like a hundred years. Luckily you lot won't have to worry about the culture shock, doubt much has changed since you died. Anyway, you'll feel alright about it when you get up there." He reassured, and Raphie nodded to herself.

"So, where abouts are you three looking to go on Earth?"

"Wherever Theo went. Where did he go, exactly?" Laine asked, half already knowing the answer before it came.

"God, it was so weird. When you say you wanna run off it's usually somewhere it's to The Bahamas, not fucking Manchester, that's for one." He laughed to himself. "And it's not even the first time someone's asked me to go there."

"So he went to Manchester?"

"He did."

"Great, take us *exactly* where you dropped him off." Laine stressed.

"Let me clarify: you're going to get the King and drag him back here?" Zero asked, rummaging around in his drawers still.

"Yeah, I mean, we need to figure out what's up with Julian first, but other than that you got the plan spot on." Raphie replied. She was still a little bit vague on what exactly they were going to do, but was under the pretence that they would just wing it once they got there. Julian lived there for like eighteen years so of course knew his way around.

"Alright guys, this is going to be a little peculiar. Are you sure you're ready?" Zero inquired for the final time as he placed a candle onto the desk.

All three gave each other cursory glances and then nodded. "You're sure we'll be able to get back when we want to?" Laine responded.

"I'm sure. Now, watch." He said, reaching to his waistcoat pocket and pulling a lighter out. The flame glowed a deep purple when he ignited it, and he used the fire to light the candle wick. Zero picked up the candle and moved to stand in front of the desk, waiting for it to melt.

Once the wax started dripping freely, he hummed to himself and allowed the wax to drip quickly onto the wood panels of the floor as he moved in a circular motion. It took a few minutes for the circle to be almost complete, and when it was at that state the mysterious man beckoned the three of them over, which they agreed to.

"When you died," He spoke to the two ex-mortals. "You weren't conscious for this part, but you will be this time, and it's going to be the strangest experience of your life, unless you've done hard hallucinogenic drugs before."

The last droplet of wax completed the circle fully, and it immediately lit up in a milky, glistening purple. "You might pass out from the whiplash or the fear, I haven't figured out which causes it yet." Zero said casually. "Do you wanna jump or am I gonna have to push you?" He asked, seriously. After a few seconds of silence, he added: "I had to push Theo, if that makes anyone here feel better about wanting me to push them."

Julian snickered. "Hold my hand, one of you." He shook his hand out in the direction of the two girls. Laine rolled her eyes. "I'm only taking your hand because you're gay, don't get the wrong idea." She smiled.

"Not to be nitpicky," Julian slurred. "But I'm not gay."

"Oh. You're bi?" The Princess asked.

"I don't really like to label myself." The human shrugged. "But now you've taken my hand I don't plan on letting go."

Laine raised her eyebrows at Julian and then turned to Raphie, who was on her right. She reached her hand out to the angel. "Come on, take it you wuss." She laughed. Raphie did so with a smile, and then Laine turned to Zero. "Alright, I think we're good to go."

"Great." Zero said. "Just so you guys know, I would usually ask for you to pay, but Theo paid me *a lot* and I felt a little guilty about charging him so much afterwards." He confessed. "Sorry, off topic. Right, good luck and I hope to see you return." He nodded, stepping back from the portal.

Laine stared down at the portal for about sixty seconds of silence before she exhaled a breath of amused air.

"One of you is gonna have to push me." She whispered softly, and about five seconds later Julian replied.

"Alright." He said, stepping closer so that his toes were on the edge of the portal. "Thanks, Zero." He said, giving a subtle nod to the man - the kind that men give to each other on the street.

"Don't call me that." The magician lectured, but Julian didn't really hear it as he had already stepped forward onto the portal and fallen through it like it was a swimming pool. The momentum of it all pulled Laine forward, who fell forwards with a yelp and into the portal. Raphie was the next victim, but she kind of jumped at the same time that Laine fell so that her entry to the portal was a little more dignified.

Through the portal was a tunnel of light. At some point Julian found himself holding the hands of the two girls harder than he had before he jumped. He kind of felt like he was floating in space with no gravity, and then at the exact time it felt like it was pulling him from all directions. He was falling, he could tell that. Maybe sideways or upwards, though. He closed his eyes tightly.

The light in the tunnel very gradually got darker, by maybe a single shade of grey every minute that they were falling and it felt like literal years that he was going towards the ground.

When he got used to the force, it was kind of nice. Julian opened his eyes slowly and noticed that he was no longer locking hands with Raphie and Laine, and in fact, he couldn't even see them. He allowed himself to relax at the feeling, staring into the slowly darkening nothingness.

Was this what dying was like? The journey to the afterlife? Sure, he was doing it backwards, but it felt really blissful and better than anything he'd ever felt before. If he'd made this trip previously, he was super upset that he'd done it unconscious. Once the fear of the fall wore off, he was content for a moment. He couldn't even form any coherent thoughts. He couldn't even remember who he was at the minute, because it truly didn't matter at all.

All that mattered was the bliss, and that he was falling, or maybe flying. The darkness came quicker as he got closer to the end of the tunnel, but Julian didn't feel the slightest bit of panic about the end of the journey.

It was beautiful. A beautiful feeling.

XVI

Knock, knock. Theo stood awkwardly at the door of the first house he'd found, hands shoved unkempt in his pockets. He tilted himself forwards and backwards, to and fro, on his toes and heels, growing even more anxious each moment that he was ignored on this stranger's doorstep. In the window to the right of the house entrance, the curtains were pulled back and a set of eyes gazed out of them very quickly before letting the fabric fall back into its original position. It took about thirty seconds after this for the door to open, but it only did so a few inches because of a small silver chain keeping it conjoined to the frame. The person pointed themselves out of the door and eyed Theo up and down.
"Hi, um, do you know someone called Vanna Thompson?" He asked, and the door was immediately shut in his face, blowing his hair back a little and making him stumble slightly. He nodded to himself, sucking on his teeth as he quickly made back down the small garden and immediately did a one-hundred and eighty degree turn back up the attached house's garden.
This time when he knocked, he was met with an almost immediate response.
"I'm not interested in donating to your charity." The resident said through the door, and Theo blinked, stuttering.
"Um, I'm not- I don't work for a charity." He said, hoping it was loud enough to be heard through the barrier. It appeared that it was when the metallic clattering of a lock being undone came through and the door opened inwards to reveal a man shorter than him, but older by maybe fifteen years. He raised his eyebrows, beckoning Theo to go on.

"I'm looking for someone, I'm just wondering if you know of her, um, her name's Vanna Thompson."

"Go to the police if you've lost someone." He grumbled.

"Oh, um, no, I haven't lost her, I just need to find her." He replied, cringing almost immediately.

"Then look her up, stalk her or something. What was your plan, knock on everybody in the city's doors?"

Theo frowned. "Um, I don't know, maybe." And the man nodded sarcastically, beginning to close the door. "Wait, sorry," Theo called, and the homeowner pushed the door open again with his right foot, encased in a black trainer. "How do I 'look her up'?" He asked sheepishly.

"With your phone? Or computer?"

"Or... what?"

The man squinted. "Do I need to take you somewhere? Is there somebody that takes care of you?" He asked, spacing his words out and taking on a very patronising tone, and Theo stepped away, shaking his head in disagreement.

"No, no, that's alright. Thanks." He called, already half way down the stranger's path, being careful to close the gate properly as he scurried away. As he felt the man's eyes on the back of his neck while leaving, he decided instantly that that was probably it for knocking on random doors.

Phone or computer. And he knew for certain there was no way he was getting the former, he knew that they were a personal thing that cost money. On the other hand, he had no idea what a computer was meant to be. A friendly looking person came walking towards him on the street and he took a gamble.

"Hi, 'scuse me, sorry, do you know where I can find a computer?" He asked, causing the man to stop.

"There's free use computers at the library, just down that road next to the park." He smiled before continuing his stride along the domestic avenue, and Theo nodded.

They had libraries in Klaevr, that was a good familiar next notion. Although, in the King's experience, the only thing they really had was books. Either way, as he was getting a little more accustomed to wandering around in search of things, it didn't take an extreme amount of effort to find the library, made of dark coloured bricks. It was obvious because it had the words 'Public Library' on the front of it.

He pushed the door open, immediately being shocked by the change in atmosphere. It was almost deadly silent, and it smelled an overwhelming amount like home. The smell of old books, parchment and mainly old people.

There were a lot of old people where he was from, or rather, people who were formally old. Most lived in their own houses, less likely to find themselves socialising. It tended to be older people who found that they'd made the most out of their lives on Earth and didn't feel the need to be so extravagant in the underworld, and it was quite the opposite with the young people. That's why the social scene was so densely populated with youth.

Theo stood at the entrance to the room taking it in. It was a big hall, with metal shelves all lined with novels and other pieces of literature. It was nothing special, and could probably use a dusting and hoovering of its cream coloured walls and dark blue carpet.

He landed his eyes on a desk and approached it, completely unsure of how this was meant to work.

"Hello, um, I'd like to use a computer." He said, looking down to the younger woman sitting at the desk. She looked up and nodded.

"Do you have a library card?"

"Can't say I do, I'm sorry." He frowned, tapping his fingers on the desk.

"That's alright, I can sign you up for one. What's your name?"

"Theo Virzor." He said, instantly thinking afterwards that he probably shouldn't have given his real name, in case they had to do some kind of check that he actually existed, which he didn't.

The receptionist typed the first four letters easily, then the space and the letter 'V'. "How do you spell that surname for me?" She asked, and Theo went through the trouble of spelling it out phonetically, opting for a 'V for violet, I for indigo' kind of system. Once that was done with, the woman pulled open her drawer and took a card out with the library name on it, scribbling his name on the back with a permanent marker and sliding it across the desk.

"You're all good to go. Just enter that number when you log in and be sure to sign yourself out when you're done. The maximum time on the computer session is two hours, then you'll have to re-log in if you stay that long." She instructed, pointing down the rows of books to the back of the building where there was a line of about fifteen decade-old computers waiting to be used.

"Cheers." Theo nodded, taking the card and making a beeline towards the computers, flopping himself down in a seat and sighing. In front of the screen, which was really weird to him, was a keyboard and a mouse.

True to the receptionist's word, there was a slot on the screen for a number to be inputted. The pixelated glow of the screen kind of hurt his eyes a little, so he just looked down at the keyboard, eyes scanning helplessly over the letters and numbers. He clicked on the first digit of his code, and then glanced up at the screen again, frowning when it didn't translate.

So, he clicked it again. And again, nothing happened, so he pushed the mouse a little bit to see if that would activate anything. It didn't but it did cause the cursor to move, which ignited a realisation that he had to click on the bar in order to scratch in the pin.

This was definitely the feeling that the older residents of Hell described when told about the advancements in modern technology and medicine. Once he'd figured out that the semi-circle made the cursor move, and the blocks of plastic with letters inscribed on them made them appear on the screen, it was pretty self-explanatory.

After traversing the absolute mission of a login page, the default display was an open internet browser. Ah, another textbox. Well, luckily Theo was now a self-proclaimed master at clicking on text boxes and typing in them. So, with a very unpracticed hand he typed the name of Julian's mother in, pressing the enter button and waiting for the results page to load.

There were apparently *a lot* of Vanna Thompsons on facebook, and Theo didn't even know what that meant, so he scrolled past all of them.

He probed around on the internet for about half an hour before finding anything even remotely like a lead. It was a website, more specifically a criminal database. The page was incredibly difficult to navigate, and became even more so when taking into account that this was his first experience with technology.

There was a page under the name of 'Vanna Thompson', and when Theo saw the mugshot picture on the right of the screen, he could easily tell that this was Julian's mother.

She had the same dark skin as him, and the same eyes too. She was a slim woman, or at least when this photo was taken she was, with short sleeve length silky hair and a tired facial expression. Theo's eyes lingered on the woman for a while.

A criminal record, huh? He wondered what exactly she had done, but all of his questions were readily answered when he scrolled down the page and found the list of convictions.

Shoplifting (3)
Tax Evasion

Child Endangerment
Child Endangerment? That could be a range of things, and Julian hadn't mentioned any siblings, so it was likely to do with him. This was actually pretty interesting, he found. But, it didn't actually get him any closer to finding the woman, so he ended up scrolling even further down on the same page.
The crimes also had the date of booking. The shoplifting seemed to date back at least ten years, same with the tax evasion. The child endangerment charge, however? It was about a week old.
Now, considering that her only child died around a week ago, it was unlikely to be a coincidence. It also had the name of the specific police station that she had been dealt at, which was definitely something useful. Theo spun around on the library chair, looking for some paper or anything he could write on. His eyes landed on the bookshelf closest to him.
Theo looked around the room, and the only other person in his vision was a teenager with large headphones on, staring down at a small laptop. He walked a few feet to the bookshelf and pulled out one of them. The edges were a pretty dark cream colour, and when he opened the front page it was revealed to him that it hadn't been issued to anyone since 2013. He nodded to himself, clicking his tongue as he walked back over to the computer he was using and pulled a blue biro from the pen pot.
Theo scribbled the police station address on the back of the book, and was about to call that a pretty successful find before he noticed another set of words and numbers.
A home address. That was certainly more of a lead than the name of a local station.
He wrote that down too, and decided in an instant that it was his best bet for the next place to go. So, he highlighted the address and copied it into the search bar. From his location to the house it was looking like an hour's walk, but there were some bus routes available. He'd have to get two, and while he was somewhat familiar with what a bus was after seeing them all sleeping at the depot earlier, that seemed like it would be one hell of a task.
However, after taking a short while to decipher his options, he came to the horrid yet inevitable conclusion that he didn't really have a choice. He had to be dropped off somewhere close to the street he was looking at, or else he wouldn't find his way and he might end up in a horrible labyrinth of houses with no escape.

The 'maps' feature also had a small car symbol that said it would only take fifteen minutes of a drive, which was significantly less time than any other method of transport. The trouble was that he didn't have a car. God, this was taking too long. It was already nearing two in the afternoon at this point, and if he wanted a chance of finding this woman before sundown he had to keep himself on the move, not sitting in a cheap chair in a decrepit library. So, he logged out of the computer with his address scribed in the back page of the book and walked back down the library.
He slowed down his pace when he approached the desk, waiting for the librarian to notice him. She did, peering up at him through her fringe.
"Did you wanna take that book out?" She asked, gesturing to the novel. Theo looked down at it and nodded.
"Where can I get a car?" He said quickly as the woman took the book, opening the front page and scanning it with her black plastic device.
"I can call a taxi for you, if that's what you mean." She said, now returning the logged book back to him. "That's got thirty days on it, you need to return it by this date next month."
He nodded (feeling a little guilty that it was highly unlikely he would be back to return it) and pursed his lips. "What's a taxi?"
"Like someone else drives you somewhere in their car. Pretty expensive though, I wouldn't personally recommend it." She shrugged. "Did you want me to call you one? We've got a landline here." She offered, and Theo agreed with himself that it was probably his best bet.
"Yeah, please."
Twenty minutes later Theo found himself sitting in the back seat of a black cab, having easily offered the address up to the driver, who thankfully didn't seem to be in a small talk mood. After the day that he'd had, the demon was in no mood to exchange pleasantries with a randomer just trying to earn a living.
The drive there was a little bumpy and windy, through some neighbourhoods and some commercial areas before they eventually arrived by a quaint little church.
"Gonna let you out here, if I enter the housing estate I'm gonna have to go all the way around the block." The driver said, turning around in the seat to face Theo. "That's twenty-eight quid." He stated, and Theo nodded, rummaging around in his pocket and eventually pulling out a twenty-pound note and a ten that he'd gotten in change at Greggs.
He just handed both notes to the driver. "Keep the change." He muttered, opening the door and stepping out of the vehicle with his bag. The cab

sped off and Theo was left standing on the edge of the road looking out at the expanse of streets, all the houses attached and made of red brick. Luckily for the King, he could see the sign for the street he wanted straight away, so he made quick work of crossing the road and onto it. He was looking for an even number, fourteen, so he made sure to be on that side of the road, which he was thankful for since it was the shady side.

Okay, there was number two, and then four right next to it. By the time he got outside number ten he could easily see the house he was after. The front window was cracked, and there was a plastic 'TO LET' sign, but somebody had taken a can of spray paint and added the letter 'I' in between the two words in hot pink.

The house itself was on the end of the street, all the houses being a direct line of brick. There was a black gutter pole in between it and the house next door. The door was on the left side of a larger window, made of wood with the paint chipping off. Above the entrance was just plain brick, but above the ground floor window was a top floor window of the same dimensions. The pavement itself was also pretty narrow, with about enough room for two people to walk side by side, or one person when the residents put their bins out.

Theo looked himself up and down, making sure that he appeared at least somewhat presentable. This was his boyfriend's mother he was gonna speak to, so of course he wanted to make a good impression. After ruffling his hair a little to achieve the shaggy look that he desires, he knocked on the door.

He looked around the road while he waited for the door to be answered, but it wasn't. She must not be home. Either way, Theo knocked again, and after five whole minutes of awkwardly waiting outside the door he grew impatient.

Although he knew it was incredibly wrong of him, he couldn't help but try the door handle out of curiosity, and he was surprised when it drifted open under his touch. Theo looked back at the street for a moment and then quickly stepped through the door into the hallway, shutting it behind him and exhaling.

Immediately in front of him was a staircase with a white wooden bannister, the stairs made of a light plastic linoleum, textured to look like wood. The floor was the same too. The interior itself was pretty well kept - there were coats hung on the edge of the bannister and an array of shoes beside the door.

Was he meant to take his shoes off? He was breaking in, so probably not, but it kind of felt impolite not to, so he did.

He cautiously made his way into the living room and it was immediately clear from the state of it that the homeowners were in the middle of moving out. Boxes were all over the floor, and there was a plastic sheet over the sofa. Theo approached one of the boxes and crouched down to look into it. It had some picture frames in them, and Theo pulled one of them out and smiled to himself.

It was a picture of Julian in school uniform, clearly from primary school. He looked to be about ten or eleven years old. His hair was actually pretty long, down to his shoulders and curling as it was in a ponytail. Then Theo saw the picture behind that one, and in that one Julian was wearing a different uniform - probably from his secondary school. He'd cut his hair shorter at this point, it went down to his squared jaw freely. After staring at the pictures for a minute (and maybe taking a sneaky glance at his older ones and finding it slightly amusing that he had dyed his hair bright blue and started wearing eyeliner in his year ten photo), Theo decided that he was being creepy and dropped them back into the box, standing and heading through to the kitchen.

There were pots and pans all over the counter, as well as a pile of envelopes addressed to 'Miss Vanna Thompson'. The kitchen table had no chairs beside it, so Theo sat on it as he picked up the envelopes.

I mean, he's already done the breaking in and looking at childhood images, it can't get much worse.

And, plus: the envelopes were already open.

Turns out that they were all the exact same thing, just with different dates. They were eviction notices, it was clear to see - written in bold red font at the top of the letter. Something about not paying rent, or being late on it too many times. Theo didn't read the whole thing, he felt a little bad about snooping in on something so personal.

He slid off the table, placing the letters back where he found them and leaving the kitchen. He was back in the hall at this point. The walls were painted white, and there were nails pounded into them with no paintings hanging on them. Theo swung himself around the bannister and jumped up the stairs.

The landing area was carpeted, and there were only two rooms plus a bathroom. One of the rooms had a succession of those wooden letters that children often have on their bedroom doors or in their rooms. The 'J' was painted orange with a jaguar curled around it, the 'U' was a unicorn, the 'L' was a lion and so on. Theo stood apprehensive outside of the door, but much like he'd done with the photos and the envelopes, he'd come this far.

Julian's room was really nice. The carpet was grey and the curtains were the same colour. The walls were that obnoxious shade of teal that most teenagers decide is the best colour in the world when given the choice to paint their bedrooms. The bed was wooden, low to the ground and had a table next to it. Loads of posters also adorned the walls, for various TV shows and films. It made Theo feel a bit ill if he was honest, simply because he realised that he was literally on another dimension than this boy whose room he was impermissible to be in.

He actually missed Julian a lot. Which was weird, I mean, he was only doing this to try and figure out what was wrong with Julian, or get him home.

It was only now that Theo realised that was the last thing he wanted. He wanted to go back home and fall asleep in Julian's arms, not having to worry about Serenity or really anything else. The warm touch of his skin and the loving look in his eyes. It was all he really wanted when he took a moment to think about it.

Theo sat on the edge of Julian's bed, dark blue duvet and black sheet pressing against his body. He sighed, exhausted. He was so tired from running around this city on some kind of wild goose chase. And now, here he was in a stranger's house. He sniffled, picking up the cute little giraffe plushie that sat on the bed and holding it in front of him.

Theo laughed to himself as he jogged the stuffed animal up and down to pretend it was walking. He stopped doing it and let himself choke a small sob out. Fuck, he was lonely here. Really lonely here. Not a single person on the Earth knew he existed, and it was the most isolating thing he'd ever felt.

He pulled back the duvet of the bed and crawled under it, feeling comforted by the idea that Julian had slept here before. He wrapped both his arms tightly around the giraffe plushie and sniffled, wetting both the pillow and the giraffe as he tried his best to stop this sudden surge of emotion as it consumed him. He could look for Vanna later, his foggy brain decided.

XVII

The impact of hitting the ground was very sudden and Julian hadn't even felt it coming until he was lying face down in the park with a mouthful of grass. He looked up, blinking. He was instantly a little confused, but the moment he recognised where he was he smiled widely and jumped up to his feet.
He was home. This was Stockport, this was where he lived. Julian turned around to see the two girls he'd travelled with still on the grass behind him. Raphie groaned, sitting up and looking at the widely grinning older boy. She looked around much as Julian had and smiled a little.
"Shit, back here, huh? It's been a while." She grinned, standing. Julian exhaled.
"Not really for me. I forgot what real grass looks like." He commented, crouching down to run his hands over it. It felt amazing.
The two conscious people then glanced down to Laine, who had been knocked unconscious during the fall. The fact that that had happened to both Theo and Laine meant that it was probably because they'd never crossed dimensions before, and the ex-mortals had.
She was in her human form, lying on her side as if asleep, and Raphie bent down to shake her shoulders.
"Wake up, sleepy head." She teased, and her friend scrunched her eyes shut before blinking them open. Laine let out a sleepy noise and pushed herself up. Then she glanced all the way around her and gasped.
"Oh my God! This is Earth. God, it's bright." She said, shielding her eyes from the sun with her right hand. She stayed sat on the ground for a few moments as Julian took a few paces around. "Why is everything so

colourful? The sky and the grass and the sun and, eurgh, I need to lie down already." She complained.

"This is so fun, I can show you guys around the town, we can go to the shopping centre and get ice creams and then sit by the river and eat them and then-"

"Julian." Raphie smirked, cutting off his stream of thoughts. "As much as that all sounds great, we do have a mission here." She reminded him, reaching a hand out to help Laine stand, which she took gratefully.

Julian thought for a moment and then conceded. "Can we go swing by my house first? I need to see my mum if we're here." He suggested as Laine brushed the dirt off her clothes with the palms of her hands.

"Fine, but we need to make it quick." She conceded. "I hope you know your way around."

And Julian nodded, squinting as he looked out over the road next to the park. "Yeah, yeah." He confirmed. "We can go over the bridge and walk alongside the river to mine, it's only like twenty minutes until the bus stop by Asda."

"Bus stop?" Laine asked, looking at the young man.

"Public transport." Raphie clarified. "How are we gonna pay for that?" She asked as Julian began to walk towards the exit of the park.

"We're young, people will give us money." He reassured, already halfway out the park. Both of the girls quickly moved to follow him, not wanting to get left behind in a town that they weren't familiar with.

Julian led them along the road in the opposite direction that Theo had gone, going up a hill and towards a pretty main road. While neither of the ex-mortals seemed to bat an eye at the traffic, Laine genuinely froze at the mass intake of these metal boxes with tyres.

She journeyed halfway across the road, to that little chunk of pavement that separates bigger streets before cars started to flow down it and Laine found herself rooted on the spot. Raphie and Julian had crossed the road easily, and when they turned back to check on their friend they realised their mistake.

Laine leant forward in stressful confusion. "What the hell are those?!" She yelled across the street, and her friends almost didn't hear because of the motor engines.

Raphie grimaced, turning to Julian and cursing herself mentally. "Forgot she's never been here." She stated bluntly, and Julian nodded with a "Yep", popping the 'p' on the end. He cupped his hands over his mouth to project his voice.

"Just run across the road when they stop coming!" He yelled and Laine looked even more terrified at that notion.

Around thirty seconds later, there was a gap in the traffic, and both of the others all-but started screaming at Laine to cross the road. She stayed put with indecision for a brief moment before just absolutely legging it across the road in a sprint. Once she got to the other side of the road, she leapt into Raphie's arms and held on for dear life, panting.

"What were those?!" She repeated.

"Yeah, that's our bad, we probably should have warned you." Raphie apologised.

"That... doesn't answer the question."

"Cars. You get in them and they take you places. We're gonna get a bus soon and that's like an extended public car." Julian said, beckoning them down the pathway towards the nearby river.

The path that went alongside the river was about a person and a half wide, but it was also neighboured by spaces of grass that they could all walk next to each other on. At this point in the day it was about 5pm, and although the sky was beginning to darken, the river was tranquil.

An elderly woman was making her way along the path towards them, and Julian grinned as he turned to the other two. "Watch this."

He inhaled thrice really quickly, and tears began to form in his eyes as he repeated the action once more. He sped up his walk slightly and approached the scarf-wearing woman.

"Hi, excuse me, I'm so sorry-" He sniffled.

"Oh, darling, what's going on?" The woman said, somewhat panicked by the crying young man before her.

"I just- I need to get home and I don't have any- I don't have any money." He cried, purposefully shaking his hands out in front of him to demonstrate his stress. The woman's face softened and she frowned sympathetically.

"Honey, it's alright. Is five pounds going to be enough? I wouldn't feel okay if I left you when it'll be dark in a few hours." She said, rummaging around in her teal purse that she'd pulled out of her handbag.

Julian looked back to the two girls who were standing in shock watching him. He sniffled to himself. "I- I have to get three buses, and you know how the prices are now. But, but, please don't worry, anything would really help." He cried, grabbing on to her wrist to comfort himself.

The woman nodded, pulling a ten pound note from her purse and handing it to him.

"There you go love, you make sure you get home safely." She nodded, reaching out to give him a hug which Julian took gratefully to fully immerse himself into the character even more.

"Thank you so much." He sniffled, wiping his eyes. "This is so kind, thank you so much." He repeated, and the woman smiled.

"That's alright my dear, be safe now." She nodded, patting his arm a few times and beginning to walk back along the road. Julian spun around so that he was facing the back of the elderly woman's head and the front of Laine and Raphie. He smiled, holding the tenner up and waving it in the air to gloat. Then, he crossed one leg over the other and did a theatre type bow, grinning incredibly widely in self-satisfaction.

When the woman was a long way out of earshot and Laine and Raphie had caught up to him, he stretched the note out in front of him. "And that, my friends, is how you do it." He laughed.

"That is so morally wrong." Laine said, looking back to the old woman as she hobbled down the path behind them.

"Not really." Julian shrugged. "I didn't lie to her, I just exaggerated my feelings. She wouldn't have given us any money if I'd approached her and said 'hey old lady gimme your cash...!', would she?"

"I 'spose not."

"Let's forget ethics and get to the bus stop, how about that?" Raphie asked, pointing in the forward direction. They both nodded and all three continued to walk along the river, the sun beginning to set and ruminating an orange glow into the sky. It was really a beautiful sight, and it kind of made Laine wish she'd had the opportunity to experience it as a human. Well, no better time than the present.

Eventually, they had to deviate from the riverside to get to the bus stop, which was next to a pretty large superstore that Julian had mentioned earlier. There was a crossroad with some shops and a bank in the area, and the bus stop was coloured black with a shelter and bench. It didn't have an electronic timetable, but there was a paper one framed. Trouble was that they had not the faintest clue what time it was, but the bus they needed appeared to come every so often.

"It's only about fifteen stops from here." Julian said, hands shoved into his pockets as he looked up and down the road. Luckily for his timing, the bus reared around the corner just after he said that. He stuck his hand out to signal it down, and the bus stopped, opening the doors.

"Hey, um, just three adult tickets please- wait, um, one sec." He said, holding his finger up as he spun around to the two girls. "How old are you two?" He whispered.

"Seventeen." Laine answered.

"Eighteen." Raphie said, before adding: "But like, I'm closer to my nineteenth."

Julian rolled his eyes, spinning around to the driver again. "Yeah, three adult tickets."

"That is seven-pounds-eighty." The bus driver said, and Julian handed him the note. "We don't give change, by the way." Driver informed, printing the tickets out and taking the ten pounds. Julian nodded silently, taking the tickets and stepping forward onto the bus, beckoning the two girls to follow him. Laine was very apprehensive about boarding this metal cuboid, but Raphie kind of dragged her.

They stepped up the stairs and Julian instantly went to the back of the bus. When Raphie sat down opposite Julian, she looked out the window and snickered. "I'm pretty sure the age for childs tickets is fifteen. Why did you even ask, do we look fifteen to you?" She teased, and Julian huffed.

"Well, I don't know! I just know you're younger than Theo."

"I'm older than him by like five months, actually." Raphie corrected, and Julian rolled his eyes.

"Guys, this is freaky." Laine said, eyes fixated out of the window. "It's like a slow train." She frowned as her eyes watched the streets blur by. "I might throw up."

"If you throw up, do it on that side of the bus, not on me." Julian said in a judgemental tone, although he was only joking. Laine groaned, placing her head in her knees.

"Wake me up when it's our stop." She said.

Despite this comment, Laine wasn't able to get any sleep in because the bus journey was only actually thirteen minutes. Julian pressed the button and tapped the girl next to him on the shoulders repeatedly, with a chorus of: "Up, princess, up, up!"

They made their way along the top deck of the bus and down the stairs, all three of them nearly falling over at the way the bus stopped while they were going down the stairs.

"Cheers." Julian called for all three of them as they exited the bus onto the street.

He smiled and ran a little towards some of the estate. "God, I've missed this shit hole." He lamented, grinning toothily as he looked back to the other two. "Come on, it's just a few roads down."

This was the happiest that Julian had been since that first time he kissed Theo, and he stood outside of his house for like five minutes rambling.

"What do I say to her? Do you think she's been to my funeral? Do you think I had one? What if she's like, just got back from my funeral and then I walk in the door?"

"Julian, just go in." Laine encouraged, a smirk breaking out on her face.

"Right, okay." He nodded, pushing the door handle down and stepping into the house. "Mum!" He echoed. "Mum! I'm home!"

He swung himself into the living room with a smile on his face, but it completely dropped when he saw the state of it. It wasn't at all how he'd remembered it, considering he was here just over a week ago. He brushed it off, moving into the kitchen and then back up towards the stairs.

"She wasn't in there?" Raphie asked, and Julian completely ignored them, rushing up the stairs and into his mum's bedroom.

Again, it was empty. Where was she? It wasn't like she went out much, and especially not in the evening. He then turned to his bedroom and opened the door, immediately being hit with a wave of reminiscence.

That was, until he noticed the sleeping person in his bed. For a moment he wondered if it was his dead body, but then he realised that it would probably smell horrifically bad if that were the case. It was only when he approached his bed that he realised it was in fact Theo asleep in his bed. He looked different as a mortal, obviously, but it wasn't at all difficult to recognise him because of his facial features and moderate lankiness. Julian smiled at how peaceful he looked, but literally how on earth had he ended up passed out in his bed, cradling Mr Longneck, his childhood teddy? Julian pressed a chaste kiss on Theo's forehead and then turned to walk out of the room, completely forgetting about his mother's absence for the moment.

"Laine?" He called out from the top of the staircase, and both of the girls appeared out of the living room doorway.

"You never told us you went emo as a teen." Raphie snickered, and Julian frowned.

"It was more of a scene moment." He shrugged dismissively. "Anyway, um, I found your brother." He pointed up the staircase, smiling smugly at his discovery.

"What?" Both girls said in unison.

"Yeah, he's uh- he's asleep in my bed. Kinda cute, probably missed me." Julian teased to himself, and the other two immediately made their way up the stairs, practically pushing past the actual boy who lived in the house. By the time that Julian had followed them, they were both kneeling by his bedside and whispering.

153

"He actually makes quite an attractive human."
"That's my brother, don't call him attractive."
"I was just saying."
"Well don't say."
Julian approached them. "Shush…! Do you wanna wake him up?" He scolded.
"I mean, we probably should, I think it's a little creepy to just watch him sleep." Laine said, looking back to the man.
"Fine, fine. You two wait in the hallway, I don't wanna scare him with a crowd, he gets touchy."
"Thanks for letting me know." Laine nodded sarcastically as she stood up and stepped out of the room with Raphie in tow.
Julian tapped him on the shoulder. "Hey, goldilocks, get up." He taunted.
"Theo…! Theo, get your lazy ass up." He tried, then he sighed.
"Sleeping beauty, get out of my bed." He repeated. "I'm the Prince that's come to wake you, Snow White." He giggled, continuously rocking Theo's slumbering body. "I can do these fairytale analogies all day, sweetheart." Theo grumbled, rolling over away from Julian, and the human shook him again, harder.
"Mmgh, go 'way." Theo mumbled, pulling the duvet over him. "I don't wanna have any mornin' cuddles, Serenity." He groaned, and Julian raised an eyebrow, getting sick of this to-and-fro.
"Theo, awake, up, now!" He said with a louder voice, and Theo rolled over and blinked up, having a groggy look on his face. It took him about five seconds to register who was in front of him, and then about an extra ten for him to register his surroundings.
"Hey, Jude." He slurred. Then about a moment later, his eyes widened and he sat up quickly. "What the fuck?!" He asked, immediately pulling Julian into a hug. "What are you doing here, how did you get here?!"
"Um, firstly, I don't think you heard my really funny joke where I called you 'goldilocks', so I just want you to know I came up with that one on my own." He told, smirking. "And, secondly, we came to chase after you because your dad is pretty upset and we had to leave Laine's boyfriend in charge, and you know he's a bit of a roadman, so-"
Someone in the hallway cleared their throat very loudly, and so Julian looked back to it then carried on. "Right, um, the point is that we're here now. Didn't actually expect for you to be in my bed, and give me back Mr Longneck." He nodded, reaching out for the giraffe that Theo was still holding.

After handing the plushie over, Theo swallowed. "So, um... If you left Nikoliah in charge I'm gonna assume that my sister's here." He said slowly.

Laine made herself apparent in the doorway. "Your sister has a name, by the way."

"Hey." Theo said, getting out of the bed properly now and embracing her. "Human suits you."

"Thanks." She laughed before pointing at the door. "Raphie's here too."

And so, the remaining person made herself apparent and she also got a hug from Theo.

"So um, do you wanna fill us in on how you ended up passed out in my bed?" Julian questioned, taking a seat on the ground, followed by everyone else.

"Right, um, right. So, I got here and made five thousand pounds." He began, gesturing with his hands as he spoke. "And then I went to the shopping centre and got a sausage roll and this shirt. And then I started knocking on doors to look for Vanna, but all of them were kind of like 'no, go away, you're a weirdo', so then I went to the library and looked her up after like ten minutes of trying to work out that weird light-up rectangle, and then I found her criminal record and it had her address on it so I came here. You know, then I got tired."

They all took a moment to stare at him after that, before Raphie leant forward. "Sorry, did you say five grand?"

"Oh God, you stole?!" Laine exclaimed, exasperated.

"No, no, I didn't steal. I took some of dad's old gold stuff and then pawned it." He replied.

Laine raised her eyebrows. "You stole... from dad? Theo, I hate to tell you this but I really don't think he needs another reason to be mad at you."

"He's mad at me because I ran off?" Theo clarified.

"Um," Laine halted, dragging out the word. "Serenity kind of tore you apart to him after she found out you were having an affair."

Theo slumped over, feeling like he was melting into the ground. "Well, that sure solidifies it. I can't go back any time soon." He sighed, defeated.

"You're fine, we need to focus on finding Julian's mother now that we have you. We were gonna do it the other way round, but here you are." Laine gestured.

"Hold on." Julian began. "You dug up my mother's criminal record? Isn't that a bit... Stalkerish?"

"Well, no."

"Kinda is."

155

"How did you guys get here then?" Theo asked in an attempt to divert the conversation away from him being a little bit creepy.

"Well," Laine began. "Us three, Niko and Serenity had a little meeting this morning about what to do, which resulted in her storming off because she was upset about Julian. Then dad showed up and she told him everything and then he took me and Serenity into one of the lounges and suggested that Serenity rule while you were gone." She explained quickly. "Yeah, I know, crazy. Anyway, I told him that since you'd left that note saying that *I* was in charge, it was my choice who was in charge and then Nikoliah and I had to present our argument to the royal council, and then the three of us went to that address and disturbed that nice couple's afternoon. Then we spoke to the blonde guy and he let us through his portal to here."

"I see." Theo breathed, kind of frustrated that he'd gone through all that trouble to get out and then to get here when they had literally just done it in the duration of a couple hours.

They spent the next ten minutes going over the exact details of Theo's 'first day on Earth' story, which also included an excessive amount of Raphie and Julian mocking him about the computer mishaps, even though it totally wasn't his fault, but whatever. After a little while, the sun had set outside and they all decided that they needed to formulate their next steps.

"I want a cuppa. Are we setting sail or is this our AirBnB for tonight?" Raphie asked, shifting her position to eliminate some of her pins and needles.

Julian nodded. "Yeah, yeah. We can crash here tonight, I'm exhausted. I'll stick the kettle on."

XVIII

"Is that my bracelet?"
Theo looked down at his right wrist, which still had the silver chain with a purple flower charm on wrapped around it. He knew he'd been caught as he sat on the opposite sofa to his sister, cup of tea in hand just like the other three in the room.
"...Sorry."
"It's fine, I'm only teasing." She smiled into her mug, taking another sip.
"If not here, where would your mum be?" Laine asked, eyes focused on Julian, who paused.
"Um, I don't know, maybe one of her friends' houses." He replied, shifting slightly in his position.
"She got arrested last week." Theo blurted quickly. "I just- she might still be in custody if she isn't here."
"Oh, yeah. Good defence in you not being a stalker." Julian nodded, smiling sarcastically. Theo scoffed.
"I'm just saying that it's probably our next best move to check that out." He defended.
"Wait, if we're trying to find out how Julian died, why don't we just… google it?" Raphie said, looking around the room for a laptop or phone.
"Right, yeah." The boy in question replied, momentarily diverting the conversation away from his mother as he stood and walked over to the other corner of the room and sifted around in some boxes, eventually pulling out a chunky black laptop. He crossed his legs on the ground and opened it, tapping his fingers on the keyboard to get in.

"What the hell is that?" Laine asked, standing and walking over to him, sitting behind the laptop.

"A world of possibilities." Julian nodded emotionlessly, typing his full name into the search bar and pressing enter.

He choked slightly, clicking on a news article that came up first. It was a very small local paper, and began to read the title out loud.

"Manchester teen dies- wait, that's so boring." He interrupted himself, sighing and shutting the laptop.

"What is? What's boring? Tell us." Theo demanded from the sofa, and Laine looked to him from where she could also see the laptop screen prior to it being shut.

She grimaced. "He died in his sleep."

"Ugh." Julian groaned. "I was hoping for jousting gone wrong or like, explosion of a caramel icing factory. That's so sad." He frowned.

"It's fine, Julian, my death wasn't very eventful either. What else does it say?" Raphie asked, curious. Laine took the laptop from his lap and opened it again, continuing to read.

"Blah, blah, obituary, blah blah, exact cause of death to be confirmed. What does that mean? They don't know?"

"Well, they must know. It's been a week, I've probably been buried or cremated or whatever my mum wanted, they can't exactly do more tests." He said, taking the laptop back. "Wait, oh my God, I'm buried like ten minutes from here. We could go on a family outing."

"To your grave?"

"Yeah. Could be fun, I always used to get sad that I'd never see my gravestone when I was younger." He lamented, before yawning. "Jeez, I'm tired."

"Same." Raphie agreed. "How are we sleeping?"

Julian thought for a minute. "Well, I guess Theo and I can take my mum's bed since it's a double, and one of you can have mine and the other can have the sofa?"

Immediately, Raphie cut in.

"There's no way I'm sleeping in your bed, you literally died in it. I don't wanna share a mattress with a dead body. No way."

"Psh. I'm not exactly gonna haunt you, am I?"

"No, it's fine, Raphie." Laine smirked in amusement. "I'll sleep in his bed, you can have the sofa."

Theo licked the dryness off his lips. "So, um, you want us to share a bed?" He asked, pointing to Julian then himself as he spoke. "Me and you?"

"Yeah, we did it all the time in Hell."

"Well, yes-, but that was more of a 'it's late and I don't wanna walk down the stairs to my room' kind of arrangement." Theo argued, nervous.

"Look, man. You can sleep on the floor if you want, but I really doubt that considering you've spent eighteen years sleeping on a prince-standard bed." Julian snickered playfully.

"No, I mean, of course I *want* to share with you, I just don't want you to feel like you have to."

"Well, good. Because I don't feel like that." Julian curled an eyebrow, standing and shutting the laptop for the second time. "It's late, we should head up if we have a whole day of gallivanting after mum tomorrow." He instructed, beckoning Theo to follow him with two fingers.

"Erm, wait." Raphie said, standing off the sofa too. She got both of their attention, and they turned to her. "Do you have a phone, Julian? I just, there's someone I want to call."

Julian pointed to the kitchen. "Yeah, there's a landline on the countertop. Goodnight." He yawned, heading up the stairs. Theo gave the same goodbye to the two girls and followed him.

They made it to the landing and Julian pushed the door to his mum's bedroom open. The walls were a light grey, and the bed had those fake-silk sheets adorned. There was a chest of drawers and a mirrored wardrobe too.

"Are we gonna change into pyjamas or anything?" Theo asked, shutting the door behind him and isolating them from the rest of the world for the night. "Nah, don't have enough. We can just take our shirts off, or you know, sleep in boxers if you're into that."

"I'm not." Theo said bluntly, scrunching his nose as he crossed his arms in front of each other and pulled his shirt off his body over his head, chucking it on the floor by the foot of the bed. He slid onto the bed and watched as Julian took his own shirt off, eyes lingering on his chest for *maybe* a little too long.

"I'm shorter than you, so I call little spoon." Julian giggled, flicking the light off and plunging them into darkness as he sat on the bed too, moving to cuddle Theo.

"Julian?"

"Mhm?"

"Are we dating? Or like... friends with benefits, or... you know. I just kinda want some clarification, I dunno."

Julian rolled over in the bed to face Theo, smiling softly to him. "Do you want us to be dating?" He asked sweetly, and Theo's eyes became a little glassy.

"Yeah. That'd be nice." He breathed.
Julian moved forward, closer to his now-confirmed-official-boyfriend, locking them together in a kiss. It lasted a few moments of just simple kissing, before it turned into more of a make-out and Julian moved to straddle Theo's waist, kissing him from above. Julian's hand moved to Theo's chest, the other one carding through his hair at the same time. This lasted for a blissful few minutes before Theo pushed the other man up a little, forcing him to break the kiss as he panted.
"I can tell you're trying to initiate something, but we are *not* having sex in your mothers bed." He whispered in a scolding manner.
"What? Why not?"
"I shouldn't have to explain, that's just weird." Theo slighted, and Julian pouted, rolling off his boyfriend and flopping down on the bed next to him.
"Fine." Julian said, voice slipping into a laugh. "Just cuddle me to sleep then, you spoil-sport." He chucked, dropping his head onto Theo's bare chest and wrapping his muscular arms around the demon's body. Theo took the hint and placed his right hand on Julian's curled hair, running his hand through it repeatedly, then taking his other hand to rub circles on the shorter male's back.
"Alright, darling."

The morning came quickly. Like most of the time, Theo woke up before Julian - probably influenced by the couple hours of napping he had earlier. He thought he could get addicted to sleeping with Julian- he felt more refreshed and well-rested than he ever had before. He sat on the edge of the double bed for a few moments, rubbing his eyes and swinging his legs to wake himself up properly.
He felt a little different waking up in a varied dimension. It felt like the air was a little heavier, or maybe that was his headache from waking up so goddamn early. He looked over to his sleeping boyfriend and decided not to wake him, instead opting to slip out of the bedroom after putting his shirt back on. He transcended the stairs as quietly as possible, hoping for a slice of toast or maybe two. However, upon entering the kitchen he saw Raphie, who had clearly taken one of the chairs they'd already packed away and was sitting beside the dining table, one leg crossed over the other as she bit her nails.

"Morning." She greeted, looking up from where she was biting her nails. Theo raised an eyebrow and leant against the counter.
"You... okay?" He asked slowly.
"Been better."
"What's up...? If you wanna talk about it of course, don't feel like you have to, I just-"
"My brother went to prison." She cut him off. "Somehow, in the time I've been dead. I'm not sure if I'm meant to call him or anything."
She looked upset as she glanced back up to the other person in the room for advice, and if Theo was being honest he was completely lost in this scenario. He decided to reply with apprehensiveness.
"What did he do?"
"Murder, apparently." She nodded to herself. "Yeah, I know." She grimaced at the face that Theo pulled. Theo took this opportunity to sit on the edge of the table in order to be more comfortable once he realised this conversation was more than small talk.
Raphie sighed loudly, placing her head in her lap. "And the trouble is that I don't know if I'm mad at him for it. He's my brother, and I don't know the circumstances."
"Well, um, maybe you could give him a call? If they allow it. See how *he* feels about it, because if he's, like, not remorseful at all then that could be an issue, but he might have changed." Theo suggested, and Raphie nodded.
"Yeah, I've had the first ten digits of the number keyed into the phone for about half an hour. I just can't bring myself to click the last one." She confessed, eyes lingering on the landline.
Theo swallowed. "I mean, I can do it if you want." He offered, feeling a little trivial.
"Okay, god, okay."
"Do you want me to leave for the call?"
"No, stay. Stay, please."
"Okay."
Theo read the number off the post-it-note on the table and stuck the last number in. After about twenty seconds of ringing, the line answered.
"United States Penitentiary Marion, what is the name of the inmate you are calling for?"
"Um, it's Alex Prendal."
Theo paused. That name, he felt like he'd heard it before. Or, the surname at least. Where had he heard that name before?
"Transferring you now, please hold."

During the incredibly repetitive hold music that seemed to be going on forever, Theo took the opportunity to inquire.

"I feel like I've heard that name before, Prendal? Is there a celebrity with that name?" He asked, and Raphie shook her head. "Alex? Alex." He repeated.

Raphie's head snapped up to look at Theo, her eyes questioning. "You probably recognise it because it's my last name." She reminded as she tilted her head in obvious confusion.

"Hi?" A voice trilled through the line, disrupting the previous mutually strange moment they were having. Raphie looked back down to the phone (which she'd put on speaker) and stuttered.

"Hey, Alex." She said kind of quietly.

Theo felt like he'd heard that man's voice before, too.

"Gracie?"

"Yeah." The cotton-candy haired girl nodded regrettably.

"What the fuck?! What the fuck?!" He exclaimed, sounding very panicked through the crackling line. "You're alive?!"

"Um, no. I was just given the opportunity to call you and thought I should."

"What?! I'm gonna pass out, Gracie, you need to clarify. Am I hallucinating? Is this what the inside has done to me?"

Raphie completely ignored the question, and instead moved to ask another.

"What did you do?" She said, voice dropping to a much more serious tone.

Julian took this exact moment to enter the kitchen, looking very sleepy and still shirtless. He yawned slightly, blinking with exaggeration. He stepped up to Theo and leant into his body so that his head was tucked under Theo's arm. Still completely focused on the phone call that was happening, Theo brought a hand to absentmindedly card through Julian's hair.

"I did it for you."

"Did what for me, Alex?" She persisted, fingers drumming against the table.

"I made sure she was sorry." He said, a distinct lack of emotion in his tone.

And then Theo realised where he recognised this man from.

"What's going on?" Julian murmured into Theo's body as he looked up tiredly.

"Kiara." Theo said, the name coming back to him as he looked at Raphie. Her eyes widened and then she narrowed them. Julian glanced worriedly between the two of them, a lot of tension having been created in the room.

"What?" Both Alex and Raphie asked at the same time, and then the former followed it up with a: "Who is that? Who are you with?!"

Raphie completely ignored her brother's plight, attention turning wholly to Theo. "How do you know her?"

Theo stuttered, looking to his shorter boyfriend as if asking him to answer, as if he could. "Um, she came to me. Just before I met Julian, she tried to appeal her position in Hell with me."

"And you-?"

"I sent her away to another kingdom." He replied simply.

"Who the fuck are you talking to?"

"Did you kill Kiara, Alex?" She asked, turning back to the phone.

"She killed you, Gracie! But apparently not because you just called me!"

Not once did Raphie look away from the phone as she continued to speak. "I did die, I'm just calling from the afterlife." She waffled slowly, and Alex groaned loudly.

"I knew I shouldn't have taken that edible." He whined.

"So, let me get this straight: you're in prison because you killed Kiara?" Raphie asked, although that fact was painfully obvious already to everyone in the room.

"You would've done the same." He argued.

"What's all this about?" Laine asked, stumbling into the kitchen. Julian turned to her and lowered his voice to a whisper.

"Raphie's brother killed someone for her."

Laine looked incredibly disorientated as she glanced between everyone in the room. There was a pause where nobody said anything.

"Are you gonna say thank you?" Alex asked impatiently.

Raphie rolled her eyes. "You're high, Alex, this didn't happen. Love you, bye." She said quickly before putting the phone down and then dropping her head to the table. She let out a long groan of frustration.

"Why did he call you Gracie?" Julian asked after a moment's silence.

"That was my name when he knew me." Raphie said, still talking into the table. "I changed it when I died." She told him, and Theo nodded.

"Hold on, can someone catch me up?" Laine said, still immensely confused about the situation from only just entering the room.

"Yeah, I will." Theo offered. "Basically, Raphie's brother pretended to be friends with this girl that bullied Raphie and then he stabbed her."

"That's a concerning amount of detail, how did you know that?" Raphie inquired, looking at the demon with astonished eyes.

"Oh, I did the forehead thing." He replied, waving his hand around in the air dismissively.

"The forehead thing?" Raphie snickered loudly.

"It's a monarch thing." Laine said, turning to face her friend. "Lets you see the whole course of a person's life in like two seconds."

Theo nodded. "Yeah, just like…" He began, moving his hand to press it against Julian (who was still leaning into him)'s forehead, as he knew it wouldn't *actually* do anything because he'd already tried the first time they met.

Only, it did do something this time.

A little girl stood outside of a preschool building, bouncing on her toes. Her mother came up behind her and placed two hands on her shoulders.

"Alright, have fun now." She whispered, sending her child off into the school.

"What's for tea t'nigh, mama?" She asked, swinging her legs at the dining table. The woman who was facing the child frowned.

"Have some of your cereal, lovely." She said, placing one of their few bowls on the table in front of her prodigy.

"No! No! I want real food!" The girl screamed before standing from the table and throwing the bowl on the floor, storming off upstairs before there was any chance of stopping her.

She danced around in her bedroom, about nine years old now. A vague One Direction song was playing on a light grey radio on the windowsill. The world didn't matter at this point, it was just her and Harry Styles against the world.

About thirteen years old now, he stood in his bedroom with a paint roller in his hand, looking up at the expanse of plain walls. His mum walked in the room and smiled. "Alright, let's get to painting then." She instructed, flicking on the radio as her son nodded proudly.

"You promise it's not too expensive?" He asked, about two or three years older now, his hair a very faded blue colour (he was going to redye it back to brown at some point, he swore). His mother frowned, taking the lid off a small vial of clear liquid.

"Nothing that makes you happy is too expensive, darling." She reassured. He was actually quite nervous – it had been a while since he'd had a shot and this was going to be a regular thing from now on.

He shut the door behind him, pushing his shoes off as he made his way down the corridor and into the kitchen – very excited about his eighteenth

164

birthday tomorrow. He was planning a party with some of his friends and the best part was that his mum had agreed to pay for it all.

"I'm going to bed, night!" He yelled out, already heading up the stairs, but he was interrupted by his mother asking for a hug, which didn't faze him much.

After bidding her goodnight and marching his way up the stairs, he pulled his shirt off, now able to do so without any stress after his top surgery about six months prior. From there, he changed into his pyjamas and climbed into bed. Something was wrong though, it was evident just from the feeling in the air.

He blamed it on his anxiety.

"That was so weird, did you see his eyes?!" Julian exclaimed, looking up at Theo in astonishment. The man was a little startled, and he involuntarily flicked back to his demon form for a few seconds as a result of the use of magic. His head pounded a little from the stress of the experience.

"Ach, oh my God." Theo choked, leaning against the wall. "Shit, I did not expect that to work. I mean, it didn't work back in the castle. That was a horrific invasion of your privacy, I'm so sorry."

"What did you see?" The other man asked, completely ignoring the previous sentiment.

"Um, you as a little kid and then you as a teen, and then you on what I'm assuming was the night you died."

"Boring." Julian scoffed, looking back to the ground.

"Interesting. Thanks for the insight into royalty." Raphie nodded sardonically.

"Alright, alright, enough showing off." Laine wavered.

"Did you see the blue hair?" Julian snickered.

"Yeah. Interesting choice, I'll say that."

"I was fourteen, fuck off. Don't act like you've never wanted to dye your hair."

"And I'm thankful that my dad told me I couldn't." Theo replied. "I had a little bit of a reputation to uphold as the Crown Prince."

Julian rolled his eyes playfully.

Raphie looked to the ground for a moment. "I can't believe my brother killed someone." She lamented, sounding more dumbfounded than upset.

Theo nodded. "Do you need a minute? We can push the stuff we were gonna do back." He suggested, trying to be compassionate. But, Raphie shook her head nonetheless.

"No, no. It's fine. Just a bit weird to think about."

"And it will be for a while." Laine said. "I'll make some tea and we can relax for a bit before we get back into the swing of mother-hunting." Raphie nodded, thankful for her friends.

XIX

In all fairness, they probably shouldn't have made so many diversions from their original mission. But, who could really blame them? Only Julian had ever been to England before, and there was *a lot* to absorb. Theo had decided that he did not want to accompany Julian to visit his grave. He saw way too many dead people on a daily basis for him to want any more of it. Laine had agreed with him, and so the group had decided to split up. Raphie and Julian were gonna go have an amble around the graveyard, and the two siblings were gonna have a walk around some of the nature and see what they could find.

There wasn't much nature back home. All of the trees and grass were dead, and it was nothing at all like what they could find on Earth. Unless the politics had a significant turn around any time soon, it was incredibly unlikely that either of them would get the opportunity to see anything like this again. Upon hearing this, Julian had shown them on a map where they could find the local nature reserve, which was also beside a set of allotments that (while privately owned) were open for the public to walk through.

But, before the group could actually break off, they had to find some way of getting back to each other again. So, an hour after leaving the house in the same clothes that they wore yesterday, the four of them stood outside a small tech shop where they were hoping to buy burner phones for little money that they could put each other's numbers on. And, thanks to Sir Dyran's gold, they had the expenses to make that kind of decision.

"No, seven-four-three."

"Seven-four-what?"

"Three."

"I thought you said seven?"

"No, just give me the phone and I'll type it in, you're useless." Julian scoffed at Theo playfully, snatching the phone from his hand as he frowned. The younger man began to punch in the phone number of one into the other.

"It's not my fault I've never used one before…" Theo grumbled, feelings a little hurt at the accusation.

"Awh, don't worry. You'll get there eventually." Raphie comforted condescending, patting Theo's back as she moved to stand next to Julian, who handed the phone back to Theo.

"Alright." Theo shushed, placing the phone in his right pocket. "Let's get going then."

"But," Laine began. "After this we really need to start looking for your mum." She reminded.

"Yeah, fine." Julian nodded. "Now, off we go to the cemetery!" He exclaimed, turning on his heel.

"Wait." Theo called, and the other turned back around. Theo opened his arms a little and beckoned Julian for a hug. The human smiled, ploughing into his body to accept the embrace.

"That was a test and you passed." He smiled before looking up to Theo and raising himself onto his tip-toes in order to kiss him on the lips with a giggle.

The kiss itself was short-lived, but it made that feeling of butterflies rise in Theo's chest again, and the energy it gave him could last all day.

"Alright, bye." He smiled, shoving the shorter man away.

And so, Laine and Theo set off walking down the road in the direction that Julian had told them to go. After about ten seconds of silence, it was broken.

"Why did you run away?" Laine asked, hands shoved into her pockets, and Theo raised an eyebrow.

"I thought that was pretty obvious."

"No, I mean, why didn't you just *talk* to someone?"

Theo took a moment to formulate his reply, eyes fixated on the ground.

"Dad would've been mad at me. And Serenity broke down when I told her I didn't want to marry her, I couldn't stay there."

"And yet Dad is still mad at you. And Serenity is still upset." She lectured as they began to walk through the entrance to the forested area. There were loads of trees towering over them, and the ground was dusty enough that when they stepped onto it, the air became hard to breathe through because of the particles.

"Well, we're having a good time, aren't we?" Theo persuaded, looking around at all of the greenery. "It's nice, huh?"

"Yeah." Laine breathed. "It's a bit sad that we've been missing out on this." She stated before a stretch of silence that lasted a few more minutes and many metres further into the woods. Theo clicked his tongue.

"Do you ever wish we were angels?" He asked, and Laine considered it. Angels were considered way better than demons, naturally. Of course there was that fact. They were beautiful and pure, and perfect on all fronts. Demons were the scum of all dimensions, and everyone seemed to know it - even the demons themselves. It seemed a little unfair though. People who were good people at heart still ended up in Hell, but it was very rare that people with bad hearts ended up in Heaven.

Theo could think of one exception.

Either way, the royal children had never done anything to actually end up in the underworld, that was just how it was and there was never any opportunity to question it. Considering how they weren't even granted the luxury of being able to visit The Heavens, it wasn't surprising how many demons seemed to escape to Earth.

That's kind of assuming that Hell was a bad place. It wasn't, not really. Some of the people were bad, or rather, misguided, but as far as places go, it wasn't *bad*. Certainly not Klaevr. They'd worked hard to build up a nice atmosphere there, and ill-behaviour wasn't tolerated. They could thank their relatives for that, but of course no matter how great they thought their home in Hell was, it could never compare to what they've been told of Heaven. And they'd never even be able to prove whether or not they were right in this assumption.

"Yeah. As unpatriotic and morally wrong as it might be to say, we'd actually get taken seriously. People like bonkers Beckett wouldn't be able to treat us like the dirt beneath their feet." She admitted.

Theo made a bit of a funny face. "That seems like a very childish nickname for a very dangerous person."

"How is it going with him?"

They came to a grassy area of the forest, where flowers of varying colours were growing. Both demons stopped to actually get a look over it as Theo considered his answer.

"It's not." He admitted. "I've been a bit preoccupied with the marriage and Julian and all, I haven't really got the chance to look at the politics side of things."

"Says the literal king. You're not the one that the politics are affecting, that's rich."

"Okay, sure. I'll get to it as soon as we get home."

"Oh, when? After you sort out your fiance?"

Theo kicked a flower on the ground in front of him. "She's not my fiance any more, I thought I made that pretty clear when I ran off."

"Dad postponed your wedding. Told the people you were ill. As far as he's concerned, you're engaged." She told him as they made their way past the meadow and towards the exit of the forest.

"When we get home I'll tell him."

"You say that, but you practically drop to your knees and beg for his forgiveness when he so much as raises his voice at you." She mocked, and Theo's frown deepened.

"No, I don't. I'll have you know I was very assertive towards him when he told me I was getting married."

"I bet you cried."

"Whatever."

By this point, the pair had made it out of the forest on the other side, and if they were being honest they'd been more focused on their conversation that reopened once every few minutes than the nature itself. It had been a while since the two of them had been able to just have a genuine conversation that wasn't clouded by other people being with them. From the exit of the forest came the opening to a small set of allotments.

"Through there?" Theo asked, pointing towards the entrance of the soiled area.

"Yeah, why not?" Laine replied, bringing herself forward to move into the allotment, and Theo followed, keeping the same pace.

"Oh, look! I've never seen where those are grown before." Laine smiled, looking at a patch of cabbages sticking out from the dirt. Of course, food couldn't be grown in Klaevr because of the lack of nature, so it was all imported from The Heavens.

"Oh, yeah. That's cool." He agreed, taking a moment to study the vegetables. If Theo was being honest, he never really understood that kind of thing, probably because he'd never been able to actually see it growing up. They continued walking through a path in the middle of allotments for a further five minutes. It was clear that they were all owned by homeowners in the area, each having their own personal touch. Some people were working on their allotments with various tools too.

Theo was very observant of everything as he walked down the path. It was the kind of path that was made by people just walking on it over and over again. Which was why, when Laine started rambling about something incoherent, Theo had to interrupt her because he'd made an observation.

"Laine."

"Mhm?"

Theo's eyes were fixated completely on one person in an allotment. It was an older woman, looking to be about forty-five or fifty. Her skin was fair, and her hair was dark and long. She had narrow shoulders but a generally heavier build with a lot of curves. She held a shovel and pushed it into the ground, standing on the edge of the metal with her right foot, clad in a dark-green wellington boot, as it lodged into the ground.

Maybe if Theo's vision wasn't so good, or if he wasn't paying as much attention, he wouldn't have made the observation that differentiated this woman from any other random gardener.

"Oh, shit."

At this point, both siblings had their eyes latched onto his woman. She continued gardening without a care in the world.

"That's definitely her, isn't it?"

"Yep."

It felt a bit like having the wind knocked out of him. Theo stood completely still as he watched this woman with intent. He felt like he couldn't breathe and had just sucked in far too much air at the same time. It was like nothing he'd ever felt before, and like every single little question he'd ever asked had been answered at the sight of this woman. Like it filled a hole that he had never noticed was empty. Although she obviously looked different to her painting in her human form, but much like Laine, Theo and Raphie were recognisable because of their facial features, she was too.

Theo and Laine looked with wide eyes at their mother for a long time.

"...Do we speak to her?" Theo asked, sounding a little upset. Even though Laine had made fun of him for crying about ten minutes ago, she wouldn't even consider it right this minute.

"I don't know." Laine spoke softly, swallowing as she did so. The only sounds in the air were their laboured breathing and the sound of dirt being shovelled slowly. They watched her for a further five minutes before Laine finally started strolling in the direction of where their mother was gardening. Theo stuttered for a moment before following her at a slightly picked-up pace in order to catch up with his sister.

Naturally, because of how close they were standing, the woman noticed them almost immediately. She leant against her shovel and looked up at them with a subtle smile.

"You guys alright?" She asked, beckoning them into the area with her hand that wasn't gripping the handle of the shovel. Theo and Laine exchanged glances before the latter decided to open her mouth.

"Yeah, yeah. We're just going for a little walk around here." She said awkwardly, and Theo decided that he wanted to die.

The gardener walked up to them at the fence, letting her shovel drop onto the ground.

"Are you two local? I don't think I've seen you around but I am getting a little old." She teased herself.

It was only from this up close that Theo got a proper look at her. She looked just like she had in the paintings, obviously with more human-features, but it was so absolutely jarring to see her in person that it felt like he was going to pass out. He was very grateful that his sister seemed to have gotten a handle on talking.

"No, don't worry, we aren't from here. Just visiting a friend." She nodded. "Oh, yeah? Whereabouts are you from?"

Laine didn't reply for a few moments, so Theo managed to strangle out an answer after regaining his ability to speak.

"Nowhere you would know." He said slowly. "What's your name?" He continued, kind of hoping she would say something that they wouldn't recognise and they could move on with their day and just admit they were wrong and maybe their eyesights were deteriorating.

"It's Aster." She smiled, reaching a hand out to shake Theo's. "It's a type of flower."

Theo reached forward and shook her hand over the fence. "Yeah, yeah. I know."

Aster looked down when shaking his hand, and she gasped in excitement, eyes latching on to Theo's wrist.

"That's such a lovely bracelet, is that an Aster?" She smiled, looking back up to Theo with a wide grin.

"Yeah, it is." He said softly. It took an enormous amount of self control to stop himself from bursting into tears and draping into her arms.

"Where did you get it? I used to have one just like that back in the day, but my husband had it custom made so I'm really surprised that you…" She trailed off right towards the end of the sentence, holding the small flower charm in between her thumb and index finger. After about ten seconds of complete silence while she ran her fingers over the purple flora, she stepped back from the two of them and looked up incredibly slowly, eyes going between the two of them.

"Oh God. You're my children."

"Yeah." Theo said for the third time this interaction, and Aster felt incredibly naive for not noticing it sooner. She frowned and then smiled, her eyes watering.

"Oh." She exhaled. "Right."

They stood for a while, just looking at each other wordlessly.

"You've grown up." She commented sadly, and Laine nodded.

"Yeah, that happens."

Aster nodded with a frown before exiting the allotment and reaching her arms out at her two children. Theo took a little bit of a step backwards at the request, but Laine seemed to immediately jump into her arms like it was the only chance she would ever get. The Princess rested her head on Aster's shoulder and sniffled.

Theo was not so happy about it.

"Laine!" He scolded, and she tilted her head to look at him as their mother did the same. "Do not hug her like you forgive her."

"Please don't be like that, Strythio." Aster frowned, continuing to hold onto her daughter for dear life. Theo furrowed his eyebrows in upset. How fucking dare she just show up and act like she'd never abandoned them? And how dare Laine to just forgive her in an instant?

"No, don't tell me how to be." He spat, pointing a finger at her. "I went- We went to your funeral. Laine, seriously?" The Princess turned completely so that she was facing Theo, but Aster's hands were still around her shoulders.

"She's our mum." She murmured.

"No she's fucking not. If she was our mother she would have been there." He exhaled, chest rising and falling rapidly as his eyes watered with anger and upset. "When I was younger I used to stay awake at night *fucking begging* the universe to bring you back! I'm not- you're not- fuck." He shook his head.

"Well, he certainly gets his anger issues from his father." Aster whispered into Laine's ear, but it wasn't quiet enough that Theo didn't hear it. He sniffled.

"You don't know me, fuck off." He said, turning around and storming off. Laine stepped out of her mother's arms. "Theo!" She shouted after him. "Theo, come back!"

As a response to this, he turned around and stuck his middle finger out towards them, continuing to walk off and around the corner. Laine

173

groaned, turning back to Aster. She looked up at the other for about two seconds before turning and running after her brother.

When Theo got around the corner and out of their sight, he collapsed onto the dirty ground, bringing his knees to his chest and just sobbing into them with no boundaries. He was leaning against a metal chain link fence and there were overgrown remnants of leaves intruding from all around him.

He hated his mother for just showing up out of nowhere. She didn't even apologise for abandoning them their whole childhoods. And he hated Laine for accepting her like she hadn't done that. He hated everyone, he hated everyone so much. He hated the universe for putting him in this situation. But more than anything he hated himself. He hated himself for being so stupid and naive and-

"Theo, hey, come on." Laine comforted from a few feet away, being mindful not to get too close, knowing that he really disliked being touched in this kind of scenario.

"Go away."

Laine sighed, hooking her hands under Theo's arms and pulling him up against his will. She all but forced him into her arms, and much to her surprise, he didn't resist it. He settled himself against her and just continued to cry. He didn't know how long he was there for, it could've been ten seconds but it could've been ten hours.

"I'm sorry, Strythio." Came a third voice, soft and regretful as both siblings turned to look at her. "I understand why you're upset. Just, let me bring you two back to my house and we can have a proper chat about everything." She offered, and Theo didn't even give her the respect of replying, just continuing to lay himself safely in his sister's arms. Aster had no choice but to stand watching for a further five minutes as Theo continued to cry into Laine's shirt. Eventually, sobs turned to sniffles and then he looked up through glassy eyes.

"No, no, go away." He persisted before turning back to Laine. "I wanna go- wanna go home." He admitted, all of the tears immediately flooding back to his eyes. Immediately, a golden-coloured pond appeared to the right of them, clearly a portal back to Klaevr. It made a bit of a whooshing noise with its appearance.

All three demons snapped their heads down to look at it. Aster instantly took a step backwards, and then she walked all the way around it and moved to sit on the ground next to the pair.

"Well, looks like we'll have to wait here another five minutes for that to go away. Wouldn't want a random person falling into it." She explained.

"Laine, I want to go home." Theo repeated on a child-like whine, looking at the portal with intent.

"What about Julian and Raphie, hm?" She encouraged, both siblings completely ignoring their mother for the time being.

"Yeah," He sniffled, "Yeah, I suppose."

"Come on." Aster smiled. "Come to mine for some lunch and I can explain everything, and you two can catch me up on what I've missed." Theo moved away from Laine and leant back against the fence. "You won't make a good king one day if you can't be just and hear me out."

Laine sighed, taking the gap in between the two others against the metal fence. "He's already the King."

"Seriously?"

Theo nodded. "Yeah, nearly six months on."

"Your father retired?" She asked, sitting up more and looking at the two of them.

"He did."

"Hold on. If you two are here," She began, tone inquisitive. "Who's looking after Klaevr?" She asked, and Theo snorted.

"Her boyfriend. Every moment I'm not back there I'm getting increasingly worried about his abilities."

"Oh? And what kingdom is he a prince from?"

"He isn't." Laine replied very quickly. "He's an ex-mortal." She admitted, and Aster's eyes widened.

"You left an ex-mortal in charge of the kingdom?"

"Yeah, dad wasn't too happy about it either."

They sat in the silence for a few moments further, and Theo's eyes just focused on the neverending swirls of the portal. It was growing smaller by the second.

"You're really the King, Strythio?" Aster smiled, looking a little nostalgic.

"Yep, and it's just Theo."

"Right, well. I'm sorry I wasn't there to see you get crowned."

"You weren't there for anything. That's like burning someone's house down and then apologising that they lost the mugs in their kitchen."

And so it fell back into silence. Theo wasn't happy with either of the people in his company, so the last thing he wanted to do was speak to them. Laine and Aster thought it best not to push his buttons when he was acting like this, so they didn't. And by this point, the portal had completely closed, only leaving the dirt and grass on the ground where it once was.

"Come on. Swing back to my house, just for some fuel and a shower if anything."

Theo looked over to his mother, jaw set sternly as he frowned.

"Please?" Laine asked, and Theo would have never even considered doing something for his mother's sake at this point, but he definitely would for Laine. So, as reluctant as it made him, he rolled his eyes.

"Fine, whatever."

XX

Aster's house was actually very nice.
It was a bit out of the way, and they definitely wouldn't have been able to find it if they weren't with her as a guide. It was tall and very modernised, looking a lot like a new-build. The windows were large and stretched out over an entire white painted wall, next to a dark door with frosted glass and many plants. It was immediately apparent that she did a lot of gardening.
Theo hadn't said a word the whole walk there, it had just been some small talk between the mother and daughter. Stuff like 'how is this person doing' and 'does this person still have that dog'. He had walked a few metres behind them the whole way, not wanting to seem like he was paying attention in case they tried to talk to him, even though he *was* paying attention.
"Shoes off, please." Aster remembered while she unlocked the door, taking her own off by pressing the front of her right foot on the heel of her left and prying the shoe off, then repeating the action with the other shoe. "I'll just take the blinds down and then you can take your disguises off." Aster instructed, walking into her living room and pulling on the chord for the blinds until they reached the floor. "You don't realise how exhausting it is to keep up until you take it off."
And then she dropped her own disguise, and it was surreal. It was one thing to actually see the woman in person, but to see her the way that she'd been depicted in all of the paintings all around the castle somehow actually made Theo realise that he was standing in front of his mother for the first time.

She had beautiful mid-grey coloured skin and the same emerald green horns and wings as Theo did. Like all the other royals, her eyes were completely blacked out. She must have noticed that they were stunned by the transformation, because she laughed a little while sitting down on her grey sofa.

"Right, we're gonna have a serious chat then. You two like red wine?" She asked, and Theo nodded wordlessly before she disappeared out of the living room, presumably in the direction of the kitchen.

Practically as soon as she had exited, Theo reverted back to his demon form and flopped down backwards onto the sofa that was against the window with a huff. Laine followed suit, stretching her wings out and carefully taking a seat next to him.

"Come on, we can at least hear her out." Laine spoke in a whisper, taking Theo's hand in hers.

"It's just-" He groaned, sitting forward. "It's just, we had to grow up without a mother and she's been here the whole time, just fucking gardening like we never even mattered to her."

"You always mattered to me." Came a voice from the doorway, and Theo and Laine looked up to see their mother leaning against the frame with a bottle of dark red wine and three glasses. "Not being able to watch you two grow up is probably my biggest regret, but I had to leave." She explained, kneeling now beside the coffee table in between the two opposite sofas and placing the glasses down as she uncorked the wine.

"I doubt that." Theo scoffed, expression annoyed.

"Okay, then. What brings you away from home?" Aster filled the glasses about half way each.

"It's complicated." Laine supplied, hand hooking around the bottom of the glass as their mother moved to sit back down on the sofa opposite their children. "Theo ran off here and then the rest of us came here to chase after him."

"Okay. So, why did you run away?" She asked in more detail, looking at her son, who exhaled.

"Well, erm, I was meant to get married yesterday. ...And I didn't want to." He said, immediately feeling incredibly dumb about how stupid that sounded.

"You had that arranged for you?"

"Mhm." He hummed, taking a sip from his glass. "And we need to find my boyfriend's mum, she lives here."

And then Aster nodded with a hum of realisation. "Right, so I assume that your boyfriend is *not* the person you were meant to marry?"

"Yeah, that's right."

"Okay so, as I take it: *you* ran away from Klaevr and left your loved ones behind, but you're upset at me for running away from Klaevr and leaving my loved ones behind?" She asked, a smirk forming on her face. Theo grumbled, not having a decent reply to that question.

"You're seventeen and eighteen now, right?" Aster moved the conversation along.

"Surprised you remember that." Theo slighted.

Aster then reached to the sleeve of her shirt and pulled it up, revealing two tattoos right beside each other. Each was a string of eight numbers, written in roman numerals in a dark black ink, although they were slightly faded as if they'd been done a large number of years ago. Laine stepped out of her seat to move closer and look at them, her eyes widening.

"You have our birth dates tattooed?" She asked and her mother nodded.

"Got it done the first week I arrived here." She nodded. "I didn't want to get your names done in case they ended up changing, which was clearly a good idea because both of you seem to have dropped letters off."

"Alright, enough." Theo interrupted, placing the glass he'd just been drinking from back down on the coffee table. "Why did *you* leave?" He asked, completely fed up with the stalling that they'd been doing. He just wanted answers.

She took a moment to think before she spoke, sighing loudly. "I suppose there's no point in lying." She admitted. "Your father was planning on divorcing me. It would have been the end of my life, I would've had to have gone back to Stonbrin and I would have been treated like dirt there. You two would've stayed in Klaevr - I wouldn't have been able to raise you anyway."

"So you just left?"

"Not exactly. You need to promise that you won't get too upset." She cringed, looking worried as her eyes darted between both children.

"What is it?" Laine asked, not making any promises, and Aster swallowed.

"Dyran and I made an agreement."

"An agreement?"

"I mean, how do you think I afforded this beautiful house and all?" She asked, and the question told a silent story that neither of the siblings wanted to say anything further about.

"He paid you to leave?"

"About the equivalent of three million British pounds. And he avoided a divorce scandal. If anything I'm sure he got a lot of sympathy about his missing wife."

The atmosphere in the room had completely hit zero, and it was deathly silent as Theo and Laine absorbed what they had just heard. Neither of them cried, or screamed, or got angry about it. They just sat on the sofa, letting it soak in. After a few minutes where Aster just watched the two of them, glass of wine in hand, Theo looked up.

"He knows you're here?"

She nodded slowly.

"I don't- I don't understand. He cried at your funeral. Who else knows?"

Aster leant back a little. "Forgive me, it's been a while." She excused while thinking. "Just him and Zero, I think."

"Zero?"

Laine leant forward, speaking for the first time in a few minutes. "The blonde bloke that does the portals." She supplied.

"Oh. He wouldn't tell me his name." Theo said, and Aster snickered.

"He tries his best."

"Dad really knew this whole time?" The Princess asked in a tone that said she hoped Aster would say no. But, she didn't. She nodded with a frown.

"I'm sorry."

Much like outside the allotment earlier, the trio fell into a complete silence. It wasn't awkward or uncomfortable, they were just taking in information and allowing themselves time to process everything. Their whole childhoods, when their dad had promised them that their mother would come back one day, he'd known she wouldn't. He was the reason she left and he had the audacity to grieve and pretend he was hurt by it all?

The stream of thoughts was interrupted by a phone trilling from Theo's pocket.

He reached down to it, pulling it out and staring at the screen. It showed that there was an incoming call, but Theo only now realised he had no idea how he was meant to answer it. He stared at it hopelessly for about three seconds before showing it to Laine with a lost expression.

"How do we answer it?"

"As if I'm gonna know!" She replied, stressed that they might miss the call. After another ten seconds of mild bickering about how to accept the communication, they heard laughter from the sofa in front of them.

"Oh, God, pass me the phone, kids." She laughed, reaching out for it.

Theo sighed hopelessly and handed the phone to her. By some wizardry or miracle, she pressed a singular button on the top left of the device, and then another just below it. Immediately, wind came through the line that was on speaker, but it wasn't so much that they couldn't hear the caller.

"Yo! Where are you guys?" Julian asked, clearly moving with the phone, and Laine and Theo shared a glance.

"I don't think you'd believe us if we told you to be fair." He gritted out.

"I'm sorry, darling, that's not a location."

"It's like, up. Up a hill from where you left us."

"The rich area?"

"Probably."

"Yikes."

Theo smiled at the interaction, and Laine leant towards the phone.

"We'll just send you the address." She said.

"Sounds good!" He replied, and then they heard Raphie's voice too.

"Julian, there is no way I'm walking up that hill."

"It's not *my* fault you're American and not used to our terrain."

"Blah blah, that has nothing to do with this."

Theo snickered a little, looking down at the device. "Alright, we'll see you soon." He said, but neither heard him over their bickering. Once the call had ended (signified by a short beeping sound), Theo dropped the phone back onto the sofa.

"That was your boyfriend I presume?"

"Yeah." Theo nodded. "He wanted to go and visit his gravestone, but we've seen enough dead people so we didn't want to."

"And what brought you to my allotment then?" She asked on a laugh, crossing one leg over another. This time, Laine took it upon herself to answer.

"We don't get any of this nature back home, and we wanted a chance to see it, I guess."

At that, Aster's eyes widened a little. "You still can't go up to The Heavens?" She asked with astonishment, and they shook their heads.

"Goodness, I expected that to have changed years ago. Why is it still like that?"

"I'm working on it." Theo explained, and Laine gave him a bit of a cursory stare. "I just need to get past Lord Beckett, and I'm… kinda scared of him."

"Beckett is still around?"

"Yeah. He hit me after my coronation ceremony because he heard I wanted to change his legislation."

"God." Was all Aster managed to say about that.
"Yeah."
"He isn't good news, Theo. You need to be really careful around him." His mother warned, serious and genuine.
"I'll try. He's scary. He told me that he- that he wanted to take the kingdom from me."
Laine raised her eyebrows. It was the first she was hearing of this.
"What?! When?"
"The coronation."
"And you haven't told anyone, why?"
"Just... never got 'round to it."
The two siblings ruminated in silence for a few moments. It was awkward, sure, but there was nothing else to say.
"Right, well, on that happy note, do you want lunch? You've got two others coming, right?" Aster asked, trying to diffuse the slight tension created.
"Mhm."
She stood, latching onto the bottle and her glass. "It'll take them at least twenty minutes to find this place, so if you two want to shower or anything like that please feel free while I cook something up." She offered. Both siblings looked at each other for a moment before they both darted off in the direction of the stairs in a race, pushing each other and laughing on the way. Towards the top of the stairs, Laine got an upper foot and elbowed Theo in the stomach, using the leverage to get all the way up the steps first and run into the bathroom, slamming the door and locking it behind her. He yelped at the unfair move and ran as quickly as he could to try and make it back, but he was too late.
Theo groaned, banging on the door. "That's not fair!" He whined like a small child.
"Life isn't fair!" She cackled and Theo turned around, sliding down the door and sitting against it. He had no choice but to admit defeat after hearing the shower turn on, so he stood and began to trudge back downstairs.
He leant in the doorway of the kitchen, watching Aster fumble around with a cookbook for a few moments before she noticed his presence.
"She beat you there?"
"I let her win."
"Alright, well come help out with the food while you wait for her to finish." Aster instructed, amused by the lie, beckoning him over to the counter. He walked there as told, leaning over the counter slightly to

look at the cookbook. It was open on a page for a vegetable pasta bake with a whole range of ingredients that Theo didn't even want to think about.

"I used to make this for you two when you were no taller than my legs." She smiled, pulling open the cupboard and grabbing a cutting board. "Can you do the pepper? It's just in the pantry." She pointed in the direction of a small open-air cupboard that had a range of pasta, sugar, vegetables, fruit and anything that you wouldn't really put in a fridge. Other than that, the kitchen was quite clutter-free and well-cleaned, with marble countertops and an island rather than a dining table. There were also large windows, but all the blinds were pulled down because they were existing in their demon forms.

Theo didn't reply, but he did walk over to the pantry and pull out a red pepper, heading to the sink to wash it before placing it on the cutting board.

"Did dad really pay you to leave?" He asked, standing against the counter without a knife to actually cut the vegetable with.

Aster halted her own vegetable cutting and turned to her son. "I'm sure he's great to you. And he was great to me too, but we just weren't happy. He didn't necessarily pay me, we just made a deal that benefited us more than a divorce would."

"I mean, he was really good to us when we were younger. But ever since I got crowned he's been really harsh on me."

"Is this solely about marriage or other stuff too?"

"He just yelled at me when I told him I didn't want to marry her, and he didn't even ask me before he agreed for me to do it. I guess that kind of sparked something, I don't know." He grumbled, starting to open some drawers to look for a knife.

"Yeah, my parents did the exact same thing to me with him. I'm surprised he would put you through that, but I think he and his mother chose me as their suitor, rather than it being mutually arranged by our parents." Theo gave up trying to find the knife and just leant against the counter to fully immerse himself in the conversation.

"What was your wedding like?"

Aster smiled, momentarily stopping the motion of the knife on the carrots as she thought about the question she'd just been asked. "It was good. I mean, I was only eighteen, but it was a nice evening. I got to wear a lovely frock, so that was a plus. Oh, sorry! Knives are in this drawer." She prompted, pulling out one of the drawers that she was standing by and handing Theo a vegetable knife.

"Thanks." He muttered, taking it and standing in front of the cutting board again.

"How about your coronation? How did that go for you?" His mother asked, returning the conversational queries while simultaneously catching herself up on some of the gaps she'd missed in the lives of her kids.

"It was okay. A lot of people. But, it was nice. I don't really remember much after the ceremony, I got a bit drunk." He said, trying to figure out the best way to cut this pepper up, and Aster laughed loudly.

"Definitely my son." She chuckled, glancing over to him. "Sorry, forgot you probably have servants that cook, I'll show you." She walked over to Theo and stood next to him, placing her own hands on top of his and guiding them to cut the pepper, one hand holding it and one hand actually doing the cutting.

Her hands were slightly smaller than his as they pressed on top of them, directing his movements. At some point, Theo stopped trying to do it himself and just let Aster cut the vegetable while using his hands as puppets as she softly explained the best method of cutting. Once the vegetable was completely done, she smiled with a hum and stepped away. It was something about the nurturing way that she leant over him and held his hands that made his eyes water. It was so caring, so loving and gentle in the way she moved her hands and offered the information to him like she was meant to teach him the world's secrets.

When she snickered a little at his lack of motion and asked if he was alright, Theo found that he had turned to her and ploughed himself into her body for an embrace, now allowing himself to hold onto her like she'd disappear if he let go for ever a moment. She made a squeak of surprise before hugging him back with a smile. "Hey, Theo." She smiled softly, and Theo didn't say anything, he only held onto her tighter.

It was like he was making up for about fifteen years of missed hugs. He had his head pressed into her shoulder, and he had to bend down a little bit to make it work comfortably, but it was okay. It felt right to be hugging her, despite the circumstances. From the position of the hug, it took him about thirty seconds longer to say anything, and when he finally found the courage to speak his mind it came out a lot meeker than he had intended, almost like a small child crying into a parent's arms after falling over on his scooter.

"I missed you."

XXI

They had just finished setting the table by the time that the doorbell rang. Outside the house, it had begun to rain quite heavily, and Theo was certainly glad that they'd come in earlier. He'd had his opportunity to shower, and had just placed down the last plate onto the marble countertop island.
"I'll get it!" Laine called from where she'd been shoving cutlery down, excessively loudly considering that the two other people she was talking to were in the room next to her.
"Put your disguise on before you answer!" Her mother called, and Laine listened, flicking back to her mortal form before pulling the door open. As a result of the heavy rainfall and uphill journey, Raphie and Julian looked a bit of a mess when Laine answered the door. Julian's hair was like a mop atop his head, and his clothes were all darkened in colour from the rain. While Raphie looked significantly more elegant in her state of wetness, she was still quite visibly drenched. They were both lucky enough that they had more clothing options with them - Julian having worn a jumper over his magenta shirt that he would be able to take off to remove most of the rain from his person, and Raphie having packed that jumper in her backpack, which she hoped was still dry (fingers crossed).
"Have a nice walk?" She teased, stepping back from the door to allow them entry.
"Ha ha." Julian mocked, entering and pushing his shoes off. "This is a sick house, did you break in or something?"
"No, we didn't break in. Theo's in the kitchen." She pointed down the hall, and Julian raced off in that direction. He swung around the door of the

kitchen and beamed at Theo in the most mischievous way. The demon smiled, and then his eyes widened when he realised what his boyfriend's intentions were.

"No, I just showered! No, agh, get away!" He laughed, trying to move away around the table. Aster quirked a smile as she watched Julian corner Theo, eventually getting to him and making great effort to smother his whole body with his completely soggy clothing. "No, agh, oh my God, I hate you." He whined with no real intention behind the words.

"No, you don't." Julian smirked, tilting his head up and kissing Theo sweetly. "Why are you all...?" He gestured up and down Theo's body, clearly referring to his demon form.

Theo snickered, gesturing over to his mother who was still watching endearingly. Julian spun around. "Oh! Hello!" He greeted, walking over to her and outstretching his hand. "Julian." He introduced, and Aster took his hand with an impressed smile.

"Aster."

Julian then turned just his head back to Theo and then to the woman he was talking to. "You look exactly like Theo but like... older and a woman." He whispered.

"I'd hope so." Aster grinned. "I'm his mother."

Julian paused for a moment, pursing his lips in thought as he turned back to Theo. "You told me you didn't have a mother."

"I didn't."

And then Laine, back in her demon form, brought Raphie into the room. She was still wearing her human disguise and gasped loudly when she laid her eyes on Aster.

"Oh my God." She choked. "That's- Hi, Your Majesty."

"Please, Aster is fine love." She smiled. "Do you two want showers? Lunch is just about five minutes off."

Julian had nodded, deciding that he could shower in five minutes, and he had dragged Theo up the stairs with him too, as they both now needed to have a rummage for dry clothes to wear. It worked out because Theo had just changed back into the shirt he wore when leaving Klaevr, since his trousers weren't very damaged by Julian's hug - and Julian was happy to put on the black jeans he was previously wearing because they were significantly less soggy by the time Julian had got out of the shower.

They made it back downstairs in about eight minutes, and the smell of the food was leaking out from the kitchen, instantly consuming their senses. Inside the kitchen, the full plates now readily in front of each seat on the island - five in total.

"Gosh, finally. I'm gonna go dry my hair." Raphie said as the two boys entered, pushing past them a little to make her way up the staircase, now reverted back to her usual form.

"An angel, huh? What's she doing choosing to spend her time with you guys?" Aster asked once Raphie was out of earshot.

"She's one of the good ones. Plus, I'm pretty sure a regular angel is like the equivalent of demon royalty so she isn't out of our league or anything." Laine replied, pulling out a stool from under the ridge of the island and sitting down on it.

"I really don't get why you guys think that angels are so much better than you." Julian commented offhandedly.

"It's more the other way around." Theo told, sitting down opposite Julian.

"They think they're better than us and who are we to say otherwise?"

"Bit harsh on yourselves there."

"Sorry, Julian, are you an angel or a demon? You're sounding a bit on the fence as to which side you're on." Aster asked, placing her elbows on the table as the four of them waited for Raphie's return.

"Oh, neither, I guess? But probably a demon because I *did* show up in Hell."

"Neither?"

Theo turned over to his mother and filled her in, gesturing his cutlery around as he recounted the story. After he was finished, she looked between the three of them with a bit of a bewildered stature.

"But, you spoke to Zero when you arrived at Klaevr?" She asked Julian.

"Yeah. He just told me it was weird I hadn't been given a demon form and sent me on my way."

"But... *he* does all of the transformation stuff."

"What?"

"Zero." She clarified. "He gives all of the mortals their demon forms at the same time as the 'you're dead' monologue. You didn't know that?" She pushed, talking down to them a little. They gaped for a moment.

"No. So, so we could have just spoken to him?" Theo asked, looking exhausted.

"I mean, he does it all, so, yeah."

"Why...?" Julian squinted, pushing his food around on the plate as he framed his sentence. "Why wouldn't he have given me a demon form? And why would he have let us come here looking for answers if he had them all along?" He pouted.

"So, you're telling me we didn't have to come here?" Theo gaped. "I hate it here, no offence. Someone called me a 'tosser' here - and I don't even know what that means but it sounds derogatory." He whined, dropping his head into his hands, and Julian burst out laughing, and he was still smiling to himself a few minutes later when Raphie came back down the stairs with dry hair and they all started eating.

Following a moment of silent eating, Aster finished a mouthful and looked up to her son. "What makes you dislike it here?"

Theo paused, not expecting to have been spoken to. He briefly choked around a piece of pasta before looking around the table. "Um, I don't know - it's just different. So many people and the weather is shit."

"Ah," Raphie interrupted, pointing at him with her fork. "Don't let that influence your whole opinion on this planet. It was always pretty nice where I grew up."

"Yeah, hey, wait-" Julian realised. "You're telling me you could've gone to live anywhere in the world and you chose Manchester? Literally why not the Maldives or somewhere?"

"Because I didn't *want* to be having a constant holiday, just a normal life." She confessed, stabbing a piece of carrot with her fork.

"Because you never had one back home?" Laine frowned.

"Yeah. I'm sure you two just want to live normally sometimes."

"Well we haven't really ever known anything else."

"Do you want to?"

No, no he didn't. Theo had accepted at a *very* young age what his life was, and that he was only being raised to look after the kingdom and then do the same and raise the next monarch. He'd never considered himself a leadership figure of any kind, but as a child, he had always imagined what it'd be like to be the King and would make Laine pretend to be one of his royal servants. He enjoyed the lifestyle, and although he was completely caught off guard by the notion of his coronation, it always felt right to him that one day he would be the King. And that was just his life, and he was fine with it. If it weren't for Serenity and Julian he would have never considered leaving Klaevr.

Laine was a little shoved by the question. Much like Theo, she'd been raised in a way that never really allowed any other options for living other than being a princess. There had been many times in her life where she'd felt useless in her role because Theo would just be the King - so, she would never really have a role other than to be second best to him. She wouldn't be telling the truth if she said that she'd never *considered* running away, but ultimately Klaevr was her home and no amount of feeling shitty about being the second born child would make her genuinely want to leave it all behind. And besides, when Laine actually thought about it, she wasn't even sure if she even wanted to be the Queen. Too much pressure. Theo was the kind of person who could live under pressure, and it made him rise to the occasion and become a better person and all of that. Laine was pretty positive she would just break down under those kinds of expectations.

"No."

"Not really."

"Not really?" Aster quirked an eyebrow.

"I mean, I guess I sometimes felt like I wasn't really needed in the castle."

"You did?" Interjected Theo, frowning.

Laine paused and her shoulders deflated. "It was just always about you growing up. I was kind of just an accessory towards you getting the throne. There as a backup if something happened to you."

"Oh."

"Hey, don't worry." Aster comforted. "I felt the exact same with my older brother, but then your father came and had me shipped away from Stonbrin and suddenly I had a purpose in your kingdom."

"That's not very reassuring." Raphie pointed out. "And I don't think 'wait for a prince from another kingdom to whisk you away' is a good moral either."

"Maybe not, but you get the point." She shrugged. "Right, now we need to actually eat this before it gets cold, hm?"

"Buckle." Aster instructed, turning around in her seat to point at the three people sitting in the back seat, one hand still resting idly on the steering wheel. They had all eaten (and the food was very good, thanks) and were now sitting in the back of Aster's car (bar Laine, who had taken the passenger seat) in dry clothes, ready to leave and face the day for the sake of trying to find Julian's mother for answers.

To be completely fair, they probably didn't need to find her anymore. They'd already figured out how Julian died, and they'd also gotten to the root of why he wasn't gifted with a demon form upon arriving in the underworld. Those were the two things that they were hoping to get closer to finding out thanks to Vanna, so although this portion of the journey was probably unessential at this point, Julian was excited about speaking to his mother again due to their close relationship and Theo didn't want to deprive him of that and they were already all the way here.

"What-le?" Theo questioned.

"Seat belt."

"What?"

"Here, ugh, I'll do it." Julian smirked, unbuckling himself from the middle seat and practically crawling onto Theo's lap on his shins, sitting up and leaning over to the left of him, grabbing the seatbelt from the top of the seat and pulling it down across his chest. "So you don't die if we crash." At the same time as this, Aster and Raphie were both showing Laine how to do her own seat belt up.

"I thought you got a taxi to my house?" He asked, clicking the seat belt in.

"I did, I just didn't do whatever this is."

Julian moved back to flop down in his own seat as Theo ran his hands up and down the material of the seatbelt.

"That's against the law Theo, you're gonna have to turn yourself in, and it's a ten year minimum sentence." He teased before doing his own belt.

"It is?"

"No, love, I'm joking." Julian giggled. "Do you have the address for the police station at all?" It appeared that the best course of action was to head to the location that Vanna had been arrested at, and so Theo reached into his satchel and pulled the book out.

"Where did you get that?" Laine asked with a turn in her seat, a little curious as she tried to read the title.

"Oh, um, I couldn't find any paper so I just took this from the library and wrote in it." He confessed.

"Ah, okay."

"Let's see the address." Julian instructed, leaning over Theo's shoulder as he flicked through the pages to the front of the book where he had scribed down the police station location. "Right, okay. It's a little far, can I stick it into your satnav, Aster?"

"Yeah, go on." The woman replied, handing Julian her phone with google maps already open. "Do you guys want any music at all?" She asked as they pulled out of the parking space and down the road.

"Oh my God, I've missed technology." Julian said under his breath while typing in the address, and Raphie leaned forward a little towards the front of the car.

"What kind of stuff do you have?" She asked, referring to the array of CDs that Aster had asked Laine to pull out of the glove box.

Laine read the album titles and artists off one by one, mispronouncing quite a few of the names because this was her first time hearing them. The whole car waited patiently as she continued to list off the ten-ish albums, but Julian interjected at the eighth.

"Yes!" He exclaimed, grabbing one of them from Laine's hand. "I promised Theo I'd play him a Beatles song when I first met him." He told everyone, opening the case. "...That was before I found out there wasn't any music in Hell, but, you know, we're here now so we might as well." Theo and Laine would be lying through their teeth if they said that they understood music. It was weird, and the former found it even weirder when Julian got really into it and seemed very excited that the two of them were having their ears blessed with the symphony of Sgt. Pepper's Lonely Hearts Club Band. It was probably influenced by the fact that they'd never heard music before and weren't really missing it in the same way that Julian does. Or at least, the way they assumed he does judging by the way he was all but jumping around in excitement.

They were on the last song of the album when they arrived at the police station. By this point in the songlist, Raphie had convinced the two siblings that they were being sour and purposeful in not enjoying the music, and they just needed to find their own specific tastes. Theo decided not to bring up that the chance he'd be able to listen to the discography of every artist before they went back to Klaevr was highly unlikely.

After helping the Virzor siblings with undoing their seat belts, the four young adults stepped out of the car from where it was parked opposite the police station. Laine leant back through the rolled down window of the vehicle and pouted.

"You really don't want to come with us back home?" Laine asked for the third time that day, and her mother frowned.

"I can't, not after all this time. Go on, get out of here." She said, shooing them away. Laine frowned sadly, walking around the car and opening the driver door, reaching out and giving a teary-eyed hug to her mother, not wanting to acknowledge that it'll probably be the last time ever, unless they plan on travelling back to sunny old Manchester any time in the foreseeable future (which was unlikely even considering the hijinks that they get up to).

After Theo did the same, Aster also gave hugs to Raphie and Julian, and then they closed the car door and began to leave.

"I'll see you guys later." She smiled, waving them away. However, when Julian was about to step out of earshot last, she called his name quietly, and he spun back around to face her and quirked an eyebrow. She gestured him over and pulled him in close while the other three milled around outside the station.

Her voice dropped to a whisper, octave a little low and honestly kind of intimidating.
"Don't you dare hurt Theo." She hushed. "You better look after eachother."
Julian nodded, blinking. "Yes, ma'am."
"Good." She smiled, patting him on the pack. "Bye, Julian."
He turned on his heel and walked along the concrete of the pavement towards where the other three were, and when he got there they all watched Aster drive off, offering a little wave out the window with teary eyes.
"Alright." Theo nodded with a sniffle as he glanced down to his boyfriend. "Are you ready to see *your* mother now?"

XXII

The building itself felt a little like a hospital waiting room and it only added to the levels of unease building in Julian's stomach. There was a row of dark blue chairs pressed evenly against the back wall, and also against the adjacent wall facing the door. Then, in the centre of the two sets of chairs was another row that was back to back with one final fourth row of chairs, allowing for a hell of a lot of seating that he doubted was ever full.

They'd come to the riveting conclusion when outside that maybe it wasn't entirely wise for Julian to just stroll up into a police station where it was likely they were investigating his death. So, he'd taken Laine's hoodie (much to the dismay of her now cold arms that weren't protected by her yellow t-shirt) and was now wearing it baggily over his black jeans, with the hood up and the bottom part pulled tightly so that his face was pretty obscured.

They probably looked like quite the gaggle when they sat down on four consecutive chairs. On the right was Laine, who was just now wearing that bright shirt and the same grey joggers as before, but right next to her was Theo, who was wearing his original shirt. It was black and had a band of light grey mesh around the centre of the torso and lower arms that was also wrapped in leather criss-crosses. Amongst this look was his brown leather boots *and* gloves (that he'd felt 'weird' not wearing) and the same black cargo trousers from earlier.

And then there was Julian, wearing his button-up magenta shirt and black mom jeans that made him look like he was going for a job interview at a Cadbury factory. Lastly was Raphie, who had stopped caring about the colour parting of her hair at this point, and had strands of pink on her blue half and vise versa, as well as the same light green t-shirt with leaves going along it from shoulder to stomach in a diagonal line, and dark blue flared jeans with trainers like the other three sensible ones were wearing.

The two sitting on the outer sides of the line leant in so that all were visible and audible as they started having a hushed conversation. The receptionist had quirked an eyebrow when they walked in, but other than that wasn't paying much mind.

"Okay well I'm not going up to the desk." Julian shook his head, eyes expectantly looking towards the other three.

Laine immediately raised her hand in the air with a flat palm. "Dibs not me!"

"Dibs not me either!" Raphie followed.

Theo scrunched his nose up. "That is *not* how we are doing this."

"You're only saying that 'cus you lost. Now go." Laine pushed his back and he had to stand to stop himself falling face first off the chair.

"What am I meant to say?" He panicked, spinning back around to them.

"You say," Julian supplied. "'Hey, I'm looking for Vanna Thompson, is she here?' And they'll either say, 'No you idiot, get out before we arrest you, or 'Yes! I will take you to her now, kind sir.' Happy?"

"Not in the slightest." He pouted, walking away from them and up towards the desk. He planted two hands on the desk and leant forward slightly. The receptionist was about a forty-year-old man with a bald patch visibly forming. He was wearing a light blue button-up with a small badge that read 'SI Meyers' in black writing.

"Hello... Mr May-ers." He read, and the man grimaced.

"It's pronounced My-ers, and that's Sargeant to you, young man."

Theo took a step back. "Right, sorry, um, I'm looking for someone that I think was arrested here."

"You mean booked here?" He asked, and Theo turned his head back around to his three accomplices who were sitting on the chairs nodding their heads vigorously.

"Yep."

"Their surname?"

"Um, it's Thompson."

He did some clacking on his keyboard for a moment as his eyes narrowed into slits, clicking his tongue in his mouth.

"Vanna Thompson?"

"Yes, yeah! That's her. Is she here?"

Sergeant Meyers paused for just a moment and then raised his eyebrows. "She is. I'm sorry, what's your relationship to the inmate?"

"Um." He said, eyes downcast to the ground. "I'm her... well, um, I'm dating her son. Was. Was dating her son." He corrected quickly. The officer frowned immediately.

"Oh, I'm so sorry."

"That's alright, um, we wanted to speak to her." He squinted, turning back around to the others again.

"Who is 'we'?"

"Me and some of my friends that were friends with him."

Meyers cringed, removing his hands from the keyboard. "I apologise, I can only let immediate family in to visit her at this stage, as she's still awaiting trial."

Theo's shoulders deflated. "Please?"

"Sorry, son."

"Please, please. I just want answers." He pleaded, making the decision to play the grieving boyfriend card, even though he was sitting about two metres away from them. The officer furrowed his eyebrows sympathetically.

"I promise you that we're trying everything we can to get to the bottom of what actually happened. If you'd like, you can leave your number here and we can give you a call if anything in the case changes."

Theo nodded with a sniffle. "Thank you so much, just give me a second." He said softly, turning away and walking back over to the seats where the others were. He sat down and sighed, dropping his voice to a whisper. "You guys hear all that?"

"Mhm." Julian frowned. "Okay, new plan. Theo, you cry a lot, right?"

"Um, not more than the average person." He replied, looking a little dejected, to which Laine snorted.

"You definitely cry more than the average person."

"I do not."

"Alright, that's not exactly the point." Julian moved away from the argument. "You've already set your story up, so now I just need you to cry."

"I'm not following."

"Ugh, okay." He complained. "You are gonna go up to that desk and make hell for that receptionist. I want you to have a breakdown about the love of your life dying and you can't even talk to the dear woman who made you dinner when you used to sleep over."

"But, I didn't used to sleep over."

"Pretend you did."
"Love of his life?" Raphie mocked. "Not egotistical at all, don't worry."
"Whatever." Julian rolled his eyes. "Anyways, you'll go and make a massive commotion about not being allowed in, and then we can just sneak past the guy."
"Right, so then, how do *I* get through after my hissy fit?"
The dead boy shrugged inside the red hoodie. "I dunno, you'll figure it out. Now, off you go, break a leg, love."
Theo nodded, shaking his hands out in front of him and taking some really quick breaths as his eyes began to water. He then made his way over to the desk and immediately started speaking before the man sitting down even had a chance to acknowledge him.
"Are you- are you sure I can't see her?" He asked, not even crying yet but still visibly upset.
Meyers sighed sadly. "I'm sorry, it's just the policy."
This would be a piece of cake. As a previous crown prince to the largest Kingdom of Hell, Theo had spoken to a hell of a lot of newly deceased in his time, and a lot of them were very upset about this new revelation. They were upset about a lot of things, like missing family or their partners or the shock of it or just generally being dead. Because of this influx in the upset about losing people, the demon had been able to pick up a few things here and there that he thought might aid him in this circumstance.
Theo planted his head onto the desk and started crying into his arms that he was leaning against. Then after a moment, he looked back up with glassy eyes.
"Please," He cried. "Please, she's all I have left of him and- and-" He interrupted himself with another loud sob-like hiccup. "She used to cook me dinner when I slept over." He properly cried, now not even making any attempt to not embarrass himself.
"Hey, I know it's difficult to lose someone, but you're only young and time will help." The man offered. The makeshift actor took this as his queue to start loudly sobbing and screaming while banging his fist on the desk.
"I miss him so much, I'm never gonna see him again!" He cried.
"I know, I know." The officer said. "Why don't you come into this back room to calm down?" He suggested, and Theo nodded.
"Mhm, yeah, yeah, thank you." He replied, taking about thirty seconds to get the words out as he found himself constantly being interrupted by his own hiccups and sniffles. Meyers stood up to open the door that

connected their small office to the waiting room, and when Theo turned around briefly he saw the other three having just snuck through the door to the area with all the cells.

He got around into the back area and had now let his dramatics subside since the task was done. For a few moments as the officer spoke kindly to him, he was kind of unsure what his next move was supposed to be. Then he saw the cleaning cupboard.

"Do you want a cup of tea or anything?"

"Just some water, please?" Theo sniffed, shoulders jerking up and down as he still came down from the high of sobbing so violently. When Meyers nodded and walked off towards a water cooler in the corner, Theo opened the door of this little cupboard and pulled one of the brooms out. Inside were also shelves of cleaning products and a mop bucket, but there was a good square metre of standing space.

"Hey, um, I think one of your shelves in there is broken. The back one." Theo pointed as the man walked back with the plastic cup of clear liquid in his hand. He frowned.

"Oh, that's weird, the door shouldn't even be left open." He said, walking into the cupboard and placing the cup of water down on the left shelf while looking curiously at the back one.

"I don't see anything." He shook his head.

"Yeah, sorry." Theo frowned before slamming the door to the small space closed and leaning his back against it. He quickly spun himself around and hooked the broom under the handle so that it was impossible (or at least would take a tremendous effort) to open. This became evident to the Sergeant as he tried to pull the handle down.

"Son, you open this door right now!"

"Sorry!" He repeated while walking away. "We'll be like five minutes." Theo continued to ignore the sounds of this man banging on the door as he nonchalantly strolled out of the back room and round into the area where the other three were waiting for him. Laine quirked an eyebrow.

"You didn't kill him, did you?"

"No, that would have been cruel. Imagine if he went to Klaevr. I don't know about you guys but I'd rather live in a cupboard than under your boyfriend's jurisdiction." He smirked, walking past them and down the corridor.

"Hey! I'm sure he's doing fine."

Her protests went unheard by her brother, who very quickly found the entrance to a room with a black plastic sign above the white-painted door frame. It read 'viewing room'. With an apprehensive glance back to

197

the others who were following him, he pushed the door open and then paused.

It was a narrow room with completely grey walls and a long rectangular window that stretched the length of the wall on the left. Through the window was another dark room with a wooden table sat in the centre. Theo's eyes lingered on the table for a few moments before he turned and walked out of the room, leaning around the doorframe and lowering his voice a little to just too loud to be considered a whisper.

"Think I found her."

"That was quick." Raphie said as she stopped walking, only to be overtaken by Julian walking to follow Theo back into the room. He made the same initial assessment that the other had done previously, but this time, when his eyes moved onto the window and what was through it, he became immobile where he stood and his jaw went a little slack.

"Yeah, that's um... Yeah."

Behind the table was a chair, and in the chair sat a woman. She was worriedly skinny and her dark skin wrapped around her bones harshly, natural hair long and still growing out. She was wearing a light grey tank top with spaghetti straps and a pair of light blue skinny jeans that were accompanied by some dirtied white converse that she was looking at under the table. Then lastly, her hands were cuffed in front of her on the table as she dawned this impatient expression.

Laine and Raphie had also entered the room now, and the two of them were both dumbfoundedly staring at her.

"Huh."

"That was... concerningly easy."

"Do we go in there?" Laine asked softly.

"No, we've come all this way to stand outside the room she's in." Theo quipped, and then he stepped forward and tilted his head around to look at Julian. "You okay?"

He nodded. "Mhm, um, I don't really wanna go in yet, so can you? Just go and maybe see if she knows anything else." He said quietly, and Theo gave a hum of affirmation.

"We're doing an interrogation?" Raphie grinned in amusement, to which Theo turned to face her and shrugged.

"'Spose so."

"Wait!" Laine called. "Raphie, lift me up on your shoulders."

"What?"

"Literally just do it a sec."

Theo watched dumbfoundedly as Raphie bent down on her knees and his sister jumped onto her back as if they'd rehearsed it before. She gave directional instructions that led Raphie to the corner of the room, where Laine reached up and yanked the security camera, taking a few tries to get it completely off the wall as it clattered down and shards of plastic hit the ground. Raphie gasped as she lowered her back down to the ground.

"You can't just do that, that's a crime!" She lectured as Laine bent down to pick up the remaining shards of the camera.

"What are they gonna do? Arrest me? I'll be in another dimension, dumbass."

"Yeah... alright, fair enough." She conceded.

Theo nodded a little and while the two of them were completely distracted, he leant down and pulled Julian into his arms, recognising the upset radiating of the younger man.

"It's okay, it'll be fine, love. Just let me know when you're ready to see her."

"Be nice to her, don't act all scary." He muffled into Theo's shirt, and the demon smiled.

"Alright, if you think I'm being too mean you can just bang on the glass." He chuckled, turning and leaving the room, going one door to the left and taking a breath in and out before he pushed the door open.

Vanna looked up immediately and rolled her eyes with intention.

"Took a while, I've been sitting here for donkey's years."

"Um, sorry." Theo said, pulling up a chair from the corner of the room and planting it opposite hers.

"You seem... young for a detective."

Theo took a breath in and nodded. "Yeah, I get that a lot." It was a little scary, like a teenager when they meet their partner's parents for the first time over a Sunday roast. He didn't want to come across in a bad way, even if she had no idea that Theo knew her son.

"So, just, erm, tell me about your son." He continued, trying to get in the role.

Vanna frowned before swallowing. "I really don't know what you guys think I did but whatever it is, I didn't, and I really just want to get home at this point. Sending in new people after new people isn't gonna make me talk." She complained, and Theo instantly felt rather guilty. It was immediately apparent that it'd be difficult to get through to her.

So, five minutes of blocking his questions later, Theo trudged back out of the door and into the viewing room.

"I give up, it's hopeless." He groaned, leaning himself against a wall.
Raphie smiled, pushing herself off the wall she was against. "Don't worry, we got this."
Julian turned around from where his eyes were still fixated on his mother through the window. "What's that supposed to mean?"
"Laine and I are gonna do good cop bad cop." She declared triumphantly.
"We are?"
"Yeah." Raphie confirmed, hands planting onto her hips with confidence.
Theo blinked. "What is that?"
"Basically," Raphie began. "I'm gonna be really kind to her, and you…!" She exclaimed, pointing to the other girl. "Get to be a bitch, and so she'll tell me everything because I'm the nice one that she can trust."
Laine scrunched her nose up in distaste. "Why do I have to be the mean one?" She asked, to which Raphie stayed silent and allowed a smirk to slip onto her face as she brought her extended index fingers up to her head and made them look like little devil horns. Laine frowned.
"Well that's just you conforming to stereotypes."
"It's stereotypical to assume that an angel is nicer than a demon?" Raphie raised her eyebrows unimpressively. Laine just pouted before conceding.
"Fine, I'll be the mean one, but I'm not happy about it."
"You don't actually have to be horrible, just stern. Now come on."
She grabbed her friend's hand and then they both exited the space and disappeared to walk the ten metres down the corridor that allowed them into the interrogation room. Julian brought his hand up to his lips to start biting his nails, eyes still fixated on his mother through the one-way glass. After a moment of indecision he turned to face Theo.
"That's enough, I wanna go talk to her." He nodded, eyes a little watery as he began to walk. Theo reached out and barred him from getting very far, making him stop his footsteps and look up.
"What?"
"Just… just hold your horses a moment. Let the girls see what they can do before we rush in. It'd probably stress her out a lot if her dead son strolled through the door." He persuaded. Julian brought his left hand up to his eye to wipe away the tear on his cheek before it even got two centimetres down.
"Fuck, I just, I feel like this is my last chance to see her and to *actually* say goodbye to her. And she probably feels horrible that she never got to say goodbye to me either, and I'm just worried that if I don't see her soon she'll disappear and that'll be it." He whined, making a great effort not to let his emotions get the better of him.

200

"I don't want this to be it." He sniffled, ploughing his head into Theo's chest because he felt vulnerable and didn't want to be seen while pouring his heart out.

"It doesn't have to be, Jude, I promise. We can come back here whenever you want." He suggested, rubbing his hand up and down Julian's back.

"I guess... I guess it was just me and her growing up. I had friends that came and went, and we moved houses loads, switched schools, and so much changed in my life and my mum was the only constant I ever had. And then I lost her. Or, or she lost me rather, but, you know."

Theo nodded. Although he didn't understand exactly what Julian was feeling, he could at least sympathise. Nothing had ever changed when he was growing up. The room that was used as his nursery became his playroom, and then it became his bedroom, and then it stayed his bedroom. Every day was the same for him, waking up and attending his lessons (most of which he never deemed necessary himself, but anything to keep his dad happy). The only major event in his life was his mother's death - if he was even allowed to call it that now that he knew the truth - and even when that had happened he had been far too young to remember her as anything other than a maternal blur with caring arms.

A *lot* had changed in the last few months. Of course, there's the whole 'king' thing, that was a big one. And then having to get married and having all those feelings about that, and then meeting Julian and having double the feelings in the exact opposite direction that he had for Serenity. And now... now he was on Earth and the home that he'd never left up until this point was being looked after by someone else, and anything could have happened. He'd also met his mother, and boy if that wasn't possibly the weirdest experience of his life. He was still trying to figure out his exact emotions on the topic.

When he actually thought about it all properly, with his newly acquired lover in his arms, his life had been completely monotone and boring up until a bit ago, and now it was like the whole weight of the world had been dropped on him all at once. After taking a step back, it was a lot. A lot.

Fuck, and he was already in the mood to cry because he'd been doing it fakely earlier.

"I didn't mean to upset you, Sparkles." He smiled, looking up through his own glassed-over eyes, and Theo took a breath in before clearing his throat. "Argh, god, no, you didn't upset me, I upset myself." He laughed at how stupid it all was and pushed the tears out of his eyes. "Just thinking about things."

"Like what?"

"Home." He stated plainly, then waited a moment before adding, "Aster, Serenity. And you."

"Yikes, you thought of me and started crying?" He snickered, pulling himself out of the hug to place his hands in the large pocket on the front of the hoodie.

"No, you know what I mean. Everything's just moving so fast."

"With us or in general?" Julian cocked his head. "We can take all this a little bit slower if it's overwhelming." He offered and Theo nodded.

"I meant in general, but that would be nice. You wouldn't mind?"

"Of course not. We literally have eternity. I'm sorry if I made you feel like you had to rush into anything you weren't comfortable with." He apologised with his eyes downcast, and Theo scoffed playfully while fluffing up the shorter male's hair.

"No, no, you didn't. I've just never been in a proper relationship before and I don't want to fuck it up because… because I really like you." He said with exasperation.

Julian rolled his eyes. "Sap." He criticised lightly, and then his hands were removed from his pocket and he held Theo's.

"I really like you too." He said with sincerity before snickering.

"See! Now you made it sound dumb. Like primary age kids getting married on the playground." Theo whined with a pout.

"Your words not mine." Julian defended, hands raised in the air as if he was under arrest. He lowered them and reached his arms out. "C'mere." This time, Julian raised himself up a little on his feet to meet Theo's lips at an appropriate angle. It was a sweet, chaste kiss that only lasted a second, but it made the butterflies in the demon's stomach wake up and start flying around like it was nobody's business. They stared into each other's eyes after pulling apart with dopey smiles, and for the thirty seconds that their trance lasted it felt like nothing else mattered.

XXIII

"I feel like I'm watching a live show of Laurel and Hardy." Was the first thing that the boys heard when they redirected their attention through the glass to the scene that was unfolding before them. "Are you guys... police cadets?" Vanna asked, bringing her hands to her lap as her eyes drifted between the two of them. Laine was sitting on the back of the chair with her feet on the part where you're meant to sit down, and because there was only one chair, Raphie was leaning forward against the desk.
"This isn't about us." Laine quipped, shaking her head exaggeratedly. "We got as far as 'back off and mind your business'. Now just cut the crap or we're gonna send you to prison for like twenty years for refusing to talk to a police officer."
"Sorry, when is my lawyer getting here?"
"Sorry about her, she's in a bad mood." Raphie smiled. "Why do *you* think you're here right now?" She asked, grinning through the side eye that Laine gave her.
"Because you think I had something to do with Julian's passing. Because apparently letting your nearly eighteen-year-old sleep in his bedroom on his own is endangerment." She frowned.
"Alright, alright. Let's rewind." Raphie suggested, pulling herself up from the desk. "Tell me about the morning you found him."
Vanna bit her lip and brought her bound hands in front of her face with a sniffle. "I don't- I don't know if I can-"
"See, you upset her!" Laine complained, dragging herself off the chair. "You're meant to be good cop and you upset her!"

Vanna looked up and narrowed her eyes in confusion. It was a miracle that she'd put up with the two of them for so long, because between them they had less police experience as a German shepherd that wasn't even associated with the forces.

"That's it, I'm done talking to you two. Can I speak to an adult?" She declared, waiting a moment before gesturing towards the door. Laine and Raphie both grumbled with each other before they reluctanty trudged out of the room, and then twenty seconds later Theo watched as they walked back into the separated viewing space.

"That went well." He teased. The girls looked a little disgruntled at the comment.

"I was super nice, I don't know what else to do." Raphie sighed. "We're wasting time, I feel like Julian just needs to go speak to her."

"So we're now agreeing to let her in on the other side of death?" Laine clarified. "I can't help but feel like that's the kind of thing we'd get in trouble for."

"I mean... Nobody has ever said anything about it, have they?" Julian asked, looking mainly at Theo, who shook his head in confirmation.

He stood stoically in thought for a few more moments. It was true, nobody had ever mentioned to him that he shouldn't go around revealing the secrets of the afterlife all randomly, but then again, he'd always been told that it was near impossible to even go to Earth. He considered it for a few moments, and then his face lit up.

"If we're telling her about it, I wanna do the thing first."

Laine audibly groaned in protest. "You're not doing the thing, she'll have a heart attack."

"It'll definitely get her to talk, though."

"Sorry, what's 'the thing'...?"

"Just, just come on." Theo smiled, beckoning them all to follow. "Julian, you stay here and if this doesn't work then you can come in." He instructed, and Julian nodded with apprehension. He was a little nervous about what these two were referring to.

They made it back into the room and Vanna frowned. "You guys again?" Theo was the first in the room, so he took the only available chair which he crossed his legs on, and the other two girls allowed themselves their own states of sitting down.

"Look, Vanna, we haven't exactly been that honest with you." He confessed, and she shifted in her seat a little.

"We aren't really police officers."

"No shit."

Theo thought for a moment longer about exactly how he was going to phrase this. Luckily for him however, he didn't even have to spend long contemplating because his sister jumped in after the first ten seconds of awkward silence.

"You just, you need to tell us everything you know about his death, it's important." She pleaded again, and Vanna just looked bored.

"This is ridiculous."

Theo rolled his eyes and took a deep breath in. "Look," he began, leaning forward to place his body weight on the table. "Your son can't properly pass through to the afterlife because we don't know how he died. So do him a favour and literally just tell us what you know." He tried, and the woman raised her eyebrows, holding the position for a few moments before she started smiling.

"Are your parents with you guys?"

Theo grumbled and glanced over to Raphie, and then to Laine. He gave a silent confirmatory nod that said he'd had enough of their back and forth over square one. So, in a matter of about half a second, Theo completely dropped his human disguise at the same time as the two young women sitting either side of him.

Now that he was in this form, Theo looked a lot more appropriately dressed, whereas Laine seemed quite the opposite in a yellow t-shirt and joggers that were accompanied by a set of rounded reed horns and a tail that began to swish behind her. The light from Raphie's halo created a glow from just above her head that she'd become accustomed too after some time. It was a little annoying when trying to sleep, but getting up for a glass of water at three in the morning had become a task of ease with her own personal headtorch.

Theo cleared his throat. Although he'd now lost his pupils in favour of a void, he maintained the stare that he had going on Vanna, and before she even had time to form any kind of reaction to what she'd just witnessed, he began speaking.

Only this time when he spoke, it wasn't how he usually did. This was one of his constantly expanding list of abilities, and although it was more on the tamer side, it was still incredibly scary for anyone who wasn't at all used to it. He was sure to speak with his teeth showing in their abnormal sharpness, and when his voice left his mouth it was like it was being layered fifty times over, being incredibly loud and sounding quite like a snake talking through a phone with the pitch turned down.

"Do you want to fucking help him, or not?!"

At the sound of the question, Raphie completely flinched away simply due to the volume, not even the horrifically sharp tone of voice. Laine had, of course, heard her brother use this ability in the past, but that had mainly been when messing around, and it sounded so much worse when it was used for its intended purpose. No matter how much she herself had tried to develop the ability of this speech, Laine had found herself constantly unable to do it - much like countless other things that Theo seemed to be able to do that she couldn't. Her dad had reassured her it would come with time, and it was a leadership thing. Theo was born to be a leader, and she wasn't, that was what she was told.

Vanna's jaw remained unhinged in genuine utter shock for a while. She wasn't sure how she was meant to react. Was she dreaming? That had to be it because there was no fucking way. She blinked, and she hadn't even realised that her eyes were welling up with emotion until it happened. Being all-but screamed at by this demon was too much. Her son. Her son, she needed to help him? It was her fault, all her fault and she needed to help him and she couldn't even do it. Her son. Her son that she loved, that she loves.

She dropped her head onto the table, her forehead hitting against the metal of the handcuffs. The second that she could only see darkness, she began sobbing wildly with a loud exclamation of "I'm sorry!"

Every single instinct that Theo had told him that this was too far and it was now time to withdraw the act and be kind to her, and comfort her. But he'd gotten this far. So, instead of being kind about her upset, he continued to pry.

"What are you sorry for?" He asked, returning back to his normal voice and it seemed almost like a whisper in comparison. Theo leaned forward closer to Vanna, and she looked up, still crying.

"It was for him. Everything I did, it was for him." She whispered, lowly enough that only Theo heard it because of how physically close he was to her. Vanna was completely frozen as she made the best eye contact possible with Theo, not even believing that she was saying what she was saying. This wasn't real, so it didn't matter. So much guilt coursed through her.

"What did you do for him?" Theo asked again, completely ignoring how upset she was, and he knew in his head that Julian would get upset at him for speaking to her like this later.

Vanna tilted her head all the way back and tried in vain to wipe the tears from her eyes as her shoulders continued to rack up and down. Now she spoke so that all three could hear her, each of the girls watching in their own silent shock and curiosity.

"We were getting evicted." She said, then breaking her eye contact with Theo to stare down at the wood on the table. "I couldn't find another place with all we have, we were going to be on the street, not knowing when our next meal would be."

She paused and took a deep breath in.

"That happened once when he was young and it was the worst few months of my life. I just felt so horrible that I couldn't do anything about it." She inhaled, squeezing her eyes shut as she continued. "And then of course we wouldn't have been able to afford all of his hormones and doctor's appointments. We stopped being able to afford them a while ago, after his surgery, but it would have broken his heart had I told him that."

With one last shake of her head, she blinked as more tears began to flow evenly down her cheeks.

"Living on the streets and having to stop being who he really was, it- it would have killed him. He was young and vulnerable, and if the lack of food or shelter didn't get to him then suicide would have without the affirming care. I-" Vanna brought her hands to her mouth to cover it. "I love him too much, I couldn't let it happen. I wanted, god, I wanted him to be in a better place."

Theo brought his whole body backwards and he leant against the back of the chair, furrowing his eyebrows in resentment. There was a silent question lingering in the air that none of the three visitors were going to ask. They didn't need to ask, because they knew the answer, but saying it out loud would have made it all the more real. The silence was deafening. Vanna burst into another fit of sobs while avoiding eye contact. She was in a horrible state of upset, unlike anything Theo had ever seen before - and he'd seen a hell of a lot. Her whole body jerked with each sob and she refused to look at any angle above the ground as she drowned in her own shame and desperation. Despite this display, Theo's mind wasn't at all focused on her. And so, without another word to the woman, he swiftly stood from his chair and stormed out of the interrogation room, leaving his sister and Raphie behind with the hysterics as he ran down the desolate corridor and back into the room that he'd left Julian.

The boy didn't even flinch when Theo pushed the door open. He just stood, body and eyes unmoving as he watched his mother break down over her actions. Theo approached on hesitant feet, not wanting to overstep anything, but it was a huge fucking revelation they'd just heard, and considering how highly Julian spoke of his mother, it definitely couldn't have been anything but devastating to hear.

It took about ten seconds of silence for Julian to turn his head and face Theo - tears welling in his eyes and threatening to fall, but he wouldn't allow it. He wouldn't allow that kind of satisfaction to the universe, it wasn't worth his time.

"You... you okay?" Theo asked, and he knew it was the dumbest question in the whole of history. Julian shook his head, taking a few moments to get his mouth to open while he searched for his voice.

"Don't do that." He said softly, voice breaking.

"What do you want me to do?"

"Just hold me."

And so he did. Theo pulled Julian into his arms, and the shorter boy slumped into them, letting all of his feelings out now that he felt protected. He was crying, and it wasn't the kind of graceful or attractive crying that you might be used to seeing in the media. It was the kind of devastating upset that gave him a headache after a minute, all the while he was hiccuping and struggling to breathe as his nose ran and he undoubtedly covered his boyfriend's shirt in snot, but it didn't matter to either of them. Theo didn't say anything; neither of them did. All that happened was the continuation of the cries as they synced with Vanna's - a wall apart. The older male's grip only tightened as the sobs increased in severity, and he knew that he wasn't going to let go for the world. Theo heard the girls enter the room, but he didn't divert his attention.

"Do you want to speak to her?" He asked in a hushed whisper as he glanced back to the woman, still sitting in the chair with a devastated look on her face. As if she hadn't processed her actions until just now. Julian shook his head without even looking up. "Not now." He breathed. "Not worth it." He let out, right before allowing the room to slip back into silence as he continued to let his emotions fall freely into his boyfriend's shirt.

Even when the crying subsided about ten minutes later, Julian didn't dare remove himself from Theo's grasp. It was too comforting, too nice to ever want to pull away from. The world stopped for a minute, but it had to restart all too soon when there was an abrupt and intrusive banging on the door. Laine darted over towards it and flicked the lock on just as the person on the other side tried the door handle with unrivalled aggression.

"You fucking kids better get out here right now before this gets any worse for you!" They heard the same man that Theo had blocked in the cupboard earlier yell, and even through the wooden door it was loud as Hell.

The four of them exchanged glances. "He's gonna arrest us when we try to leave!" Raphie whisper-yelled before she started pacing. "We took way too long here."

"Shit, okay, what are we doing?" Theo asked, and now that Julian was a little calmer (momentarily) he was able to contribute.

"I don't know, you're the magical one, do something magical!" He instructed, throwing his hands around in front of him as the banging and yelling got louder.

Laine was the kind of person that completely crumbled under pressure, as previously established. And so, she just managed to worm her way into one of the corners of the room with her hands over her ears because Officer Meyers wasn't getting any quieter.

"Fuck, I don't know!"

"Open this door right now!"

Theo looked around desperately. There was no window in the room, other than the one that led into the viewing room that Vanna was now speaking to an actual police officer in. He heard the man jangling with a set of keys.

"I'm unlocking this door and you guys are in serious trouble." He warned, and Theo's panic increased tenfold.

Laine kept her hands shoved over her ears as this all unfolded, but as she watched her brother, his boyfriend, and her friend panic in a little triangle. Then, as the door handle got rattled even more, Laine moved her hands away from her head and looked to the ground in the centre of the other three as she made her exclamation.

"I want to go home!" She yelled quickly, making the other three fall into complete silence as the golden portal materialised on the ground. A wide grin formed onto Theo's face.

"Laine, you genius!" He said.

"Are we going then?" Julian asked hastily, panting through his anxiety. The sound of a key being shoved into a lock on the other side of the door sounded out, and Raphie looked at it.

"We don't have much of a choice anymore." She realised, reaching her hand out towards her friend. The Princess took it quickly and stepped closer towards the portal. Theo nodded as he drew a sharp breath and wrapped his hand around Julian's wrist. Julian pulled the King's wrist down so that they were actually holding hands.

At this point, they fully realised that their time was waning and they had about five seconds left before they were destined to serve two years for trespassing and assaulting a police officer.

"Come on, let's get home." Theo nodded, mainly as a reassurance to himself as he stepped forward and fell through the portal, pulling Julian down with him. About a second later, the two girls followed. After, the portal closed up completely in a matter of blinks - not having a purpose since the summoner had gone through it.

They were lucky for that too, because it was only a matter of a few more seconds before a very bewildered and angry police officer was gaping at an empty room.

XXIV

Not to toot his own horn or anything, but Nikoliah thought he was actually doing an okay job looking after the kingdom. He had never realised how many boring meetings he would have to sit through, and he thought he'd definitely look at Theo with a new level of respect after this. He genuinely thought that it *was* going well, and it was, which was why he was so disoriented when he was disturbed during his sleep on the second night of his time as acting king.

Nikoliah only stirred a little when he heard his name for the first time. By the fourth, he was awake (albeit groggily) and sitting up with a tired look on his face.

"Sir, we need you like right now!" One of the servant boys called from his doorway, shaking and looking incredibly distressed.

Agh, what was so important that it couldn't wait two more hours until sunrise?

He swung his legs over the edge of the bed, not dignifying the intruder with a response just yet.

"There's um- there's people, there's-" The boy started, but he was completely pushed aside as Sir Garrah's silhouette appeared in the doorway, his hand on the sword against his hip.

"Amadeus Beckett is here with his troops and he wants the kingdom. You get your ass up and take control of your men." He said, all too calmly despite the actual internal feelings he was having. A wave of panic flooded through Nikoliah's body as he choked a little.

"Seriously?" He asked, already having ripped his shirt off while getting ready. Garrah did not look impressed.

"It's your call, are we fighting them?"
Nikoliah turned to the servant boy who was still shaking on his legs. "You, go get everyone up. I don't want any of that shit you pulled with me. You bang on their bedroom doors and scream the castle down." He instructed sharply, and the boy nodded with a meek "Yes, Sir!" before disappearing off down the corridor.
"Are they trying to fight us?" He asked, turning back to Garrah as he continued to dress himself with haste.
"Seems that way. It makes sense he'd attack when the whole royal family is absent, we know he's had bad intentions towards the kingdom for years."
Nikoliah nodded to himself. He'd trained his whole death for this exact moment, it would be fine. He hoped. He looked all around his bedroom, in a quick worry-filled glance, and then it dawned on him.
"Shit, my sword is in the Princess' bedroom." He said to himself, and Sir Garrah frowned like a disappointed parent.
"As is your dignity apparently. Run." The man scolded, pointing out of the room and down the corridor. Now, realistically, Nikoliah should not have taken orders from this man, because *he* was of a higher rank. But, it didn't matter at that exact moment.
"Please, please, get everyone to the courtyard!" He yelled, hand instinctively falling to where his sword would have been attached to his belt as he started running. He hadn't meant to leave it in Laine's room, he'd just ended up keeping it there rather than his own bedroom, and he'd ceased all of his sword training these last few days in favour of the Kingly duties, so he hadn't needed it.
He ran as quickly as he could, legs struggling to keep up with the rest of his body. Many people were also dashing around in panic, but he ignored them all in favour of skimming through one of the servant's passages that lead out just before her bedroom. In the few minutes it had taken him to traverse the length of the castle (the soldiers' and staff's quarters being on the other side than the royal wing), the atmosphere had morphed completely.
Everyone was fully aware of what was going on at this point. Out of the biggest window, Nikoliah could see loads of angels in the streets of the village closest to the castle. It was scary, as silly as that thought was coming from an adult. While it was true that they weren't exactly going to die, already being dead and all, they could most definitely get hurt. They could get hurt badly, especially pureblooded demons, as they were more susceptible to injury. Nobody had ever got a blade close enough to

any pureblooded demons to simulate a life-threatening injury, so nobody *actually* knew what the consequences to one of them 'dying' was.

Nikoliah pushed his way into Laine's still vacant bedroom, and his eyes landed on his sword leaning up against the back wall. It was a long, silver piece with a black leather handle and cotton-blue coloured leather accents that matched his horns and tail. The grip was moulded exactly around his hand - he had had it custom made just after he received his knighthood, as per tradition. He grabbed it, and it instantly felt *right* in his hand.

If he'd made the mistake of leaving his sword in a room that wasn't his own during his training, he would have been bollocked beyond belief and failed instantly.

He was glad that he had authority now.

He left the bedroom as quickly as he could, being stopped on the staircase by a panicked-looking Kougan.

"What are we doing? What's the plan?" He asked quickly, not wanting to waste the knight's time. Nikoliah exhaled with a determined look on his face.

"If you want to fight, then get to the courtyard. I don't care if you have training, if you want to fight, then fight. If you don't want to fight, I highly suggest you try your best to get out of here." He instructed, marching himself off down the stairs, and if Kougan had asked him any follow-up questions, he hadn't heard them in spite of his hurry.

People were yelling random scattered commands and queries left and right, but the acting king opted to ignore them. He had to get to where he hoped his men were waiting.

This was bad, bad. He'd been trusted to look after the kingdom and he'd allowed all Hell to break loose in the dead of night. In actuality, Nikoliah was very well equipt to deal with this - he just, god, if he fucked this up and they were defeated, he would never be forgiven.

To his tremendous relief, his soldiers were all formed up in the internal courtyard with their armour (dark grey leather, traditional of Klaevr) and swords, looking incredibly tired. This courtyard wasn't outside the castle, but rather a square of concrete ground in the centre of two wings. It meant that they were protected while they took a moment to strategise, although they wouldn't take it for granted as they had no idea how long they had until Beckett's men made it through their initial defences.

When the knight ran in, they all started murmuring. Nikoliah didn't waste any time, and he wasn't going to bother with all of the proper drill that had been ingrained into his head.

"Alright! Shut up!" He yelled, projecting his voice across the sea of demons with a range of different coloured horns. In an instant, they all fell dead silent and looked at him with apologetic worry. "This shit is serious, I hope you all remember your fighting drills, because those angels outside definitely remember theirs."

"What's going on, Sir Nikoliah?" A girl at the front of the group asked impatiently, fingers drumming along the handle of her sword. At the question, a lot of others started murmuring in agreement.

He inhaled. "As per my understanding," He began in a booming voice that hushed everyone up quickly. "Lord Amadeus Beckett and his army of halo-wielders are after the kingdom. Of course, it makes sense in King Theo's absence that now is an appropriate time for him to attack. Questions?" He asked, and he didn't even wait a second before swiftly moving on.

"Good." He said, when nobody even had the time to raise their hand or interrupt. "If you find yourself face to face with any of them, you *do not* make the first move. I want it to be completely clear to them that we are not engaging unless provoked. If they come charging at you with a weapon, obviously stop them - but you are not to initiate. Understood?" They all gave a chant of 'Sir', as conditioned.

"Alright, I understand there hasn't been much time for you to prepare for this. So, I'll offer now, and this is the only time I'm going to offer." He continued, taking a cursory glance back to the doors of the castle which were still partially visible from their location.

"If you don't wish to participate in the fighting and would much rather just get out of here before it all kicks off, I suggest you leave now." He extended the notion, raising an eyebrow, and about five or six of the at least four-hundred people fell out of their ranks and promptly exited.

Sir Garrah ran into the courtyard as these people were still filing out. He was panting and red-faced, stressed to the extent that nobody should ever have to be.

"Time's up." He panted, keeping his voice in a whisper so that only Nikoliah could hear it. "They're taking people's houses, everyone's trying to get to the station but without any defence from us they aren't getting there."

Nikoliah nodded, putting on a brave face. One of his main principles as commander of the soldiers was that he would never be the kind of man to lead from the comfort of an office or cosy fireplace. If he was making his people fight in the front lines, he'd be there too.

So, he turned back to the rows and rows of demons waiting for his instruction.

"Well, shit, this is it." He said to them, "Follow on."

He grabbed his sword from the right of his hip, unsheathing it with a metallic sound that told even those who couldn't see him that they needed to do the same. So they did, all pulling their swords (which were all the same mid-length blades with dark grey leather the same as their armour wrapped around the stubby handles) and holding them to their chests to keep them away from others and the ground. They wouldn't want to dull the blades before they even got the chance to use them. Nikoliah took an incredibly deep breath, turning to the man who he'd appointed his advisor. "You coming?" He asked, and Sir Garrah took a glance towards the exit.

"Wouldn't miss it."

Theo's knees hit the ground first, and then he slumped forward onto his forearms, gasping in air as he thumped against the wooden planks of Zero's basement. He groaned at how suddenly he'd hit the ground. It had felt like he'd only been falling for ten seconds before he was met with the harsh reality of oak.

Julian yelped loudly as he landed on top of Theo's ankles, coughing as the dizziness flooding his brain began to subside. Theo let out an exclamation of 'ouch!', before spinning around and sitting up. He took a deep breath in. "God, I missed the air here."

"Agh!" Came a scream from above them, and then Raphie landed a few metres away from them on her back, incredibly shortly followed by Laine. They all took a long while to catch their breaths and regain control of full consciousness, the room being only filled with heavy breathing. Theo eventually climbed to his knees and then stood fully, leaning against the wall.

The room itself looked exactly how it did when they left (minus the four teenagers in various states of exhaustion), apart from Zero's drawers all being open and empty. Following a few minutes of bewildered complaint about the sudden nature of their return to Klaevr, Theo ran a hand through his hair.

"Come on, let's go see how Nikoliah's surviving." He said.

"Yeah, okay." Laine groaned, taking another moment before standing up.

Julian sat up cross-legged and reached his arms out towards Theo. "Babe?" He smirked, drawing out the last syllable. Theo rolled his eyes. "Fine." He conceded, leaning forward and grabbing Julian's hands to pull him up. Julian brushed the dirt off his lap and smiled, perching up onto his tip-toes to press a kiss to his boyfriend's lips.

"Ew." Laine scrunched her nose up and walked past them.

"Oh, as if you won't be frenching your boyfriend the moment you see him." Julian retorted, grabbing Theo's hand as he himself made a face of disgust at that thought, following Laine up the stairs, both of the other two in tow.

Unlike the basement, the actual house up the stairs did not look how they remembered it.

The usual neat organisation of their geometric kitchen had been completely interrupted - with the chairs all over the ground and even smashed plates strewn on the counter. The glass cupboards had been all smashed, and so had the light bulb.

"God, what happened here?" Julian asked into thin, unknowing air. Nobody responded to him, and Theo unhooked the hand of Julian's that he was holding, picking his pace up a little bit and walking towards the door of the house.

He peeked into the living room to see that the front window had been broken.

"What the fuck?" He mouthed to the other three, and then he looked up the staircase. "Hettie? Elsie?" He called out, but was only met with silence.

Laine pushed past Julian slightly to get to the bottom of the staircase, and then looked past Theo up the staircase too.

She started to jump up the stairs and Theo gave a call of "Wait!" before following her. They both got to the top of the staircase and were met by three doorways. The upstairs of the house looked pretty much unscathed.

"Hey!" Julian called from behind the two siblings. "What the hell is going on?"

"Yeah, that's what we're trying to find out." Theo replied, taking a step down the corridor and beginning to scan one of the bedrooms.

It was a nursery, clearly, probably used when the homeowners' daughter, Leila, stayed. There was a small child's bed in the corner, and an array of blankets all around. It was completely empty, and there was a small teddy bear sitting atop the light yellow pillow.

"Guys!" Raphie yelled, panicked from her tone of voice. Theo turned and made his way to the voice, which happened to come from the largest room upstairs.

Inside the room, Raphie was crouched down on the ground, a good ten feet away from them with her hands up in the air.

In front of her, were two figures, Hettie and Elsie, both leant against the edge of the bed. Each of them had their hands tied with beige rope, and Hettie had a black eye right beside a bruise on her cheek. Elsie was leaning into her chest in the bleak darkness of the room, eyes closed as she sought after comfort. Theo flicked the light on and both women looked up to him, fear in their eyes.

"What happened here?" He asked, sticking a thumb in the middle of the first woman's knot and untying her wrists.

"I don't know, but they seem pretty scared of me." Raphie observed, looking them up and down again. Theo looked at her and then back to the couple.

Elsie allowed her eyes to flutter open and she swallowed, recognising the concerned panic corrupting Theo's features. She tried her best to provide an explanation, but found her ability to speak falling short.

"Angels, they..." She trailed off, now with her hands free as she moved to wrap them around her wife.

"They what?" Theo asked impatiently.

"They took Zero somewhere," Hettie provided in spite of her situation. "And they said they were gonna hurt us. They told us they'd wait here for you until you got back so they could catch you off guard." She paused her explanation to deliver some heavy breaths. "We managed to convince them you were planning on being gone for far too long for them to wait."

Theo swallowed with an understanding nod, looking up at Raphie - who vigorously shook her head. By this point, Laine and Julian too had made their way into the room, watching the situation unfold with stressful eyes.

Julian didn't understand what was going on. He didn't know anything about this kingdom, or the lifestyle or anything. But, what he could tell was that his boyfriend was very distressed - his chest heaving up and down as he tried and tried to get answers from these exhausted women. He looked out the window, the bedroom being at the front of the house - having a perfect view of the whole kingdom.

The whole kingdom, which did *not* look how he remembered it.

"Um, Theo?" Julian tried.

"Yeah, one sec." He dismissed, looking back at the injured women. "Do you know why? What they want?"
"Theo!"
"What?!"
Julian cocked his head to gesture to the window, and saw that Laine was looking out of it with wide eyes. He stood quickly and walked over to the large pane of glass.
He could see the outline of his kingdom from where the house sat on top of its hill. It was night time, maybe about four in the morning and so all was dark apart from the fact that there were halos illuminating nearly all of the streets, and fire, a lot of it. It was actually a beautiful contrast against the dull colours of the buildings and sky. He stood completely motionless for a moment as he took the whole sight in.
"Fucks sake, Nikoliah." He muttered, turning ninety degrees and quickly rushing out of the bedroom, down the stairs, down them quickly and out of the front door - completely leaving everyone else behind. Maybe they yelled after him, maybe they didn't; he wasn't listening.
And then he was running down the hill. At some point, he didn't know when, his wings had expanded out behind him in brushstrokes of viridian green. Since he was on a downhill sprint, he was able to push himself off the grass and allow his wings to completely catch him, allowing him to move through the air at a rate two times faster than he would usually go at.
When he reached the outskirts of the city, the noise became easily apparent. There were screams ringing out from all directions, and metal hitting metal.
Theo landed, or attempted to land, but actually ended up falling forwards and doing a half-roll before skidding to a halt on his knees. He stood back up as quickly as his body would let him, running through the first street he could make contact with.
He was so completely blindsided with panic and anger that he didn't even notice he was being watched until a sword pressed up against his throat horizontally from behind him. He yelped slightly and skidded to a halt, his skin grazing against the metal uncomfortably. He couldn't see the sword, or the person wielding it, but he could tell it was an angel from the glow he was seeing coming from behind him into the nighttime air.
"Welcome back, Strythio." A taunting voice came in his ear. They sounded young, maybe in their mid twenties, but certainly not anyone

that Theo would have recognised. "You didn't miss much, don't worry." They grinned through their own schadenfreude.

Had Theo been in possession of a sword, he'd have been perfectly capable of disarming this angel. But, he wasn't. He was totally unarmed and he tilted his head backwards to ease the pressure of the blade against his pale skin.

"God, wait until the boss hears I got you. I'm gonna get promoted, Your Highness." They laughed a little, clearly teasing the title. Theo tried to move a little, but the flat side of the sword only got pressed deeper, to the point where he was struggling to breathe.

And then he heard a clattering, and the sword dropped to the ground in front of him.

Theo spun on his feet just quickly enough to see the angel fall to the ground unconscious. And, standing behind him was Nikoliah - holding his sword by its blade, obviously having used the handle to knock them out.

The soldier looked like he'd been through Hell and back, which he'd only actually done the first half of. He had a fresh wound on his forehead that dyed his light brown hair crimson, and dripped down his grey skin onto his collarbone and shirt. His cotton-blue tail curled itself around his torso protectively, which was something that a lot of demons did instinctually when scared. His hands were shaking and bloody, and neither him nor Theo knew whose blood it actually was. He had clearly been wearing leather armour that had served him well - as it was tattered and ripped in many places, exposing his undershirt.

He blinked at Theo for a moment, and then he slowly lowered his shaking arms, along with the sword. Then, he found himself stumbling himself into the King's arms, burying his head deep in the demon's shoulder.

"God, Theo." He whispered. "I never thought I'd be so happy to see you." He admitted, holding onto Theo's body so tightly, in a way that would've gotten him fired in an instant this time last year. He was crying, he realised. Actually, he'd probably started crying when he sustained the injury that was currently causing his blurry vision.

"I'm sorry, I'm so sorry." He whined, and Theo pushed him away slightly to get a proper look into his eyes.

"You're hurt." He frowned, more clouded with concern for the knight than concern for his material possessions probably being looted from his bedroom.

"Everyone's hurt." Nikoliah swallowed, looking back towards the centre of the kingdom. "Everyone's hurt." He repeated. "You need to get to the armoury, Theo, he wants to kill you."

"I don't think that's possible." Theo replied softly.

"Better to assume it is than it isn't."

There was a pause.

"What happened here?" The King asked, just praying, begging, that it would be something a little better than what he was anticipating.

Nikoliah looked to the ground. "Beckett, that's what."

"Lord Beckett did this?" Theo asked. He felt sick with the wave of guilt that hit him. He knew that Beckett wanted to do this. He didn't say anything to anyone - he had been too stressed, too busy.

"I mean, who else?" The knight bent down to pick up the sword off the angel on the ground, sizing it up. "He has more soldiers here than we have demons in our whole kingdom."

"Where are all of ours?"

"Fighting. Dying, probably. If they could."

Theo reached out and took the angel's sword from Nikoliah's hand. He spun it around a little. "Okay, I'll go to the armoury and get *my* sword, and you just, well, you just carry on." He bluffed, waving his hands around in front of him.

Theo was about to turn and leave to run off towards the castle, but he was instead interrupted by the three people he returned back to Klaevr with. Julian came around the corner on the path, panting. He made eye contact with Theo and ran up to the demon, hugging him suddenly.

"You can't run off like that, I was worried." He frowned, voice muffled by his lover's shirt.

"I'm sorry."

Laine followed, and she spent a good few seconds staring right at her bloodied, exhausted boyfriend. He turned and noticed her, dropping his sword onto the ground and wrapping his arms around her. It was incredibly dangerous for them to be acting so vulnerable at this time, considering that now neither of them had any weapons.

They didn't say anything to each other, just hugged. Nikoliah himself had honestly never been so scared. He was worried that during the invasion, Laine had maybe come back and gotten herself hurt. The thought of her getting hurt and him not being there to protect her was really upsetting - and he didn't get upset much. He hadn't been upset when the initial invasion had started, he hadn't even been upset when his model solar system didn't win their year two design competition. But, he was definitely upset now - and he'd never felt so weak.

Whereas, it was almost the opposite for Laine. When she'd first looked out the window from the bedroom of that house, her first thought had been that Nikoliah was in charge. And, if he was in charge and the invaders were everywhere, they must have done something to him. She was so relieved to see him that she wasn't even phased by the fact he looked half-dead and more exhausted than a hamster that had been running on a wheel for hours.

It was hard to properly see in the dark, but that was okay.

Laine was just so happy to see her boyfriend, to know he was safe.

For now, at least. They were safe.

XXV

Raphie rounded the corner last, and at the time that she did so, Nikoliah pulled away from Laine and he moved down to retrieve his sword, hand going to hold it defensively in front of himself - chest heavy and movements skittish.

The angel stuck both her hands up in surrender, cringing as her eyes cast down towards the unconscious angel. Nikoliah groaned, not even bothering to stand back up from where he had grasped his sword. He just sat down on his knees and looked at Raphie, accusatory.

"You need to figure out what side you're on." He instructed. "This is *your* kingdom attacking ours. If you're with us, I suggest you find something to differentiate yourself from the rest of your sparkly-headed friends, and if you're with them, I'll give you a ten second head start."

Laine frowned and crouched down in front of him. "Niko." She sighed. "Calm down."

"Don't fucking tell me to calm down, Laine."

He brought his knees up to his chest and ran his right hand through his hair, wet with his own blood and sweat. His whole body was shaking. Laine looked at him with worry, and then to Theo - who shared the same expression.

"I think he's delirious from blood loss." Julian raised his eyebrows.

"He's not- I'm not delirious." Nikoliah replied, annoyed. "I just- fuck, I need to go fight."

He looked like a rabid animal, tense and injured as he flinched away from his girlfriend's touch. There were some hurried footsteps in the distance that made the soldier stand - reacquired sword close to his chest.

Sir Garrah rounded the corner, his only injuries being some scrapes on his hands. He stopped completely in his tracks.
"King Theo." He sighed, smiling. "Crown Princess."
"And Sir Nikoliah." He gestured. "Look, you need to get back out there and organise the strategies. It isn't going to end well without you." He instructed seriously, and it had Nikoliah nodding hastily. He turned back to Laine and gave her a half-hearted hug with one arm.
"Yes, yeah. Alright." He said, sticking his sword back on his belt as he ran away down the same path that the other knight had come down.
They all managed to take a back route towards the armoury that kept them out of most trouble, so, there were no real issues other than a few particularly bold angels that they managed to easily overpower without undue effort.
When they made it to the castle, it was chaotic. Light and darkness collided in every corner, and since Theo and Garrah were the only two with the swords, it became increasingly stressful as they realised the sheer scale of the operation that Beckett had running.
Julian ducked to the side, standing helplessly behind Theo at the bottom of their grand staircase, while he fought off an older man. Their swords clinked together, and Theo winced as he was struck just above his elbow.
"You guys go on, I can hold these ones off." Garrah yelled loud enough that they could all hear - and they did exactly as he said. Theo broke connection with the angel he was fighting, ducking under his sword and spinning so that he was suddenly bolting in another direction with Julian on his heels. It felt like an eternity of panicked sprinting that they finally made it to the armoury, and Laine (being last in) slammed and locked the door shut behind them all.
The room itself had dark, maroon walls - each and every space available honing some kind of sword or dagger, or crossbow, or similar. The King and Princess both had their own swords, taking pride of place right in the centre of the room.
Theo's had quite a short blade, as per his own personal fighting style. Whereas, his sister's was longer and more sleek. They both looked fairly similar to Nikoliah's in the sense that they were fashioned with black leather, accessorised by the colour of their horns, wings, and tails. On the handle of each of theirs, inscribed into the leather were the letters 'VRZ' - indicative of their surname.
"Woah, that's cool." Julian mused, picking the sword up before Theo even got the chance. "It matches you." He noticed, holding it up next to the demon.

"Yep." Theo replied, taking it off the shorter man, and Julian could only pout. "Julian, Raphie, just go ahead and pick any you like the look of, and we can get out there and help our people as soon as possible."

Julian seemed pretty excited to get his own sword, even despite the circumstances. He bounced over to a large rack and started touching and fumbling with every handle before he found one that he was happiest with, pulling it out of its hold and bringing it to toss it between his hands playfully. Raphie, however, kept her eyes downcast. Her body language was very closed off, and Laine waved a hand in front of her face to get her attention.

"I don't know, it seems wrong for me to take one of your swords." She confessed her thoughts as she bounced up and down on her toes with anxiety.

"No, it's fine." Theo replied as he walked over to the rack to pick one for her. "You're fighting with us, so it's fine."

Raphie didn't say a word to that. She looked up to Theo with guilty eyes, taking a step back on the concrete ground.

"You're fighting with us, right?" The King asked again. Laine's head snapped to look at her brother - offended by the insinuation that her best friend would ever go against them. Especially at a time so dire, especially after all they'd been through.

"I'm sorry." Raphie whispered with a subtle shake of her head. Her lip quivered as tears began to well up in her eyes. "It's not about you. You're losing. We can all tell. Even you can tell, Theo, you're losing, your men are losing." She spoke wobbly. "I don't want to take the fall for something I wasn't even meant to be involved in."

Laine's heart dropped to her stomach.

"Raphie." She pleaded. "We, we crossed dimensions together."

She nodded. "I know. And, now I'm gonna cross dimensions again and go back to *my* home." She croaked. "I'm sorry. I love you guys but I'm not taking the fall with the rest of your kingdom."

Theo raised his eyebrows as he looked her up and down with a huff.

"You're a fucking coward." He accused, voice low and bitter. "You can't just run away to your little safe haven when it gets difficult!"

Raphie took another step backwards, fidgeting anxiously with her hands. "I'm sorry." She repeated.

"No, no, you aren't sorry. If you were sorry, you would stay- you would-"

"Look, Theo, I'm not sorry for leaving." She confessed, actually looking up at him when meeting his eyes. "I'm sorry that you did a shitty job looking after your kingdom. I'm sorry that you ran off and left your land defenceless, but I don't want to be held responsible just because I'm friends with your sister." She whined, clearly upset despite allowing the truth of her thoughts to slip through her clouded speech.

Theo didn't have a response to that one. Nothing snarky, or angry, or even upset. He just watched in awe, in betrayed awe, as she rubbed her eyes and turned towards the door, taking up Theo's previous offer and grabbing the sword closest to her on the way out.

"Um, good luck." She nodded to herself, making painful eye contact with Laine that said a thousand words she didn't even want to attempt to absorb, pulling the door open and slipping through it - exiting the room, leaving the other three agape in a stunned silence.

And, it remained like that for a long while.

Theo ran down the corridor, ducking and diving and ducking again. He grunted as he was slammed into a wall - hard. He had the wind knocked out of him almost instantly, and his first reaction was to kick wildly at the angel, sending him tumbling onto the ground. He breathed heavily, stumbling away from his position and grabbing his sword off the floor. The angel regained his original stance, charging at him with their sword outstretched. Theo yelped, moving into a defensive stance as his body skidded to a halt with the force of their sword against his. Theo used this pressure to his advantage, kicking his right leg up into the stomach of his opponent. The angel gasped and fell onto the floor. Theo bent down and took his sword into his free hand.

"Mercy, please, please." The angel chorused, sitting up onto his elbows - defenceless. Theo swallowed. He didn't want to hurt anyone. So, all he did was shake his head. He swallowed, then bringing down the angel's sword in between his feet and into the carpet - dangerously close to seriously injuring him. The man gasped loudly, and Theo gave him a dangerous look of warning before he walked away.

The castle was basically theirs now. Theo had cleared the whole right wing, and was now about to walk past his bedroom. After that, it was only up the staircase that Julian had been sleeping atop of. He was actually feeling quite optimistic about this now.

That was, until he made it to the doorway of his bedroom.

It felt so good to lay his eyes on his bed. Red sheets and his black mesh canopy, God, how badly he wanted to collapse into it. He walked into the room and felt like a weight had been removed from his shoulders. It was blissful, almost.

And then, he noticed the figure curled up in his bed. Small, and dainty in their figure, dark orange hair swirling out of the covers and onto the pillow.

Serenity.

Shit, why hadn't she left when he had? What the hell was the point of her having stayed, knowing very well that Theo wasn't going to suddenly come home and drop to his knees begging for her forgiveness and hand in marriage?

Theo approached with apprehension and peeled back the duvet. She was curled in on herself, eyes closed with discontent. Her chest was rising and falling at an exaggerated pace - bruises all over her bare shoulders and even her jaw. She was wearing a magenta-coloured tank top and pair of pyjama bottoms, which made sense considering it *was* the middle of the night. Theo could only assume that she had been caught off guard during the fighting and had stumbled back to their bedroom as the only location of comfort that she knew in this kingdom.

"Serenity?" Theo mused, shaking her shoulders lightly so as to not startle her. "Serenity, wake up." He tried again, but it was decidedly futile after the third call. He glanced over to the doorframe - mahogany door still wide open, making them both helplessly vulnerable. The demon knew he couldn't leave her here, no matter how troubled their relationship had been. And so, he sheathed his sword back into his belt and hooked his hands under the sleeping woman's knees and elbows - hoisting her up bridal style.

He held her close to his chest, worried that she would fall or get hurt even more if he didn't take perfect care of her. Her orange hair dropped beside her like flames running down a trail of gasoline, and the closeness in bodily proximity gave Theo a much better look of her whole body. She looked hurt, that was for sure. Her tank top was stained with blood, but it was crimson, not blue like that of purebloods. When Theo pressed his hand to the area, he found it completely void of any moisture. He hiked her shirt up a little just so that he could see the skin under where the blood was - but there was nothing at all.

So it *must* have been someone else's.

God, he was wasting time. He slinked his way out of his bedroom - not bothering at all to try and arise any emotion about being back home. The corridor was completely barren, so that angel he'd knocked down earlier must have scampered off somewhere. He began to walk hastily down the corridor, but found himself having to stop at one of the sights.

The paintings - the ones that were of all previous monarchs. They lined the wall elegantly, picture frames golden and ornate.

They'd all been slashed. Slashed with swords no doubt. Big crosses disrupted the paper that the painting was on, leaving them peeling off from the centre and completely ruined. Theo's feet stopped moving under him.

He was suddenly very grateful that they were waiting until after he was wed to do his portrait - considering that it would have been of him and Serenity together. It definitely would have hurt a lot more if his own portrait had been damaged so, just like his father's, and his grandmother's, and-

And his mother's.

It would've been a lot more of a stab in the heart had he not recently been granted the blissful confirmation that she was okay. If he didn't have that reassurance, he thought he might have broken down at just the sight of it. But, he didn't. He couldn't. Not when he was being relied on.

So, he persevered past, keeping his head up and looking straight forward. If he wasn't under threat, he probably would've kept his head down to avoid looking at any more of his home destroyed. He ran down the stairs, not sparing Laine's room any glances. Luckily for his sanity and exhaustion, there was a distinct lack of their opposition.

He realised then that he was probably the only person in the castle. Well, besides Serenity, but she wasn't exactly talking company. Julian and Laine were both outside holding their own, and Theo was about to be doing the exact same the second he stepped into the main outdoor area. He stopped and took a deep breath.

The front courtyard was busy. Far too busy.

Firstly, the main gate had been completely closed - restricting anyone from entering or leaving. It appeared that most (if not all) of the commotion was going on in this area, as the streets now just looked busy and panicked. Theo could easily pick out certain people that he knew - like his sister, and his boyfriend, and his sister's boyfriend, and even some of the castle staff that weren't even soldiers to begin with.

The angels were all dressed in a natural beige coloured armour, but it kind of bordered on grey in the nocturnal light. The kind of colour that middle aged parents paint their walls to feel exhilarated, when we all really know it's just white with a fancy name like 'Ibizan Pebble' slapped onto it. They had large, but elegant swords which they held with only one hand, different to the way that the soldiers in Klaevr were trained. And then, in the centre of it all, stood nobody other than Amadeus Beckett. Theo had to admit that maybe he was a little bit impressed that the man had taken the time to actually come down in person. It happened more than often that people like him would just send their men to do a certain job, not actually bothering to lift a finger themselves. He was dressed differently to the rest of his posse - shimmering silver metal armour over his purple-blue toned light skin, and the way his halo shined down on it made it seem almost ethereal. Dangerous.

Theo looked down at the unconscious princess in his arms. He had to get her out of here. His eyes darted around hastily. There were demons ravaging through the streets on the other side of the bars, trying to get to the train station no doubt. He ran, ran, ducking under swings of people's swords - needed to transverse the courtyard as easily as possible.

About ten times during his sprint did he think he was going to fall onto his face from the sheer weight of his head, and how loudly it was pounding in his ears. He latched one hand onto the black metal bars of the locked gate, eyes swimming and digging through the crowd.

Then his pupils latched on to Elsie and Hettie, having seemingly made their way out of their house and they were following the major drift of the crowd toward the train station. He called out their names a few times, to no avail because of the loud noise consuming all their senses. On the third or fourth chorus, Hettie turned her head towards him, making eye contact for a brief desperate moment. She tapped her wife on the shoulder, turning and beginning to traverse in the opposing direction of the crowd, being pushed as she fought her way towards the monarch.

"Please, please." Theo chanted, loudly so that she could hear him. "Please, can you take her?" He asked, begged, gesturing to Serenity. "To Vaemunt. To her kingdom, please can you just make sure she gets there?"

Hettie looked down to her, and then up to the panicked demon holding her. "How?" She asked, gesturing at the large metal bars splitting them apart.

Elsie appeared from the crowd, only barely managing to get out of the wild current. She watched as Theo shifted his position to be fully supporting Serenity with just his left arm, using the right to hoist himself up on the bars - taking full advantage of the divots in the metal. Eventually, he got high enough that he could look over the bars, gripping onto them with his life. Hettie did the same, using Elsie's hand as a leg up.

She reached up and took Serenity carefully from Theo's hands, holding her tightly. She stirred a little - and Theo was honestly amazed she was yet to wake up in the chaos.

Theo's arms felt a little empty after they were devoid of his (technically) fiance. He jumped down from his position on the fence in one swift movement. "Thank you." He breathed, barely sure that he was even standing from how dizzy he felt.

"Yeah, yeah, of course." Hettie nodded, pulling Serenity against her hip in more of a maternal stance. "Good luck, okay?" She offered, but Theo had already zoned them out now that he didn't have anyone else's safety on his shoulders. Well, he did. He had his whole kingdom - but it wasn't like a specific person that he was meant to be caring for, like in Serenity's unfortunate circumstance.

He spun around and turned to face the scene before him. And, he was incredibly fortunate to have done so - because the moment he was facing outwards a shorter, green-haired angel came charging at him, slashing against his torso with intention. Theo stuck his left arm out in front of him, his right arm going to pull his sword from its holster.

He yelped as his whole body was thrown onto the ground, porcelain skin scraping against dirt and gravel. He felt this horrible stinging pain on the right side of his stomach, and when he pressed a hand to the area he confirmed his suspicion that, yes, he was in fact bleeding. His hand came back coated in a royal blue, dripping down and onto the ground beneath him.

He barely moved his sword over his body quick enough to block the angel again, scrambling to his feet and pushing his own weapon against his attacker's arm with an upwards motion. She screamed out as blood, dark and red and dangerous, started channelling out of the wound - leaving a helping of it along the blade edge of Theo's sword.

"You dick!" She accused, dropping her sword completely as she cradled her injured arm. "That fucking hurt!" She all but whimpered, dropping to her knees.

Theo took a step towards her with confused indecision.

"Oh, um, um, I'm sorry." He hesitated, not really sure of how to react.
"You attacked me first, though."
"Yeah! Because I was ordered to, you asshole! This is gonna scar!"

Theo leant down to her level, completely ignoring his own injury. He looked at the angel's arm, and, yikes. He had really hurt her. The wound was deep and bleeding excessively, flesh and skin were all torn up around the edges.

His eyes widened a little and he lost all ability to think for a moment. He had never wanted to hurt anyone, that had never been his intention.

The woman started to sniffle and Theo directed all his attention to her, trying to make up for his actions even a little. He felt compelled to do so. That was until the green-haired angel suddenly jumped up and kicked him in the jaw. It hurt like a bitch, and he was propelled back against the dirt all over again. The angel was up immediately, pleased with having duped the demon. She stabbed her sword down, and if Theo hadn't slid out of the way quick enough it was likely he would have been impaled through his torso.

He had all of the wind knocked out of him initially, so that when he came to his senses he realised that his sword was *not* in his hand, but rather on the ground where he'd absentmindedly put it down to help the angel. He began to crawl over to it, but the angel grabbed the back of his shirt and yanked him backwards, holding her sword against his chest.

Fuck, fuck. He'd trained for this. He totally had. But, it was just, God, he'd never assumed he would actually need it. He tried to think, think like his life depended on it. He ended up just elbowing her in the thigh, and she just chuckled.

And, God, he did not like that.

He latched onto the edge of the sword in front of him, slicing his fingers open as he pulled down. The angel was caught off guard by the motion - her whole body shifting forwards, which gave Theo the opportunity to yank her whole body forward.

She fell over him with a groan, and Theo lept up through his blurry vision. He ran past her, grabbing the sword that was his off the ground. And he kept running, leaving a trail of his blue blood along the ground. He ran faster than he thought he'd ever run before, with no intention of stopping.

XXVI

The only experience Julian had ever had with fighting was from when he was about fifteen years old.
He had been walking home from his then girlfriend's house at about ten o'clock at night in November, his electric blue coloured hair shining out against the blackness of the night. The streets around where he lived were narrow and dimly lit, brick buildings towering over him as he kept his head down.
He was at a kind of still point in his transition. The awkward period of time where he didn't pass as a boy, but he got really weird concerned looks in women's restrooms, and even one time got asked to leave one by a middle-aged woman. He was only about a month on testosterone. To get straight to the point, it left him walking around the streets of Manchester late at night looking visibly trans and queer, despite his hoodie and black jeans shielding him.
He'd been walking along the street, headphones in, blasting Queen to drown out his thoughts when he'd suddenly hit the ground. A group of four or five boys, all dressed in tracksuits surrounded him. He panted, music fading lowly out of the headphones that were now on the ground as he pushed himself up against the wall.
One of the boys muttered something unintelligible, but Julian hadn't even heard it because of the blood rushing in his ears. They were towering over him in a semicircle, pressing his back to the wall. One of them grabbed the messenger bag off his shoulder and tipped the contents out onto the ground, which was only really a sketchbook, water

and his wallet. His phone was in his pocket, but he had a feeling that it wouldn't last very long if this kept up.

So, he'd done the one thing that his mother had always repeatedly taught him to do if a man ever attacked him.

He kicked the guy closest to him in the crotch, and he groaned loudly in extreme pain. The rest of the posse didn't seem to like that at all, because he easily found after that they were hitting him and grabbing him and before he knew it he was on the ground once more - yelping and crying out in pain as he was kicked against the wall while a range of various colourful words were yelled at him.

It was a horrible feeling - one of the worst in the world. In that kind of moment there was nothing he would have rather had than the mercy of death. But, he wasn't so lucky. All he was able to do was lay still as he was hurt, defenceless and weak against his assailants. And they didn't stop for a while, not even when he started crying, or when he started coughing up blood onto the pavement.

It was weird - trainers shouldn't hurt that much. They aren't exactly made of strong material or anything. Maybe it was the idea that he seemed so helpless and vulnerable that they thought they could make a target out of him that hurt more. He'd always hated that about himself if anything - the way he was so frail and weak all the time. Which was why after that day, he'd made a specific point to spend more time at the gym in an attempt to aid the work of the hormone replacement treatment giving him more muscle mass.

And he'd looked like shit afterwards too. People in the corridors at school avoided him for a long time, and his girlfriend didn't even kiss him for a solid few weeks while he still had a massive cut along his lip. She'd told him that it was because she didn't want to stop it healing properly, but he knew deep down she just thought he looked ugly all bruised up.

Thinking back to it, the boys hadn't even been much stronger than him. They were around his age, maybe in the year above or even below (but that would be a million times more embarrassing), and they were still growing like he was. It was just that they'd been cocky and confident and he was a shy little thing that was still trying to discover himself, let alone learn how to be a fearless young man.

And all the while they were hurting him, they were chatting to eachother like nothing was even going on. Like it didn't matter to them what they were doing, like it was their regular evening routine - and maybe it was. They had stopped eventually though - they would have gotten too tired at some point. But no, that wasn't the case. They'd only stopped when a

police cruiser had heard Julian's screaming and halted on the curbside to check it out. Obviously, they'd played a game of chicken and sprinted off in the easiest direction possible, taking his wallet with them - but nothing else other than that, except maybe Julian's ego.
He'd spent the rest of the evening in A&E with a few broken ribs as his mother fawned over his well being.
But, this time, he was three years older, and had gained a lot more muscle and confidence. He kicked an angel right in the stomach, and they tumbled to the ground as he smirked in satisfaction. His back was pressed tightly against Laine's as they together fought off attackers in a 'Charlie's Angel's' type position. Each time Julian hit an attacker, he was pretending that it was one of those boys from that evening. He wondered briefly if they'd heard about his death and felt bad about it, but he highly doubted that.
Laine moved forward a little to deal with one specific angel that just kept bouncing back. She stepped to the side to get a slash in from an alternative angle, but was completely thrown off when the angel jumped up behind her and grabbed her horns, pulling her whole body backwards. She used her right hand to fling her sword towards her own back, and it hit the angel in his side directly. He gasped, dropping off her body and onto the ground where he promptly hit his head and lost consciousness.
"Fuck, how many are there?" Julian breathed, stepping next to her and looking down in their moment of freedom from the fighting.
"Apparently a lot." She replied with a grimace. "Menphe is a big kingdom." Laine looked around. "...so I'm told."
Julian hadn't really ended up using his sword much in the fight. It wasn't exactly standard for random English kids to get training in how to fight with swords, but he did know somewhat about fighting physically because he'd been mates with a lad who liked boxing quite a bit. He'd even brought him along to a few training sessions, which had really helped Julian learn to defend himself.
Considering that the two of them were standing in the centre of a whole pile of unconscious angels, having done their fair share of fighting, most others stayed away from them while they caught their breath - instead finding another demon to go for; a lone demon.
Like Nikoliah.
He skidded along the ground on the opposite end of the courtyard, fighting about four people at a time. He was already pretty badly injured, which made him even more of a target. He was lucky for his extensive training, because he was fighting incredibly well. Each time he managed

to do rid of one angel, another would appear amongst their peers – so frequently that by the time he'd beaten all of the original four, another completely new set were in their places, swinging their swords at him. He hadn't seen Theo yet – which was both worrying and comforting. It was worrying, because he might have been absolutely destroyed in the castle and was just bleeding out or something all alone. However, the fact that he was yet to appear outside did mean he was in a much safer position than anyone else was. Outside, it had begun to feel like a bloodbath. Not that anyone had been killed yet – they couldn't have been, but people were hurt, and there were unconscious angels and demons lying all around. It would be a big clean up for them when they won. Nikoliah briefly worried about how many people could be bedded in the infirmary at once.

As it felt like he was just about to get the angels all down, he went for one last strike towards the upper body of a rather tall one. But, he wasn't able to swiftly complete this movement, because he had an angel come up from behind him and quickly crash their sword into one of his legs. They instantly connected with bone, which stopped the movement of the sword. Nikoliah gutturally screamed at how much it hurt, and he fell onto the floor in a slow, agonising movement.

"Filthy sinner." The angel smirked, moving to stand next to the person they'd saved. "What should we do with him?" They asked, spinning their sword around in their hand. Nikoliah lay in a relaxed seated position, but he was anything from that adjective. There was blood oozing out of his leg, and his hands were shaking violently. He didn't think he would be able to get up if he tried.

"I don't quite know. It would almost be merciful to knock him out. Maybe we could go again at that leg wound? Each have a go until we break through the bone and it's just hanging on by the skin and muscle?" Nikoliah nearly retched, trying to sit himself up on his hands. He scanned around for a way out of this, eyes latching desperately on to the one person he thought could protect him. Sir Garrah was just about finished dealing with one specific angel on a further side of the courtyard. He looked around for a next possible attacker, eyes stopping when they saw a tall angel pressing the tip of their sword into Nikoliah's chest, not breaking skin yet. Yet.

Immediately, he took off in a run towards the younger soldier. Although Nikoliah had been of a higher rank than him these previous few days, he still felt a strong paternal connection to protect him. Garrah's own, actual son had been an infant when he had died, and as far as Nikoliah knew, both his parents were too still living. Garrah had always seen himself, his younger self, in Nikoliah. In a brave, independent young man that's too ambitious for his own good. Full of pride and hubris and easy to make mistakes.

Garrah picked his feet up, moving as quickly as he could. The angels noticed him approaching. They heard his footsteps and spun to face him, readying their battle positions. The chief charged at them with his sword. One of the angels went around behind him, trying to hit him with their sword, which they did successfully once.

It was fortunate enough that Garrah was more successful - managing to slam his body into the tallest angel. They immediately fell to the ground, and it gave the second ten times more incentive to fight. Garrah didn't even falter in his movements, though. And while he was doing that, Niko was able to push himself back up to his feet, albeit wobbly and with a concerning leniency on his non-injured leg. And so, he joined in too. Because the angel was completely faced towards Garrah, Nikolah was able to give a strong hit with his sword to the angel's upper arm, inspired by the tortuous words that had come out of their mouth earlier.

The angel clearly wasn't expecting that, because they gasped out and stumbled around to face Nikoliah. From this position, Garrah was able to hit them over the back of the head with the handle of his sword, and they too fell to the ground.

"Shit, thanks." Nikoliah breathed awkwardly.

"Come on, you need to sit down." Garrah instructed with a strict, caring tone of voice now that the danger had passed.

"No, no, I don't- I don't, it's fine, I swear, just got a little in over my head." Garrah shook his head sternly. "You're bleeding. A lot, you need to stop." He said, placing both arms on Nikoliah's shoulders to steady him. He blinked drearily, looking over the courtyard. There was still a lot going on, a lot of fighting to get through. He had to help, it was his duty. His purpose in Klaevr. The only reason they'd kept him all this time.

"No, I have to- I have to keep going." He shook his head, swaying dizzily on the one leg that he was supporting his whole body weight with. Garrah spun Nikoliah around so that he was fully leaning into the body of the older man, tilted to the right so that Garrah's arm was hooked around his back.

"You've done so well, I promise." He praised softly, not letting his grip falter. "But that's enough now." He bent down, pulling Nikoliah down lower to the ground with him so that he wouldn't hurt himself any more when he inevitably fell. The injured young man gave a lot of pleas and choruses of 'no, no' and 'need to fight', but Garrah opted to completely ignore it.

"You've worked so hard, everyone is so proud of you, but you've done enough. You've done enough." He repeated, and Nikoliah nodded slightly through his blinking as his vision began to blur. Garrah pulled the overcoat off one of the unconscious angels, completely dropping Nikoliah onto the ground slowly and carefully, sitting up on his knees as he wrapped the fabric around the wound on the demon's lower leg, attempting to cease the bleeding.

Nikoliah groaned at the tightness of the wrapping, but found eventually that it didn't matter and he didn't care, because god, the idea of sleep sounded so perfect right now. So amazing and relaxing that he just closed his eyes in exhausted acceptance and let it happen, slipping into a desirable slumber.

XXVII

Theo stopped running when he heard his name, his full name. He spun around in a sort of stumble and looked up towards where the voice had come from.

"Strythio!" The voice called again, and his eyes darted directly towards Lord Amadeus Beckett. He was standing about twenty metres away, but walked forward as he spoke. "I was hoping you would show up. Did you have a good time on Earth?"

He didn't look at all hurt, rather, he looked like he'd just woken up from a long nap, had a shower, and done his whole skincare routine including moisturiser. He was very tall with broad shoulders, and he had the sword to reflect it - thick and elegant with a streamlined appearance as he held it casually in his left hand. He adorned a shit-eating grin that was basically a massive brag about the way he'd descended the Klaevr into anarchy.

"I thought I told you that you aren't welcome here." Theo slighted, holding his sword out directly in front of him for protection. Beckett walked closer, and Theo took a hesitant step backwards.

"I must've not received that message, not when you were so hospitable towards me. You know, leaving the kingdom completely void of anyone senior. Even *after I warned you*. Almost as if you were begging for someone like me to arrive."

Theo continued to step backwards, leaving a continuously maintained five metre gap between them. That was, until he took one more step and found himself hitting the back wall of the courtyard. His wings extended wide, curling around his body slightly to instinctively protect himself. The wound on his lower torso had stopped bleeding now, just leaving a gash in his clothing surrounded by dried, dark blue blood. When Theo hit the wall, Beckett stopped his advance.

"You don't have to get hurt." He reassured with a sympathetic tone. "I bet you're so tired."

Theo decided that he wouldn't be that easy. He ducked quickly under his own sword to the left of Amadeus, striking him with the edge of his sword. The man quickly retaliated, clashing the metal together.

"We can fight if you want to." He gritted out, using a lot of force. Each time he went to strike, Theo moved his sword under to block it - and then he took off in a run. He was young and quite tall, so he could move pretty quickly. His sword slowed him down a little because of the sheer weight of it, but he'd become pretty accustomed to holding it by now. And, he was pretty convinced that he was going to get away.

He felt a sharp pain in the left side of his chest, being thrown onto the ground by the force of how hard he'd been hit with the sword. When he made contact with the gravel, he skidded along it and ended up on his back, with a massive gash where he'd been hit. Beckett took two steps towards him, blood now on his sword.

"You do realise that this courtyard has been closed off, right?" He chuckled, both at the question and the terrified expression on Theo's face.

"Why- why are you doing this?" He breathed out.

Beckett leant down and grabbed the collar of Theo's shirt. "I promise it'll all make sense eventually." He said, then he released his grip on the shirt and sent him hitting the ground once more. He grunted, hand still gripping onto his sword. He swung it at Beckett from his low position, and the man must not have been expecting it, because the hit landed really well, drawing blood from his shoulder.

"Little shit." Beckett muttered with a pained hiss, but Theo was already on his feet and darting off in the other direction by the time the angel had recalibrated.

Because of this new injury, Theo was not running as quickly as he had been previously. He ran back through the area he'd come from initially, making it to about the centre of the courtyard before he couldn't physically breathe anymore. He stumbled as he tried to continue running all while he coughed excessively, panting over and over again. He wasn't paying any attention to his surroundings until he felt metal pressing against his neck, the whole length of the sword restricting his movement. He stopped moving, and then the sword shifted to be under his chin, and he stumbled backwards, back once more to a brick wall.

The blade of Beckett's sword was outstretched, the sharply pointed tip digging into his throat. The man tilted the metal up, forcing Theo to look at him through his exhaustion.

"You're so naive, Theo. So fucking naive." He teased, now standing about two metres away from him with the tip of his sword pressing into his skin, threatening serious injury as his back was pressed completely against the wall.

Laine breathed out, absorbing the silence that was newfound by the recent defeat of the angel she was fighting. She looked around to see if anyone needed help, eyes going wide and panicked when she quickly noticed her brother being very badly hurt by Lord Beckett. She wasn't that far, so she took off in a sharp run straight in the direction of the men.

Beckett grinned at Theo as he whimpered in pain. Then, he took a glance around and raised his cocky eyebrows at Theo's sister.

"Princess Laine, if you get any closer than that I *will* drive this sword through Strythio's neck." He threatened loudly, and she stopped about twenty metres away from them. The people all fighting around began to slowly end their battles, all their attention focusing on the scene being created.

"Let him go! What do you want?" She screamed, shoulders inflating and deflating up and down with her heavy breaths.

"This doesn't have anything to do with you, I suggest that you protect yourself." He warned. And then, Julian pushed himself through the crowd of angels and demons, who had formulated themselves on opposite sides of the courtyard in a kind of horseshoe shape.

Julian skidded across the dirt, pushing out of the semi-circle and making his presence known. Beckett turned towards him and grinned.

"Oh! You must be the boyfriend I've been hearing about." He paused his speech and smiled. "Come here." He ordered, beckoning with his free hand. Julian looked around, beginning to move forward on hesitant feet.

"Drop the sword for me, Theo." Beckett told him, adding a little more pressure that had the King gasping and releasing his grip on the sword involuntarily. Laine gasped sharply. He had just disarmed the King, which had very strong implications as far as battles over kingdoms go. It clattered to the floor and Beckett tilted his head to the left.

"I apologise, I'm being rather rude. Your name is?" He asked Julian, who looked around, mainly to Laine, who nodded approvingly, silently permissing him to cooperate with the man.

"Um, it's Julian." He stuttered.

239

Beckett dropped his voice to a whisper. "Do me a favour, Julian. Can you go and grab Strythio's sword off the ground?" He asked. Julian nodded carefully and walked the distance between the two of them. It was now deadly silent in the courtyard, everyone just watching the scene unfold. Theo had his head tilted backwards, an uncomfortable expression on his face. Julian made it towards him and bent down, picking the sword up. "What do I do?" He asked in a whisper, as quietly as possible. Theo couldn't articulate much, not being able to open his mouth more than about a centimetre at the risk of slicing his throat open.

"Do what he says." Theo replied, voice strained, hurried and whiny. Julian nodded with a mutter of 'okay', turning and walking back to Beckett with the sword.

Amadeus smiled, and when Julian got close enough to him, he wrapped his arm around Julian's torso. Julian yelped and dropped the sword at his feet. Amadeus released the sword from Theo's throat, swinging it around and bringing it up to Julian's body - completely trapping him in place between his only body and the blade. Now that the pressure was completely gone, Theo found it incredibly difficult to stay standing. He stumbled forward a little, dropping to his knees as he rocked back and forth dizzily.

"Alright Julian, I think you've probably ruined his life enough, don't you think?" He asked, and even if it wasn't rhetorical, Julian would certainly not have indulged in answering. "You should probably go home."

He circled his hand around in a quick motion, and just a few feet to his right appeared a large purple hole in the ground, shimmering and moving like water.

Julian's eyes widened at the implication. "No! No, fuck, no!" He screamed, thrashing his limbs about. Theo looked up. He inhaled, pushing himself to his feet shakily. Beckett almost laughed at the desperation.

"Just, make a good life for yourself, kid. Forget about this place." He told, able to fully pick Julian up from his collar, leaning his body over the portal as the younger man held onto his arm and expressed a string of pleas not to do it.

Laine brought her hand up to her mouth in shock, and could only watch helplessly paralyzed with fear as Theo ran towards them. At the moment that Theo was about five seconds away from reaching them, Beckett released his grasp and gave Julian a push. He screamed Theo's name and fell, body dissolving into the portal completely. The moment he went through it, it completely evaporated, leaving only the gravel and dirt on the ground - as if it were never there.

Theo fell onto his knees again, collapsing onto the ground where the portal had been.

"No! No, please! Please, I'm sorry!" He begged, hands desperately scraping at the ground. He collected dirt under his nails as he clawed at the gravel in anguish. "No, no! Fuck, no, please." Theo cried, completely shameless and pathetic.

"You can have the kingdom, please, please get him back." He sobbed, wailing as his chest heaved.

Beckett gave a sympathetic frown. He crouched down to Theo's level, pressing two fingers under his chin and tilting it up to look at him properly.

"I think we're long past the point where you try and bargain with me, hm?" He cooed condescendingly.

"How did you do that?" Laine said, at a very normal volume, but because it was completely silent as about three hundred people watched in shock, everyone heard it. "Only Zero could do that, he-" She paused, stepping forward accusatively. "What did you do to him?"

"Nothing I didn't have to." He replied, calloused as he stood up, leaving Theo on the ground at his feet. "Actually, Princess Laine, you're very important right now."

"I am?"

"Yes, where's Sir Nikoliah? Your father told me all about you and him." He stated plainly. Laine took another step forward.

"My father?"

"Oh! Yes, that does remind me." Beckett teased. "Something I wanted to tell *you*, Strythio." He said, bending down once more to be eye level with the King, who was still crying in a mess on the gravel. "I told your father about my plan to come down here and do this a few days beforehand." He confessed, and Theo met his eyes. "And you know what he did when I told him?" He asked, waiting a few seconds for nobody to answer before he did it for himself.

"He left."

Beckett waited a few moments longer. "He heard I was going to fight you, and he left the kingdom, back to T'kota. He had absolutely no faith in you *at all!*" He smirked, and Theo had basically stopped crying now, just watching the angel with stressed confusion and puffy eyes.

"I digress, where was that boyfriend of yours, Laine?"

She stayed completely silent upon realising that she had no idea. She knew he'd been fighting, but she hadn't seen him since they'd first reunited after they'd been to Earth. She looked around, becoming incredibly panicked. What if he'd gotten hurt? Badly hurt? She'd already just seen Julian get thrown into a portal, and she was already so preoccupied with worry for Theo that she hadn't even thought about him; it hadn't even crossed her mind.

Sir Garrah pushed himself out of the crowd from just behind Laine, holding Nikoliah's unconscious body bridal-style. "Laine." He called softly, and she turned around. Her eyes widened and she hurried over. Theo too noticed this, and he tried to stand to follow Laine, but Beckett pushed down on his shoulders so that was immoble.

"You stay right here." He instructed.

Laine sniffled, pushing Nikoliah's bloodied hair out of his face. "Is he okay?"

"Nothing some time in the infirmary won't fix, I promise." He nodded. "Sir Garrah, you come up here too." He decided. "In fact, any of Strythio's staff are requested."

As far as personal staff went, it was genuinely just Nikoliah, Garrah, Jaymie and Kougan. All three of the conscious people on that list ended up standing in the semi-circle also. It was clear that both Jaymie and Kougan had been fighting - covered in patches of blood, and Beckett didn't miss the way that Jaymie walked with a bit of a limp.

"Oh! You two are the stylists, right? You made his coronation outfit?" Amadeus asked with a smirk, and they just nodded wordlessly. "Yes, I liked that one. It was a bit queer, but I did like it." He said. "I'm going to keep all of you."

Theo looked between them with a sob-influenced hiccup.

"Come here, Princess Laine." He directed, and she certainly visibly hesitated, so he laughed. "I'm not going to throw you through a portal if that's what you're worried about. Like I said, you're important."

She looked around and slowly walked over towards him, keeping a few metres distance. She looked down to Theo while she was close enough, frowning at how horrible he looked. He was bleeding in multiple places, eyes puffy from crying and whole posture exhausted.

"I spoke to your father about this, Laine, and we were both very impressed by you. You know, you're confident, and well-spoken, and a very good fighter as it has appeared." Beckett told her, speaking over Theo's head.

He walked up to Laine, very close, so that they were within touching distance.

"But I feel so bad for you." He sighed. "You have so *much* potential."

Laine looked around a little. "I do?"

"Yes. You've just never had the opportunities to showcase it. I pity you, really." He frowned. "Your father agreed with me. The kingdom would be far better off if you had been the eldest. Strythio is... mediocre at the best of times. I don't hold any respect for him. But, you, Princess Laine. I do."

Laine blinked. Was that really true? Her father thought she was more deserving of the throne than Theo was? Part of her hoped it was true, because she'd spent her whole life being viewed as second best to Theo, and maybe, maybe it would be nice to have that change for once. But of course, no, she could never *want* that to be true. That would ruin Theo, he would never get over it.

Still, a part of her couldn't help but feel proud.

"What do you mean?" She whispered, silence prevailing throughout the courtyard. Theo tilted his head completely up to watch the interaction. "I don't have any children. So, I'm naming you and Nikoliah as my heirs, provided you stay together. Of course, if not, then it'll be just you and whoever you marry. When I retire, the kingdom will go back to you."

Laine's mouth dropped open in a kind of shocked 'o' shape. She looked down at Theo, who met her eyes. Beckett noticed this interaction and sighed. "Don't worry about him, he's out of the picture." He reassured to Laine. "You'll have the crown one day. But for now..." He muttered, looking around. "Ah!"

An angel left through the main door of the castle, walking gracefully as she held out a dark green coloured cushion in front of her body, and on the cushion was a crown. Theo's crown.

"Please don't, please." Theo whispered, unable to even stand from how weak he felt.

"Well, Strythio, I do believe that the law states that should someone disarm and defeat the monarch, they can take the crown. And, you do look pretty defeated right now. Do you feel defeated?" He asked, smirking as he leant down. Theo shook his head repeatedly.

The angel carrying the crown kneeled as if she were proposing, head bowed, and Lord Beckett peeled the crown off the cushion, dismissing the angel quickly. Theo's breath hitched as Beckett put the crown atop his head, the halo above his head reflecting beautifully onto the gold. He stood in front of the now six in the morning sunset, smiling cockily. Then, he stepped behind Theo, hooking his hands under Theo's arms and pulling him up onto his knees, facing the whole crowd of angels and demons. Laine stood behind them with Sir Garrah, Jaymie and Kougan. She was sniffling, lip quivering as she tried to make sense of this.

"Now, this is what I've been waiting for." Beckett announced. "The public trial of Strythio Virzor."

He walked a few paces around, beckoning the same angel who had delivered him the crown. She stopped just next to him - her dark teal coloured skin contrasting beautifully with deep blue hair that fell just to her lips. She had a sword holstered in her belt, and was notably still wearing rose gold jewellery over her armour, which dangled upon her wrist as she held out a rolled up ball of rope.

"Thank you, Fiducia." Beckett smiled. "You can do the honours."

She grinned silently, nodding and kneeling down behind where Theo was sitting. She reached around and grabbed Theo's wrists, yanking them behind his body.

"Ack, get the fuck off." He protested, weakly due to his heavily injured and emotionally distressed state. The girl, Fiducia, grabbed him by the hair and pulled his head backwards. He let out a gasp of pain, completely immobilising him while Fiducia conjoined his hands behind his back, wrapping them in a thick rope and tying a knot.

She released her grip on his hair, standing wordlessly and scampering back over to where Beckett was standing.

"Thank you." He smiled. "You can stay here and assist." He told her, and she gave a genuinely joyous grin. He clapped his hands together in front of him.

"Right." He announced loudly, stepping so that he was standing just behind Theo, back a few metres from the wall so that the whole courtyard could see them. "During Theo's coronation, he took an oath. Do you remember what promises you made in that oath?" He asked, looking down towards Theo. "I sincerely hope you do."

He did remember. But it was stupid, it was just one of those things. Like, when you get married and you promise all that big stuff about forever, even though a good portion of people get divorced. It was just like that, just like, 'yes, I accept this responsibility, blah, blah, let's get to the fun part of the evening'.

"As king, Strythio vowed to act in the best interest of the kingdom, and to serve and protect his people."

He paused for a moment, letting the whole crowd absorb the information.

"But he didn't, did he? He got a little bit scared and literally crossed dimensions to escape his responsibilities. And when he did that, he committed a crime against his kingdom. Treason. Treason, because he allowed his people to get hurt. His people, or the people that used to be his. My people, now. I take extreme offence to the fact that Strythio has hurt *my* people, made them scared, destroyed their homes. I can't let it go unpunished."

Theo's eyes widened, and a series of noises erupted from the crowd. Some of them being pleased shouts and claps from the angels, others being worried gasps mixed with angry shouts from the residents of Klaevr.

"I grew up in the nineteenth century, and people were hanged or beheaded for treason back then." He announced. Theo looked around panickedly, and if he had been able to turn his body all the way around he would've met eyes with his sister as she started to cry. "But I won't be so merciful. Do you keep your dungeons clean?"

"Please, please, don't- please." Theo cried in a whisper. "I didn't do anything to you."

Beckett laughed. A genuine, hearty laugh. "Goodness, you're naive. It's not about you, it's about what you *have*, and what you've taken for granted. Klaevr deserves a ruler that gives a shit about them." He nodded, kicking Theo's back with his dominant leg, and because his hands were bound behind him, he had no way of defending himself as he fell forward onto the dirt. "And that isn't you."

Theo had begun to sit himself back up when Beckett kicked him in the side of his head. He wasn't that far from the ground, so the impact of the force was a lot stronger than it would've been otherwise. The moment his head hit the floor he was knocked out, vision flickering to a dizzy haze of darkness. It was at this point that Laine broke out of her paralyzed stillness and ran over towards them, skidding to the ground with a halt. She pulled his head into her lap.

"You aren't- you aren't actually going to put him in prison, are you?" She asked gently, looking up at Amadeus, who groaned.

"No, not here, at least. But, you are more than welcome to relinquish your title as a Princess and join him if you have objections." He said. "In fact, the same goes for all of you demons. You're either on my side or his, and considering he's on the ground covered in his own blood right now, I hope you can make the right choice."

Laine grabbed onto Theo's hand that was still tied to the other and held it tightly. She knew the choice she had to make, and she knew exactly what her brother would tell her to do. That didn't make it easy though. She pulled Theo into her lap protectively.

The light was beginning to shine through over the skyline of Klaevr as the sun rose. The air was cold and crisp against the orange sky,

courtyard completely silent other than the shifting of feet against gravel. Nobody could say anything, only watch with their eyes fixated on the Princess as she held her brother in her arms and started to cry.
Beckett had turned away at this point, beginning to walk towards the castle. Fiducia gave Laine a sadistic smile as she approached, bending down to her level and prying Theo from her arms.
"No, please, just a minute." She whispered, but the angel girl completely ignored her and hoisted him up into her arms, his own body dangling limply.
She followed the direction that Lord Beckett walked in, and it left Laine sitting cross legged on the ground, tears flowing down her face. She scrambled to her feet and stumbled back to the edge of the crowd where Sir Garrah and her boyfriend were. All eyes were locked onto her shaking figure. The Princess made it over to them and took Nikoliah from the older soldier's arms, holding him close to her chest as he stirred a little. This time, she wasn't going to let anyone take him from her. Not for anything.
The double doors on the second floor balcony of the castle opened - the balcony that monarchs used to address the kingdom, as it overlooked the whole courtyard from the centre and could also see over most of the kingdom. The noise of the doors opening created enough attention that both the angels and demons alike looked up to it.
Beckett stepped out of the doors, making his way all the way up to the railing. From his position, he could see everything. He could see his own soldiers, happy in their success and believing they had saved the kingdom from downfall. He could see the demons, distressed and panicked. He saw Princess Laine sitting on the ground, cradling her boyfriend - and he thought for a moment that he should ask Fiducia to start preparing the infirmary for the injured that he cared about.
Everyone was looking up at him, expecting something, like a speech. Instead, he breathed out, looking over the kingdom and his successes. There were still many demons that weren't fighting in the town centre, probably oblivious to what had happened. But, it didn't matter - he would get them back.
The sky looked beautiful. In fact, with some houses still on fire, lifting plumes of smoke like waterfalls in the sky, the whole kingdom looked beautiful.
He looked down at his watch. Six thirty. About the time that the festivities would usually start, the servants would start getting up and

sorting things out, preparing breakfast. He exhaled. Everything seemed to have worked quite well. He was pleased with himself.

It was a new day for Klaevr.

TWO YEARS LATER

XXVIII

Nikoliah rolled over, hand searching around in the dark for the off button on his alarm clock. It screamed incessantly at him for a prolonged amount of time that he was certain would wake up the whole castle. He slapped the bedside table like it had wronged him a few times before he hit the top of the clock, silencing it for the next twenty-four hours.

He groaned, staring up at the ceiling for a few minutes. He didn't want to get up, because the minute he got out of bed he knew he wouldn't be able to get back into it for at least another eighteen hours, if he was lucky. His mind relayed the events of yesterday, and the day before, and how today was gonna be pretty much the exact same. All of a sudden, the patterns on the ceiling felt very interesting. Then, he felt a soft kiss on the top of his head, accompanied with a whisper. "Come on, love, you're gonna be late."

With another reluctant groan, he nodded and sat up, rubbing his eyes in the darkness. "I don't get it, why can't we just push the day back two hours and finish at ten?" He complained, looking over to the clock that was, in fact, not playing a trick on him, and did correctly read five forty five AM. Laine giggled and rolled over.

"Someone's jealous." She teased, pulling the duvet back over her head.

"Yeah, I am jealous." He huffed, pushing his pyjama bottoms off and starting to get changed into his casual day uniform. It was just really a pair of dark grey trousers and a button-up light grey shirt, with a cotton-blue stretch of fabric tied around the torso of the shirt - a leather sword holster attached to it. All the other knights had the same uniform, just with different coloured fabric to match the colour of their horns and tail.

He leant down on one knee in a proposal position, tying the laces of his black boots up. When that was done, he looked up back to the bed. Laine was sitting up properly, wearing a red tank top that was visible over the duvet. Her hair dye had faded out now, leaving it completely naturally brown. She held Nikoliah's sword out towards him, because he'd left it on her side of the bed.

"Thanks." He muttered groggily, taking it and slipping it into the holster. He walked into the bathroom and splashed some water on his face,eyeing himself up in the mirror.

God, he looked exhausted. He'd been keeping his hair short, not letting it grow past his ears (mainly because it was easy to keep, but also because a certain blue-haired angel he worked with had kept teasing him that it looked scruffy). His light grey skin was rough and uncared for, also observable by the stubble beginning to protrude from around his jaw and neck that he hadn't bothered to shave yet. Laine had made a joke that it made kissing him more interesting, and whatever the Crown Princess says goes, he supposed.

He fidgeted with his shirt collar a few times. Then he untied the blue cloth around his waist, moving it up a little and redoing the knot so that he was sure it wouldn't slip. But, it didn't look right, so he did it again. Then he noticed a scuff on the tip of his right boot, and he tilted his head back with an annoyed huff as he came to the realisation he'd have to re-polish them. Not now, though. He was already dangerously late. He spared a glance at his watch to confirm that.

It was bang on six as he left the bathroom, stretching his arms out above his head. He then leant down towards his girlfriend on the bed, with the intention of a quick goodbye kiss. But instead, Laine wrapped her arms around his shoulders and gave him a deeper kiss on the lips, before moving to pepper kisses all along his jawline. He smiled at the action, and Laine used the advantage of him leaning down to pull his whole body onto the bed in one swift movement.

Nikoliah chuckled as he was pulled completely on top of her, rolling to the side so that his sword wouldn't brush against her exposed skin. "Stop it, I ironed this shirt!" He laughed, trying to playfully wriggle out of her cuddly grasp. Laine then rolled over on top of him, to be sitting over his torso, legs either side of him.

"Well, it isn't my fault it fits you so well." She smirked. When she leant down to kiss him again, he grabbed her waist and pushed her off of him back onto the thick mattress, to which she gave a yelp.

"The next time Beckett yells at me about punctuality I'll attribute it to you." He accused while smiling, sitting up on the edge of the bed. "Now get some more sleep." He instructed, pressing one last kiss to her forehead with a hug.

"Alright, alright. Have lots of fun. I love you."

"I love you too."

Nikoliah swung the door to the room open, stepping out into the corridor. He brushed his shirt down a few times, but it was pretty much too far gone for him to try and unwrinkle it with his hands. The moment he did so, Laine flicked the bedside lamp off and curled up again - something he desperately craved at this ungodly hour.

But, no. Instead, he made his way along the corridor - down the spiral staircase that he was *technically* not permitted to use, because it was for servants only, but he was in a little bit of a rush, and this time six years ago he *was* a servant, so maybe he was just staying humble. It was a bit of a trek towards his office, as his and Laine's bedroom had been moved to the West wing, where it had previously been in the East. This was mainly because it was more convenient position wise (having a window that overlooked the whole kingdom, being right atop the ballroom etc, but kind of also because one too many servants had found Laine sitting on Theo's bed, usually silently as she picked cotton off the duvet. She'd taken to doing that a lot, and it had worried a lot of people.

Nikoliah had gently suggested that they moved a little further away. For her sake.

He got to the ground floor quickly, tapping along the wooden planks of the corridor, lined with paintings and cream-coloured wallpaper. He made the journey along the hallway as efficiently as possible, but he had to stop about three times when someone of a lower rank would salute him. It was tedious, sure, but he couldn't say he didn't like the power rush.

Those who were not of high enough rank to get saluted did wear the same thing as him, just without the band of coloured cloth around the midsection. Instead, they wore black cloth, which made it pretty easy to identify knights by the (usually) bright colours alone. He did eventually get to where his day would start, that being his shared office - the fifth door on the left of the corridor.

He pushed the door open carefully, looking at the ground as he shut it behind him.

Fiducia was leaning back in her chair, one leg crossed over the other with her eyebrows raised. She was wearing the exact same thing as Nikoliah, instead with a mid-dark blue strip of cloth around her torso. She, of course, was an angel (one of the few that permanently lived in Klaevr still), so didn't have a signature colour like Nikoliah did. Therefore, she got to choose her own, and she chose the same colour as her hair - which had now grown out to her neck, looking strikingly vibrant against her teal skin. She always kept it back in a ponytail, with just her messy fringe not tied up.

She pulled back the unbuttoned sleeve of her shirt and tapped her watch twice in quick succession.

Nikoliah rolled his eyes and flopped down in his chair. "Yeah yeah, I'm late." He admitted, dropping his arms onto his desk as he leant forwards as if he was going to collapse onto the wood. It was still dark outside, so the room was lit with candles both on his and Fidcuia's desks, which were actually just the same square table that they'd metaphorically split in half with their possessions. They had a big pile of paper and an ink pot which they too shared. But, other than that, it was mainly combat stuff kept in the room.

One corner was completely full with swords and shields on the wall (which were mainly decorative), and the other had just a wall of shelves, all full of different boots and assault vests and everything they could possibly use to do their jobs.

Fiducia slid a sheet of paper over towards him - a schedule for the day. He scanned his eyes over it briefly. "Beckett gave you this?" He asked, and she nodded. Fiducia brought her hands up to the level of her chest and began using sign language to communicate her next words.

'I bumped into him in the corridor. He's concerned about this evening, wants us to make sure it's gonna be okay. Which is unlikely.'

"Ugh." Nikoliah gave an extended groan. "He's always got something to be concerned about... And it's always us that have to run around after him." He complained. Fiducia snickered at him.

'Not to sound invalidating but that is what we get paid for.' She argued, standing from her seat and walking to lean over her work partner. She pointed at the first timing on the sheet, being about five minutes from the current time. Nikoliah's eyes scanned over the whole morning routine.

6:15 - Reveille for all soldiers, practice fighting drills and castle defence

8:00 - Breakfast for unranked soldiers / Street and house searches in city centre
10:00 - Breakfast for ranked soldiers
10:15 - Swordsmanship training for young apprentice soldiers (Fiducia to lead)
12:00 - Lunch for all soldiers

 "He expects too much of us." He complained. "And why did he specify that *you* get to lead the sword shit? I'm really good with my sword!" Fiducia grinned with a bit of a chuckle. '*I kick your ass every time we spar, and he watches nearly all of them. I could fuck you up if I wanted to.*' She signed, moving to sit atop Nikoliah's desk.
"That doesn't mean I'm bad, it just means you're good!" He bargained, voice ending on a child-like whine. She rolled her eyes.
'*Remember that time you got disarmed by a thirteen year old?*'
"I let him win." He defended. "He was having a really bad confidence day, he cried to me the morning before practice! So I let him win and now everyone won't stop bringing it up." Nikoliah pouted, crossing his arms and leaning against the wall. Fiducia slid off the desk with a glance at her watch and swung the door open.
'*Whatever you say.*'

Nikoliah took a deep breath in as he overlooked the large dining hall. He was so hungry, but it was only eight o' clock. Him and Fiducia had been running around all morning trying to train their soldiers, but considering that the latter didn't speak at all, he had resided to do most of the shouting. Which made them like him a lot less than her. He really just wanted to collapse onto a table and shove a full English down his throat, but he still had two hours until it was his turn.
He was not happy about it.
Fiducia stepped up next to him, trying so desperately to ignore the smell of cooked food and porridge that they couldn't have. They would be eating later, with all of the higher-ups. It was mainly because the real 'big dogs' didn't like to be up so early. (He knew that it was mainly for Laine's sake that the important people ate later, and he would never berate her for it, but it was a little annoying to watch the regular soldiers eat).
They were all lined up, sitting along columns of wooden benches as they dug into their meals. Nikoliah averted his gaze.

'Go and take a piece of toast if you're gonna be grumpy about it.' Fiducia told him, flat expression on her face. 'They can't exactly tell you off for it.' He nodded as he conceded, stepping slowly over to the long buffet table with a stack of toast on the end. Without a moment's hesitation, he grabbed a slice and began to tear off the crust.

Fiducia looked away from him with an amused smirk, staring at the clock on the wall for a moment. And then, an unranked older teenager came scampering up to her.

"Ma'am, I think Sir Renton is stealing." He said with a timid point towards the table, and Fiducia laughed out loud, bringing her hand to her face afterwards to conceal how funny it was.

Firstly, it was funny because Nikoliah was acting *exactly* like he was stealing, glancing around suspiciously before snatching food off the table and holding it behind his back. Secondly, it was funny because this young soldier had used Nikoliah's "proper" title, replacing his first name for his last when referring to him. That was funny because he *hated* it. She'd heard stories about him being very grouchy when he was young, because it wasn't his place to correct any seniors on his name.

But ever since he'd become a knight, he'd been outwardly resenting people addressing him with his surname. Fiducia wasn't sure how this young man had become accustomed to it, but, boy, was it hilarious.

She regained her composure and signed a quick 'thank you', feigning that it was very important to her. It was entertaining at least - all of the castle soldiers respected her significantly more than they respected Nikoliah (she assumed that was either because she was an angel or he was a dumbass), but the general public liked him a lot more. Which she assumed was because she was an angel, full stop.

The boy nodded and went to sit back down, just as Nikoliah returned, still chewing on a mouthful.

'Better?'

"Mmhmhm." He hummed, drawling around his mouthful very unprofessionally. After he'd finished swallowing, he crossed his arms in front of him. "What's next for us?"

Fiducia pulled her schedule out of her pocket and highlighted that they would have to go into the city centre to confiscate any illegal-looking items. God, what a walk.

"I don't know what the King wants from us, I can only carry so many flares." Nikoliah said, exasperated. Fiducia smiled in amusement and gestured towards the door.

'*You're taking the lead on this. They like you the most.*' She bargained. Nikoliah rolled his eyes at that, pushing the door open and holding it with his foot as she walked past, out of the bustling dining area.

"They like me better because I don't have a glowing ring of light above my head." He teased, following her out of the room, catching up so that they walked side by side down the corridor.

'*Touche.*' She signed, more to herself, because Nikoliah couldn't see it since they were walking side by side.

It had been like that a lot in Klaevr as of late. Hate towards angels. Which was exactly why Beckett was so worried. Beckett had been so unbelievably harsh as a king for the first year, and people began to grow sick of his behaviour. It was the two year anniversary of when he'd taken control over the kingdom, and on this exact date last year, there had been a massive riot from the civilians. A riot that Nikoliah had been pushed into with a harsh instruction of 'stop them'.

He had not stopped them, despite his best efforts. In fact, they had only stopped when Fiducia had come out. They were all pretty scared of her. Because of this anniversary, Beckett had been full of paranoia - convinced the same thing would happen. So, he'd been sending his two best soldiers running around trying to find things out about any plans going on underground. Nikoliah had personally opted *not* to tell Laine that this was going on. She wasn't very good with dates, so was pretty oblivious as to what day it was, and she only got upset when anyone brought it up.

He hated seeing her upset, so he might have been telling little white lies about the work he'd been doing as of late.

They made it all the way out of the front doors of the castle, still walking side by side as Nikoliah made small talk about his evening yesterday, and Fiducia just nodded along as she inputted the occasional raise of her eyebrows or light snicker at something dumb. It wasn't until they reached the actual body of the town, about half an hour later, that their conversation was cut short.

"King Beckett's lackeys are here!" A teenage boy called from where he was leant behind a market stall. The street was lined with them, most quiet because it was only early morning. At the shout that the teenage boy made, people started to murmur and direct their attention towards the two of them, scattering and going to stand nearer to the doors of their houses.

Nikoliah dug his black leather boots into the ground, halting and frowning a little.

"Put the shit away, put it away!" Someone whispered, ducking underneath her stall. Another girl snickered loudly.

"Conspicuous. Really fooled them there, good job." She laughed.

"Um," Nikoliah started, glancing between the fifty or so people. Fiducia was already walking over to the girl who had originally whispered, pulling boxes out from under her stall. "Do you think we could... maybe not tonight?"

There was a dead silence that followed and the second of the girls bit her lip. "Look, Nikoliah, I'm sure-"

Fiducia cleared her throat loudly.

"Look, *Sir*," She corrected with an eye roll. "I'm sure you mean well, but you were pretty close with King Theo, I don't know why you're trying to pretend you weren't."

"I'm not trying to pretend I wasn't, but I have to deal with the aftermath of whatever you plan." He sighed. Fiducia came over with a handful of fireworks, waving them in the air as a 'okay got evidence we were here, let's go' kind of signal.

"Alright, well, you've tried, so just go back to Amadeus and tell him you tried, but we aren't letting anything slip." She said, leaning against the stall selling apples. Nikoliah rubbed his eyes and glanced over to Fiducia, who clicked her fingers twice and pointed down the road and started walking.

"Well, you guys aren't the only street in the kingdom, so we kinda have to go around a little more than this." He explained, and then cursed himself for how stupid he sounded explaining his instructions to these random people. He looked down at himself and took a deep breath in. "Um, okay, have a good day guys."

He began to walk away beside his partner, and they got a few steps down the street before one of the girls called out towards him.

"You realise you walk with a limp, right?"

Nikoliah flicked his head around, spinning completely to face the girl a moment later. He was completely positive that he *did not* walk with a limp. After those angels had hurt his leg pretty badly, he'd spent six whole months in which he wasn't meant to lean on it - but he had far too much pride to use crutches or anything, so maybe there was a small possibility it hadn't healed all that well. He stared at her dumbfounded for a moment and then he responded.

"No, I don't." He argued in response, eyes flicking down to his legs and back up.

There was a chorus of murmurs in agreement from the crowd. A chorus that had Nikoliah furrowing his eyebrows. He choked a little in exasperation. "I don't, do I?" He asked again, looking towards Fiducia. She thinned her lips out and held her hand up, waving it flatly, like an instruction of 'a little', accompanied by a tilt of her head as she bit her teeth together.

He swallowed, absorbing the silent point being made towards him. "Well, that's just because I'm ageing." He fumbled. "My joints aren't as good as they used to be." He said slowly, and a few people laughed. The younger of the two girls raised her eyebrows and crossed her eyes.

"What are you, like twenty-five? You aren't exactly a senior."

Nikoliah frowned deeply. "I'm twenty-one, but..."

The girl grimaced. "Yikes, you must get stressed pretty often. You look older."

He blinked a few times in quick succession. Fiducia hit him on the arm and he turned to look at her.

'They're teasing, come on, we have shit to get done.' She signed. He nodded and spun back around to the direction they were heading, one hand holding onto his sword through its holster as he tried to brush their words off. They walked away from that street (and those particularly upsetting girls), but as they walked to the next one, Nikoliah couldn't help but keep sparing glances down to his leg.

Maybe he did walk with a limp.

XXIX

Laine sat on her bed, brushing her still-wet hair slowly in front of the ornate gold mirror on the wall. She was well rested now, and had been woken up by red sunlight streaming through the curtains about thirty minutes ago. She was wearing one of her favourite dresses - dark green with lace sleeves, falling down to her knees. She paired it with some traditional black heeled shoes the same colour as her headband and eyeliner.

The truth was that she was procrastinating going downstairs for breakfast. Which might have been selfish, because she knew they wouldn't start eating without her. It was just that her father had chosen to visit the kingdom today, and she hadn't spoken to him (or even sent him a letter) in a good few months. She hadn't wanted to, not after what she found out about her mother, and certainly not after he returned to the kingdom acting all buddy-buddy with King Beckett after the fight was over.

She fastened her earrings with a deep breath in, glancing herself over in the mirror once more. Her bed reached out to her, but it was unattainable until at least the weekend. She tried her best to remain grateful that her day didn't start at six AM like her boyfriend's.

Much to her delight, she made it down to the smaller dining room by nine fifty-nine. It was the same dining room that she'd first been told about Theo getting engaged, so a sour feeling generated in her mouth every time she walked in.

Already sitting at the table next to Fiducia, Nikoliah seemed to be deep in a conversation with Dyran. He'd been trying really desperately to repair a good relationship with the man that he hoped would be his father-in-law one day. He'd had a very rocky relationship with the ex-king, but as of late it seemed to be looking up.

Despite this, his expression morphed to one of relief the moment Laine walked in. Dyran raised his eyebrows.

"You'd really choose to wear that on today of all days? What is it, like a political statement?" He asked with a frown.

Laine glanced down to her outfit. "What?"

Nikoliah kicked Dyran's foot under the table. The man frowned instantly deeper and snapped his head to look at the soldier. He leant forward, raising his hand over the left side of his face to block Laine from seeing his mouth move as he whispered.

"She doesn't know."

Dyran's face flickered from one of anger to confusion to realisation. "Nevermind, honey, come sit down." He smiled, outstretching his arms. Laine frowned and glanced over to the three others in the room. Did they know something she didn't?

Either way, she moved to pull her chair out and take a seat next to her father, who pressed a kiss to her forehead. Nikoliah was opposite her, and Fiducia to his left. The room was completely silent in an awkward lull for a few moments, but it was broken when the doors opened and King Beckett walked in with a straight set jaw and overconfident composure. Instantly, both of the knights in the room shot to their feet and stood at attention with a forty-five degree bow of their heads, the exact same way they would address the man had they bumped into him in the corridor. Laine rolled her eyes as Beckett's smile grew.

She thought it was dumb as hell. It made them seem lesser than the others in the room, like a patronising display of inferiority. And she *did not* like it when people undermined her boyfriend just because he was ex-mortal.

It was so stupid, because Beckett was also ex-mortal. But he had this kind of sense of superiority because he's been dead for a long time, or he's powerful, or whatever.

"Thank you." The King nodded, instructing them to sit back down, which they did. He sat at the head of the table, looking at his watch with a frown. "I told those servants ten on the dot. Remind me to fire them before lunch time." He laughed, and so did Dyran.

Once he'd come down from this high of amusement, Beckett leant forward. "Goodness me, how have you been, Dyran?"

Laine completely tuned the conversation out - not even bothering to listen to the small talk being made. She didn't care about it. Suddenly the grains of the wood felt really entertaining to her as she swung her legs under the table. There were considerably less people seated around the table as of late than there should, or would have been.

Most of the higher ranking soldiers had given their titles up when it was demanded that they work under King Beckett, just opting to live regular deaths as normal residents of the city. Anything but obey a tyrant angel. Sir Garrah had been one of these people who had refused to work for Amadeus, and it had hit Nikoliah pretty hard having to lose the only guidance he'd ever had. He hadn't spoken to him in almost eighteen months now, which had both caused his independence to grow and his confidence to fall. Laine knew deep down that Nikoliah would have definitely resigned from his position had he not been in a relationship with the Crown Princess, but she was also secretly glad he had chosen to stay. He wouldn't have really been able to have a life afterwards anyway, and the strain would have almost certainly meant the end of them being together - yeesh, imagine trying to integrate back into society after dating the future queen.

Maybe she was getting a bit full of herself. She wondered briefly if it was immoral for her to have kept her role after the fall too, but it wasn't like she was faced with much choice.

She must have really zoned out, because she looked back down to the table and there was a plate in front of her. An egg, two sausages, a piece of bacon and a hash brown. Full English - minus the beans, because she didn't like them, but everyone else on the table had them.

Fiducia smirked at the way Nikoliah was eating slowly, pushing his food around his plate like he wasn't hungry. She kicked him under the table and they both started snickering just below the conversation of the older men. Laine felt a twinge of jealousy grow in the pit of her stomach at the way they were obviously laughing about some kind of inside joke she wasn't in on. She shuffled uncomfortably in her chair and angrily cut the corner off her hash brown.

Nikoliah raised his eyebrows at the sound of the knife digging into the plate. Putting his cutlery onto the table, he cleared his throat.

"Laine?" He called, and she looked up with a smile. Sir Dyran and King Beckett looked over to him also, despite the fact that Nikoliah hadn't intended for them to be involved in the conversation. "I was thinking that maybe we could... I don't know, maybe we could go out for dinner tonight. There's a new restaurant that opened in Stonbrin last week."

Laine grinned. "What's the occasion?" She teased, voice light and airy.
"Well, you know, I've been so busy with work recently, and so have you. Just kinda feel like we deserve a nice evening out." He offered.
Beckett dropped his cutlery suddenly, causing the whole room to tense up as they looked at him.
"I hope you are aware that you are working tonight, Nikoliah. It would be a real shame if you got put on unpaid suspension for a week because you want to have an evening off without booking it in advance." He warned, body language confident and cautionary.
Now, it wasn't as if Nikoliah and Fiducia were given much time off. They were entitled to a week's total of paid leave over each year - provided that they only worked six day weeks - alternating between days on weekends. It was the kind of thing that they couldn't really argue, and could just learn to live with for the sake of their positions. It isn't very often that your job gives you free meals and housing.
"If you feel that is necessary, then so be it, Your Majesty. I would like the evening off to spend with my girlfriend." He replied, voice not wavering.
Fiducia hit Nikoliah lightly on the arm.
'*You cannot seriously leave me alone tonight to deal with the riots.*' She signed, and Nikoliah was the only one who could actually understand it. He'd gone about a month of working with her before he had asked that she teach him, simply because he got so bored of having conversations with a wall. She would never ever admit it, but Fiduca had been really glad he had wanted to learn sign language. Nikoliah didn't want the others at the table to understand their conversation, so he replied in the same manner.
'*I wasn't any help last year, and I need to get Laine out of the kingdom so she doesn't remember the date and get upset.*'
"Enough." Dyran said rather suddenly. "It's quite rude to exclude us from your conversation. Apologise to the King so that we can finish our meal." He instructed, and this is where the young man he was talking to made his first mistake.
He rolled his eyes.
"Right, Nikoliah, get out." Beckett snapped, pointing towards the door with his fork in his hand.
"What?"
"How dare you talk to me like that!" He raised his voice. Nikoliah shrunk back in on himself as he noted his second mistake. "I am *not* happy with you, young man. Go and sit in my office and we can have a talk about your behaviour later."

He swallowed and glanced down at his still-full plate. Laine felt anxiety build up in her chest. She loved her boyfriend, she really did, but he was quite stubborn and he *did not* like being bossed around. She looked up at him worriedly as he blinked.

Beckett grew impatient very quickly. "Nikoliah, out! Now, before you lose your rank!" He yelled. Fiducia frowned at the yelling, although considering she had worked for Beckett for about three years now, she had grown quite accustomed to it. Nikoliah swallowed and pushed his chair out, walking behind the other knight and out the room, abandoning his plate of food.

"God, it's like disciplining a child." He groaned. "I apologise. Although, you'll be lucky, Laine. He certainly won't be doing any work this evening." Dyran shook his head. "Honestly, Amadeus, I'm not too sure why you keep him. He's seriously gone downhill these past few years. He was one of my best when I was king, but, ever since he started messing around with my daughter, he's just-"

"Dad."

"But hey, at least you've got this one." Dyran continued, gesturing to Fiducia. "I've never heard her run her mouth like he does."

Beckett laughed. "Goodness, maybe I'll have to cut that boy's tongue out. He's a fine soldier but he talks far too much." He suggested, no actual intention behind the words, but it had Laine downcasting her eyes and sharing a knowing glance across the table at Fiducia. There were no words involved in the exchange, but it said enough. This was going to be a long meal.

Laine and Nikoliah held hands as they stepped out of the train station and into the city centre of Stonbrin. The latter hadn't yet detailed to his girlfriend exactly what Beckett had said to him inside his office, but what he did leave with was the evening off and the next two weeks of his work unpaid.

He seemed like he didn't want to talk about it, so Laine didn't push it. It wasn't like he would have spoken about it anyway, considering the sheer amount of people swarming them. Laine was a princess, and since her mother had come from this kingdom, she was *technically* a princess here too. But, that was iffy, as she had never even spoken to the King and Queen (her auntie and uncle, she supposed) and didn't plan to.

It was fine though, because they'd only just arrived, and Nikoliah had been careful to make a reservation in a nice restaurant near to the train station. He had changed into a dark blue suit with a light blue tie, the same shade as the dress that Laine was wearing.

The restaurant itself was classy. Overhead lights looked down upon black tables in dimmed warm tones. Each table had a vase with black roses atop it, as well as pre-laid out silverware and heavy marble chairs.

The server led them to a secluded booth in the corner, one that Nikoliah had specifically asked for because he knew Laine got anxious easily when in the public eye. The moment they sat down, she pulled her notepad out.

"Can I get you two any drinks?"

Laine leant over towards Nikoliah to look at the drinks menu. "That one looks alright." She said, pointing to a rather expensive bottle of red wine." Nikoliah hummed in agreement. "Yeah, we'll get this one please." Laine finished with a smile as she rested her right hand on Nikoliah's under the table.

The server frowned with an 'awh' sound. "God, I can't believe you're old enough to drink. I remember when you were born. Nineteen years, huh?" She reminisced, all the while scribbling the order down on the notepad she had.

"Yeah, I know." She laughed, trying to be polite, but she couldn't even count the number of people that had said that exact thing to her on one hand. "Can we also get some garlic bread to share?"

"Of course! That'll be out as soon as possible."

The moment the server was out of sight, Laine slumped down backwards in her seat - abandoning all 'ladylike' posture with a sigh.

"You alright, darling?" Nikoliah snickered with amusement.

"Long day." She drawled. "And I've got that meeting tomorrow morning. You mustn't let me drink too much this evening."

"Is this the kind of meeting that I'm meant to be at?" Nikoliah asked, and Laine sat herself back up.

"No, don't worry. It's just something all the heirs to the thrones of all the kingdoms do. Kind of like a youth club but we talk about politics and leadership strategies." She announced, doing a little sarcastic set of jazz hands. "It's only annual, and the one I went to last year was boring as anything."

"Sounds fun." He replied, equally sarcastically. "Glad I don't have to go, though. I don't think I could sit through something like that."

"Mhm. You sit through enough droning from Beckett as it is." She laughed. "Proud of you for standing up for yourself today, though."

The server came back into view, one hand balancing a tray of glasses and the other hand holding a dark-coloured bottle. She set the glasses down in front of each of them.

"I'm not sure it's a good sign if my big victories consist of rolling my eyes at my superiors and then getting screamed at for it."

The server chucked as she poured the wine. "I hear that. My boss is an asshole too." She confided, placing the now half empty bottle back on the table and dismissing herself.

Laine picked the glass up and took a small sip. "Did he really *scream* at you or is that a hyperbole?"

"In front of my soldiers." Nikoliah nodded, watching as Laine's eyes widened.

"No shit, seriously? The younger ones?"

"Yep." The knight nodded once more. "He dragged me outside to where they were doing their swordsmanship stuff with Cia, made them all stop and watch as he yelled at me for ten minutes."

Laine cringed, reaching across the table and taking his hand above it.

"God, they're never gonna respect me again. They won't forget that, and neither will I."

"That's what alcohol is for, love." Laine joked, swishing the crimson liquid around in her glass. "Here," She began, raising her glass to the centre of the table. "To rolling your eyes at my dad." The Princess toasted. Nikoliah laughed and clinked his glass with hers before they both drank.

"To be fair, I probably shouldn't have." Nikoliah groaned. "He was starting to like me, too."

Laine frowned. "He's just been... a little passive as of late. It's kind of worrying."

"What do you mean?"

"I mean, all he does is follow Beckett around and agree with him. I could have sworn he used to have a personality." She joked.

"Think he's just getting old, babe."

"I think he's scared of him."

Nikoliah blinked a few times. "You think your dad is scared of Beckett?" He clarified, and his girlfriend nodded.

"He wasn't, he didn't used to be. I think what he did to Theo really got to him. Psychologically. He's embarrassed that his bloodline has been disrupted by an ex-mortal, right? But after Beckett retires, it goes back to me and all is well."

Nikoliah gave her a slightly confused look.

"He wants to stay on Beckett's good side so that he doesn't change his mind about passing the crown down to me. He can pick someone else at any moment. Hell, if I mess something up he's probably gonna give it to Fiducia."

"So Dyran has kind of evolved to be exactly how King Beckett wants. Survival of the fittest, but he's doing it for you."

They paused the conversation briefly as the server placed the sharing platter of garlic bread in between them. Nikoliah reached for a slice as Laine replied.

"I don't think he's doing it for me. He's doing it for the Virzor name. I mean, nobody even *asked* me if I wanted to be the Queen one day."

"Do you?"

Laine inhaled with her thoughts. Over the last couple of years, it had been something that she'd really grown to accept would just be the case. The first few months it hadn't felt real, and even though she had been the heir to the throne while Theo was king, they were only a year apart so it wasn't like it would ever actually go to her.

"I mean, yeah. Yeah, it'd be cool." She started, tearing off a piece of garlic bread. "I would feel a lot better about it had Theo abdicated. I'm not sure, it feels like I'm stealing from him."

That was simply because the throne was never meant to be hers - and Theo had known it was meant to be his, and he was happy with it. Laine didn't think that Theo had been a bad king, just had some bad circumstances. She felt a lot like she didn't deserve the crown at all. Nikoliah had spent a long time trying to convince her that she did.

"Would he have wanted you to be the Queen?" Nikoliah asked, serious expression on his face. He could easily answer the question himself, but he wanted Laine to say it and truly understand it. However, she didn't, opting to completely deflect.

"I hate how we talk about him like he's dead."

Nikoliah nodded, acknowledging his mistake of using the past tense. It had been what most people had started doing. Nobody really wanted to talk about him as if he were a real person, more like an ideology or political statement about carelessness. Nikoliah hummed around his mouthful of garlic bread.

"Okay, sorry. Would he want you to be the Queen?"

"Yes, you know he would." She grumbled.

XXX

Their meal continued quite pleasantly - ordering their food and digging into it the moment that it arrived, laughing and talking over the now empty bottle of wine.
"And she seriously said that?!" Nikoliah laughed out, covering his mouth with the back of his hand, clutching a piece of steak on his fork. Laine nodded, banging her hand lightly on the table to regulate her laughter. It took them a few minutes following that to calm down, and they settled into a comfortable match of giggles.
"I love you so much." Laine smiled as she brushed her legs against her boyfriend's under the table.
"I love you more." He replied, leaning his chin against his hand. "I know it's been difficult the last two years, but if there was anyone I would want to spend a difficult couple of years with, it's you."
Laine smiled lovingly. "God, has it seriously been two years?"
Nikoliah hummed in recognition, slowly.
"When is the anniversary? It must be soon, right? I feel like I should do something for it."
He eyed up the ridges of his plate. "Yeah, it's probably soon. Um, did you wanna think about getting another bottle?"

Laine furrowed her eyebrows and picked up the drinks menu again. "Deflective much."
"Sorry," Nikoliah replied. "Just thirsty is all."
Laine responded with a cursory glance as she beckoned the waitress back over. Without much undue effort, they ordered a second bottle to

their table. The server gave a polite nod and spun on her heel to walk away, but the Princess interrupted her with a question.
"Um, wait, sorry." She called, and the woman turned back around.
"What else can I do for you?" She smiled warmly.
"Do you know what today's date is?" Laine asked, tilting her head to the side. "Our calendar keeps falling off the wall, and at this point we just decided to get a new one in the new year."
The server gave an appropriately charged chuckle and glanced down to her watch, which also displayed the date on a rotary system.
"It's December third, dear." She offered before abruptly striding away.
Laine's gaze remained fixated on the space of air that the waitress had walked away from as the information she had been given began to set in. Her smile completely dropped. Nikoliah grimaced.
"Darling, I didn't-"
"No, you didn't." She replied quickly, turning to look at him through glassy eyes as she realised that he had conned her. "You knew it was today. I can't believe you lied to me."
Nikoliah's heart dropped to his stomach. He didn't want to have an argument with his girlfriend, it was supposed to be a nice evening out.
"I didn't want you to get upset like you did last year." He rationalised.
"Oh!" She exclaimed, hitting her hands against the table. "Shit, sorry! I didn't realise that you knew better than me."
"You know that isn't what I meant."
"You think I'm stupid? Just getting me out of the kingdom so I don't get upset about it? I have every fucking right to be upset about it! I can't believe you thought I would just forget." She yelled quite loudly, making a large portion of the restaurant tune into their conversation. Nikoliah glanced around anxiously and lowered his voice to a whisper when replying.
"I don't think you're stupid, I just- I hate seeing you sad." He bargained to no avail.
"And that makes it okay to deceive me? To control me? I bet you love being able to control me. Feeling superior because I'm all innocent and fucking stupid and I don't remember the anniversary of the worst day of my life."
"I didn't say any of that, love, please calm down."
Laine reached over to her right and grabbed her handbag from the seat.
"Don't tell me to calm down, fuck you." She instructed sternly, standing and walking quickly out of the restaurant. Nikoliah cussed under his breath, pulling his wallet out and slapping a number of bills that he didn't

count onto the tablecloth. He stumbled up out of his seat and tried following her out of the building, too preoccupied in Laine to be worried about the embarrassment all the eyes on him should have caused.

He'd fucked up, really badly. He probably should have known that this would happen. He should have known she would find out eventually, and now she was probably going to hold this grudge against him for a while. Maybe she would even break up with him over it. He would definitely lose his job if that happened (which would be awful), but more importantly he would lose the one person that he knows he can trust. That he loves.

He couldn't let that happen, so he picked up the pace.

It had started to rain whilst they were in the restaurant, so that by the time Nikoliah made it out after Laine, her hair was completely drenched and her makeup was running down her face - either from the adverse weather or the way that she had started to cry.

"Laine! Laine, I'm sorry." He yelled after her on a whine. She spun around to face him and shook her head.

"You aren't sorry; you don't get it!" She yelled back. "Of course I'm going to get upset that someone I love got banished! I haven't been allowed to speak to him in two fucking years, Niko! And *you* are supposed to be the person that I can talk about it with! You're meant to comfort me, not distract me or deceive me, god!"

Tears spilled from her pupil-less eyes, staining her face to be equally as damp as her hair and dress, which was clinging to her body uncomfortably. She could hardly even see her boyfriend from both the rain and the dizziness. He might have called something else out to her, but Laine completely ignored it as she stumbled up the steps of the train station.

Inside the walls were dark red brick, candles lining them to illuminate the building in the dead of the night. There were two attendants working in the station, both older looking men with warm smiles.

The first of the two immediately showed concern upon Laine's entry, asking her quickly where she wanted to go and if she was safe to get home. She sniffled for a moment, about to produce a reply when Nikoliah entered the building - hair and clothes dripping wet and a panicked look on his face.

"It's him." She panted, looking over at her boyfriend. "I don't know him, and he's been following me around all night trying to get me to go home with him."

At that information, the second of the workers began to approach Nikoliah with an aggressive stance. His eyes widened.

"Laine, you can't-!" He began, before yelping as he was pushed. He took a step backwards and put his hands in front of him where they were visible. "No, you don't understand, she's my girlfriend." He pleaded. Laine shook her head and let out a sob.

"I've never met that man before, please, I'm scared." She choked, watching in satisfaction as the second of the men pushed Nikoliah against the wall and held him there. He tried his best to rationalise with the men, but it was to no avail.

"It's alright, young lady, let's get you home. You're the Crown Princess of Klaevr, right?" He asked softly, leading her away from the door and towards the carriages. Laine nodded. "I thought so. Well, don't you worry, he'll be lucky if he's allowed back in your kingdom after something like this. I'll make sure he gets dealt with." The man promised. The Princess nodded once more with a sniffle, still riled up and angry at Nikoliah for lying to her.

It wasn't until the private carriage she was in had already left the station that she let herself cry.

She was properly crying in a way that she hadn't allowed herself to do in a long time. Loud wails and sobs wracked her body as her hand clutched strongly against the handle of her handbag. She wanted everything to stop, it was all so shitty and stupid. Stupid dinner date, stupid boyfriend, stupid train.

It was fine though, it would be fine. Fine because she was on a train going straight home, home where she could go back to her normal routine.

Her normal routine. God, it seemed jarring.

Wake up, smile for the people. Wear something nice - you don't want people to think you've given up. Be polite, be perfect - you have a reputation to uphold. Eat breakfast. Hate it. Talk to people you hate, report to people you hate. Share a home with someone you hate. Someone that stole everything from your family. Smile, pretend it's fine. It's fine. Sit through meetings. Do everything you need to do. It's your job, you wouldn't want to upset anyone. You are so lucky to have the life you do, why can't you be more grateful? You're selfish, you don't deserve anything. Eat lunch. Dissociate through the afternoon. Eat dinner. Finally relax. Get some downtime to spend with your boyfriend. You deserve this, you've been working so hard. Fall asleep in his arms. Feel happy there for a fleeting moment. Wake up, smile for the people.

She wasn't going back there. Not tonight. Especially since the one thing she looked forward to at the end of each day (spending time with Nikoliah) was officially off the table.

So, she got off the train at Klaevr, as it was direct, but instead didn't leave the building. It was late at night and therefore the building was quite desolate, only homing a few people who seemed very exhausted and disinterested in her departure from the locomotive. Laine had taken the time to fix her makeup on the train also, so nobody was giving her unjust stares for her depleted appearance.

She decided that her meeting tomorrow could suck it. She wasn't going. Twenty minutes later she was on another train, and three hours following that they began to pull into the next station.

the Kingdom of Nesbryn. A barren area right on the outskirts of Hell, only accessible by the railway and completely devoid of visitors almost all days of the year. It stood off the coastline of the main land mass that was referred to as 'Hell'. Smaller than all other kingdoms by at least a third, constantly plagued by dark days and even darker nights. The train carriage rattled over the dark brick bridge that miraculously made the connection between land masses, and Laine looked out the window.

Into darkness. It was terrifying, unlike anything she'd ever seen before. No stars in the sky, no clouds or anything; only darkness was left in its wake. The actual kingdom came into view, and it was clear that it had been neglected. A mainly completely flat kingdom with houses propped up on rotting wooden beams, grass growing long and uncut around gravel pathways.

Around a thousand years prior to the Crown Princess' journey to Nesbryn, it had been set up as a method of protection for all other members of Hell. A community for those too far gone to be rehabilitated, home to a small population of about fifty, known by wider society as 'The Banished'.

Around two years prior to the Crown Princess' journey to Nesbryn, a very powerful angel had banished her brother to this land, condemning him to being *one of them*. When angels decided that somebody was too dangerous, they sent them down to Hell. But, when demons decided that somebody was too dangerous, they sent them to the lonely Kingdom of Nesbryn. It was a decision that could only be made by monarchs, and when a monarch made a decision about it, nobody could argue the choice.

Laine had a thought that it was silly that it was referred to as a 'kingdom', considering it had no king or queen at all, rather functioning more as a level playing field. It didn't matter what happened in Nesbryn. It was nobody else's problem.

It hadn't truly hit her that she had made the decision to go to this place until they were all but pulling into the station. She had been lucky that she was of royal status, because trains destined to cross the brick bridge to Nesbryn only departed from stations upon official business and very specific requests. Really, all it had taken was some teary eyes and a stack of money from her handbag, but she would like to think to herself that the people protecting her kingdom from the rail network could be held to higher standards.

That was the issue, though.

She wasn't allowed to be here. Nobody was, not unless it was decided that they would be banished there. Beckett had made sure of it, especially keeping a watchful eye on the Princess - we wouldn't want any fraternisation with the enemy, would we?

The King had trusted Nikoliah to look after her, and she had separated herself from him and run off to a dangerous kingdom that she had been strictly prohibited from visiting. He would probably have to beg on his knees to keep his job, and for a moment she felt a little bad. But then she didn't, because he had been a dick and she despised the notion that he only serves to protect and look after her.

So what if the kingdom is 'sketchy'? She can look after herself, goddamnit.

She brushed down her soggy dress as the train squeaked to a halt, standing and wobbling a little on her heels. In her own mind she made the decision that she was never going to get dressed up for her boyfriend ever again, because at this exact moment it felt dumb and impractical. The carriage that she was in itself was quite small, just six seats wide. Nobody would even really notice if it went missing.

Laine swallowed the thought down, stepping off the doors of the now motionless train and onto the concrete of the platform. She didn't look back at where she had just been standing, too scared that something might be behind her.

The station was tiny, as was the whole kingdom. Dimly lit and led out onto a street of almost pitch darkness, despite it only really being an hour or two past sunset.

Growing up in Hell had meant a lot of things for Laine. One of the main ones was that she had quickly become accustomed to the concept of death. Death, destruction, morality, eternal punishment and all things associated with it. Despite this, no childhood experience could have prepared her for what the atmosphere in Nesbryn was like.

Cold - that was the first thing. Cold, but not in a windy way. In the kind of way that happens when you sit in your bedroom late at night on a winter's evening, and despite the fact that all the windows are protecting you from the rage of the weather, you're still cold - no matter how many layers you put on. The chill ran down her whole body, feeling more like it was under her skin than on top of it.

The second thing she felt was the fear. A heavy weight pushed down on her chest, immediately instilling a chemical reaction of adrenaline to course through her veins. Fight or Flight. She closed her eyes and took a deep breath in.

The land in front of her didn't have any people on it. However, it did inhabit a series of tall buildings either side of a gravel path. She didn't quite trust that nobody would jump out at her if she went down that way, so she looked to her right.

A smaller path, clearly trodden away by repetitive footsteps. It lasted only about five metres before opening up onto a gravel square, about a hundred metres by fifty metres wide. Houses and other buildings lined the edges and corners of the square, but most notably a large rectangular building with lights on in all four square glass frosted windows.

That looked promising.

The dark sky overlooked her as she stumbled across the uneven surface of the pathway. It was so deadly silent that it almost felt like there was a ringing in her ears. Maybe there was.

As Laine got closer and closer to the entrance of this luminous building, the noise of grateful chatter and evening hurrah became even more apparent. Silhouettes were starting to form like ashy images of souls tapped out. It was obvious that this was some kind of tavern, or a pub in which people socialise, and they must have been quite engrossed in their evening because it took about thirty seconds of Laine hovering in the doorway before they noticed her.

There were about five or six demons of all genders huddled around a round table in various states of tipsy. The tallest of them all honed a pair of highlighter orange horns and crimson hair, clearly dyed, against dark grey skin, right hand encased in a pint glass, set upon a mahogany table, much the same as the chairs surrounding it. Laine found that it felt quite bright inside the tavern in contrast to the darkness outside, squinting to avoid feeling blinded.

"Oh! A'right love?" The orange-horned one called towards her. Xe tilted xer head to the right in confusion as xer eyes notably scanned up and down her outfit. "You aren't from here. What's the occasion?" Xe teased, bringing xer hand off the mug and up to rest on xer chin. The rest of the table directed their attention towards Laine also with a set of giggles and grimaces.

"She's a princess." One of them sing-songed, blowing a kiss to her in the air.

The original demon smirked and rolled xer eyes behind xer dark red fringe. Laine swallowed with intimidation for a moment.

"I, um, I'm looking for Theo?" She said, although it was more like a question with the way she winced at the end.

A broad grin spread across the demon's face as a few others reacted. Particularly, a demon with a chin-length bob and sharp teeth.

"If you're looking for Princey and you have pureblooded eyes, that makes you either the ex-fiance or his sister. And for your sake I really hope it's the second one." She said, pursing her lips.

Laine wanted to leave, but she pushed the feeling down.

"Um, I'm his sister, yeah." She nodded. The demon with the orange horns stood and walked up to the bar with xer glass.

"You'll be miffed then. He was gonna be here tonight, but he cancelled because he was tired or some shit." Xe said, opening a little gate and stepping behind the bar. "Do you want a drink, pet? It'll help you deal with the atmosphere around here until your body adjusts."

It was clear to Laine that this demon owned the tavern with the way xe was walking around the back of the bar and uncorking a bottle of wine with xer teeth.

"No thank you, no, I'm alright." Laine replied, deciding that it was very important she kept her senses as high and alert as possible.

"Suit yourself. You up for a game of poker or shall I just point you in the direction of Princey's house?"

All of the eyes in the room were on her. "Just his house, I'd rather get there before it gets any ...darker." She cringed, realising how dumb she sounded in front of these people.

"Okay, so you're gonna leave here and take a left, keep walking along the edge of the square until you reach a sidestreet. It's the second road off the edge of that sidestreet, third house down on the right. Should have a green door, but they'll probably all look black in the dark."

Laine nodded repeatedly, circling the instructions around in her head.

"Alright, well good luck. Don't talk to strangers." One of the demons at the round table shooed, clearly rather interested in re-engaging in their previous conversation before it was interrupted.

"Yeah, thank you." Laine muttered, nodding to the orange-horned demon before leaving the tavern quickly. The conversation ignited again and the Princess tried not to die from how awkward and embarrassed she felt. Was everyone who lived in this kingdom so confident and cocky like that?

Despite her fear, the interaction had given her two positives. One, being that she felt slightly more relaxed with the idea of the residents of Nesbryn (considering that they were yet to try and hurt her), and two being that she now had directions to her brother's house. Left. So, she turned left, cursing herself again for wearing heels. If she was wearing socks she probably would have just taken the shoes off and walked on the gravel, but it would be much too uncomfortable barefoot, so she didn't.

As the sounds of the demons in the pub faded away, that ringing in her ears came back. It was starting to feel a lot more real. Goosebumps littered her arms, but she just focused on repeating those directions in her head. Second road off the sidestreet, third house with the green door.

Second road off the sidestreet, third house with the green door.

XXXI

She did find the house eventually, and after six minutes of fidgeting outside the door, her hand came up to the knocker - shaped like a great dane and made of black painted copper. A metallic click-clack of internal locks being undone protruded through the wood, before the door swung open at a moderate pace.
Before she could even register that she was standing in front of her brother for the first time in two years, he had grabbed her by the arm and yanked her inside the house, abruptly shutting the door behind her and pushing a metal lock on the ground down with his right foot.
"Don't you ever do that again." He hissed, words sharply spoken and accusatory. Laine blinked for a moment.
"What...?" She asked, dumbfounded.
"Come here! At night, presumably *alone*! Wearing that. You could've gotten hurt." He winced, the corner of his mouth curling upwards at the unpleasant thought as he interlocked his hands in front of him and fidgeted.
"It's good to see you too, Theo." She whispered back, tears welling in her eyes. For a moment the other demon just stared at her.
He had changed a lot.
He was somehow even paler due to the lack of sunlight he had been getting, which also meant that his freckles all but vanished from his face. His dark auburn hair had grown out just past his jawline, looking considerably scruffier and less cared for than it once did. As well as this, he was a good few inches taller and skinnier too. Almost too skinny.
There was an assortment of scars slashed across his visible neck and

sharper jawline. Some old, some new. His wings were floating idly behind him along with his tail, dejected and probably not used in a long time. His teeth were sharper, more evolved, and his nails looked as if they hadn't been cut in a while - dirt so far under them that it would be near impossible to get out. Finally, his eyes were slicker with a layer of redness beside his eyelashes.

He was wearing some light grey jeans, ripped so much so that Laine could see more of the fabric fraying than the denim of the jeans, as well as a dark green hoodie. She didn't miss noticing the flower bracelet still wrapped tightly around his left wrist.

His house was dimly lit, the only light being via a few candles that scented like cranberries. They were placed on the square light oak table standing on three legs in the centre of the main room, adjacent to a light blue sofa and matching coffee table. A kitchen island made of some kind of stone was against the other back wall, and then also another door that led presumably to a bedroom and bathroom. There were notably no windows, and only one floor.

Theo frowned softly. He took a hesitant step forward and carefully pulled Laine into his chest in a desperate hug. He didn't say anything, and he didn't cry like he might've this time two years ago. After about twenty seconds, he pulled away, hands still on Laine's shoulders and voice dropped to a whisper.

"How did you get here?" He asked.

Laine bit her lip.

"Train."

Theo rolled his eyes. "Okay, fine. Why did you come here?" He rephrased.

The Princess frowned for a moment and squeezed Theo's wrist that she was now holding tightly. "Nikoliah took me out for dinner so that I wouldn't realise it was December third and get upset. I realised anyway and got upset at him, then I, um, I left him in Stonbrin and just kind of… missed you all of a sudden, I don't know."

Theo gave a light chuckle.

"The implications of that story are that this is the first time you've missed me? I know you don't feel emotions very strongly but has it really taken you two years to get sad about me being gone?" He teased, not actually offended.

Laine rolled her eyes at the insinuation. "You know it hasn't, but it was just like, I had no way of seeing you until today so it was kind of in vain. Beckett's like a hawk over me." She replied, watching as her brother walked over to the table and drummed his fingers against it as he took a seat.

"You're still his heir?"

"Much to father's delight." She responded bluntly, pulling out the opposite seat and sitting down too. Laine noticed Theo's sleeve ride up to his wrist and her eyes widened.

"Is that a tattoo?!" She almost yelled. Theo instantly tugged his sleeve back down.

"No."

"Dad would kill you." She said poignantly. "Do you have any more?"

Theo sighed and pulled his sleeve all the way up to his elbow at that, unveiling one which was a large orchid running from his elbow all the way down to his wrist and hand, where the vines on the edge of the stem wrapped around his wrist and thumb. It was positioned to weave around the markings down his forearm. It was made of a simple black ink, matching the smaller skull and crossbones tattoo that he had almost like a stick n poke on his lower neck, which he revealed alongside a larger geometric design of overlapping triangles down his collarbone as he pulled the top of his hoodie down.

"Gosh, that's beautiful." Laine said quickly to avoid seeming like she was judging Theo. "Who did them?"

"Oh, um, I did." He said slowly. "I do that now, um, as a job."

"You're a tattoo artist? That's sick."

Theo smiled slightly in a way that was rare of him. He let go of his shirt and pulled his sleeve back down. "Thanks." He breathed. "I just, I have a steady hand, and the people here are quite... alternative."

Laine laughed. "I guessed as much. One of them had bright blue hair."

"Oh yeah," Theo nodded. "That's Axel, he's harmless really." He informed before pausing. "When did you meet them?"

"Just now. At the little pub place near the train station." She said, and Theo's expression flattened.

"Ah. Sorry if they were a little weird." He replied, voice quieting until the room was in a somewhat awkward silence. Now they'd gotten all the small talk out of the way, the atmosphere felt thick and heavy. The room remained silent for a few minutes following, in which the two siblings seemed to have nothing to talk about despite having so *much* to talk about.

Theo swallowed.

"I'm sorry."

"For what?" Laine asked softly, eyes not yet disconnecting from the table.

"Everything. The shit that happened, leaving you alone to look after the kingdom. Both times. I imagine you've been pretty upset with me about it."

Laine smiled to herself in reassurance. "I couldn't be upset with you about it. I'm upset that it happened, not because of you. It wasn't your fault."

"Whose fault was it then?"

One of the doors that extended off the kitchen-living-room gilded open and hit against the wall on the other side.

"It doesn't take that long to answer the door, did you get mauled by something?" The demon asked, voice high and playful. He then flattened his expression with an "Oh."

Theo groaned and rolled his eyes, pressing his hand over his face to hide his embarrassment. After a few moments of silence, he flopped his hand back onto the table and directed his gaze to the third person in the house.

"Isaac, this is my sister. My sister, this is Isaac." He gestured.

The demon that had appeared out of the doorway, Isaac, bent down a little and held his hands up in a gesture that could be interpreted as either jazz hands or surrendering. He had very light hair, kind of white coloured but in reality it was more of a bleached blonde. It was a buzz cut that had grown out for about two weeks, still incredibly short. He had a thick layer of eyeliner surrounding his eyes, and dark yellow (almost golden) horns curling out from each side of his head. Overtop a pair of baggy beige cargo trousers, he wore a black corset and see-through black dress shirt.

He smiled, all the way up to his ears as he gave a little courtsey. Then, Isaac pranced over to be stood in front of the guest, holding a hand out.

"Nice to meet you, Elaine." He smirked, grabbing her hand and shaking it.

She hesitated for a moment before returning the favour with her correction.

"Oh, um, it's Laine. Without an E." She supplied.

"He knows your name, he thinks he's funny." Theo excused with a roll of his eyes.

"Oh." She said quietly, watching as Isaac walked towards the sink and filled the kettle up with water. "Does he live here?"

"No."

"Yes."

"He *doesn't* live here." Theo repeated. "Just likes to pretend he does because I actually bother to keep my cupboards full." He accused, turning

280

his head to watch as Isaac flicked the kettle on and spun around to lean against the wall with a sickening smile.
"Accurate."
Isaac drummed his fingers against the edge of the kitchen counter for a few moments. "Well, I *have* heard a lot about you, Laine. I feel as if I need to properly introduce myself. God, this is like meeting a reality TV star." He thought aloud, pulling another chair up to the table, but rotating it one-hundred-and-eighty degrees and sitting backwards, legs spread either side of it.
"My name is Isaac and I'm Theo's boy-toy." He beamed, leaning very heavily forward on the wood of the table.
Theo frowned.
"We've talked about you referring to yourself like that." He said flatly.
Isaac only grinned more.
"You're the one who refuses to let me call myself your boyfriend."
"Because you aren't my boyfriend."
The kettle screamed that it was done boiling, and Isaac hopped out of his seat, taking a few steps backwards and beginning to pour himself a cup of tea. Once the noise of the kettle whistling had completely blown over, he brought the piping hot liquid to his mouth and took a sip, tilting his head backward to allow the burn to travel down his oesophagus generously.
"You can keep telling yourself that." He hummed. "I have the rest of eternity to get it through your head."
Steaming tea still in his right hand, Isaac waltzed towards the door of the house.
"I'll be at Ayale's. Let you two catch up without me eavesdropping." He said, opening the door almost too carelessly.
"Wait, hold on." Theo said quickly, standing up and walking to the kitchen counter where he pulled a drawer of junk out and started sifting through it. Eventually, he pulled out a single bank note and three coins. "We have that unpaid tab from last weekend." He explained, dropping the cost into Isaac's outstretched arm. "If I speak to xer tomorrow and xe tells me xe didn't get anything from you then you've lost expensive tea bag privileges. Tell Ayale I'll get the rest to xer after Livvy pays me for last week's tattoo tomorrow."
Isaac nodded repeatedly. "Yep, yep, yep." He chorused, slipping the money into his right hand pocket. "I'll see you later." He said, winking.
"Be safe. And bring that mug back."
"No promises."

The door clicked shut and Theo re-locked it.

"Sorry. Kinda forgot he was here."

Laine smiled in slight amusement. "S'alright. At least he put the kettle on. Can I try out one of these 'expensive tea bags'?" She asked, crossing her right leg over her left. Theo nodded and pulled two mugs from the top cupboard.

"Is he really your boyfriend?" Laine whispered at the ceiling.

It was later now, maybe about two or three o'clock in the morning. All the lights in the house were off, only a single scented candle towering in between the two siblings as they lay in the living room. Laine was on the sofa with a light coloured blanket draped over her, and Theo had dragged his mattress into the living room so that he could keep her company. It was a lot like when they were younger, really young, and he would sneak past the royal guards into her bedroom so they could have a 'sleepover' and whisper in the dead of night.

Laine had done most of the talking thus far. She'd caught him up on all that had gone on in Klaevr and beyond these last two years. The people of Nesbryn didn't get any newspapers or similar. She'd told him about how her and Nikoliah were doing, about how their dad had been sucking up to King Beckett. About how half of their staff had left in protest, only to be replaced by angels who could do their job better than them. About how Raphie hadn't come back since the battle in which she left. Not even sent a letter or anything - she had just completely disappeared, and because Laine couldn't go up to Menphe, she had no way of knowing what her old friend was up to without her. About how Serenity has gotten engaged again, to a prince from one of the other kingdoms. She had been fine after the battle, mainly thanks to Theo ensuring her safe exit, and now she was carrying on with her life. Theo was relieved to hear as much.

She told him about how much pressure she was under. They'd been able to relate to each other that much. The stress of being an heir so young. Of course, when Theo was king, Laine *was* technically the Crown Princess, but it hadn't been taken at all seriously due to the fact that she was only a year younger than Theo and would realistically never be monarch. With Beckett, it had been different. So much more had been expected of her, all the meetings, all the paperwork, all the training, all the expectations. Theo hadn't really confided in anyone what all that had

been like until this evening. He'd had those kinds of pressures since he was old enough to listen to them being spewed at him. Now he had something that brought him and Laine closer together. They had relatable experiences outside of growing up in the same family for once.
"Maybe. I don't know." Theo replied while he blinked. "He likes me a lot more than I like him."
Laine felt a little bad for Isaac for a moment.
"Why do you entertain the idea of him, then? I mean, why not just stop being friends, or whatever you are, with him?"
The question lingered in the air for a while, before Theo look a large gulp of the glass of water beside him.
"It gets lonely here." He admitted, lying down on his mattress and rolling over to look Laine in the eyes. "There's only about fifty people in the kingdom, and at least forty of them are complete social recluses that have been here longer than grandma has been alive." He breathed. "...It's not like I have many options."
Laine nodded. She hadn't considered that much. Being shunned from society as he was must've been hard for him.
"That's why everyone here is so close with each other. We all share a common denominator."
Being unwanted, right.
"Nobody has forgotten about you, you know." Laine said softly.
Theo shook his head. "It wouldn't matter if they had. Just feels a bit shit going from having everything to nothing in like, what, a week?"
"A week between when?"
"The wedding was meant to be on November thirty-first. I met Julian a week and a day before then. So, more than a week. Nine days."
Laine sat up on her elbows, a lot more interested in the direction of this conversation.
"Do you blame him?" She asked carefully.
Theo thought for a moment.
"No. No, I think that I would have ditched the wedding either way. I'm more angry than anything." He said softly. "Angry that I allowed myself to be blinded by him."
"How so?" Laine prompted.
"I was in love. Head over fucking heels. I didn't realise it then, but I was. So much so that I blocked everything else out. Didn't care about the consequences of my actions so long as I was with him. And now I have nothing and I'm not even with him." He confessed. "Don't think I've ever admitted that before."

"Admitted what?"
"That I was in love. I can't even remember what it felt like anymore. Sometimes I think of him when I'm kissing Isaac, but don't you ever repeat that."
Theo groaned and rolled over, pulling his second pillow over the exposed side of his head.
"That's really bad, Theo." Laine replied quietly with a little bit of a giggle.
"Yeah." He breathed.
Theo looked back up at Laine after a few moments had passed.
"On that day, when we got back from England." He started softly.
"Beckett was using magic, right?"
Laine nodded quickly. "Yeah. Wouldn't have been able to do what he did to Julian without it."
"How?" Theo replied almost immediately after. "I've been thinking about it a lot. How did he do that? He shouldn't have been able to."
Laine thought for a moment. It *had* been remarkable. Beckett was an ex-mortal, and they couldn't do magic, not at all. It was a trait that was specifically honed by pureblooded demons.
"Unsure. Probably related to the mysterious disappearance of Zero."
"He's not back?" Theo sat up quickly, worried at the implications.
"No." Laine replied bluntly. "Beckett refused to talk to me about it. Dismissed me to my room when I tried to push it. Hettie and Elsie don't even know, but I've only been able to speak to them via letter since I'm not allowed into town unsupervised for the very reason of stirring conspiracy."
Theo swallowed and fell into silence as he laid back onto the mattress, pulling his duvet up over him. They had a lot to think about - the Virzor siblings. A lot to say, and a lot to think about. But it was late. It was late and he was tired. It had certainly been the most interesting day that Theo had ever spent on Nesbryn. And now, with Isaac spending the evening at Ayale's tavern, just having some time alone with his sister, he felt relaxed.
It was something he would have easily taken for granted a while ago. Playfully shoving her out of his bedroom for the sake of getting back to his spell practising. He lay down and exhaled, feeling an idle sense of security wash over him as he listened to Laine's breathing.
He closed his eyes, and for a moment - just a moment - it felt like he was at home.

He remembered that he was in fact *not* at home when he was awoken only an hour later by a loud clamouring growl. He knew it all too well, and was immediately brought to reality by the sound. It had come from the main square near the tavern, loud enough that the whole kingdom was likely to hear.

Within ten seconds, Theo was cursing to himself and lacing his boots up whilst another growl sounded out. Laine groaned and squinted as she was brought to her own state of consciousness. She leant up and watched her brother stumble around in his kitchen before he found his longsword (one that Laine didn't recognise, not the same one he had used in Klaevr) and gripped it tightly in his hand.

"Where are you going...?" She asked blearily, just before a louder, more intentioned growl echoed through the foundations of the house. Theo snapped his head to look at her.

"There." He supplied quickly. "Stay here, don't leave until I get back." He instructed harshly before he disappeared out the door in an instant.

Right, well, she wasn't taking that.

Laine kicked her duvet off of her quickly, still wearing her green dress. She didn't want to put her heels back on, but found that there was another pair of older, more beat up brown leather boots by the door that she could easily slip on. So she did, and only about thirty seconds after Theo had left, she was running down the street after him.

The noise was a lot louder outside, so much so that Laine had to stop running for a moment because she was paralyzed by fear and indecision. Ahead of her by about fifty metres, Theo was around the corner approaching the square that the tavern was adjacent to.

"Fuck, there he is." Ayale pointed, allowing xer eyes to move away from the creature to look at Theo.

"Sorry." Theo replied quickly, skidding to a halt beside Isaac, who was holding his sword in front of him. "How are we doing this?"

The seven demons in the square stood in a sort of makeshift semi-circle. Theo was closest to the left, with Isaac next to him. Next to Isaac was Livvy, then Fern, Toby, Ayale and Axel. Livvy was quite short, and had a lot of tattoos that contrasted against her mid-grey skin and pastel purple horns. She had a light brown bob that was well-brushed, despite them being six hours into drinks before the creature had arrived. Fern's hair was darker and long, all the way down to her hips with a pastel pink streak on the left side. She was tall, about six foot four if you included her light green horns, with broad shoulders that made her fighting stance impressive. Toby was shorter, with dark grey skin that wasn't quite as dark as Ayale's, but still dark so. He had black hair in a scene fringe, and purplish pink stubby horns. Lastly, Axel was down on one knee tying his shoelaces, a dark blue mop of hair (of which some blonde roots had grown out a few inches) covering his eyes. He'd dyed his hair the same colour as his long, pointed horns. Axel's right horn had been severed from about half-way up, leaving just a stub of colour until where it would have continued.

In front of the seven, about a hundred metres away, was a creature. A dragonish, dog-like thing that stood on four short black scaled legs, and a large torso plated with hard rock scales that were almost impossible to penetrate. All five of its eyes were completely blacked out, analysing the every move of the demons that were about a third of its height.

It roared again, head and mouth directing a blast of white-coloured fire tumbling at the ground. Toby screamed and skidded backwards as his feet were nearly burnt off. The demons had scattered either side of the flames.

"What the fuck is that?!"

They all quickly directed their attention to Laine, who was standing on the edge of the square with a shocked expression of panic over her face.

"I told you to stay in the house!" Theo yelled back over the noise that was simply the creature breathing.

"It's a creature of Perterruit." Ayale said quickly. "If you're helping kill it, then help. If you aren't, then you should leave."

Theo extended his wings out behind him and hovered a few metres off the ground to look above the creature.

"She is not staying!" He repeated, catching the creature's attention as it turned and began to bound in the direction he was flying, away from the rest of them. Theo yelped as the creature jumped up on its massive hind legs and blew a breath of fire out at him. He dived to the side and rolled against the ground to avoid the flames - sword still held tightly in his right hand as it dragged against the dirt to stop him slowly.

"You were fighting way worse creatures when you were her age last year!" Xe called back while running underneath the view of the creature.

"Plus, if she's half as good at her spells as you are, we can get this done a lot quicker." Fern had to yell to be heard.

"If she gets hurt I'm never forgiving you lot." Theo gritted, running along the gravel towards Laine. The other six continued to fight the creature as they had with others many times before. Any amount of drunk they had been from their night at the pub was completely dissolved by the harsh reality of this beast.

"What actually is it?" Laine whispered to Theo as he slid to a halt beside her.

"It's one of the creatures that is supposed to guard Hell." He replied, not wanting to waste any time. "Sometimes they go a bit rogue. And when that happens they always end up here. Where all the other rejects are. Rather, instead of building a lovely community as we have, they try to burn us to a crisp." He breathed, panting excessively from all the running already. "I'm the only one with the appropriate magic that can get this job done in less than an hour. Do you know your projectile blasting drills?"

Laine thought for a moment. "Maybe. Sounds vaguely familiar."

Theo replied somewhat exasperatedly as he grabbed her hand. "Whatever, just copy me."

He pulled her up towards the air, wings flapping excessively to carry both of their weights. Laine's dark red wings then extended out behind her as she started to carry her own weight.

"We have to get it's head." Theo said softly, watching as the rest of his friends on the ground scrambled to keep it occupied, slashing it with their own swords and other weapons. Axel managed to get an arrow right in one of its eyes, although it was mostly futile considering the thing had four more lying around spare. "It's gonna fall, probably onto its back. Don't waste time."

Theo took a deep breath in with his eyes closed. The swirling, jagged markings on his arms began to glow under his hoodie, getting brighter and brighter by each second as a mass of dark green light began to form in the palm of his upturned right hand.

"No rush, we aren't about to get flambéed or anything!" He heard Fern yell from below, which he completely ignored. It would put him off. Once he had a full expanse of glowing light in his manipulation, Theo looked over to Laine, who was lightly doing the same to a much less practised extent.

"On my count." He said, and she nodded.

Theo counted down from three and they both used the light motion of their fingers to project their light towards the head of the creature. It growled and took a series of quick leaps out of the way of the magic, which slammed against the ground and dissolved into nothingness. Theo frowned.

"Okay. I'm gonna hold it in place, you're gonna get a hit in. Don't fuck it up." He said sharply, in a way that scared Laine. She had never seen that kind of side of him before, but he was clearly feeling very stressed.
"Alright, yeah." Laine nodded quickly. Theo swooped himself down to a lower level so that he was standing next to Ayale and Toby.
"You're letting her do it?" Toby asked sceptically.
"She's competent, and it's gonna keep moving if I don't do a paralyzation." He replied, pressing his two hands together and circling his fingers in a specific motion, signing shapes into the air. Eventually, a box of green light was created. He pushed it towards the creature that was thrashing around at Isaac, Fern, Axel and Livvy on the opposite side of the courtyard. His markings glowed intensely as the green light tied like a rope around the creature's legs. It began growling and making an effort ten times stronger.
"Laine!" He yelled up towards her. She was nodding vigorously, trying to summon the magic that she needed. She was so out of practice, as it hadn't been mandatory for her to continue her spell casting training. Beckett hadn't wanted magical competitors in the castle, so he didn't permit it.
She closed her eyes tightly, and the markings along her arms started to faintly flicker as a spindle of dark red light began to wisp itself out of the air and towards her hands.
She was worried it wouldn't work. So worried that she pulled her hands all the way back and pulsed the light outwards towards the creature. It flew quickly and struck the beast very strongly in the head. Theo released his grip on the beast, immediately breaking into a sprint towards it with the others.
The creature itself was knocked completely off its feet and onto its back in a loud thud.
Axel leapt upwards and then down in a swift movement, using his sword to slice the back right leg off the creature. In one swift movement, the limb slid off, leaving bone and muscle in its place. Laine thought she might throw up.
Ayale, Fern and Toby had done the same to the other three legs, leaving the beast completely immobile as it began to recover from Laine's blast and growled a breath of fire out.
Theo jumped up onto its torso, catching the sword that Isaac had thrown at him, since he had left his on the ground when practising the magic. He leant down on his knees and drove the blade right through the beast's heart.

For a moment, it writhed. And then it stopped, falling completely dead in front of the eight demons.

"Where the hell was that fighting level two years ago?" Laine asked Theo, who was still staring idly at the sword digging into the creature, exasperated as she flew downwards and planted her feet on the ground. Theo leant back on his knees as he let go of his sword, breathing in and out quickly.

He looked down to the deceased creature's fur for a moment before a soft sniffling sound rang out across the courtyard. Ayale gaped as xe leant against xer sword.

"Is he crying?!" Xe almost laughed.

Theo sat back cross legged, bringing his knees right up to his chest and plunging his head in between them. His sword was still sticking out of the beast as his cries grew more noticeable despite his best embarrassed attempts to muffle them.

"I haven't seen him cry since he first got here." Livvy commented slowly, cocking her head and frowning with her lips parted to show off her pointed teeth. Laine pulled up and climbed the creature, approaching Theo carefully in front of the other demons all crowded around it. She stopped and pulled his shoulders backwards, away from his knees. She knew that it was too much for him, all of this at once, so she didn't say anything that would overwhelm him more. He blinked and turned to face her as tears continued to pour down his face. Laine knelt forward and pulled him into a strong hug.

He was so glad to have her back.

XXXII

It was just about three o'clock in the afternoon the next day when Laine returned to Klaevr. After being woken up at such a ridiculous hour for a task that sucked all the energy out of her, she'd slept in until at least noon. Theo had been up since nine, being somewhat accustomed to lack of sleep, and when she had woken up he had been huddled around the kitchen table with a cup of coffee and the lad with the pink horns that she was too tired to remember the name of.
She had said goodbye to him just around one, promising it wouldn't be the last time. In fact, she hadn't really wanted to leave and face her responsibilities, but Theo had consistently tried to persuade her that the last thing she wanted to do was optionally stay in Nesbryn, especially considering the life of luxury and happiness that was waiting for her a few kingdoms over.
Theo had walked her to the train station and given her a brief hug, not wanting to prolong it, since that would make it feel more like it would be a long time. He wanted it to be like a 'popping to the shops, see you in ten' kind of hug.
She had nodded and began to walk away, turning a little in curiosity when Theo didn't follow her further up into the actual building.
"Not going to walk me to my train?" She teased, crossing her arms in front of her body. Theo opened his mouth to respond, but then only let out a slow sigh.
"No, I um, can't." He replied. When Laine only looked at him with discontent confusion, he dropped his arms to his side and took a step closer, eyeing the ground with intent.

"What are you doing?" Laine asked as she moved to stand next to him.
"Just, just stand behind me." He said gruffly, pulling the edge of his sleeve over his hand. He glanced back to Laine and then stuck his arm out a few feet ahead of him. Nothing happened, so he took one more step forward. This time, about half way through the step, Theo's hand connected with an invisible wall that hadn't been there until he had touched it. Instantly, a wave of orange flames dispersed out from his fingertips and splayed upwards over the sky, painting it in copper gold very momentarily. The heat was scarily close, as if the sun had been put right in front of them for about half a second before disappearing into the darkness of the blanket above them.

Theo flinched backwards with a yelp of pain, cradling the hand he had reached out with. The edge of his sleeve was singed back and emitting light amounts of smoke as it was still being consumed by the flame. He hit the sleeve with his other hand a few times until the fire went out, leaving only a sickening smell of burning and a scuffed piece of fabric around the base of his wrist as he let it fall back into place. His tail wrapped around his torso for a few moments, but he seemed to notice and correct this unconscious action quite quickly.

"Ouch." Laine cringed a little. "That's why you can't leave, then."

"Well, yeah. I didn't just get dumped here and immediately decide that was it for the rest of time. Obviously if there wasn't some kind of border, I would have just come home." He stated on a little bit of a wince.

Laine frowned. "Seems to be a lot of things here trying to set you on fire."

Theo nodded. "Nothing's gonna kill us, so it's kind of the next best thing. Getting burnt fuckin' hurts. The fire is probably some kind of metaphor for eternal damnation."

"Do you get burnt a lot? Surely you'd be kind of desensitised to it if you don't mind me saying so."

"Only twice so far, so not that much." Theo responded in a quick manner. "Other than little ones like that. One when I first got here and learnt that running at it doesn't make it disappear, and the other when I first fought one of the creatures of Perterruit. Before Fern made me somewhat adequate armour. I, um, that's what tattoos do, for most of us at least. Covers up the scarring."

Laine looked back to Theo's collarbone, where the top of his geometric pattern tattoo was visible. And, sure enough, the skin underneath the ink was visibly rough and red-toned beyond the usual very light colour of his skin normally. She looked at it for a moment while blinking.

"Why do you feel the need to cover them up if you *all* have them?" She asked, genuinely curious although in her tone it may have come across a little condescending.

Theo thought for a moment about his answer, crossing his arms in front of him in a naturally defensive position. "I guess it's like, would you rather have the same scars as everyone else or an interesting design over it? We sort of treat it like a mark of courage, or stupidity, but that depends on who has it." He smiled, as if recounting a past memory.

Laine nodded, kind of understanding the significance. "But, I don't get it. Could you not just… get tattoos without getting hurt first?"

Theo's face dropped to one of exaggerated annoyance. "That would ruin the fun." He pouted, before taking a glance down at his watch. "Agh, you need to go home. People are going to worry."

So, much to her own reluctance, she nodded, and gave him one last hug that lasted longer this time. She cherished it, and then watched as he stood immoble with a slight smile tugging at the corner of his mouth as she hopped up the steps and towards the train station.

"Bye!" She called for the last time as she approached her train carriage. Theo smiled while snickering.

"Enjoy the sunlight for me."

It seemed that maybe a *few* people had noticed she was missing.

They had obviously been quite worried, considering what happened the last time one of the royal siblings vanished into the night.

"Where the hell have you been?!" Nikoliah whined as he ran into the train station. He'd been contacted the minute she was spotted back in Klaevr. "I've been so fucking worried." He replied, almost as if he was going to cry as he wrapped his dishevelled arms around her shoulders.

However, Laine didn't hug him back. Instead, she shoved him away a little and watched as he stumbled a few feet away with a dazed look on his face.

"None of your business where I was." She said bluntly. She had decided in her sleep-fogged mind that she was going to break up with him. She had made the decision shortly after defeating the creature. What if she had died, or something, and she had never let Nikoliah know how much he had hurt her? What if he went to her funeral and told everyone they were a perfect couple? It was obviously not going to happen, but it made her realise that she had to tell him how she felt.

Guilt tugged at Nikoliah's chest as he glanced around. A lot of people were watching them, people who had been instructed to find Laine and now wanted to be the first to report new information to the King.
"Can we please not do this here?" The knight whispered, understanding that she was clearly still pissed at him. Laine raised her eyebrows.
"Why can't we do this here, Niko? Did you do something wrong that you don't want people to know about or something?" She asked in a loud, sarcastic tone.
Nikoliah stuttered slightly, fighting the instinct to place his hand on his sword at any sign of conflict. "Let's just, let's just talk about this in our bedroom. When you're safe back home and without a crowd." He said nervously, stepping a little closer to Laine in order to lower his voice. She looked for a moment as if she was considering it.
But, he had lied to her. Lied right to her face because he thought she was stupid enough not to remember the date. And the worst part was that she *was* in fact stupid enough. He made her feel dumb, made her feel like a horrible sister. She wasn't going to forgive him for that just because he felt a little worried.
"I won't see you in *my* bedroom." Laine replied, again trying to be loud. He deserved to feel bad about this. "We're over, Nikoliah. I'm not dependent on you and I hate that you act like I am."
Nikoliah's heart dropped. His head started pounding and his chest heaving. Laine walked past him, knocking into his shoulder as she did. He was completely certain that he was going to die. He'd built his life around the Princess, he didn't have anything else.
Everyone was looking at him, expecting him to say something. He'd just been given the worst news of his death, and he watched everything he had as she walked away. His heart exploded inside his ribcage - he didn't know if he was breathing or not.
It was the second worst thing he'd ever been told.

The first worst thing he'd ever been told was considerably a lot more serious. But it was exactly the same feeling.
He was sitting beside his mother, aged twelve, bouncing his right leg with anxiety over the edge of the thin mattress he sat atop. She reached over and grabbed his hand, holding it tightly. The walls in the room were white, and it led outwards onto a busy hallway full of doctors, nurses and patients. From the hustle and bustle, his dad walked in with two brown

paper cups of tea, handing one to his mother before he too sat down beside Nikoliah.

They didn't say anything for a while. Not until an older woman in a light blue button up shirt and long white coat knocked on the already wide open door.

"Good morning, again." She smiled easily, sitting down on her black swivel chair. She moved forward slightly and gave another smile. "We need to have a little chat about these test results. Nikoliah, would you rather you stayed here with us or just your parents and they can tell you the important parts afterwards?"

He looked up to his mother, and a spike of panic shot through him. If the test results were good, she would *not* have said that. He suddenly found that he couldn't speak.

"Nick, darling? Do you want to wait outside?" His mother asked again, and this time he could at least hear her through the blood rushing in his ears. He shook his head quickly. He was by far old enough to understand what a doctor might be telling him.

The doctor nodded and glanced back down to her clipboard. She sighed. "Alright then, Nikoliah, I need you to listen very carefully." She said. His mother squeezed his hand. "The tests that we did earlier this week helped us to look at your bone marrow, and then we used that evidence alongside the MRI to complete our diagnosis. We believe it's already progressed to stage four."

His mother was crying. He wasn't exactly sure why. The doctor hadn't even said anything bad yet.

"I need you to know that we have a really super range of support for both Nick and you two, Mr and Mrs Renton."

"You know this is your fault, Nina." Came his father's voice, harsh and unforgiving. "You knew your father had it and you still waited so long to take him here to get tested when he started showing signs."

His grandpa? Nikoliah had never even met him, he'd died before he was even born, so he wasn't too sure how the man was relevant. His mother only cried more, clutching his hand tightly.

"What's the prognosis?" His father asked, blunt and uncaring to the distress radiating off his mother.

The doctor straightened herself back up. "At this stage, even with chemotherapy, he has about a 0.5% chance of making it longer than two months. I'm so sorry that it wasn't caught sooner."

Nikoliah blinked. What the fuck did she mean? He had asked to stay and now the doctor was still talking as if he wasn't in the room.

"What?" He managed to ask softly. The doctor gave a really gradual, sympathetic smile.
"You have Leukaemia, Nikoliah. Do you know what that means?"
And his world had shattered around him. He felt like he was the only person in the world who was actually there, able to hear and see him. He couldn't hear anything, only able to watch as the doctor's mouth continued to move. Suddenly, there was nothing. Nothing for him, no future, no hope, no happiness, no support.
It was the worst feeling he had ever felt.

It was the exact same feeling that Nikoliah had as he watched Laine walk away. Nobody dare say anything to him - they had all just watched him get broken up with by the literal princess. He was probably not in the kind of mood to be spoken to. He was standing desolate in the train station for a whole five minutes before he snapped out of his haze.
He looked up from the ground and it felt like the whole world was staring at him.
"You have jobs to do, go away." He said loudly, not making eye contact with anyone in particular. After a thirty second interval in which people only stared at him, he grew a lot more impatient.
"I said go away before you lose your fucking jobs!" He yelled a lot louder that time, and the people watching scrambled to leave under the threat of getting on the bad side of one of their superiors. Nikoliah headed straight for the castle, wanting to just get into the safety of indoors before another person could whisper something and snicker.
He was approached the minute he entered the castle, by Jaymie Newman - the stylist who had stayed on and was now generally doing most of Laine's wear as well as Nikoliah's when they did public events together. She stopped right behind him.
"Yo, is it true Laine broke up with you?" She asked quickly.
Nikoliah stopped in his walking and turned down to look at the older woman.
"It's true that you need to mind your fucking business." He replied easily, striding away. Jaymie frowned, unimpressed by the answer as she moved to follow him.
"You realise that if you don't tell us anything then us staff will be gossiping about just her side of the story, right? So, spill." She persisted, standing in front of him.

"Jaymie." He said strongly, willing himself not to yell at her. The stylist rolled her eyes.

"Fine. Beckett wants to see you in his office then." She told him, before dropping her voice to a low whisper. "I think your job is on the line after the things Laine said about you when she walked in that door."

Nikoliah took a deep breath in. He could find Laine later, make it up to her and all of that. Prove the stupid gossiping staff members wrong. But, for now, he was already late to a meeting with the King that didn't even have a time - just the sheer fact that Jaymie took about a minute to actually tell him he needed to be there, Beckett was probably expecting him about now.

So, he didn't reply to her, slightly pushing past her even as he walked away down the hallway. He walked past him and Fiducia's office, noticing that she was hunched over her desk writing something in there. He was glad that she didn't take the care to glance up - that would've been awkward, even though she already knew about the drama.

He made it outside of the King's office as quickly as he could. When Dyran and then Theo were kings, such a room hadn't existed, but Beckett was a politician and had worked his whole death behind a desk, so he much preferred it to speaking to people from atop a large throne.

Nikoliah knocked on the door quickly, waiting for a response from inside.

"Come in."

He pushed the door open slowly and bowed his head towards the King, who was reclining in front of a set of bookshelves - his halo casting light into the room. He was wearing his usual attire, consisting of light grey trousers with a white button-up shirt, and a tie the same tone as his light purplish-blue skin.

In front of him were two chairs made of dark wood. The one on the right was empty, and in the one on the left, Laine sat with her hand on her lap as she sniffled. She looked up to him through glassy eyes as he entered.

"Sit down." Beckett said sternly, and so Nikoliah did, trying not to look at Laine for too long.

"Right." He began. "I will *not* have the two of you creating petty drama in my walls. If you have an issue, you will sort it out in private. The whole kingdom is undoubtedly talking at the moment." He said quickly, and Nikoliah felt a sense of righteousness at the fact that that was exactly what he had tried to tell Laine.

"I understand that you are both high on emotions at the moment. Princess Laine, I want you to take the rest of the day off from your duties. We will discuss your disappearance overnight tomorrow

morning. Are you one-hundred percent certain that you no longer have an interest in pursuing a romantic relationship with Sir Nikoliah?"
Nikoliah's head snapped over to look at her. She was upset, and she looked it. Still wearing the green dress that she had left in the night before. Nikoliah managed to score eye contact with Laine as she bit her lip.
"Darling, I'm sorry-" He tried again, not willing to let her walk away under circumstances like this.
"Yes, I'm sure." Laine sniffled and cut him off, breaking their eye contact.
"Very well." Beckett replied in a slightly judgemental tone. "You will not spread anything to anybody outside of this room about this. If you wish to make a public statement about this change you may do so any time after tomorrow. Am I understood?"
"Yeah." Laine nodded, wanting to curl in on herself and die. Maybe she had been a little harsh on Nikoliah, but then again, she really hadn't. She was a princess, for God's sake, she deserves someone that doesn't lie to her.
"And you, Sir Nikoliah? Do you understand?"
"Yeah. Yes. Yes, Your Majesty." He stuttered through his anxiety. He was going to cry. He never cried.
"Good. Laine, you are dismissed. Nikoliah, stay here for a moment."
Laine nodded and stood from her chair, not even bothering to spare Nikoliah a glance before she was out of the door and closing it behind her. The room lingered in silence for a moment, but it was fleeting.
"I hope you realise that I don't need you." Beckett said, leaning forward over his desk intimidatingly. "Fiducia can do what both of you do in her sleep, she's just courteous. Hell, I had to send her to Stonbrin to pick you up because you weren't competent enough to make those guards believe you. In fact, I think I only kept you on because of your relationship with the Princess."
Nikoliah nodded. He knew that. He had known that for a while. He decided to bite the bullet.
"Are you firing me, Your Majesty?" He asked quickly.
Beckett smirked, and then he smiled, and then he laughed. He reached up and pushed his hair that had grown out away from his eyes, despite the fact that it was about an inch away from even touching his eyebrows. It returned the slicked-back style he was going for.
"You want to keep your job, don't you? Want to keep your rank?" He asked.
Nikoliah nodded.

"Okay." Beckett continued. "I hope you understand the consequences of this. You've forfeited all rights to the throne." He lectured, eyebrows raised.

"I wasn't dating her for the throne." Nikoliah replied quickly. His tone was a little harsh.

"It's just us here, Nikoliah. Man to man. We both know you were in it for her status." He smirked. Nikoliah's eyes widened.

"I was not." He protested.

"You'll undoubtedly try and win her back."

"Because I love her."

Fuck. Fuck, fuck everything. Everything was shit, fuck it all. Everything was blurry. He didn't know how much time was passing.

"Stop crying. You're a fucking soldier. You're acting like a little girl."

He nodded. Fuck, stop it. Weak. He wiped his eyes with the back of his right hand. Beckett watched him, straight lips and eyes cold as he recomposed himself.

"Right, Nikoliah." He started after the knight had dried his face. He was still sniffling, allowing his lip to quiver in order to hide his emotion. He would have a good cry in his bedroom later. Or, he would when he found a new bedroom.

He always did this. Something bad happened and he would pretend it wouldn't until it was too much. He should stop. Laine was trying to make him more vocal about his feelings as of late. Fuck, Laine.

"You can keep your job, despite... all this." King Beckett gestured with his hand, circling around his face and upper body with a disgusted look on his face. Nikoliah nodded, and was about to start profusely thanking him before the King added another condition.

"I will allow you to keep your job." He repeated, clearing his throat and glancing down at his notebook, still illuminated by his halo. "Under a few circumstances."

XXXIII

Raphie hadn't missed Hell much. Hell was grotty. It was dark, and gloomy and all-round unpleasant to be in. She *knew* that. That's why it was below Heaven. That's why demons were below angels.
Still, something was tugging at her.
At first she thought it was because she missed Laine. Which was true. She had felt pretty bad when she first heard that Theo *had*, in fact, lost the fight against Amadeus. But also, she was kind of relieved. If he had won it would have been super awkward for her.
Her own kingdom had changed a lot too. Mainly in the absence of Beckett. He had moved to Klaevr permanently after his first six months as king there. Of course, he was never king of Menphe, hence why he sought the power out elsewhere, but he still had a massive influence that was missing. She had never brought herself to go back to Klaevr, but she had heard that it was doing okay. Politically, at least. The citizens weren't happy, but she'd heard that Laine was, which was more than she could say she'd heard about Theo.
Still, despite how the gossip had been spread, something was nagging at her to go back. It had become so entwined in her daily life for the first few years after her death that it felt unnatural to not feel that unnerving shift in atmosphere when getting off the train. However, she had told herself she couldn't go back. Not after leaving them during the big fight. She didn't need Klaevr, not really. She had friends in Menphe, friends who were angels, like she was. The kind of people that you *want* to be associated with.
Raphie had decided that she wouldn't ever be returning to Klaevr. Not unless something gave her a really good reason.

Two years and four days after she had stopped visiting Hell, something did give her a reason.
The reason came in the form of an awkward knock to her bedroom door.
"Yeah?" She called out in a raised voice, completely expecting it to be one of the other girls that she lived with asking her for her hair straighteners or something. She lived with four other girls, kind of like a sorority, but it was more that none of them had parents and they all got along. Of course, they had their own individual bedrooms, but one was barely used because two of the girls were dating and ended up mooching into the same room over time.
In the last two years, Raphie had cut her hair shorter - down to her shoulders - and dyed it all cotton candy blue, disregarding the split dye of her past. She was wearing a pair of white, wide-leg jeans and a black, tight-fitting cropped shirt, all over her light pink skin.
Her bedroom door shifted ajar, and one of the girls of the house was illuminated by both the fairy lights above her head and her halo.
"Raph, there's some kid looking for you." She said sleazily. Raphie looked up from her sketchbook curiously.
"What?"
"Yeah." The girl repeated. "Some kid. Short lad, looking for you at the door."
Raphie groaned when she realised she would have to get up off her bed. But, she did. She got up off her bed and was sure to blow the candle on her bedside table out before she left. The floorboards creaked under her and she descended the wooden staircase, following in pursuit of the girl that had knocked on her door. On the next floor of the house, the girl veered off into her own bedroom, with a quick mumble of 'good luck'. Luck? She wasn't sure why exactly she would need luck. It was very likely one of those door-to-door advertisers that she had made the mistake of giving her address to.
The front door was open. Open slightly, so that anyone could push it with minimal force and just waltz right into their nordic-inspired hallway whenever they wanted. Nobody had, thankfully.
Upon pushing the door open with her foot, she found that there was in fact a boy at the doorstep.
A boy she recognised.
He looked different as an angel, sure. Dark purple skin and a glowing ring of light floating above his head. He was wearing some light grey joggers and a black t-shirt. He looked disorientated. He looked like... Julian.

She didn't have time to double-check her assumption with another glance before he was in her arms, hands locked tightly around her back as if she'd disappear if he let go.

"I'm so glad I found someone." He muttered, sniffling a little. His hands were shaky and his breaths heavy.

Raphie blinked. She looked back into her empty hallway. Right, okay. She supposed this was probably where she earns her good deed for the day.

Five minutes later, Julian was sitting on the sofa with a mug of tea in his hands. He was still sniffling, watching Raphie as she shut the door and walked towards him with her own cup, sitting next to him.

They waited in silence for a moment.

"What brings you here, then…?" She asked slowly. The last thing she had heard through the grapevine was that Julian had been sent portal-bound back to Earth by King Beckett. Apart from that, she hadn't heard a thing.

Julian took a grateful sip of his tea.

"I died, I think. Again."

"So you were living again?" Raphie replied, eyebrows raised.

"In Massachusetts." He confirmed. "I just, I kind of appeared in a country. Didn't speak English, but it wasn't European." He said with a squint of his eyes as if trying to recall it. "Forget what it was called now, but I was alive. Had a pulse and all."

Raphie looked at him more interestingly now.

"I didn't think I could go back to England because they would have a record of me being dead. So, I went to America. Made a bit of a life. Applied to university, but it's the summer before I'm gonna start now."

Raphie wasn't going to correct his use of 'gonna'. She leant backwards on the sofa, exasperated by the idea.

"Why are you here then? In Menphe? When, before, you were in Klaevr?"

Julian shrugged. "New life, new sins, I guess." His dark hair brushed over his eyes.

"How did you die?" Raphie asked, and maybe it was intrusive to have asked so suddenly after he got here.

Julian thinned his lips for a moment. "Um," He began with a squint. "I think a car hit me. I… I kind of remember being in hospital. Vaguely. I might be wrong, don't take my word for it."

"Right." She nodded. "Anything else eventful? How did you find the states?"

"Alright. A lot of interesting people." He nodded. "I missed the afterlife a lot." He lamented.

"I probably would too. Honestly a little surprised it took you two years to end up back here. I probably would've offed myself to get back."
Julian went quiet. He buried himself in his mug of tea.
"You did?" Raphie asked quickly.
"Tried to. Once. I didn't, um, I didn't know what I was meant to do without Theo. And then, when you *know* what's waiting for you... It's just. Yeah. They didn't believe me when I told them about Klaevr, obviously. Tried to diagnose me with psychosis. Spent a month in a psych ward over it."
"Well, shit."
"Didn't do it again after that. I just decided to let nature do its thing." He continued, and Raphie hummed in acknowledgement.
It took a few minutes of processing that information for Julian to ask his next question.
"Can you take me to Theo?" He said quickly, eyes scrunched shut in anxiety. "He hasn't married or anything, has he?"
Raphie bit her lip. She doubted it, that was for sure. But, really, she didn't know the slightest thing about the man and how he was doing nowadays. He could have ten children by now, and she would be none the wiser. Of course, he *probably* didn't have ten children, but, you know. So, now she had to figure out what to tell Julian. He looked so hopeful, so desperate for any sliver of information about Theo. Information that Raphie couldn't give him.
"I don't... know." She confessed.
Julian frowned. "What do you mean?"
God, where to start? Obviously, he knew about the whole 'abandoning them in the height of their battle' scandal she had started, because he was there. What he didn't know was anything that happened after he got whisked back to Earth. Since a whole two years had passed, it had been quite a lot.
"Well, um. He lost the fight against Lord Beckett. King Beckett, now. Or so I heard. He got banished to Nesbryn and I haven't heard anything at all about him in two years. I don't think you're gonna be seeing him any time soon."
Julian's heart dropped. For the last two years, it had only been '*get through this lifetime and you can see him again*'. And now he'd made it back to the afterlife and he can't? He had no idea if Theo even still thought about him. He's a king, for God's Sake, he probably has men lining up for him to look at them. And, ew, *King Beckett*? It didn't exactly roll off the tongue for him, in fact, it quite repulsed him to think about.

The King, *his* king, had been dethroned and taken over by some snotty, posh, politically inclined tyrant? And for what? This was unfair. Utterly unfair.

"We need to go there, then." He decided quickly as his thoughts continued to race laps around his head. Raphie gave a silent groan at the suggestion. She didn't have the time for this, she had her own life now, a life without that land. "To that place that Theo is. Nesburn?" Julian clarified upon her silence.

"Bryn."

"Nesbryn."

Raphie frowned as guilt tugged at her heart. "We aren't getting to Nesbryn, Jude, sorry. It's not the kind of place you just pull up to like you would with Klaevr." She cautioned. Julian set his mug of tea on the ground.

"Then let's go to Klaevr. I didn't cross dimensions five times to be told no, Raphie."

Raphie's body tensed. She remained silent for a good few moments before regaining her voice. "We can't go there." She admitted quietly. She suddenly felt quite silly for having left them two years ago.

"Why not?" Julian asked, getting straight to the point instantly.

"...I still haven't gone back. You know, since... since you last did."

Julian swallowed. "Right." He acknowledged. That would certainly make things harder... "No time like the present?"

Raphie could only roll her eyes. "I have a life here. I've kind of forgotten about Klaevr, if I'm honest. I'm not sure what goal you were hoping for when you knocked on my door, but it can't have been this."

The newly-dead boy gaped. It was! It was this, how dare she? He had every right mind to let her know just how out of line she was being right now. He would rip right into her about loyalty and courage and all that. At least, he wanted to. In reality, all that came out of his downturned mouth was a weak whine of "Please?"

The last few months, the idea of returning to Klaevr had been pulling at her. But, every time the thought arose, she would shush it back down with a promise of 'I'll go if I have a reason'. Even through the embarrassment, and the betrayal and the tainted memories, she couldn't deny that, well...

This was a reason.

Laine was almost done with hanging her clothes up. The spaghetti straps of one of her tank tops kept slipping off the wooden hanger she was trying to wrangle it onto. She pulsed it up again, bringing her hand away and watching for a moment. And then, like all previous attempts before, it slipped off. The article of clothing fell onto her carpeted floor.

She groaned in frustration and threw the sandalwood hanger. It slammed against her bedroom wall and then collapsed onto the ground. Laine flopped backwards onto her bed and kicked her legs out in front of her with another groan of frustration. She couldn't have one good thing, could she?!

Her door was knocked on. Again.

"Go away." She grumbled. People had been bothering her nonstop the last few days. They think she's gone absolutely crazy or something. Another knock was pressed against her door and she felt like yelling. Reluctantly, she slumped up from her bed and took a few stumbles over towards the door. She wrapped her hand around the handle and took a deep breath in before swinging the door open.

If you had asked Laine to name the top one-hundred things that she reckoned could have been outside of her door, she would have named all hundred before she got to anything remotely similar to Raphie and Julian looking sheepishly hopeful.

She gaped for a moment, taking the sight in.

Raphie looked older, like she was. Two years ago, she was only eighteen, and now she was a proper adult - so there was that much. Then, she had dyed her hair into one solid blue colour. Her fashion taste seemed to have evolved too - as she was sporting a crocheted white bralette-style crop top with a brown denim short skirt that wrapped tightly around her waist. Then, a pair of white leg warmers over brown boots.

Julian was an angel. That was strange, firstly. He had completely vanished through a portal in a way that nobody knew what had happened to him. And, then, here he was, standing on his own two feet - maybe a few inches taller - with the same mischievous smile that she remembered. His hair looked exactly the same, if not slightly shorter, but the same colour.

"Surprise!" Julian smiled with a toothy grin as he bounced on his heels. "It's super good to see you." He grinned again. Raphie looked a little like she wanted to die on the spot. Laine blinked a few times before looking left and right along the corridor.

"Come inside before someone sees you." She said quickly, ushering them into her bedroom and clicking the door shut. Julian perched on the edge of Laine's bed, which left the two girls standing adjacent to each other.
"Hey." Laine said softly, making proper eye contact with the angel for the first time in two years. "You didn't visit."
Raphie swallowed. "I know." She admitted. "I, um, felt bad, so I... I don't know." She whispered.
"You missed my eighteenth birthday."
"Well, you did miss mine." Raphie snickered a little.
"It wasn't *my* fault that you decided to share a birthday with my mother! You knew my dad liked to take us to Stonbrin to celebrate." She slighted back. It was a fond memory.
"I had to get drunk alone! On my eighteenth!" Raphie smiled through a laugh. Laine laughed too.
Once they had calmed down, they were both left smirking in the ideas of their past. Raphie felt a warmness in her chest at being back with Laine again.
"Are we good?" She asked slowly.
Laine blinked a few times. "Leaving us was kind of shitty."
"I know." Raphie admitted. "I'm sorry I did that to you guys, but I was fucking terrified."
The Princess definitely understood that much. "I get it. And, to be fair, you were right. We did lose."
"So, um, can we call it a truce? I've missed being friends with you." Raphie said quietly.
"Yeah." Laine breathed. She had missed it too. "We're good." She nodded, and they remained looking into eachothers eyes for a moment longer.
"Oh my god! Just kiss already."
They both snapped their heads over to the bed, where Julian was swinging his legs slowly.
"You can't say that, she has a boyfriend." Raphie lectured, glancing over to Laine for confirmation of that statement. The Princess shook her head slowly. Both visitors to her bedroom gasped.
"He broke up with you?! What a dick." Julian remarked from the bed.
Laine shook her head again in the exact same way, and Raphie gasped.
"You broke up with him? When? What did he do?"
Laine rolled her eyes. "Earlier this week. And, just because I left *him* doesn't mean he did something. Maybe he just got annoying to be dating." She shrugged as she sat down on her vanity chair.
Raphie raised her eyebrows. "I'll ask again. What did he do?"

"Actually, no!" Laine replied with her chin in the air. "You don't get to interrogate me. What the hell are *you* doing here?!" She squeaked, pointing to Julian with an outstretched arm dramatically.
"Died."
"Yeah, no shit." Laine groaned. "I mean, like, what happened in the two years between last time I saw you and now?" She asked. Julian frowned.
"I already told this to Raphie, do I have to do it again?"
The girls both looked at him as if he had just put spaghetti in a pan without water and it was about to set on fire.
"Fine, fine, yeesh." He conceded. "Got portal'd back to Earth, moved to Massechusets. Stayed in a hotel for a bit and got a job as a barista. Missed Theo. Tried to kill myself, didn't work. Finished school, applied to uni. Stepped into the road too quickly without looking."
Laine looked around in the silence. "Makes sense...?" She said after a moment, although it sounded more like a question. "And, I guess... Beckett gave you a new life. So you went to Heaven because you didn't do anything that bad since you got your new life."
"I prefer the term 'respawned', actually." Julian laughed. "But, yeah. I guess so."
Laine looked down to her lap and fidgeted with her hands for a moment.
"Um, Julian?"
"Yeah?"
"You know... You know that Theo's not here, right?" She asked anxiously.
Julian's previously giggly demeanour faded. He swallowed and nodded cautiously. "Yeah. But- but, I was hoping you could take me to him."
Laine grimaced a little. "I would like nothing more. You're way better for him than that Isaac guy. But I'm kind of in some trouble."
"Isaac?"
"What trouble?"
"I saw Theo like four days ago. I snuck to Nesbryn without telling anyone, and King Beckett is *not* happy with me over it. He's got people on all corners making sure I don't try and go back." She admitted.
"Who is Isaac?" Julian repeated, exasperation leaking through his voice.
"Just some boy. Isaac thinks they're dating and Theo thinks they're friends with benefits."
Julian's jaw dropped.
"He has a boyfriend?!"
Laine grimaced. She definitely should have been more careful with the way she said that.

306

"He doesn't actually love him. He- um- He told me that he thinks of you when he's with Isaac if that makes you feel better?"

"It doesn't." Julian deadpanned. "Gah. I have to win him back now, too."

There was another knock on Laine's bedroom door, but rather than waiting for a response, this person just knocked and then opened the door after about half a second's wait.

"Laine, I left my good belt in here. Can I- Oh. Hello." Nikoliah stopped about a foot into the door. He was wearing his full kit - his good quality cargo trousers and elbow, shoulder and knee pads over his light grey shirt and cotton blue sash. He looked tired, but determined. He blinked a moment at looking at the two visitors.

"Niko, mate, what did you do?" Julian immediately asked with a narrow of his eyes. Nikoliah's eyes locked on Julian and widened slightly as he recognised him alongside his voice. The knight's eyes cast back over to Laine.

"I really hope you can find a way to get him out of here in the sixty seconds it's going to take me to walk to the King's office." He said bluntly as he walked over to Laine's closet and picked up a black leather belt with holsters on it from the bottom of the cupboard.

"Oh, come on!" Laine breathed. "You do not have to tell him."

Nikoliah stood back in the doorway. "His majesty."

Laine grimaced at her ex-boyfriend. "You don't have to tell *his majesty*." She mocked slightly. Nikoliah took no notice.

"I work for his majesty, not for you, Crown Princess." He said easily. "Sixty seconds."

He shut the door behind him after that, and the three left in the bedroom could hear his boots treading against the carpeted floor down the corridor towards King Beckett's office.

"What the hell is up his ass?" Julian asked quickly. "Swear to god he was not that much of an uptight prick two years ago."

"Touche, he wasn't. Is he okay?" Raphie raised her eyebrows.

"He's trying to get me back for breaking up with him by inconveniencing me every way he can, don't worry too much." Laine replied softly with a roll of her eyes. "Having said that, we *should* be worried about the King marching in here in about two minutes."

Julian stood and brushed himself off as if he'd been eating.

"Well, *Crown Princess*." He teased. "Looks like we're going to Nesbryn to escape him." He smiled mischievously, willing Laine to agree. Raphie turned to look at Laine with a raise of her eyebrows. She hadn't done anything genuinely exciting since they went back to Earth. Laine stood and grabbed a cardigan off the back of her chair.

"I suppose if we're sneaking you out of here either way." She decided.

XXXIV

The original idea of climbing out of Laine's window would not have worked, simply because the fall would probably have broken their legs. Raphie had dismissed the idea quickly, just on that basis.
Their next option was to leave Laine's room, and use one of the staff staircases to get onto the bottom floor. They could get out of the window from there. The issue was that the staff staircase led down into the hallway that held the King's office, where he was likely to come out when looking for them.
Discussing this plan had already taken about forty seconds. They needed to go quickly. Luckily for them, nobody was in the corridor at all, so they could make a quick dash across it into the passageway with the staircase.
"This is small as Hell, what if I was claustrophobic?" Julian whispered with a giggle as they stepped hastily down the spiral staircase.
"You'd get over it." Laine snipped back, leading the way down the passage. Raphie dared to laugh and was promptly shushed by her friend with the reminder that they were *sneaking* out.
The staircase was dimly lit, only by overhead candles that were way too high on the wall to be effective. The walls were unpainted - just raw stone bricks that lead onto a thin wooden door. Laine, being at the front, got there first and pressed her ear against it to listen.
Silence prevailed.
She decided to stop beating around the bush and push the door open. Huh. Empty hallway. They were in some serious luck.
"Okay, quick, come on." She said, scurrying out, stepping towards the window at the end of the hall. It had an ornate black frame and the same

ugly curtains that Theo had wanted to replace around the time he was first crowned. He never got round to it, obviously.

Raphie hooked her hands under the edge of the window and tried to push it upwards. It didn't budge at all.

"Who locks a window?" She exclaimed as she tried to pull the handle open.

Laine cursed under her breath.

"I can- I think I can do a spell to get it open, but no promises." She said, rubbing her hands together. Ever since she had helped Theo kill that creature with her magic four days ago, she had become a lot more invested in practising it and actually utilising it effectively. Through the cotton of her cardigan, the markings on her arms began to glow and some red light started to form in between her two hands.

Someone at the end of the corridor cleared their throat.

Beckett stood with his arms crossed in front of him. His eyebrows were raised and he had a look of anger on his face as the two angels and demon turned to look at him.

"Laine, I swear, you open that window you're renouncing your title as heir." He cautioned, voice thick and confident as he stepped closer to them.

Laine focused on the magic brewing in her hands even more. In the rush of adrenaline and fear, she had a realisation. She didn't even want the title anymore. Not after everything. She would happily succeed Theo as an heir, but Amadeus Beckett? Under his conviction?

She pushed the ball of light towards the lock.

It snapped open with a trail of smoke moving off of it. She quickly pulled it open and urged for the other two to go through.

"I don't want to hurt you. I just need the boy." The angel approaching them cautioned, lips tight in a thin smile as he picked up his walking pace and began to charge some magic in his hands. He needed Julian. If he had Julian, he could stop anyone from attacking him under the threats of hurting the man. He knew that was Theo's one weakness: love. It probably ran in the family - two birds, one stone.

"Quickly!" Laine basically yelled at them. Raphie hopped through and kind of rolled on the other side, landing on some concrete-infused gravel. She leapt to her feet afterwards and reached her hands through the window towards Julian.

Beckett had started to run, and he was incredibly fast. In his hands, he charged a ball of white light, which he threw at the newly deceased angel.

Julian quickly threw himself through the window with a scared yelp, being half-caught by Raphie and therefore able to stay on his feet. "Don't you dare!" Beckett yelled. Laine looked back at the man running towards her and leapt out of the window in a haste-charged stumble. Her skin scraped across the gravel and she was incredibly grateful she hadn't chosen today to wear that new skirt she bought.

The recovery time from actually getting out of the window and stumbling back to their feet had to be quick. The obstacle itself gave them at least a thirty second head start, because if the King decided not to climb through it, he would have to go around the long way before he could even tell any of his soldiers to stop them.

"Okay, follow me." She breathed, bringing herself to stand in a rushed manner. She broke off into a run along the edge of the corridor, and ignored a vague groan of athletic protest from Julian.

This should have been terrifying. The mere concept that the most important person in the kingdom was incredibly angry at her and would probably do anything to get the three of them back. It should have made her skin crawl with anxiety and fear. But, it didn't. The only extra neurological chemical Laine felt was adrenaline. Sheer, pure adrenaline. Exhilaration.

It was so exciting to be doing something *wrong*. She had spent the last two years conservatively smiling under Beckett's instruction, unable to express any discontempt at all.

But, now, she felt so free. She smiled broadly into the rapidly travelling wind. She even dared to laugh. It was an *amazing* feeling.

They collapsed onto a set of four seats towards the front of the train with heaving breaths. It took until they were ten minutes into their journey before they had calmed down enough to hold a proper conversation.

Because of how scarce the trains to Nesbryn were, they only operated upon request. Maybe it was taking advantage of her power, but threatening to take the jobs of the people operating the train station made them act pretty quickly. And since Julian had never been on a train all on his own before (bar his friends, of course), it was really exciting to him. Once he had regained his energy, he was running up and down the carriages like a madman, both enthused with the idea of going to see

Theo and being able to do socially unacceptable things like cartwheel (or, attempt to cartwheel) down the centre of a train carriage.
"You're going to tire yourself out." Laine lectured from her slumped position. Her feet were up on the seat opposite her, and Raphie had done the exact same with only her right food in her position next to Laine. Julian laughed.
"Keep complaining and I'll break out my year two gymnastics club routine." He chided, stopping his movement and placing his hands on his hips. "Do you have water?"
"Do I look like I have water?" Laine deadpanned, gesturing to her itemless upkeep. Julian frowned and sat down on an empty seat.
"Well, is there water in Nesbryn?"
Raphie brought her foot off the chair and sat up, looking at him.
"No, the eternal punishment for them is unquenchable thirst." The angel replied, and Julian took no notice of the sardonic slight. He sat down properly and began to bite his fingernails.
"It's... kind of dark." He whispered as he peered out of the window. He sounded like a small child to the two girls, who looked at him with mild concern.
"Yeah. There's no sunlight in Nesbryn." Laine recalled quietly, still watching with intention as Julian looked out of the ever-darkening window.
His eyes remained latched onto the glass. It was... really dark outside. And cold. Was there heating on this train? He rationalised that, probably not. "You okay?" Raphie asked slowly. Julian nodded quickly in dismissal.
"Are you... Sure?" Raphie confirmed.
Julian blinked softly.
"What if he doesn't want to see me?" He whispered.
"What?"
"I mean, is this the right idea? He- he has a life, his own life without me. We dated for like a week two years ago- I- I don't know, is this... the right thing to be doing?"
Laine stood up from her seat in the train and made the two-step journey towards where Julian was aimlessly looking out the window. She sat beside him - entirely blocking his view of the window. She tucked a loose strand of her hair behind her ear and looked at him as the newfound distraction in front of his view forced Julian to do the same.
"I'm not going to make any promises I can't keep." She stated bluntly. "But I saw him four days ago and he spoke about you completely unprompted.

I didn't even bring you up, he just started talking about you." She reassured, and Julian nodded slightly.

"And hey!" Raphie called from them, a few metres away. "If he's over you, everybody that's ever died is a fish in the sea." She grinned. Her attempt of helpfulness did nothing to calm the nerves of the anxious boy sitting on the train, but it did seem to give Laine a feeling of mild amusement, signified by the way she rolled her eyes with a small snort.

Nesbryn was just as cold as Laine remembered it.

Despite the fact that it was about six hours earlier in the day than it had been last time, you would expect maybe even a cool afternoon breeze to be flowing generously through the streets. But, no. The wind blew just as viciously as always, doing wonders to the hair that the Princess had spent brushing for ten minutes this morning.

Julian had to grab onto Raphie's shoulders to stop himself being blown over. Of course, it was more psychological than genuine chance he would really get blown over, but out of all the fear manifesting inside his chest, it was probably the least of his worries.

The pub had been closed. Naturally, it wasn't evening yet, and day drinking was not a habit that the people of Nesbryn wanted to grow accustomed to. It would be all too easy, considering their circumstances, to drown their sorrows in booze. So, Laine had so valiantly led the way towards Theo's house, taking them diagonally through the courtyard that they'd fought that creature in.

"See, this is a lot more akin to how I pictured Hell as a kid." Raphie whispered. And, she was right. It was desolate and decrepit, all alone and lightless. The kind of place that people come to die. Just the mere atmosphere had Julian standing at each corner for a few moments in case someone (or something) jumped out and mauled him. Each time, he would promptly scurry to catch up with the much more fearless girls he was travelling with as they made another semi-snarky comment about his fragile masculinity.

It was only when they got to the top of Theo's street that Julian's fear began to self-rationalise.

There was a tapping. A faint tapping of feet on stone. The darkness made it difficult to make anything out than a blurred silhouette. Laine shushed them and all three stopped under a cold-toned streetlight. The sound got closer and closer, louder and louder. Julian found his fingers digging into someone's arm (he didn't know nor care whose) and undoubtedly leaving nasty fingernail indents.

Out of the dark mist appeared a demon that Julian had never seen before. He crossed his arms and raised an eyebrow.

"Isaac." Laine tried to smile, voice light and airy.

Isaac raised his eyebrows.

"I think you're the first person who has ever visited here and made the choice to return, Laine. Unless you've slept in the train station this week." He laughed.

Julian flashed an uneasy eye towards the man, who noticed. "You angels oughta be careful here. Wouldn't want something to happen to you because you chanced on dirtying yourselves with our demonic filth." He warned, and for a split second, it sounded like a threat.

Laine swallowed. "Haha, um, is Theo home? Looking for him, as per usual." She smiled. She was unnerved very apparently.

Isaac smiled with the corner of his mouth. "It's the middle of the day, he's at work. I can show you if you'd like."

Laine nodded quickly. "Yeah, um, yeah. Thanks."

"No worries. This way then. Who are your luminescent friends?" He asked, walking alongside Laine back towards the square. Raphie and Julian exchanged a fearful glance, but still followed with appropriate vigour.

Laine chanced a glance behind her to confirm that they were in fact following. "Right, sorry." She said sheepishly. "Isaac, this is my friend Raphie." She gestured, pointing towards Raphie.

She gave an awkward wave, which Isaac returned with the same energy. "And, who is short, dark and moderate over there?" He asked, gesturing to Julian.

"I'm not that short." He replied on an offended note.

"Teasing. Sorry." Isaac smirked, hands falling into his pockets. "And you are?" He asked once more, turning to face Julian as he continued to walk, just backward.

The angel risked a look over at Laine.

"Julian."

Isaac stopped walking.

"Julian? As in, Theo's Julian?" He asked, eyebrows raised in concern.

"He's talked about me?"

"Sometimes. Nothing interesting, mainly complaints." Isaac replied quickly, turning back around and continuing to walk. The air became a little thicker.

"Really?" Julian asked, smirking a little. He was clearly getting under this man's skin. "You seem tense. Are you sure? Is it something else?" Julian pestered, walking closer to Isaac.
"Julian." Laine warned lowly.
"Are you jealous?" Julian pushed. He liked this feeling of powerfulness. Isaac set his jaw square.
"He's never just *randomly* brought you up, you know. I had to ask him. And even then he seemed embarrassed of you." Isaac spat.
Julian raised an eyebrow. Now we were talking. "And you're what? His pretend boyfriend?"
"I've been his 'pretend boyfriend' for a year and a half." He replied, narrowing his eyebrows.
Julian retaliated quickly. "I bet he thinks of me when he's with you."
Isaac's strong footsteps halted against the gravel. "Do you want me to take you to him or not? You need to lose the fucking attitude, because, quite frankly, he's *my* boyfriend, not yours. And you'd be an idiot to consider trading an eternity in Heaven for a boy. And he'd be an idiot to let you do so." He grunted, anger set on his face. "Don't say another word to me or I will just walk home and go to sleep in *our* bed, and you can find your own way there."
Julian found his temper incredibly humorous, but for the sake of wanting to find Theo, he silently vowed to keep his mouth shut for the remainder of the journey. Which he did, even impressing himself. Laine had made idle small talk with Isaac, who still spoke as if he was mildly irritated, and Raphie just kept a slow pace beside Julian. It was strange. In every other kingdom she'd ever been in, being an angel had made her feel more powerful or better than everyone else. Here, however, her halo made her quite self-conscious. It made her a target.
She still felt quite self-conscious when they turned down a small alleyway where an orange light was glowing out of a glass panelled building. There was a small darkly-painted door on the right, and the window was frosted over so you couldn't see in. Adjacent to the door was a torch lit and attached to the wall. If he were alone, Julian probably would have lingered awkwardly outside for upwards of ten minutes. But, he wasn't alone, and so Isaac made no hesitations to push the door open.

XXXV

Theo was hunched over his desk with a fineliner pinched between his index, middle finger and thumb. He was tracing the outline of a small black cat. The door swung open somewhat suddenly and he messed his line up with a sudden jerk of his hand.
"Shit." He muttered, pulling his sleeve over his hand and dipping it in his glass of water before trying to wipe the page. When the ink only smudged, he frowned and slid the paper off his wooden desk and into the bin.
He looked up easily.
"Hey." He breathed. He dropped his pen down onto the desk.
"Hey there. Hope I didn't interrupt too much." Isaac smiled slightly.
"No, not at all. It wasn't going well anyway. I feel like something's off, nothing's been working today." He complained, standing up from his desk and walking around to sit on the front of it.
He was wearing a black hoodie with fishnet sleeves over a pair of light grey jeans, the same colour as the rusting necklace fastened around his neck. The inside of his little store was quite simplistic, honing just some wooden floorboards and dark blue floral wallpaper on the back wall, whilst the rest was just darker wood than on the ground. The walls were also decked with an array of posters. There was a small dark sofa and two chairs next to it. And, lastly, a small glass cabinet was home to a set of tattoo equipment, including ink of all colours of the rainbow.
"Well, you've got some visitors again." Isaac told him.
"Laine?" Theo asked, trying to peek his head round the door.

"And company." Isaac replied, stepping backwards out the door. "Well, come on then." He said somewhat impatiently.

Laine walked through the door, dragging Raphie behind her. Theo sat up a little straighter and his eyes widened.

"Shit, Hello." He said, eyes floating up and down Raphie.

"Hey." She replied in an awkward manner. She clearly felt some kind of remorse or embarrassment about the nature of the last time they saw each other. Theo rolled his eyes.

"I've been here too long to hold a grudge, come here and give me a hug." He smiled, leaping up off the table and meeting her in the middle in an embrace.

Raphie held it for a while. "I'm sorry." She muttered.

"Don't be." Theo shook his head. "You were being smart. I like the hair."

"Thanks. I like the tattoos."

Laine had taken a few steps forwards, and once Theo and Raphie disconnected she snuck in for a hug with her brother also.

"What brings you here again?" Theo asked after a moment's silence.

Laine smirked. "He's nervous." She giggled, galloping over towards the door. Theo watched as she reached her hand out and seemed to struggle to pull someone into the building. Eventually, said person gave in and stumbled awkwardly towards the door.

Julian's halo illuminated the air around him. He looked up and made wishful eye contact with Theo, who did the same. Their eyes locked in a battle of earthy tones. Theo's hands dropped to his sides and his lips parted slightly. Seeing Julian felt like the feeling of untying a knot. Of waking up five minutes before your alarm. Of finding money in your wallet that you didn't think was there.

His shoulders deflated and his body untensed. The room remained silent until one of them would make some kind of move. Theo blinked and suddenly Julian was in his arms. He didn't remember when he'd gripped onto the man and buried his head in his shoulder, but he had, and now he was crying.

The whole room around them disappeared as they held each other. Julian sniffled and pulled his head away, looking up at Theo happily.

"God, what the fuck are you doing here?" Theo smiled through his tears, sniffling with a grin on his face. Julian giggled and pushed his head back into Theo's chest, pulling back after a moment and tilting his head upwards towards the demon.

"I missed you. A lot." Julian said quietly.

And then they were kissing. Careless and like it was the last time they ever would, not worried about the other people in the room at all. Theo was pushed against the desk as they continued to show their appreciation for each other, the kisses only getting more desperate by the second.

All of a sudden, the contact was gone completely. Theo watched Julian stumble backwards, barely having time to process it before he was slapped across the face harder than he had ever been slapped before. Harder than King Beckett had slapped him at his coronation.

"You fucking prick!" Isaac yelled, tears welling in his eyes. "You asshole!" Theo hissed in pain and slid off the desk. "Shit, I'm sorry, Isaac." He breathed, tilting his head sympathetically.

Isaac looked furious. He wouldn't take that. He had been completely and utterly betrayed. He had been told over and over again that he was good, he was fine. He didn't need to be stressed about losing Theo, it was just them after all. To be told that and then shown up for some random angel? He was angrier than he had ever been. He had tried so fucking hard to play nice, but, no. No, this was the final straw. He wasn't going to let this happen to him.

"You told me I didn't have to worry about him! You said you were over him, you were done! Fuck you!" He yelled, pushing Theo's chest and sending him stumbling a few steps backwards. Laine and Raphie didn't dare say a thing as they watched the situation, keeping close to each other and backing towards a corner.

"Well, obviously, I thought he was in a different dimension, didn't I?!" Theo yelled back, chest heaving up and down. He'd realised that he'd fucked up to do this in front of Isaac. Isaac was a nice guy, sure. But his emotions flipped like a coin. Say one thing wrong and he was screaming like you'd murdered his whole family. So, in that kind of situation, Theo could only do what he had been taught. Fight fire with fire.

Julian stepped backwards a little as Isaac's face contorted between rage and devastation.

"No!" He yelled, almost like a child having a temper tantrum. "No! You don't get to do this, Theo! I'm not a fucking puppet for you to throw away when something better walks in the door!"

"We would never have even been anything if we weren't stuck in this shithole together! We don't love each other, Isaac, we love feeling loved. We're desperate, not in love. Don't pretend we ever were."

Theo stumbled out of the way as Isaac tried to punch him. He retaliated with a sharp elbow to his ribcage, which left the other demon groaning in slight pain.

Isaac shook his head. That was his breaking point. He stepped dangerously close to Theo and shoved him against the wall.

"Don't lie, don't you fucking lie." He cried, body jerking in sudden movements. "You love me, Theo. You love me!" He repeated. Theo could only shake his head.

"I never loved you, you knew I didn't." He swallowed.

Isaac used his forearm to push Theo against the wall again, trapping him between his body and the wood. Being already the perfect height, Isaac pressed his mouth against Theo's - grabbing his arms to prevent him from pushing back. Theo gasped as his lips were stolen into the kiss. He couldn't breathe, he was going to die and he was sure of it. He pushed Theo against the wall with more vigour. Isaac slipped his right hand up into Theo's hoodie as he deepened the kiss, determined more than anything to prove how much they loved each other. He pressed his whole body against Theo's as he continued. His hand trailed down to the waistband of Theo's jeans. He couldn't breathe. He was going to die.

And then Isaac was away from him. He gasped and coughed for a taste of the fresh air, sliding down the wall as he struggled to find himself again. His eyes were watering as he spluttered, unable to think or see anything other than the disgust he felt towards himself. He felt dirty, he felt like a slut. He was going to throw up. He was going to have a breakdown.

"Fine." Isaac gritted, shoving Julian, who had just punched him in the jaw. "You're a fucking dick, Strythio Virzor." He said, and then he looked over to the other man. "When his next fucktoy arrives to replace you, you'll be fucking sorry." He yelled. The demon took one last furious look around the room and stormed out of the store.

Theo pulled his knees up to his chest and buried his head in between them. Someone was talking to him. A soft voice was saying things. Things that he couldn't hear or reply to. His voice had been robbed from him. He blinked, and blinked again. When he looked up, the lights were off. The two halos in the room were providing a dimmed light that wasn't too overstimulating. Julian was leant down on his knees a few feet away from him on his right. Raphie was on his left, and Laine was right in front of him. He was a dick - Isaac was right. He was a fucking horrible person to have led Isaac on like that. His thoughts were interrupted by his sister.

"He's gone, I promise. He's gone." Laine chorused in a whisper. "You're okay."

Theo nodded to show that he'd heard this time. He reached out to his right and put his hand on Julian's. The angel squeezed his hand back and leant in a little closer. Theo's arm wrapped around Julian's torso in the darkness and pulled them together. The embrace felt like safety.
"What do you want, love?" Julian whispered. Theo shook his head.
"Just stay." He replied. "Please, just stay."
"I'm not going anywhere." He reassured, and he meant it.

The forcefield surrounding the Kingdom of Nesbryn had been strongly standing for the last seven centuries. It reached up as high as flight was possible, and stretched tightly around the walls of the island, locking those imprisoned there by society away for an eternity of abandonment. The forcefield was held up by a crystal. A three-dimensional hexagon of ruby, blood-coloured stone. Said crystal was kept inside a secure vault a few hundred metres underground T'kota. Since T'kota was the central kingdom, and far out of reach of anyone subject to living in Nesbryn, it was deemed the most secure location to hone all of this power. The crystal was, despite popular belief, accessible only by a door. A door that held challenges, yes. But a door nonetheless.
It was heavily guarded by many layers of magical security. It was the kind that needed a lot of power to be broken through. And, in terms of 'a lot', it actually meant the power of four pureblooded demons. This was a tried and true theory. Three was too little; there wasn't enough power between just three. The last band of four that had ever attempted it had been shunned, stripped of their titles and banished to Nesbryn themselves after being so, so, desperately close to breaking all social order. They had gotten past the magic, but legend said that the stone itself was too heavy to dislodge from its podium. This had been about five-hundred years before Theo had become the fifth pureblooded demon to be banished to Nesbryn.
About three-hundred years before Theo's banishment, one lone demon had attempted to break the forcefield. She had been the young Crown Princess of Klaevr, feeling a little trapped in her role and hoping to break social injustice through large-scale rebellion. Because she was only young, Cordelia Virzor had not been doomed to the same punishment as the previous demons who had attempted. Rather, she had just been sworn to secrecy about the scandal. It was the kind of thing that had stayed between the royal family for centuries.

Cordelia had told Laine about it when she was around seven. It was the kind of meaningless anecdote that didn't have any leverage to a young girl. In fact, until Ayale had brought the legends of the stone and its attackers up, she had completely blacked it out of her mind. The realisation had been powerful, and Laine had immediately decided that she could be a great help to them.

And, she already lived in the same kingdom as the stone.

Okay, so, as far as getting Theo out of Nesbryn went, they had two demons. That was the plan - to break the forcefield down.

"Well, we don't know any other purebloods. Not other than dad, and from what I hear, he's not on the table." Theo pouted, chin resting on his hand as he drummed his other fingers against the table. They had stayed in his tattoo parlour for a good hour before ambling back to the tavern to properly talk and figure out what their next move was.

Laine raised an eyebrow. "We do know one other." She chided, and Theo gave her an exasperated look.

"We're not asking her." Theo replied instantly, defences going up. "End of."

"Oh, come on." Laine rolled her eyes. Julian, Raphie and Ayale stayed mostly silent as they felt the tension in the air grow. "You'd seriously rather stay here forever than swallow your pride from a failed engagement two years ago?" She asked rather loudly.

"Oh!" Julian gasped, slapping his hands against the table. "We're talking about Serenity." He breathed. "Sorry, I was a little lost."

Ayale furrowed xer eyebrows. "The Vaemunt princess? Swear she's married now."

"Engaged." Laine corrected with a point across the table.

Theo dropped his head onto the wood so that his voice was muffled. "Exactly, she's moved on. I don't want to intertwine our lives any further."

"She's the only one that can help." His sister continued to push. God, she was annoying.

"Also," Raphie began. "You won't even have to see her. We can go ask her to help. If she says no, you'll never have to see her again because you'll be stuck here. And if she says yes, then it's all good between you, right?"

Theo pushed his empty glass towards the centre of the table and closed his eyes.

Laine stood instantly and her chair made an uncomfortable scraping sound against the ground.

"Come on, Theo." She groaned. "You cannot seriously care more about your own ego than your people. They're fucking suffering under

Beckett's rule, and they'll continue to suffer all because you're a little embarrassed about some girl you used to kiss! Get over yourself."

Theo blinked and looked up at her. "They aren't *my* people, Laine. They're yours. If you care so much then figure it out yourself. It's not *my* fault you ran away and got yourself in trouble with him." He grumbled, leaning back on his chair and sinking into his hoodie.

The tavern went completely silent as the other four people in the room looked at Theo. He, however, was paying them little to no notice. That was until he felt a hand push under the bottom of his chin where it rested against his arms on the table. Julian pulled his head up as he leant over the wood, forcing the other man to make eye contact with him.

"You listen here, mister." He lectured, jaw set tight. "I don't know if you think this act of not giving a shit about your life is cool, but I did not die twice for you to tell me that you can't be arsed! You're scared that you aren't wanted back in Klaevr, right? So rather than cease the opportunity to go back and live your life how it was, you'd seriously rather stay here and sulk like a fucking child? Get over yourself and start acting your age, I swear to God." He growled. "I love you. I'm not going to let you do this to yourself, get a grip."

Theo's head stayed in the upwards position it was pulled into even after Julian moved his hand away. His mouth was hung open in slight shock, pointed fangs visible inside his mouth before he shut it again when he realised how stupid he probably looked. `

"Uh, yeah. What he said." Raphie pointed subtly towards Julian. Theo pinched the bridge of his nose between his thumb and index finger and sighed.

"Fine, fine. Go to Vaemunt and beg Serenity to help you. But she won't." He said.

"Good attitude. That's bound to get you far." Ayale smiled and rather violently patted Theo on the back twice from where xe was now standing behind him.

Theo ignored xer and stood from his own chair. He strolled over to Julian and wrapped an arm around his chest.

"Julian stays here. That's my condition."

Julian grinned a little at the idea of being the one thing Theo wanted most.

"Okay." Laine nodded. "I'll go to Vaemunt alone. I'll recruit Serenity and her fiance, hopefully, and then we'll go to T'kota and speak to grandma. With any luck she'll agree to help us break the forcefield down. In the meantime, you can get all of the demons here to prepare themselves.

The second that thing goes down Hell is going to break loose. I'll meet you back here and we can go to Klaevr ourselves and show King Beckett how we feel. Sound good?" She beamed somewhat unsettlingly.

Theo looked around the room at the others. When he woke up this morning this was probably the last thing he expected to be doing. Planning to get out of Nesbryn and take his throne back with his arm wrapped around his *actual* boyfriend? Hah, funny idea. Never going to happen though.

But, it was. It was. He didn't know if he was ecstatic or appalled at the idea. Raphie, Ayale, Laine and Julian all had their eyes set on him as he underwent this emotional shift. With a swallow and semi-reluctant roll of his eyes, he nodded.

"Sounds good."

XXXVI

Laine arrived in Vaemunt about two hours later. The atmosphere was pleasantly surprising - nice and breezy with a warm glow from the sun against her skin. She, despite her royalty, had never actually been to Vaemunt before, and she had to admit that it was really nice. Almost as nice as Klaevr was this time three years ago. Nicer now. The people seemed cheery, but all gave her disapproving looks when she walked past.
It made sense, she supposed. Theo was likely quite infamous in this kingdom. They'd lost their second born princess to an engagement with her kingdom's first born. That immediately made her more high of status, if she would marry to be the Queen consort. But, obviously, she didn't. Laine hadn't spoken to her since before she left for Earth with the others, so she had no idea about Serenity's feelings towards the whole situation. She could only hope that there were no grudges being held. Besides, she was happy now - engaged and thriving back in her own kingdom.
The man who had ended up properly putting a ring on her finger was also a second born. The Prince of one of the smaller kingdoms, in the south west of Hell. His parents were both still on the throne, so, aside from his elder sister, he didn't have much purpose staying in his home Kingdom of Atroka.
Laine had met him once, only briefly. At the group she had been forced to go to, in which she spoke relations with all other potential future monarchs. He'd seemed nice enough. Quite stern, but nice. The kind of guy that shook your hand and said 'pleasure to make your acquaintance'.

Although, Laine reasoned, that may have been his parents' influence. They were known for being quite uptight in their rule, which did make sense considering that Atroka was the kingdom for the worst people in Hell - other than Nesbryn.

Naturally, because they had met before, Laine recognised Prince Vercobrix when he came down the stairs to greet her.

He was a tall man. Older than Serenity too, about twenty-five. His features were slender and his skin dark. His hair was shortly braided and slicked back behind his ears, which held his dagger-shaped earrings. He wore dress shoes underneath dark trousers, which had a mid-blue coloured dress shirt tucked into them. Over that held a light grey waistcoat. His lavender-coloured horns were of impressive size, in the same shade as the expensive wristwatch on his left arm.

Vercobrix raised an eyebrow.

"Good afternoon, Princess Laine." He said easily, flicking away a few of the guards that had come to see if she was a problem being in the castle. "What brings you here?"

Laine smirked at his formalness.

"Afternoon." She smiled. "I was hoping I'd get to talk to you and Princess Serenity. In private, ideally."

He nodded and looked back towards the staircase. "Yes, of course. I think we can accommodate that." He said, holding his hands together and fidgeting with them in front of him. His nails were sharpley trimmed.

"Do follow." He instructed, turning on his heel and beginning to peruse towards the stairs. Laine followed him quickly, trying not to let his serious upkeep psych her out. The castle that they lived in was similar to the hers - wide hallways and dark coloured carpet illuminated by the warm glow of fire torches attached to the wall.

"So, how are the affairs going in Klaevr?" He asked as he slowed down to allow Laine to walk beside him. "Still good, I hope."

Laine noticed that he rarely blinked.

"Um, good. Yeah. I mean, I don't really... Do much for it. King Beckett does all that formal stuff." She said, voice trailing off as she felt incredibly small.

Vercobrix's lip curled upwards. "Eurgh." He gritted. "I would prefer if we weren't to use that man's name inside these walls."

Laine quirked an eyebrow as she realised that this was pretty good for them. "You dislike him?" She asked carefully.

"I do. As does Serenity. I sincerely hope you won't sing his praises to me now I've said that." He replied, gaze narrow as he turned to look at Laine. She felt a little paralyzed under his gaze, like a deer in headlights.
"No, no, of course not. He ruined my life. I just, he is the King of my kingdom, so he does play a big part in my belonging." She rationalised.
Vercobrix hummed in acknowledgement as he continued to lead the way down the corridor. Eventually, they stopped outside of a set of double doors.
Vercobrix leant against the wall and knocked on the wood.
"Yeah?" Came Serenity's voice from inside. Vercobrix suppressed a smile and turned towards it with his hand on the doorknob, which was the same colour as the golden band of the ring on his ring finger.
"Wait here a moment." He told, before opening the door and disappearing inside. The wood was only thin, so Laine could easily eavesdrop on the conversation.
It was stunning. Vercobrix's voice dropped an octave and became sweet and charming as he spoke.
"Hey, lovely."
"Hey, you." She giggled back, and Laine heard the sound of them exchanging a quick kiss. "Who was at the door?"
"Laine. The Klaevrian princess, Strythio's sister." He replied softly, and Serenity snickered.
"Yeah, I know who she is; you didn't have to mansplain her family relations." She laughed a little. "What did she need?"
Vercobrix didn't laugh, but Laine could tell through the tone in his voice that he was at least humoured. "Alright, alright. She wanted to speak with us. That okay?"
"Yeah, of course. Is she outside?"
"Yeah."
Serenity raised her voice slightly. "You can come in, Laine." She instructed playfully. Laine was caught a little off guard by being addressed through a door, but entered anyway.
"He has a lot of faith in those doors." She smiled warmly. Vercobrix rolled his eyes and sat down on the edge of their bed.
The inside of the bedroom was a lot different to how she had imagined it from outside the door. The walls were a light yellow - only a few shades lighter than the blanket at the end of the bed. There was a large ornate mirror with a gold edge, which also matched the bed frame. The sheets themselves were just plain white, whereas the curtains were black. There was a lovely chandelier which was also gold above them, and a

swirl-patterned black, white and grey rug on the ground atop white carpet. Laine noticed a stain that looked like orange juice peeking out from under the rug.

Serenity's hair was a lot shorter now, just down to her jawline, but still the same fiery orange as how Laine remembered it. She looked happy. Not only in her smile, but the glow of her skin and light in her completely blacked-out eyes. She was wearing light blue jeans that hugged her hips, as well as a short-sleeved white dress shirt with the top button undone. Serenity rose from where she was sitting on the bed. "Can I hug you or would that be weird?" She asked wearily.

Laine gave her a reassuring smile. "We can hug." She confirmed, and Serenity blinked before pulling her into a quick hug.

"It's good to see you." She said, leaving one hand resting on Laine's shoulder for a moment. "I, um, I know we didn't end things on very good terms before you left for Earth. So, I'm sorry for the things I said about you and Theo. They were untrue, I was just angry."

Laine blinked. She didn't even *remember* what Serenity had said, let alone care enough to still be upset about it.

"No, no, it's okay." She reassured. "You had every right to be angry." Serenity sighed and sat down on her bed. "Maybe." She muttered. "How are you? How are things?" She asked, subconsciously resting one of her hands on Vercobrix's leg.

"That's actually why I came here." She explained, sitting down on an oval chair in the corner, about two metres away from them on the right of their bed. She pulled the corner of a blanket into her lap and began to run her thumb and forefinger along the seams.

"Okay." Serenity replied with a subtle nod of her head. "You want our help with something?"

Laine nodded. She felt like she was being interrogated. She was in their home, in their bedroom, at their mercy.

"We want to break Theo out of Nesbryn. Hopefully take our kingdom back." She said, cringing immediately afterwards.

"Who's the fourth?" Vercobrix asked quickly. He leant forward in a more assertive position and Serenity snapped her head to look at him. Laine's eyes danced around the room for a moment.

"My grandmother, hopefully. She tried to do it when she was young, but failed."

"Seems to be a recurring theme in your family." Vercobrix smirked a little. "I apologise. You are aware we would be breaking many laws?"

"The fourth?" Serenity asked immediately after, the confusion ruminating in her voice.

"A crypt, darling." Vercobrix replied. "That needs the combined magic of four pureblooded demons to break through. Laine, you, I, and her grandmother. Correct?"

Laine blinked. "Yep."

Serenity watched with a look of bewilderment as Vercobrix brought his hand up to his chin.

"I can't help but feel as if some people are put away for good reason." He said.

"You think Theo deserves to be there?"

"I don't think *he* does. I think that the rest of them do. We would be unable to bring the forcefield down without letting all of them out, it seems unbalanced."

"Have you met them?"

"Have you?"

"Yes, actually. I have. And they were almost all very nice."

"I concede that you may have met them, physically. But I highly doubt you've actually met them. You know what they are really like, behind the facade. People don't get thrown in that place for nothing, Laine." He warned.

"Honey." Serenity asserted in a cautious voice. "You're being inconsiderate. Let's take it down from a five to a three." She suggested calmly. Vercobrix huffed and his eyes darted between the two girls.

"Okay." He said. "Laine. I can understand why you would want us to help you with this because it is a cause close to your family. However, I feel as if the consequences may outweigh the benefits in this scenario." He tried again, his words slower and more calculated. Once he had finished speaking he glanced over to his fiance, who grinned at him and nodded a few times.

"You just told me earlier that you don't like Beckett. You want him gone, and so do we. It's the same cause, I promise." She begged.

Serenity's face contorted to one of sympathy. "I feel horrible about what happened to Theo, he didn't deserve it at all. But, I just- we've moved on with our lives. It isn't anything to do with us, we don't gain anything from this. Why should we risk getting our titles revoked and ending up in Nesbryn ourselves for someone I haven't spoken to in years?"

Laine was stunned into silence for a moment. She allowed herself a moment to process the words as Vercobrix hummed in agreement. She wasn't quite sure what her argument was. Please? Because we want you to? In fact, her preparations for this request had been very lacklustre. That was, until she remembered a detail.

"He saved you." She pushed. Both of the pairs of eyes in the room snapped to her. "He carried you out of the castle when you were unconscious and covered in blood. I'm pretty sure it was the last thing he did before he got attacked by Beckett. Maybe if he hadn't, he would have had more time to prepare."

Serenity bit her lip. She suddenly looked as if she was flooded with guilt.

"He did?" Vercobrix asked. "You told me you got out yourself."

Serenity kept her eyes downcast to the ground.

"That woman told me. I forget her name, the one with the little angel girl. I came to on the train back here and she told me that he had, but it was just... embarrassing. To have to have been saved by the guy who pretended to love me. I wanted you to think better of me." She muttered. "I'm sorry."

Vercorbrix looked hurt for a moment, and then he nodded. "I understand. I wish you had told me. There are things we could have done to repay him."

"Repay him now." Laine said quickly. "Do this for him, please. And when we get Klaevr back, and he's king, I promise he'll give you whatever you want as a thank you." She said.

Serenity nodded softly. "Okay."

"Okay?" Vercobrix questioned almost instantly.

"It's gonna be fine, I promise. It's been so boring around here recently, come on." Serenity pleaded, grabbing onto his hands and pulling on them. A smile tugged at Vercobrix's lips.

"Okay." He finally agreed. "Because you want me to. Not because I think it's right."

Laine breathed a sigh of relief. "Thank you."

"Did you want us to go now? Or do we have time for lunch?" Serenity asked, already unbuttoning her shirt to put something more practical on.

"Yeah, just, get whatever you need together." Laine nodded.

"And so, the plan is that you get Theo out and he helps to fight Beckett, yes?" She confirmed, slipping a dark blue cotton t-shirt over a long sleeve black turtleneck. Laine nodded. "Alright. I'll ask my sister if we can borrow our soldiers for the day. They'll help."

"What?!" Vercobrix exclaimed, nervous and frantic.

"Well, if we're helping them, we're helping them." Serenity replied. "They don't have an army. Maybe even your parents could send some men over, Vee."

Vercobrix bit his lip and slipped his hands into his trouser pockets. "I'd rather not involve them, let's just- we can- No, sorry. I don't think they would be able to accommodate that. Not with how unruly the people of my kingdom are, and-"

"Hey, hey. It's fine." Serenity laughed, pushing herself up on her tiptoes and bridging the gap between them. She pressed a delicate kiss to his mouth as her hand pushed some of his loose hair out of his face. "I get it, I don't like your parents much either."

"In-laws, haha." Laine vaguely laughed as she tried to lighten the mood. "Sorry." She muttered when all she got was confused glares. Vercobrix squeezed Serenity's wrist and traced out patterns against the skin.

Once her fiance moved his own hand away, Serenity clapped her hands in front of her. "Right, okay." She announced, spinning to face Laine. "We can get our stuff together, I'll talk to my sister. Rendezvous in thirty?" She suggested. Before they could even say yes she was out of the door and fleeing down the corridor.

Vercobrix's eyes lingered on the door for a moment before he looked back to Laine.

"You okay?" She asked, eyebrows raised in concern. He nodded quickly.

"Yes. Just so long as she keeps in good time." He sighed, sitting down on the bed again.

"You sure? You seem antsy." Laine pushed, not sure if it would pay off or not.

Vercobrix swallowed. "I have very strong routines that I like to follow, um, I dislike when things are unplanned or too sudden. Not your fault, of course." He diverged, gesturing towards Laine. "Serenity has been so kind to me about everything, I'm not sure what I would do without her." He continued, running his finger along the edge of his engagement ring.

"I'm glad she found someone." Laine smiled genuinely.

"I'm glad for it too. I would likely be homeless if it weren't for her." He said, eyes downcast.

"You're a prince, Vercobrix, I doubt you would have been homeless." Laine laughed, humoured by the idea.

"I mean, I was twenty-four when I met Serenity. My parents were very angry that I wasn't in a committed relationship by my age. They told me if I didn't move out in the next month I would be on the streets. Serenity's sister agreed to let me live here until I found somewhere, but then I met her and... I don't know. She's the first person that has ever understood me. I've been told I'm difficult, but she never thought so." He lamented, small smile lines forming at the edge of his mouth.

Laine smiled at that. She was genuinely really happy that it had worked out for Serenity the way it did. It would have been awful if she remained depressed and alone. Not that she *needed* somebody to exist, but she seemed like she wanted somebody.
"You really love her." Laine stated, voice breathless. She wondered for a moment what Nikoliah was thinking about her right now.
"I can't wait to marry her." Vercobrix confirmed with a smile. The first one Laine had seen from him ever.
"How long have you been together?" Laine prompted, trying to form an internal timeline of the previous few years in her head.
"Eh, a year? Maybe a year and a few months. Which isn't very long in hindsight, but royal marriages happen very quickly. I mean, her and Theo were like a week."
Laine hummed in agreement. It was true. It was pretty rare that couples consisting of royalty stayed dating for very long, usually because they wanted to become official monarchs together, or because they would be taken more seriously. It was a tradition that had stemmed from the time when every single royal wedding was arranged, because those typically had very short durations of intervals between meeting and exchanging vows.
"I thought you would have married that knight by now."
Her eyes met his for a moment and then she looked away.
"Yeah." She agreed, not bothering (or wanting) to elaborate any further. She was well beyond tired of all this talk about him. She wasn't even in the same kingdom as him, why does he keep getting brought up?
In reality, this was only the third time it had been brought up to her. She was just... thinking about him a lot. In the back of her mind. Which was weird, because she had made the decision to end it. And, he had been a dick the past few days. Really uptight and kneeling at Beckett's feet every movement. It wasn't the same man that she loved. It was the man she had first met, when he was only fifteen, all strict and serious about his responsibility. Maybe she had broken him. Maybe that was what she wanted.
"Something happened." Vercobrix inferred from the way her mood shifted. "You broke up?"
Laine nodded.
Vercorbix could tell in her way her shoulders hunched that it was a little bit of an uncomfortable subject, that he shouldn't have pushed it. So, he dropped it.

"Do you want to borrow a jacket? You must be cold in a short sleeve like that." He diverted after clearing his throat.

Laine raised an eyebrow. "You ask about my boyfriend and then offer me one of your jackets?" She teased. Vercobrix spluttered a little.

"No, no, you just- you look cold, it wasn't related."

The Princess' smirk grew into light laughter as she listened to his rambling. "Relax, dude. I'm kidding. A hoodie or something would be great. Serenity's would probably fit me better, I'll ask her when she gets back."

The Prince nodded as he fiddled his fingers together on his lap. He took a quick glance down to his watch.

"Only twenty-six minutes until then." He reported with an exhale. "I'm going to make a cup of tea, would you like one?" He asked, standing from the bed and ambling over to the door.

"We're about to break every law ever made and your priority is a hot drink?" She snickered. "Is there nothing else you want to do?"

The Prince looked humoured by the question. "Alright, two cups of tea coming up." Vercobrix smirked, turning on his heel so he was facing away from Laine and slipping out of the room.

XXXVII

"Uno!" Julian grinned, slamming his card onto the deck.
"This isn't fair." Theo pouted. "I don't get this game, it's dumb."
Julian leant over the table and narrowed his eyes playfully. "You can sulk after my next turn. Play your card." He demanded with a smug smile.
Theo pulled a red number 'six' card from his hand and laid it atop of Julian's previous red four. In actuality, the cards were all made of paper and mediocre colouring with crayons, since they didn't have a real pack of cards.
Julian practically threw his final red card onto the table. "I win!" He cheered, and Theo leant back in his chair as he carelessly dropped his remaining hand onto the table.
"You've had practice. I've never played this before." He complained.
"Sore loser." Julian scoffed with a smile on his face still.
He was still smiling as he collected the makeshift cards up and slotted them back into their pile on Theo's kitchen counter. He turned to look at Theo and frowned sarcastically.
"Hey, it's okay. There's always next time." He teased easily.
"You said that three games ago." Theo replied with another pout. He stood from his chair and crept up behind Julian to wrap his hands around his boyfriend's shoulders.
Boyfriend.
He liked being able to think that again. My boyfriend.
Yes, of course, the last two years he had had Isaac. But that ship had long sailed, especially after what had happened earlier that day. There was no real flame with Isaac, though. Every time he laid eyes on Julian a new giddiness formed in his stomach as if he was about to ask out his primary

school crush. He'd never felt that kind of passion for anyone else, and he didn't think he ever would again.

Julian giggled and spun around, still held in Theo's arms as he pressed his face into his chest.

"I missed you."

Theo repeated the affirmation, letting the other man stay in the comfort of his arms for as long as he wanted.

"Hey, uh, stop me if you don't want to talk about it, but, did anything else happen with your mother?" He asked. It had been irritating him a little, that they had got as far to see her in a police interview seat but the loose ends had never been tied.

Julian bit his lip. "Yeah. I considered showing up to the trial just to spook everyone, but then I didn't."

"Trial?"

"Yeah." He nodded again. "She pleaded guilty and got twenty years."

Theo raised his eyebrows. "God." He muttered. "Are you okay about it?" He asked as they moved the conversation towards the sofa.

"I don't know. I mean, she might have... killed me and all, but, but she's my mum." He said softly. "She taught me how to ride a bike, taught me how to fight off boys when their eyes lingered too long." He laughed a little as he finished his sentence.

"Oh yeah?" Theo asked with a raise of his eyebrow. "And how would you manage that?" He intrigued. Julian rolled his eyes. He stayed still looking at Theo for a few seconds, right before pouncing onto him and starting to tickle him. He laughed boisterously and began to squirm away, ending up on his back on the sofa, with Julian atop him - in an even more vulnerable position than he had been to begin with.

"Alright!" He laughed, trying to swat his boyfriend's hands away. "Message received!" He continued to laugh uncontrollably. After a moment of enjoying the sight, Julian stopped his attack and flopped himself down onto Theo, so that he was effectively using the taller man's chest as a pillow. He sighed in playful exhaustion.

It had been a while. A long while, since either of them had felt truly content. And, even though they were about to wage a war with their own kingdom, and even though there was every chance in hell it could go incredibly wrong and ruin their lives all over again, there was nothing to worry about for the moment.

Julian allowed Theo's body heat to seep into his skin, soaking up the warmth and care. He closed his eyes as he felt a soft hand start to card through his hair carefully. With all of his worries at ease for the moment, he allowed himself to fall asleep. It wasn't even another ten minutes before the hand running through his hair slowed before falling limp as well.

The wind was brisk and the clouds heavy. Theo took great care in watching where he stepped, having not had enough coal to take his own torch out whilst still considering the sake of his fireplace and being warm once the cold of the night truly set in.

He had left his boyfriend asleep on the sofa, having not slept for long and decided to walk to the main square area to see if he could find some coal that would eliminate the goosebumps maintaining themselves on his arms. Through the darkness protruding around him, Theo walked carefully.

He heard the growl before he saw it, having only just had time to react before the creature was swooping down past him, quite literally nearly taking his head off. He cussed quite loudly and his hand darted down to his hip, where his sword would *usually* have been holstered securely. Only, it wasn't this time. He had left it in his house, expecting a short walk and was quite distracted by watching the angel (both literally and metaphorically) sleeping peacefully on his sofa.

The creature wasn't quite as large as the one he had met earlier in the week. This one was medium-sized and more reminiscent of a dog than anything. Well, a dog with four eyes and large wings stretching across the sky. It was just about as tall as a two-storey house, and just about as wide as one too.

Since Theo was only really half-way towards the main square, he was immediately concerned with this *thing* breaking the peace in the residential areas. More specially, Julian waking up and leaving the house to investigate. He drew a deep breath in and broke into a run towards his initial destination.

The creature seemed very interested in him. It snarled and began to bound after him, so much so that if it weren't for the large wings expanding from his back, he might have been flattened like roadkill.

By the time he made it to the main area, he could feel the heat of the creature's flames against the back of his neck, skidding to a halt and holding his hands together a few metres off the ground - trying to summon his magic.

"You've got to be fucking kidding me." Came an annoyed voice from the ground. Theo looked down and made reluctant eye contact with Isaac, who had undoubtedly been in the tavern probably drinking his sorrows away, even if the thought was a little harsh to imagine so.

"Where the hell is everyone else?!" Theo called back, lowering himself a little as the creature reared itself backwards at him, immoble for the moment but dangerous and growing more so each moment he remained idle.

Isaac had to yell over the growls to even be heard by Theo. Luckily, he *did* have a weapon on him, and he unsheathed it.

"They took your angel friend to the forest to get more coal!"

"All of them!?"

"Yeah, she was-" He interrupted himself to allow the creature's growl to ring out before he continued. "Fuck, she was nervous about something attacking them in the forest, so they all went." Isaac explained eyeing the creature with a fearful face.

Theo rolled his eyes. Good, great. That was great.

The creature decided it was done waiting around, and so it pushed itself off its feet and began a sharp sprint towards Isaac, who could only run between its legs and around it, aiming a sharp slash to its underside. Not enough to hurt it, though.

The creature turned around, snarling with its whole teeth. A large helping of spit landed on the ground at Isaac's feet, some even making its way onto his jeans. In any other situation, he probably would have been grossed out.

Theo's eyes widened as the creature drew a deep breath. Isaac looked up at it, paralyzed with fear and completely unable to run away in good enough time to save himself from being burnt.

Thanks to the distinct lack of weapon gracing his hands, Theo had both of his arms free when he swooped himself down towards Isaac. The creature's mouth was like a living flamethrower as it exhaled, barely having the opportunity to start melting the rubber on the tip of Isaac's shoes as he suddenly found himself thirty feet off the ground and in Theo's arms. The gravel singed into a sickening black. Isaac was pushed slowly away from and back towards Theo's body as his chest heaved up and down.

From their position in the sky, with Isaac bridal style in Theo's secure embrace, they had a moment of raw, unadulterated eye contact.

"...Thanks."

"Are you okay?" Theo asked, breathless.

"Yeah, yeah." Isaac nodded, tears pooling in his eyes. "Please don't put me down." He whimpered, hands clutching tighter onto Theo's shoulders and neck. His sword was now too not with them, rather being on the ground just under where the creature was looking at them and snarling. Its wings expanded out much like Theo's, which made both of the demons panic.

Theo glanced around, able to propel himself through the air and right towards the rooftop of one of the buildings surrounding the square. The building itself was tall, about five stories and topped with dark red tiles, some cracked and others completely absent. He planted both of his feet onto the terracotta, although it was unstable and slanted. The creature reared its head around a few times, eventually deciding it had lost sight of them and starting to pace around the square, expectant for its next prey to return from the forest.

Theo put Isaac down onto the roof tile also. From their position, they could almost see the whole kingdom. The houses all of uniform ugliness bunched up like strangers on a crowded tube. The forest off to the edge of the kingdom. And, of course, the edge of the island that transcended into pure dark abyss.

The wind blew generously, causing both men to have to hold onto the chimney to avoid getting rocked too hard and tumbling to the ground. Isaac's hands shook as he reached up and rubbed the tears away from under his eyes. Theo looked up at him and for a second, almost pitied him for being so afraid.

"That thing you pulled in the tattoo parlour wasn't cool." Theo asserted, swallowing as the wind pushed his hair in front of his face.

"I could say the *exact* same thing to you." Isaac replied, voice wavering and wobbling with each word. "You really never loved me?" He asked again.

Theo paused for a moment. "I did. Maybe. I don't know if it was love or excitement." He muttered with a shake of his head.

"Excitement?"

"You know. Here for eternity and there was another queer guy my age. You helped me feel less alone, you helped me pass the time." He admitted, understanding how wrong and unfair it sounded instantly.

"Pass the time?" Isaac clarified. "Is that what I am to you? The back page of your fucking schoolbook that you doodle on until class is over? Fuck you." He spat, voice cracking with upset.

"No. No, that's not- not what I meant. I'm sorry." Theo tried to reason. His wings folded back into his back. "You- you must have had someone. Someone when you were alive."

Isaac shook his head slowly. "Not other than my English teacher. But he was more of a hallway crush."

Theo smiled sympathetically for a moment. "I promise, Isaac, there's someone for you." He bit his lip. "But it's not me. It's not fair to you."

Little droplets of rain began to pour down from the looming grey clouds, wetting the roof under the men's shoes.

Isaac's feet stumbled a little against the tile, and he gripped onto the concrete chimney tighter. "That's the thing, Theo. We're stuck here. Here there is nobody. Nobody but you. It has to be you." He whined, trying not to cry. The rain had picked up to a moderate pace that made it almost difficult to properly see.

Theo shook his head. "It doesn't, it doesn't, I promise. We aren't good for eachother, we're a product of circumstance, not genuine emotion." He confessed. And, this time, Isaac nodded. "When my sister gets this forcefield down, we'll get out of here. You'll find someone. And, if you don't - people die every day. Your person might not be here yet. But they might be this time next year."

Isaac's eyes watered relentlessly, but he looked up at Theo- eye contact desperate and painful. But he was right. God, he was right. It was so unfair that he was right. With a deep breath, and a collection of his thoughts, Isaac nodded.

A large gust of wind hauled above them, followed not even half a second later by the creature swooping above them, dangerously close. The growl combined with the physical proximity of the thing and the rain lubricating the terracotta meant that within the span of a second, Theo had completely lost his footing on the roof and fell downwards, grabbing onto the ridge at the end of the roof as he screamed.

Isaac ducked downwards, holding onto the chimney still. Theo tried to pull himself back up onto the roof, but with no proper grip, he struggled. Isaac leant down closer to him as he watched.

"Use your stupid wings!" He yelled, stressed and exhausted.

Theo's breaths heaved as his knuckles began to turn white from gripping onto the ledge. He flexed his back muscles a few times, trying so desperately to summon his wings out behind him.

"I'm fucking scared! They don't do shit when I'm scared, fuck!" He yelled, his boots scraping against the wall of the building in an attempt to push himself upwards. His hair and clothes were completely drenched by the rain, although it was the least of his concerns.

Isaac took a deep breath in and began to edge his way down towards the ledge. "Don't make me regret this, Theo." He warned, slowly moving downwards. Theo groaned and released one of his hands from where he was gripping the roof, outstretching it towards Isaac. The demon did the same, their hands meeting. Isaac pushed his feet against the tile and pulled as strongly as he could.

The rain slammed down harder onto them. A single clap of thunder rang out over the kingdom, the noise being so unbelievably loud. Isaac flinched and his feet slipped on the roof. He scrambled to regain his footing, eventually unable as he stumbled again. The rain assisted him as he fell off the roof, his grip on Theo's wrist meaning that the other demon was also yanked from the sanctity of his grip. Both screamed and clung onto each other as if it were life or death.

The air moved quickly around them, as did the rain and continuing thunder. Theo's eyes focused on the ground. He brought his hands together around Isaac's shoulders, only connecting his palms for about half a second before they moved away and flashes of green light hurried towards the ground.

The two streams collided with the gravel. One of them shot back upwards towards the two men as they fell, hitting them and enveloping them in the light. Not even half a second later, they hit the ground, completely protected by the magic cast around them.

Once they were lying against the dirt, the magic disintegrated.

Theo pushed himself up to his feet to look around for the creature. His eyes met the thing just quick enough to watch the second beam of light lit the beast straight through its head, above its eyes. Although, this time, it didn't writhe or growl in pain.

It stopped moving completely for a few moments, and then sat down like an obedient dog on its hind legs. Isaac sat in a half-attempt of cross legged, legs shaky and breaths rushed.

"What the hell?" He asked with a distressed whisper, watching the thing just sit still. The rain began to die down, just stilling to a reasonable drizzle. Theo looked back at Isaac, reaching a hand down to help him stand. Isaac took it with an unsteady grip and pulled himself to his feet with the help of the other demon.

With extreme caution, Theo began to walk towards the creature. He hadn't noticed it before, but when he looked down he noticed that the

jagged and swirled markings on his arms were still glowing under the fishnet sleeves of his hoodie. That was... strange, to say the least. He didn't know why that was the case - he wasn't performing magic. He could hear Isaac's slower footsteps behind him as he continued to advance closer and closer to the creature. Under no circumstance did it move, just staring off indirectly at the sky. Theo furrowed his eyebrows.
"Why isn't it attacking us anymore?" Isaac asked, bewildered. Theo narrowed his eyes untrusting.
"I don't know." He admitted. He raised a hand up towards the creature and frowned as it did nothing at all.
With a concerned and frustrated groan, Theo dropped his hand in a sudden movement.
The creature jerked its body downwards roughly, bracing itself against the ground. Theo stepped back quickly. He brought his hand slowly back up to his chest height, and the creature moved back up onto all fours. He took a glance back to Isaac, who watched him with bewilderment.
"Do it again." Isaac whispered. Theo pulled his hand backwards and then pushed it forward, and the creature began to bound straight ahead. He panicked and quickly opened his palm and jerked it backwards a little. The creature stopped with a skid.
"You're telling me all we've had to do this whole time is have you hit its brain and mind control it?" Isaac said, exasperated. Theo kept his lips tight and eyes latched onto the creature.
"I wonder if..." he began to mutter, before raising his voice. "Hey, c'mere!" He called, hands still limp beside him. The creature turned around and started running towards Theo. He panicked for a moment, not expecting it to have worked. "Okay, stop!" He yelled, and it did so almost instantly. "Just, just sit." He commanded, and once again the creature did so. Theo turned to look at Isaac. "We can use this, right? If we're fighting." Theo stated.
"For sure." He agreed. "It's like your pet. You need to name it." Isaac suggested, most of his stress was diluted by this new revelation and Theo's control over the previously life-threatening beast.
Theo raised an eyebrow. "Name it?"
"Yeah."
The creature almost looked warm under the light of the moon, calm now. "Well, it's- it's a creature of Perterritus. What about... like, Terry?" Isaac suggested. Theo scrunched his nose up. "No, that makes it sound like a middle aged man who cares too much about football."

Isaac snickered. "You're getting pretty good at these earthly pop culture references."

"Thanks." He replied. "I do try."

"Okay, okay. What about... Peter?" Isaac suggested again. "Just sounds like it went to a private school." Theo dejected again. "Alright, I have one." He added quickly. "What about Perry? That's cool and urban, right?"

Isaac raised his eyebrows. "Like the platypus?"

"What?" Theo replied on a laugh.

"No, nevermind. Perry is good, I like Perry." Isaac nodded.

Theo smirked. "Perry, go to sleep. We'll wake you up when we need you." He called at the creature. It looked at him curiously for a moment.

"That's you, you're Perry!" He yelled, laughing at how stupidly ridiculous he was sounding. The creature opened its mouth in a yawn-like motion before settling down, lying with its head on its front legs in the middle of the square.

They would have a bit of explaining to do when the others got back.

XXXVIII

As far as she expected it to go, Laine thought her mission was going about as well as it could be. With little argument or question, Serenity and Vercobrix had agreed to help them - even having offered their whole army to help them re-invade Klaevr and take their kingdom back. Laine had been incredibly grateful for it, and even got to speak to Serenity's sister herself. She was super nice about it, and the plan was that they would come back after going to T'kota to get the soldiers who would go to Klaevr with them where they would hopefully meet Theo and company.

Travelling in a pack of three purebloods did get them quite a bit of attention when they were on the train. One young boy had asked them for their autographs. So, needless to say, they were quite relieved when they arrived in T'kota and were able to soak up the tranquil atmosphere. It was actually mildly sunny, which was a nice surprise. It was like a weight was lifted off their shoulders as they arrived in the kingdom, since nobody there really cared at all about their status. They didn't have a monarchy in T'kota, but of course, there were demons of royal descent living there.

"We should be coming here for our picnics, Vee." Serenity thought out loud, turning to her fiance.

"Yeah. It is nice." He conceded, eyes cast to the red-pink toned sky. "I'm not sure why you don't visit your grandmother more, Laine. I would if I had relatives living here."

"Well, I would if I had *pleasant* relatives living here." She replied easily. She hadn't seen her grandmother since Theo's coronation, where they barely shared ten seconds of obligatory small talk. The last time Laine had actually visited Cordelia was at least five years ago. She hoped that the woman wasn't holding a grudge over it, but knowing her, she probably was.

Laine was honestly surprised that she still recognised her grandmother's house, but she did. Maybe it was the nostalgia hitting her like a tidal wave. Her and Theo used to sit in her front garden and throw mud at each other. Father would usually get rather annoyed at them for it, but they didn't care all too much.

Serenity and Vercobrix opted to wait at the bottom of the set of steps leading up to the house, while the Princess they were with hopped up the steps and fidgeted with the edge of the hoodie that Serenity had let her borrow. She knocked twice quickly. For about thirty seconds, not even the sound of reluctant footprints rang out in the hallway.

"Is she... home?" Serenity asked apprehensively. Laine turned with just her head and shoulders to look back, not replying in favour of turning again and knocking. This time, Laine was only able to knock once before the door was violently swung open.

Cordeilia looked pretty much the same as she remembered from the coronation. Dirty blonde hair curled around her face, kept short and tidy, laying as a nest to her bluey-green coloured horns.

"Oh. Hello, Elaine." She greeted, keeping her body between her visitors and the door. "I see you've finally washed out that horrific hair colouring."

Laine had to bite her tongue to stop herself from making multiple comments about those sentences. But, no. She desperately wanted to be on the good side of this woman.

"Haha, yeah. Well, teenage rebellious phase and all." She breathed with an awkward laugh. "Um, speaking of those, do you remember when you-"

"Oh! Hello Prince Vercobrix." She smiled, looking a little surprised. She pushed past Laine and left her granddaughter standing awkwardly in the doorway of her home.

"Hello, Ma'am." Vercorbix replied in a serious nature.

"Oh, please. No need for formalities. Your parents and I go way back." She said happily, almost *laughed*. Laine gaped in the doorway for a moment.

"I'm sorry, dear. What is your name?" She asked, looking over to Serenity.

"Oh, um. It's Serenity." The Princess smiled back.

Cordelia leant forward in interest. "Ah! Strythio's Serenity?"

Serenity's face dropped. "Not really, no." She shook her head. Vercobrix turned to her and offered a glance. It wasn't much, but between them it was a great reassurance.

"Well, to think. If things had been different you could have been my granddaughter-in-law." Cordeilia gave a weary grin and turned back to the Princess' fiance.

"I'm so sorry, where are my manners? Do come in." She offered, arm outstretched towards Vercobrix. She turned on her heel and brushed past Laine, who gave a cursory look towards the other two. Vercobrix shrugged slightly and took Serenity's hand, leading her up the steps after Laine.

Much like the woman herself, Cordelia's home was the same as Laine remembered it. It was large and spacious, quite minimalistic. The hallway was adorned with paintings of various flowers - something the ex-queen used to indulge herself in in her spare time. She lead them into the first room on the right,

In the centre was a decorative green rug, aligned beside a singular grey sofa and an armchair of a slightly darker fabric a few metres opposite. The walls were an unmatched cream tone, and stopped for a moment to make room for a rectangular window.

"Are those the same curtains we used to have in the castle?" Laine asked upon seeing the familiarly ugly pattern.

"They are." Cordelia replied as she remained tight-lipped. "Over half of my decorations are things that I nicked from the castle when I moved out." She replied, and Laine swore for a minute that she looked like she was going to smile.

Cordelia went right for the armchair, which left the other three demons standing in the centre of her living room a little awkwardly. Eventually, Serenity perched herself onto the edge of the sofa. Instinctually, Vercobrix moved to be next to her - which left Laine little choice but to also squeeze in. They were uncomfortably close together, but they doubted they would be here long anyway.

"Well, go on then." Cordelia clapped her hands in front of her. "How are you parents, Vercobrix?"

"Good."

Cordelia rolled her eyes. "Fine. Be like that if you'd like."

Vercobrix looked confused for a moment before his mind caught up. "Oh, no. I wasn't intending to be rude or monotonous. They're just good."

"What do you three *want* then? I don't suppose you just came here for a posey." She commented snarkily, crossing her left leg over her right.

Laine sat up straight in order to feign confidence.

"Well, grandma. I'll keep it simple." She began, hands shuffling together in her lap. "We want to break down the forcefield around Nesbryn so that we can get Theo out and take our kingdom back properly."

Coredelia just looked at her granddaughter for a moment, and then she laughed. Laughed.

"Goodness, if only the King and Queen of Atroka could hear that you've roped their son into this." She smirked.

"So, you want my advice?" She asked expectantly.

Laine shook her head. "We want you to come with us."

"Right, I understand." Cordeilia nodded. "This is *your* idea, Laine, and you've roped these two poor dolls into it. You'll no doubt throw them under the bus when you get caught."

"I will not." Laine argued, kind of annoyed by the insinuation. "You can just say no. You don't have to be rude about it." She huffed, standing and walking towards the door.

"I never said I wouldn't do it." Cordelia added, posture straight and voice overconfident. Laine's head snapped back to look at her. "I mean, come on." She continued. "I'm old. What are they gonna do to me? At my age? It'd be community service to put me away, they wouldn't dare. I'd be more worried about you three." She gestured towards them. "Life in Nesbryn would mean a lot to you."

"Getting Theo back would mean more."

Cordelia raised her eyebrows and smirked slightly. "Well, I respect your dedication to him. Most of his supporters faded away when they realised of his incompetence."

Laine raised her eyebrows from the doorway. "He lost one fight."

"A fight he should have been prepared for."

"He wasn't even in this dimension."

"He should've been."

"You're saying you agree with Beckett?" Laine asked, anger seeping through her voice.

"I'm saying that he acted selfishly. No monarch doesn't make sacrifices for their people. If he had done that, Klaevr would likely be prospering with a king and queen right now." She said, sparing a glance to Serenity, who swallowed with anxiety.

"It would have been anything but prospering if it were ruled by people in an unhappy marriage." Laine raised her voice.

"He had it in him to make it work, if only he'd tried harder instead of loving that mortal boy."

"At least he has it in himself to love somebody."
Cordelia tightened her jaw.
"You've come to my doorstep to beg me to help you. You aren't acting much like you want my help. Maybe you should leave." She snarled threateningly. Laine's eyes widened as she observed her surroundings. Vercorbix had his right hand wrapped around Serenity's own hand, eyes cautious and worried. Serenity leant back on the sofa, legs tight together with the right one gently bouncing up and down.
She knew she'd lost, and her grandmother was right. She needed Cordelia a lot more than Cordelia needed her.
"Fine. I'm sorry. Please can you help us out and show us how to do this?" She pleaded.
"I will." Cordelia replied after a moment. "I don't aim to be harsh to you, Laine. But I'm your father's mother. I *care* about you. I didn't care enough about your brother - was too easy on him. Made him think it was okay to slack. I won't let the same happen to you." She lectured, eyebrows raised. Laine had to stop herself from scoffing. Vercobrix's parents were incredibly strict, and he just ended up constantly anxious about doing the wrong thing. He'd never said that, but Laine could tell from the way he acted.
"Right." She nodded. "God forbid I turn out like him." She commented sarcastically.
Cordelia sighed and stood from her armchair. "I love you. And I love Theo also. Which is why I'm going to do this for him. I want you to be happy, and you clearly aren't so long as that angel is on the throne. Let's get him off and things can go back to normal." Cordelia reasoned, reaching a hand out and placing it onto Laine's shoulder in a comforting notion. Laine nodded. God, she hated it, but her grandmother was right. Again.
 "Yeah, okay."
"Good." Cordelia nodded. "Sit back down and we can talk through it."
So, the Princess did. She sat back down on the sofa semi-reluctantly, bunching up closely with the other two.
"Right, I assume somebody told you about my teenage escapade. Who?" She asked, clearly curiosity fueled. Laine spluttered a little. She hadn't really been expected to have to answer interrogations about it.
"Um... some demon from Nesbryn. Called Ayale, I think."
Serenity moved her hand on top of Vercobrix's and squeezed it as he snapped his head up in interest, eyes narrowing. "Ayale Johnsen?"
Laine looked around. "I don't know, I didn't catch a surname." She shrugged.

"What?" Cordelia asked, slightly humoured by his sense of urgency.
"No, nothing. Sorry, carry on." He dismissed.
"Well, I certainly haven't heard of this person, so it must have been through word of mouth." Cordelia mused. "Well, of course, we were young. Maybe around your age, Serenity. How old are you? Early twenties?"
"Twenty-two." She nodded.
"Yes, that's about it. About a year before I had Dyran. My parents had become increasingly fed up with me and I threatened to run away in the same way that every child does when having a strop. They didn't take me seriously. So, I wanted to do something that meant they *would* take me seriously."
"Letting all the demons out of Nesbryn?"
"Bingo." She nodded. "Of course, we were naive and didn't know much about it. We were lucky to have been heirs." She admitted, nostalgia glowing in her eyes. After a moment of careful reminiscence, she looked back up at the three younger demons sitting on the sofa. "Have you all eaten? Gotten enough sleep?"
"Yeah, we just had lunch like two hours ago." Serenity nodded, running her thumb over her fiance's knuckles as he held her hand tightly.
"Good, you'll need it if you want your magic to be consistent. Do you keep up with it?" She asked, and Serenity shrugged.
"A bit. Vee does it more than I do."
'Vee' tilted his head slightly to look at the woman seated next to him before nodding. "My parents, they're very big on it. I feel like one day they're going to visit unannounced and expect me to show them what I've been practising."
Cordelia snickered a little. "It's a good skill to have. Especially considering there's less than fifty in Hell that can even wield magic. What about you, Laine?"
She had honestly zoned out the past few moments, so when she heard her name, she flicked her head up and tried to recall the question. "Um, a bit." She mumbled. "Killed a creature in Nesbryn with magic."
"More than I expected of you. Good. Good practice." Cordeilia nodded. She felt quite honestly impressed that Laine had even had it in her to try and attempt a fight using her magic. It wasn't the kind of thing that was necessarily taught a lot. She wouldn't have been able to spar using magic with anyone other than Theo, but Dyran had banned them from it after the concussion incident of their early teens.

"Well, if you want to go today we should do it now. It'll be dark before we know it and that's double the amount of danger." The older demon realised, glancing to her lilac-strapped watch. "Are you one-hundred percent sure you want to do this? Big risk, you know that?"

Laine nodded profusely. She was sure. In fact, she didn't think she had ever been so sure of anything. She had ruined everything with Nikoliah, and with Beckett too, probably her father also. If she didn't have Theo on her side, she didn't have anyone. And she wasn't going to get Theo on her side without this. He can't take the kingdom back if he isn't anywhere near it.

Serenity sighed in exhaustion. "Yeah." She agreed. "As much as he fucked me over, Theo deserves happiness. And Klaevr deserves a better monarch than Amadeus Beckett." She droned, already disgusted by the idea of the man. She looked over to Vercobrix for his own confirmation. He bit his lip.

"You're right about that much." He hummed. "If we get caught doing this, Ren, I'm not explaining it to my parents, or to your sister."

Serenity rolled her eyes. "She's chill, she doesn't care. And, unlike some, I'm not scared of your parents." She jabbed playfully, leaning forward and pressing a kiss to his mouth. "They don't have to come to the wedding." She whispered, playful and teasing. Vercobrix rolled his eyes.

"You make them out to be worse than they are." Cordelia almost smiled from her seat.

"Well, I'm sure they're mighty pleasant at the formal dinners you look at each other from across a large table at." The Prince retorted back, voice dropped to a low hum as Cordelia stood from her seat and began to slip her arms into the sleeves of her white coat that was previously hanging on the back of the door.

"It's a forty minute walk to the threshold of the route down there." She changed the subject quickly. "I expect you three to start warming up your magic as we move. When we get ten minutes away, I will stop you and we can start acting more stealthily."

She waited by the door for the three younger demons to scurry up and out of the house with varying degrees of enthusiasm and small talk, twirling the set of her keys in her hand. Once they were all out and a considerable distance down the path, Cordelia locked up and caught up to them in longer strides. They slowed down to facilitate this change, remaining anxiously and awkwardly silent aside from Serenity and Vercobrix's low occasional whispers.

From the time Laine, Serenity and Vercobrix got to the end of her garden path, Cordelia was well ahead of them. Despite the fact that they had let her get ahead because she was the only one who knew the route, she turned around on her heels and raised her eyebrows expectantly, ready to lecture them on tardiness or something.

"Don't fall behind." She said, stern eyebrow raised and flat yet solid shoes making consistent taps against the ground as she led the way quickly.

XXXIX

Perry's sleep was only *nearly* interrupted when the remainder of the demons (and one angel, sorry) returned from their hunting mission in the woods. It was curled up under the still prevalent moonlight, guarded by Theo and Isaac as they dealt a hand of cards between them to pass the time.

"What the fuck?!" They heard Ayale's voice as xe led the group back into the main courtyard. Both men looked over at them all, defensive stances honed. The only light really on them was the torch that Fern was holding and the halo of light above Raphie's head as her eyes widened with fear at the massive beast she was seeing.

Theo leapt to his feet almost instantly, holding his hands out in front of him and scolding them.

"Shh!" He yelled. "It's sleeping."

"Well, yeah, I can see that…!" Xe whisper-yelled back, walking a little faster to be closer to Theo. "Why haven't you killed it?"

"What the hell is that thing?" Raphie asked, exasperated as she caught up and stood behind Ayale with a semi-disgusted expression. "It's creepy."

"That's Perry."

"You gave it a name?!" Ayale expressed xer anger and panic. "Theo, what the fuck? I know you've been a bit sad, but I didn't think you were sui-homi-cidal!"

Isaac approached the three of them, standing beside the man he had fought the creature with. "It's fine, dude, Theo's like, totally it's daddy."

Theo snapped his head to the side to look at Isaac with a sigh. "I thought we agreed on puppeteer." He frowned with a whine in his voice.

By this point in the conversation, the remainder of the four demons had walked over and joined the interaction so that they were now standing in a semi-circle before Theo and Isaac, who were trying to justify not killing the creature.

"Just, just, I'll show you. Nobody hurts it, okay?"

That question was met with various stares of confusion, but eventually Toby moved his hand away from his sword and ran it through his dark blue hair.

"Right, we can at least hear him out, can't we?" He tried to reason. Axel swallowed, but kept his hand gripped onto the handle of his sword.

"We're trusting you here, Princey." He hummed, shoulders deflating.

"Yeah, yeah, it's fine." Theo nodded. "Perry!" He called across the square like he was beckoning a child off a playground to go home. All of the spectators flinched when the creature's head snapped up. It looked right at Theo as the demon's arm-markings began to glow. He felt a tense hand wrap around his upper arm, and looked to his right to see Raphie was standing closely behind him as if he was going to protect her.

"You okay?" He whispered. She squeezed her eyes shut and nodded.

"I don't like that thing one bit." She admitted. Theo nodded despite the fact that she couldn't see him.

"Keep your eyes shut then."

Theo brought his hand up in front of him and then slowly pulled it towards his chest. Perry instantly poised onto its feet and started bounding at a moderate pace towards the controller.

"Hey, slowly." He warned as a response to the obvious panic that shot through those with him. The creature slowed down to a walk.

Ayale, Toby, Fern, Axel and Livvy could only watch in a worried awe as the creature made its way right up to Theo, and upon a signal from the ex-king's hand, sat down before him and leant its head to be at the same height as Theo's. It was about two and a half times Theo's height, and just as proportionately wide, which made him look really weak and breakable beside it.

"See, it's harmless." He whispered, bringing his hand up and running it over the creature's dog-like muzzle and glabella. After a moment, Theo smiled and kept his eyes locked on the beast.

"Raphie, I'm going to let go of you, okay?" He informed, removing his hand from Perry and prying the angel's gripping fingers from his arm. Raphie opened her eyes and squeaked at the proximity of the creature, taking a few steps backwards.

Theo hovered off the ground, hooking his hands around the large curled horns on the creature's head, and using them as rungs to climb up onto it. Perry snorted and layed down with its head still up, Theo sitting cross legged on its head, wings elevated to keep his balance.
"See? This thing is my bitch." He smirked, running his hand over its fur repeatedly.
Isaac rolled his eyes. "Alright, calm down, *Icarus*." He scolded, looking up at Theo before he turned back to the others. "We just thought that Perry might be able to help us fight." He explained.
Ayale took a few steps up to it. "How did you do this, though? It's so... tame." Xe remarked, completely astonished. Theo moved and slid off the head of the creature, using his wings to catch the impact of the jump as he landed on the ground again.
"I tried to hit it in the chest and missed, so I hit it in the brain and it just started doing whatever I said or did."
"I didn't know these things even have brains." Livvy raised her eyebrows and squinted slightly. "It's weird." She remarked, a hesitant hand moving to do the same that Theo had, stroking Perry like a domesticated pet.
Theo nodded. He hummed, glancing back at the demons and angel standing around him. "A lot of things around here are."

The tavern felt a lot more full of life that afternoon, despite the fact that it was only about 3pm. A small record player in the back corner was droning underneath the excited voices of the people all huddled around the table, playing some classical music that was really not that good, but it was better than nothing at all.
Raphie and Theo had comfortable seats beside each other, watching as everyone gave amused cheers when Fern and Toby started dancing with their arms interlocked.
"Don't let me get that drunk." Ayale slighted behind xer glass, still taking a sip despite the contradiction being imposed.
They had all sort of paired up at this point - as they let Perry sleep outside and waited for anything further to reach them from Laine's end. Isaac had wandered out quietly after Julian awoke from his nap and arrived, so quietly that Theo didn't even notice his ex was gone until he was. Livvy and Axel (who Theo was pretty sure had some kind of romantic situationship developing, but he wouldn't dare bring it up) were sitting close together, engulfed in a conversation that nobody else could

even hear over the music and cheering. Julian perched beside Ayale, with Theo on his other side. Even considering the past two years, Julian and Theo had kind of run out of things to catch up on - other than meaningless anecdotes about things prior to their meeting. And so, Julian entered into a comfortable rhythm talking to Ayale over his own pint.

The idea of a glass of beer had made Julian scrunch his nose up at first, but after being told it was quite literally *all they had*, he elected to give it a try at least. The subtle waft of the meat that they had found hunting earlier being cooked in the oven floated around the room too.

"Raph." Theo called, turning to face the angel.

"Mhm?" She replied, moving away from shuffling the deck of cards in her hand and placing her hands on her lap as she looked at Theo.

"Um, okay, if this is too personal you can like... hit me or something, but-"

"Oh, god, what is this about?" She snickered, planting her elbow on the table.

Theo squinted a little, trying to drown out the music that was growing louder. He didn't want to be rude or invasive, but ever since Raphie had come back, there was something that he wanted to talk to her about. Something he had meant to, but didn't, and then he didn't see her for two years and it all kind of got in the way. He swallowed and allowed his eyes to drift over and meet hers.

"Why did you kill yourself?"

Raphie blinked. She wrapped her hand around the cylinder of glass holding her alcohol, and took a generous swig from it.

"You know why. We talked about it in England when I phoned Alex." She supplied. Her voice was quite flat and disinterested.

"No, I know *why* you felt shitty." Theo rolled his eyes, noting his mistake. "But, why did you *kill yourself*? Was there no other option or was the prom queen thing just the cherry on top?"

Raphie leant back a little. "That's weird. Weird that you know that. This is weird and feels like an invasion of privacy." He mumbled. Theo nodded.

"Sorry, forget it." He apologised, scanning around the room and allowing the two of them to fall into silence for a good five minutes.

"Are you okay?" Raphie asked, voice tame and hushed. "...That was worryingly nonchalant."

Theo raised his eyebrows - pulled back into the conversation. "No, yeah. I'm sorry. I guess death doesn't really phase me that much. Guess I don't get it. Never tried it before - never will. Just something that other people get."

"I'm not sure that 'get' is the appropriate descriptor for dying. At least not in the book of most living people."

Theo slumped down onto the table, chin resting on his arms which were poised against the wood. "Two years, Raphie." He mumbled into his sleeve. "Ten percent of my life, one-hundred percent of my adult life."

Raphie frowned.

"I'm pretty sure the point of this place is to make you suicidal. Not sure how you haven't become weak and reclusive simply from the lack of sunlight and vitamins. If not depressed then definitely mauled by one of those *things*." She slighted, furrowing her eyebrows when Theo didn't really have a reaction.

"Do you regret it?" He asked after a moment, only his eyes moving towards her, head still buried onto the table.

Raphie exhaled. "I killed myself because I couldn't see a future where I was happy. It wasn't *just* her, it was everything." She breathed. Theo remained silent. "Why didn't you ask your boyfriend? He tried to kill himself, too."

Theo sat up. "He didn't want to *die*, he wanted to be here. It's not the same when you know there's something waiting for you."

Raphie swallowed. "What brought this on?" She tried to dismiss. Theo frowned.

"If this doesn't work. If Laine can't get the forcefield down, if *I* can't defeat Beckett. I couldn't the first time."

"You're worried this place will be forever?"

"Already feels like it has been." He muttered. "A minute is an hour when all you can do is stare up at a starless sky."

"My biggest mistake was thinking those feelings would last forever." Raphie said. "Because they didn't." She added, turning to look at Theo right in the eyes. He smiled for a moment.

"It's just- when people on Earth feel that way, it's because they can't do their existence on Earth anymore. They don't know what's next for them, maybe it's a kind of hope. Longing for what could be. But, I just- I *know* what this is. This is it. No third stage, no hope for anything else. If I feel hopeless here, then when will I not?" He grumbled, slumping backwards in his chair and bringing his right leg up onto the seat so that he could rest his chin on it. "It isn't fair."

Raphie didn't really know what to say, in all honesty.

"And I can't even talk about it with any of this lot. They're all so... happy with this place. Content, I should say. They're assholes and they don't care."

"Do you *know* that's how they feel?" Raphie whispered as her pupils ghosted all of the demons. "Have you asked them?" She questioned again, but was only met with silence. "Vulnerability is a dam, Theo, if you all act tough and never chip away at the wood, everything's going to stay the same."

Theo looked up towards her and blinked. He supposed she was right. His eyes pursued the other demons in the tavern, all still having their own little moments. It appeared that Fern and Toby had tired themselves out with their antics, and were now slumped down on the sofa talking tipsily.

"Why did you change your name?" Theo asked, not dignifying actually sitting up, but at least tilting his head towards the angel next to him.

"A lot of questions today, hm?"

"Maybe, yeah." Theo hummed in agreement. "Just don't remember the last time I spoke to *you*. Just you, without Laine there."

"Okay, well, why did you change yours?" She asked, shifting in her seat as she turned the question on him. Theo raised an eyebrow.

"I didn't. Not really."

"I would argue you did. Most people treat it like you did."

Theo did sit up this time, releasing his hand from its grip on the edge of the table.

"I don't know. My birth name is so... formal. Like, when Julian first came to Klaevr I told him my name was Theo and he didn't believe me. Then, when I told him it was Strythio he did. I don't like the idea of being a stereotype, being conformist."

"You don't like the idea of being conformist, but you changed your name from a lovely unique Latin name to one of the most common boys' names in English-speaking countries?" She asked, laughing a little. Theo rolled his eyes.

"I always felt like I was in trouble when people called me Strythio. My dad still does that. He doesn't do it to Laine, though, so maybe it's just me." He sighed. "My mum once said that she liked Strythio because she could make a lot of cute nicknames out of it. Like Theo." He recalled, squinting as he tried to recollect his childhood.

"So it's about her?" Raphie asked.

"Maybe. Maybe not. I don't dislike my birth name, I wouldn't actually have it changed formally or anything, it's just pretentious, though."

Raphie could agree, even if it was a little impolite. It was quite a pretentious name.

"Well, to answer your question: I guess I changed my name because I wanted to disconnect myself from the girl I was when I was alive. I don't like Gracie, she wasn't a particularly cool or pretty or adventurous girl. She was just there. But, I want to be more than there. I want to do stuff, as my own person. Raphie was my middle name, so really, it wasn't that drastic."

Theo nodded. "A lot of dead people say that."

"Say what?"

"That they wish they'd done more in life. That they want to reinvent themselves for their death. I don't think I've ever spoken to a dead person that was genuinely content with everything they got to do in life." He explained. "People never live to the fullest until it's too late. And then they feel sad about it. It's a pretty depressing cycle."

"God, okay." Raphie snickered. "You should write a book about all these profound thoughts."

Theo had zoned out a little, but was brought back to himself when his vision completely disappeared and he felt a pair of cold hands press themselves over his eyes.

"Guess who." His boyfriend giggled. Theo huffed and reached his own hands up to pry Julian's off his face.

"You aren't funny, you know that, right?" He entertained, leaning backwards to look at Julian upside down. The man in question smiled playfully and leant over Theo's shoulder.

"What's going on over here? You guys look cheery." He commented sarcastically.

"Theo's being angsty."

"I'm not being angsty. I just wish things were different sometimes."

"Different?" Julian repeated, leaning fully over Theos' chair by now. "Different how?"

"I just..." Theo started, before groaning loudly. "Everything sucks. I wish I wasn't here. I wish my mother had stayed. I wish I liked girls. I wish I had my home back. I wish I was back home. I wish I hadn't grown up."

Julian leant forward and pressed a kiss to Theo's hair as he simultaneously wiped away the single teardrop falling from his eye.

"I wish I didn't cry so fucking easily, fuck." He sniffled, throwing his whole head onto the table, into his arms to hide his face. "It's you two and Laine showing up. You've made me all emotional again."

Outside of the tavern, a loud howl sounded out. Everyone's attention turned to the windows, where it appeared that Perry had woken up and was in some state of emotional distress. It was thrashing around and whimpering like crazy. Slowly, every person who had now had their evening interrupted turned to face Theo.

He looked up from where he had buried his head, tear tracks streaming down his face and the markings on his arms glowing brightly.

He took a deep breath and pushed his chair out, causing a horrible scrape of the wood against the floor. In complete silence, all except for the still-droning classical music, Theo stood up and walked towards the door of the pub, all eyes falling upon him. Nobody dared to go after him, not when he was in complete control of a beast like that and was upset.

He yanked the door open and stepped out into the moonlight. He used his sleeve to wipe his face and stared up at the creature.

"You really get it, don't you?" He mused, watching as Perry stopped moving and looked down at him. It moved forward and nuzzled its nose against Theo's shoulder and neck, making him stumble back a few steps. Theo reached his hand up and stroked Perry's head, down to its nose as it tried to comfort him.

After a few moments, he nodded and sniffled. The air was cold on his skin and it only served to make him tear up more with the shivers he was experiencing. The fresh air had also helped him to calm down a little, which allowed his 'pet' to do the same.

He sighed, running a hand through his hair and then shaking it out in front of him to alleviate his stress. "Alright, Perry. Go back to sleep."

XL

"We're here, be quiet now." Cordelia whispered. They had walked for about forty-five minutes, mostly through the urban areas until they reached an off-track desire path which interrupted the usual structural integrity of the gravel on the ground. That route had been about ten minutes, and opened up onto an area that looked like something out of a rural Scandinavian countryside.
The grass was alive. It was bright and lucious. Even better than the kind that Laine had seen on Earth. Fresh, growing, living grass was something that Serenity and Vercorbix had only seen drawings of. They had it in Heaven, but they had never been - and the same could be said for Earth.
"Woah." Serenity gaped, stopping in her tracks.
"Woah, quietly." Cordeilia scolded, beginning to march through the grass as if it were her hallway that she knew like the back of her hand.
"Is this what they have in Heaven?" Vercobrix asked, kneeling down in a proposal position and running his slender fingers through it.
"Not sure why you're asking three demons what they have in Heaven." Laine criticised. "But I think so."
"That is pretty cool." Serenity appreciated, taking the handful that her fiance had just ripped from the ground and reached out towards her. "Weird texture. I'm not sure why I expected it to be less smooth."
"Kids...!" Cordeilia called out, and the three *adults* still standing on the edge of the gravel-grass border looked up to her. She had made her way all the way over to the wooden shed-summerhouse-gazebo looking structure that was in the centre of the grass. It was made of an orange-toned wood, and although it was rarely approached, it looked

just as if it had been installed yesterday. "Come here, the grass will still be there when we're done."

"She's getting really into this." Laine whispered to Serenity, eyes narrowing at the uncharacteristic traits being displayed before her.

"I think that anything slightly rebellious gives old people like a million adrenaline rushes at once." The other princess snickered back, dropping the grass in her hand and following the other two towards the building themselves.

It wasn't very big - really only the size of your average conservatory. The door was too wooden, and the kind you would find in a regular garden. It was actually a little unsettling just how normal all of it appeared. Were they sure this was the right place?

It was, though, and that would become apparent to them sooner rather than later.

Cordeilia looked back to check that they had followed her instruction and approached the wooden structure too.

"Is there some kind of puzzle to get in?" Vercobrix asked, eyes running over the ridges of the wood.

"No, it's a door, love." Cordelia smiled in amusement, wrapping her hand around the doorknob and pulling it open towards her. Serenity snorted and gave Vercrobrix two strong pats on the back.

She stepped aside and gestured for the other three to walk into the seemingly empty room. It was just the same wood on the floor and ceiling. Not even a light.

"Well, isn't this anticlimactic?" Vercorbix asked sarcastically.

Cordelia rolled her eyes. "You'll see, young man." She lectured briefly. "Are you all completely sure that this is what you'd like to do?"

Laine answered with affirmation almost instantaneously. Vercobrix just looked at Serenity.

"Well, we've come this far. We'd be cowards to back out now." Serenity shrugged.

"You three are very lucky to have my guidance. The first time I did this all we had was what we had read in the library, and even that was vague." She commented offhandedly, stepping inside of the structure herself and shutting the door almost all of the way, still leaving a little gap.

"Ready?" She asked for the final time.

"Yeah."

"Yep."

"Yes."

"Okay, just step away from the walls a little bit." The older demon told them, which resulted in an awkward shuffle a few centimetres forward. It ultimately did nothing, but, really, it was more placebo anyway.

Cordelia clicked the door shut all the way and the room was plunged into complete darkness - all except for a quick flow of white light that ran its way along the edges of the building for a second before dying out again. For a fleeting moment, it stayed just like that. Only the heavy breaths of nervous young adults occupied the room - although it only lasted about two seconds before Laine felt the floor completely disappear from beneath her feet.

She must've screamed pretty loudly, because it was all she could hear as she plummeted down this newly-created freefall pit. It was light. She didn't see the others. Her eyes were squeezed shut. This was how she was going to die. God, nineteen years of being immortal and it's a fucking garden shed?

Her body plunged into the water and she was immediately pulled back to her senses. The water was cold. Super cold, and flailing her limbs around to find the surface could only do so much so quickly. Water flooded all of her senses as she pried her eyes open and was able to make out the blurred light above her. She moved her hands upwards and then towards her in order to move herself up, and found that she was eventually able to breathe again.

She gasped as she inhaled, kicking her legs and thrashing her arms in a panic-induced attempt at treading water.

She appeared out of the water about five seconds before Serenity did. The other Princess' hair was completely soaked, as was the rest of her - eyeliner running. She gasped for air, and once she could breathe again she relaxed slightly as she tread water.

It was no longer dark, rather the space they were in was illuminated by some kind of glow from the edges of the room. Towards the two women's left, there was a ledge which signified the edge of the water-area.

Another large splash to the side of them sent them rocking in the waves. Only out of the corner of their eyes did they see the blurred colours of Vercobrix hit the water, but it was enough that Serenity was able to process it with a loud exclamation.

"Oh, shit!" She called, voice panicked.

"What?" Laine replied quickly.

"He can't swim."

"Why the fuck can't he swim?!"

"Well, Atroka isn't exactly known for their blossoming leisure facilities,is it?!" She argued back. "Fuck!"

Laine didn't have time to suggest that Serenity go and save him before the redhead was already back underwater.

Serenity swam downwards, immediately throwing herself into another fit of panic when, despite the light, she was still unable to see him. Her lungs *burned* from lack of air, but she kept swimming, even as the increase of water pressure numbed her ears. Thankfully, it was only another twenty seconds of swimming before she was able to spot the lavender of his outstretched wings curled around his unconscious body. She felt so dizzy.

God, if she passed out now too that would not be good.

She hooked her arms under his, trying to hoist him up by his shoulders as his head tilted back heavily. Swimming upwards was difficult enough, let alone if she was dragging another person (a person heavier than her, too) up with her.

It became immediately apparent that she couldn't do it. Maybe two minutes ago, but now she was getting weak from the lack of oxygen. So weak that the idea of sleep sounded amazing - even underwater.

She felt a strong shove from behind her, blinking back into herself and turning around to see Laine. Her hair was flowing up all around her from the water, and she moved to swim on the other side of Vercobrix.

She lifted just underneath his knees as Serenity continued to hold his underarms, and they both pushed off the ground of the lake so that they were on an upwards momentum. With two of them and only once of him, it made everything a lot easier, despite the desperate need to breathe. The light became in sight, and it was that final stretch that was the most difficult.

When they got to the top of the water, the relief was like nothing they had ever felt before. They gasped, choked, coughed, spluttered for air. Because of their route of swimming, they were towards the ledge now, which meant that Serenity could push her fiance's unconscious body onto land. She gripped onto the edge of it and pushed herself up in spite of her weakness.

Vercobrix looked a mess. His wings were outstretched, completely soaked like the rest of him. His hair was messed up - the water having ruined the slicked back-look and now it just looked scruffy and soggy.

"Vee!" She called, shaking his shoulders hastily from where she knelt beside him. Laine still breathed heavily from the edge of the water, holding onto the ledge for dear life.

Serenity moved behind him and picked him up from behind, pressing her hands to his abdomen and pushing upwards. Then, she did it again. And, again. And, on the third try, Vercobrix's eyes snapped open and he coughed. He coughed and at least a pint glass' worth of water was vomited up out of his mouth and onto the previously dry ledge. He gasped for breath, shoulders and chest heaving up and down. He coughed as he tried too quickly to take in air. Serenity stayed in her kneeling position and pulled Vercobrix into her arms and subsequent lap, holding him closely as if he were a child as he heaved for air.

From the rectangular shaft that they had plummeted down, Cordelia came flying down leisurely, using her wings to support her journey. "Goodness, what happened to you three? You look like bathed cats." Serenity's eyebrows scrunched up in anger. "Why didn't you tell us we were going to get thrown into a pool at a hundred miles per hour?!" She gaped, watching irritatedly as the older woman stepped down onto the ledge, completely dry as she folded her wings away.

"The whole point of this is that it's difficult for you. If I told you everything that was going on you would find this to be a walk in the park." She argued.

"He could've died!" Serenity yelled back.

"You know very well that he could not have died." She sighed. "Besides, most people who aren't able to swim can at least usually keep themselves afloat for long enough. You should work on that, Prince Vercobrix."

He swallowed. "God, you're a bitch."

"That comes across as rude, darling. That was like an eight." Serenity whispered with a smile, humouring herself at their usual dynamic.

"Calm down." Cordelia scolded. "That was by far the most physically dangerous segment over with."

Laine pushed herself out of the water and sat on the ledge, leaving her feet to still dangle in the wetness. She turned towards the two engaged demons. "Are you okay?" She asked, and, even though she could conclusively predict the answer, she wanted to be nice at least.

Vercobrix nodded, swallowing again. "Yeah, thank you." He breathed, shifting to try and stand himself up. Serenity kept her hands poised on him and lightly pushed him back down into her lap.

"Stay here a little longer." She whispered kindly. "We have plenty of time, don't overexert yourself."

From each corner of the room, the light that was keeping them visible began to grow. It detached from the walls and swirled around in the centre of the room, eventually forming into a figure.

The figure made of white light faded to a more light green, grinning widely. Their face was warm, and they made the room smell of apples. They didn't look like a typical human. They had a pair of horns atop their head, yet long hair that went down to their elbows and a very masculine, wide jaw. Their whole body was translucent. They were wearing quite an old, traditional cloak with no shoes - only knee-high socks as they floated in the air.

"Gosh! Hey there." They chirped, eyes fixated on the demons. "Long time no see!" They floundered, before giggling. "See, it's funny because I've never seen you before." They told, before gasping as they pointed their outstretched arm at Cordelia.

"You! I *have* seen you before! You've aged!"

Cordelia raised an eyebrow. "That is what time does to you."

"Sure does!" The figure nodded with a broad grin. They raised an eyebrow and their pointer finger moved over towards the dark-haired demon who was now sitting next to his fiance. The figure smirked and then looked back at Cordelia.

"Their son." She said, and the figure brought both their hands to their mouth and gasped excitedly.

"Awh! That's so cute." They nodded, kicking their feet in the air under them before their eyes went wide. "Sorry! My name is Willow, or Will if we get close. I look after this place! And you three are...?"

"Confused." Vercobrix replied, looking at Cordelia with a fixated stare.

"No, silly. You were meant to say your name!" The figure, Willow, encouraged.

"Vercobrix." He said slowly. Willow nodded vigorously and then pressed their hands together in front of them before pointing them forward at the redhead next to him.

"Serenity." She said, smiling a little, entertained. Willow then bounced their hands to point at the last of the three.

"Um, Laine." She said.

Willow hovered down closer to them - so that they were only a metre away. They moved to sit cross-legged before the three, so that they were hovering above the water.

"So. Vercobrix, Serenity, Laine. And... c'mere Cordelia, you're involved too."

The older woman walked over and leant back against the wall behind the three others.

"There." Willow smiled. They clasped their fingers together and leant their chin forward onto their hands. "Vercobrix, Serenity, Laine and

Cordelia. Let's have a nice chat. Heart to heart. Why are you here?" They asked, and it was the first serious thing they had ever said. The first time their voice hadn't sounded fifty octaves too high.

"My brother." Laine answered quickly. "He was the King, and then he wasn't the King anymore and he got banished to Nesbryn. But, we want to take our kingdom back and we need him out of there to do it."

Willow raised an eyebrow. "Why do you need him out to do it?" They asked.

"Well," Laine began, pausing to think. "Because it's his throne. He's the only one capable of taking it back."

Again, Willow pursed their lips.

"Who said that?" They questioned, eyes narrowed. "Who said that *he* had to do it? Why don't *you* do it? Are you not good enough without him?" They said, sounding genuinely mean for a moment. Laine frowned.

"It's not that. I don't want to be queen. And he *does* want to be king." She explained. Willow nodded.

"Okay, I'll take that answer." They smiled, flipping back instantly to their cheerful personality. "Serenity! Why are *you* here?"

Serenity was a little scared to answer after what they had just said to Laine.

"I owe him something, I guess."

"What do you owe him?" They enquired with a tilt of their head.

Serenity bit her lip. "Alright, so, like two years ago I was arranged to marry him."

"I'm listening." They nodded.

"So we went out for like five days. And then it turns out that he's actually gay and he was having an affair with this British lad."

Willow gasped. "Drama, drama. Go on."

"So I was very upset about it, and after he decided to run away I stayed at his castle. Then while he, the King, was gone, his kingdom got attacked."

"This just gets worse and worse for you." Willow grimaced.

"Yeah. And so I did fight for a while, but I could only do so much. When he came back in the middle of the fight he neglected immediately helping himself and made sure I got out safely." Serenity swallowed, looking a little guilty. "Even though the last thing I said to him was quite horrible."

Willow narrowed their eyes.

"Serenity, it feels to me like *he* owed you a favour." They stated plainly. "He lied to you. And then he made up for it by saving you."

Serenity blinked. "I dunno, maybe."

"Okay, so I pose this to you." Willow began. "When you hopefully get him out of Nesbryn, what favour are you going to ask back?"

Serenity thought for a while.

"I don't think I need one." She finally responded. "I'm happy now."

Willow smiled. "Awh! Well, I do like hearing about the kindness of people's hearts. Fine. Your turn!" They continued, looking over at Vercobrix, who tensed a little.

"Why are you here?" They asked for the third time.

Vercobrix remained silent and just pointed at Serenity slowly.

"What about her?"

"She wanted to do this and needed me to do it too. I love her so I said yes." He shrugged.

"Oh!" Willow exclaimed. "Are you two together?"

"Engaged." Serenity confirmed with a smile.

"That's amazing! So you don't have any drama with this guy?" Willow asked.

"No, I haven't even met him."

"Well, I think that's very kind of you to be doing this despite that." Willow admitted, and then their chin tilted up to look at the final demon.

"Cordelia! Why are you here? Again."

"I'm here, Willow, because these kids wouldn't be able to do it without me." She said vainly. "And, also, Strythio is my grandson. I would be lying if I said I didn't care for his well-being a little. The same with my granddaughter Laine here. She will be happier if we do this. So will he."

Willow clapped their hands together in front of them. "This is so adorable." They breathed. "I'll give you the lowdown on what's going to happen." They explained, snapping their fingers. The water completely disappeared and was replaced with more grass.

"One by one, in an order you decide, you'll be challenged with a scenario that will be created by magic and tailored to your own personal thoughts and feelings. If you can fight it successfully, you'll be able to get a hold of a key. All four keys will unlock that…" They snapped their fingers again and a grand metal door appeared on the back wall. "…door. From there, you're on your own."

Laine nodded to herself. "What kind of challenges?"

"Emotional ones." Willow answered easily. "You'll have a difficult memory from your past replayed to you. That's all I can say." They admitted honestly. "Who's going first?"

"I suppose I will." Cordelia volunteered. "It'll likely be the same scenario that I faced those years ago."

The other three nodded. They were okay with the arrangement, and it gave them some time to dry off before their eventual turns.

"Be careful." Laine warned softly. She didn't even know if it was heard, because if it was, her grandmother paid no attention to the words.

"Good luck!" Willow called, turning slightly.

"I won't need it." Cordelia affirmed. "But thank you." She said, just before stepping off the concrete ledge onto the grass. Immediately, she faded away into golden light that eventually evaporated.

XLI

It was not the same scenario as the last time she had visited. Last time, Cordelia had been fifteen years old, and it had been a fight with her parents. The memory that she recognised this time had occurred when she was only twenty-three. After her last attempt of breaking down the forcefield. She watched it all play out like a third-party viewer - instantly recognising herself about two-hundred years ago, and also the doorstep that she was standing on.

Cordelia pressed two knocks to it quickly. It took around ten seconds for the door to open up.

"You can't start coming to my house. People will talk." Replied the younger, Oliver Garrah - also in his early twenties.

"We need to talk." Cordelia replied quickly, ignoring the argument and pushing her way into his house. Oliver looked out onto the street and then pulled the door shut, watching as the then princess floundered down onto his sofa.

"About what?" He asked, sitting down on the armchair opposite her.

Cordelia took a deep breath in. "You have to promise not to get angry or storm off. We need to talk properly."

"Well, I can't promise anything if I don't know what you're on about."

"Just promise, Oli."

He rolled his eyes. "Fine, promise."

Cordelia nodded. "I'm pregnant." She blurted, leaning back a little.

"Excuse me?" He replied, eyes wide and panicked.

"Yep. We need to get married before it starts becoming obvious." She said, hastily.

Garrah spluttered. "How do you- you don't know it's mine! You get around."
"It's definitely yours. You're the only guy I've been with in the last six months." She replied regretfully. "And we need to get married."
He set his jaw strongly. "We're not fucking getting married."
"It's your responsibility!" She yelled. "My parents are going to kill me! I'll- I'll tell them it was you. They'll have your head."
"You're acting like I tripped over and suddenly you're pregnant! Everything we did, we chose to do it *together*. You cannot pin this on me alone." He argued, hands shaking. "I don't love you enough to marry you."
"Of course you don't love me! I don't love you either, Oliver. They were stupid fucking hookups, but now we *have* to get married or my whole future is gone! I'm a princess, I'm going to be queen. And I am *not* raising this child alone!" She screamed, beginning to cry.
"Yes you fucking are. I'm not uprooting my death because we couldn't keep it in our pants." He said back.
"So god help me, Oliver Garrah, I will ruin your life."
"You don't have the guts."
"Look, do you care about me and our child or not?!" She asked, voice upset as she continued to cry.
Garrah sighed. "...Of course I do. I won't marry you over it, though."
"I'll get you a job." Cordelia suggested quickly. "I'll get you a job, a job working for my parents in the castle. I can deal with them yelling at me over this, they dislike me as much as it is."
"You want me to work for you?" Oliver asked, in shock that she had the audacity to suggest that.
"You're young. You died young. The main thing that people who die young do is join the army. I can get you a job, maybe as a soldier, or a paperwork boy. You can live in the castle and be around our child when they grow up."
Garrah swallowed. "We aren't going public about this." He said strongly. "Nobody knows. Not even the kid. It would ruin my life."
Cordelia was still upset by this, but she was happy she could find a compromise. "Fine. Not even the kid. But, this way at least, you can still be around and make sure they stay safe."
"Fuck, okay. Now get out of my house." He instructed.
The older Cordelia watched as the memory flashed to a different one. One from only a week later.
It took place in the same house. Only this time, twenty-three-year-old Cordelia didn't knock. She barged into Oliver's house, in tears.

"Oli!" She cried, leaning against the sofa. The bedroom door opened and he peered around the doorframe. He didn't say anything as she wailed. "We have to get married. I know, I know I said it was fine- but- but it's not fine! It's not fine!"
"What... happened?" The other demon asked slowly.
"My- my parents told me- they told me that if I don't find the boy that did this and marry him before the kid is born then they're gonna disown me! They're gonna throw me out- out onto the street."
"I'm sorry. This is obviously going to be much harder on you than it is on me, but, your parents don't mean that. They're trying to scare you."
"I really can't do this alone, Oli." She pleaded.
Oliver looked right at her for a moment, right before his body began to mutate. His eyes went completely white, and this sickening smile appeared on his face. His horns grew larger with a horrible crunching sound, the same with his height. In an instant, Cordelia's consciousness was flicked into that of her twenty-three-year-old's body.
Watching the memory had been difficult.
But this would be worse. She remembered it from the first time.
"God, you're a needy whore." The alternate version of him insulted, voice distorted. "Can't even stick up for yourself. You're scared, aren't you?! You weren't so scared when you came onto me. What happened? Fucking pathetic. And you've come here expecting me to do what you say. As if I care about you in the slightest!" He yelled.
Of course, it wasn't the real words of this man. It was a projection of her innermost thoughts.
And then Garrah went to attack her. He lunged forward and shoved her against the wall, throwing a strong punch at her. She ducked under him and kicked his side, making him growl and stumble backwards in his primal form.
"Can't even fight properly! Weak little thing, aren't you?" He asked, voice dripping with hatred. He kicked at her chest and shoulders, which made her fall to the ground with a scared yelp.
"Oh!" Garrah yelled, voice still many octaves too deep and distorted. "I shouldn't hurt you too much. Might kill the baby." He smirked. "But, you'd like that wouldn't you? Then you could tell people that you miscarried and it was all a tragic upset. Deep down you'd be glad to be rid of that parasite. He ruined your life, didn't he?!"
"Shut up!" Cordelia yelled, stumbling against the wall as she tried to stand.

"You could've had a life. A good one. You could have married and found love. You could have had a legitimate child. But nobody wanted to entertain the idea of dating a slutty princess that managed to get herself knocked up illegitimately."

The woman ran right at Garrah, screaming as she charged into him and knocked him to the ground. From there, she just hit him. She hit him over and over and over again, until his face was bleeding and he was unrecognisable.

She breathed out quickly. Her shoulders hurried up and down in panic. He had stopped moving entirely. Underneath her, his body faded away completely - only to be replaced with a bronze key - ornate and decorated with golden gems. That was it. She picked it up, grasped it in her hand, and all of a sudden, she was kneeling back on the grass - reverted to her past self.

"What the fuck?!" She heard Laine basically scream from where she was sitting. Cordelia looked over. Both Serenity and Vercobrix too had their mouths hanging open. Even Willow had the audacity to grimace.

"Sir Garrah is my grandfather?!" She yelled.

"Sorry." Willow hummed. "Forgot to mention that you can see each other's memories too. Oversight on my part."

Laine's eyebrows furrowed in shock and anger. She stood from her seated position immediately with the intent of marching over to her grandmother and giving her a good talking to.

"Ooh, Laine! Careful!" Willow called, but it was too little too late.

Laine went bounding across the grass. But she only got two steps along the magical grass before her own body dissipated into the golden light, and it appeared she had taken her turn.

She watched herself standing in the throne room of their castle. She still had her streaks in her hair, but this had been a good few years before her father retired - and the streaks in her hair were light blue. She was fourteen - standing opposite her father.

He sighed.

"We've been over this a lot, Laine. The answer is no."

She frowned. "But it isn't fair! It's not fair, dad."

"I get that you want to go, I do. But it isn't your job." He told her, trying to be patient.

The door clicked open, and a sixteen-year-old rendition of Theo stepped around it apprehensively.

"...What are we fighting about?" He asked slowly.

"God, you're so nosy!" Laine insulted him, frustrated and angry.

Dyran took a deep breath in before he spoke. "Laine is upset that I won't allow her to go to that, that ball thing that you are attending next weekend."

"Well, you wouldn't be allowed to go anyway, Laine." Theo said, and it sounded a bit like he was mocking her. "It's for the heirs."

"It isn't fair!" Laine yelled, looking over at her dad. "He gets everything! He gets to do everything, all because he was born first. I hate you!" She yelled, quickly.

"Well, you're far too young to be fraternising with potential suitors anyway." Dyran argued. Theo blinked a few times and turned to face the door.

"Alright, good luck, Dad." He whispered, walking back out of the door and leaving the two alone.

"That was unnecessary." Dyran lectured, looking down on her. "You can't be so rude to your brother like that. You know that this is just how things work." He said easily. Laine shook her head.

"But why?! Why is that how it works? It's never me! It's always him. I get that he's your favourite, but you could try and make it a little less obvious." She grumbled before spinning on her heel and walking away down the carpet in the throne room.

"Laine, come back here." He demanded. "This is why Theo is more responsible. He doesn't throw a hissy fit every time he doesn't get his way!"

"Because he always gets his way! He's never had to try for anything, you hand it to him just because he's your eldest." She replied, equally as angry.

She turned around, just in time to be flicked back to her fourteen-year-old body as she watched her father grow deformed and monster-like. His shoulders got broader, eyes rolling back in his head and turning completely white as his height grew also.

"We both know that you're never going to amount to anything compared to your brother." He said, voice distorted in the same way that Garrah's had been. "I don't know why you try."

It was terrifying for her to be standing face to face with such a terrifying version of her father. She stood paralysed for a moment, just staring at him.

"If Theo were here he would have already defeated me by now." Dyran smirked. Laine shook her head.

"No. No, you're lying." She affirmed, pushing back into a fighting stance and running at him.

371

Dyran reached out his arm and pushed her away, sending her rolling onto her side on the ground. She groaned and leapt back up. Standing next to him, this version of her father was tall. Taller considering that she was in her fourteen-year-old body. He towered over her, almost enough to make her cave and give up.

She tilted her head up to look at him, daring not to break eye-contact first.

"You are *nothing*. I don't know why we bothered to have a second child, all you do is complain and get in the way." He spat. He was so close up to her - pushing her against the wall like a skyscraper.

Laine pushed her right hand upwards and punched him in the jaw. His head snapped to the side, and he growled. Dyran picked her up by the throat and pulled her off the ground, leaving her feet dangling in the air as she panicked for breath. Laine's hands darted up to the one holding his. At her newfound height of being pushed against the wall, her legs were at perfect height to deliver a set of strong kicks to his chest.

He released her, and as she was falling, her body tilted upwards and she used her right foot to kick the underside of his chin. As soon as her foot collided with his skin, Dyran's body disintegrated entirely.

Laine hit the ground on her knees at the same time as the key did. Relieved and eager to get back to her interrogation, she grasped it quickly.

And then she was back on the grass in the same position. Her grandmother was still on the grass too, knelt about a metre away from her. Laine looked up.

"Does Dad know?" She asked, making painful eye contact.

"Of course not." Cordelia replied. "And you'll do well not to tell him."

Laine narrowed her eyes.

"That's why he quit in protest of Theo being banished. Because he's his grandson."

Cordelia gave a strained smile. "He told me, Laine, his only regret is not being able to keep watching over you, looking after you. He told me he trusted Nikoliah would do it well."

Laine frowned. "You still talk?"

"When we need to. He does have his own wife now, let's remember."

"Does his wife know?"

"I believe she does."

Laine fidgeted with the grass under her hands. Her voice dropped to a betrayed whisper.

"Why didn't you just tell us?" She asked. "As a family secret. Why did you let him grow up believing his father didn't care?"
"Secrets don't stay secret if you tell them to more than one person." Cordelia replied quickly. "It wasn't something we could risk. And you're fine. Your father turned out fine."
"I'm telling Theo."
"No, you are not."
"You at least have to let me tell Nikoliah. He's like a son to Garrah, he'd be thrilled to hear he could actually be a grandson-in-law to him." Laine pleaded with a pout.
Over from the ledge a few metres away, she was interrupted by Vercobrix's voice.
"I thought you broke up." He stated, confused and not really appreciating the tone of the conversation Laine blinked.
"Well, we did. But-"
"You still love him?" Vercobrix asked, as if he were asking a teacher at school for clarification about the time of an exam. It was so casual and almost just a statement.
"I didn't say that."
"You implied it."
"Alright!" Willow beamed. "Let's move on! Come back here, you two."
They smiled, beckoning Laine and Cordelia back over towards the rest of them. Both women stood and started to move over, albeit a little reluctant with their moods slightly shot down.
"You won't be telling Theo, and you certainly won't be telling Nikoliah." Cordelia whispered. "Especially not if you're no longer together." She continued. "You can tell him if you marry him."
Laine rolled her eyes. "You're not the only one who can keep secrets, you know."
"I'll take your word for it."
The room was filled with a heavy tension that wasn't there moments before.
Willow hovered to the side to allow the two returning demons to get back onto the ledge, holding their keys firmly in hand.
"Which of you two is going next then?"
"Can we not have some more time to talk about all this?" Laine asked, a little bit fed up of feeling rushed.
"The sun sets in four hours." Willow chided. "Talk all you wan't, but remember that."

Laine slumped back down on the concrete next to Serenity and Vercobrix.

"You all right, Laine?" Serenity asked, turning over to face her.

"Yeah." She replied. "Yeah, yeah all good. Just thinking. How are you gonna decide who goes next?"

The two fiances looked towards each other slowly, before smirks spread onto their faces. Vercorbix rolled his eyes and reached his hand out in a fist next to Serenity's.

"Rock, paper, scissors, shoot."

Serenity played paper. Vercobrix played rock. He dignified his loss with a groan at the same time that his fiance lightly cheered.

"You're going first." She instructed.

"You guys are in your twenties." Cordelia judged.

"It's how we decide everything." Serenity rationalised with a smile.

"Did you do rock paper scissors to decide whether or not you were going to say yes when he proposed?" She mused.

Serenity rolled her eyes. "I proposed, actually. And then we did rock paper scissors to decide whether or not *he* would say yes." She joked.

"You proposed?" Laine interrupted.

"Yeah." Serenity confirmed. "I love him but he never gets anything done. We'd talked about marriage before but just never asked properly."

"Alright, we don't need a detailed run down of our relationship." Vercobrix said, slightly amused as he stood up. Serenity followed suit and wrapped her arms around his shoulders.

"Good luck."

"I'm not going off to war." He said, kissing her quickly before turning towards the grass. "Do I just... go?" He asked, looking over to Willow.

"Yep!" They affirmed. Vercobrix took a deep breath in and stepped onto the grass.

XLII

Vercobrix's stomach dropped the minute he saw where he was watching. It was his bedroom, back at his parents' castle in Atroka. All dark coloured walls with a window on both the back and left ones. His double bed was shoved into the corner, adjacent to a dresser which he used as a bedside table. The walls were mostly plain, other than a small memorabilia board on the wall side of his bed - which consisted of a corkboard and various things like train tickets, receipts, pieces of fabric and letters glued onto it.
He had taken the board down about a month after his eighteenth, but he hadn't gotten those patterned purple curtains until that birthday, which placed the memory he was about to relive in a very short space of time. The room was empty, even the candles that would usually keep it light were burnt out.
He heard his own voice from the corridor, loud and upset. The door swung open and eighteen-year-old Vercobrix stormed in, leaving the door open behind him for the second voice to chase him.
He looked obviously younger. His hair was longer, and this was way before he had it braided, rather just being curly. He was wearing the traditional thing that a prince would walk around in - which for him and his family, was a dark grey button-up shirt tucked into black slacks. He was breaking the dress code a little in the minutely rebellious form of his Doc Marten style boots and jewellery.
"Well, maybe you should try harder!" He yelled, spinning around and facing the door as the other person walked through.

"I should try harder?! Are you fucking joking?!" A more practised-looking, nineteen-year-old Ayale Johnsen yelled, following him yet stopping just after xe had cleared the doorway. Xe was wearing less formal clothing - just jeans and a black t-shirt. "You have never had to work for a thing in your life, and you're telling me that I need to try harder?!"
Vercobrix rolled his eyes.
"You knew damn well when we started talking that I'm wealthy, I don't know why you're yelling at me like you didn't know that."
"You're supposed to be my boyfriend!" Ayale replied, voice angry and overexaggerated. "But you won't use the mountain of money you're lounging on to help me fucking live!"
"It's not my fault that you make bad life decisions! I didn't make you poor, you did that to yourself." He spat, crossing his arms.
"I can't believe you. You make me feel so shit all the time because of this power imbalance."
"I just don't see why I should be giving you *my* money because you can't be asked to work yourself."
"You say that as if you work! The only thing you put effort into is running to your mommy and daddy when you get upset!" Xe criticised, taking a step closer to Vercobrix as he narrowed his eyes and set his jaw. "You're an entitled brat! You're the youngest child to some of the richest parents in the whole of this dimension, and you refuse to help me heat my house. I hope they fucking die so you can get a taste of the real world."
Vercobrix took a really deep breath in and exhaled with a shudder of self-control.
"It was you, Ayale, that was throwing rocks at my window since we were fifteen. You pursued me *knowing* I was a prince, and now you're mad at me that I'm a prince? Sounds like you only went after me so that you could leech off my wealth."
"I'm not mad at you because you're a prince." Xe retaliated quickly, stepping another half metre closer. "I'm mad at you because you're fucking controlling. You constantly use your status to get what you want from me. You make me feel like I can't disagree with you because I'm just so much less than you are."
"You are." He replied plainly. "I'm not being horrible, that's just how it works."
"No it isn't!" Ayale yelled back, voice raising once more. "You're so toxic! This is the first time I've ever tried to tell you that the way you act upsets me and you're yelling at me!"
"You're yelling at me!"

"You're nothing but a selfish, entitled brat, Vercobrix, get the fuck over yourself." Xe accused, venom in xer voice as xe leaned up towards xer boyfriend.

Ayale nearly fell over from the force at which Vercobrix slapped xer. "Don't you dare talk to me like that." He scolded. "I might be your boyfriend, but I'm still your Prince, and I expect you to treat me as such." Was he fucking serious? There was no way.

Ayale looked back at him, betrayed.

"What on earth is going on?!"

Ayale spun around to be looking right at Vercobrix's mother - the Queen, Ola. Vercorbix shrunk back in on himself and cast his eyes at the ground. "Nothing, Your Majesty. I'm sorry." He replied, sounding so much more small and vulnerable than he had just twenty seconds ago.

"Should you lie to me one more time, young man, I will have to wash your dirty mouth out with soap." She replied. Vercobrix winced. "So, I shall ask again. Why are you two yelling?"

Her son didn't reply.

"Prince Vercobrix just hit me, Your Majesty."

The Queen remained expressionless, tilting her gaze over towards Ayale. "Well, why did he do that?"

Vercobrix replied before Ayale could.

"Ayale said that xe wishes you would die." He said quickly. The Queen looked angry. "And some really horrible things about me and our whole family." He sniffled, playing into the role.

The Queen rolled her eyes. "You are adults. Act like it." She scolded. "Having said that, I will *not* allow that kind of behaviour from someone courting my son, Ayale. From the sounds of it, his physical retort was a natural instinct to protect his family. Is that right, son?" She asked, gaze softening as she tilted her head sympathetically.

Vercobrix nodded quickly. "Well, yeah. I was scared that xe would hurt me."

Ayale's jaw dropped. There was no fucking way.

"Fine." Xe said. "Fine, if you want to be like that, then you can be like that." Xe gritted. Ayale was so angry. This was so unfair.

So xe hit him back. Harder. Hard enough that he fell over completely, although he might have done it on purpose to make it seem worse in front of his mother. And then Ayale kicked him, kicked his side on the ground.

Vercobrix's mother screamed with a step away, before scurrying off along the corridor calling her husband's name.

This was when Vercobrix's twenty-five-year-old consciousness was thrown into his eighteen-year-old body, in this situation. It was instantly recognisable when he took this change, because he started to hyperventilate on the ground.

It wasn't real. He tried to tell himself. *It's not real, it's not real.*

Ayale's body had begun to mutate by now, making xer taller and broader and a lot more dangerous. He knew that he had to get up. He had to get up and fight xer, but he was in such a distressed state after watching that part of himself play back that he couldn't. It was too much.

Ayale reached out for one of his bedposts, ripping it from the frame with a sickening crunch of wood. The wooden canopy above Vercobrix's bed collapsed.

"You don't deserve love." Ayale spat. "You're just like your parents." Xe slighted, raising the wooden beam above xer head.

Vercobrix tried to sit up, but he couldn't. He couldn't move. He was pretty sure he was having a panic attack.

Ayale smashed the beam downwards. Vercobrix was back on the grass. He was clutching his still-wet sleeves and struggling to breathe. He sat himself up. All of the others in the space were looking at him like he was some kind of monster. He pulled his knees up to his chest and cried. He couldn't breathe.

Within ten seconds, and after confirmation from Willow that it wouldn't send her into her own scenario, Serenity was on the grass, kneeling next to Vercobrix.

"Hey, hey, darling, look at me." She said, keeping her voice low and quiet. "Come on, you remember what we talked about with Sophie? What you talked about with her?"

Vercobrix nodded and looked at Serenity. He felt sick.

"I'm sorry, I'm sorry."

"Don't be sorry." She replied easily. "Come on, come back over onto the concrete and you can calm down."

It took Serenity a further ten minutes to get him from where he was curled up on the grass back to the ledge. He sat down against the back wall next to her and leant his head in her lap as the others watched.

"That was... Intense." Laine said, trying to shift the mood a little. "You dated Ayale?"

Vercobrix looked towards her. "For like three years." He confirmed. "I- I was a really bad person back then. Really bad."

Serenity brought a hand to the back of his head and started to run her hand through his hair. "He's been trying really hard to work on himself, it's not his fault, not entirely. His parents, they-"

"Ren." He whispered. She looked down at him. "I don't want to talk about them right now."

"Okay." She replied, nodding.

Laine furrowed her eyebrows. "But... if Ayale was living in Atroka with you like, what, six or seven years ago, what happened? Why did I meet xer in Nesbryn?"

Vercobrix sat up, but kept his hand interlocked with his fiance's.

"That memory. The one we just watched. It didn't end there." He said, eyes fixated on the ground. "Ayale hurt me. Really badly, I couldn't walk for like two months."

"So your parents banished xer."

"Yeah." He breathed. "Even though I deserved it. I haven't spoken to xer since." He lamented, feeling guilty.

"That's why you were so defensive about doing this. If we do this successfully, you'll have to speak to xer again."

Vercobrix sniffled, leaning back towards Serenity so that his head was on her shoulder.

"Who is Sophie?" Laine asked. "Last question, sorry."

Vercobrix bit his lip. "She's just this woman that I talk to sometimes. Talk about stuff with her, we both do."

Laine raised an eyebrow. "She's your therapist?" She questioned, not really understanding why he was acting like he was ashamed of it.

The Prince swallowed. "Yeah, I guess."

Willow blinked through the uncomfortable silence. They had just been watching this whole time, unsure of really what to say.

"Alright! Are you gonna get back in there, Vercobrix? You only get three lives, and, ding! You just lost one." They asked, voice way too cheery.

"Can we just have a minute first?" Serenity asked. Willow nodded.

"I don't think I can." Vercobrix shook his head. "I really don't think I can."

"Yes, you can." Cordelia chimed in for the first time. "I know you can. The past is the past, Vercobrix. It's already happened, it isn't going to change. So, you can't let it define you."

Vercobrix shook his head. "I can't fight xer."

"That version of Ayale is not real." The ex-queen replied. "Right now, the *real* Ayale is rotting away in Nesbryn. And if you don't defeat xer right now, then xe's going to stay in Nesbryn forever."

Vercobrix kept his eyes trained on the ground.

"I know that you can do this." Cordelia continued, leaning down on one knee to be closer to his eye-level. "Your parents did this with me, two-hundred odd years ago. Don't let them be better than you. If you can't do this, they're better than you. Don't let that happen."
Vercobrix looked up. "They did?"
"Yes." She replied. "They got through their scenarios. I couldn't do mine. That's why we failed." She admitted, voice soft and caring. It was unlike anything Laine had ever heard before.
"You couldn't do it?" She clarified. "But, but you seem so confident."
"Come on." Cordelia said, ignoring her granddaughter. "Get your head in the game."

It was another twenty minutes before Vercobrix found himself ready to try again. He had to watch the whole scenario from the beginning, but at least this time he could anticipate Ayale's first move.
The second that he was thrown into his body, he was alert. One hit with the wooden beam was enough for it to be over for him. If he could do the same the other way around, that seemed like an incredibly easy way to finish this. He stayed on the ground for long enough for Ayale to pick the beam up, but quickly darted out of the way before it could hit him.
Xe dropped the beam and turned to face Vercobrix, who was now standing up. He darted beside the bed and further away.
"Yeah, run from me like you run from everything." Ayale practically growled.
The first time he had fought this fight, back when he was eighteen, he had lost. Lost badly. His mother had run off to get his father, who had come and pulled Ayale off of his son's long unconscious body. Vercobrix hadn't woken up for a week. And when he did, coddled by his family in the infirmary, he hadn't left that hospital bed for another month. He doesn't remember much from that time. Just *ouch, fuck, shit, that hurts.* His parents became a lot more protective after that. A lot more overbearing, suffocating. They hardly let him stumble out of his room without a guard.
Even though he believed now that he deserved it (and was kind of glad for it, as it had given him quite the reality check), it still sucked.
He lost a good six months of his life to those injuries, and a former three years to his relationship with Ayale. Time he would never get back. It had been so painful, emotionally and physically.

He was sure to channel his anger about the whole thing when fighting Ayale.

Vercorbix skidded across the ground, kicking the back of xer knees and sending xer falling to the ground with an annoyed grunt. Vercobrix's hands were shaking as he grasped for the beam on the ground.

Ayale's demeanour changed.

"No! No, no! Please, please don't hurt me!" Xe pleaded, beginning to cry.

"Please, you've already ruined my life, please, stop it."

The Prince froze.

"You aren't- you aren't real."

"I was real when you manipulated me for years."

Vercobrix dropped the beam. He was sorry, he was really sorry. He hit the ground quickly, this distortion of Ayale sitting atop him and completely immobilising him. He didn't realise it had happened until he was helpless.

"You forced me to keep quiet, you made sure that I couldn't talk to you about shit." Ayale hissed, voice still deeper and more exaggerated than usual. Xe pushed xer hand over his mouth to muffle his panicked screams. He had messed up, he shouldn't have fallen for it.

"You deserve *nothing*." Xe slighted, mouth very close to his ear. He couldn't hear anything else. "You don't deserve to have gotten away from your parents. You don't deserve Serenity. You realise that you're just going to end up doing the same to her as you did to me? People don't change that quickly. Just wait until she realises it and leaves your deceitful ass."

Vercobrix bit down on the hand in his mouth. He had caught xer off guard, and as Ayale moved xer hand away with a yelp, he grabbed onto it and yanked forwards. Ayale fell back down onto the carpet before the Prince, who, no longer restrained, climbed to his knees and picked the beam back up.

"Vercobrix! Vercobrix, stop it! Stop it, you're a monster, you're hurting me!" Ayale's projection screamed, covering xer face with xer forearms. Vercobrix hesitated. He wouldn't make the same mistake again. He shook up to his knees and hauled the beam up with him.

"Please, not again, please!"

Vercobrix threw the beam down, hard. For a moment, a horrible sound like bones breaking and skin and organs squelching happened, but it was gone before the Prince could register it. On the ground, only the remnants of still-fading golden particles and the key that he was after was left. He reached forward and grabbed it with his shaking hand.

The grass felt a lot better under his knees when he knew he was successful. He grasped onto the key for dear life, still shaking horrifically.
"Awh, bless." Willow cooed, their voice spreading around the whole area. "Poor lamb."
Vercobrix looked up towards them, frowning at their patronising words. He stood himself up and stumbled back over towards the platform, and right into his fiance's arms.
"Well done." She whispered. "Well done, my love. I'm so proud of you."
Willow smiled. "Right! You're up, Serenity. I don't think it can really get much worse than that, so I wouldn't be too worried." They grinned.
Serenity looked over to Laine and Cordelia, who were sitting nearby.
"You'll look after him while I go and face my scene?" She asked, softly.
Vercobrix felt completely and utterly humiliated that he was being spoken about like a young child who can't stay home alone.
"Of course." Laine replied easily. "That was really amazing, Vercobrix. I don't think I could have done that."
"...Thanks." He said, muffled by his face in his girlfriend's chest as her arms wrapped around him.
"Okay, I need to go now." Serenity snickered, pressing a quick kiss to Vercobrix's forehead.
He pulled himself away and leant against the wall. "Good luck."
"Good luck, Princess Serenity." Cordelia encouraged softly. Serenity smiled to herself as she teetered on the edge of the platform. She looked back at them briefly, and Willow gave her a hearty thumbs-up from where they were hovering. Serenity nodded to herself and stepped onto the grass.
Out of all of them, she had the most recent memory by far.
She was walking through the streets of her kingdom, just under two years ago. It was her first public appearance since coming back from Klaevr, and all she wanted to do was walk to the market to get some bread.
It had only taken her about twenty steps out of the sanctity of her castle grounds before a group of teenagers noticed her.
"Hey, look. It's the *fairy princess*." One snickered, loud enough that Serenity heard it, but she could pretend that she didn't.
"Oh, shit, yeah." Another smirked. "Swear down, she turned him gay."
"Yeah, that's what Ben was telling people."
"If I was forced to date her, I would start kissing men too."
She didn't even know how they had heard. Theo hadn't necessarily had the chance to go public about it, although she assumed that considering

the scene that Beckett created with the two of them in the courtyard, word had kind of begun to travel, even more spurred on by the fact that he ran away from their wedding.

She kept her head up, and strolled past them to the best of her ability. It was only when she was actually walking past them that she found herself unable to do so.

"Oi, fag hag!" The loudest one yelled, and she stopped in her tracks. All of the other teens began oo-ing and such. "Is it true that no straight men would date you, so you had to get a poofta to pretend to? Someone told me that you knew the whole time." The teen grinned, maintaining ruthless eye contact.

"She knew that fake love was the best she would ever be offered." Another snickered.

Screw the bread, she could get one of her workers to go and get it. Despite her upset, Serenity was sure to not start crying until she was back towards the castle. She got inside, and into one of the long hallways on the second floor, where she leant against a wall and dropped down onto the ground in tears.

And then her current self was in her body. She looked up quickly and blinked, wiping her eyes. When watching it, she was under the impression that she would be fighting the teens. But, now? They were up to a mile away back in the town.

She pushed herself to her feet slowly. It was quiet. Really quiet, which she supposed meant that in this memory it was just her and whoever she was fighting. But still, nobody was near. She couldn't hear anything. She walked along the corridor, brushing her hand against the wallpaper. Before she could get to the corner, where the corridor diverged into meeting rooms, she heard footsteps in front of her.

She spun around, back the way she had game, but found that the corridor had completely shut itself off, now just a wall where the staircase would be. When she turned around again to go the other way, he was standing right before her.

This version of Theo looked just how she remembered him, shorter hair and more organised look. His eyes were completely white, horns double their size and more muscular. Other than that, not much had really changed. He grinned. His fang-like canines were definitely sharper.

"Where are you going?" He asked, voice distorted. "You can't get away from me." He laughed.

Serenity swallowed. This was unfair. He wasn't even actually there in real life, and she still had to fight him? Suddenly she preferred the teenagers.

383

She took a few steps backwards, and then a few more as Theo moved forward. She gasped when her back hit the wall that she had forgotten was there. Theo leaned right over her and bared his teeth.

"No matter what you do, Serenity, where you'll be in a hundred years, people are *always* going to remember you as *my* ex-girlfriend." He said, smiling. Serenity felt trapped by him leaning over her.

"The one that nobody could love organically." He said. "The one that turned him gay. The one that wasn't enough. The one that made him sneak off and go *fuck some boy instead.*" He whispered. "Because she was that undesirable."

Serenity had kicked him. Kicked his stomach, although she was aiming a little lower. He stumbled backwards and hissed in pain. He charged back at her, running quickly as she dived out of the way. Theo hit the wall where she was just standing, seeming to have all the stamina in the world as he immediately charged back.

"How was that for you?" Theo asked. "All alone on the morning of your wedding. How did you tell your parents?" He mocked with a teasing frown. "They must have been so disappointed. Your sister, the Queen. She's so amazing. They finally managed to find someone so desperate that they would date you, and it didn't even work out. I feel bad that only one of their kids could be successful."

That was it for Serenity. He was spewing all of her greatest insecurities at her. Each new word set another wave of rage coursing through her veins.

She ran up to him and punched him in the side of his head. It made him dizzy, which allowed her to push him forward and deliver a strong kick to his chest. He landed on his back, breathing heavily. Serenity moved over to him quickly, looking at his stupid face. The man that ruined her self-esteem, the man that obliterated all of her respect.

She jumped off the ground and directly onto his chest. She definitely heard his ribs crack, but she jumped again, and again, until she was just jumping on the carpet. She felt the key under her shoe and looked down, grabbing it.

When she had stood back up, she was on the grass, victorious.

XLIII

"Well, I'm certainly sorry for underestimating your combat skills." Cordelia said. "That was remarkably quick."
"Always nice to be able to release some pent up anger." She smiled back, walking over towards the ledge.
"I didn't realise it was that bad, Serenity. I feel like I probably could have done something to help." Laine said, feeling a little guilty. Although, realistically, she had had very little to do with their relationship.
"People will always talk, no matter what you say to them." She reassured, coming back onto the concrete. "And, it's fine. I'm pretty much over it now. But god, that was cathartic." She sighed. "Sorry, probably shouldn't call me trying to kill your brother cathartic, but it was."
"It's chill, he's not in the room with us right now."
Vercobrix was smiling a little bit. Serenity narrowed her eyes, amused.
"What are you smirking about?" She asked.
"Just thinking about how crazy our next session with Sophie is gonna be. She's gonna love to hear about that." He said, quietly, before turning his head towards Laine. "Sorry."
"Again, fine."
Serenity rolled her eyes playfully. "Oh, sorry Cordelia. Forgot you were his grandmother for a second."
The older woman smiled in playful amusement. "It's not a big deal, I would feel the same way if a man had done to me what he did to you."
"Awh, well done guys!" Willow said, elated and happy. "You all did so well!" They cheered, hovering higher off the ground and moving in the air to express their joy. "You gonna go for the big door now?"

"What's behind it?" Laine inquired. Willow made a motion of zipping up their mouth with a muffled 'zrrp' sound.

"My lips are sealed. It's all you from here." They said.

And so, keys in hands, the four demons began to walk across the grass. The thing about this was that they had also run out of guidance from Cordelia. She hadn't gotten this far last time.

The door itself was about twice the height of Vercobrix, who was the tallest of all four of them. It was wooden, with grey metal edges and a handle of the same colour. Below the handle, were four vertical keyholes.

"What happens to you now, Willow?" Serenity asked, turning back to look at where they were standing on the grass, feet a few inches off of it. They shrugged, still smiling.

"Whatever happens, happens!" They grinned. "I'll see the next set of demons that try this."

"What if nobody does after us? What if we do it, what then?"

Willow sighed. "I really appreciate the care, I do. But, I'm not real. I'm not a real soul, just a protector of this place. I'm created by the same magic that holds up the forcefield. When it goes down, there's no use for me anymore." They said.

Laine frowned. "If we break the forcefield down, you'll die?"

"I won't do anything, I just won't be here."

"Why do you help people then? Surely you should be misleading them."

"Not real, Vercobrix. I'm not real."

The sound of the lock jangling made the youngest three demons look down to where Cordelia had already put her key in.

"We don't have forever, guys." She warned.

Laine looked away and back at the glowing figure. "Thank you for helping us." She said easily.

"Of course." They replied, voice quieter and sympathetic.

Once all four keys were placed in the door, just their handles sticking out, each demon held onto theirs, agreeing that they would turn them at the same time.

"Ready?" Laine asked. They affirmed her.

Laine turned her key clockwise, and so did the others. For a moment, nothing happened. Then, the door shifted ajar, creaking open slowly. Willow waved them goodbye, and they went inside slowly.

Once all four had made it into the room, the door slammed shut behind them quickly. The room was only about three by four metres. It was completely dark, no light at all - apart from the centre of the room.

On a podium was a glowing red gemstone. About as large as a football, and in a hexagonal shape that was extended to be three-dimensional. Around the gemstone, beams of light flew out of it in all directions, through the walls of the room.

"So, I assume we have to knock that off the podium? It's the source of the magic." Vercobrix stated, reaching forward and touching it with one finger. He yelped and drew his hand back.

"Fuck." He grimaced. "It burnt me."

Laine raised an eyebrow. "Yeah, yeah. That makes sense." She rambled. "The forcefield in Nesbryn, it burns them when they touch it. And this is linked to it."

Vercobrix shook his hand out in front of him. "Ach, so how do we do it if we can't touch it?"

Cordelia rolled her eyes. "I don't know if you guys have ever been taught this before, but if you put your hands together and rub them with an intention, you might get this glowing light that can do things for you!" She gasped sarcastically, before dropping her face back to unimpressed.

"Ah, right."

"No, look." Serenity pointed out, leaning closely to the bottom of the gem. "It's connected to the podium." She said. Laine moved closer to it and looked with her. True to the Princess' word, it was. Little metal rods pushed into the gem, glowing in the same red as the beams.

"So how do we get it off?" Laine questioned, stepping back.

"Probably something in the room." Cordelia hummed, beginning to walk around the gem and inspect the walls, despite the dim lighting.

"Ceiling!" Serenity gasped, head tilted all the way back to look at it. On the ceiling, a small verse was carved into the concrete.

While three will leave, one will stay. They will release the banished from further away. One's two hands on the stone will break all ties, but only those connected by magic will hear their cries.

"What the hell does that mean?" Laine breathed, reading it over again and again, muttering it under her breath.

"Someone has to put their hands on the stone? To break the connections." Serenity observed. "But, we can't do that. It'll burn us."

"If someone's hands are burnt they can't use magic." Cordelia whispered, her stomach dropping at the realisation. She kind of pushed Laine out of the way to get a proper look at the words. "We have to leave someone here." She stated, looking down at the others.

"What?"

"Three will leave, one will stay." She repeated. "That one charges magic in their hands and puts them on the stone to break the connection between it and the podium." She continued, cogs turning in her brain. "Their hands will get burnt, and they won't be able to use magic to lift the stone off the platform."

Vercobrix narrowed his eyes. "Only those connected by magic will hear their cries." He whispered, reading off the ceiling. "'Their' in reference to the banished?"

"You have to have a magical connection to the stone when it gets pushed off to get out of here." Laine said finally. Her heart was beating out of her chest.

"Oh." Serenity breathed, her hand finding Vercobrix's as she held it tightly. "We don't all get to leave?"

"Now would be a good time for rock paper scissors, you two." Cordelia joked, smiling a little as she looked at them. Vercobrix and Serenity just gave her absolutely mortified glances.

"I'm kidding." She said, incredibly amused by their reactions. "Obviously, I'll stay."

"What?" Laine asked, voice breaking a little.

"Those two are getting married next year." She said, gesturing to them. "Lord knows they deserve it after what they've been through. And you, Laine. You haven't lived yet, you're so young. I've been here for hundreds of years. My baby is all grown up, and my grandbabies are all grown up too."

Laine frowned. "We'll come back for you." She breathed. "After the fight."

"That's another point, I won't be much use in the fight."

"You were amazing in your memory earlier." Serenity replied, not really knowing if this conversation was one she could be inputting on, but she did anyway.

"I fought well in my twenty-year-old body. I couldn't now."

Laine ran up to her and wrapped her arms around her grandmother in a tight hug. Cordelia leant into it and returned the gesture.

"I know I was never the nicest you and Theo when you were growing up, so, take this as my act of kindness. Don't expect anything from me for as long as we're on speaking terms."

Laine nodded as she pulled away. "Thank you."

"But, how did you and my parents get out when you were unsuccessful?" Vercobrix asked. "Surely nobody came to rescue you."

Coredelia shook her head. "Willow teleported us out."

"Oh, but they won't be here after we do this."

"Well, that's okay. We'll come back." Laine repeated.

"If you can. I don't know what'll happen to this place if we're successful." The older woman replied. She pushed a strand of loose hair behind her ear. "No matter, let's get this done. It'll get dark if we aren't quick."

The room was deadly silent as she formed the magic in between her palms. The markings on her arms began to glow very subtly. Once the glow of light pink had formed properly, she separated her hands and held them out in front of her.

"Just- agh- be careful." Laine whispered, earning herself a cursory glance.

She quickly pressed her hands onto the gemstone, and for a moment, she felt nothing as her magic was absorbed into it. The bonds holding the stone to the podium shattered with a high-pitched sound, followed straight after by the searing of skin. Cordelia screamed and leapt backwards. Her palms were red, skin bubbling as it melted away. Serenity had to physically look away to stop her breakfast from coming back up.

Laine screamed and lept backwards. "Fuck." She gasped, unable to take her eyes off the inflamed skin on her grandmother's hands as she shook them around wildly. Vercobrix brought his hand up to his mouth with a gasp, turning to watch his girlfriend crouch down on the ground with her eyes screwed shut as she retched.

"That's at least second degree. Maybe third. Can you feel your hands?" Vercobrix interrogated, ignoring his fiance for the moment and kneeling down beside where the older woman had sat on the floor.

"I can feel that- that it hurts, yeah!" She replied, sounding annoyed at him. If he noticed, he didn't show it.

"That's good." He said quickly. "Only because it means you haven't severed your nerve endings. I didn't- I didn't mean that it's good that you're hurt, sorry." He rambled, eyes fixated on the burns. "Okay, just don't brush your hands against anything at least until tomorrow. If they touch the walls or something then the salvageable skin might get ripped off."

Serenity clasped her hand over her mouth while muttering, although it was muffled. "Oh my god."

Vercobrix looked back at her and cringed a little. "Sorry."

Laine walked a few metres over to Cordelia, hesitant and on wobbly legs. Vercobrix stood and moved away so that Laine could be with her. He walked back over to Serenity and sat beside her on the ground, whispering reassurances as she continued to look pale.

Laine kneeled down in front of her grandmother and hugged her again, careful not to brush against her charred hands. She prolonged it, not wanting to think about the consequences of leaving her here. Suddenly, in the moment of their embrace, anything this woman had ever done or said to her during childhood completely melted away in favour of genuine care and familial love.
"Alright, get off and go." Cordelia snapped. Laine frowned and nodded wordlessly as she climbed back to her feet.
"Okay, so, do we just... knock it off?" Laine asked the other two. They looked to her before Serenity stood, leaving Vercobrix on the ground for the moment - although he quickly moved to stand at the same time so that their held hands didn't disconnect.
"I guess so." She shrugged, pulling her hand away from her fiance's and putting them together in front of her. Vercobrix followed her lead.
"What if we aren't strong enough, though? I know our magical abilities are exceptional, but I don't think they make us physically stronger." He asked. Laine shrugged.
"If we aren't strong enough then, oops. Nothing we can really do, so let's just try our best."
Vercobrix hummed, not completely satisfied with the answer. Then, together, the three young people charged their magic. Laine had all that she wanted first, so she swirled the ball of red light around her hands and pushed it towards the gemstone. The magic split apart and huddled around the gemstone. Moments later, Serenity's dark blue and Vercobrix's bluey-purple light did the same. They each had to focus very intensely to keep the grip on the stone.
The three of them stood in a triangular position around the gemstone, hands turned outwards as beams of coloured, glowing light transfixed to the gemstone, holding it like several yards of unbreakable rope.
"Okay, I'll count down." Laine said. "You ready?"
They both nodded.
"One, two-"
"Wait," Serenity interrupted. "On three or after three?"
Vercobrix snickered and turned his head to look at her. "I don't think it matters all that much."
Laine smirked, humoured. "On three, I guess."
"Alright, thanks." She smiled. "Gosh, I was just getting clarification!" She laughed, looking at Vercorbix. "You don't have to look at me like that." She defended with a smile.

"If I have to watch another second of you two ogling over each other I think I'm going to succumb to my injuries and die right here." Cordelia said, voice flat and uncaring from the corner of the room.

"Noted." Serenity nodded, eyes focusing back on the gemstone.

"Okay, one, two," Laine went on, squinting at the glowing light to practise all her intention into it. "Three." She finished.

Her hands curved upwards, immediately feeling the horrific strain on her arm muscles.

"You remember when I said we should start working out together?" Vercobrix asked, voice strained as the beams of light he was manipulating tightened. Serenity rolled her eyes with an exasperated groan. "And you said," He continued, shifting his voice pitch as best he could to do an impression of his fiance. "No, Vee, that's a waste of our time and we could never commit to it."

Serenity snickered. "You sounded so gay just then."

"Ooh, god. That's derogatory." Vercobrix grimaced, eyebrows raised.

"No, you know I didn't mean it like that." She laughed. "And my voice is *not* that high-pitched."

"You've never even met a gay person that talks like that. You've picked that up from too much socialisation with ex-mortals."

Serenity rolled her eyes. "Well, maybe you're being derogatory, generalising a whole species like that." She fought back playfully.

"Task at hand!" Laine raised her voice, eyes darting between the two lovebirds. Their eyes flickered to her before ceasing their communication to focus once again on the gemstone.

"Hold on, which way are we pushing it?" Vercobrix asked after a moment.

"Right." Laine replied.

"Oh, I was going up." Serenity confessed.

"I was going right." Vercobrix then added.

"My right or your right?" Laine clarified.

"Well, my right, obviously."

"Yeah, well, I was also going to my right, dumbass."

"Kids." Cordelia interrupted again, and once more, they all turned to look at her. "Just push it in the direction of the corner opposite this one." She said calmly. "God, and you're supposed to be the rulers of the next generation." She muttered, shaking her head and tutting. Laine rolled her eyes.

"Okay, onetwothreego." Laine slurred quickly, jerking forwards suddenly as she invested all of her body weight into pushing the stone. It shifted an inch, and then another. Pretty soon, all three were straining themselves to push it.

"And... one last big push for me." Cordelia teased them, sounding like a primary school teacher talking down to her students. Laine glanced back at her, frustrated by her belittlement, but she still pushed herself that little bit harder. It hurt like hell, and she was pretty sure she would need a ten year lie down after this.

That extra momentum from all three of them had the gemstone moving even more, and then it teetered on the edge of the podium.

It fell off incredibly quickly, breaking all of the beams of light shooting out of it. It hit the ground and shattered like glass, into an uncountable number of pieces. Laine went to jump backwards in self-defensive shock, but before she had the opportunity, she was falling.

They had all only each been teleported about two metres off the ground, so it was only a matter of seconds before they hit the grass on the surface.

Laine shielded herself and gasped for breath, rolling onto her back and looking up at the orange sky as her chest inflated and deflated with the weight of her breathing. She tilted her head up momentarily and looked around for the sight of her grandmother, but she was just as absent as expected. Serenity yelped when she hit the ground, landing on her side. Vercobrix landed on his front, letting out a long groan of pain as all three of them were spewed out on this grass - still in the same triangle formation that they had been in previously.

"Is that it?" He breathed, coughing. "Did we do it?"

There was a loud clap of thunder. They all turned to look at the sky above them, specifically the direction which the loud clamour had come from.

A dark, black, smoke-like colour began to flow into the sky from the West, like blood into water.

Laine sat up, and then struggled to her feet as she kept her eyes fixated on the colouration.

"Seems so."

XLIV

If one thing was abundantly clear to her, Fiducia knew that King Beckett was *not* happy. The door to her and Nikoliah's office hit the wall behind it so hard that she thought it might come off the hinges, startling her.
"Both of you, get the fuck up, now." He commanded. She squinted a moment, confused. It was late, like six o'clock in the evening. She was meant to be getting off work soon.
"May I ask, why? Your Majesty." Nikoliah asked, standing to his feet at the same time as Fiducia.
"The forcefield around Nesbryn has been broken down." He continued sternly. "Which is something that can only be done by magic-wielders. I can think of one." He said, eyes pinning Nikoliah to his position. "You wouldn't happen to know anything about that, would you?"
Fiducia looked over at him nervously. Would Laine have really done that? And, if she had, would she have told her ex-boyfriend about it?
"No, Your Majesty, I wouldn't." He said effortlessly. The King scowled.
"Fine. Go and prepare your troops. I have a feeling that we might run into Strythio tonight."
Nikoliah grabbed his sword from the holster on the side of the wall, and then he grabbed Fiducia's too, handing it to her.
"Don't let me down." The King instructed angrily, spinning on his heel and exiting the room. Fiducia ran her hand over the handle of her sword anxiously. She looked over at Nikoliah and frowned at the vacant look in her eyes.
'Are you okay?'
He blinked at her as if she was confused.

"Yeah, of course."

'*Okay.*' She signed, not fully convinced.

"Okay, let's go then. We have a job to do." He gestured to the door, eyes set on it. Fiducia nodded and walked out first while attaching her sword to her hip. Rally the troops. Right, easy enough.

The thunder was louder than anything they had ever heard before. It was a singular clap, and despite storms being a regular occurrence, everybody in the tavern could identify it as much more than a regular occurrence.

They all pretty much leapt out of their seats, completely abandoning the plates of cooked meat that had been served about half an hour prior in favour of getting outside.

The sky looked like it was melting.

The darkness was seeping out into the red sky now that the dam had been broken. Theo looked at the sky with wide eyes. The usually completely straight border between the dark sky and the red one had been completely shattered.

"Woah." Raphie breathed, looking up at the marble.

"She fucking did it." Theo said, astonished. He spared a glance to Julian, and then to Ayale, who was standing beside his boyfriend. Both demons smirked a little before they bolted off in the direction of the train station. It took about two seconds for Axel, Fern, Livvy and Toby to scramble out of the building too. They ran right at the forcefield - too amazed to contain their excitement.

"Like kids to a candy shop." Julian snickered.

"Hey, you would be the same if you were any of them." Raphie chided, watching with raised eyebrows as Theo and Ayale made it to the usual border of the forcefield. It was instinctive that they stopped there, just before the marked out line on the ground.

"Right, who wants to see about losing a hand?" Axel grinned, skidding to a halt in the line with all of the others.

"Dibs not me." Toby replied instantly.

"Wuss." Fern teased, taking a few steps back and gearing up to push him. His eyes widened and he yelped, trying to move out of the way. He didn't, not in time, and so about a second later, Toby and Fern found themselves on the other side of the border after being pushed and pushing respectively. They crossed it like it was nothing. Fern laughed, eyes widening in excitement when she realised that there was no forcefield anymore.

Theo felt an immense wave of relief crash over him as he himself walked over the line.

He wanted to scream, and to cry, and to jump around all at once. But, in reality, nothing came out. All he found himself able to do was stand still and look around as his friends - the people that had grown to be his friends over the last two years - celebrated.

Someone leapt beside him and wrapped their hand around his shoulders, pulling him towards them. Once they let go, he stumbled forward with a surprised smile, turning around. Ayale grinned widely, catching Theo completely off guard when xe pulled him into a hug.

"Oh my god, I love your sister so much." Xe grinned into his shoulder. "I'll hug her when she gets here."

Theo smiled. These people that he had grown to know had always been so… miserable. Not necessarily in how they acted, but just their whole demeanour. Theo didn't think he'd ever seen them look so genuinely hopeful for the future. It was a fire in their eyes that had always been absent.

"Right, um, we need to get ready then." He said, trying not to slaughter the happiness gained. Livvy pointed at Theo through her smile.

"Yes! God, I'm excited to fight something that can't breathe fire."

"Ah, ah!" Axel reached a hand up at Livvy. "It's right there, it might hear you." He laughed, looking over at Perry, who had not yet been stirred from its sleep.

Theo rolled his eyes. "Come on, we need to go and get weapons and armour and such. Before my sister gets here, and I give her thirty minutes."

"Boo, you suck." Fern called. "Can't we just leave now?"

"No, 'cause the Princess girl is gonna come back with the other ones she did the thing with." Axel retorted. "Then there's more of us."

"The 'princess girl' has a name." Raphie reminded them from where she had strolled back up to them. Julian was walking with her and then he skipped over to Theo and stood beside him, tilting his head to the side and allowing his taller boyfriend to press a kiss to his cheek.

"Oh my god, we get it, you have a crush on her." Axel droned back. Raphie rolled her eyes.

"What the hell is going on over here?" Isaac asked slowly, blinking at everyone else. "Is the forcefield down?"

"Yeah! We're gonna gear up and then we can go fight that guy that Theo doesn't like." Livvy grinned.

"Well... why do we need to do that? Can't we just... leave?" Isaac said, looking around at all of the demons.

Theo walked back across where the forcefield would have been and closer to Isaac so that he could hear. "If we don't defeat him, then we have exactly zero chance of not getting thrown back in here. If we win, I get to be the King of Klaevr again. Which gives me the legitimate power to banish people, and therefore gives me a standpoint on the debate about if this place should even exist."

"Yeah, and then he can give us all knighthoods for our tribulations." Toby joked with a smile.

Isaac nodded to himself. "Okay. Well, should we go to the armoury then?" He asked, slowly gesturing in the direction of the building.

Laine, Serenity and Vercobrix got back to the train station in T'kota as quickly as they could. It seemed, though, that it wasn't quite quick enough. It appeared that the underworld had kind of gone into panic mode, which included the people operating the trains.

"Sorry, kids. No more passenger trains until *that* is resolved." One of the guards said, pointing up at the poisoned sky. Laine frowned. She really wished that people would stop calling them kids when they were all very clearly adults.

"Please?" She asked, sweetening her voice as best she could.

"No can do I'm afraid." He replied again. "Where were you hoping for anyway?"

Laine bit her lip and glanced over at the other two. It probably was *not* in their best interests to tell this guy where they were hoping to get back to, considering the circumstances. A whistle blew across the platform, and one of the trains began to close its doors.

"Where is that train going?" Laine asked, diverting the question. The guard turned around and looked over to it, dismissing her with a wave of his hand.

"Just over to Nesbryn with some guards. Nowhere that you three want to go, that's for sure."

Laine cringed, looking at the departing train with annoyance.

"We're totally gonna have to run after that, aren't we?" Serenity whispered next to her. She nodded.

"Excuse me?" The guard asked.

"Sorry." Laine offered, just before she kicked him in the side of his legs. He fell over to the ground and she took off running down the long platform that the train was leaving from. She heard various shouts behind her, which she ignored.

After a moment of shocked hesitation, Vercobrix took off following the two girls that had already made their starts. He was going to be in so much trouble, he could sense it. But, he wasn't doing this for himself. If he was doing this for himself he would have stopped the moment Laine appeared in the entryway of their castle. He was the tallest, with the longest legs, and so he caught up easily.

"What exactly are we gonna do when we reach the end of the platform?" Vercobrix struggled out while keeping a steady pace. They weren't even in proximity of the train and they had about ten more seconds of sprinting before they would lose the platform from under their feet.

Laine turned her head over towards him. "Well, I would show you, but I think they would hit you." She said, leaping off the platform and extending her wings. They caught her in the air, and she used them to continue moving through the air after the train. Serenity pushed off afterwards, allowing her dark blue wings to paint the sky around her. She turned around slightly to watch Vercobrix do the same.

The two of them hadn't really done much flying with their wings. It wasn't entirely necessary. Despite this, it was very impressive to every ex-mortal who had been chasing after them. They knew, of course, that it was possible - but most had no reason to need to fly anymore. For most, it was their first time seeing something like that.

Vercobrix propelled himself into the air using his wings, moving them so that he could keep up with Laine, who seemed much more practised in her flight.

It wasn't long until Laine had reached the back of the train, her hair blowing in the wind as she fought against the natural air resistance. The whole thing had two carriages, and Laine managed to get about a metre past the first one before she tucked her wings in, losing the leverage that she had and dropping onto the roof of the vehicle. She planted both her hands onto it, as well as her feet, and then to her knees. She breathed heavily, manoeuvring around to face the direction that the other two were still flying.

Vercobrix, being stronger, had gained some momentum on his fiance, and it only took him about ten more seconds to drop himself onto the train with a grunt of pain, ending up further to the front than Laine. He didn't dare retract his wings - considering that they were the only thing keeping his balance. He moved to his knees slowly and crawled closer to Laine so that they could speak.

"That was the worst thing I've ever done." He breathed. The train began to pick up speed as it fully exited anywhere near the station. They were surrounded by houses all nestled together, as well as sections of forest (all made up of clusters of dead trees and dark overhang). The sky had begun to darken significantly from the black colour bleeding into it.

"Guys, I can't- agh-" Serenity called, still flying desperately, but with the way the train was picking up speed, she wasn't optimistic.

Laine looked back over to Vercobrix. "Can you hold my ankles?" She asked quickly.

"What?"

"Just hold them." She instructed, sliding over to the back of the carriage. Vercobrix followed her, starting to worry for Serenity too. Laine knelt on the edge of the carriage, steadying herself with her hands. Vercobrix quickly understood her intentions, wrapping his hands around her ankles, just above her trainers. He assumed a position that gave his body a good grip of stability on the train, kind of straddling it. Laine extended her wings fully, leaning forward. She wished she had a hairband to tie her hair up right about now.

"Don't you dare let go." Laine warned the demon behind her. He nodded profusely, eyeing his fiance as she put all her effort into keeping up. She leant forward, reaching her hands out. It gave Serenity one metre or so less to fly forward. Her legs moved in the air below her despite the fact that it didn't actually do anything.

"Grab my hand!" Laine yelled, but the wind made sure that Serenity couldn't hear a thing, only making stressed eye contact with Vercobrix as she pushed herself as hard as possible. She understood anyway, and outstretched her arm, grabbing onto Laine's wrist.

Vercobrix kept one hand firmly on Laine's ankle, and then he moved the other to meet Laine as she leant herself back up to pull Serenity closer. He wrapped his arm around her waist and pulled her backwards.

Serenity was pulled further towards them, and in one swift movement, she planted both feet on the top of the train carriage and sort of fell forward. She landed on the top of the train, relieved and exhausted as she slowly dragged herself to a sitting position.

"Fucking Hell." She said, swallowing.

"You okay?" Laine asked.

"Yeah. Can we please get inside the vehicle, though?"

Vercobrix reached out and grabbed onto Serenity's hand. "Let's remember that this train is transporting guards." He said slowly. "Are we ready for another fight so soon?"

Laine crawled towards the back of the train. "We don't really have a choice. If we don't get them now, they'll get Theo and everyone else in Nesbryn."

"We were kinda dumb not to bring swords." Serenity observed. "We'll have to use our magic again."

"Which is fine." Vercobrix added, more reassuring himself than anyone else.

A large gust of wind blew, which had them gripping onto the metal tightly. The train was going really fast now, as it was completely direct. Her hair blew behind her as she pushed herself to the end of the carriage and planted down onto the ledge at the back of the train. There was a door on the back of the carriage with a small window.

Through the uncleaned glass, she could make out the figure of just one person, an older man. He held a cigarette between two of his fingers and was watching out of the window idly. He did have a sword, but it was leant against the wall a few metres away from him.

On top of the roof, Serenity and Vercobrix had diverted all of their attention towards the hatch on the carriage next door. They must've made too much noise in hijacking the vehicle, because the hatch opened up and a woman dressed in armour poked her head out. Vercobrix made eye contact with her and they kind of just stared at eachother like deer in headlights for a moment.

"Are you two gonna come down?" Laine called, pulling herself up a little. She looked back over the carriage and made eye contact with the demon looking out of the hatch, and then back to Vercobrix, who had turned to look at her. She blinked a few times. "I'll get the guy in this last carriage then meet you in that one." She said quickly, dropping back down onto the ledge of the train.

"Is there any chance we can negotiate this with our words?" Vercobrix asked hesitantly. The woman raised her eyebrows and turned back towards the inside of the carriage.

"You were right." She said. "But it's a pureblood. Are we, like, legally allowed to fight them?"

From inside the carriage, he heard a gruff voice.

"If it's on my fucking train then you knock it off. I don't care."

Serenity pulled herself to her feet, leaning on Vercobrix, who was still on one knee to avoid compromising his balance. The guardswoman nodded and pushed herself onto the roof, where she was followed by another guard, who handed her a sword.

"We don't want to hurt you." She said, holding on hand out towards them. Vercobrix scrunched his face up and raised his eyebrows.

"It sounded a bit like you do when he said 'knock it off, I don't care'." Vercobrix replied.

The man that had climbed out of the carriage with the other guard took a quick glance to his colleague and began sprinting at them. For a moment of quick indecision, Vercobrix stood completely still.

The man running only got half way across the train before a ball of dark blue light struck him in the side and sent him flying off the train and onto the forest floor. Vercobrix looked over his shoulder at his girlfriend, who was breathing heavily and still charging her magic in between her hands.

He nodded quickly. "Okay, yeah. Okay." He said, standing up himself and extending his wings all the way out to assert dominance.

"Going to need back up!" The guard called, donning a fighting stance. The next of the soldiers began to climb out of the carriage as she began to approach them, flailing her sword. It was clear that she was well trained with the way she approached, but you can only have so much training - especially against magical beings.

She swung quickly, with malicious intent. Serenity ducked under the first, but she hit Vercobrix's arm with a slight tilt of the sword. He quickly stepped backwards, shooting a beam of light towards her. It wrapped around the handle of her sword and tugged it from her, straight into his hands.

Serenity had stood back up at this point, threatened by the wind in the air. The guard looked dumbfounded, unsure of what to do now that she had been disarmed. The next guard who had crawled out of the carriage ran up in defence, standing in front of his teammate. Serenity moved backwards, giving Vercorbix a few steps advantage to bound towards her. She held her hands out and interlocked them at the level of her knees.

Still holding the sword, Vercobrix planted his right foot onto the makeshift step. Serenity pushed him upwards, and he propelled back off of it into a backflip over the top of the other two on top of the train. His sword pushed into the first guard, completely knocking her off the edge of the train like her successor. He planted his feet back on the roof of the train, facing Serenity with the newest guard in the centre. The man spun around, eyebrows furrowed in anger. He raised his sword and went to hit the Prince, who retaliated by clashing his own sword with it as if they were fencing.

He fell off the train - suddenly falling victim to Serenity's magic.

"That was badass, Vee." She grinned, high on adrenaline.

"Yeah." He replied glibly. "I hope they aren't hurt properly."

Some grunts and strained noises came from inside the carriage. Vercobrix was pretty close to the opening, so he glanced into it. Laine was having a battle with one last guard, pressing against his sword with magic. He tilted his head towards the hatch to gesture to Serenity that they should go and help, before taking a few steps towards it and climbing down.

Laine glanced behind her. "You're bleeding." She said quickly.

"I know." He replied, handing Laine the sword. She raised it above her head and thwacked the other man's sword. It clattered to the ground in an instant.

"Bitch." He grumbled, keeping his eyes locked onto her as he reached down to grab it. Serenity clambered down off the roof now too, feeling incredibly relieved to be out of the wind. She looked through the connecting door to the rear carriage and saw one lone guard unconscious in the centre of the aisle between seats. By the time that she looked back, the final enemy was in the same state, with Laine breathing heavily above him. She dropped the sword onto the ground and moved to sit on one of the tables on the right side of the carriage. The only injury that she had sustained was a bruise to her shoulder, which she frowned at before beckoning Vercobrix over to where she was. He had a singular, long cut on his upper arm, which was dripping deep blue blood.

"This'll make it look like you've done the most work when we get to Nesbryn." Laine smirked, pressing over it with the sleeve of her jacket to stop the bleeding.

"My big strong man." Serenity teased, sliding onto the table next to him and wrapping an arm around his shoulder, despite his chagrin at the name. "Laine, you should've seen us fighting up there, we were so good." Laine raised an eyebrow, moving her hand away from the wound and deciding that she was satisfied that it had stopped bleeding, although it had stained her sleeve a dark blue.

"Excuse me, I was fighting alone, I think that I was so good." She bargained.

"We were all good. I'm exhausted, can we please maintain a nice atmosphere for the next ten minutes so I can pretend to be asleep?"

Vercobrix asked, clambering into the chair by the window and laying his head flat on the table in his arms.

Serenity snickered. "Alright, darling." She entertained. "We'll whisper."

XLV

Their journey to the armoury was swift, and the demons of Nesbryn arrived back at the train station area not long before they heard the squeaking of breaks against the old, uncared for track. Theo grinned and dropped his sword (which he probably should have not done in hindsight), leaving it on the ground and bounding up the stairs of the train station. He had changed into his very best (least ripped) pair of blue denim jeans, with a loosely fitting black hoodie that only had elbow length sleeves. Underneath it, the long, green sleeves of his undershirt stuck out. He had both knee and elbow pads, as well as a brown leather belt with his empty sword holster attached. Finally, he wore dark brown leather combat boots - the same as his fingerless gloves.

He had left everyone else, still sorting themselves out, down on the ground. It had taken Julian ten minutes of trying things on to find an outfit and accessories that he was confident he could fight in. Raphie had been a lot less indecisive, and since all of the other demons already had things tailored, once they'd gotten over the hurdle of scrambling stuff together for their guests, they were fine.

Laine pulled the door open just as Theo stepped through the entrance of the train station. She looked tired, and less composed than usual, but more than anything, she looked relieved.

A grin spread across her face. She ran into Theo's arms easily, wrapping her arms around him tightly. Theo buried his head in her shoulder and smiled.

"God, Laine." He whispered to her. "You're so amazing. I love you so much."

"I love you too." She replied. "We're actually gonna do this." She said, hopeful. She pulled away and gave him a prideful look before disconnecting their arms and turning around as Serenity and Vercobrix followed out of the carriage.

Serenity and Theo both looked very different from the last time they had seen each other. Serenity's hair was shorter, whereas Theo had allowed his to grow out to look a lot more shaggy than previously. For Serenity, seeing him again was kind of akin to how Laine had felt. He didn't look very good, health wise. He was skinnier and clearly bordering on malnourished, as well as looking extremely tired. Serenity looked happier - that was the first thing that he noticed. She had a glow in her eyes and a certain excitement about her. Although, it was somewhat stunted by the prior events of the day.

For a few moments, they just made eye contact.

And then Serenity smiled at him. She reached her arm out and beckoned him over. He accepted the hug gingerly. No words needed to be exchanged between them; just being in each other's presence was enough of an interaction to say everything that they needed to. After thirty seconds, Theo moved away slightly and looked her directly in the eyes.

"Thank you." He said.

"You're welcome." She replied. "It's good to see you, Theo."

"Yeah." He breathed.

He turned to Vercobrix and shook his hand without hesitation. A smirk slipped onto his face as he narrowed his eyes.

"Don't tell me your name, I do know it." He said, and Vercobrix raised his eyebrows as he waited. Theo spared a glance over to Serenity, who laughed. "Well, I know who you are." He defended. "You're King Aasir and Queen Ola's son."

"Yep." Vercobrix smirked.

"Agh- don't tell me." Theo cursed himself. "It begins with a V, doesn't it?"

"It does." Vercobrix nodded slowly.

"See, I *should* know this." He said quietly. "Well, it's been two years of me just having to remember the names of six people."

To his right, Serenity and Laine were laughing hysterically. Theo pouted.

"Just tell me, man." He conceded, shoving his hands in his pockets.

"Vercobrix." Came an angry voice from the steps of the train station. Vercobrix snapped his head over to Ayale and his eyes widened.

"Yeah, that's it." Theo said timidly, stepping backwards as he recognised the tension.

Ayale wasted no time in storming up to Vercobrix and kicked him right in the stomach. Vercobrix yelped in fear and fell backwards onto the ground.

"I was hoping I'd paralysed you." Xe spat, voice loud. "You have some fucking audacity showing up here." Xe yelled, delivering a strong kick to his side.

"Ayale, Ayale, Ayale." Serenity chanted, sticking her arm in front of xer. "Please don't hurt him."

Ayale turned to look at her with an exasperated expression. "Excuse me?" Xe said, eyes darting back to xer ex-boyfriend on the ground, looking particularly frail and terrified. "Are you fucking crying?"

Vercobrix sniffled and brought his sleeve to his eyes to destroy the evidence. "I'm sorry, I'm sorry."

"You're- what?"

"I'm sorry, Ayale." He whimpered, sounding so incredibly vulnerable.

"'Sorry' doesn't give me back the last seven years, asshole."

Theo turned his head over to look at Laine, who mouthed 'later' at him. Unsatisfied by this explanation, he took a few steps back to stand next to her so as to not be in the way.

"He's changed a lot, Ayale. I promise." Serenity said, bringing her hand down.

"Sorry, who the hell are you!?" Ayale replied.

"Oh, um, his fiance. Serenity." She tried to smile.

Ayale rolled xer eyes and looked down at the feeble man on the ground. Xe knelt down to his level and whispered.

"I get the feeling you want to talk about everything rather than fistfight me right now." Xe said. Vercobrix nodded frantically, uttering a raspy "Please." Ayale wasn't happy about it, but xe nodded. "Fine. Just us, though. I don't want this ginger girl defending your honour while *we* are having a conversation."

Xe grabbed onto his hand and pulled him up. "Prince Vercobrix and I are going to speak with eachother alone. Will you manage without us for five or ten minutes?" Xe asked, looking at Theo, who nodded.

"Yeah." He swallowed, a little intimidated by this demon that he had always known as quite kind.

"Good." Ayale replied, walking out of the train station, hand gripping Vercobrix's and dragging him out. Julian, Raphie, Fern, Toby, Axel, Livvy and Isaac were all watching in slight worry. Of course, the latter five had heard all about Vercobrix - as telling stories about their lives or deaths was really all they had to pass the time. Julian and Raphie scampered up

405

into the train station to greet Laine, going past the two ex-partners as they walked across the square.

"Where are we going?" Vercobrix whispered, a little worried about being so far away from everyone. If he screamed for help, it was unlikely they would hear him.

"Almost there, you'll see."

They walked past Perry, who was still asleep, just at the same time as they heard Serenity's distant voice ask the others 'what the hell that was'. If he had the capacity, Vercobrix would have done the same, but he felt like a small child getting dragged off to their bedroom after misbehaving, and he really didn't want to be on Ayale's bad side during this conversation. Especially since he didn't think he had it in him to fight back if anything were to happen.

Ayale kicked the door of their tavern open and released Vercobrix's arm, slinking into one of the booths at the back and gesturing annoyedly for Vercobrix to follow. Once they were both seated, Ayale narrowed xer eyes.

"Why are you here?" Xe asked, venom in xer tone.

Vercobrix bit his lip. "I, uh- well, Serenity and I helped Laine get the forcefield down and then we just kind of came here to help fight and all."

"That's very out of character for you."

"What?"

"Helping people. Out of your character."

Vercobrix nodded. "It was the least I could do."

"You're engaged, then?"

"Yeah."

"Does she know?"

"Everything."

Ayale looked taken aback. "Why is she still with you?"

Vercobrix looked down at the table. "I've really been working on it. I moved out- away from my parents. I've been going to therapy for the last three years. My parent's idea originally, but I carried on when I moved."

"Why did your parents put you in therapy?" Xe asked, not even acknowledging anything else that he had said.

"I had a breakdown." He said easily. Something was compelling him to be transparent. "About myself, about you, about my role in Atroka. Stopped eating, didn't get out of bed for days at a time. They gave me two years of professional help and then told me if I didn't sort myself out they'd throw me onto the streets. Then I met Serenity. And she was so kind to me, when I didn't deserve it at all."

"Did you tell her that you were a manipulator before or after you fucked her?"

Vercobrix frowned. "I fell in love with her. And she with me, it wasn't like that."

"When did you tell her?" Xe persisted.

"I lived in her castle for months before we started dating. So, I told her like five months into us knowing each other and a month into our relationship."

"And she stayed with you?"

"She understood. She was hesitant, she made me go over everything for like two hours. Took me to a couples therapist, but she understood."

"Sounds like she's naive."

Vercobrix leant back in the seat and closed his eyes. He took a deep breath in, counting in his head. When he got to five, he held his breath for another five, and then exhaled, eyes opening to look at Ayale again. "It's not really your business." He said calmly.

"Fine." Xe replied, looking at him coldly. Xe ran a hand through xer crimson hair.

"Ayale, I'm sorry. I know it's not an excuse, but my parents weren't very kind to me and I was projecting onto you." He explained. "Our relationship was really bad, I shouldn't have treated you like that. I'm sorry."

"Okay."

"Okay?"

"Okay." Ayale repeated. "I accept your apology. But I don't forgive you. You fucked me up. I still can't imagine dating anyone, or ever feeling safe around men. Sometimes some of the guys here raise their voice or make sudden movements and I think they're going to hurt me and I have panic attacks."

Verobrix pressed his lips into a thin line as he cringed. He felt horrible. He wasn't sure what he expected.

"Is there anything I can do that would make you forgive me?" He asked.

"No." Ayale said effortlessly with a shake of xer head. "But that's okay, Vercobrix. I don't forgive you, and I never will. But it doesn't mean we can't be civil."

Vercobrix nodded. He could accept that much. "I really am sorry."

"I can tell." Ayale replied. "I remember you being a lot tougher. Makes me feel a bit sorry for you."

"Do you think we could start again?" Vercobrix asked. "It's been seven years."

"I'm not going to forget about what you did. But I can acknowledge your development." Xe said, placing xer chin on xer hands.
"Can we be friends?" Vercobrix asked, and Ayale laughed.
"No." Xe replied bluntly. "Not in any universe."
"Alright." The Prince nodded. "Can we have a mutual relationship in which we co-exist in the same circles but don't hurt each other?"
Ayale looked a little apprehensive, but xe sighed and looked him in the eyes sharply.
"You promise me you've changed?"
"I promise."
"So God help me, Vercobrix, if you slip up *at all*, I will cut your fucking head off."
"Understood." He swallowed with a slow nod.
"Good." Ayale said. "Then, we can manage that, I think."

"Yikes." Theo grimaced. "I'm at least honoured that you guys went through all that effort for us." He said, sitting on the ground in a makeshift circle with all the other demons, Raphie, and Julian. The two princesses had just finished their dramatic retelling of getting the forcefield down, even as far as running after the train. And also, the Vercobrix and Ayale affairs. "Especially you, Serenity. Thank you."
She smiled at him. "That's okay. I felt like I owed you that much. I'm just glad we're both happy now" She admitted, sparing a glance to Julian and offering him a smile. He was sitting next to Theo, leaning into his side with his arms wrapped around Theo's right arm.
"What did I do that made you owe me?" Theo asked, shifting his position so that Julian could properly lie on his shoulder, letting his eyes slip shut in the knowledge that he was safe beside his taller boyfriend.
Serenity pursed her lips. "I didn't treat you very well after you came out to me. And then you still helped me during that fight."
Theo nodded. "No, it's fine. I kind of deserved it."
Serenity cringed. "I don't want you to think I'm like, homophobic or anything. I was just upset."
"You weren't upset about the gay thing, you were upset about the lying." Theo clarified.
"Yeah. I mean, my future-husband is bisexual. So, I couldn't really be homophobic." She said.

"I didn't say you were." Theo snickered. "You're really defending yourself here." He said, amused as a smirk slipped onto his face.

"I just want to make sure." The Princess laughed, smiling too. "Oh! Speaking of him." She noticed, looking over to where Vercobrix and Ayale were walking back over from the tavern. They had about a metre of distance between them, appearing a little uncomfortable, but they were talking too.

"I kind of hope they haven't made up." Axel grinned snarkily. "Was looking forward to beating that dickhead."

Serenity frowned. "Why is everyone here so violent?" She whined, now hoping that they *had* made up.

"Being in a place like this does that to you, princess." Fern drawled. "A lotta pent up anger. Especially towards those who put us in here." She said bluntly, turning to look at Vercobrix as the pair were still a good ten metres away.

"He feels bad enough." Serenity pouted.

"We'll beat both of your posh royal asses in a minute." Axel retorted.

"Hey." Theo frowned, furrowing his eyebrows and looking over at them.

"That's okay, Princey, you're one of the good ones." Isaac mocked. All of the others (bar Raphie) laughed at the sarcastic comment. Even Julian snickered from his position slumped against his boyfriend.

"What are you lot laughing about?" Ayale asked as xe got close enough to hear.

"Our oppressors." Toby replied.

"Oppressors?" Theo raised his eyebrows.

"Yeah, well, only the monarchs have the capability of banishing us to this place."

Ayale rolled xer eyes. "I assumed you were talking about our luminous friends." Xe said, eyes falling onto the two angels. Vercobrix walked and sat down next to Serenity, offering her a short explanation under his breath as she listened. Ayale knelt down next to Isaac.

"Hey, I thought we were all good." Julian said, looking right over to the demon. His tone of voice was less offended and more humoured.

"We are. I'm joking. If we weren't good I would have left *you* in that forest." Ayale replied, looking at Raphie. She blinked a few times.

"Well… I'm glad you chose not to?" She said back, a little worried.

Ayale nodded. "And besides, we all need to get along if we're going to do this." Xe said, looking over at Vercobrix once more. "*All of us*. Vercobrix and I have talked and it isn't anybody else's business. We can handle ourselves."

Axel rolled his eyes, but agreed.
"Um, before we go, can I make a request?" Laine interjected whilst she had the chance. All eyes fell on her, and she continued. "Please can we not hurt any of the Klaevrian soldiers too much? Most of them are quite young and they don't really have that much of a choice working under King Beckett."
"People get hurt in war, Laine. You know that, right?" Fern asked.
"Yeah. But, I just feel bad for a lot of them."
"Well, you're their princess, you would."
Laine looked over at Theo. "They're your people too. Don't you feel bad?"
He sighed. "Of course I do. We'll be as gentle as possible, but we aren't going to get through to Beckett by walking up to him. They're going to fight us too."
Laine understood that, of course she did. She just felt like it was wrong in some way.
"We should probably get out of here before they send another guards' train over." Vercobrix said suddenly, changing the subject.
"Right." Theo nodded as he stood.
When they got to the carriage, Laine opened the door and peered inside with a grimace. "What are we gonna do with the bodies?"
Fern rolled her eyes and stood beside the door. "I'll drag 'em." She said, grabbing the man in the front carriage by the ankles.
It was quite astounding to witness this muscular woman dragging this equally muscular man out of the train like it was nothing.
"God, what did you do to him?" Raphie cringed, taking a step back.
"Nothing, he's fine. He'll just be confused when he wakes up." Laine defended. "There's one more in the other carriage."
Once all of the unconscious guards were no longer in the train, the demons moved out of the train station and into the train. It consisted of only two carriages, side by side. There was no engine on the front or back, as it wasn't a traditional train. It was powered by magic, and served the intention of the riders.
There were four tables in the carriage, each with the ability to hone four people. Then of course, there was the plain second carriage which it seemed the guards had been using to smoke. They didn't use it, though, as sixteen people could fit in the first - more comfortable - carriage, and there were only twelve of them.
Around one table, Ayale sat with Axel, Toby and Livvy. On the other, Fern and Isaac were sitting on the edge seats so that they were very close to

the rest of them. Serenity and Vercobrix sat next to each other on their own table.

"Oi, Theo, c'mere." Ayale called from the table, gesturing that he should sit with them. He thought for a moment, and then he glanced over at Laine, Raphie and Julian all huddled around one table with a vacant seat. "I have some catching up to do with them lot. I'll come and speak to you all before we get to Klaevr."

"Alright, have fun with your boy-fie." Xe smirked, being recognised with laughter as Theo rolled his eyes playfully and slouched into the seat next to Julian.

"They scare me." He whispered.

"It's what they're best at, don't let it get to you." Theo replied easily. "God, I can't believe we're doing this."

"It's gonna be fine. If we've gone this far and it doesn't work out, I'm not gonna be happy." Laine added, taking Theo's hand across the table to reassure him. "Oh!" She called.

"What?" All three others asked quickly.

"I found something out about grandma, but you can't tell her I told you." Theo raised an eyebrow. "What is it?"

"Okay, don't freak out."

"Good start." Raphie muttered with a smirk.

"I found out who our grandfather is. On dad's side."

"I thought you said it was just like a random guy." Julian said quietly.

"It was a random guy at the time, yeah." Laine nodded. "Don't freak out, okay?"

"Just tell me." Theo replied quickly.

Laine leant back a little in her seat and closed her eyes.

"Sir Garrah."

Theo's jaw dropped. It suddenly made a lot of sense to him. Why he'd always been so protective, why he'd taken extra care into monitoring his actions. Why he always looked so nostalgic when talking to him or during any major life events. Theo had just assumed it was because he'd been working in the castle a long time, but- it made a lot of sense.

"Oh, are you telling him about that?" Serenity questioned from the table adjacent to them. Her voice was humoured and high-pitched. Theo just looked over to her and then back to Laine.

"What the fuck?"

"Yeah, I know." Laine agreed. "And grandma only gave him a job in the castle so that he could be involved with watching dad and us grow up without anyone thinking it was weird and realising that he was the baby daddy."

"Don't ever say the words 'baby daddy' again, please." Raphie cringed.

"Oh my god." Theo said, hiding his face in Julian's chest, who laughed and began to run a hand through his hair.

"We're gonna have to talk to him when we get to Klaevr. He's definitely gonna wanna help us fight when we tell him that we know." Laine bargained. "Besides, we need someone to command all of our fighters. If he were here, I would get Nikoliah to do it, but he's gonna be doing it for the enemy."

Theo nodded and pulled away from Julian. "Fine, fine. Yeah. We can speak to him. Just us, though. We aren't dragging our whole posse there. I think he'd have a heart attack."

"Did your grandma tell you this?" Julian asked.

"No, it was her memory that she had to face in the crypt. Like, them talking about how she was pregnant with his kid."

"I didn't even know that they had ever been a thing." Theo said, exasperated by this information.

"I think that was the point of them hiding it." Laine replied.

The train began to move with a clacking sound, and a large cheer erupted from the table with all of the residents of Nesbryn. Theo flicked his head away from the conversation he was having and watched them, and they looked happy. It wasn't something he'd seen from them before. He was glad for it.

XLVI

Laine, who had now made this journey multiple times, could tell when they were nearing back home.
Serenity and Vercobrix had gotten off the train when they were passing through Vaemunt, so that they could find Serenity's older sister, Queen Luciana, and hopefully collect their soldiers who she had offered them.
It was nerve-wracking to nearly be back. Under such different circumstances than usual, too. For Theo, it had been over two years since he had stepped foot inside the kingdom, which was incredibly ironic considering that it was supposed to be *his* kingdom. And then of course, for the likes of the Nesbryn-dwelling demons huddled around the table at the back of the train, it was their first time in Klaevr *ever*.
Theo didn't think that the sight of that stupid dead-tree-infested forest would ever make him feel so good.
"We should probably start rallying. Figure out what our exact plan of action is for when we get home." Laine said, drumming her fingers on the table as she admired the view from the dirty glass window.
"Home." Theo muttered softly, head falling into his hands.
"Well, it won't be if we don't sort ourselves out." His sister replied sternly. "We need to go and speak to Garrah. What are you two and the rest of them gonna do?" She asked, gesturing towards Julian and Raphie and then the rest of the demons on board.
"Do you know where he lives?" Theo asked.
"Vaguely." Laine replied absentmindedly with a nod of her head. "Niko dragged me to his house one time last year to collect this old notebook

that they used to write about the state of the kingdom in. He wasn't actually there, but his wife gave it to us."

Theo nodded and looked over his shoulder at the demons on the other table.

"What are the people like back home?" He asked. "Like, do they...like Beckett or whatever?"

"I'd assume not. I mean, they had annual anniversary riots about it. Nikoliah and Fiducia get treated like shit by the townspeople for working for him."

"Who is Fiducia?" Julian said with a scrunched up nose. "Weird name."

"The blue one."

"What, like from Avatar?"

"What is that?"

Julian rolled his eyes. "Nevermind."

"Okay, well, maybe they could, like... go around the streets and get people to join in. If we're taking our kingdom back and it's something they already want, then the civilians might want to fight too." Theo suggested.

"Yeah." Theo nodded. It wasn't implausible. "Okay, so they can do that. What are you two gonna do?" He asked, looking to the half of the table where Julian and Raphie were perched.

"Can't we just go with them?" The former asked, lazily pointing at the demons in the corner who were making *quite* a lot of noise.

Laine shook her head immediately. "Definitely not." She protested.

Raphie raised her eyebrows. "Touchy. Why not?"

"Because you're walking flashlights." She replied. "We're nice about it, but considering the enemy is one of you, it's not a good idea."

"One of us? Sounds a bit discriminatory." Julian frowned.

"I don't care." Laine stated bluntly. "They don't want to see angels ravaging their streets; the last time they saw angels ravaging around their streets their kingdom got attacked and their houses got burnt down." She said, and it was so stern that it took about ten seconds for anyone to reply.

"Okay. What then?"

And Laine blinked for a few moments. She wasn't too sure what. Theo sensed her hesitation and jumped in.

"Well, the last time Beckett kicked our asses it was because he had that portal magic. So, maybe we should go about trying to find how we can stop it?" He suggested.

"Where do you two get your magic from, then?" Raphie asked, leaning forwards on the table as the train continued to clack through the forest.
"I don't know, genetics?" Theo replied, unsure of himself.
"Right. So, where does Beckett get his magic from if he's not pureblooded?"
"Zero right?" Julian said. "The portal guy. He used to do all that."
"Yeah, then he disappeared and Beckett started being able to do it." Theo continued for him.
"So we have to find him." Laine concluded.
"Out of all people, Laine, you're the one who would know the most, so if you don't know then it's probably a lost cause."
"I did ask. Beckett just got annoyed at me whenever I did. Hettie and Elsie don't know anything either, the guy's just vanished." She replied.
And, it was true. Since they had been to the couple's house on the night the kingdom was attacked, nobody had heard a word from Zero at all.
"We know he can't be dead." Theo said. "Because people don't do that here. So, he's got to be *somewhere*."
"Well then, that's your job." Laine inferred, referring to the two angels. "We won't be at Garrah's long, just long enough to recruit him, so you can do some snooping in the castle - try and find information."
Julian groaned and covered his face with his palms, agonised by the sentiment. "How do we do that, exactly?" He asked, unhappy with the idea of having to navigate the castle alone.
"Start with Beckett's office. He'll undoubtedly be running around like a headless chicken following all this, so I don't think he'll be there. Look for paperwork, journals."
The screeching of brakes resonated throughout the carriage.
There was an immediate mood shift in the space - everyone becoming more determined and adrenaline-filled.
"Yo, princey?" Ayale raised xer voice across the carriage. "What's the plan, man?"
Theo stood up from the table, and for a moment he debated whether or not it was unsafe to stand on a table inside a moving train, and then he decided that what he was about to do would be way more dangerous - and so he clambered onto it.
"Okay! Plan of action is as follows," He began, rocking a little on the table as his combat boots squeaked against the material. "I want you guys to go around and let the people know what we're doing. Like, knock on doors and get people that care to fight too."

"Sick." One of them replied, and they all seemed content with the notion. Theo turned his attention over to the table that he was previously occupying.

"Raphie and Julian are gonna do some snooping in the castle whilst Laine and I go and recruit our grandfather that we didn't know was our grandfather to help organise everything. We'll reconvene around the castle gates if everything hasn't already descended to chaos. Cool?"

"Cool." Axel spoke for all of them.

"Good." Theo confirmed. "It's kinda likely that they'll be expecting us, so, let's be pretty hasty and not bring too much attention to ourselves until we're well away from the train station."

Theo hopped down to sit on the edge of the table just as the station began to consume the edges of the train. He looked down to his sword and made sure it was sturdily attached to his belt, but when he gazed back up his boyfriend was standing beside him.

"Oh, hey." He said. "You alright?"

Julian nodded wordlessly and perched himself on the edge of the table.

"Are you gonna get hurt?" He asked quietly.

"Probably." Theo replied, realising a little too late that it was not the response Julian was hoping for. He recognised this fear and corrected himself. "What I mean, Jude, is that everyone's gonna get a little hurt, but it's gonna be fine."

"Well, you don't know that." Julian replied somberly.

"You're worried about me getting hurt?" Theo asked for clarification.

"I'm worried about leaving you." He replied, leaning his body into Theo's. "Last time I left you it was the last time I actually got to speak to you for two years. What if the same thing happens, and that's it?"

Theo heard the concern, but he didn't have a response. He turned his head to look Julian in the eyes.

"I can't promise that won't happen, but I can promise that I'll do everything I can to make sure it doesn't." He said softly. Julian nodded, but he didn't look reassured. Theo wrapped a hand around his waist.

"The second we're done talking to Garrah, I'll find you, and I won't leave you ever again." He promised. "I'll fight with you, and I'll win with you, and then I'll marry you and make you my consort, and I'll never let you out of my sight. But, please? Just for these next few moments?"

Julian looked up at him, and it was with the most adoration he had ever felt for a person.

He smiled softly, leaning up and kissing Theo affectionately. It didn't last long - it was sweet and chaste, but it was enough to solidify the vow.

"Thank you." He whispered. "You mean it?"

"Forever."

And there were the butterflies swarming in his stomach again. They were all-too familiar, and they had Julian transported back to the day that he and Theo first met. He was instantly reminded of those first feelings that he was so undeniably out of reach - and they had him feeling all the more intensely grateful for what he and Theo had now.

He wouldn't trade it for the world.

And as he peered up at his boyfriend with doe-like eyes, Julian knew he wouldn't have to.

Their bodies rocked as slightly in place as the train came to a final halt at the terminus station in Klaevr. Theo was instantly snapped out of the haze, breaking eye contact with Julian and sliding himself off the table assertively. He quickly turned back around and pressed a kiss to Julian's forehead, before moving to where Laine had stood up and held one hand on the sword hoisted to her hip.

The rest of the demons seemed quite enthralled to be out of Nesbryn, getting to take all of their grievances out - especially onto someone like Beckett.

"Alright." Theo declared, standing towards the back of the carriage as all of the demons crowded the door, awaiting his instruction. "Let's make all hell break loose."

Having said that, Theo and Laine had to get one thing out of the way before they themselves could participate in the fighting.

It took just five minutes of hasty running for them to reach the doorstep of the house that Laine claimed to be Garrah's. Just streets over, they could hear the shouting of Ayale, Livvy and Fern in particular.

Theo wasn't sure how he felt about being home. He was back in Klaevr, but it wasn't the same place that he had been thrown out of two years ago. It felt different, the air was heavier and more tense. It was clear that there was a distinct lack of happiness - which was something that King Beckett had grown to believe about Hell and the demon inhabitants of it. They didn't deserve to be happy, because they had obviously done something back in their mortal lives to warrant Hell.

He, obviously, fundamentally disagreed. However, he had the kind of feeling that Beckett hadn't been enforcing sorrow actively, but rather it was just the way that he governed.

Having thought all of this, it was the streets that he knew so well, and a part of him felt incredibly relieved to be standing in the same streets again, not worried that a fire-breathing monster would appear from anywhere and attempt to scorch him.

Laine knocked on the door confidently, and Theo suddenly got a seizing feeling in his chest. It had been two years, and one of the last conversations that he had had with Garrah had been about how shit a job he was doing at ruling. Part of him felt like he deserved what happened to him.

The door swung open, and it wasn't Garrah who opened it, but rather a woman around his age with cropped grey hair and dark grey horns to accompany it. She looked pleasantly surprised to see Laine.

"Oh!" She chirped, and then her eyes cast over to Theo and they widened a little. "Oh. Good to see you, Princess Laine. And …Theo."

Theo smiled slightly. He could appreciate that he didn't look his best, and also it was a bit of a shock to see him after so long.

"Is your husband home by any chance, Daisy?" Laine asked quickly.

"He is. What's the occasion?" Daisy replied, curious.

"We're leading a revolution and we want his help."

Daisy nodded determinedly. She turned her head slightly and angled herself towards the stairs behind her.

"Oliver!" She called. "There's royalty at the door for you!"

A few thuds of feet on floorboards and stairs later had the man emerging from behind the door, wearing dark blue jeans and a t-shirt. He had an immediate reaction to the sight of the two siblings on his doorstep.

Daisy politely excused herself before the three could start talking.

"I was expecting that I might see you here today, Theo." He said quietly. "And you, Princess Laine, it's good to see you both. How are you?"

"As good as I can be." Theo replied.

"Yeah, we're alright." Laine confirmed. "But, we wanted your help with something."

"Okay. How can I help?" He asked.

"We've got a handful of the friends that Theo made in Nesbryn, and some of the townspeople. Trouble is that we don't have any trained soldiers to help organise everyone and lead the fight."

Garrah appeared indecisive for a moment. "And what about Nikoliah? Can he not?"

Laine grimaced. She felt bad all of a sudden. "No, uh, I broke up with him. He's not very happy with me so he's doing Beckett's bidding like he was born for it."

The man frowned at the news. "Okay." He acknowledged. "It's just, I don't really do this anymore. And, as much as I have nothing but the utmost respect for you two as royals, I don't know if I can-"

"We know you're our grandfather." Laine blurted desperately. Garrah's eyes widened in shock. "And, we understand, we don't wanna make anything awkward, but we're worried that without your help we won't be able to do this. If you aren't doing it because you care about your royalty, do it because you care about your grandkids, please." She pleaded.

The man looked like he had seen a ghost. "Did your grandmother tell you that?" He asked, sounding somewhat betrayed. "Does your father know?"

"Both no." Laine answered, knowing a lot more about it than Theo. "When we broke them out of Nesbryn we had to watch each other relive difficult memories, and hers so happened to be you and her discussing her pregnancy. You know, with our dad."

"I didn't mean to hide it from you." He said. "Your father was born in different times, and I didn't want to marry her, but if it got out that I had had premarital relations with the future Queen as an ex-mortal I think my head would have been on a spike outside the castle gates."

Theo nodded. "Look, we didn't come here to guilt trip you or to try and hold you accountable for it, we just could really use your help."

He faltered a moment before sighing. With a quick glance outside, to the rise in noise, and then back down the way that his wife had just walked, he nodded. "Okay. This once, but after this I've retired properly." He told himself, striding back up the stairs. "Give me five minutes."

The siblings heard him, and they took a few steps away from the door while waiting.

XLVII

Raphie and Julian hadn't the most optimistic viewpoint when approaching the castle, but it was made instantly clear to them that there was no way in all seven Kingdoms of Hell that they were getting in there without being clocked.

It was visible that the castle was on some kind of high alert, with soldiers parading around the courtyard and standing by all viable entrances and exits.

And also, it didn't help that they were quite literally luminous and therefore pretty easy to spot.

"Okay, so... Now what?" Raphie asked, standing behind one of the pillars that held the main fence around the castle. Julian looked indecisive for a moment.

"There's no way we're getting in there with our lives."

Raphie glanced through the metal of the bars constructing the fence.

"Not through a main entrance, that's for sure."

One of the guards looked in her direction, and she flicked her body back behind the pillar quickly.

"It's a guarded castle, Raph, it's not going to have any side entrances." He argued back, stressed.

"Alright, don't get yourself worked up over it."

"No, because, because if we can't get a way inside then we've already lost." He said, exasperated and overwhelmed. He was feeling antsy and incredibly worried about all the pressure on his shoulders. Raphie could definitely tell.

"Hey, it's fine." She tried to reassure him. "Let's not rule everything out because of one bump in the road."

Julian shook his head, eyes watering. "No, no. I'm not doing this shit again. We can't do this, we're hurting ourselves."

"Julian."

"What?"

Raphie grabbed his hand and started leading (or, more appropriately: dragging) Julian along the dirt ground around the edge of the castle fence. He quickly became flustered, yanking his hand away but failing to cease the movement of his legs as he kept up with Raphie.

"If you decide to just give up because you're scared, then we have quite literally got a zero percent chance of success." She said firmly, keeping her eyes planted on the edge of the building as he walked, rather than the distressed young man following her. "But, if we at least *try* then we have a greater than zero percent chance of doing this."

Julian knew that she was right, of course she was. He swallowed and kept his eyes downcast on the ground.

"I know." He frowned. "I'm sorry. It probably won't help our cause if I have some kind of anxiety attack."

"We just need to keep ourselves grounded." Raphie said, half talking to herself as well as her company. She continued to walk with intention, prompting Julian to follow in the same way. It wasn't long before they had made their first quarter of the edge of the castle walls. Raphie's feet dug into the ground as she stopped and her eyes locked onto an oversight.

"The window." She pointed out in a hiss, putting her hand out in front of Julian to stop him walking. He bumped into her arm and brought his head up before looking at Raphie and then turning his head towards the direction that she was looking in.

True to the angel's revelation, they had left the window open when clambering out of it.

It was still slightly ajar, the lock melted off even visible from the far distance that the two angels looked at it from.

"Okay." Julian agreed. "More than zero percent chance."

Raphie nodded. "Unguarded, too."

"Not to be a negative nancy, but there's no way we can scale this fence. Not without the purebloods and their flight."

Now, above them, the sky had completely mixed colour to a deep red. A blood red.

From around the corner, the figures of two soldiers appeared, having some kind of hushed conversation. The glow of their halos caused Nikoliah and Fiducia to notice them quite quickly. The former locked his eyes onto the two of them with a determined gaze. Fiducia turned to Nikoliah slowly and scrunched her nose up. Her colleague frowned. She kept her right hand on the handle of her sword, so was unable to sign anything to her colleague. Instead, she turned quickly on her heel. From where they were standing, Raphie and Julian were unable to hear the thing that Nikoliah said to her, but they could infer pretty easily that it wasn't a good idea for them to stay after being caught.
Nikoliah and Fiducia disappeared back the way they initially came.
"We should go."
"Yeah."
And so they moved off, back towards the front area of the castle. Now knowing that people knew they were here, they were slightly less cautious in travelling discreetly. A couple minutes into their retreat, they found Theo and Laine skittishly skidding down the path towards them. Theo smiled when he saw them, opening his arms to allow Julian to dive into them.
"Assuming you didn't get very far, then." He said, somewhat humoured.
"Lots of guards out. I get the feeling they know we're here." Laine observed.
"Yeah." Raphie agreed. "We found a way in, but Nikoliah and that angel he was with saw us scouting it out."
"How long ago?" Theo asked, not missing a beat.
"Five minutes tops." Raphie replied and Theo nodded, looking over to Laine.
"It might be the only way in." She supplied. "If we go now we can probably get through before they have the time to realise."
Around them, it was definitely evident that things had started happening. The siblings had waited until Garrah was ready and escorted him to where the hoard of demons were still doing their best efforts at breaking down all social order. To be fair to them, they were doing well. There was a lot of noise from all the streets. It was clear that the people were ready for a revolt.
It's an age old fact, that even if everybody wants something, it takes one person doing it first for everybody else to join in.
"That okay with you, Jay?" Theo asked, looking down at Julian, who nodded.

"Yeah, sorry." He said, pulling away from his chest, but keeping his hand locked into Theo's.

"Okay, quickly." Raphie instructed, guiding them back the way that her and Julian had just come.

"Hey, it's fine." Theo whispered to his boyfriend as they fell back a little.

"I know." He replied quietly. "I can't shake the feeling that something bad's going to happen." He admitted.

"Which is normal in a situation like this." Theo reassured. "Especially one where we've been here before and something bad *did* happen. It doesn't mean anything, I promise."

Julian squeezed Theo's free hand tighter. "Yeah."

"We're on a time limit here, lovebirds." Raphie spun around and called back. Neither men had noticed how much of a gap they had created by dawdling.

Theo rolled his eyes but still picked his pace up, not letting go of Julian's hand and dragging him along too. "Yeah, we're coming."

He landed on the ground on the other side of the fence with a slight thud, cradling Julian in his arms bridal style to hoist him over also.

"Okay, okay, put me down now." He laughed, having made quite the fuss out of it. Theo snickered and carefully released the boy onto the dirt. He flexed his back muscles and folded his wings away, turning towards Raphie and Laine for further instruction. They had crossed the fence first and were now ready to infiltrate the building.

"Okay, come on." Laine whispered, striding carefully towards the window. Around them, they could all still hear the sounds of panic and frustration. It was clear that no actual fighting between sides had begun yet, but they were definitely gearing up towards it.

Time was sparse.

It was instantly so much warmer the second that Laine made it through the window and into the corridor. Theo followed after her, having to stop for a moment once he entered.

It smelled like home.

He absentmindedly brought his hand up to place it against the wallpaper. And then to the curtains. Those stupid curtains that he had hated the pattern of when he was growing up and first coronated. Those disgusting curtains that made him happier than he'd felt in years. He suddenly had no desire to change them.

423

Theo's eyes followed Julian as he climbed through the window. He felt completely paralysed in place, overwhelmed by the feeling of nostalgia. The corridor was long, and it only took about five seconds before the quartet heard some light humming from one of the side entrances to the corridor.

"Shit." Laine whispered, grabbing Theo's hand and yanking him into one of the nearby disused offices as his eyes stayed glassy. He was quite startled by it, still wobbling on his feet as the two angels followed them in.

Theo stood closest to the door that was still open, back against the wall. When the person heading along the corridor strolled past, he quickly leapt out and grabbed them from behind, pressing his hand over their mouth so as to muffle any distressed sounds.

Kougan yelped and looked up at them as Theo shoved him towards the centre of the room. His eyes widened behind his ginger fringe.

"Oh my god!" He practically yelled. Immediately, he was harshly shushed by all four members of his company. "...Sorry, sorry." He apologised, before following up with: "What the fuck." - still in a whisper. "You're back."

Theo kicked the door shut behind him and leant against it.

"Nice to see you too." He drawled.

"You're in a lot of trouble, Laine. You know that right?" The man said. "King Beckett is quite unhappy with you."

"I don't expect anything less." She replied easily.

"Oh." Kougan said, looking over at Julian. "You're the boy."

"Is that what they call me around here?" He asked, somewhat amused.

"You aren't very popular with the people of this kingdom. Heard a lot of talk that they blame you for all this."

Theo snarled and pushed himself off the door, taking a few steps over to Julian and hooking an arm around him. "Look, dude, we're trying to find someone. And maybe you could help. A constant monologue isn't necessary."

Kougan grimaced and looked over to Laine. "What did they do to him on Nesbryn? Swear to god he didn't used to be so... snappy."

Theo narrowed his eyes. "He's in the room, you know."

"I think he's just feeling a bit overwhelmed with being back here, he doesn't mean it." She reassured the man. Theo's instincts screamed at him to retaliate, but he knew deep down that it wasn't worth it, and his sister was right - as much as he detested the idea.

Kougan nodded and then looked back over to Theo and Julian briefly.

"Who are you looking for?"

"Blonde guy that Beckett's getting his magic from. We think he's probably here somewhere." Laine replied. "You obviously work here, so if anyone would know it's you."

"You also have lived here for the last two years."

"Yeah, but Beckett always made a point to not tell me anything. I don't think he ever really trusted me." Laine replied. Kougan nodded.

"He had a handful of construction-esque work done within the first month after being crowned."

"He did?"

"Over in the east wing. I only know because he kicked me and Jaymie out of our office for like six weeks when he was having it done."

"Well," Raphie interrupted. "That could be anything. He could have installed a hot tub." She said with a slight smirk. Kougan crossed his arms in front of him.

"You guys asked." He replied, walking over towards a dust-ridden desk in the corner and perching himself on it. "Are you fighting today, then? Should I tell people?"

Laine raised an eyebrow as she placed a hand on her hip. "Has King Beckett not told people?" She asked.

"Not us." He replied. "Maybe he's told the soldiers, but not us bottom tier workers. Although it would explain why Nikoliah and Fiducia have been looking particularly stressed this morning." He said, swinging his legs slightly as his burnt orange tail floated behind him.

Laine nodded. "If you or any of the staff want to help fight on our side, then you can go and find the rally of people who we've already recruited swarming around the town. We'd appreciate it."

Kougan nodded and slid off the desk. "Yeah, will do. I hope you guys can do this. Lord knows we need it around here these days." He said, pulling the door open and disappearing easily.

Theo took a deep breath and tilted his head back, staring up at the ceiling as he spoke.

"So, I suppose we should go and check out his construction work." He inferred, bringing his head back down and making strong eye contact with his sister, who nodded.

"Yep. And we really don't have time to lose."

Julian blinked a few times. "Do the people here really not like me?"

"They don't even know who you are." Theo said, looking down at the shorter man. "It was a secret for a reason, I don't think they know your name."

"Yeah, and besides, causation is tricky." Raphie tried to comfort him. "We could go back really far and say that it's Theo and Laine's dad's fault for having kids."

"And we aren't going to get the last two years back by blaming people." Laine added, striding towards the door. "Come on, before we run out of time and Beckett finds us." She said, pulling the door open and glancing down the corridor.

"She's right, you know." Theo whispered, pulling Julian close to him. "I hope you don't feel responsible for any of this."

"No, it's fine." Julian smiled. "I just want the people of this kingdom to like me, especially if we get married someday."

"And they will." Theo said. "Promise. Now, let's go before we get left behind yet again." He said, following the two girls who had only just left after seeing an empty hallway.

XLVIII

The end of the hallway was dusty, clearly uncared for by any particular person. As the pair walked at the back, Theo and Julian were chancing occasional glances behind them to assess the state of their safety just casually ambling the halls.
"I don't know." Julian said kind of quietly. "Feels like a trap."
Theo nodded in acknowledgement, but he made no effort to change any of his mannerisms to actually accommodate the worry. A few metres ahead of them, Laine tripped on a ridge in the carpet and stumbled forwards slightly before catching herself. She turned around and looked down at the thin carpet placed over the wooden floor.
"Ouch, firstly." She grumbled, leaning down towards it.
Her brother stepped a little closer and used his right combat boot to push the carpet backwards, causing it to wrinkle around an obvious part of metal jutting out of a wooden compartment. Raphie hummed in curiosity and pulled it all the way back, revealing a dark wooden trapdoor on metal hinges.
"Now, that definitely feels like a trap." Julian confirmed. Laine looked up at him with a slight noise of agreement.
The wall to signify the end of the corridor was only a few metres away from where the trapdoor was placed. It was at the end of a corridor that only had the office of the stylists (not their studio which they do the fittings in, their actual offices which they draw up designs in), and was therefore pretty significantly neglected. No wonder Laine had never noticed it, but despite that, she cursed herself.
"I'll go." Theo said quickly. Julian's head snapped up to look at him.

"You have no idea what's down there!" Julian argued.

"Could be a dog." Laine teased. Theo rolled his eyes.

"Ha, ha." He gritted. "We don't have much time. Wait until I tell you that you can follow me to come down."

Theo crouched down and pushed the metal lock on the outside of the trapdoor, a lot of pressure going onto his thumb and index finger, indenting the skin slightly. It clicked open with a metallic sound, and he placed his hand around the handle. As the trapdoor opened, it let out a rusty groan.

The young man looked down into an abyss of darkness, staring into it with his eyes of the same nature.

On the left side of the opening, the top rung of a metal ladder stuck up slightly.

"Be safe." Julian said lowly. "Please."

Theo nodded wordlessly, meaning it as he slid off the ground and hooked one of his feet onto a rung a few metres down.

His hands wrapped around the metal uncomfortably, and Theo plunged himself into the sheath of darkness as he continued to descend the ladder with shallow breaths steadily increasing in speed. He was swallowed by the lack of light, even as he moved his right foot down to the next rung and hit concrete on the ground. Steadily, Theo moved the other foot to the ground and stood, rubbing his hands together to deter some of the soreness from the harsh metal.

He swallowed, looking back up at the light, where he could see his sister peering down the trapdoor, although he knew that she could see him no longer.

The light around him remained nonexistent, but as the seconds turned into about a minute of him standing indecisively, one hand replanted on the closest rung of the ladder for comfort, the darkness alleviated slightly as his eyes adjusted. He could at least make out walls around him.

For a moment, it looked like he was standing in a narrow room with no windows or lights, or anything. But, then, after a few blinks and a chance of a couple steps forward, he noticed that the room diverged to the left and he wasn't in a room at all, but rather, a corridor.

Theo bit his lip and looked back towards the entrance that he'd just come through. His hand slipped off the metal bar and he trekked forward with caution.

"Zero?" He whispered into the sparse air, taking a look down the corridor as it turned. No response came back at him. He began to feel a pit of dread in his stomach at the realisation that this was fruitless.
Or, he did, until he noticed the meagre warm light deep at the end of the hall.
Hand firmly holding onto the handle of his sword, still attached to the belt on his hips, Theo took another step forward - repeating the name of the man he was looking for as he went.
The corridor seemed endless, but with the pitch black consuming Theo, he had no way of really knowing the distance other than the rough estimation of how big his strides were. The light got closer and closer, until he could actually see the glow pouring out of a small doorway and hitting the adjacent wall, making the concrete shine slightly.
Theo took a deep breath in and stepped again, peering wearily around the doorless-entryway to this litten-up area.
His eyes landed on a person, a demon who was illuminated by multiple burning torches on each of four walls.
A tall man. Legs folded up in front of him. His hair was a light blonde, greasy and grown out past his shoulders, almost disguising the rich purple horns sitting atop his head. He had an untrimmed beard, the same blonde as his hair, if not slightly darker. He was wearing a pair of dark trousers and a shirt that Theo could tell was once white, but had been stained in various manners that he'd rather not think about.
Zero appeared asleep, his tail wrapped around his torso as he rested his head on a folded up cloth. His right ankle had a metal shackle around it that was attached to the back wall.
Theo allowed his eyes to absorb the information, before he felt his hands begin to shake. He stepped backwards until he hit a wall, the wall behind him. He couldn't even make out the end of the corridor, but he was moving down it with all possible haste until he reached the original confining space.
The light in the above him was still there, and it shone a glow onto the ladder that made it easy for Theo to find, grabbing onto the metal and hoisting himself up. He scaled the wall quickly, making it to the top of the ladder and pulling himself out.
Julian was watching him with intent, a look of relief washing over his face as he saw that Theo was fine. The pureblood turned over to look at the side of the trapdoor where Laine and Raphie were looking at him expectantly. Theo's chest moved up and down quickly as he swallowed.

"Found him." He huffed. "Come on."

Theo reached a hand out to Julian whilst the other stayed gripped onto the top rung. Julian nodded and took the hand, scooting on the ground. Theo began to move back down, letting Julian clamber onto the ladder above him.

"Is he okay?" Julian asked.

"Don't know. We'll see." Theo replied unintentionally bluntly as he rapidly moved back down the ladder, this time skipping the final few rungs to plant his feet on the ground and step backwards, eyeing down the corridor to where he could once again see that low light.

"It's really dark down here." Laine said, able to step off the ladder after Julian.

"There's light this way." Theo said, voice directing them to follow.

They were lucky that Julian and Raphie had halos floating above their heads, because it provided a significant amount of light that really did help the visuals.

"What? What way?" Laine asked, blinking in the darkness.

Theo reached his hand out towards Julian's. "Take my hand. Laine, take Julian's. Raphie, take Laine's." He said, quieter this time. Julian took the outstretched hand of his boyfriend, and the other two followed suit.

Theo led them along the corridor as efficiently as he could. They had nothing else to say to each other - there was too much tension in the air, worry and danger.

Zero was, of course, still unconscious when they got back to him. Once the light was sufficient, Theo dropped his hand, segregating it from Julian's as he slid onto the ground - to his knees next to Zero's upper body.

Being so close to him, Theo was suddenly overwhelmed with the need to care for this man.

Laine gasped from the doorway as she looked at the clearly malnourished man. Raphie felt the need to take a step forwards to help, but Laine stuck a hand out to stop her as she watched her brother feign over the man. Julian stood on the other side of Laine, completely stuck by the adrenaline coursing through his veins.

"Zero." Theo spoke loudly now, hands on the man's shoulders and shaking them lightly. "Zero, Zero, wake up." He pleaded. "Wake up, I swear to god, Zero, wake up." He repeated, and repeated again.

After a rough ten seconds of the fiasco, the man on the ground let out a low groan. Theo removed his hands instantly, eyes fixed on Zero's face as he pried his eyes open and blinked up.

"Theo?" He mumbled blearily.

Theo nodded. "Hi, Zero. Hi. Are you okay?"

The man's eyes wandered towards the other three visitors that he had. He pushed himself up so that his back was against the wall and he sat up, watching them. He looked at Theo for a moment, and it took a following thirty seconds for him to process who he was in the room with.

"What are you four doing here?" He said. "This isn't safe."

Laine crouched down beside Theo. "We know. We need to be here, though."

Zero looked up at Julian for a moment. "That halo is new." He remarked.

"Yeah." Was all Julian could reply with a light nod. He looked over to Raphie and they both moved to sit down cross-legged with the other three as well.

"Zero, we need to defeat Lord Beckett." Theo said bluntly.

"I had assumed that was basic knowledge." The man replied with charisma.

"We can't do it because he's using magic."

Zero eyed them with caution.

"Magic that we think is yours." Laine clarified, pushing a loose strand of hair behind his ear. "Is that right?"

The blonde man frowned. He looked upset for a moment, and then he nodded.

"How did he get you last time?" The man asked.

Julian fumbled with his hands. "He threw me into a portal to Earth again."

After a pause, Zero flicked his gaze from Julian to his boyfriend. "And how did that stop *you*, Theo?"

Theo swallowed. It was embarrassing to say out loud.

"Well, I- I, um." He stuttered a moment. "I was upset."

"You were upset?"

"I thought I was never going to see him again. I was upset, and my judgement was clouded and I couldn't defend myself." He explained quietly.

"I know." Zero replied with a nod. "I heard all about it. You had a moment of vulnerability, but you have to accept that if you want to be able to do this again."

"You know?" Theo asked, confused.

"Amadeus Beckett told me all about it. He had quite the evil monologue." He seemed to smile a little at that, as if remembering. "You aren't going to win this fight if you can't accept that he's bested you before. You're quite used to everything getting handed to you on a silver platter, but no today, Theo. You need to put the effort in."

Theo nodded, and he would. He was prepared enough to do so, so he would.

"How long have you been down here?" Raphie asked in a moment of silence. Zero looked dazed for a moment while formulating a reply.

"As long as it's been since he invaded. Since I last saw Elsie and Hetts." He said, longing coming right through his voice. "Are they okay?"

"They're worried about you." Laine replied easily. She knew, of course, through the letters that they had been exchanging. Zero nodded.

"I can understand that."

It was deadly silent in the room for a few moments following, before Zero looked away.

"I'm sorry, Theo." He said. And, when the ex-monarch gazed at him with disorientation, he continued. "I should never have let you leave."

Theo shook his head. "No, it was my decision, you couldn't have known."

"It's been plaguing my mind for what feels like centuries. I did know." Zero said anxiously.

"What?" Laine asked, suddenly engaged.

"Not exactly!" The magical man defended instantly. "I, part of my ability, I can sense auras. The auras of people and what might be waiting for them. When you came to me and asked me to let you leave, Theo, your aura was bad. It felt like dread and pain. I still remember how it felt, it was something I won't forget."

Theo blinked a few times. "I don't understand." He said.

"I knew that something bad would happen to you if I let you go. But you were so... trapped. If I didn't let you go, you would have married Princess Serenity, and I had no way of knowing how that would turn out." He confessed. "Of course, I tried my best to interrupt your engagement before it even happened, but it didn't seem that she cared about your romance being fabricated, or about your affair."

Theo narrowed his eyes with a glance over to Julian.

"What do you mean you 'tried your best to interrupt' it?" He asked, sounding worried.

Zero shifted where he was sitting. He moved slightly to be poised more confidently, looking deep in thought, obviously trying to figure out the best way to phrase what he was about to say.

"I made the decision not to give you a demon form, Julian, because I knew it was the only way that you would find Theo."

Julian faltered. "You, you- what?"

Theo's head snapped towards Julian and then back to Zero.
"You showed up in Klaevr, young and had your life wrongfully cut short too soon. Your aura, it felt like hope. It felt like hope, and when I focused on it, the hope tied you to the King. As an overseer of all the feelings in the kingdom, Theo's aura had been bothering me for a while. It was wrong, it felt like deceit and hurt. And then, Julian, you arrived. And all of it went away. I could feel like there was an invisible string between you two. I had to connect the string, it was the only way I could sense any prosperous future for the kingdom. But I knew that you wouldn't get to see a random ex-mortal, Theo. People die everyday, he wasn't special."
"So you made him special." Theo muttered, feeling so incredibly stupid.
"You were playing cupid." Julian said, feeling bewildered. "And it worked. That's like a punch to the stomach." He remarked, a frown tugging at his lips.
Zero shook his head. "I connected you two because I *knew* for a fact that you were supposed to be together. I wouldn't have done it if I wasn't sure that it would work. I hope you don't take offence to it, I wasn't trying to force you into the relationship."
Theo nodded to himself, moving a little bit closer to Julian and taking his hand.
"You had all of this built up emotion, Theo." Zero carried on explaining. "And then I sent Julian out into the wild to be found. Less than an hour later, this massive weight evaporated off my chest. All of this negativity in your aura, all of this repression, these feelings that you were pushing down further and further - towards breaking point. The same feelings that I could feel would ruin your life, they were completely gone. And, for the first time since you were old enough to feel, I felt happy with your aura. It was cathartic for you; a catharsis that you deserved so strongly. Like you finally had it in you to be the person you were meant to."
Theo felt a way he had never felt before. He had wanted answers so badly. He'd gotten them and yet, he had never felt more confused.
Julian reached up and wiped the tears away from Theo's eyes. Tears that he hadn't even noticed he had let slip out. Instead of moving away from the action, Theo leant forwards into Julian's touch, and then all the way into his arms until he was crying, properly crying, into his boyfriend's shoulder.
Julian held him tightly, and in that moment, nothing in the world could persuade him to let go.

Theo sniffled and pulled his head up out of the fabric of Julian's clothing, making eye contact with Zero, who looked very guilty. The magical man was right. Without Julian, his life would have been horrific and miserable. "Thank you." He whispered, but due to the size of the room, everyone heard it. "That doesn't explain why the forehead thing didn't work the first time I tried it." Theo realised.

"Ah," Zero listened. "That would have been me also. I assumed that it would tell you something about what happened to him, so I put a spell on his psyche that made his memories impenetrable to reading."

"Oh." Laine understood. "And then, it worked on Earth because we were in a different dimension where your magic couldn't reach him."

The man nodded and smiled slightly.

"Exactly. I hope it wasn't too invasive. I can only apologise about your kingdom." He remarked. "I had thought that allowing you to marry Princess Serenity would have brought your kingdom certain doom, but it seems that the certain doom happened either way." He breathed. "It doesn't seem like Nesbryn treated you very well, and, for that, and my responsibility for it, I am truly sorry."

Theo closed his eyes and then nodded. He pulled away from Julian, staying connected to him, just not as closely.

"I don't think you should be apologising for how the last two years of *my* life have been." He said croakily. "You've been... here."

Raphie acknowledged the statement, and it sparked her own set of questions.

"Why did he keep you here?" She asked. "If he's taken your magic, why does he keep you here?"

Zero raised an eyebrow. "He hasn't taken my magic." He said. "He's borrowed parts of it, yes. But he can't take it from me."

"He can't?" Laine asked.

The demon nodded in confirmation.

"For him to fully have my magic transferred to him, it has to be a willing passover, to the right person. He kept me down here so that he could harvest my magic. I refused to give it to him, and I couldn't if I wanted to, so he's only been able to take parts of it. My lack of magic right now is why I can't get out of here. I'm far too weak." He explained. "But he can still use my magic in the way that I could. The day of the fight, he used it to create a memory haze that meant that you two, Laine and Theo, conveniently forgot you had magical abilities when fighting him. Did you ever wonder why you never used magic against him that day?"

"Oh." Laine said, blinking as she realised. "It just never came to mind."

Theo furrowed his eyebrows. "Can't you take it back from him? The magic."

"I can't. The only way he would stop having his magic is if-"

A loud clanking sound came from down the corridor. It was the same sound that Raphie had heard when she shut the trapdoor earlier that day.

They all tensed up. Clear footsteps came from down the corridor, getting closer. Louder. There was hardly any time for reaction other than mild panic spiking in their chests.

And then, the footsteps rounded the corner and Nikoliah froze in the arch of the doorway as he saw them all.

He took a double take, blinking silently. Laine's eyes widened. Did he know? Had he known the whole time that Zero had been down here, and he hadn't told her?! Was he a part of this?!

Zero looked up at him with a mild curiosity, and then, the second that he tried to turn away to likely get someone to help him, Zero reached his hand up, outstretching it towards the knight.

Suddenly, a beam of light was connecting Zero's hand and Nikoliah's chest. The soldier spun around to face them, and then Zero gave a tug. Nikoliah's head fell backwards and he gaped in pain. Laine watched with wide eyes as Zero pushed his hands together before him, causing more of the light to weave its way out of Nikoliah's body and towards him - forming a ball in his hands.

As quickly as it began, it was over.

The last strand of light was pulled from Nikoliah, and his head fell back to its forward position, along with his whole body slumping to the ground.

"Poor thing, bless him." Zero cooed, moving on his knees to tilt Nikoliah's head up. Theo couldn't tell if the sentiment was serious or sarcastic.

"What the fuck was that?!" Laine asked, exasperated.

"I'm sorry." Was all Zero replied. "I know he's your friend, but I had to get it out of him."

Laine's gaze flickered between Zero and Nikoliah. "Get what? What?"

Nikoliah groaned into the concrete on the ground.

"Hey, look at me." Zero instructed. "You're alright. It's alright."

He blinked himself back to consciousness, eyes trying to focus on the man in front of him. Instead, he could make out the silhouette of a girl. Long, brown hair. Deep red horns.

"Laine." He mumbled.

Zero nodded enthusiastically. "Yes, that's Princess Laine. Do you know anyone else?"

Nikoliah pushed himself up on his elbows as everyone watched him. He felt like shit. There was a massive headache throbbing behind his eyes, and his whole body felt sore.

"What the fuck?" He whined.

"Do you know who you are?" Zero asked seriously. "What's your name, young man? Can you tell me?"

Nikoliah frowned. Patronising, but whatever. He looked around the room, and his eyes widened.

"It's, it's you. Theo. You're here." He said lightly.

"How do you feel?" Zero asked, completely ignoring his observations.

"Definitely like I'm having a weird dream." The soldier replied. "You're all… fuzzy. And, Laine's here, and Theo's here, so this must be some made up scenario. And, and, Julian, you- you definitely are not an angel. And, Raphie, she- she left us during our fight. Laine told me all about it. She wouldn't be here."

Laine frowned. He knew that Julian and Raphie were here. He had seen them, hadn't he? And then he'd scurried off to tell Beckett. It hadn't been that long ago. It had been earlier that day.

"Okay." Zero nodded. "What's the last thing you remember?"

"What the fuck is up with him?" Julian asked under his breath, but again, due to the silentness and size of the room, it was audible to all.

"Just, give me a moment." Zero instructed.

Nikoliah thought about it really hard. The last thing he remembers.

"I was at a train station, maybe. No, I was in trouble. Someone was unhappy with me."

"Who was unhappy with you?"

"Blonde. Scary, blonde angel." He murmured to himself. "King Beckett. He was unhappy with me."

"Why was he unhappy with you, Nikoliah?" Zero asked, and the soldier squinted. He knew for certain that he had not told this guy his name. He tried to picture why he was in trouble, and he did find it, but he couldn't grasp a hold of the words. Instead, he pushed himself up a little higher and pointed a finger at Laine.

"Me?" She asked, raising her eyebrows.

"He asked me something. He asked me if I wanted to keep my job, and I said yes."

"Why did you say yes?"

"I didn't have anything else. Not without Laine, and if I didn't have my title and my rank and my job then I was nothing. So, I had to keep it. I had to."

"Carry on." Zero prompted quietly. "You're doing so well, there has to be more."

"I, um." Nikoliah squeezed his eyes shut and thought for an extended period of time. "I was allowed to keep my job. But, he said only if I let him help me do my job better."

Zero hummed. He sat up again.

"We're in the basement area of the castle, Nikoliah." He said, before turning to Laine. "How long ago did you leave him with Beckett?"

Laine thought about it properly. These last few days seem to have all blurred into one.

"No more than a week." She finally remarked. A look of relief washed over Zero's features.

"It's only been less than a week, so you're going to be fine. Do you understand what's going on?"

Nikoliah shook his head slowly. He wanted to wake up, this was a weird dream.

"From what I can gather, you agreed to let King Beckett plant a seed inside of you that allowed him to grow some magic that took over your body for a little while."

Nikoliah rubbed his eyes. "I let him mind control me?"

"Well, I was looking for a less scary way to say it, but, yes."

"This isn't a dream?"

"It's real. Touch my hand, experience the senses. It's real. You're very lucky that you came down here. I could tell from the minute you appeared that your aura wasn't your own, and I was able to pluck the intruder out of you. If this kind of thing was left untreated, you could have lost all of the thoughts you've ever had."

Nikoliah felt like his brain was picking words up and a quarter the quickness they were being said in. It felt like he was rowing through sludge.

"What the fuck is going on?" He whispered.

"It'll make sense soon enough." Zero assured. He then looked around at the others. "I really need him to be coherent as soon as possible. Can someone just give him some kind of contact? Physically or emotionally, he just needs familiarity and grounding."

And having heard those words, Laine's arms were on him in an instant, just pulling him closer to her in a hug as she whispered. She might have broken up with him, but he looked so vulnerable, and *of course* she cared about him.

Zero swallowed. "I'm sorry, we were saying something important before he arrived. What was it?" He asked into the air, as if saying it aloud would remind him.

"How Beckett can stop having magic." Raphie recalled softly, seeming to be the only person in the group able to think after the events of the last ten minutes.

"Oh, yes." Zero confirmed. "Well, he's harvesting magic from me. If I were to give one of you my magic willingly, then I would have no more magic for him to harvest, and he would lose it all."

Theo's eyes widened. That was outrageous. "You would give your magic up? For us to have a fractionally better chance at winning this fight?" Every set of eyes in the room was on Zero. He nodded eagerly. "I can't be of any use to you in this state, here. You all can be."

"So- you- you want to give it to one of us?" Laine asked, flabbergasted by the insinuation. Zero waited for a moment before he continued what he was saying.

"That's the thing. I couldn't physically give it to you, Laine, or to you, Theo. Because you both already wield magic. And, I couldn't give it you either of you two angels, because this role you would take on is as guardian of Klaevr, which you aren't from." He explained. "The only type of person I could give it to would have to be an ex-mortal from Klaevr." Nikoliah realised what the blonde man was insinuating about five seconds after everyone else in the room, so when he looked up, they were all already looking at him.

"Me?" He asked, but was only met with a resounding silence. "So, so, hold on. Julian, you, you're back. And you too, Raphie. And then Theo got out of Nesbryn, and now you're all here, and you want to defeat Beckett by taking the magic that he used against us last time. But the only way you can do that is if I take it?"

"You've made a very quick recovery from the mind control if you've pieced that all together." Zero said. "You're right."

Nikoliah immediately shook his head frantically. "I can't. I'm not the right kind of person." He said hastily. "That's a really bad idea."

"Forget if you think it's a good idea. Do you want to? Would you be willing?" The man asked seriously. Cogs whirred in Nikoliah's head.

"I guess, yeah."

"Okay." Zero replied. "If Beckett was mind controlling you, then he likely knows that we're down here. So we need to be quick."

"Wait." Theo interrupted. "Nikoliah, are you on our side?" He asked, narrowing his eyes.

"Theo." Laine frowned.

"It's a genuine question." He defended. "He might not have been in control of himself the last few days, but he's spent the last two years working for the man we're trying to defeat."

"Of course I'm on your side." He replied, a little hurt at the insinuation. "I worked for your family for a total of like eight years before Beckett took over. I only stayed working for him because my girlfriend was the heir, I never supported him."

Theo judged the sincerity of the comments for a moment, and then he noticed the pleading look in his sister's eyes and conceded. "Fine."

"Okay. Take my hand." Zero said, now that he had permission from all parties. Nikoliah reached forward and connected his hand with Zero's in a stationary handshake. "This is a huge responsibility, do you understand that? It won't go away after this fight; you're going to be doing this job forever, or until you pass your magic on to someone else and start again."

Nikoliah nodded. His mind felt less fuzzy now.

"Did someone give you your magic?" He asked.

"Someone did. A very long time ago, though. It took me at least a decade before I had properly gotten the hang of it."

The soldier was not the biggest fan of the idea that he would be *thirty* before he properly understood how to use his magic.

"Can't you just teach me?" He questioned.

"That isn't how it works, I'm sorry." Zero replied. "Nikoliah, you still feel responsible for what happened to this kingdom two years ago. You feel like you failed to protect it. And no amount of me trying to convince you otherwise will change those thoughts. But if you feel like you failed to protect it last time, then protect it now." He said, determinism in his eyes as he looked at Nikoliah. "Now, quickly. Are you ready?"

Nikoliah turned slightly and looked at Laine, who smiled some kind of encouragement whilst the other three seemed to just watch in awe.

"I'm ready." He breathed steadily, looking back at Zero.

"Okay, close your eyes. I need you to think really far back. Do you remember the first day you had in this kingdom?"

"Yeah." Nikoliah replied.

"When we first met, do you remember that?"

"Yes."

A band of purple light began to grow out from Zero's chest, travelling down his arm steadily.

"You were young, I remember feeling horrible. I always feel horrible when children appear here. You were very upset. Frantic, wondering where your parents were. Telling me that you had school work to be doing. They had sent it to you digitally so that you wouldn't fall behind while you were in hospital. You really didn't want to fall behind, did you?" Nikoliah shook his head without replying.

"And you arrived here, and you were immediately distraught. You were upset that you hadn't done everything you had wanted to. You wished you'd lived more as if every day was your last. Your biggest accomplishment was winning your year 4 spelling bee. You wanted to have done more. Do you remember that?"

"Yeah." He breathed.

"And so I suggested that you look into something military. You had felt horrible during the last few weeks of your life, because you were weak and could hardly lift the glass of water that you kept on your bedside table to your lips. So, you assured me that you wanted to do something that would let you run around and make the most of your strength. You wanted to make something of yourself. Do you still want to do that?"

"I do, yeah. I do." Nikoliah nodded.

"Good, that's really good. Just think about that. Think about your purpose in this dimension. What are you here to do? What have you done? What haven't you done yet?"

The purple light got past the connection of their hands, and Nikoliah's breath hitched in pain as the light penetrated his skin, entering his chest. The magic began to swirl around him, crossing through his head and his heart.

"Open your eyes. Look at me." Zero said quickly. Nikoliah did so.

Zero looked pained. A strained look on his face even as the magic flowed out of him. The light began to leave his chest, at the end of its trail. It reached towards his wrist, and just as it was about to completely leave him, he opened his mouth to speak.

"You're going to be amazing at this, Nikoliah. I know you are." He said with sincerity. "Trust yourself, and the rest will work itself out."

The light disconnected from Zero's arm, leaving him completely void of any magic. The purple light swirled around Nikoliah and slowly faded to the same cotton blue as his horns and tail, swirling around him and taking the whole room up before suddenly imploding inside of him. Nikoliah screamed from the pain of it, but it had completely subsided in about two seconds.

All of the light dissipated, leaving Nikoliah breathing heavily.

He looked in front of him and was horrified.

On the ground before him, Zero lay completely limp. His jaw was hanging open off its hinges, and his eyes were completely absent from his skull. His head was bent and snapped in a way that definitely wasn't possible. Laine screamed the loudest. She jumped towards Nikoliah and hid her face in his shirt. Raphie just stayed staring at the corpse in silence. Julian's mouth was hanging open in shock.
Theo leapt forward, hands grasping onto Zero's shoulders.
"What the fuck!" He yelled. "Get the fuck up!"
"Theo." Julian whined. Theo shook his head.
"No, no. I don't- I don't know what to do." He panicked, hands shaking. "I've never- I've never seen a dead body before. Is he dead? Fuck, fuck." He rambled. Theo pushed himself to his feet and kicked the side of the lifeless figure. "Zero! Get the fuck up! That's not how this works, that's not- You can't do that!"
The body did not move.
Theo dropped to his knees again and started shaking the shoulders of the body. "Please, please." He whined pathetically.
"Theo! He's gone. Stop it." Julian protested, grabbing Theo's hand. The demon turned and looked back at his boyfriend.
"He's not- he wasn't meant to fucking die! That's not- that's not how things work here. What happened to him?!"
"Theo, I think he knew that was going to happen." Laine said quietly. She was crying, he noticed. "The way he said that to Nikoliah, like he knew that he wouldn't have a mentor. If he knew it would happen and he brought the idea up... then, he must have been at peace with it."
Theo shook his head. "No. No, he- he can't-"
Julian was suddenly behind him, wrapping both arms around him and pulling him into his chest. And Theo cried. He cried in a way that he had never before. He wailed, and screamed like a little child.
He had always thought it was so stupid. So silly, the way that ex-mortals get so upset over death. He'd always been above it.
Laine sniffled. She turned over to Nikoliah, who was sitting to her right. "Are you okay?" She asked.
He nodded.
"I feel weird." He muttered. "Really weird. There's a lot of emotion in this room and I can feel it on my chest." He admitted. "I feel really strange."
The Princess nodded. "Raph? Are you okay?"
Raphie's eyes disconnected from the body and looked at Laine.
"Shocked." She replied. "I didn't expect that, that's all."

"Yeah." Laine agreed, nodding. She stood and moved so that she was sat in between Nikoliah and Raphie. Theo was still audibly distressed, very much so.

If they had wanted to talk, they wouldn't have been able to hear each other. So, instead, they just sat. Julian was looking after Theo, he would be fine.

The comfort of being near another person was enough.

XLIX

It was only a minute later when circumstance forced them to push the events of the past twenty minutes behind them.

Nikoliah suddenly inhaled a deep breath.

"What?" Laine asked, worried.

"Are you angry?" He asked, before shaking his head. "No, it's-" He muttered to himself, looking over at Julian and Theo. Theo was sniffling now, looking at Nikoliah anxiously as Julian held him still, appearing concerned.

Nikoliah furrowed his eyebrows. And then all five of them heard the creak of a floorboard above their heads. Nikoliah's eyes widened and he looked up through the ceiling. "Fuck." He cursed.

The floorboards creaked rhythmically above them, the sound getting closer and closer to where the trapdoor was.

"Angry, he's angry. Murderously angry - we need to leave." Nikoliah rushed out, looking panicked like a deer in headlights.

"How are we meant to do that if he's fucking right above the only exit?!" Laine yelled in distress.

"I don't know! Please calm down."

Theo looked around, wiping his eyes. "There isn't another way to leave." He said, swallowing.

Julian shook his head. "No, the portals. Zero could make portals, can you make portals?"

"I don't know!" Nikoliah said, alarmed. "How did he do it?!"

Laine closed her eyes, trying to think.

"He did that thing with a candle." Raphie remembered for her friend.

443

"Oh." Theo reacted. "He didn't use a candle when he did it for me. He just kind of," He began, gesturing in front of himself with his hands.

"In words, please." Nikoliah pleaded.

"He put his hand on the ground and drew a circle with it." Theo said. "But, like, you need to do it with intention, as with all magic. It won't work without intention."

The same noise that they had heard when Nikoliah and entered rang out again, but it was louder. And then the sound of heavy shoes against the ladder. Nikoliah closed his eyes and tried to focus, They needed to leave. To get outside the castle.

"Strythio Virzor...." Beckett called from the bottom of the stairs. Theo paled at the sound of his voice. "I know you can hear me. Come out here and fight me like a real man would."

He could hear the footsteps getting closer and closer, so Theo leapt up with a hand on his sword.

"Theo!" Laine whispered.

"I'll buy you time, help him make the portal." He instructed, looking around at all of them as he continued to whisper. Julian didn't look happy, but he didn't protest.

Theo stepped over Zero's body with a grimace, and then out into the corridor.

Beckett was holding a torch, which he pushed into a holster on the wall. He looked different to when Theo had last seen him. His hair had grown out a little, not too much, and he appeared more muscular, but with the same amount of stubble as he remembered. He stood confidently, holding a sword that was longer than Theo's.

Beckett hissed sympathetically. "You've really let yourself go." He snarled. "Have you not been eating properly?"

Theo rolled his eyes. "Fuck you." He spat. "You have some fucking audacity talking to me like that."

Beckett cooed. "Awh, sorry. I should have guessed, you're like, hardcore now, I suppose. All grown up."

"Yeah." Theo replied with resentment. "I suppose I have grown up." He said, stepping forward slightly.

Beckett nodded. "So you've come for your revenge?"

"I was a child, Amadeus. You took advantage of me being vulnerable."

"You were hardly a child. It was two years ago, don't be dramatic." He scoffed. "You're twenty now, right?"

"Awh, you remember my birthday. That's so sweet." Theo teased.

"Twenty years ago, Strythio, I had already been given my Lordship, and I was passing legislation that is still in effect today. You are *nothing* to me, because I know what hard work is. I did everything myself to get to where am I today, and I won't be letting a nepotism baby like you try and best me."

Theo narrowed his eyes.

"The truth is that you're still a child mentally. Compared to me, I mean, I have about 300 years on you. You're a weak little child who just throws tantrums when he doesn't get his way. You're the dirt I walk on, don't act like you aren't."

Theo pulled his sword out of his holster. "You act like your political career is some kind of accomplishment." He remarked. "In fact, you spent decades just constantly spewing about how little my whole species is compared to your species. And yet, here you are, acting like you're one of us. I suppose I don't really understand it."

"It isn't for you to understand." Beckett replied.

Theo shook his head as he grinded his teeth together. He hated this man, he ruined everything. But if he had learnt one thing, it's that under no circumstances could he show vulnerability. He had to appear confident. He raised his sword above his shoulders, slicing downwards as he leapt forwards.

Beckett was shocked at his composure and boldness, only having scarce time to respond by blocking the hit with his own sword. The metal clashed together loudly.

The angel rebounded and hit back at Theo, who moved his sword with both hands on it. He had to step backwards and he hit the wall.

He couldn't risk the angel seeing the others in the room, so he bounded forward again and attacked. This time, he got a decent hit that had the King hissing in pain. It seemed to only serve to make him angrier, so the next hit was hard. The edge of his sword pierced into Theo's neck, but because Beckett had to get so close to administer the hit, the demon was able to kick his leg up, directly into the angel's stomach, which sent him stumbling backwards rapidly.

"Theo!" Julian's voice came from his right, and he looked over to see that Laine and Raphie had gone, leaving just Nikoliah and Julian, watching from in front of a slightly oddly-shaped, light blue portal.

Theo looked to where Beckett was still recovering from the kick, and then, without a moment's hesitation, he stepped through to his right and took Julian's hand.

The younger man pulled him through the portal, and for a second he felt like he was floating through a tunnel of wind, and then suddenly he hit the ground, getting dirt on his clothes.

He coughed, groaning and sitting up just in time to watch Nikoliah land on the ground next to him. The portal completely disappeared in a black-hole style animation. He blinked, trying to absorb where they were.

They were outside of the castle walls, in the courtyard. Julian still held his hand as he groggily came to his senses.

"Theo, you're bleeding." Laine noticed, sitting up onto her haunches and reaching a hand towards his neck. When she pulled it away, her hand was stained with dark blue.

"Yeah. But I hit him first, so–"

"Doesn't matter, he clearly has a better sword than you." She interrupted, looking down at her cardigan which was already stained by Vercobrix's blood earlier. She slipped it off her arms and folded it up, pressing it against Theo's neck as he frowned.

"Distracting him like that was really kind of you, thanks for doing that for us, Theo. Even though you didn't have to." Theo said sarcastically imitating what he wanted to hear. Laine rolled her eyes.

"I'll say thank you when I'm not worried about you bleeding out."

"I can't believe I just did that." Nikoliah said, frowning. His hands were shaking in front of him. He looked around momentarily to check that they weren't being watched before he continued speaking to the other four. "Hold on, can I please get caught up a little?"

Raphie was the only one not incredibly pre-occupied, considering that he other two were fawning over Theo's injury.

"Julian died and was put in Menphe, and then he found me and we came down to here because he wanted to find Theo. So, we came to the castle, and Laine had nothing else to lose, so she took us to Nesbryn, where we found Theo. And then Laine met up with Serenity and her fiance, and the three of them broke the forcefield around Nesbryn down. So, we went back there and came on a train here in the hopes of defeating Beckett."

Nikoliah nodded. "We, we need to get out of this area, we're unprotected."

"Alright, calm down, Daisy." Julian scoffed playfully.

"Daisy?" He asked, confused.

"Yeah. Like, from 'An Inspector Calls'."

"What?" He asked, snickering a bit.

"Because your surname is Renton. And you were suggesting that we leave here right now, which is a suicide mission."

"I don't think anyone gets the joke, darling, sorry." Theo said, wincing in agony when speaking put pressure on the wound.

"Okay, I get you three not getting it. Because you didn't grow up in England. But, you're British, Nikoliah! You must have read 'An Inspector Calls'! For GCSE english lit, right?"

Nikoliah shook his head with a smirk. "I didn't get that far, sorry."

"What?" Julian asked.

"Yeah, mate. Died in year eight."

Julian groaned and stuck his head in his hands. "Okay, fine, forget I ever said anything."

Theo snickered. "Okay, that's enough, Laine. I'm fine." He said, moving away from her bunched up cardigan. His blood was dried around the wound, sticking to his skin.

"Might need stitches." Laine murmured.

"Okay, well, let's just focus on right now." Theo retaliated, standing up and looking around. "Now that we've done the magic part, we should find everyone else again, right?"

"Right."

"Everyone else?" Nikoliah asked.

"God, you really have missed a lot, haven't you?" Raphie raised her eyebrows. "Don't get broken up with next time."

Laine rolled her eyes. "The other demons that Theo made friends with in Nesbryn. They're here too, helping us." She supplied.

Nikoliah nodded to himself. His thoughts were racing as he still tried to make sense of everything.

Theo extended a hand out to Julian, which he took and pulled himself onto his feet. Raphie stood too, and before anything, they were ready to set off again.

Serenity and Vercobrix made it back off their train into Klaevr as quickly as they could. They were still dressed the same as before, having been lucky to get on a train at all - although it was completely down to their status as royalty.

They could tell as soon as they arrived that things were already going on. There was an array of loud noises, mainly yelling. Some doors of houses were wide open, and there were market stalls empty and tipped over.

Everything was darker than usual because the black sky had seeped into the usual brighter red, which meant torches and lampposts were the only sources of light.

"I hope you remember the way around." Vercobrix said in a whisper. He had been particularly stressed about coming and *fighting*.

"The lack of light isn't helping at all, but we can just follow the noise." Serenity reassured, squeezing his hand tighter.

She moved with an agile grace, leading her fiance along the dirt paths with a good level of urgency. They were lucky that Serenity was able to navigate the most efficient route to the castle area, because it was only a couple of minutes before she spotted Theo flinging his sword at a soldier around his age.

He had definitely improved his fighting skills over the past few years. His swipes with his sword were all very purposeful. His feet moved in the perfect way to support his body. Around him, others were engaging in the fight that had broken out. They were all hovering around the entrance to the castle.

Theo slashed his sword around his waist height, hitting the person fighting him in their torso and sending them stumbling backwards and onto the ground. He took another step forward. The soldier shook his head and scrambled to his feet, scurrying away into the night air.

Theo breathed out, and when he did, the condensation from his breath was visible in the atmosphere, like steam.

"Theo!" Serenity called, walking a few paces towards him. He turned towards her and smiled.

"Hey." He smiled. "You guys alright?"

"We're good." She confirmed, glancing back to Vercobrix as he nodded. "Are you?" She asked, eyeing up the scar forming on his neck.

"Oh." He said, absentmindedly bringing his hand to the wound. "Yeah, yeah. The others should be down there. We ran into some guards and my fight happened to escalate up here."

Theo was conscious to look around and make sure he wasn't letting his guard down. He flicked his head to the right. "Come on, let's go find them." He instructed, turning ninety degrees. As they began to walk, his hand still gripping to his sword like it was his only lifeline, he watched the surroundings.

"Assuming you didn't get any help from your sister?" He asked, eyes on the silhouette of the castle gates. Serenity frowned.

"No, I'm sorry." She admitted sheepishly. "She changed her mind. She was worried that if she gave us help and then we lost, she would have started a war between my kingdom and yours."

"Which, to quote her," Vercobrix began. "She doesn't 'need on her plate right now.'" He grimaced.

"Sorry." Serenity said again. "I did ask her a few times, but she was pretty distressed by it. I think seeing the border come down made it real to her."

"Not the first authority figure that hasn't believed in me." Theo replied a little quieter. "Seriously, it's fine. We're equipped."

They walked along the path in a comfortable silence, but there was an interruption before they could return back to the others.

"King Theo!" Someone called. He turned around and felt his chest seize up with guilt at the sight of a short-haired blonde woman and her taller, curly dark-haired wife.

He smiled. The blonde woman was bounding towards him, and then (in a way that would have been weird to even think about this time two and a bit years ago) they were hugging.

"It's good to see you, Hettie." Theo whispered. She pulled away and grinned, stepping backwards to leave room for Elsie to come and offer him a hug too.

"Are you okay, have you been okay?" She asked, hands on his shoulders like a concerned mother.

"I've been fine. Have you two?" He answered quickly - dismissively.

Hettie blinked a few times and then her mouth drew up into a saddened smile. She looked at Elsie and then replied for both of them.

"Yeah. We've just had a lot on our minds. It hasn't been nice around here since he took over." She said solemnly.

Theo turned towards Serenity and Vercobrix for a moment. "Um, you guys can go on and find the others. I need to talk to these two alone." He explained.

"Alright." Vercobrix replied. "Be safe."

"Yep." Theo said.

"Okay, bye." Serenity bid him farewell, and the couple moved off behind Theo and down the longer path. Theo looked back towards the couple and shuffled a few feet towards the side of the path.

"What's up?" Elsie asked, leaning on her right leg and jutting her hip out.

"Um, okay. I know you guys have been, like, worried a bit. About, um, about Zero."

Both of their faces dropped instantly. Elsie's eyebrows contorted to sympathy as she wrapped her arm around Hettie's shoulders.
"Oh." Hettie said, voice breaking. "Oh. He's- he's gone, isn't he?"
Theo bit his lip and tried to look anywhere but their faces.
"I'm sorry."
"Who did he give the magic to?" Elsie asked, pulling her wife into her chest for comfort.
"Nikoliah." Theo said. He found himself completely unable to articulate further than his monosyllabic replies.
Elsie nodded. "Hey, Hets, you hear that? The nice kid with the good work ethic. The Princess' boyfriend."
Theo didn't correct her. Hettie nodded and looked back up with tearful eyes. "Were you there, Theo? When he went?"
"Yeah." He breathed. "I was." He told, and then after a second, he thought. "I, um, you seemed to get what I was trying to say pretty quickly. Had he, like, talked to you about it?"
Hettie held her arms in front of her. She looked like she was going to be sick, but she nodded.
"Yes, he did." She said. "We knew it would happen soon. He knew too. It was like, *god*, it was like when my grandmother died when I was seven and my parents sat me down to *explain* the concept of death to me."
"He knew it would happen?" Theo plucked out of the sentence. Hettie sighed.
"Can we find Nikoliah for this conversation? Please." She asked. Elsie nodded.
"Yeah, yeah. Of course. Um, follow me." He said, leading the way down the path.
Behind him, he could hear Elsie and Hettie talking.
"I had a feeling the minute he got taken that that was it. I wish I could have said goodbye."
Theo turned his head around. "Um, sorry to intrude. And, tell me to shut up if it isn't my place, but, I only really got to speak to him for five minutes. And, he asked about you. He wanted to make sure that you were okay."
Hettie sniffled. "Thank you, Theo. It's just- a lot. He was like my dad, he really cared about us, even if he pretended he didn't."
"Yeah." Theo nodded. "I mean, I'm probably not the best person for comfort, considering that I've never really lost anyone to death. Both times my loved one reverse-died and then I found them again, so-"
"What?" Elsie asked. "Julian's back?"

450

"Yeah."

"Who was the second person?"

Theo paused. Oh, right. He had kind of forgotten in the past two years that his mother being alive would be a big deal here. In fact, other than Julian and Raphie, they hadn't told anyone. Not even their dad. Theo understood why he didn't have the opportunity, but Laine hadn't even told anyone that she knew about the dark secret that their family was built on.

"Oh, um. I'd rather not get into it." He confessed. "We're thinking about Zero. And, speaking of..." He trailed off. Laine, Raphie, Julian and Nikoliah were still fighting two final soldiers. Theo walked up to Nikoliah and called his name, pulling him away from the fight and leaving the other five to deal with the final enemy as the second fell to the ground unconscious.

"Yeah. What's going on?"

Theo stepped to the side and allowed Nikoliah to look at Elsie and Hettie. "Niko, this is Elsie and Hettie. Elsie and Hettie, this is... Yeah." He stepped away. Nikoliah looked at Theo, confused.

"Well, uh, yeah. Nice to meet you two. Who are you?" He asked, a little worried about the appearingly serious tone of the conversation.

Hettie moved forward and hugged Nikoliah. He squeaked in surprise. "Hi?"

"Hi." She mumbled. "It's nice to meet you."

Nikoliah looked incredibly confused. Elsie approached. "Hi, Nikoliah. My name is Elsie. I'm Zero's daughter-in-law."

Nikoliah blinked a few times and then looked down towards the woman in his arms. He pieced it together quickly and wrapped his arms around Hettie tighter.

"I'm really sorry." He whispered. "If I hadn't come down into the dungeon... there would have been nobody for him to give his magic to, and he would still be here."

Hettie pulled away instantly and shook her head.

"No, no. You don't understand. It's- God, I don't know how to phrase this." She debated. "Just, do you remember why you went to the dungeon? I'm assuming that's where he was."

Nikoliah shook his head. "I don't remember before then. I was being mind-controlled."

"Well, how did you die?" She asked.

"I've known you for like a minute." Nikoliah said quietly.

"Just, how?"

"Cancer."

"Was it... at all sudden?"

Nikoliah bit his lip. It had been. His family had hardly had time to accept the diagnosis before they started planning a funeral. They had started planning a funeral while he was *still alive*. It had been pretty dreadful for him. He had been given a Make-A-Wish, but he had wanted to meet Taylor Swift and she was quite a busy woman.

One day he went to school, and then the next day his whole world got flipped upside down. He didn't go back to school for one day in the two weeks he had. He never said goodbye to his friends, and now, nine years later, he would be surprised if they even remembered his name. He wanted to articulate this, wanted to tell them about how upset he was that it had been so sudden. He couldn't.

"Yeah."

"This might upset you a bit, Nikoliah." Hettie said. "But, the guardians kind of operate on a reincarnation system."

"Sorry?"

Hettie cringed. She stepped a bit away, and Elsie brought her hand back onto her shoulder. The fighting close to them had ended by now, so only the murmuring of conversation ten metres away from them could be heard.

"I think it's possible that you were taken so quickly so that you could be here. When he moved on." She said.

"You- what?"

Elsie sensed that he needed it explaining to him properly, so she stepped in. "Zero was a reincarnation of the last guardian. The magic, it works in strange ways. If it could sense the end of its lifespan, sometimes it takes matters into its own hands to ensure that there will always be a protector of the kingdom."

Nikoliah looked as surprised as Theo felt. He had never heard any of this before. It was a lot.

"That's not- he chose to give it to me, it was a choice."

"Was it a choice that he knew he had to make?"

Nikoliah took a step backwards. "You're trying to tell me that I died to be here? I was only born to be dead?"

"You died young, didn't you?" Hettie asked. There was no reply - she knew the answer. "And yet you still ended up in Hell. Have you ever thought about what you did to get here?"

452

He had always just assumed that he had accidentally hurt people. Maybe it was the girl who asked him to their year 6 disco that he rejected. He had never thought of there being an actual reason.
The silence said everything.
"But, he- I'm not- I might not be the *one*, he might have just thought I was."
Elsie removed her hand from Hettie's shoulder and took one of Nikoliah's. "I know it's difficult. But, we spent a lot of time with Zero. And he told us a lot about the magic. It doesn't transfer to the wrong person, Nikoliah. If you have it, then you were meant to have it." She said in a low volume.
The knight didn't say anything. He pulled his hand away from Elsie's.
"If anything, Nikoliah, take this as a reassurance. It doesn't change what has happened to you, and what will happen to you. The fact that you were meant to have this ability shows that you have nothing to worry about when it comes to wielding it."
It was supposed to be something that made him feel better. But it didn't.
"Look, I'm sorry for your loss." He said, voice breaking. "But, I- I can't do this right now." He whined, blinking his tears away. He took some steps backwards and he was gone in an instant.
Theo looked back at the two women, who both looked a little guilt-ridden.
"Is that true?" He asked.
"Yeah." Hettie replied. "It is. And, I hope you remembered that. You're likely going to have to give that talk to the next one."
Theo swallowed. "Okay. Okay, I'm sorry, I'll speak to you guys later. I need to..." He gestured towards the direction that Nikoliah left in with his hands.
"Of course. Make sure he's okay." Elsie said, holding Hettie once more.
The demon nodded, and in a moment's notice he was running after Nikoliah. He went past the others with a quick mumble of "Just wait here."
 Slightly further along the path, he found the young man sitting on a ledge of stone. His face was buried in his arms, which were resting on his knees. He was crying. It caught Theo off guard.
He had known Nikoliah for so long. Since he had first died, even. He had never been one to show extreme emotion. Not around him, at least.
"Niko?" He said softly, sitting down beside the man.
"My whole existence." He whispered. "My whole existence has been made up to get me here." He said, the realisation hitting him like a truck.

453

"Carry on." Theo whispered with encouragement.
"I, I had dreams. I wanted to be a footballer, like most young boys did. And then, I came here. And, I wanted to be a soldier. And then I had to start working with Fiducia, and I just wanted to be believed in. I put so much effort into being where I was." He said, crying. He leant into Theo's body and rested his head on his shoulder.
"But, none of it mattered. I could have done dogshit with my life and I would still have ended up here, accepting Zero's magic. I worked so hard for nothing. Nothing mattered at all." He breathed. "Which is probably a good thing. I wouldn't have gotten this far without whatever divine intervention this has been."
"Of course you would have." Theo said. "When I was growing up, Nikoliah, I used to think of you as like a cool older brother. And then, obviously, we grew up and I started feeling resentment towards you because you had all the skills that my father wanted me to have."
Nikoliah looked up. "You really felt that way?"
"Every day." He admitted. "It didn't help that he used to treat you like a son. One time he made a joke to me that you were his favourite child and I cried in my bed that night." He laughed a little. "It's complicated, but everyone thinks you're amazing. I get the feeling that Beckett undermined you and made you feel like you're worse at your job than you are. Which isn't true."
Nikoliah smiled slightly. "Thank you." He said. "Does this mean I have to stop being a soldier?" He asked.
"I mean, a lot of responsibilities will definitely make themselves clear. But, I think you can juggle it if you really want to. You can do the 'welcoming the recently-deceased thing' from the castle."
"And what if we lose?" Nikoliah asked. He thought for a moment. "I'd have to go into hiding. Beckett would want me dead. He'd do to me what he did to Zero."
"Well then we aren't going to lose." Theo said with determinism. He looked up when Laine cleared her throat from the clearing of the area they were sitting in.
"Sorry." Theo apologised. "Do we need to move on?"
Laine shook her head. "No, I just wanted to see if he was okay."
Theo's mouth dropped open in an 'o' shape. He looked down at Nikoliah's upset frame and stood up, looking at the ground as his sister walked past him and took the seat he was previously sitting in. The last thing he saw was her pulling his hands into her lap as they started to speak.
Theo walked around the corner back to where the others were.

"What's going on?" Julian asked, walking up to him.

"Nikoliah's just having a hard time coming to terms with everything. Are you guys okay? No injuries?"

Julian shook his head.

"No, we're all good." Raphie answered for them all. Theo noticed that Serenity's sword had a little bit of a blood stain on it, and he kind of smiled at the idea of her protecting herself, and clearly her boyfriend too, from the way he was standing behind her like a scared child.

It appeared that Hettie and Elsie had retreated, probably back to fighting with others. And, speaking of others, it seemed that they had finished their rally.

"There you are!" Ayale called, bounding down the hill with the other five demons from Nesbryn in tow. "We're having a blast. Are you ready to get serious and like, go invade the castle or something?"

Theo grinned at the enthusiasm. "Yeah, yeah. Are you guys okay?" He asked, eyes scanning them over for any potential injuries.

"We're great!" Livvy beamed. "Never felt more alive." She stated.

"Yeah. I've seen more people in the last thirty minutes than I have in the last ten years." Fern said, a large smile plastered on her face.

"And I got to fight something that couldn't burn me." Toby said.

"Yeah!" Isaac actually seemed happy. "I pretended some guy trying to hurt me was you, Theo. Very therapeutic."

"Oh!" Theo laughed. "Thanks for letting me know."

"Right, are we going anywhere? Where's your sister?" Axel asked. "Ten quid says she died."

"Unlikely." Ayale snorted.

Theo looked back in the direction that he had left Laine and Nikoliah in. "Yeah, one sec, I'll get her."

He trekked along the path towards the clearing in the shrubbery. He approached slowly, ready to tell them that they were ready to leave. When he looked around the corner he saw them sitting close together. Laine had one leg hooked over one of Nikoliah's - her hand on his chin as they kissed, gentle and caring. Theo immediately stepped back away out of view. He blinked a few times to process the sight before he walked back down the path. The distance was a meagre fifteen metres, and so he returned to the others and raised his voice.

"Okay! Just about time we head off somewhere else!" He said loudly in their direction. Julian raised an eyebrow at him.

Ten seconds later, Laine and Nikoliah came stumbling out of the bushes. They walked with a gap between them, looking like they were making idle small talk, although they both had slight smiles adorning their features. Laine bounced towards Theo and ended up beside him as Nikoliah had to awkwardly introduce himself to the demons of Nesbryn. Theo looked at her with a low whisper. "That's how you should have handled it when you found Julian and I." He slighted, making eye contact with her at the end of the sentence. Laine looked caught off guard. She rolled her eyes.

"You can have the brother of the year award." She said sarcastically. "Thank you." She said eventually. "I guess. Just, don't think I owe you anything." She warned.

"Wouldn't dream of it." Theo said, hands up in mock defence. "Now come on, let's get our hands dirty. Once and for all.

L

Theo snickered, giggling and feeling giddy like he was drunk. He was walking through the corridors of the castle with Laine. In some regards, it was nice. As if they were kids again - playing hide and seek. They have to be quiet, or else one of the staff members might hear them and send them to their rooms for playing past their bedtime.

The truth was that they had entered the castle from that same side window as earlier. They were looking for his crown. The one that Beckett had taken from him before. The others had been more than happy to split off from them and begin the fight that they had already started in the courtyard.

Julian had not wanted to leave Theo, so he had come with them. He was walking next to Theo, and both men were kind of relying on Laine's knowledge of the halls - since it had been a while.

"This is the kind of thing that's going to get us hurt." Julian laughed. "You aren't even trying to be stealthy."

"Neither are you." The other man giggled back, wobbling slightly.

"Boys, come on." Laine warned. "We have a destination."

Theo and Julian have each other an exasperated look, but they accepted the caution.

The castle was far too quiet for what was going on outside, but Theo supposed that it did make sense. All of the soldiers were out there, since nobody knew that the three of them had entered the castle (and if they did, nobody had made any move to show it).

The destination that Laine was referring to was the throne room. When Theo was king, he had never kept his crown there, because it felt showy-offy, but showing off was exactly what Beckett had wanted to do. Seeing the crown any time she wanted to speak to him had honestly made Laine feel a little ill.

Just before they could get there, one of the doors from the rooms on the side swung open.

Theo wasn't surprised to see that his father hadn't changed much. He was, however, surprised to see him general.

He had the same brown hair, and his beard was still shaped the same way. He hadn't grown any taller, but he did look more reserved in his movements. He was wearing traditional clothing, and holstered a shortsword on his belt. He had stayed in the castle after Laine ran off, just to watch over her.

He stopped and looked at the three of them.

"Oh! Dad." Laine said, surprised. Theo stopped and sucked in a harsh breath as his eyes scanned up and down the man before him.

Julian looked between them and his eyes widened in realisation.

"Oh, you're- you're Theo's dad." He smiled, stepping forward. "We never actually properly met. Julian." He introduced, reaching a hand out towards the man.

Dyran raised an eyebrow and gave Julian a look as if he was some mouldy bread left out on the counter. Julian pulled his arm away after a moment.

"Come on, Julian, let's go get it." Laine whispered, sensing the need for the two of her male blood relatives to talk. She grabbed the older one's hand and pulled him away into the throne room through the large creaking door. It left just Theo and Dyran standing facing each other.

For about ten seconds after they disappeared, Theo stayed completely silent as he looked at his dad.

"Son."

"Don't call me that." Theo replied. He whispered, maintaining eye contact with his father.

"Theo." He tried again, sighing. "I'm glad to see you."

"Makes one of us."

Dyran's shoulders deflated a little and he shook his head. "You cannot seriously be upset at me over everything." He said. "Not after all this time."

The other man took a deep breath whilst he formulated his response.

"You left me for the wolves." Theo stated. He kept his stance strong and as confident as possible.

"You shouldn't have let the wolves get you, then." Dyran responded as if he was talking to a young child. "I gave you everything you needed, Theo.

458

A prospering kingdom, a beautiful princess to marry, all the staff you could ask for. And you still managed to land yourself in this position. Blaming me for any of this is plain wrong."

Theo scoffed.

"You- you forced me into a box. You should have been there to support me."

"Theo, I never would have had an issue with your sexuality. But, you didn't *tell me*. When you were struggling to manage everything while running the kingdom, you didn't *tell me*. I would have been there for you, because you're family. You're my son. I would have done anything to help you, but you never gave me the chance."

"Am I family in the same way that my mother was family?" He asked. The question was cold and curt. Theo realised that, *right*, he was doing this right now.

"What?" His father asked, distressed at the mention of her.

"Well, I must be. You abandoned her to save yourself too."

Dyran responded with a petrified stare. He had no words. He was certain that Theo was making things up, because there was no way in the seven kingdoms that he-

"Yeah. When we fucked off to England, we found her. And she told us everything." He spat. "You let us grow up without a mother because you didn't want a bad reputation?!" He began yelling. He was angry. All of those feelings about growing up alone, and having to deal with the sympathetic glances that he received in public after her disappearance.

"Now is not the time for this." Dyran responded. His jaw was set strongly.

"When is the time for this, then?"

Dyran shook his head. His son, his only son, was talking to him like this. He didn't even have words to describe the betrayal that he was feeling. But, he found them in the form of rage.

"What the hell happened to you? You aren't the same son I remember having. You- you've got fucking tattoos! I did not raise you to be the kind of boy that gets tattoos." He said, gesturing to Theo's shoulders and down to his arm where his large flower tattoo was visible where his sleeve had ridden up.

"Your son died in that courtyard." Theo replied, frowning in mock empathy, before straightening back to his calloused emotions from before. "And then he got socialised with some of this dimensions' most tortured souls. So, I don't know. Forgive me if I didn't turn out how you had dreamed." He grinned, rolling his eyes as the smile slipped off his face and he shook his head.

459

"I didn't have big dreams for you." Dyran admitted, lowering his voice. "I just wanted you to do what you were supposed to. I don't know why you were so insistent on being different."

"Well, I wanted to fix things." Theo whispered.

"Fix things? Like what?" The ex-king asked, moving back a little in a defensive stance.

"Oh, I don't know, maybe the way that the angels systemically treat us like the dirt under their shoes with their laws. I wanted to do something about it, dad. Because you never had the guts to stand up for yourself." He accused, crossing his arms in front of him. He had put his sword back in the holster on his belt.

"And *you* standing up for yourself seems to have gone well."

Theo rolled his eyes.

"What you don't understand, Theo, is that your role as king involved sacrifices. Sometimes you have to smile and wave at your oppressors because challenging them will only make things worse for you."

"I disagree. That rhetoric is why things have stayed the same. I wanted to change that."

"Well, you certainly are one to talk about disliking angels. Seems that found yourself one." His dad said, raising his eyebrows and loosely gesturing towards the throne room that the two of them had gone into.

"Don't bring him into this." Theo replied harshly.

"You brought your mother into it." He retaliated snappily. "You know, I don't know why you did that."

"Did what?"

"Why you started fooling around with him. It's just, I just, I didn't care about it being boys. But, out of all the boys you could have fallen in love with, did it really have to be an ex-mortal?"

"He's my soulmate. Literally."

"He could have been the King of the world on Earth, Theo, it wouldn't matter." He gritted. "I could have set you up with someone else if I had known." He said, snapping his fingers to remember his next point. "That Prince from Atroka, he was queer for a bit, wasn't he?"

"He has a name, and he's engaged."

"To your sloppy seconds."

"Don't you fucking dare talk about her like that." Theo spat, stepping even closer to his dad so that they were only about a metre apart. He could deal with being ripped into himself, maybe. But, the minute that his dad started attacking people that he knew and cared about, that was the line.

"I just think it's unfair that you seem angry at me for your own mistakes." Dyran said sincerely, looking up at his son who had now grown slightly taller than him.

"I was hoping that you would come here and we could reconcile and I could be proud of you for defending yourself. But, if I'm being completely honest, son, I'm disappointed in the man you've become."

And, ouch. That hurt more than the scar scabbing over on his neck. Theo went completely silent at that, swallowing and looking away. He wasn't going to cry, that would prove everything right. But, despite his mind's protests, he had to bring his hand up to his face to push a tear away. He sniffled, completely turning away from the man he was talking to.

"Theo." He said sternly. "Our relationship isn't as good as it should be, but we can't fix it by arguing." He frowned, feeling slightly remorseful.

"Oh, sorry." Beckett said from the other end of the hall. "I didn't mean to intrude on a family reunion."

Theo spun around like a whippet, turning to see the man that he hated smirking at him. The demon took a few steps backwards so that he was kind of level with his father. He tilted his head towards the man and spoke as quietly as possible.

"If you want to prove to me that you care, then pick the right side here." He said, and then he ran towards Beckett, sword in the air.

Beckett reacted quickly, clashing against the sword with his own.

Theo drew his sword back and then down immediately towards Beckett's stomach, but he was kicked to the ground before he could make the impact, having the wind completely knocked out of him as he fell onto the carpet. He kept his sword in his hand as he groaned in pain, tilting his head up to look at Beckett as the tyrant stood on his sword.

"I saw you seem to have killed Zero." He chuckled, crouching down towards Theo's face. He shook his head incessantly. He realised in that moment that Beckett must not yet be aware that he had lost his magical abilities, because Theo was certain that if he was aware, there would probably be a sword plunged into his heart by now.

He tried to stand, but Beckett pressed the tip of his sword to Theo's throat. In the same way that he had before.

"You know, Strythio, I was being merciful when I let you go to Nesbryn." He drawled. "You should have been thankful, but you took my generosity for granted and had the audacity to come back here trying to get the better of me."

Theo narrowed his eyes, pushing his legs up against the floor. The angel towering over him pushed the sword further down, forcing him to tilt his head backwards to avoid it piercing his skin, accompanied with a pained whimper.

"Give me one valid reason not to slit your throat like I should have done two years ago."

Amadeus gave a yell of pain as Dyran slammed his body into the side of him. The angel was shoved to the floor a few metres away from where he was previously threatening Theo.

The youngest man breathed heavily at the sudden movement, scrambling to his feet the minute that he was free. He watched as his dad leant over the angel on the ground, even as Beckett quickly regained his stance and let out a noise akin to a growl.

"You're going to regret that." He said deeply.

Julian and Laine pushed the door of the throne room open. In Laine's hand, she held the golden circle of the crown. It was clearly heavy in her grasp, weighing her hand down with gems of assorted colours.

"Sorry. ...Glass was hard to break." Laine said, pausing when she looked up and absorbed the scenario.

"Princess Laine." Beckett smirked. "And, Strythio's side piece. I had a hunch you two were around." He teased. "Oh, Julian. I love this new angel thing you have going on. You're one of us now, you realise that? You don't need to be with a sinner like Strythio, especially not down here."

"Fuck you." Julian said with venom. He stepped closer to Theo and allowed the taller man to grab his wrist protectively.

"Did I just hear you swear at me? Because, I think really, you should be thanking me. I mean, I gave you that halo, after all." He boasted with an obnoxious smirk.

"Don't retaliate." Laine whispered. "Come on, we got what we wanted. We need to leave."

"Ah, ah." Beckett hummed, holding his sword up between his body and the wall that they had to walk past to exit. "You don't get to show up, take what's mine and leave."

"There's four of us and *one* of you." Laine said, narrowing her eyes as she tightened her grip on her sword.

"Dyran." Beckett said, raising an eyebrow at the man before him. "I'll give you that choice again. I can attribute your little outburst just now to paternal instinct, but here I'll give you another opportunity to choose the successful side." He offered. "So, is it me or him?"

Dyran bit his lip and scrunched his face up, turning slightly to look at Theo, who took a sharp intake of breath.

"It's him."

Dyran pulled his sword back and hit it at Beckett's torso. The angel quickly moved his arm up to block the attack with his sword, but he was a little slow. Dyran's sword left a deep gash in his forearm. Beckett screamed in shock and pain, stumbling backwards. He regained his footing quickly and raised his eyebrows with the fury of a raging fire. Theo leapt forward protectively as Beckett raised his empty arm.
"Bad decision." He lectured venomously. Immediately after, Beckett threw his hand down quickly, towards Theo's feet.
Nothing happened. And he did it again.
Theo's face grew into a shit-eating grin as he realised what Beckett was trying to do.
"Awh. Are you having some trouble with that?" He ridiculed, smirking with pride. Beckett's eyes widened with absolutely unstoppable rage.
"You have seriously fucked up, Strythio Virzor." Beckett said. His voice was dangerously cold, gritting his teeth together as he committed homicide with just the look he was giving the demon.
He ran directly at Theo, who dived to the ground to avoid being impaled in the stomach by the sword that stabbed into the wall where he had previously been standing.
"Go. Go!" Theo shouted at Julian and Laine, flicking his head towards the hallway that led to the exit. He yelped as Beckett thrusted his sword at him, once again hitting him in the same shoulder as before. He dragged his sword back up, having his next hit blocked by the harsh metal of the angel's sword. Dyran had disappeared down the corridor quite quickly, trusting the instruction of his son, who had made it clear that he was in charge.
However, Julian stayed cemented to the ground. "We're not gonna leave you here!" He shouted back over the sound of metal hitting metal.
"Yes, you fucking are." Theo strained, throwing his sword at Beckett's torso.
"Listen to your big strong boyfriend, Julian. He knows you can't protect yourself." Beckett stated plainly. Theo blinked in surprise at the comment, which left him completely off guard when Beckett flung his sword at Theo's upper leg, cutting through the material of his trousers and making him stumble against the wall at the end of the corridor.
Julian lunged his sword down at Beckett's hands. He pulled them away quickly. Not quick enough that it didn't leave a blood red scar along the upside of his right hand.
"Julian, leave." Theo instructed, pressing his hand to the wound on his leg, hand shaking as it came back covered in dark blue blood.

"No, Theo. I can help."

"He said that to make you stay so that he can hurt you as an ultimatum!" Theo explained, pushing off the wall. "Just like last time, Jude."

Julian swallowed.

"No," Beckett responded before Julian could. "I'm just being honest with you, kid. You know he doesn't think you're capable. Why else would he tell you to leave when the action begins?"

Julian narrowed his eyes. He felt paralyzed in position. Amadeus smirked. Then, Beckett raised his sword over his right shoulder and slashed it downwards towards Julian. In half a second, Laine had extended her wings out behind her. Her right wing pushed out in front of Julian, blocking him from a potentially deadly hit of the sword. The metal dug through the feathers of her wing, leaving a large gash down the centre of it.

Laine bit her lip to stop herself from screaming with the pain. Her eyes watered.

She quickly pulled her wings inwards slightly, leaving her room to grab Julian's hand and immediately begin running down the corridor - dragging him along with her.

"He can hold his own, I promise." She said, and Julian remained silent from the shock of nearly being badly hurt, only able to tilt his head back and observe the expression of relief on Theo's face as he saw they were leaving.

Laine dragged him down the corridor, both disappearing down the grand staircase.

"That was brave of your sister." Beckett remarked. "Clearly she got all of that trait."

Theo rolled his eyes. "You're weak for bringing him into this, when you know it's between us."

"You brought him into it when you dragged him away from Heaven to come and fight for you in this shithole." Beckett spat as Theo ducked under his sword.

"He came here himself. But, you wouldn't know what having someone do something for you because they love you feels like, would you?" He snarled, jumping up and gripping his sword in front of his body.

"Well, you wouldn't know much about ruling a kingdom, would you? Considering you only lasted, what? Three months? Before you caved and ran off?"

Theo had to concede that that had been a mistake on his part. He didn't have a witty response.

"Well, I suppose the past is the past." Beckett mused, attempting to lunge his sword at Theo, who ducked and spun slightly, hitting his back with it. He hissed slightly, but showed no further symptoms of pain. "This is making me nostalgic. I'm getting deja vu." The King grinned. He pushed Theo against a wall with one swift movement of his forearm. Theo felt completely at his mercy against the wall, beginning to wish that he hadn't sent his sister and his boyfriend away.

Suddenly, he felt a tingling sensation running all down his arms.

From the parts of skin that weren't covered, he observed the glow of the golden markings up and down his skin. He blinked a few times, confused. He wasn't using magic.

And then he remembered.

Theo hooked his leg around the back of Beckett's knees, making him buckle at them, falling forward a little. In the half a second of time that this bought him, Theo slipped out from underneath Beckett's towering grasp, sprinting down the corridor as the angel yelled at him to stop being a coward. He ran, his lungs burning like he'd never run before.

At the top of the grand staircase, Theo skidded to a halt. Beckett was running after him.

He made sure to grab hold of his sword as strongly as he could fathom, leaping up onto the bannister on the right side of the staircase and sliding down it. In just a couple of seconds, he had breezed along the wood, being thrown off by momentum at the end and planting his feet on the ground safely.

He was already at the door to the castle when Beckett reached the top of the staircase.

Outside of the castle, the kingdom had descended into chaos.

Theo could notice pretty much every single person that he could name fighting, and it appeared that nearly all of the kingdom's residents were either doing the exact same thing or watching from outside the castle gates. He knew that they were watching, because when he exited the castle, there was a lot of noise made in his favour.

For most civilians of the kingdom, it was their first time seeing him in years. He was like a symbol of hope to them, and despite knowing that he was around from word of mouth, seeing him in the flesh was like a beacon had been shone from the heart of the courtyard up into the neverending sky.

They cheered at him, some even shouting his name or just generally giving shocked gasps towards his presence.

But Theo ignored it all. He ran across the courtyard, spinning around just as Beckett exited the castle with wrath on his face. They were both bleeding in their respective, opposing colours.
He could definitely see Beckett's mouth moving, but with the uproar of the crowd and the clamour of fighting, he didn't hear a thing.
The sensation and light levels in his arms began to increase quite rapidly, and Theo looked up at the sky.
He beamed with an unfathomable sense of pride when he saw the silhouette of Perry flying against the blood red canvas.
People started screaming at the sight of it. All of the cockiness melted right off Beckett's face, and some of the fights around them began to naturally come to a close just so that they could take this in. In a dimension where animals weren't really an everyday occurrence, seeing something as large, fantastical and mystical as a creature of Peterruit was incredible. Jaw-dropping was a severe understatement.
Perry came closer and closer, making people naturally create a big circle of space where it was going to land. Theo didn't move at all.
And then, with a ground-shaking thud, Perry landed in the courtyard. He skidded along due to his natural momentum, ploughing through the gravel. Just a mere two inches from where Theo had his hand raised with a single finger up in front of him, Perry stopped.
"Hey, boy." He whispered. "Did you come to protect me?"
The dog-like thing moved its head up and down, nuzzling into Theo's shoulder and nearly knocking him to the ground.
"Thank you." Theo said with a smile. Perry moved its head back and whimpered as it took in the sight of Theo covered in his own blood.
"What is that?!" He heard Beckett yell, no, scream, from across the courtyard. It made everything and everyone else go deadly silent.
"This is Perry. Do you want him to come say hi?" Theo teased, speaking Loudly. He puffed his wings out behind him and hovered a metre and a bit off the ground to ensure that he was out of the creature's trajectory. Beckett looked mortified.
"Klaevrian soldiers!" He called. "I want every ounce of your focus on killing that thing!" He instructed as loudly as he could. Much to Theo's dismay, there was a decent reaction from the troops he was talking to. Theo flew up to hover beside Perry's head.
"See that tall guy with the halo?" He asked. Really, it was silly, since he was deep down commanding the creature with his thoughts and arm movements, but it was something he could entertain for his own sake.
"He's bad news."

466

Perry growled in Beckett's direction.

"I don't want you to hurt him too badly. No fire makes contact with his skin, okay? That shit hurts, and I want to hurt him myself." He grinned. The creature pulled back on its heels, ready to pounce under Theo's instruction. Nonchalantly, Theo flicked his wrist in Beckett's direction with a grin-riddled instruction. "Go on."

Theo pulled his wings back in and dropped to the ground. He watched intently. After Perry had gotten the first four or so metres from him, he felt someone hug him from his side. His eyes flicked down to Julian.

"Are you okay?" Theo asked, wrapping the hand not holding his sword around his boyfriend's shoulders.

"As long as you are." Julian replied easily. "You're bleeding a lot. Are you sure you aren't going to pass out? Do you feel dizzy?"

Theo felt his chest fill up with warmth at the care. "I'm okay. My blood isn't the same as your blood. It takes a little more than a few scratches."

People screamed when Perry breathed out the fire for the first time. In an instant, it seemed that the fighting had resumed - a side effect of the anarchy that Perry's arrival had reinstated. Most of the soldiers wearing Beckett's uniform were aimlessly following the beast around. The ones that weren't were either pre-occupied by a different fight, or they were soldiers that had switched sides at the start of the battle. Those ones had taken their waist sashes off their uniform to show their rebellion.

"Um, you know that what Beckett said wasn't true, right?" Theo asked, a little worried that Julian was genuinely upset. "I know you can defend yourself, I just get a bit protective."

Perry made its way over to where Beckett had been standing. There were soldiers swarming it, most looking panicked but frantically trying to attack the creature, although they fell short when Perry would so much as look in their direction. Theo wasn't worried.

"I know." Julian replied. "And, if we're making confessions about our feelings," He began, looking up at Theo, right in the eyes. "I can never tell if you're looking at me or not."

"What?" Theo snickered, completely caught off-guard by the nature of the statement.

"Well, you- you don't have pupils? And, it's like you're constantly wearing sunglasses. Like, right now you could be looking at me, or someone on the complete opposite side of the courtyard. It- just, it bothers me sometimes, I don't know if you're talking to me or not. Noticed it the first day I met you."

Theo laughed out loud. "It's taken you two years to tell me that?"

Julian blushed and rolled his eyes. "I just thought you should know. It's creepy. You're creepy."

"You really know how to charm a guy, don't you?"

"Shut up."

Then, Theo hit the ground hard. He had gotten distracted, and when he looked up, Beckett was standing over him. His right hand was wrapped around Julian's torso.

"Hey! Get the fuck off me!" He yelled, thrashing and kicking his legs.

Theo's blood ran cold. Where was Perry?

"You knew deep down that you could only run for so long." Beckett said, pouting at Theo.

"Let him go, now." Theo warned, clambering up to his feet.

From behind Beckett, Perry gave a wail. Theo looked to the side of the two angels in front of him to see the creature, *his creature*, struggling on the ground as a sword was plunged into his body and soldiers held its limbs down. The glow of his arms wasn't quite as bright.

"Did you get a little distracted? Let your dog get hurt?"

Theo took a sharp intake of breath. If he didn't manage to get over to defend Perry in the next minute or so, it would lose. Frantically, he looked around the courtyard.

Laine was with Raphie, both fighting a much older demon who seemed to have them in a good fight.

Nikoliah was fighting a man around his own age, and just a few feet away from him was Oliver Garrah, who was combatting a yellow-horned woman.

Serenity and Vercobrix were together, seeming to have nailed a duelling technique in which they used each other's best abilities to battle.

Ayale, Isaac and all of the other demons from Nesbryn seemed to have completely scattered. Honestly, they were doing really well protecting themselves, even winning a few of the fights.

Hettie appeared to be tending to a wound on Elsie's arm, all the way on the other side of the courtyard.

His father was fighting with two demons at once.

To make a long story short, Theo had no back up. At all.

He took a quick step forward, but stopped as quickly as a deer caught in headlights when Julian gasped in pain and tilted his head backwards as Beckett dug his sword into his neck and tore his skin open in a straight line. Julian gasped in pain.

"Stop! Stop it!" Theo yelled, instantly stepping backwards. Beckett's sword began to appear coated in blood that dripped down Julian's neck and stained his shirt red as he screamed and whimpered in agony. Beckett laughed loudly.

"Stop! Stop, stop, let him go. I'm sorry!" Theo pleaded, unable to move at all because of the sword at his boyfriend's throat.

There was a loud roar-like scream. Perry writhed on the ground, legs flailing. It tried to breathe out fire in protection, but the effort only slowed down its movements as it went limp as another sword drove right through its skull. The tingling sensation in Theo's arms completely dissipated along with the light.

Perry was dead. He'd waited too long.

Theo charged at Beckett. He swung his sword over his shoulder and hit the angel backwards. Beckett dug his sword into Julian's skin and then released it in a slicing motion as he fell backwards. Julian cried out and fell onto the ground - blood pouring out of his neck.

Theo looked back at him. Instantly, he was at Julian's side, dragging his weakened body into his lap.

"Oh my god, oh my god. I'm sorry. I'm so sorry." He rambled pleas as he pushed his hand down on the wound with tight pressure. Julian gasped in pain and then groaned as he brought his hand out and gripped Theo's wrist with it.

"Oh, goodness!" Beckett taunted loudly. "Did your darling get hurt because you keep fucking up?"

Theo's tears mixed with Julian's blood as the crimson substance got all over both of their clothes. Beckett grimaced. "Ouch, Theo. That looks bad. Lots of blood, maybe even an artery."

Theo shook his head. It was clear that below him, Julian was trying to speak, but he couldn't. Instead, he squeezed Theo's wrist where he held his strong grip.

As a result of the King's loud ridiculing, most of the people in the courtyard and even outside of it had stopped fighting. Instead, they watched intently. For many of them, it was something they felt that they had seen before.

Raphie skidded to a halt before Julian and Theo. She dropped to her knees and took her hoodie off.

"I'll take care of him, Theo." She said in an urgent whisper, pressing her jumper to the wound on Julian's neck as she made Theo remove his hand. "Go and get him." She commanded.

Theo was kneeling with three angels around him now - sticking out like a sore thumb as he nodded. He released his grip on Julian, who was now lying on the ground blinking hazily. Theo would have said something to his boyfriend, but if he had, the younger man would not have heard. Theo leapt up, more fuelled by rage than he had ever been in his life. He made eye contact with Beckett as devastated tears pooled down his face. His whole outfit, and nearly every expanse of light skin had been plastered in blood, both his own and Julian's - which mixed together around his collarbone to form a purple tone.

"Oh, good idea. Leave him to die so you can get some petty revenge on me." Beckett scorned sardonically, readying his sword in his hands. It felt like the whole world was watching Theo, but to him, he didn't care one bit. He could have let Perry go. But, Beckett had sealed his fate the minute that the edge of his sword broke Julian's skin.

Theo narrowed his eyes. He was past the time to retaliate verbally. Everyone watched as Theo bolted at the angel that had ruined his life. He flung his sword at Beckett. Their two weapons clashed. Theo's wings extended out behind him and he used to leverage to propel himself upwards. The new angle gave him an effective hit on Beckett, which ripped right through his shirt. Theo landed on the ground on the other side of the angel, who spun around.

Theo kicked Beckett in his stomach, slashing his sword through his torso with as much brute strength as he could muster. Beckett yelled, stumbling backwards.

In the moment of opportunity that he had been given, Theo hit his sword at Beckett's hand. His fingers spasmed, and the angel's sword fell out of his hand and to the ground with a clatter that halted all the movement in the courtyard.

Disarmed, Beckett's eyes widened.

Theo was close enough that he could kick the man right in the chest, hitting him to the ground easily. He walked right up to Beckett and looked down on him.

"Well, Amadeus, I do believe that the law states that should someone disarm and defeat the monarch, they can take the crown." Theo mocked, getting really close to Beckett's face as he repeated the exact words that had been playing through his head for the past two years.

The courtyard was completely silent. Everybody was listening.

"You have not defeated me." Beckett protested, voice still strong even from his weak position.

Theo looked over at Julian. He was still on the floor, appearing as if he was about to pass out. Raphie looked very pale and ill at the sight of him. Laine was with her too. He was hurt. Badly.

The demon took two steps to stand right before Beckett's chest, one leg on either side of his body.

He plunged his sword downwards.

Everyone in the crowd screamed or had another verbal reaction to the gore. Beckett's blood spurted up out of his chest and splattered all over Theo's face and shoulders. It was nothing compared to the rest of what was on him.

The angel gasped in suffering as he found himself unable to speak, and with a would be fatal wound.

Theo yanked the sword up - causing a squelching noise. He spat down on the wound, taking a few steps away. He looked up angrily at the crowd that were watching.

Nobody had considered the once feeble Crown Prince capable of such brutality. It was shocking.

Theo breathed heavily, still crying. He didn't even remember why anymore. He took a few steps away, vision blurred. He couldn't move, but his eyes were set on Julian. If he went over there, the wounds would become real. He couldn't let them become real- he couldn't.

"Theo!" Laine yelled.

Theo looked up just in time to see that Beckett had stood up. One hand clutching the gaping hole in his chest, he dashed towards Theo. The anger etched into every crevice of his face was the most dangerous thing he had ever witnessed. Theo found himself stuck to the ground. He was about to die, he could feel it.

Beckett got closer. Theo snatched his arm up over his head to protect himself. About five inches from his body. Then, four.

A portal appeared right in front of Theo, vertical. One that Beckett, spurred on by his momentum, ran right into.

And then the portal closed and he was gone.

And Nikoliah stood a few metres away, hands out before him and shock imprinted on his face. Theo felt relief rush over him as he realised that he was fine.

Beckett was gone, and he was fine. He looked up at Nikoliah, his eyes saying a million words before he was darting off in the direction of his boyfriend now that all the danger had passed.

Theo stumbled over and collapsed to his knees before Julian, taking him off Laine and pulling him into his lap as the man below him blinked away his last fragment of consciousness.

Over the other side of the courtyard, somebody screamed.

Fiducia brought her right hand to her mouth as she processed what she had just watched.

Nikoliah snapped his head over to look at her. She brought her hand away from her face and to the handle of her sword. The soldier took a few steps closer to Nikoliah, pulling her hand away from her sword to sign something to him really quickly.

'Traitor.'

She grabbed her sword from her holster.

"Hey, hey- Cia, we can talk about this." He tried to rationalise, but she was not having it. He had robbed her of the one man who had ever actually believed in her. Who had seen something in her despite all of her difficulties that she had faced in her life. She had cared about Nikoliah, and had been so kind to him. She had spent months after months teaching him sign language, for fucks sake!

Fiducia slammed her sword down towards Nikoliah, and in an instant, they were duelling. Just like they had done as lighthearted practice for two years.

Nikoliah was exhausted. He'd been through a lot today. Still, he thwacked his sword as much as he could, although he was riddled with guilt.

His colleague did not feel the same. She was furious. She hit with real intention, trying to kill Nikoliah if she could. He was an untrustworthy coward, just switching sides when it was convenient to him.

And, Nikoliah put up a really good fight. But it wasn't good enough - not against someone like Fiducia, and certainly not after the day that he'd had.

Fiducia got an amazingly lucky angle, and hacked her sword at Nikoliah's side. The metal collided with his arm, just below his elbow. It went right through the skin and first layer of muscle, hitting bone instantly. Nikoliah screamed and fell to the ground on his front. Fiducia wanted to cause him pain. Real pain, for backstabbing her and his honour as a knight.

So, she stepped onto his back. He couldn't move as his injured arm was outstretched, dirt getting in the bleeding wound. Fiducia snarled as she raised her sword and hacked at his arm again. He screamed louder. She did it again. So much so that his forearm was barely hanging on.

"That's my fucking boyfriend, you bitch!" Laine yelled, hitting Fiducia from behind with the hilt of her sword. The angel's sword fell out of her hand as her eyes rolled back into her head and she passed out from the strength of the hit. She fell to the ground right beside Nikoliah, who was still very much awake, in pain, and screaming.

"Alright, you're alright." Laine said, bending down onto one knee. She nearly retched at the sight of the mangled mess that Fiducia had made of his arm, but she used all of her self-control not to make it obvious how bad the injury was.

Nikoliah was picked up. Laine held him tightly to her chest, one hand hooked under his knees and the other around his back, holding onto his arm. She moved quickly over to where Theo was cradling Julian, and gently placed Nikoliah on the ground, leaving Fiducia on the ground, unconscious.

"I'm sorry." Theo cracked, voice hoarse from crying.

"Don't be. He's going to be fine." Laine dismissed. "Is *he*?" She asked, looking down worriedly at Julian. The crown that she had been holding was on the ground by Theo's knees.

Within one minute, it felt like everybody that had been on their side was crowded around them. Theo didn't know. Julian had passed out at some point, and this blood was drying all over his neck and shoulders. The sun was beginning to rise. They had been fighting all night.

Theo felt a hand on his upper arm, and he turned his head back to look at his father.

"We'll take him to the infirmary. We'll take everyone that needs it." Dyran reassured. Theo nodded whilst sniffling. "You did it, Theo. You're okay."

Theo nodded and pulled Julian closer as he looked around. The courtyard was so quiet now.

LI

"We're going to be late at this rate, hurry up!" Laine said playfully as she slung her nicest cardigan on over her light purple dress. It had spaghetti straps over her shoulders, which met the horizontal top of the dress. Underneath it, she was also wearing a long-sleeve black cotton t-shirt so that she could take her cardigan off if she wanted to.
It had been three months since the fight. Three months since Theo took his crown back.
"No, we aren't. Don't be dramatic." The King scoffed. He clipped his necklace around the back of his shirt, turning around to look at Julian - who was sitting on his bed, having been ready for at least thirty minutes now. "Are we?" He asked.
Julian raised his eyebrows in amusement, looking down at the watch on his wrist. He looked back up and tilted his head to the side, wavering his hand to signify that, *maybe*.
"Probably." He said, voice incredibly hoarse and quiet.
"Ack, shush." Theo instructed, pacing over towards him and looking down at him with an entertained smile. "Still no talking, remember?"
Julian rolled his eyes. "You asked." He strained, voice obscured by the large scar along his neck.
"Well, I apologise for asking." Theo snickered, pressing a kiss to Julian's temple and wandering back over to his mirror to grab his boots from the feet of the desk. Laine and Julian watched in amusement for about a minute before saying anything else.
They were all comfortably getting ready in Theo's bedroom now. It was the same room that he had had growing up, albeit redecorated. Laine

and Nikoliah had kept their room on the other side of the castle, which it turned out had been pretty good for their personal space now that they were both fully grown adults. And, also now that they were both in relationships publicly, it meant that they had more privacy and general comfort. About a week after the fight, Theo had gone back to Nesbryn with some of the others that lived there to get loads of his stuff that he had become attached to. His room felt a lot more grown up now, and definitely more reflective of himself.

After having settled back in, Theo had done an address to the kingdom as per protocol when a "new" monarch is crowned. But, he'd already done one two years ago, so, this time, he took Julian out onto the balcony, held him close and kissed him in front of the whole kingdom. It definitely had put an end to any rumours circulating about them.

It was also the best thing that Theo had ever done. The best feeling he had ever felt.

"Right, we're leaving. You're going to have to wear one shoe." Laine said, referring to the way that her brother was still half way through lacing his first boot up. Julian huffed and slid off the bed, grabbing his boyfriend's other shoe and manhandling it onto his other foot.

"I can put my shoe on myself." He protested.

"Evidently not." Laine said, opening the door. "Come on, Niko. We're leaving." She yelled down the corridor. She hoped that he had heard - because the corridor was incredibly busy. There were a lot of staff members hustling and bustling down it.

"Yeah, okay!" The knight-turned sorcerer yelled back from where he was moving up the staircase. Nikoliah was wearing a formal grey suit with a purple tie the same colour as Laine's dress. His jacket was made of expensive cotton, and it cut off just above the elbow of his right arm. Below that, there was nothing. He had lost his right forearm to Fiducia, due to a mix of it being mostly unsalvageable and the wound becoming infected pretty quickly. It had taken a while for him to adjust to, but by this point, one of his limbs was something he had begun to feel content with sacrificing for what he has now.

He walked into the bedroom and raised his eyebrows with a snicker.

"You cannot wear that many accessories to someone else's wedding." He said, amused.

Theo groaned. "You're jealous. I'll take one off."

Nikoliah naturally moved to stand next to Laine. He narrowed his eyes in thought whilst looking at Theo.

"He's nervous."

Theo snapped his head to look at Nikoliah and rolled his eyes. "I wish you would stop doing that." He complained, and Julian laughed.

"What are you nervous about?" Laine asked.

"Well, you know." Theo mumbled. "People are gonna stare."

"Are they?" She asked.

"Yes! They think I'm some kind of psychopath."

"Eh." Julian hummed, not disagreeing.

"Hey, no. I don't need you in on this as well."

"Theo." Laine said, planting her hands on his shoulders. He was still sitting down on the stool in front of his desk. "Maybe some people think you're a bit deranged," She said, and he scoffed. "But, you haven't exactly killed anyone or anything. You know that Beckett is fine. He just can't leave Menphe now." She explained, before sighing at his expression. "See. When I say that he's fine and you pull a face like that, it kind of feeds into the 'psychopathic' speculation."

Theo laughed, finishing lacing his second boot up. "Okay, I'll be sure to show no emotion today." He joked.

"And," Nikoliah added. "This is your first public appearance since you took the crown back. So, eyes will definitely be on you. This is your opportunity to prove them wrong. We're going to have a great time in Vaemunt today, I can feel it. Just enjoy yourself, chill out for once. Lord knows you need to."

"Yes, right." Theo conceded. "Now, off we go."

"Uh! Strythio Virzor!" Jaymie called when Theo got to the bottom of the stairs. He halted, scrunching his nose up and looking over at her. "I'm pretty sure I told you to tuck that shirt in."

"I don't want to, it looks too formal." He protested weakly. He was wearing a black, long sleeve button-up with the top two buttons undone, and loosely tied dark green tie, underneath a dark grey suit jacket and semi-formal jeans.

"You're a grown adult man. And, I let you wear the stupid jeans. Tuck your shirt in." She lectured, watching as he grumbled and did just as she said, tucking the edges of the shirt into his black leather belt.

"See, Julian wore his how I told him to wear it." She observed, looking at his light grey trousers and white shirt tucked into it, with a black blazer over the top. The jacket had a dark green lining that was visible when Julian walked or stuck his hands in his pockets.

Kougan laughed, emerging from one of the doorways off the side. "You know she tried to make me bet money that you would modify your outfit." He said.

"Unsurprising." Laine agreed flatly.
"Right." Jaymie said sternly, pointing at the Princess. "You're on make-sure-king-Theo-keeps-his-shirt-tucked-in duty. Okay?"
"Okay." Laine nodded.
"Very important." Kougan mused. "If you lot go there and look bad, that reflects on us."
"Yes, we get it." Theo complained lightheartedly. "You care."
Julian hit Theo's shoulder, and he turned around with a raised eyebrow. Julian brought his arm up to his chest height and tapped his wristwatch a few times.
"Right, yes." Theo understood. "We best actually leave."

"Ah! You look so good." Raphie whooped, all but jumping off the train into the station. She bounded over and hugged Laine quickly, moving onto the other three afterwards.
"As do you." Theo replied. "You dyed your hair."
"Flattered that you noticed." The girl replied, pushing a loose strand of her newly-vibrant cotton candy pink hair behind her ear. It was tied up in a half-up half-down style, and she had dyed a few streaks of white into it too, and Laine struggled to grasp how much time that must have taken. When she had done her red hair when she was sixteen, she had had to bleach it twice before the colour began to stick for longer than a few washes.
Raphie was wearing a long, light turquoise skirt that went all the way down to her ankles, having little daisies embroidered on it. She wore a beige coloured halter top, and earrings that dangled down all the way to her shoulders with clear crystals on them.
"How are you guys?"
"We're good." Nikoliah replied.
"Good. How's the whole 'guardian of Klaevr' situation treating you, dude?"
Nikoliah nodded. "Better than I thought it would."
"He's been making paper stars." Laine giggled. "For each person that he welcomes into the kingdom. Little bright ones that he's nicked my post-it-notes for."
"Hey." Nikoliah pouted. "You told me you thought my star-jar was cute."
"It is. Very cute, love."

"Mhm, and I use different colours for different people. Blue for kids, pink for teens. Yellow for adults."

Raphie listened with an amused smirk adorned on her face. "Well, they say that everyday is a vacation if you love your job."

"I do." Nikoliah replied. "It feels right. Which, I guess, is anticipated."

"Wasn't on my bingo card for this year." Julian said with a smirk. His voice was quiet, but in the small circle they stood in, everyone heard perfectly well. "Hostile ex-soldier dabbles in origami."

And then, a younger-sounding voice came from the ground, right beside the group's legs.

"How do you make stars if you only have one hand?" The girl asked curiously. She was about as tall as Theo's waist, and had blonde hair in a bob at her shoulders, as well as light purple skin and a halo floating above her head. Nikoliah snickered and bent down on one knee to talk to her.

"Well, how do you reach the high-up cupboards in your kitchen?" He asked.

"'Cause I'm tall. And I can always reach." She proclaimed proudly. "And sometimes my mummies help me a little bit." She murmured with a cheeky grin as she looked at Laine. "Does the pretty princess help you reach the cupboards?" The girl asked.

"She cuts the paper for me." Nikoliah said in a playful whisper.

The girl grinned and nodded.

"Oh my god, I am so sorry." Hettie apologised, rushing up to them from where she had just stepped off the train. "Sweetie, remember how we talked about approaching strangers?"

Leila looked at the floor guiltily. "They aren't strangers." She protested. "I know, like, two of their names."

"Oh, there she is!" Elsie said, sounding relieved. "Sorry about her."

"Nah, you're good." Nikoliah reassured. "How are you guys?"

"We're pretty great, actually." Hettie smiled, pulling Leila close to her.

Theo couldn't help but let his mouth break into a smile just looking at the young girl. "God. She's grown up, hasn't she?" The King commented, looking at the wives nostalgically.

"Sure has. She's seven now. Feels like we were on Earth when she was born just yesterday."

"Seven and three quarters!" Leila yelled up at her mother.

"Seven and three quarters." Hettie corrected herself.

Leila nodded with pride. She waddled over to Theo and pulled on his suit jacket. He looked down. "Hey, Leila. You okay?"

"Yeah, yeah." The girl affirmed. "I just wan'ed to say thank you."
"For what?"
"You, um. My mummies said you helped us a lot, King Theo. 'Cause they used to not be allowed to come to Menphe with me, but now they do. And they said that you did that. And I like getting to see them more. Now we sometimes stay up there and we sometimes stay down here." She said, voice quiet and sincere. Theo thought for a moment that he might pass out from how happy that made him. It hadn't been easy. And, maybe it had been just a little bit to do with his very public relationship with an angel. Then, maybe it had also been a bit to do with Amadeus Beckett losing his political title and jurisdiction over the law.
Really, it had only taken like three meetings with himself, some other monarchs from Hell, and a handful of them from Heaven too. Theo had entered the meetings expecting to have to fight his corner super hard, but it turned out that most of the rulers shared his ideology - and it had just been powerful people like Beckett that had stopped them before. With him out of the way, Theo was really happy to abolish the law that demons couldn't enter any Kingdoms of Heaven.
"That's okay, kid. You know, your mummies helped too."
"They did?" She asked, wide-eyed.
"Yeah. They were super brave."
Someone tapped his shoulder, and he looked up to see Julian. The man waved at Leila briefly, and then flicked his head in the direction of the train that had just arrived.
"Oh! That's us, Leila." Theo said.
"Where are you going?" She questioned, stepping back and grabbing Elsie's hand.
"Two of my friends are getting married today, squirt. Ceremony starts in an hour, so we really have to get going or else we might miss it." He noted.
Hettie cleared her throat. "Yes, sweetie. And we have to go too. The ice-cream place closes in forty-five minutes." She remembered, and Leila immediately gasped.
"Oh, no! Okay! Bye, King Theo! Bye, Princess Laine! Bye, star-boy! Bye, pinkie-pie! Bye, fluffy-hair-boy!" She called, before skittering off in front of her parents, who too bid farewell to the group.
"We are genuinely so thankful, Theo." Elsie said, holding Hettie's hand. "For the legislation, and also for the kindness. Towards us, and to Zero. Really, towards everyone. Abolishing Nesbryn was a big one. We thought that was great."

Theo nodded with a smile. It had been a lot of work, but he and others had been able to testify that the idea of monarchs being able to just banish people whenever they felt like it was an abuse of power, and it had led to the whole concept being done away with. A lot of more traditional politicians and higher-ups called him stupid for even wanting to attempt something so big, but he had done it eventually. Ayale, Axel, Fern, Livvy, Toby, and Isaac had been grateful. He'd been making sure to catch up with them when he found the time.
"Did she just call me pinkie-pie? You guys better not let that nickname stick."
Laine beckoned Raphie towards the train. "Come on, pinkie-pie." She guided.

They were relieved to find that, despite their tardiness, there was still a short queue to get into the venue when they arrived, about fifteen minutes before the ceremony was to start. They were inside the castle, lined up outside the entrance to their grand hall. It was a royal wedding, so, mainly important people. Monarchs, ex-monarchs, their kids, knights, noblemen and noblewomen. About the same crowd that Theo had at his coronation.
There was a vast number of guards milling around, protecting all entrances and exits and everything in between. It was nothing short of typical for an event like this.
Julian clung to Theo's arm like a child who was worried they would get lost in the supermarket. He was clearly feeling a little bewildered by it all. Theo turned to him and smiled reassuringly.
"Just smile and wave, Jude. You're actually kind of lucky, you don't have to speak to anyone if you don't want to."
The angel nodded with a little smirk. He supposed that, yeah, he could use his injury to his advantage - just for today. He had almost lost his ability to speak completely, so, today, just for today, he was taking the recovery of his severed vocal chords *very* seriously.
They made it to the front of the queue in only five minutes. And, gosh, was the ceremony hall beautiful.
It was a very large room, with ten rows of wooden white chairs, each with five seats on each side of the aisle. There were flowers all along the walls in wreaths, and a large marble platform at the front of the hall, on which stood an altar in between the curve of a large arch that was made

up of artificial blue peonies and purple roses. The ceiling had some kind of ethereal painting on it, and the walls were a light yellow colour.

"Hey, guys." Vercobrix greeted from where he stood beside the doorframe. "Thank you for coming."

"Hi!" Laine chirped, hugging him as carefully as she could so as to not get any creases in his suit. It was a slim fitting outfit, coloured in a dark grey that appeared light against his dark skin. He was wearing a cobalt blue waistcoat over a white button-up shirt, and then a windsor-knotted tie in the same colour as the waistcoat. He looked really good. But, then again, it *was* his wedding day. So, anything less would be unacceptable.

"This place looks amazing." Raphie grinned, taking it all in. "I feel super out of place though. No idea how I managed to worm my way into a royal wedding."

"You're not the only ex-mortal here, Raph." Theo reassured her lightly.

"I think I'm the only one here that's not in a relationship with a pureblood." She observed looking around. "Oh, no. There's a few. Knights and people." She nodded. "Sorry, lovely wedding. Good luck." She said to Vercobrix, a little embarrassed that she had gotten distracted. He just smirked a little and nodded.

"Hello." He said, shaking Nikoliah's hand. They had never formally met, so it was now that they did all the formalities.

"Prince Vercobrix." He nodded. "How are you feeling?" He asked, studying the Prince's face.

"Good. Really good, actually."

"Good. Glad to hear it." Nikoliah said to himself. He could tell that they were going to be really happy together. That they already were happy together. He would've said it to the Prince, but the only people that he really did the aura-readings with were his close friends and Laine. Because, they found it playful. He could understand that some people would just find it a little violating.

"King Theo." Vercobrix smiled genuinely. He had done a lot of fake smiling at guests that he didn't really know so far, but he was seriously happy to see Theo. He felt a lot better knowing that Klaevr was in safe hands.

"Prince Vercobrix." Theo replied in high spirits. They hugged, which was something that Vercobrix would not have even allowed to cross his mind this time three months ago. But, things were different, and everyone involved in them taking Klaevr back had been through a lot together. It was a special kind of bond that couldn't be fabricated.

Vercobrix also hugged Julian for the same reason. After that, they quickly found their seats - three rows back from the front. The bride and groom's families had the front rows reserved, and the second row was traditionally where monarchs sat. Technically, Theo could have sat in the second row, behind Serenity's parents, but it would mean that he would have had to separate himself from the four others that he came with. Serenity looked beautiful in her wedding dress.

It was long, trailing all the way to the floor. White, and the whole of the shoulders and sleeves were made of a transparent lace. The dress was tight-fitting down to the waist, where it splayed out and led into a long train that dragged behind her. Theo would never admit to anyone that he cried watching the ceremony. He was really happy for them.

After the vows, they all made a little column and threw flower petals as the newlyweds came down the aisle.

It all happened in a flash of time, but before they knew it, everybody had filtered into the reception room and were told that they had about twenty minutes of time to mill around before the bride and groom came in and the meal would commence.

After Laine and Nikoliah had wandered off with Raphie, and Julian had scampered off to the snack table, Theo was left alone, leaning against a back wall and watching the room. He must have zoned out a little bit, because the next thing he knew someone was talking to him.

"King Theo." The woman smiled, bowing her head a little. "It's good to see you again."

Theo blinked a few times and looked over at her. It was a woman older than Theo, maybe about twenty-eight to thirty. She had long, red hair and freckles as a result. She was dressed very formally, but, most prevalent of all was the crown that sat atop her head.

"Oh, Queen Lucianna!" He recognised, bowing for her and then looking back up. "Thank you for having us in your kingdom. It's very beautiful, Your Majesty."

"Please, Lucy is fine."

"Yeah?"

"Yeah."

They both nodded to each other, and for a few moments, they stood watching the crowd side by side.

"Of course, I would come and speak to you anyway, but I do have a reason for this particular conversation." Lucy admitted. Theo felt his stomach churn with anxiety momentarily.

"Okay, shoot."

"I just- I know that Serenity had originally told you that I would help you out when you were fighting against Amadeus Beckett. And, then, I didn't. I just- I want to make sure that you know that I didn't do that maliciously. I was just quite worried about starting a war and-"

"Hey, it's fine. I'm not holding that against you. And, it was all fine in the end." He disputed her anxieties with a kind-sounding reply. Then, he narrowed his eyes. "Were you worried that I was angry at you about that?"

"Slightly." She admitted.

"Why? Do I seem like the kind of guy that holds a grudge? Serious question."

Lucy opened her mouth to speak, and then closed it before thinking a little. "Well, I had people describe to me in vivid detail about the way that you stabbed your sword through Beckett's chest in front of your whole kingdom. And apparently you didn't even flinch when his blood got all over you."

Theo nodded. "Ah." He noted, looking to the ground. "I did do that, yeah." He acknowledged. "But, I feel like that was justified."

Lucy snickered a little. "He would have died if you two were mortals."

"I would have died the first time we fought if we were mortals." Theo replied solemnly. "That wasn't why I was so angry, though. Like, sure, he imprisoned me in a sunlight-less island for two years whilst he stole my kingdom from me and made all the residents miserable. But, then we were fighting, and it was between *us*. And he *really* hurt my boyfriend. Just to hurt me. And it worked. He still hasn't recovered, and the doctors said that he won't for at least another four months."

"I understand." Lucy replied. "I mean, I don't have a partner, obviously - I don't really do that kind of thing - but, it's like, my little sister has only been married for an hour and I am already prepared to murder Vercobrix if he ever hurts her."

Theo laughed.

"And, if it makes you feel any better: I heard that Beckett is still bedridden whilst recovering." She said. Theo knew that, of course. He also knew about how Beckett's former right-hand, Fiducia, had retreated back to Menphe with him. Which, he felt, was a little bit of a shame. Nikoliah had been convinced that she had potential for redemption, but when she had woken up from her unconscious state and gone right back to violence towards them all, he realised that she didn't.

"My sister told me not to make any faces or comments that will make me appear psychopathic." He replied with a smirk. Lucy found that quite funny.

"Right, well, I'll imagine what you would have said."

Theo nodded. He could definitely do the same.

"And, besides." The King continued. "I think that you screwing me over with potential backup kind of makes up for me pretending to want to marry your sister, and then leaving her alone."

"Yeah, that was shitty." Lucy agreed. "But, the past is the past. She's okay now, she's married very happily. And you seem happy too."

"I am."

Lucy smiled and reached her right hand out towards Theo. "So, are we good?"

"We're good." Theo replied, taking her hand and shaking it. Lucy nodded contently and bid him goodbye, moving away to socialise with other guests.

Theo rolled his eyes. "You know, you could have come over." He told Julian, who was hovering a few metres away during the whole last minute of their conversation. Julian shook his head. He approached Theo and bowed dramatically, sweeping his hands towards the ground in an exaggerated movement, bringing his body back up with an entertained grin on his face.

"Yeah, fair enough." Theo conceded, wrapping his arm around Julian's shoulders and pulling him close. They couldn't seem to get any silence, because it was only ten seconds before they were approached again. This time, it was someone that Theo was not so stressed to talk to.

"Hey, grandma." He said, smiling at Cordelia as she approached.

"This place is nice." Was her reply.

"It is, yeah." Theo agreed smoothly.

Laine had gone back to the stronghold after the battle was finished, where she had collected her grandmother that they had previously left. The woman was very relieved to see her. As predicted, the translucent, green-tinted spirit that had helped them break the forcefield down was gone, which was a shame. Laine would have liked to have said thank you. Still, they had made it back to her home in T'kota, where she had been given medical care for the burnt palms that she had given herself. Still, on Serenity and Vercobrix's wedding day months later, Cordelia wore gloves that protected the wounds as they still healed.

"Julian." Cordelia said. "I don't think we ever properly met. My name is Cordelia, I'm Theo's grandmother."

Julian smiled. He liked feeling accepted by Theo's family. He reached his hand out, expecting a handshake, but Cordelia shook her head.

"You're going to marry my grandson one day, kid. We can hug." She said, opening her arms. Julian fell into them quickly and then, once he pulled away, Cordelia continued to speak. "Actually, that's something your father and I have been wondering. Now, do stop me if it's an intrusion, but why have the two of you not gotten at least engaged yet?" She asked. "You seem very serious about each other."

Theo looked down at Julian, who made eye contact with him and nodded, as if to say '*yeah, fine, tell them. Whatever*'.

"We're just... taking things slow." Theo admitted. "Our relationship started pretty quickly, and we didn't have much time to actually talk about things, or think about things. So, I guess, we're making up for lost time and just kind of... Not putting any pressure on ourselves right now. We are what we are."

Cordelia raised her eyebrows. "God, you're in the honeymoon phase."

"Are not." Julian protested with a light smile.

"It's not a bad thing!" Cordelia defended. "In fact, I'm glad that you're taking time to figure yourselves out. I think that one of the biggest mistakes that royals tend to make is rushing into things with love. I know I did."

"Oh. Yeah. Have you told dad about that?" Theo asked, as if it was casual.

"Not yet. I trust you and your sister to keep a secret. But, if I do, I need to talk with Oliver about it first. We last spoke like, a month ago. And that was about you two finding out, not even delving into your father. He's married, he's happy. It would be a big decision."

"Yeah." Theo agreed. "Well, if you do tell him, let me know. I want to be there."

Cordelia raised her eyebrows as Julian giggled.

"Oh, and, also, we don't want to get married whilst we're both still recovering from the fight. Both emotionally and physically."

"I want to say my vows without sounding like an eagle that's screamed too much." Julian stated. Theo turned his head slowly to look at his boyfriend.

"Yeah. And you want that to be possible in the future. So, hush up. Lovingly." He said. Julian shook his head with a mischievous smile. "Plus, you sound like that anyway." Theo teased.

"Wow." Julian drawled out, shaking his head jokingly. "Transphobe. Making fun of my scratchy testosterone voice."

"Oh, shut up." Theo bit back with the same level of jest. "You're currently ruining that 'scratchy testosterone voice'; I literally cannot keep telling you to stay quiet."

"Well, how else am I gonna convey my feelings? I can only gesture so much, sparkles."

"Nikoliah told you that he would teach us sign language, you just can't be arsed."

"Touche."

Cordelia blinked at them. "You guys are really cute. I'm going to refill my glass." She said, looking down at the empty goblet in her hand, now devoid of the red wine she was previously drinking. Then, she walked off.

"This place is a hotspot for people approaching us. Let's walk around a little and look busy." Theo decided, taking Julian's hand.

"Theo! Julian!" Someone called from a few metres away.

"Spoke too soon."

He turned around. Serenity had changed into a reception dress that was still white, but she was much more able to move in it. She had a massive grin on her face, and bounded over.

"I haven't gotten to speak to you guys yet, how are you?"

"Livin' la vida loca." Theo replied. He glanced over to Julian hesitantly, and the angel nodded enthusiastically. "We've been working on pop culture references. That's a song."

Serenity nodded slowly, entertaining the fantasy that Theo at all understood what he was trying to pick up. "That's great, sounds great." She laughed. "I'm really glad you came. You and everyone. It means a lot to have so many people here."

"Yeah, of course." Theo said. "You look amazing."

Serenity looked down at her outfit. "Thanks. I feel amazing."

From the right, a brunette woman with mid-toned grey skin and very bright red horns approached. "Serenity, there you are." She sighed.

"Vercobrix is looking for you."

"Oh! Thanks." She replied. "Um, Theo, Julian. This is Sophie. Sophie, this is Theo and Julian." She introduced. "Alright, I'll talk to you two later." She confirmed, and with a content smile, she walked off to find her husband.

"It's good to meet you, Theo. I've heard a lot." Sophie said, extending a hand to shake, which Theo took. As she also shook Julian's hand, Theo registered what she had said.

"What?" He asked, a little under his breath.

"Oh, my apologies. I'm Princess Serenity's therapist. So, um, heard a lot."
Theo cringed. "Bad things?"
"Feelings." Sophie countered. "But, I'd rather not let that be the nature of our relationship. Don't think of me like that. I don't take anything that we've talked about in our sessions as a reflection of you personally."
Theo nodded, looking at Julian and then back to Sophie. "Okay." He accepted. "Well, it's nice to meet you, regardless."
"Yeah." Sophie nodded. "Alright, I need to get back to my partner. I'm worried that they're going to get lost. This place is huge." She said, and then she turned and began to walk away.
"Um, Sophie?" He called, cringing. She looked back around and took a few steps closer.
"Mhm?" She hummed in response, and Theo tightened his grip on Julian's hand.
"Do you, um- like, is Serenity the only person you speak to, or-?"
"I see her once a week, Theo. And others, of course. Why? Do you… maybe need someone to talk to?"
Theo immediately shook his head. "Erm, no- not really- sorry. Forget about it."
Julian hit him lightly. Sophie raised an eyebrow.
"I just thought, that, you know, maybe *you* might want to." He said, looking down at Julian. His boyfriend sighed, but he understood. So, he looked at Sophie and nodded.
"Okay." Sophie smiled warmly. "I can come and see you, Julian. And, Theo, if you happen to be around, then I can speak to you as well." She said.
"Thank you." Theo replied. Sophie nodded, a silent message of *'it's okay'*, and then she disappeared into the crowd.

All of the girls at the wedding gathered together in the centre of the ballroom excitedly. From the sidelines, Theo, Julian, and Nikoliah watched with amusement as Serenity stood a few metres in front of the crowd, holding her bouquet.
She swung it downwards and then up a few times. Each time the crowd cheered a little louder. Then, on the third swing, Serenity threw the bouquet into the group. There was an excited scream. Laine used Raphie as leverage to jump up. She extended her arms out and caught the bouquet, landing on the ground with a large grin on her face.

Raphie cheered along with everyone else, hugging her. Theo snickered and turned his head towards Nikoliah.

"Oh!" He said, voice high-pitched. "That's *my* girlfriend."

"Sure is." Theo laughed. Laine looked over at Nikoliah and waved the bouquet at him. She bounced over quickly and launched herself into his arms.

Theo didn't know what the two of them had said to each other when they were sitting together in the bushes on the day of the battle. He didn't know what they had said since. But, he could tell that they were trying for each other, and they were joyfully dating again. He was happy about it, because he trusted Nikoliah not to make the same mistakes again.

"Alright!" The organiser called. "Can everybody please take their seats for the meal to commence?"

From their left, Dyran approached and looked quite amused at the recent events of the bouquet toss.

"I found our table, over here." He instructed, gesturing for the five of them to follow along. They did, and they quickly arrived at the round table, with seven seats on it.

In the centre of the table was a glass vase. All of the tables for guests had either the purple roses or the blue peonies. However, in their vase, there were some flowers of a different shade of purple. Lighter, and with a bright yellow centre.

Theo looked at the Asters and smiled inwardly. He could finally look at them as something positive. Of course, he, Laine, and his father still had *a lot* to work through together in regards to his mother. And, they would. Not right now. And maybe not even for the rest of this year. But, they would figure it out eventually. He knew that the future wouldn't be easy, but, for once, he wasn't pushing anything down. He felt equipped to deal with whatever life threw at him next.

Theo sat down at the table, pulling Julian's chair out beside him too. It had only taken about ten seconds of sitting like proper adults before Laine pulled a deck of cards out of her bag. She handed them out to each member of the table, sharing a smile with Raphie sat next to her, ready for it to be the entertainment until the entrees arrived.

Theo looked at Julian next to him, who quickly brought his cards to his chest with an excitable chuckle to avoid any potential cheating. Theo smiled at the gaiety and pressed a kiss to Julian's forehead. His eyes cast around his closest family and friends, all with him, exactly where he wanted to be. He grinned, slinging an arm around Julian, sentimentally allowing his boyfriend to rest his head on his shoulder. The game commenced.

Theo looked down at the cards that he had been dealt.

He had a good hand.

More from James P Conway:
www.jamespconway.com